# RISE ABOVE HATE

# RISE ABOVE HATE

## *May God Save the King*

KHALID M. ALI

Genre: Religion Spirituality and New Age

Rise Above Hate: *May God Save the King*



Printed in the United States of America
ISBN 979-8-88945-358-1 (sc)
ISBN 979-8-88945-359-8 (e)


2023.09.06

Brilliant Books Literary
137 Forest Park Ln,
Thomasville, NC 27360,
United States

# Prelude

S o I haven't left the country since the spring of nineteen ninety-eight. Visited Spain with a few friends from work, it was the greatest trip ever. But one gloomy thing did happen the Chairman of the Board passed away. I'm busy globetrotting outside of North America and we lost another hero. Fast forward to two thousand twenty-two since that bad omen still ain't left the country. I'm punching a clock @ the historic Fontainebleau, Miami Beach Florida back residents side. I'm working K solo out there all alone every time I think I gotta breather the phone rings or multiple families show up to window requesting their vehicle.

I'm flying Zoom Zoom, beep beep, Arriba Arriba, andale, andale, all over the place in total control of the operation. Past high noon closing in on one p.m. and residents who left in the morning are starting to come back home. Papi Chulo & Maria pull up in the Porsche truck cool as the other side of the pillow. Outta respect I don't even look at or flirt with his girl. On this day they park close to the edge too far left and forward almost blocking garage door. (I grab the keys) Right behind them residents guests pulls up in a silver Chevy equinox parking the same way too far to the left and directly behind the Porsche bumper to bumper. (I grab the keys)

Next up is the man himself not saying any names. It's a Rolls Royce big boy but he parks it so that nothing can touch it. In his gravelly voice he lets me know "the keys are in the car" and disappears inside. This is all happening so fast I don't have time to put any keys in the office plus cars are behind the Rolls and a traffic jam is starting to form. That simply cannot happen I jump into the Porsche and move it forward and to the right. Hop out in a split second climb into the Equinox and do the same now traffic's flowing as the car passes I turn to my left and in the passenger side beyond the window one inch away from the suit jacket is a white dress shirt. I look up better yet pan backwards and I see him laughing, clapping right at his neck hysterically like he's at the funniest comedy show ever. Automatically I smile big big smile teeth showing and chuckle . . . SINATRA!!! As the car a Chrysler Pacifica North Carolina blue paint, mirror tint old body style passes by.

Check the camera's February 22nd, 2022.
Khalid H. Ali

# TABLE OF CONTENTS

STOP
THE
WAR
START
IMPEACHMENT
MINORITYX.COM

# "Welcome Back"

"Love is patient, love is kind. It does not envy, it does not boast, it is not proud. It is not rude, it is not self-seeking, it is not easily angered, and it keeps no record of wrongs. Love does not delight in evil but rejoices with the truth. It always protects always trusts, always hopes, always preserves."

—1 Corinthians 13:4-7

A TOOTHACHE CAN BE ONE of the most painful experiences you ever have to face as the nerves inside your mouth riddle from your gums to your brain and the pulsing ache quakes away at your jaws and the only thing that can save you is a trip to the dentist, the tooth doctor and as patients sit with mouths wide open the last thing they want is an interruption in the operation but that is exactly what is going on as the door gently cracks open and two heads go poking through to peek inside. "I have to find my mom so I can get the keys to the car." And like children they search room to room through the dentist office. "I can't believe we are checking every room this is crazy, just call her on her cell phone." She turns around and face to face at Lid and says "I tried to call her it's off, don't you think I already thought about that?" "He air whispers to her "gimmie a kiss" and grasp forward to kiss the best ever but she quickly turns back around and continues to search from room to room. Fed up with the games he takes his right hand and smacks her on her backside as hard as he can and all you hear is smack echo throughout the quiet dentist office, she turns around with her full blushing caramel cheeks smiling away and says "I'm going to get you" surprised of her reaction since they've never been this playful with each other he pushes the envelope even farther and ask "Can I please have a kiss?" This time she turns around and just stops and looking right into each others eyes the window to their souls lock and they finally kiss. Lid wraps his hands around the bottom he just smacked and she wraps her arms around his cut and toned body courtesy of working out all summer and they kiss, when finally they come up for air still interlocked in eye contact he goes back for seconds when Sister Kareema finds them. "What are you two doing back here?" He bust out in a smile and she turns to her mother and says "Mom I'm looking for you to get the keys for the car." "Here "she hands Jasmine the keys and Lid comes over to give her a hung "I'm leaving in a few hours to go back home, Mrs. Kareema so thank for everything and it was nice spending the summer down here with you." The always pleasant Mrs. Kareema smiles and says "It was nice to have met you Lid; it was no problem you just stay out of trouble up in Philly and finish school o.k." "I will" They hug Lid and Jasmine walk out the dentist office hand in hand whispering to each other "You better call me as soon as you get home" "I will" they walk outside and stand in front of Mrs. Kareem's white Jaguar, when Lid's phone rings, he answers and say "Yo I'm at the dentist office on Carrolton in front of a white Jaguar, gotta go" and quickly hangs up. "That was T Money?" "Yeah he on his way I don't wanna leave babe" and like that Jasmine goes from glamorous girlfriend to your best friend and she smiles with full cheeks blushing away and says "You better go silly I'll be home next week and you better get your butt to New York every weekend." "I will can I have another kiss?" Jasmine says nothing but her brown eyes tell it all as they flare up and she leans up to kiss Lid. Lost Lid doesn't even answer his phone as T Money is calling him and the sound of the hot boys blaring from T Money's ride doesn't distract them as they kiss. Finally coming for air Lidkisses Jasmine on her hand and steals one more quick kiss from her. "You have to go silly, I love you." "I love you to" and Lid hops in the passenger side of T Money's ride when he remembers "Oh shit my luggage!" "Jasmine! I gotta get my luggage out ya mom's car. She smiles and puts her fingers to her forehead and using the keys pops the trunk of the car, Lid grabs his luggage and puts it into T Money's trunk, and Lid gets back into the passenger side, Jasmine still standing in front of the dentist office says "Call me as soon as you get home babe." "I will" she blows him a kiss as they pull off. "Dog I don't know what you did that but last semester you two where ready to kill each other and now y'all hugged up like Adam and Eve, what happened?" "I don't know essence fest T Money, Teena Marie I don't know but since she been down here this summer we been inseparable."

"But y'all was trying to kill each other last semester?" "I got her number from her girl friend Portia and called her during the spring time we started talking all summer I'm buying phone cards apologizing about everything that happened, it was crazy. But we used to talk every night when the phone got turned off I was calling on phone cards at the Piggly Wiggly till my cell phone was back on. Since she been down here it's been like a dream." "When she goin back to NY?" "Next week" "You goin right up to see her?" "You better believe it I need her yo, you know how many years that kiss was in the making. Like two years man I can't wait to get back home and be like two hours away." "Can't believe you leaving man?" "I gotta go tuition too high, plus I gotta see if I can save my house in Philly man." "Man that house is gone, I know why you leaving." "Yeah me too, this shit better work out or I'm going to loose it up north." T Money turns up the music and when they get to the airport the two old friends shake hands and hug "Thanks for being there T Money, first week of school we was in the same group forty niners fans yo, that's crazy, I'll be back." "Nigga I'm gonna never see you again!" Lid smiles "never say never", and walks into the airport carrying his two bags of luggage disappearing into the crowd. The last time he was in Philly was the previous year the summer of 2000 and before he left he asked his moms not to sell the house. She assured him that she was not selling the home she kept her promise and two months later she did not sell the home she just abandoned it. Eighty thousand dollars down the drain, but that's what happens when you lack true male leadership from a husband, and you're not financially savvy. Lid now regrets leaving Philly for New Orleans but back in ninety eight he had to get away from Philly his plans to marry his childhood sweetheart foiled as she found another husband, Lid just wanted to get away and New Orleans seemed the most remote and far out place. New Orleans was fun but he lost his religion falling into drug, and alcohol abuse, Muslims don't smoke weed, or drink but being away from his family and Philly Lid forgot about God and forgot about his contract with God. Prayer five times a day, forbid what is wrong and stand up for what's right, give charity, and being humble. The changing political climate also intrigued him and getting out of the south seemed like the smart thing to do, everyone knows that the Presidential election were stolen, driven by his ambition to please his father the forty first President of the United States , forty one his son forty three made a deal with darker figures to win the

White House. No one took to the streets, Americans did not stand up against clear election fraud, and everything was put to rest when the United States Supreme Court ended the recount. What kind of future did America have in front of her? We all just kept going with our lives, going to work, paying bills, watching television, on our own pursuit of happiness when the republic that we should hold dear fell into the hands of the neo republican party. What made us all continue our normal routine and not take to the streets as a whole did we stop caring about our country and started caring more about money? Coming back home to Philly were everything started for Lid and the city where it all started for America in 1776 the declaration of independence marked the birth of a new nation. He thinks about his family, his half brother Sharif's finally home after spending the past ten years behind bars in up state Pennsylvania. Life's always been tougher on Sharif they share the same father but different mothers which made a big difference in their upbringings Sharif's mother was slipped a date rape drug in a bar of North Philly when he was just a toddler. The experience alone of being rapped had devastating effects on Mrs. Jackie, but the date rape drug had lasting effects on her brain and she took her pain out on her new born baby, her son Sharif. When the authorities finally took him away from her, in public she was beating him up punching him in the face closed fisted mercilessly while the three year old was being choked to death with a leather belt. How could you value human life after a gang of brothers decided to rape you? The state took Sharif away and the streets have raised him every since. Lid looked forward to finally spending some time with Sharif running the streets of Philly with his notorious older brother. Word has it that he is that Sharif is a knock out street fighter, a man of honor and respect and would fight you three times in one day to get his point across, but all the memories Lid has are just pure legend since they've spent more time seeing each other in a visiting room as apposed to out in the free world. One day while his baby sister Adesha was playing with the kids in the neighborhood one of the knuckle head boys had pushed her onto the ground busting her pretty face up on the concrete. He's always had a very strict rule about the girls not playing with the boys and this was exactly why. From the back porch of another neighbors house Lid jumps down and smashes the kid for pushing Adesha on the ground. Then he began beating on the kid, when it was all said and done the kid had caught a pretty bad beat down. He was member of the Davys family and they had a pretty big crew like six boys and one girl, and Lid immediately sought out the oldest brother Hakim, to let him know exactly what happened. Hakim agreed that his younger brother was out of order and assured him that he was even going to beat his little brother up for pushing Adesha to the ground. But later that day things changed as Mrs. Davys demanded that Hakim defend his family's honor and so a show down was brewing and as Hakim went around the neighborhood collecting a gang to beat Lid down he just sat on the porch with a baseball bat and his best friend Bilal. And as the day turned into night the gang of six came around the corner and down the street and right before they made it up the front steps one of the neighborhood's old G's brother Muhammad drove by and asked "What was going on?" After both parties explained their sides Muhammad bluntly said "Y'all don't touch him his brother is Golden and this whole city owes him because he kept his mouth shut when he could've talked and brought the whole Black Mafia down." That was it Hakim went back home and Lid went back to his porch. But just off the reputation of his older brother a lot of people didn't mess him and being sheltered a true home body the streets was something he knew very little about. Most niggas will go after money quick drop out of school, get busted for selling drugs, whatever but most don't make it to twenty without a criminal record or better yet without getting a chick knocked up. I always stayed out of that kind of trouble trying to lay the ground work down for his younger sisters and cousins seven girls in total. Being what I believed was a good Muslim. The closest he came to the streets was the occasional nights out with his Uncle Sha, another old G of days of earlier ages always ahead of the trends and at this point of his career his twist was the white collar thing travelers checks, credit cards, and fake bank checks, he always says "They count the time in months with this stuff, it's a no brainer." Optimistic  about the future with a new love and new possibilities things are looking up as he stars out the window of the airplane looking down on God's creations of the blue sky, and white clouds.

The plane lands and patiently he waits for the other passengers to depart. Flying as student has its advantages it's cheap but you must wait for availabability, and most of the time you usually end up in the back of the plane. Once off the plane, he moves through the crowded airport heading towards baggage claim, turning on his cell phone, calling his mother and greeting her with words of peace "As-Salaam Alaikum Mom" "Wa Laikum Salaam baby, did you get off the plane yet?" "Yes I am on my way to baggage claim meet me at arriving flights, did you bring the girls?" "Yes they are with me" In the background Lid hears his sisters yell I'll Lid! "I'm going to kiss the ground when I get outside" "You are so over dramatic". At baggage claim Lid checks the scene out in his bright yellow leather jacket flamboyant as always he casually flirts with some females in baggage claim. Once his luggage comes around he grabs his bags and heads out the automatic doors. Immediately he sees his mom and two sisters, and notices their not wearing the traditional hijab covering their hair. Before he crosses the street true to his word Lid drops his bags, falls down and kisses the ground. And loudly shouts "I love this town!" His sisters meet him half way in the street. They exchange hugs and the 1st son of the 2nd daughter meets his mom's sister Halima on the other side of the street. "As-Salaam Alaikum mom" "Wa Laikum Salaam son boy you are such a drama king this is not Ghost Busters." Like most African American females sister Halima has raised her children alone. She and her husband split when the children were very young and the strength of a race is shown by the actions of its community. At first  alone Halima got help from her family went to nursing school found full time work after graduation and paid all the bills, clothed herself and her children, ran the Sunday school at the mosque, and took care of all the needy children in the neighborhood. The strong African American women did it with three children no boyfriends, and no Halima time if she wasn't at work she was home caring for her children she was caring for others. His father Raheem left his family when they were only six, the old G from Germantown did time up Graters ford prison with the higher ups in the nation of Islam Imam Malik and Chris Valentine and after getting released he was quickly married to sister Halima at the historic Sister Clara Muhammad school by Imam Malik, like so many African American males Raheem was unfaithful to his wife and his family, and the horrible shadow of domestic violence over shadowed their marriage towards the end "truly if I grant you old age you will be reversed in nature" And for sure that is exactly what Raheem did after the divorce completely neglecting the children he brought into this world spending his time chasing joy and fun. They all get into the car and as always since the girls abandoned their home there is a sense of uneasiness as that conversation still looms over them.

"What's the new house like?" "It's got three floors; you and Raquiaa have to share the room on the third floor. Replies Adesha. "Mom why don't the girls stay on the third floor?" Adesha interrupts "Because I get my own room" "It really doesn't matter because I am moving back to Philly in a few months anyway." Lid sharply responds "What's up with the old house?" It's gone, some Korean family moved into the house they got it for sheriff sale for like three thousand." I still can't believe y'all walked away from the house that was equity for our school loans. I asked you if you were going to move, I would've transferred schools or something." "Look boy we are not going to talk about the city was getting way too dangerous and I was worried about Adesha she was falling in with the wrong crowds." "Yeah well that's eighty grand out the window, WOMEN!" "That's enough of that cause I'm ready to put you right back on a plane to New Orleans!" And with that statement Lid shuts his mouth on the ride back from the airport Lid scrolls through his phone calling friends letting them know that he is back in town. His childhood friend Omar is the first person who answers. Omar has done well for himself dropping out of college he's made a name for himself in Delaware and Philly getting arrested on campus shooting somebody, and getting into a few shootouts in Wilmington. Childhood friends since the days of elementary school at Sister Clara Muhammad, they reconnected in high school and the combination of the two drove teachers so mad that by there sophomore years the faculty had arranged it that the two of them would only have home room together and nothing else. The teachers actually got their schedules together and made sure the two of them did not have any classes together. "As-Salaam Alaikum, Omar?" "Wa Laikum Salaam, yo you still down south in Louisiana somewhere?" "Naw I'm back in town the money got funny down there and I had to transfer schools." "So you dropped out?" "Naw I'm at Delaware s State your old school" "Aw man you don't want to go there that's a party school." "Yo I just gotta graduate that's all, plus I wanted to be closer to my family and that stuff with Forty Three yo everybody know he didn't win those elections." "Here you go always got some conspiracy theory or something. It doesn't matter who the President is it's not going to change shit in your world or my world." "I wish you were right but some things up" "Whatever it is boy you ain't gonna stop it, you got some money saved up?" "Yeah but I have to hold on to it for school, and if I don't have to pay them I am going to hold on to it and go up New York."

"Whats up the rotten apple?" "This girl I know" "Nigga its millions of girls in Philly what's your problem?" "You know how I get waited two years to get with Aisha in high school." "Yeah you did and you got her too, so were you staying at?" "At my moms in Delaware." 'What happened to the house uptown?" "We just was arguing about I don't even want to start talking about it." Well Delaware nigga's are sweet; I took an entire block from them in Wilmington in no time." "Yeah well that's not my kind of party they got minimum mandatories and federal sentencing guidelines for that stuff." "Scared money never made no money." The conversation takes a brief pause "I'll be up there this weekend yo, in shah Allah until then be safe cuz As-Salaam Alaikum." "Wa-Laikum Salaam." He hangs up the phone and taps his sister Raqayya "Yo you heard from Ra-Zen since he's been out?" Jokingly she say "Don't be touching me, he's in Philly out of the half way house and I heard he is already in trouble." "You got a number for him?" Sister Halima breaks up the conversation "You know your brother is nothing but trouble, and you are going to end up in jail along with him if you start hanging out with him." "Mom he's not in jail anymore and I am grown my decisions are my decisions." "Well you will not be bringing that nonsense into my house?" "Aren't you renting you walked away from your house, and how are you going to believe some cop?" "The probation officer said he's suspected of killing a few dozen people for hire?" "Yo he's not even supposed to be telling you anything like that." He turns around and begins to continue talking with Raqayya "Can I have that number for him?" It's his girls number Elaina I think he is staying with her. The number is 215-471-3120." "Thanks Lid saves it to his phone, the rest of the ride is pretty quite as Lid reflects on his time in New Orleans, changing his major from Biology to Public Relations, how he lost himself being away from his family picking up bad habits using Marijuana, and drinking conduct so unbecoming of a Muslim, how he stopped making prayer and he thinks about what the future could be reconnecting with Philly and educating his people. They pull up to the new house and the three story town house looks nice from the outside, but unlike the brick built row homes in Philly the houses in the burbs are made out of plastic and Lid is not impressed. Once inside he takes a look around and his mother ask him "So how do you like it?" "How much is the rent 1200.00" "That's fourteen thousand a year, utilities included?" "Nope, that's why y'all better pay rent on time where's my money?" She puts her hand out and Lid quickly says "I need my money to pay for school." "Stop lying boy I heard you on the phone you said you were going to New York to see some girl." Lid smiles that's only if they don't ask me for any money during registration." "Don't worry honey I won't collect anything from you until you get a job." "Thanks mom" Exhausted from the flight Lid falls asleep on the couch. The next morning Lid awakes and makes Fajir prayer, a few hours later the family is all in the kitchen having breakfast. Lid has plans to go to Philly so as soon as she comes downstairs for breakfast he ask "Mom can I hold the car and drive to Philly today? There are some people I would like to go visit and I really would like to go to grandma's house too." "Don't use my mother to soften me up." Just to be in his business she ask him "Who else are you going to see?" "I want to see your brother Uncle Sha and Omar. I'm home mom; I've been gone for an entire year I just want to go see Philly." "She opens the kitchen drawer cabinet and pulls out a pamphlet, "Here boy this is the train schedule for the R2, and I'll drive you to the train station in an hour." Just to be smart Adesha then ask for the car "Can I hold the car to go to the mall later?" "Yes Adesha bird just put gas in it. Lid says nothing he just smiles and goes upstairs to get ready for his train ride. As an adult Lid understands he must have his own and he should never get upset when someone say's no regarding holding something that is there's. Lid also understands the relationship between Adesha and their mother, for years it was just the four of them but things changed after the divorce and the birth of Adesha was like the emancipation of Halima. Soon after his mom and father were not even on speaking terms and Rashad slowly their father was out of their lives. A lot of pressure was put on Halima and Lid to help co-manage the household at the young age of seven. His responsibilities were no linger about himself, he had to take care of his two younger sisters and adhere to pretty much anything his mother asked of him. The quote un quote man of the house syndrome fell on his shoulders like so many African American males, what was different was Halima who stuck to her Islam and never had any relationships for six years until she remarried. During that time period there was no other man in this family's life so with no challenges Lid had established his presence leading prayer, and being a good Muslim. To the best of his ability Lid did what he could washing clothes, dishes, ironing clothes, making breakfast, school lunches, doing homework basically taking over some of the homemaker role which used to belong to the wife as the husband would go to work. But in America the oppressor the rich and powerful have designed a system that changes these rules making the African American female the money maker. The key to conquering a race is destroying the male and because of the inhuman practices of slavery and segregation the American White man has accomplished just that. Lid and Raqayya represented a failed marriage and the pain and turmoil that followed Adesha represented her independence, so Lid walked upstairs feeling hurt but understood exactly what just happened and complaining would not change a thing. Still in the kitchen the women begin to talk amongst each other and depending on the topic of conversation it can be a good thing or a bad thing. "Mom I don't know how long this is going to work the two of us sharing a room on the third floor." "It's only been one night and he didn't even sleep upstairs last night." "There's not enough room for the two of us on the third floor it's only one room." "He knows he has to move soon y'all better make the best of it and no fighting!" Tee finally adds her two cents "Well you are not coming down to my room" Raquyya snaps backs "Well if I wanted to I would!" Sister Halima breaks the whole argument up and says "He will be out in his own apartment by next semester." Upstairs Lid is getting washed and dressed; he gets dressed and throws a change of clothes in a city blue bag. Minutes later Lid trots down the steps and lets his mom know "I'm ready to go to the train station." Sister Halima grabs her keys and they are on their way out the door. As Lid is getting into the car he calls his Uncle Sha. Sha lives by the famous words "I've been everywhere but to work" And that's the truth a member of the nation of Islam and Black Muslim Mafia Sha has been involved in everything from Cocaine sales, real estate scams, pager and cell phone scams, fake check cashing, fake travelers checks, credit cards, and the one time he did try to work it was in the asbestos removal business and he along with a few others swear that they were the first to come up with the idea. Be that as it may Lid really looks up to his uncle Sha because his father has not been in his life and the opposite goes for his uncle Sha who lost his son when he was only fifteen. "As Salam Alaikum Uncle Sha?" "Wa Laikum Salaam nephew I heard you were back in town." "Who told you my moms?" Uncle Sha wakes up and clearly says "Come on brother you I get the information raw and uncut from Shirley." Yeah well I'm going to tell Grand mom you called her by her first name." "Lid you will do anything to get in the good list with her?" "You better believe it the pancakes and ice tea is enough." They both laugh "I'm in the car right now on my way up the city I have to catch the train so I should be there in like an hour and a half." "Man it's early you calling me before twelve o'clock is in total violation, you know how it is around here two o'clock on the weekends if that." "Yeah I'm sorry, so what's up you gonna get me from the train station?" "You gonna stay with us all weekend?" "Yeah I guess so" "I have to run it by Miko but they miss you so it should be cool. I have some things to do this weekend so you can drive, what train station are you getting dropped off at?" "University of Pennsylvania right across the street from Penn Field, I should be there around two o'clock." See you then and don't call this early again As-Salaam Alaikum" he laughs "Wa-Laikum Salaam" On the way to the train station Lid and his mother finally have a chance to talk without the girls being present. He takes the time to confront her about the old house and how it was abandoned. "Mom you know I had plans to fix that house and sell it to pay off my college loans. Why did you lie when I asked you if y'all were going to move and just leave the house?" "Lid I told you Adesha was falling into the wrong crowds and we had to get out of Philly." "But I asked you the summer before if y'all were going to move and you said no." "I would've transferred schools and moved back home then that's equity yo!" "I only paid eighteen grand for that crappy house, it needed a new roof, the back stairs were falling apart and I decided to leave it." "But you lied mom, I asked you if you were going to move and you said no, when you brought that house it was just for you, you and dad brought that house for you and your family" She coldly interrupts "Don't be bringing your dad into this he has had nothing to do with y'all since he left, I paid those bills and took care of y'all buts for years, and I'm still doing it now!" "You wouldn't be if you kept the house I went to college out of state thinking I could return home and sell the house, now it's gone in sheriff's sale and my debt is going to be out of control. Just walking away from the property was stupid." "That's enough boy you better watch your mouth or you will be walking to the train station the rest of the way and you better stay your ass up there in Philly." "Why you cussing at me." "Because I can" "That's no way for a Muslim sister to behave" "You don't see me wearing my scarf anymore, I got news for you I'm not going to part of no hislam." Taken aback Lid is really shocked when he hears this from his mom as they continue to now argue about the house. "You thought wrong, it was my house and I left, you got a problem with that you can just kiss my booty butt."

Lid Just smiles and turns away, his mother is not the same women she was in the old days, she's lost her Islam, her guide with him away in school they missed their prayers and stopped covering their hair, American feminism has turned her into a different person, a person foreign to Lid almost like a rebellious child trapped in the body of a middle aged women. The trust and respect that kept them close in early years was no more feminism caused her to let go of her Islam with no husband or male guide in the house the women went adrift. She no longer lived for the safety and advancement of her children but for herself she felt betrayed by God after being so devout and not once but twice loosing husbands Hadiah had here faith shaken and the foundation of Islam had crumbled. Knee deep in debt, without any equity, his most trusted advisor now reverted back into a teenager the rest of the ride to the train station is silent until Lid brings up a story. "Remember the summer of 1999 when I came back home after college and stayed in the house for a month before moving down to Uncle Sha house?" "I told you boy I don't feel like talking about the house anymore!" "I'm not talking about the house one night when I was sleeping down stairs on the air mattress I had a nightmare. You know how you wake up and you can't move your body but you can see everything around you?" Still upset Halima snaps back "What's your point, that's when a witch has you." "Mom you know we don't believe in anything like that." "When I was younger that's what we used to call it." "I was downstairs on the airbed and I could not move anything except my head and look around. I was laying down so everything was upside down, when I looked in the dining room beyond the dinning room table and up against the wall I saw a shadowy figure, in the dark I thought it was fluffy but on four legs it had these red eyes and was a little bigger than the cat." "Lid what are you talking about?" "When I finally could move again I went to the basement door thinking let me let the cat downstairs, but when I opened it fluffy was at the top of the stairs with this look her eyes were wide open and she had this look like I was trying to get up here and let you know something is up there." "Shut up boy what are you saying you saw a demon in 961?" "That's the year I left and went to college, y'all stopped making prayers right? Why not then no one is making prayer in the house that could lead to a Jinn coming into the house you have the book you know." "I don't believe in that hislam anymore boy you better get yourself together because you have to get out of my house, and figure life out for yourself." Lid says nothing and as they pull up to the train station he graciously gives his mom the greeting's of peace "As-Salaam Alaikum mom, and even though she says she does not believe she still responds out of familiarity or because inside she really knows the right way for her is Islam "Wa-Laikum Salaam." As Lid leaves the car he contemplates to himself is she even still Muslim? did a jinn take hold of his family? Is there anything he could do to save them or himself for that matter?" The train ride on the R2 is quick and crossing into Philly is like a long awaited dream for Lid who has been away from his home town for a year. He sees the city skyline, the back yards of the row homes, center city, and everything is so familiar to him, looking out the window he just smiles, and gets ready to run the streets with his Uncle all weekend. Once off the train he gives his Uncle Sha a call "Yo! As Salaam Alaikum, I'm at the university of Pennsylvania stop you on your way?" "Wa Laikum Salaam for real hahahaha well hold up there a few minutes good brother. I told you it was early for me." "You went back to sleep?" "Hold your horses Sundance I will be there in fifteen minutes." "Alright I will see you when you get here." As-Salaam Alaikum?" "Wa Laikum Salaam" They both hang up and now Lid has to sit at the train station and wait for his Uncle, if he knew he was going to have wait 30th Street would've been much better because it's more crowded. It's pretty desolate at this stop, and other trains stop off at the station the ticket men asked Lid "What train are you waiting for?" Being African American draws a lot of attention especially at Penn even if there are only a few people at the stop, top priority in this part of town is protect the white people, but Lid patiently waits and takes the time to talk to a few friends on the phone. "As Salaam Alaikum Omar? I'm in the city." Still asleep Omar grumble's "Wa Laikum Salaam Cuz you still in Delaware?" "Naw I'm in Philly I got the train and came up here" "Yeah well its early man the only thing I'm talking about is business you copping, cause I got pounds for five?" "I have to talk to my brother about that." "He's home?" "Yeah" "How long did he do?" "Like ten years up state, you know they wanted him to snitch but he didn't so they roofed him." "I know some people in Delaware they could set you up with a corner and everything." "I'm cool but we can talk about that in person at a strip club or something this weekend." "Sounds good were you staying at?" "Out west at my uncles" "Alright I have to go to Wynnefield in the morning he live close to their, you know I don't know shit about no West Philly." "Yeah he's on the other side of the bridge" "See I don't even know what bridge you talking about?"  "Yeah you do right before you get to Overbrook anyway just call me and I'll give you directions As Salaam Alaikum." "Wa Laikum Salaam" They hang up and Lid decides to give Jasmine a call, they met in New Orleans during his second year at Xavier on the way to class in the morning he used to pass an all white Lexus ES with Pennsylvania tags. Now Lid and his friends were the only guys from Philly during their freshman year, and arrogantly he thought he knew all the new freshman during his sophomore year, so every morning he would pass the ES and wonder whose car is this and why don't I know this person? And finally after talking around the camp fire with the rest of the dogs he was put to shame when he admitted he did know who Jasmine was, and from that point on he was on a mission to meet her and find out what all the talk was about. It wasn't until spring semester that he finally found out who this mystery person was. Lounging around in the administration building before class Lid and his friends were just talking messing with girls, having fun when all of a sudden the crowded hallway split like the red sea, and everyone moved out of the way as Jasmine walked down the hallway. Almost walking right past Lid on the way to class completely out of character stopped her and asked a question he already knew the answer to, "Is your name Jasmine?" "She stopped and her brown eyes light up and she graciously replied "yes" Lid stuck and not knowing what to ask just took a moment to capture her beauty, her smile was so genuine and she used every bone in her cheeks and face, the dark blue dress and her caramel skin went together perfectly and Lid was truly at a loss for words. Surprisingly he did not have to do anything as she began to hold conversation with him. "And you are?" "Lid I'm from Philly, and I know everybody from Philly and I don't know you so you must not be from Philly?" Surprised he challenged her about her home town she gives Lid a little attitude and says "I'm from Philly and you don't know me so I guess you don't know everyone from Philly." "What high school did you go to?" "Milton Hershey" "That's not in Philly sweat heart, you ain't from Philly." Taken aback Jasmine smiles and says "I have to get to class." "Bye" A lot of eye contact was made in just seconds and before she walks away she smiles and says "nice to meet you" "Same here we'll be watching" As she walked away Lid does not look as the rest of the guys take a look at Jasmine's rear assets. From that point on he chased Jasmine like Captain Ahab in Moby Dick all over campus, and she played along until the summer break when both of them went home to Philly.

The phone rings and rings and finally her answering machine picks up, and Lid leaves a message "Hey I'm back home; I'm going to catch the bus to New York next weekend." As he leaves a message the phone clicks on the other line and its Jasmine calling him back. "As Salaam Alaikum I'm leaving a message on the other line babe. She replies softly Wa Laikum Salam" I just got home last night, can I catch the bus up to see you next weekend?" "You can come up on the bus right now silly, I don't know how much time we can spend together because I have to work, and we have group study sessions tomorrow." "On a Sunday, that's crazy" "I know but it's the only day everyone can get together outside of class. "Next week would be better but it's up to you babe." "I'm waiting for my Uncle to pick me up at the train station now and as usual he's late." "The one whose house I went to and he said look what Santa brought me when he answered the door?" "Yeah that uncle, it was cracking up when he told me that upstairs." Jasmine sharply replies "Well it wasn't funny the way you were acting though, how could you turn so cold and stop talking to me." "You had another man in the bedroom; I could've killed dude and you for that matter" "I thought we were not going to bring that up." "You brought it up in the first place!" "I'm sorry I just wasn't ready to be with just one man, it's my life and I can do whatever I want to do." "That's where ya wrong it's not just your life it's our life and you didn't take me into consideration coming home and seeing things like that." "I'm sorry, so when are you coming up here today or next week?" "Next week" "I will see you then babe I love you" "Ditto As salaam Alaikum" "Wa Laikum Salam" They both hang up the phone and in such a short period of time Jasmine and Lid had a lot of history and when they went home in the summer of 2000, she took him in like a stray dog and like a special edition comic book it was Batman and Wonder Women teaming up for a limited engagement. Lid would accompany Jasmine everywhere which really made things awkward because she couldn't pick up any guys, and as the summer went along she stopped talking to or about any other guys and it was just the two of them. The problem was intimacy both being Muslim they knew the rules you have to be married and just having

Lid around like that was wrong, but both of them showed restraint until Jasmine brought some guy home. On evening after work Lid comes home and Jasmine is home in the bedroom with what sounds like another man. Lid grabs the bottle of Puerto Rican rum and storms in the room and to his dismay she's in the bed with some Puerto Rican guy. Heartbroken Lid steps into the bedroom door and calmly ask "What are you doing?" whatever was going on had stopped as he turned the bedroom light on and the guy immediately gives Jasmine a hug and leaves. Jasmine goes on through the night trying to explain what happened how she was attracted to the guy because he was an ex con and how this was her apartment and Lid had no right to open the front door with his key and come inside without calling. Then SShe goes on to explain how they would never be a couple because Lid is light skin he doesn't even fit the criteria of the man she's attracked to. Everyday and night together for a whole summer and that was her story? Lid says nothing still heartbroken he finishes the bottle of rum and falls asleep on the couch, in the morning he packs his things, and with the reality that she might be losing him her story changes. Mikhial lies and says that he was coming right back but in reality he knew and she knew as well that was the last time they would share the apartment and those memories and as he walked out the door Jasmine started to understand that when dealing with Lid there will always be consequences to her actions. Fighting the guy wouldn't of made any difference the responcibility fell on her shoulders not to let him get that close, that fast and the only way that happened is if she wanted it to happen so here is the consequence you loose Lid and so she did until Portia gave him her numbers the following spring semester after she transfered schools and moved to New York.

Lid takes a look at his watch and twenty minutes have gone by, and he begins to walk upstairs to the street level and once up top he calls his Uncle Sha and no one answers, and just as Lid is about to leave a message a gold mini van pulls around the corner and talking on his cell phone while eating a sandwich Uncle Sha smiles through the semi tinted window at his nephew. He jumps into the passenger side of the mini van and gives his Uncle the greetings "As Salam Alaikum?" "Wa Laikum Salam black man, what are you staying for a week you packed a big bag?" "Man I gotta change clothes for tonight were going to work later right?" "No I'm going to work, your just going to look cool and hang out with all the gangsters, and flirt with girls." "Yeah well that's what Sinatra did y'all better start calling me old green eyes." They both bust out in laughter, then whoever Uncle Sha is talking to on the telephone comes back on the line. "No way man! Its two parts the two's have thirteen numbers and the three's have fourteen numbers. Only fifty seven work out of the eighty that you got after a week of having the box! Meet me tonight at the social club!" Shamp's hangs up the phone, and finishes his sandwich, with food still in his mouth he begins to explain the faults we have as African American s regarding business especially illegal activity. "Nephew stay legal because you can be as sharp as a razor on your end but the people you deal with are a mess and never have anything together. And that will lead to both of y'all getting locked up. It takes this guy two days to get this box over to me, for two days he's like he is going to bring it after having it for a week. The other day it was the kids, yesterday it was some other stuff and he just stopped answering the phone. He finally brings it over to me and in a week you would think he had five hundred numbers on it and it only has eighty numbers. And fifty seven of them work. Time nephew black folks have no commitment to time and efficiency everyone thinks it's a game. I could've gave that box to Dee and he has this girl works at Fridays and would've been had it back and filled with numbers. "Confused Lid just ask "What box?" Uncle Sha laughs and replies "O yeah you've been gone for a year the last thing you remember is the American Express checks, I'll show you when we get to the lab." "You had boxes of checks like five hundred thousand in traveler's checks man that was crazy!" "Yeah I had to tone that down for a while FBI had a special investigation niggaz buying them from me using them in Philly to buy stuff, Philly the fraud capitol of the country! I tell them every time to take those checks out of state or down south and nobody wants to listen." "Yeah well that's the life, they just better not be snitching on you. So what's the agenda for tonight?" "Hold up lets talk about school. You didn't drop out or anything did you?" "No I transferred to Delaware State." Uncle Sha rolls his eyes and exclaims "Oh lord that's a party school I know that." "What happened down South?" "A few things I went there because I wanted to be a doctor, but that stuff did not work the chemistry was on a whole nother level. So I'm paying all this money to major in public relations at a school that is not even known for its communications department? Then mommy left the house uptown and there goes my equity." 'Yeah my sister made a real dumb move walking away from eighty thousand in property value. She should've called me I would've at least got her fifty thousand for it minus my cut." "Yeah well I needed that Unc that was part of my decision for going to such an expensive school." "So what about my Christmas gift where is she at?" Lid just bust out laughing I was just talking to her on the train platform and we brought that up." "What she's down there waiting for the train?" And uncle Sha quickly motions to make a u-turn when Lid stops him. "No No No I was talking to her on the phone, she's in New York I'm going up their next weekend." "Oh because I ready to make that u-turn" "I see, we spent some time together in New Orleans over the summer, but that's not why I transferred." Uncle Sha frowns his face as if to say stop lying "Alright she had a lot to do with the decision moving back up here especially after the last few weeks we were together in New Orleans. We went to the essence fest concerts together, and spend the days together, I was spending the night over her moms house, the whole nine yards the last night I put Frank on and it was a done deal. A'int nobody ever played no Sinatra for her, then "Summer Wind" came on and I kept playing that we feel asleep outside all hugged up touching is so crazy yo, the summer wind was blowing I'll never forget that night. The morning I leaving for up here, so she had to go to the dentist so we at the dentist office like kids yo, love punches, I'm smacking her on the but, nibbles on the neck, then finally when I was ready to leave she kissed me, I kissed her it was like magic, pure, like we kissed before a thousand times in past lives, and finally things were right and we found each other again." "Damn nephew she really moved you?" Lid exhales "Yeah she had a lot to do with me leaving New Orleans and moving up here, the elections, and money issues too." "Well there's nothing wrong with that nephew just don't put all your eggs in one basket women change like the wind brother." "Thanks for the advice Unc. What's up with the mini van yo? What happened to the big boy Benz?" Uncle Sha lets out a big exhale and deeply sighs Miko crashed it up going to work in the morning, a fucking tire falls off a tractor trailer!" "What a tire came off the tractor trailer!" "Naw the truck was carrying tractor trailer tires like a flat bed and one of those tires for the tractor trailers falls off onto ninety five. She tries to avoid it you know she has whip game and crashed along the divider between ninety five south and ninety five north." "Is she alright?" "Yeah the Benz for that matter was wrecked, I mean wrecked." "So y'all got insurance, they ain't pay for it?" "Yeah the damage was way too much they cut us a check and I picked up an Expedition and this mini van." Lid begins to rap "I pull up in the expedition and the girls be like no no no no no he didn't." "The trucks hers, she took the Benz thing pretty hard. I'm stuck with this but it's like "Get Shorty" hey it's the Cadillac of mini vans." They pull up to the house and waiting at the front door is Lid's younger cousins Naim and Khadejah. One year apart Khadejah is eight and Naim is seven, like younger versions of their parents the kids have pretty much ran the house from day one, one of their earliest adventures involved them pushing over the spring water from the tank and lying in the spring water as it poured to onto the floor. When their parents finally awoke and found the kids playing in the water they proclaimed they were taking a bath. But the kids have always been pretty self reliable and trustworthy, and after not seeing their big cousin for a year they took off out the door at first sight of Lid. "I thought I told y'all to stay in the house when no one is home?" Uncle Sha pleas go on deaf ears as Lid is already out of the car and giving Khadejah a hug, always happy she exclaims "It's been like forever since the last time you were here, were you been at?" "You know I was in college, your getting tall Miss Lady" Naim interrupts and shakes hands with Lid "As Salam Alaikum?" "Wa Laikum Salaam" "What she means is you usually come home in the summer time man what happened?" "You better ask your Aunt Halima about that one Naim, but long story short I'm back home now and that's it." "So are we going to play Star Wars master Jedi?" "I don't know man I'm getting a little too old to be running around the neighborhood with broom sticks and the Star Wars soundtrack playing in the background." Naim shattered by his cousin's responds say's "I know man Star Wars is getting corny" "Come here Khadejah, so what's going on with you grown lady?" She smiles and they march upstairs and into the house. Lid and Khadejah have a special bond he's her only older male cousin and when she was born Lid spent a lot of time at the house taking care of both Miko and baby Khadejah. Uncle Sha was on the other side of town with his girlfriend Angela, and he and Miko got very close like brother and sister outside of Uncle Sha Miko too has never really had another trusting male in her life. She had a very rough child hood and rumor has it she used to jump out of her fathers window to run the streets all night with Uncle Sha when she was a teenager. Uncle Sha heads upstairs to the third floor Lid continues to kick it with his little cousins for a while. Sitting down on the couch watching television Khadejah is the spitting image of her mother, Lid has a seat next to her and lowers his voice to almost a childlike tone. "So what's going on in your world Khadjah?" She smiles as if she was waiting for him to ask and begins to run off a list of girly things. "Well mom is taking me to the hair dressers today I think I am going to cut my hair." "Don't do that it's so beautiful long the way it is." "Yeah I know but I get tired of having to do it all the time. I might get my nails done, the hamster Bubbles died inside the ball, hahahaha we lost him in the house one day and then he turned up dead inside the ball. Were getting a Guinea pig from the pet store tomorrow. I'm the best at double Dutch on the block, and my mom is taking me out for new school clothes, she brought me some clothes last week you want to see them?" "Maybe later, your birthday was in July I missed it." She sighs "I know but I have some gifts you could buy me." And out of nowhere she pulls out the circulars from department stores, toys r us, target, Wal-Mart, and Macy's, and starts to point at possible gifts. Lid starts to laugh "I'll get you something from Toys R Us the next time we go". Naim excited about hearing toys r us mentioned loudly interrupts "Toys R Us!" when are we going?" "Not today!" Lid gets up and darts towards the stairs, "Where are you going Lid?" "I'm going upstairs to the lab to talk with your dad. "Is your mother home?" Naim replies "No she's at work" And Lid takes off upstairs, out of Islamic tradition and respect Lid makes sure his aunt is not home before he goes running through the house, upstairs the lab is decked out with six different computers, three desk top computers and three high end lap top computers, on desk top is connected to a gigantic forty inch monitor uncle Sha uses the giant screen to get close ups of check duplication's because when recreating checks he needs very precise details. In one corner stands the two towers each machine can make up to sixteen DVD's or sixteen cd's at on time so that's thirty two copies made in minutes. The cheetah machine used for creating identity cards like state id's, or driver's licenses, and credit cards. Lid looks around the office and then begins to scurry around things like a kid in a candy store he keeps asking his uncle what does this do?" "Uncle Sha say's nothing and concentrates on his work he has to focuses on the drivers license, it must be perfect to fake out store clerks, cops, and bank tellers the drivers license must be a complete replica of a real one complete with hologram's and all. Lid continues to scurry about the office and goes into the closet, this action catches the eye of his Uncle Shamp's and he stops what he is doing. "Stay out of the closet!" Startled Lid answers back "The guns are in the closet aren't they? Let me see the M-16 please?" "I don't know what you are talking about but stay out of that closet! All this equipment a t-shirting printing press, a cd duplicator, the internet on every computer with every design program imaginable and the first thing you do is mess with my machine guns." "So you still do have an M-16." Uncle Sha just start to laugh and goes back to his computer for work. Lid takes heed to his uncle's warnings and takes a seat next to him by the computer. "What are you doing?" "Duplicating this driver's license the cheetah allows me to make a license with the holograms just like the real versions." "What programs are you using?" "Photoshop" Uncle Sha grabs a book off one of the printers and hands it to Lid. "Photoshop for dummies, alright I'll read it." Sick and tired of looking at books Lid brushes past a few pages after being engrossed in text books for the last three years the last thing he wants to look at is another text book at least until school starts back up. Uncle Sha phone rings and he starts yapping away, there's a knock on the office door and Naim appears holding two broom sticks and has a grin on his face "Do you remember the force master Jedi?" Lid searching the room looking for a weapon to defend himself with and in the corner he sees and old mop, he jumps up and grabs the mop, and Naim tries to stop him almost smashing his cousin in the head with his two broom sticks, but Lid dodges it. "Young Jedi your training is incomplete you should've struck me when you had the chance." All of a sudden they are exchanging fast and furious attacks at each other. Uncle Sha stops his phone conversation and yells at both of them "I know y'all must be crazy none of that stuff in my office!" Without breaking stride Naim and Lid move out of the office and into the hallway of the third floor, back and forth they go click clang click, "The force is strong in you young Jedi, but you are too aggressive." Naim answers back "you are not the boss of me" The two cousins continue to furiously clash down the winding stairs down the steps and back up again click, clash, Naim takes a wild swing that Lid dodges but the blinds on the window don't share the same fate. They both stop and give each a shocked look as the blinds been knocked off the window, Naim not knowing what to do thinks about what his mom is going to say when she gets home and sees the blinds destroyed. Lid takes a wild swing a Niams knees taking advantage of the opportunity "Ahhhh!" Screams Naim "Your thoughts betray you young Jedi. We are not finished with your training." Upset about the cheap shot Naim losses all control and unleashes a fury of attacks on his cousin, Lid trying to dodge all the attacks slips up and Naim nails him right upside the head. "Ahhh!" Naim has no reaction as he keeps attacking and the two move down stairs into the living room, where they battle right in front of the television blocking Khadijah's view, "Get out the way dummies!" Exhausted from fighting Lid finally calls a quit and exclaims "Your training is over for now young Jedi." They both drop the broom sticks and Lid heads to the spring water fountain. "I gotta get something to drink I'm exhausted." "What are we going to do about blinds? My mom is going to get mad when she sees that." Khadijah jumps off the couch "Oooh what did y'all break!? I'm telling" Lid and his cousins run upstairs to examine the scene, "The blinds fell, but the window is o.k. I'll just pick these up and put them back on the window." As he hangs the blinds up his stomach begins to turn as the lower part of the blinds are completely shattered and pieces are falling to the floor. "I'm telling mommy when she gets home!" "Come on Khadeja stop being a snitch" "Yeah I'll take you to seven eleven if you don't snitch." She contemplates and agrees to the deal with a slight head nod. Lid goes back upstairs to his uncle's office, and as soon as he hits the door Uncle Shamp's exclaims "Are y'all done acting like fools?" "Yeah Unc you know I have to play Star Wars with my little cousin, he ain't seen me in like a year. Plus all those years of having no boy cousins to play with I've been waiting for this for years." "Yeah well y'all better not have broken anything because Miko is on her way home and she is going to flip if y'all did." Lid and Maim look at each other and smile, "So young nephew what's the buzz tell me what's happening on college campuses? Besides the girls?" "You know they had some young boys on campus trying to your thing using a laminator selling ids for twenty bucks a piece. Mid way through the semester they got busted though, and I'm still chasing Jasmine." "You told me." "Besides that the main thing we talk about is the elections Unc." Lid gets very serious as he speaks about a subject he holds dear. "I still don't believe Forty Three won, as always I watched the election night coverage and I was excited because I saw Florida go Blue and I thought to myself this is a done deal, it's no way Gore is going to lose. I sat in my apartment and watched Florida go from blue to white, and by morning it was red. But it was how it happened I've been watching election coverage since 88, and I've never seen a state called wrong. I went to sleep after they called it blue, and then in the middle of the night something woke me up and I turned the television on and it was white too close to call, and by morning it was red. Then the whole issue of the hanging chadds, the recount, and then James Baker got off an airplane in Florida and everything stopped. Now he was Forty Three seniors secretary of state and during the Forty Two years he was out of sight out of mind then all of a sudden he shows up in Florida and the recount is halted the Supreme Court then stepped in but the tide turned when the news showed Baker get off that airplane and from that point on George W. Forty Three had won the elections. That's it we did not take to the streets, revolt, or even question what was happening nothing." "So what does that have to do with you nephew?" "Everything that's election fraud man, I had a conversation with some students at school old New Orleans money and they were all messed up talking about they were going to vote for Forty Three . I told them he was a puppet for the industrial military complex you know what Eisenhower warned us about in his last speech. If elected the military would be back in action and this country was going to go down a dark path all for corporations and less and less concern for people and the environment for that matter. I also told them that corporations would take power over the government and a new age would dawn, a new America not the policing force or peace keeping force of old days but the sole super power of the world playing the antagonist." "Impressive, what did the students say?" "They listened and did some research on Forty Three his work history, education level, and a few days later they came back and agreed that Forty Three would be a puppet President and they said they were going to vote for Gore." "But Forty Three won anyway?" "I know Unc that's part of the reason I am up here something's going to happen. I read a political satire cartoon in the news paper when I was down south it had Russian President Putin and Forty Three together and the caption read "Summer Camp is Over" something's going down." "Like what Lid?" "I don't know but I really want to be close to family, I miss my family, and Jasmine's closer so that's a bonus." Lid and Sha conversation is interrupted by a very unpleasant and loud "What the HELL is going on in here!!!! What happened to my blinds!!!" It's Miko and she immediately yells for her children NAEEM, KHADEEJA!!! Get up here now!" No one moves, Naim tries to hide in the closet but his father tells him otherwise "You better get down there" his face frowns up as he is about to hear the music for breaking the blinds, and Khadejah trots up the stairs and starts whining to her mother already upset because this is cutting into her cartoon time, she folds immediately keeping her promise that she would tell she spills the beans "Naim and Lid were playing stupid star wars mom I didn't do anything." "Who?" "Hi Miko!" Lid yells from the office and Naim proceeds to come down stairs to face the music, "We were playing Star Wars mom it fell it was an accident." Miko immediately comes upstairs to the office not as upset her voice is lowered and as she walks into the office she lets Lid know "You paying for those blinds nigga." All attitude Miko snaps her neck and points her freshly painted finger at Lid, uncle Sha goes back into his computer and instantly transforms from cool Uncle to loving husband. "I told y'all to stop that didn't I? What did they do to the blinds Miko?" "That nigga broke them the whole bottom part is cracked all up they got pieces of the blinds all over the floor. I brought them from IKEA; I bet they don't even have them anymore. What's wrong with you man?" Lid just smiles, and Miko tries to stay mad but after a few seconds she just smiles too "It aint funny" "I'm not laughing" replies Lid and softly he says "I'm sorry". Miko walks over to her husband and takes a seat on her lap and the two of them engage in husband and wife love talk. Lid turns his head and smiles wishing for the day he could be in love like that. "How was work love?" "The same old mess it's a mad house on Saturdays." "Do you like my hair?" She tosses her long thick black hair around "It looks beautiful dear" they share a few kisses and during a break Miko exclaims "I want snow crabs tonight for dinner" "Anything you want love" Uncle Sha is completely under her spell but who wouldn't be half black, half Filipino the mix of genes have produced a very unique women with big brown eyes, light skin, and long straight black hair, with legs and hips like a sista Miko is the total package.  Feeling a little out of place Lid gets up to leave the office and give them some privacy but before he is clear his aunt asked "Where are you going?" "To seven eleven why you guys want something?" "Look at you if we didn't ask you wouldn't of said anything. Niggas" "I was trying to give y'all some alone time and creep out of the room." "Well bring me something back from the store and we will be square about the blinds." "I want a Klondike bar, two bags of hot cheese popcorn, and a red bull." Uncle Sha reaches in his pocket and pulls out a roll of bills and gives Lid a crisp twenty. "Alright hears my order a big bag of Utz honey BBQ chips, a can Pepsi, a pack of kool milds, entamins cinnamon rolls a four pack, and get the kids something." Lid grabs the twenty and writes down the orders, "Hold up don't give him any money he just broke our blinds he has to pay for that." "Come on Miko I'm in college I don't have any money." "Stop lying you know you are stacking boy." "Naw I have to pay for registration and buy new books." He quickly changes the subject so that's cinnamon rolls, a Pepsi, a pack of kool mild's, BBQ chips." "Naw don't forget the UTZ honey BBQ chips." "Yeah two bags of hot cheese popcorn, a Klondike bar, and a red bull?" They both say "Right". Lid leaves the office and heads downstairs as he passes the second floor he sees Naim in his room cleaning up. "Where you going?" "To seven eleven, I guess this was your punishment for Star Wars?" "Yeah, are we going to play later?" "You better believe it." They both smile, "Do you want something from seven eleven?" Naim stops cleaning "Yeah I want five laffy taffy's, a bag of hot cheese pop corn, a bag of cheese curls, and five bazooka Joes. I have some money let me get it." Naim closes the door and goes into his secret stash seconds later he appears with a hand full of change. "How much?" "Just give me a dollar in quarters and we will be square, why did you close the door it's not like I am going to raid your change stash." "I know but I can't let Khadijah find out where my secret stash is at and if you know then you'll tell her you're a sucker for those sighs." Naim's telling the truth so Lid doesn't even argue and just says "Whatever" as he trots down the steps. When he gets downstairs Khadejah is on the couch still watching television "Where are you going?" "To seven eleven wanna come?" Excited she smiles and says "Yes, you gonna buy me something?" "You don't have any money?" using her skills Khadejah sighs and makes a somber face and solemnly says "No". Lid folds just as Naim called it seconds ago "I'll buy you something come on." Lid walks towards the door and Khadijah goes to the mirror behind the living room closet to fix her hair. "Girl if you don't come on who are you going out to impress?" She smiles "nobody but I can't be outside looking a mess." "You like eight, uh excuse me but I'll be nine on my next birthday." "Yeah next year come on girl." They both exit the house together and walk to the store Khadijah can never walk to the store alone, she always must be escorted, protected so she takes this opportunity to complain about not being able to go to the store alone. "You know they don't let me go anywhere by myself, it's not fair I can't even walk to seven eleven alone and it's only down the street." "That good Khadijah we have to protect you and keep you out of harms way anything could happen to you out here in just a few seconds you are very beautiful and good hearted and this world is full is evil hearted human beings who would definitely try to hurt, plus we don't want any dumb boys trying to talk to you." "I'll boys I hate boys" "Right now you do but in time that will change." As soon as they get inside the store she takes off for the slur pie machine, Lid just rolls his eyes knowing this is not going to be the last thing she wants from the store. Lid begins to grab the food a Pepsi, the Klondike bars, the cinnamon rolls, the honey BBQ chips, and three bags of hot popcorn and cheese curls. He then proceeds to the checkout line and in perfect harmony Khadijah is finished making her slur pie and right next to him in line. "Yeah let me get a pack of kool mild's and a pack of Newport's" "I'll cigarettes nasty." Yeah I got to quit one day, oh yeah go to the candy aisle and get ten leafy taffy's and five bazooka Joes for your brother." Can I get a pack of Mike & Ikes please?" "Go ahead just hurry up" She quickly returns with way more candy and drops it all on the counter "I thought you said just some Mike&Ikes?" She smiles and as usual Lid smiles back and just says "Whatever". "Alright the total is going to be twenty six seventy eight." That's a little more than the twenty dollars Uncle Sha gave Lid and Lid goes into his pocket dipping into his stash pulling out a ten dollar bill. After the cashier gives him his change Khadejah grabs the bag of candy and Lid grabs the other two, and they leave the store and begin to walk back home, Khadejah is preoccupied sipping on her slur pie and eating candy, and Lid is thinking about the ten dollars he just broke in the store knowing he has to pay for college registration next week. When all of a sudden as they cross the street walking towards them is a pretty young thang on a collision coarse with Lid. She's so slender but her tight light blue jeans poke out her ass and hips, and her beautiful brown skin just resonates with the sunlight, her lips are so bold and perfect they make you want to just hang on to her bottom lip for dear life after a kiss, and her big brown eyes are staring right at Lid as she tries to act like she's not. Her neck and shoulders are all out in the open and she has to be a young girl because her tithes look new, and she is coming right at Lid. Usually shy an not very aggressive Lid would be a fool to pass up this opportunity and as she passes by they exchange a slow stare down of glances but as he smiles she rolls her eyes giving off an impression like why you sweating me and Lid keeps going, then he takes a look back to check out her booty and even though she's a young girl she's fucking because that thing is plump and phat. The tag on her blouse is sticking up and Lid uses this opportunity to say something to her, and he darts back towards the girl and gently taps her on the shoulder and softly ask "Excuse me miss?" The girl ignores him and keeps walking he's persistent and again opens his mouth to let her know "Your tag is up on your shirt." Embarrassed she stops, and her next motion is breathtaking as she constructs those perfect lips to form a smile and says "thank you". "What's your name?" "Sequita" she replies "You have a boyfriend?" "No", "Were you going to seven eleven?" "Yeah I have to get groceries for my grandmother." "Oh thank heaven" they both share a giggle "Can I walk with you?" Seeing he has bags in his hands she ask "didn't you just come back from the store?' "Yeah but I wanna walk with you, so we can talk some more get to know each other." Flattered Sequita's face blushes again and with bags in hand the two of them walk side by side. Khadejah and after thought is well ahead of Lid and Sequita and she comes back laughing away at her cousin she ask "You want me to take the bags?" "Yeah I will watch you cross the street, and go straight into the house." Lid and Sequita watches as Khadejah crosses the street and then jogs up the steps into the house. "So what grade are you in?" "I'm in the eleventh I go to Saint Mary's school off Tabor Road in German town." "Good I like Catholics, I just transferred from Catholic school in New Orleans they were very nice to this old Yankee." "So you in college?" "Yeah I go to Delaware s State now." "Oh that's a party school."Lid laughs "I know everyone keeps telling me that." The two continue to walk side by side exchanging glances on the way to the store "So are you in the game?" "No way Quita I'm in college, I help out when I can but money isn't everything plus my brother just got out after doing ten, my cousin upstate doing ten, my other cousin is down south doing a twenty five year bid somebody has to stay home in the free world." "What about you're Uncle? What happened to that Benz he used to have? And what's up with that girl he's with who is she?" Shocked by her bluntness Lid answers the later question first "That girl is his wife" "she's young" replies Sequita, "yeah well I have no comment about that. The Benz was totaled in an accident and no comment bout my Uncle and the game." Once inside the store she grabs her groceries and Lid gets a soda and when she puts her groceries on the checkout counter right before she is ready to pay Lid steps in and gives the cashier a twenty to pay for everything. "What are you doing?" "I'll pay for the groceries, chivalry not dead." The cashier smiles and Samantha says "Thank you" and again treats Lid to that heavenly smile. And on the way back home they once again exchange glances and finally Lid ask "Can I have you… Oh I mean can I have your number? May be we can go out to the movies or something?" "O.k. but don't be calling me all kinds of times at night." "I'm not crazy I wouldn't do that." Lid gives her his phone and they giggle together as she tries to work the phone, and put her number in it." "Alright Sequita I'll see you soon." "Where you gonna take me?" "I don't know the movies or something; you're kind of young so I'll have to call you my social worker case." "You better not; I've dated guys older than you." Only in the hood, only in the hood hey you didn't even ask me my name?" "It's Lid; the kids scream it up and down the block all the time, that's how I know he's your uncle." Lid smiles she's been checking him out for years, "Can I have a hug" "No, I just met you." Lid frowns and shrugs his shoulders, "Come here boy, and Sequita and Lid both grab each other and share a hug, she smells great like bath and body perfume, and after a few seconds they let go of each other." He gives her the I'll call you motion by closing his three inside fingers, leaving out the pinky and thumb and places them to his ear. Lid jogs across the street and trots up the stairs and true to form before he walks through the front door he jumps in the air and taps his heals, happy about his latest conquest.

The night befalls Philly and after working in front of the computer all day designing bank checks, driver's license, and credit cards, the hard part is completed and now it's time for fun.  Up in the office Uncle Sha and Lid prepare to make a mass exodus out of the house, as the kids are asleep and Miko is in the master bedroom filled from her snow crabs and half asleep. Quietly Lid ask "What time are we leaving for work tonight?" "Soon take my suitcase and put it downstairs in the living room and you better get ready now because when I come out the bathroom I'm going to be fully dressed and I'm going straight down the steps and out the door, I don't want to wake her." Lid nods his head and ask "can I have some Versace blue jeans cologne?", "Just a little bit that's my favorite but I wouldn't want to do anything to mess up tangerine man's night on the town." Quietly they both laugh he gets up to go the bathroom, completely changed from earlier in the day Lid has on orange and black Bo Jackson Nike's, dark blue polo jeans, orange polo t-shirt whose words are written in blue matching the jeans perfectly topping everything off is his orange fitted Phillies baseball hat with the matching blue P. Inside the bathroom he brushes his teeth one more time trying to loose the cigarette smell from his breathe. He grabs the bottle of cologne from the medicine cabinet and grabs the cologne and sprits on his wrist, neck, and chest and then leaves the bathroom. When Lid returns to the lab the computers are all off and Uncle Sha gets up out of his chair for the first time since he left to pick Lid up from the train station and stretches. "I'm a genius I should've went to MIT." He hands Lid the suitcase and comments "I said you can have some not take a bath in it" "It's my favorite man?" "Mines too I hope you didn't use all of it." "Naw it's some left" laughing Lid grabs the suitcase and heads downstairs as Uncle Sha makes his way to the bathroom. Naim and Khadejah are asleep in their bedroom, Khadejah has her own room on the third floor but she still sleeps on the bunk beds with her brother because she hates sleeping alone upstairs. Miko is asleep in the master bedroom, with the television still on, Lid creeps down the steps trying not to press down to hard on the wooden floors and cause them to creek, but all his effort is wasted when the old steps leading to the living room cry out like a hungry infant needing a bottle. "Sha" Miko says quietly half awake and half asleep, Lid says nothing and continues downstairs. He sits on the couch  and patiently waits for his uncle, about a fifteen minutes later Lid hears the bathroom door open on the third floor and in seconds Uncle Sha is down the steps and on the second floor as he passes the master bedroom Miko yells "Sha!" but by the time the last s is sounded he is already down the steps Lid takes the Q and with suitcase in hand opens the front door and out the door he goes, followed by Uncle Sha and right before the door closes you hear Miko say again "Sha!" as he locks it shut.  Lid immediately goes to the Expedition and stands next to the driver's side, "The Van nephew, it's like Get Shorty". "Well I'm DJing this party" Uncle Sha unlocks the doors and Lid hops in the passenger side. Uncle Sha follows in the driver's side and reminds Lid "don't mix your cd's with mines because they will disappear." "Yeah I'm still missing my funk flex big kap cash money""Cool" and Lid breaks out his cd's a little NAS, Biggie, Jay-Z, and DJ Clue." Cruising to the music the two are off and the first stop is Dona's on 52$^{nd}$ and Market streets. The old heads bar of choice the outside is a big boy Benz's convention as the parking lot for KFC, and around the bar is full of nothing but four hundred series Benz's and up. Dona's has the best drinks in West Philly, they have the most liquor which of coarse makes them the best drinks, plus with the older crowd there's no riff raff and violence everyone is just out to have a good time. At the door stands Mr. Barry who as always is dressed like a gangster from the nineteen thirties. Draped in a three piece suit and hat to match he greets Uncle Sha. Eyes deadlocked with Uncle Sha he says "What's up Sha?" and then he cracks a smile, they share a common bond like most African American males he too has been everywhere except to work and he gives Uncle Sha a hug. "I'm chilling trying to make another million, how bout you?" "It's all good, who's this?" "That's my nephew he's back from college he's studying to be a lawyer gonna be my Tom Hagen." Mr. Barry laughs and them proceeds to pat down Lid once finished he opens the door and commands Lid to "Enter young blood". Inside Dona's Uncle Shapes is already being met with hands shakes from the old heads and hugs and kisses from the older ladies, dressed in sharp evening gowns. You would think there was some kind of banquet with all the suites and dresses but in reality this is the way everyone always dressed on the weekends just for a few drinks and fun. Shaped like a horse shoe the bar sites in the center, and just about every seat around it sits a patron. In the corner there are a few poker machines an in front of them reminiscent of Atlantic City sits two old ladies, and Uncle Sha take the moment to say "This must be the off night for AC." As he steps a few paces ahead of Lid still shaking hands and giving out hugs. Towards the back of the bar sits two giant sixty inch televisions and surrounding the screens on goers check out the boxing match on screen and sports center on another, sitting in the corner keeping company with the two best looking women in the place is the owner Mr. Hill sipping a bottle of champagne, and as Uncle Sha makes his way to him Mr. Hill helps makes a space for his long time acquaintances. Lost in the ruckus Lid catches the eyes of a few cougars at the bar, and a few seconds later he catches up with his Uncle who is now chit chatting with Mr. Hill. "Hey this is my nephew Lid" "Hey you doing sonny, what's a young guy like you doing in a place with all these old heads?" "It's to be here at least you know there won't be any dumb stuff with you guys." "Smart man" replies Mr. Hill and they shake hands, "Call me Mr. Hill but loosen up kid and relax your making me nervous." Mr. Hill calls over the bar tender

"Hey get these guys some drinks!" Lid steps forward to place his order "Hey you got any Guinness?" "You have to speak up honey." "DO YOU HAVE ANY GUINESS?!" She frowns her face one because Lid spoke really loud, secondly because Lid's the first person ever to ask for a Guinness, so make things easy she just runs down the list of available beers. "We have Heineken, Coors light, and Budweiser." Getting inpatient she stands in front of Lid with one hand on her hip, and Lid asks his Uncle "Yo what are you getting?" Uncle Sha turns around and says "Donna knows what I am drinking" completely embarrassed because the bar tender actually owns the bar and it's name in lights out front Lid turns around and just says "I'll have the same thing he's having" "Two V-O and cokes then." Donna comes back with the drinks and tells Lid "that will be eight dollars" Lid reaches in his pocket to pull out some money, when out of nowhere a hand gripping a twenty cuts in front of him, it's Uncle Sha and he just shakes his head at Lid letting him know that as usual the drink are always on him. Lid gets out of the way and Uncle Sha goes to the bar "Hey Donna you see those two fine young ladies over there get them whatever they want, as long as it's no champagne I aint that crazy" And pulls out another twenty Donna gives him the change back from his drinks and he accordingly gives it right back to her in tip money She smiles, and Uncle Sha lets her know with an air whisper "You know I love u". Lid stands in front of his uncle stiff as a board looking more like security than a party goer, and Mr. Hill reminds him again "Loosen up young blood." As he shakes his own shoulders to add extra emphasis to his orders. "I'll be right back and Uncle Sha heads to the back of the bar towards the bathroom where a group of men are huddled around in a circle and every few seconds one goes in as another one exits. Feeling completely out of place Lid just takes in the scenery and blows kisses at the cougar whose eye caught when he first walked in. Surprisingly she blows one back and he erupts in laughter, curiosity however calls him to go check on his Uncle as a few minutes have passed by and there is no sign of Uncle Sha and Lid walks through the crowd exchanging looks with the old heads, but as he gets closer to his uncle the pleasantries change to hardened grimy looks and Lid thinks to himself whatever's going on around here I'm not supposed to be back here. He gets close enough to tap his uncle on the shoulder and when he turns around his nose is redder than Rudolph the rain deer, eyes popping out the front of his head he quickly ask "You finished with your drinks?" Lid nods his head, "Here get another round and make sure you tip Donna, I'm almost done here." Lid walks back to the bar and orders "Donna can I have a V-O and Coke and a Coors light?" "Cool sweet heart." Lid pays Donna and tells her to "keep the change." By the time she comes back uncle Sha returns just in time "Man you gonna get in trouble busting up our sessions nephew, feeling twice as better than before he's now dancing to the music and chit chatting with all the ladies. "What sessions Unc?" and in his best Spanish accent he says "Cocaine" Lid just smiles, both men continue to check out the scene and gulp down there drinks and a few minutes later they begin to head out the door around the horse shoe shaped bar. Once again handshakes and hugs are given out and this time even Lid gets a hug from the cougar he blew kisses too earlier. The moment is broken up when Uncle Sha tells his nephew to "Give me your phone" and standing in front of the two ladies he brought drinks for Uncle Sha puts there numbers in Lid's phone. As they leave the bar he lets them know "I'll call y'all later" while he hands Lid back his cell phone. A few minutes past one which is still early Lid ask his uncle "What's up next?" "The social club brother I have that meeting and I think you will have some more fun there because the crowd is about your age." They pull off in the minivan and go up 52nd street, from Market Street it's only a hop skip and jump to Haverford where sitting on a corner next to Small Park is three store front row homes converted into one giant castle. The windows are all covered in black but the bottom of Lid's feet thump away as the concrete on the outside jumps from the music being played on all three floors inside. The premier hot spot for all the neighborhood hustlers and hoes, Lid is stricken with anticipation as they walk through the front door, and once again met by security. This time tougher and up with the new times "As Salaam Alaikum Sha" "Wa Laikum Salaam" They both get frisked and once inside they pass the pool hall Sha gives a heads up the pool players and continues on Lid following up a straight flight of stairs. On the second floor you can hear the music blasting and thumping away and Lid's heart just jumps with anticipation as to what's behind the door. And finally from the other side the door opens, and yeah the crowd is much younger, than at Dona's but just like Dona's Uncle Sha is greeted with hugs and handshakes from all the young hustlers and hoes. Keeping form Uncle Sha introduces Lid to everyone and jokingly lets everyone know "that's my Tom Hagen!' Filled with premium ghetto booty the dance floor is more like a love making session that just requires some clothes as apple bottoms are slowly grinding up against the dicks of all the neighborhood hustler's this is their reward for holding down the blocks hustling all day and all night dodging cops like a regular nine to five the weekend is a time to just relax and have fun and inside the social club everyone is having a great time. As they move through the crowd inhaling the clouds of weed smoke, Lid takes a look at the circular bar which is stationed in the center of the next room. Again packed with people sitting at the stools and more people crowded behind them trying to order drinks Uncle Sha finds a seat at the end of the bar, directly in front of the kitchen which must have some very good soul food because the aroma is in the air and the line to buy food rivals the crowd buying drinks. As soon as they sit down a voice screams out from the crowd "Yow what's up old head!!?" Uncle Sha and Lid immediately turn around in the direction of the voice and Uncle Sha just smiles and replies "Just trying to make it another day Blackman!" The man approaches Lid and Uncle Sha brown skin with corn rolls and a scrappy beard, this is different than the other shout outs its not just being friendly Uncle Sha genuinely is happy to see this guy. "Damon AKA the white rat! Where you been man I thought you were dead." They hug and shake hands "I was" replies Damon "I just got back out a few weeks ago they had me up in Grater ford. I need some work old head, I know you got the connections hook a nigga up?" Side tracked by the two women accompanying Damon Lid is paying no attention to what they are talking about. Completely dazed and confused Lid's mouth just drops. One of the girls is a red bone sister with shoulder length black hair and auburn streaks, she has on black daisy dukes only compliment her ass and hips which are poking out from every direction with red fish net stockings, the short red tube top exposing her shoulders and belly Lid just reads her shirt which says "Spank Me". In awe Lid glances over and next to her is a much slender but just as beautiful brown skin with jet black hair cut real short her skin is just glistening as most of her body is exposed as she dons a piece of cloth that doubles as a dress, with open toe sandals that wrap all the way up her leg, Lid goes into shock when their eyes meets and sees that she has a pair of hazel eyes that blend in perfectly with her green dress or piece of cloth. Damon introduces the two women "this is my baby boo Katrina as he wraps his arm around the light skin honey, "Y'all better not get any ideas about her." "Aw Come on ain't no fun if the homies can't get none. Exclaims Uncle Sha, inpatient for an introduction Lid exclaims "Who's that?" "Slow down, this is Danielle she's Jamaican. Sha kisses both women's hands and introduces his nephew, star struck Lid just grins like a school boy and smiles. Both women laugh and say "You are so cute and immediately Danielle speaks up "Are those your real eyes?" Blushing Lid says "Yeah, they yours?" She nods and comes a little closer to Lid." In her heavy Jamaican accent she ask "So what are you mixed or something?" "Naw I'm from Philly" Needing to talk to Sha alone Damon sends Lid and the girls to go get drinks "Here nephew take and the girls go order us some drinks." He pulls out Benjamin from out of his mitt of cash Lid looks over at his Uncle Sha to make sure it is o.k. to leave, with a head nod from Uncle Sha Lid darts off with the girls and Damon and Uncle Sha begin to discuss business. "Sha you know I just got out of prison I need some work man I have like three thousand, and I need some help from the white girls right now." White girls is a code word for cocaine, and Uncle Sha keeps a connection on how to score weight in cocaine "Look man I know somebody who can get you what you want but it's going to be more like five thousand. Now I can out the other two grand up but that's all I'm going to do I have no time for DEA problems or crazy young boys. I heard you already got in some trouble with those young boys over on Hoops Street?" "Naw Sha that thang is cool, them niggas not saying nothing just a bunch of talk I've been living on my moms block forever now. Go away for a while and they are trying to box me the fuck out!" I just need the work and watch it's my block again so what's up?" Uncle Sha exhales "Alright call me tomorrow in the afternoon and I will take care of it." The two men shake hands to solidify the agreement. "Now let me get back to Katrina before your nephew steals my girl." "Yeah he's good at that they love the I'm a lover not a fighter act." "You mean he's acting Sha?" "Damon that nigga is insane but aren't we all?" At the bar Lid is in the ear of Danielle as he respectfully takes heed to Damon's warning and stays away from Katrina. Uncle Sha and Damon come over and Lid gives his seat up at the bar to Uncle Sha, and starts handing out drinks. "V-O and Coke for you Unc, Damon the girls said you wanted a glass of Alize." "Yo I'm not drinking no sweet ass Alize, yo bar tender get a double shot of Hennessey! Fucking bitches lied to you so they could drink this Alize themselves. Nephew where is my change?" Lid reaches in his pocket and pulls out a mitt of bills a twenty and a few tens. Lid goes back to finishing his drink, and Damon shuffles through the change "Yo what did y'all get?" "The girls got all kinds of drinks that was like fifty dollars, sitting at bar the girls have an assortment of glasses as they giggle away. "I just got a Guinness and a shot of Hennessey." Not upset Damon just proclaims "Both y'all bitches fucking me tonight!!" The whole group laughs as they all check out the scene Lid reminds Uncle Sha that they are here on business and ask "Yo you see fat boy yet?" "Naw he's not here yet let me call him." He does do and a few seconds later Uncle Sha has an answer "He's on his way. Go get the suitcase out of the trunk, no just bring the large envelope, bring a suitcase in here they might think you have a bomb or something." Lid grabs the keys and before he gets past Danielle she grabs him wrapping her hand around his waist, and she ask him "Were you going cutie?" "I'll be right back I'm going to the van, we still gonna dance." He walks off and as he gets to the dance floor he looks back at Danielle and she blows him a kiss. As he walks down the stairs he thinks to himself this is exactly what he was missing down south running the streets with his uncle, picking up hoes and stunting at the bar's like he was a made man. Once outside he takes a glance he takes a glance over at the Chinese store still open three o'clock in the morning Lid notices two young boys standing out front of the store dressed in shorts and long sleeve hoodies Lid thinks nothing of it and as he goes to the Mini-van he exchanges glances with the young boys. Using the brush that he keeps on the side of his hip Lid adjusts it as if it was a gun as he passes the young boys, then he goes into the mini van and grabs the envelope from the suite case. Once back at the door security reminds him "All this running in and out is not a good idea." "My apologies, I had to do something for my Uncle." And brings the envelope plain view as if it is some top secret document, once back inside Lid jogs up the stairs a little tipsy from the Hennessey he has to concentrate so he doesn't fall up the stairs and once he is inside he quickly hands Uncle Sha the envelope  and its back to Danielle. Back in her ear he says "I told you I was coming back". She smiles and inspired by the reggae music playing she grabs his already hard dick and drags him to the dance floor, since she's Jamaican she has an unfair advantage, and to even things out Lid turns Danielle around and grabs his dick placing it ever so gently between her ass cheeks, if they were naked they'd be making lust. As close as they can possibly be to each other without actual intercourse they dance song after song as he softly kisses her on the cheeks, neck, and shoulders as she sweats away tearing up the dance floor. Occasionally her hazel eyes and his green eyes meet when he turns her around and they meet face to face speaking the language of lust without saying a word. Lid glances over at his uncle who is now speaking to a group of men. Damon and Katrina aren't at the bar and Lid wonders where they ran off to until a load voice yells in his right ear. "You two are tearing this club up, looking like y'all making a porno in here." Lid just smiles and continues to dance.  A few minutes later Danielle calls it a quits after bumping and grinding with Lid for like twenty minutes. "I need a drink", closer and more intimate than when they first left the bar on the way back Lid is draped all over the backside of Danielle trying to conceal his hard dick poking out his pants he whispers sweet nothings into her ear as they approach Uncle Sha at the bar. "Damn nephew I saw you two on the dance floor, y'all need a room." "They all laugh "Were did fat boy go?" "They left you missed that part good thing too he gets all paranoid about new people." Damon with Katrina draped all over him come over "I don't know what y'all started on the dance floor but all of a sudden it turned into hedonism out there." They all take a look at the dance floor which is filled to capacity and everyone out there is dancing the night away, lustfully, slowly and as the night wines down everybody is looking for somebody to go home with. "We are about to go down to the after hours spot y'all want to come with us? You and Danielle are all over each other come on?" Danielle makes her request "Come on red it's going to be fun". Lid looks at his Uncle and Sha just shrugs his shoulder giving him and I don't care look." But Lid thinks otherwise "Naw I'm going to stick with my uncle we still have some running around to do." Danielle sighs and proceeds to write down her number on a napkin at the bar. Once finished she puts the napkin in Lid's pocket and gives him a soft kiss on the cheek. "you better call me tomorrow boy" " I will" upset about passing up spending the rest of the night with some prime Jamaican booty Lid order's another drink as he watches Danielle, Katrina, and Damon walk away from the bar and struggle to get through the dance floor crowd. "I can't believe you passed up on that ass?" "Me neither, I got her number though." "She was all over you nephew I thought you knew her from somewhere before." "Naw man I just be getting them like that." "Stop fronting nigga now you Hugh Hef or something like that,  come on the nights still young you know those two I pulled at Dona's they are still on the menu we can get a room or something." Yeah this is what Lid was missing the D.J.'s the girls, the gangsters, the bars, the city, the DJ is playing Fat Man Scoop's who's fucking tonight as the social club goes crazy partnered up everyone is fucking tonight as they raise their glasses of liquor and beers up in the air Lid loves it and just takes it all in for a few seconds the harsh realities of the hood rear their ugly head in the form of violence. BANG ,BANG ,BANG ,BANG ,BANG ,POP ,POP ,POP, POP!!!! Stunned the DJ stops the music and parts of the crowd head to the window only realize that they can't see anything, others fall to the ground anticipating shots that might come through the window. The noise of the gun shots are broken with a brief split second of silence and then the screams of a women yelling in pain out of fear, and in fear AAAAHHHHHHHHH!!!!!!! Lid begins to leave the bar when Uncle Sha grabs his arm shaking his head "Wait they could still be shooting." A few minutes pass by and outside you see the glaring lights of red and blue from the Philadelphia police department. The club goers begin to usher out from the second floor and on to the street, police tape already up Lid is shocked when he and Uncle Sha finally get outside. A white Chrysler 300M riddled with bullet holes, and inside laying lifeless in the drivers seat filled with bullet holes is Damon, Katrina is on a stretcher and paramedics race to save her life, and Danielle is crying being attended to by paramedics and surrounded by cops, "Oh Jesus! Oh Jesus! Crying she screams I can't believe they killed him." Uncle Sha and Lid move to the mini van and Uncle Sha gives the explanation, humbled he says "I have to go tell his mother around the corner on Hoopes street, I just talked to him about this the young boys were not playing." "What just happened we were all just dancing?" "Damon was trying to move out on his old block and he had been going through some beef with the young boys down there." "They handled it though punk ass mutha fuckers." Lid has never seen Uncle Sha cry and he is not about to do it tonight but his voice and words are humbles as he explains to Lid what happened. "I don't that just happened we were all just together I was about to go with them." "Good thing you didn't because I would've had a bigger problem on my hands." Uncle Sha gets on the phone as he zips around the corner to Hoops street and parks up the block from Damon's moms house. "Stay in the car" Uncle Sha gets out and Lid looks around thinking about how blessed he was not to go with them, and reflecting on the neighborhood he's in. Hoopes street his mom's sister Halima grew up down here with Uncle Sha and their family. From the days of the old gang wars when people could not leave their neighborhood in fear of being beaten up and or murdered, to the emergence of the nation of Islam and how that movement changed all that reorganizing the streets and providing everyone from whatever part of the city you were from some dignity and organization. Damon was uncle Sha young boy in those days, his mother and Lid's grand mother knew each other and in a way they all were family like the European immigrants in the beginning of the century, these families former slave families migrated to the north in the thirties during the great depression looking for freedom and opportunity. Lid watches from the mini-van as the old women just falls to her knees in the doorway of the house, and Uncle Sha catches her mid way to the ground and hugs her a few minutes pass by and more family members begin to show up at the house and soon Uncle Sha leaves. Inside the van he exclaims "That's enough action for one night, these niggas are crazy out here." The ride back to the house is silent no music, no phone calls, and once at the house Lid crashes on the couch and Uncle Sha begins to go upstairs when he ask " You know you almost went with them tonight? What changed your mind?" "I came with you Unc. I leave with you, even though I spent some time down the way it's still not my neighborhood. Plus my whole purpose is being an extra set of eyes for you out there." Uncle Sha nods his head "For a book worm you're a pretty stand guy nephew, see you in the morning As Salaam Alaikum." "Wa Laikum Salaam."

# You gotta be kidding me?

I's MID SEPTEMBER AND after spending most of the money he had saved up over the summer  to register, Lid is one week into classes at his new university and he is thinking to himself that leaving Xavier was a big mistake. But maybe things will pick up as with most universities the first week of class is usually orientation with students making sure they are in the right class, and teacher making sure they have the right students on role. Excited about his black politics class, because this week Dr. Kwabla has promised that they will talk about the 2000 elections and why the supreme court of the United States of America stopped the recount in Florida and awarded the elections to George W. Forty Three . The students at Delaware State are much different than the students at Xavier where most of Lids class mates where from the best high schools in New Orleans, or private schools they seemed more attentive in class and ready to learn. Coming from public schools the Delaware State crowd is quite different and come off as if they really don't want to be in school and have better things to do. He knows he will have an advantage over them and looks forward to succeeding in class, as things might be a little bit easier than the heavy reading fast paced of learning at Xavier. The bus ride to Dover is very peaceful the rural scenery, is quiet the farm land and it's animals, the silence is a break from the hustle and bustle of city life. But as the bus pulls into campus this Tuesday Lid could never anticipate what was about to happen next, and the rest of the world would never be the same. His first class is in the ETV building and still new to the university Lid takes the long way to class as he walks through the university he catches the eyes of two ladies dressed in bajamas who must be on thier way to breakfast in the cafeteria, Lid smiles and continues to class. Soon he is in the ETV building the headquarters for the Political Science department, the Math department, and parts of the Communications department; the ETV building has a complete television studio and radio room used to house the on-campus radio station. But as he walks through the automatic doors to his surprise about a half dozen students are huddled around the television and filled with curiosity Lid takes a look at what causing all the commotion. But before he gets in view of the television a girl screams out from the crowd "OH My GOD!!" The rest of the crowd gasping, Lid moves through the crowd and takes a look at the television screen and to his dismay he sees the most unbelievable, horrific acts he's ever seen on live television, as smoke and fumes drift into the sky and like a fighter with a black eye the New York City sky line is filled with black smoke. Still unaware of what just happened Lid just watches the screen until ABC news shows a replay of how things got that way, and like a missile an airplane just flies into the skyline and crashes into one of the world trade center buildings, and immediately burst into flames. The crowd screams in disbelief and Lid just watches in horror as what used to be fiction found in episodes of the X-files just became reality and news anchor Peter Jennings begins to speak "We don't know if a plane flew off course but an airplane has crashed into the World Trade Center in New York City." Still anguishing over the replay of what just happened faster than before another airplane comes crashing into the second twin tower and BOOM! All in one the crowd screams in terror and fear, and now the tears begin to flow from the eyes of female onlookers and an already sad situation turns to melee as students try to deal with the sheer emotion of what they just saw. One students proclaims "Did that just happen?", some students just huddle up and begin to pray as the crowd gets larger from students naturally going to their first class, but unnaturally seeing the most horrifying events in American history unfolding on television. "Why would someone do something like this?" Cries out one student, speechless Lid takes a look at the carnage ensuing around and the carnage in Manhattan as people begin to hurl themselves out of the buildings and immediately thinks of Jasmine who is in New York and not too far the twin towers. Inside he gets a sick feeling as his stomach tightens up and gripped with fear he grabs his cell phone to call her but the automated operator comes on and lets Lid know "All circuits are busy right now." Quickly he exits the ETV building and outside students and faculty are all huddled up in circles praying tears flowing down the eyes of all students and what was a peaceful morning just minutes ago has now transformed into something out of Pearl Harbor the movie as people just run and cry and scramble across the campus. Lid remembers that during registration there were a few land line pay phones in the Martin Luther King building on the other side of campus, and speedily walks across campus. The university is filled with students and faculty crying, shaking their heads in disbeliefs and as Lid walks into the MLK building the pandemonium from outside only doubles as hundreds of students stand mesmerized in front of the television screen, completely out of sorts, never has Lid so many people grief stricken, confused, and scared. A female student walks up to Lid her mascara running down her face from the tears she's crying just ask "How can something this happen to us?" "I don't know I'm at a loss for words." He gives her a hug as together they watch mayhem together, remembering his mission Lid parts ways with the young women and heads to the pay phones which in reaction to the loss of cell phone service has accumulated pretty long lines. As he waits students usher into the building with updates and quickly they spread throughout the building, there's a plane heading for Philly!" "There's a plane heading to D.C.! and finally the unimaginable "The news said the Pentagon just got hit by a plane." Finally it's Lid's turn to use the pay phone and immediately he calls Jasmine, and still gets no answer as the cell phone service in New York is disconnected. Then he calls his mother "As Salaam Alaikum mom" "Wa Laikum Salaam" "Are you watching the news, I can't believe this is happening." "I know honey are they going to close your school?" "I don't know yet, they said the Pentagon just got hit what's going with that?" "The news just keeps showing smoke coming out of the building." "Has anyone claimed responsibility?" "No, the news just keeps showing the buildings getting hit; they said there are two more planes out there." "I don't know how anything like this can happen, mom those buildings are going to fall on New York city mom do you know how many people are going to die and how much damage that is going to do?" Unaware of what's already taken place Halima updates Lid on the gruesome attacks "Lid honey one of the buildings already fell." Shocked Lid's heart just stop a beat and the grief and horror of the attacks shakes his insides thinking that the building fell over and imagining the carnage done Lid ask "When it fell over how damage did it do to New York?" "No, it didn't fall over it imploded and made a mushroom cloud like a construction site." Intrigued by that response Lid continues worried about the backlash something like this would have on the Muslim community. "They are going to start locking Muslims up like that movie with Bruce Willis or what happened to the Japanese during World War II where are the girls at?" "Adesha's and Ruquayya's schools have canceled classes Ruquayya is on her way back and Adesha is on the school bus coming home." "I'm on my way back home I love you mom As Salaam Alaikum" "I love you too Wa Laikum Salaam honey." As soon as he hangs up the phone a few campus security guards are talking with students close to the main doors and students emerge from the conversation screaming aloud "Classes are cancelled until further notice." The crowd cheers no matter how bad things are the announcement of no class is a sense of relief for all and the cheering continues as Lid takes off to the bus stop and once outside he sees that the bus ride is going to be pretty full as students and faculty crowd the bus stop. People are somber fear stricken with tears in their eyes some have a look of anger in others a ghostly glare of disbelief. And suddenly as Lid stands waiting for the bus stop a man just walks up to him a begins to talk "I don't know what kind of people would do that to us, the Americans in the airplanes, and up in New York city? This is so horrible." "I know this is not like Pearl Harbor we just watched the whole thing on television and from what I understand this is just the beginning." "I know I heard that to on the news Jack Mathews." He extends his arm to shake hands with Lid "I work for the state of Delaware, they sent everyone home that worked for the state and from the looks of the crowd they closed the school too." "Yeah schools out too, my name is Lid Islam, I transferred up here from New Orleans. I really don't believe this is happening." They shake hands but not even two hours after the horrible attacks the ramifications of September 11th start to take effect, and once Lid tells Mr. Mathews his name automatically the older man frowns his face and a fearful angry look overtakes the modest gentleman. Lid immediately picks up on it and tries his hardest to quell any fears Mr. Mathews may have about him. "I can't believe the stealth's did not shoot those planes down before they hit the towers?" They can get anywhere in the country in ten minutes it just doesn't make any sense." Mr. Mathews adds "And where the heck is the military all you see cops and fire fighters in New York but no military." "I don't know man but this is crazy." The two of them stand next to each shaking their heads in disbelief as the bus comes around, like a good Muslim or good human being for that matter Lid stands clear as he lets the women get on the bus first, some men are less polite and just get on, but after all the women get on the remaining men and Lid board the bus. As he pays the bus driver politely says "Thank you". Only hours ago Lid was riding the bus coming down to school and everything was so peaceful but now he looks out the window up in sky filled with terror and fear of what used to be the friendly skies. Once home as soon as he opens the door his mother greets him urgently giving her son the greetings of peace "As Salaam Alaikum" Lid quickly replies "Wa Laikum Salaam. Were the girls at?" "Up stairs Adesha's in her room crying she doesn't understand what's going on. Raquayya's upstairs too trying to call her friends in New York." "There's no service in NY I been trying to call Jasmine for hours but I can't get through. We need to make prayer mom." She nods her head in agreement and then begins to give Lid updates both buildings fell over; people were jumping out of buildings committing suicide. It was this smoke cloud that just engulfed New York it moved through the buildings and people were running from it, look on the TV every is covered in ash and they probably are going to die from asbestos poisoning." "You better believe it." "But then all the buildings around the world trade centers started collapsing." "What!" "Yeah when they fell they didn't fall over, they collapsed like and implosion and the buildings around them started to implode as well. The news is saying that it might be explosives in the garages or the shock from the twin towers falling down might've caused it." "Why did they fall down like that, the steel is on fire it should've started melting and fold over that why I was worried about the buildings falling on New York." "They didn't do that they imploded?" What's going with the pentagon?" "It was hit by one of the airplanes; they're showing much just smoke coming from the building the news said the plane was destroyed completely by the flames." "Where's the President, where's Cheney?" "Forty Three  is on air force one he's coming on TV in a few hours, to address the nation, and visit New York when things settle down if things settle down?" Cheney is at an undisclosed location." "What's that?" "They won't say probably an old fall out shelter or something. All the planes in the sky are being grounded, Lid this is so insane how could something like this happen to us?" Filled with anger as the images from the news project images of fear, crying, terror, death, and complete carnage, the assault on Lid's cool and calm demeanor, has taken its toll and in a burst of fury he screams "I SWEAR TO GOD IF MUSLIMS DID THIS IM JOINING THE MILITARY AND WE

ARE GOING TO NUKE THE HELL OUT OF THE DESSERT!!!!" Sister Halima tries to calm her son down "Lid stop cursing and calm down pay attention to what is going on here. I know you are upset but cursing and swearing is not going to change anything, did you talk to your friends mother may be she has talked to Jasmine?" "What kind of SHIT is this I was going to go up there this weekend, who does anything like this mom?" "Calm down lets make prayer like you said earlier, come on." Raquyya comes down stairs "whats all that screaming Lid?" "Nothing we bout to make prayer so get Adesha and grab some scarves to cover y'all hair." As she covers her hair and lays the prayer  rugs out sister Haleemah opens up and tells her son "I'm thinking about going up there to help they said they need nurses and doctors to tend to the injured and wounded." " I'll drive you up there but I don't think I can get into the island." "No son that's out of the question you have to drop me off in New Jersey and then I have to go through all the security checks." "Are you guys ready?" From upstairs his sisters scream "No we are still making wudu." "And Lid takes the opportunity to give his Uncle Sha a call on the house phone "As Salaam Alaikum, unc are you watching this?" "Wa Laikum Salaam I don't have a choice its on every channel you better watch what you say on this line all that Arabic is not a good thing now, you know they are going to start locking those A-rabs up." "I thought about that earlier do you believe this man they are going to blame this on the muslims, I hope we had nothing to do with it." "There you go with that we I'm a jewish-muslim Shalom Alaikum." Lid cracks up laughing a good break from the anger and fear that has gripped him for most of the day. "Unc you crazy, like right after Oklahoma city they tried blaming the muslims on that thing but come to find out it was some good old country boys behind and it was a different story." "Yeah you right" They girls come down the steps and with hair covered line up next to sister Haleemah to begin prayer, and now his mother reminds him "Lid we are ready." "Alright Unc you crazy man about to make prayer man gotta go As-Salaam Alaikum" "Wa-Laikum Salaam brother." Lid hangs up the phone and shares with his family the joke "Yo Uncle Sha said he is not muslim anymore he's a jewish/muslim talking bout Shalom Alaikum." "The girls giggle, but sister Haleemah as always is very serious about salat and tells Lid stop playing boy and call the athan for prayer." And Lid does so. Since he is the only male in the house he's always led the family in prayer, going to Sister Clara Muhammed school as a youth he learned the proper ways to perform salt and at an early age learned enough sura's out of the Holy Quaran to make salat. If a male is r=present women cannot lead salt, and Lid takes great pride and admiration in leading his mother and sisters in prayer five times a day. When he went away to college there was a struggle taking place between his mother and he as she started to drift away from Islam and was very adamant about Lid leaving the house and going away to college, when he went away he missed salat, and they too had no one to lead them in salat and they drifted away from the religion. However the tragic events of September 11, 2001 if anything has reaffirmed faith in this family as what was though impossible twelve hours ago is a reality and GOD is the only one they should refuge with in such confusing times. "Allahu Akbar, Allahu Akbar, Allahu Akbar, Allahu Akbar/ God is the greatest, Ash-hadu an la illaha illallah, Ash-hadu an la illaha illahah/ I bear witness that there is no deity except GOD, Ash-hadu anna Muhammad dan rasulullah, Ash-hadu anna Muhammad dan rasulullah/ I bear witness that Muhammed is the messenger of God, Hayya alal salah, Hayya alal salah/make haste towards worship, hayya ala l'falah, hayya ala l'falah/come to true success, Allahu akbar, Allahu akbar God is the greatest, La ilaha illallah/there is no deity except God." The prayer they make is Zhur prayer the midday prayer consisting of four rakkas taking about seven minutes when the family is finished the television comes right back on and CNN has now announced that the terrorist group Al-Queda has claimed responcibility for the attacks. "Mom how could something like this happen who in the world is Osama Bin Laden?" "Shush honey listen they have the father of one of the highjackers one the phone line now. The television turned up the father of Muhammed Atta is in Egypt and on the line live with CNN." "My son had nothing to do with this, I was with him yesterday here in Egypt." The news quickly turns off the interview with Muhammed Atta's father and once again show the horrific images of the airplanes hitting the twin towers, and the Pentagon on fire. And together the family discusses what is going on, "Grandmom said she is o.k. she is watching the news and here is the number to cousin Sherlys." "Thanks Raqayya" Adesha ask "are you serious about going to the military?" "I don't know a few hours ago I was ready for war, but now I don't know that's way too much information too fast. How do they know all the highjackers involved already, we already have a terrorist watch list, and if you have any criminal record the camera's at the airport do retinal  scans on your eyes, why didn't they stop these people?" Sister Haleemah agrees and add " Remember on Broken Arrow with John Travolta he said the stealth bombers can get anywhere in the country in ten minutes, why didn't they shoot the planes down?" "Weird, mom that's all I have to say, the buildings are falling down all around the twin towers and they didn't even get hit." Lid then gets a call from Sister Aisha Jasmine's mom and after a few minutes on the phone with her he is a little relived when he gets off the phone he lets everyone know "That was Jasmine's mom she's o.k. sister Aisha said she's with friends far away from all the mayhem. She also said that someone found the passport of one of the highjackers on the street in NewYork." In complete disbelief the girls all say "That's crazy!" "Lid I have three words for you honey Wag the Dog!" "I'm starting to believe you mom, the news still hasn't shown any footage of an airplane actually crashing into the Pentagon, they just keep showing the footage of the planes hitting the towers but from the same angles." Ruqayya adds "I don't understand why the buildings did not bend over y'all steal bends they imploded." "Just pray son for all those in New York, the people who commited suicide jumping out of building, the NYC police and Fire department, and the world in general because is never going to be the same after this." "O.k. mom" His thoughts and mood completely changed from this morning when he was ready to join the military upset and angry about attacks on U.S. Soil as the day passes and more information is revealed there seems to be more to the story. How did the highjackers get on the planes in the first place?" "How did they gain control of the airplane by using box cutters that seems a little far fetched? Why haven't we seen an airplane hit the pentagon? Why are the buildings around the World Trade centers collapsing as if they are being imploded? Why did the Twin Towers implode like a staged demolition site and not bend over and fall? And why did such an earth shattering and  unbelievable event take place during the Presidency of George W Forty Three  a man who appointed by the supreme Court of the United States? By the days end Lid and the country is faced with more questions than answers and instead of making any rash decisions like joining the military Lid begins to wonder what if the military had something to do with this? What if this was an inside job? What if America was changing into a country that takes the lives of it's own citizens to achieve a greater goal? What if Muslims were seen as the new communist party? His life, his family, his career, his future would all be in jepordy sitting outside his mothers house smoking away at a cigarette Lid worry's about his future in a country that has shown a new face in this new century.

Wednesday September 12th, 2001 the first day of the new America unlike days of old the cable networks all have twenty four hour news channels and this leviathan fuels the airwaves with anti-islamic propaganda, and rumors of more immenant attacks. The new enemy is being created not a ideology but a theology a religion the religion of Islam the rhetoric from the White House is that "They hate our way of life" And fueled by the propaganda relayed on television the footage missing persons being posted all over New York, the constant images of airplanes crashing into the World Trade Center and Americans running from dust clouds in the streets of New York all comes together when the United States Senate convenes on the steps of the capital building in Washington D.C. to sing God Bless America. A hero emerges in a white cowboy hat , rolled u sleeves, and a hard hat, a hero who weeks before failed to get the budget passed, who years before failed at all his business ventures, who without the help of the Supreme Court, a fraudulent election, would've failed at his bid to be President promised us that he would search the ends of the earth to find the people responsible, when the people responsible were looking at us right through the camera devilishly smiling on the inside. Thursday September 13, 2001 and its back to school, different than just a few days ago the campus is riddled with fear and the frusteration would all come to head in Dr. Kwabla's black politics class. Class opens with Dr. Kwabla giving warm words for all the victims "I think all of our prayers should be with the families and victims those who have fallen or are missing from the horrible attacks on Tuesday." There's a moment of silence in the classroom and after about a half minute a young lady with tears falling down her eyes and a heavy north jersey accent says "I can't believe those rag heads did this to us my sister is in the army and we are going to go over there and kick some ass!!" The classroom erupts in cheering and applause, and her statement is followed by a brother with a New York accent "I'm from Brooklyn and my cousin is missing he was in the World Trade tower, he worked there and I don't understand how something like this could happen. But I just ask everyone in the class to please keep us all in your prayers cause New York is a mess, right now. I mean how did this happen? Were was the military, and how come the government didn't know about this?" He sits back down and some female students comes over to consol the male student. Then Lid raises his hand sitting in the front row Dr. Kwabla clearly sees Lid and he calls on the new face feeling very uncomfortable , should he say some warm words for the victims, should raise some serious questions? H does both "My name is Lid Islam, I think we all should take a few moments throughout the day to remember and the victims the fire fighters, and police officers, the people who just was going to work, and it ended up being there last day on earth. But as Americans we need to take a closer look at what happened on Tuesday and how did those people get passed security and board those planes? Why didn't the military shoot down the airplanes?" Did anybody actually see an airplane hit the pentagon?" The classroom erupts in confusion "He said what!?"/"He's right"/"May be he is one of them?" Dr. Kwabla gets control of the classroom "All those questions and more will b answered sooner or later but today we have to opn our text books up to chapter one." All at once the classroom wines together "All Man!" When class is over a student pulls Lid to says "That was brave of you to say that." "Yeah thanks but I don't think I made too many friends today." The students shakes Lids hand "You got a friend in me." "Thanks yo." The rest of the day he walk alone, but in each class the topic of discussion is September 11th, on the bus ride home he shares the back seat with a women and after they share a few moments of eye contact she finally says "I can't believe something like this happened to America, my name is Nicole." "I know this is crazy yo people were just jumping out of the windows on to the street killing themselves it's crazy., he extends his hand my name is Lid." And just that fast the events of September 11th begin to change the world around Lid as Nicole pulls here hand back and her face is riddled in fear." Just because his nam is Islamic, the events from Tuesday will forever shape, his relationships, his career, and his future."

At home sister haleemah sits in front of the television with the news on "As-Salaam Alaikum" "Wa-Laikum Salaam mom." "Are you going to Jummah tomorrow?" I don't know, the FBI and the state police are probably going to b all over the place." "They are probably going to think that you are one because isn't this your first time at this masjid?" "Yeah the foreigners have to deal with this drama, I have to worry about you, my sisters and myself and make sure nothing happens to us." "Lid you have nothing to do with what happened on Tuesday don't let that kep you away from Allah, I raised you better than that." "O.k. I'll go but then I have to go job hunting afterwards and then I have to go to the train station to go to Philly." "Your going to spend the weekend at my brothers?" "Yes" "He only cares about money, you know that?" "Well he can still get paid there's going to be room for dissent because right now everyone is going to take the news for face value. That muslims highjacked American airplanes and crashed them into the World Trade Towers, and the Pentagon. We should start doing some research getting the facts together it's going to b very important to see which direction the country goes towards over the next few months, but I have to find out the truth because something like this would not've happened if Al Gore had won the White House." "Kiddo it send chills up my spine to say it but I believe you, I really believe you." The next day Lid catches the bus over to Christiana mall and a folder full of resumes and he goes into stores like Macy's, footlocker, radio shack, electronic boutiques, and circuit city, requesting to speak with the manger and asking if they are hiring, only days after 9/11 Lid's actions seem very foolish but things don't start to sink in until he starts handing his resume over to mangers and their eyes open wide when they read his name. And out of their mouths rolls the worst phrase any job seeker can hear "We are not hiring right now." But for what it's worth he gave the job hunt a shot and around twelve o'clock his mother picks him up from the mall. "Look boy you better learn how to catch the bus, I am not going to be your taxi." 'Alright mom it's just isn't like the city Septa does not run all over the place down here, I don't even know were the buses are taking me." "I'm not trying to hear it, so how did the job search go?" In disappointment he shakes his head and says "Not good everybody told me they were not hiring, and I got this feeling like once they read my name that was it, it was different than before you kow people usually ask you were you name from or how do you pronounce it, they were just like now way dude." "Well may be you can talk to someone at the masjid about it?" "May be but you know how they get with that white superiority stuff looking down on us like they so much better."As they pull up to Masjid Ibrahim fir Friday prayer it is reminiscent of the movie "the Siege" parked outside is th estate police, and the streets are linned with protesters with signs that read "Go home rag heads" "We don't want you here!" This is the first time at thi Masjid and he is one of a few African Americans at the service, during the service the iman speaks about this being "a very important time to hold true to our beliefs, he also gave the crowd some information about the now infamous O'Sama Bin Laden. He was trained in Afghanistan by the CIA during the nineteen eighties, they trained these fighters to go to war against the Soviet Union teaching them bomb making skills, and how to use surface to air missles." "Mom I think there is more to this then some struggle between two countries or religions for that matter." "Calm down boy things will cool down you will see. Did you talk to Jasmine?" No I still haven't talked to her I was planning to go up there this weekend but I've only talked to her one time since I been up here and that was the last time I was at the UPenn train station so for good luck I was waiting until I got there again to see if it worked again." "Well you still can't get up to New York the national guard is still stopping people in New Jersey . Go to Philly son and talk with my brother yeah he's money motivated but we were once revolutionaries and I think you have some good idea's he might want to get involved with investigating. Now you know you are going to get black listed but at this point the truth is what matters." Lid leans over and gives his mom a kiss, a drastic change from the last time she took him to the train station and the argument about the house overshadowed the entie trip, if anything September 11th brought their family a little closer understanding that in a blink of an eye and that the loss of a home, or building is nothing compared to the loss of life.

# Cadillac Black, Malcom X, and Strip Clubs

THE AMTRACK STATION IN Wilmington is filled with local police, amtrack police, and K-9 dogs. The police have automatic weapons and not the usual pistols, and they have a look of zero tolerance. "Can I have one ticket for Philly please?" "Can I see your I.D.?" He grabs his wallet and shows the cashier his identification. "That's going to be five-twenty-five." He pays the cashier and receives his ticket and once he is on the platform there are more cops with automatic weapons and they look ready for a raid, and the whole atmosphere is more like an occupied state. When he arrives to Philly he gets off at the University City stop and like last time he gives Jasmine a call sitting down on the benches the phone rings, when finally she picks up. "Hello?" "As-Salaam Alaikum Jasmine you all right what's going on up there?" "Everything's good, the first day it was crazy we had to run out the building my apartment's and we running to different buildings, people were so scared then the light's went out and we all had to stay in this apartment it was like thirty people crammed up in this one apartment, she laughs it was so wild." "But you o.k. huh?  Can I come up there?"  There's a pause and then Jasmine flatly says "I met someone too" "What? What about us?" at that very moment Amtrak police who are present on the University City platform walk up to Lid and says "If you are not waiting for the train then you have to move you can't stay on the platform." Lid motions to his phone and cop flat out says "Move!" He gets up and tells Jasmine "I'll you right back, As-Salaam Alaikum." And she replies "bye" and hangs up the phone. Lid goes upstairs where Uncle Sha is waiting for him and once inside he takes the opportunity to talk to his uncle about September 11th in person."Before h says anything to his uncle he quickly gives Jasmine a call abck, and she does not answer the phone as it just rings and rings. "As Salaam Alaikum Uncle Sha" "Wa-Laikum Salaam" they shake hands "Can you believe what just happened?" "Yeah I believe it's the government they have everyone thinking this is some holy war." "Do you think they are going to start locking us up?" "If they have not done it yet, I don't think so. What had to be done is done look around you nephew cops are everywhere, the people all are frightened and the government is standing there looking like heroes. When in fact they let this shit happen if I could put money on it I would say the army flew those planes into those buildings." "You know Uncle Sha I never saw a plane hit the pentagon man, the news always shows the Pentagon just on fire and smoking." In Germany the Reichstag building was burned down and the Nazi party blamed it on the opposing political party, which most members where jews and that's how the Nazi's took complete control of Germany, this is the same thing I bet you were thinking about joining the armed forces?" "Yeah until like five o'clock that afternoon and the news reset, with full dossiers on the high jackers. You and I both know if they had information at five at night they had the information at seven that moring." "What are we going to do about it Unc?" "We? I'm going about my normal business this place is about to change and I want no parts of being on the wrong side of the government especially this type of government." "Yo you are the king of White Colar crimes, what are you talking about?" "That's one thing nephew, taking them on as they reshape the future is another." "I was thinking about a website, there's going to be a lot of people who stand up against this hypocracy." "Where's the money in that Lid?" "People will ome to the web site for truth. You can get paid for clicks on the websites and advertising, come on man it will be fun." Uncle Sha exhales "I'll think about it but your going to have to do your part get on the web and find proof." "I'll start with the laws because the president is talking about changing the laws already." "Go get the information nephew and I will think about it. How's your girl up their?" "I don't want to talk about it." As soon as they get to his uncles house, they both go straight upstairs to the office. Lid jumps on the computer and starts to search for the closest airforce base to New York city, pictures from the crash, the hijackers, and so on until the night falls "I found that stuff about the Reichstag fire, the whole country was in an uproar and the Nazi party blamed it on the communist, they passed this emergency decree to overcome the crisis "For the protection of the people and the state" The emergency decree stated "restrictions on personal liberty, on the right of free expression of opinion, including freedom of the press, on the rights of assembly and association, and violations of the privacy of postal telegraphs and telephonic communications on property are also permissible beyond the legal limits otherwise prescribed" "Wow, that basically says the people have no rights and because of the emergency, you can't express yourselves,  your conversations are tapped, and you didn't have the right to assemble or protest for anything." "That will never happen here Uncle Sha we have the Constitution man that protects us from a police state like that." "That's where you wrong when we protested for civil rights the police broke it up, they sent dogs after us and sprayed us down with water hoses, so you can't put anything past this government." "This is a different generation, we are not having that crazyness, can't assemble, secret police, Americans turning against other Americans, no way this generation is the generation that completes the American vision, the dream, all people, all religions, all walks of life." "I hope you are right nephew but with Forty Three  in office anything is possible." "We going to work tonight Unc.?" Uncle Sha shakes his head "Naw I've been playing the day time since Damon got murdered, I went to the funeral your Jamaican girl was there. She asked about you why didn't you call her?" Lid exhales "I was going to call her but on Tuesday that stuff went down, plus I really messed up with Jasmine, I was supposed to been up there to see her, but I been calling her and calling her and she didn't answer, I finally talked to her a couple minutes ago and she is like she met someone." "Ahhh scandalous nephew I told you about them like the wind they are." "Yeah well that's life that's what all the people say your riding high in April shot down in May." "Focus on Philly your doing the right thing most guys your age would not think twice about investigating or even looking into what happened on Tuesday." "Lid scrolls through his phone and finds Samantha's number and decides to give her a call. An old women picks up the phone "Hello?" "High ya doing Mrs. is Samantha home?" "Hold on, and the old women yells SAMANTHA!!!!" And a few seconds later Samantha picks up the phone "Hello", Hi Samantha it's Lid I met you a week ago, I walked you to seven eleven rember?" "I know who this is I thought you were never going to call." "I'm sorry Sam I had class and then this 9/11 stuff happened I just got sidetracked." "Yeah I don't believe people would do something like that Fucking crazy Muslims. People were jumping out of windows killing themselves live on television." "Sam I don't think these people being muslim had anything to do with this." "Well that's not what the news said, they said Bin Laden planned the whole thing and they all live in Afghanisands" "Afghnistan Sam" "Whatever they did it cause they hate Americans and this is the beginging they attacking through the mail sending stuff to Congress. It's going to b more, that's what the news said. Jokingly she says "Hey you muslim you sure your not a terrorist?" A little hurt by her words he just says "Cool out Sam and stop playing there is more to this than meets the eyes." "Like what inspector gadget?" "I can't talk about it over the phone but come around the corner and lets sit out on the steps." "You got some weed?" "Naw but I can get some just bring a dutch from the Rican store and I got you." "You better have some green or I'm through with you?" I got you Sam just come around the corner." "Aright I'll be there in like fifteen minutes bye." They hang up the phone and Lid runs in the house upstairs to his uncle's lab. "Hey Unc you got some weed for sale?" "Yeah in bulk how much you trying to get?, you about to go smoke and earase everything you learned in college." "It relaxes my mind you know I have all kinds of thoughts racing through my head, prepping for conversati0ons that haven't even taken place yet." "Yeah yeah yeah tell it to the judge we had weed in my day, the stuff you guys smoke has got all kinds of chemicals in it. Go in the closet and grab then ammunition case the weed's in a plastic bag in there and just take a little bit that supposed to be sold in bulk smoker." Lid gets up and grabs the ammunition case out of the closet embarrassed by his uncles bluntness about his addiction h tries to change the subject. "You know Wolferwitz and Cheaney used to be on Reagans staff in the eighties, they called the Afghans our friends back in eighty four in the fight against the communist." " You found all that on the web?" "Yup you gotta kno how to ask the machine the right questions to get the answers you are looking for." "Good job now you are going to go smoke some pot and forget about all of it." Lid laughs "I'm going outside to see my young jawn holla back!" He throws up the peace signs as he runs out the door, down the steps and outside on the porch, as he waits for Sequita to come around the corner. And he is not disappointed with her hair fixed up in micro braids her face glows and once again her blue top reveals her kneck and shoulders , her skin tight blue jeans gives him an idea of what her but looks like as she covers it up with a white hoody wrapped around her waist. Lid just melts as he checks out her rebooks admiring Sequita from head to toe, her skin just shines and as soon as she decides to make eye contact with him, she reveals the best part of herself and that's her smile. Lid jumps off the porch and hugs Sequita "How you doing Sam what's the deal?" Still smiling "I'm fine" as she pulls out a vanailla dutch, "Yes you are" "Whatever boy as she flags Lid away still smiling they sit down on the steps and begin to talk as Lid hands her a hefty napkin full of weed. "Damn this alotta weed, how much this cost?" Not wanting to let an outsider know his uncle has weed he just says "I gotta a connect, just roll the dutch so I can watch those lips work." "Coul you just gut this because I hate the way that shit taste." Carefully using his thumbs and finger nails he splits the cigar in half and dumps the insides out on the ground, when he's finshed he gives Samantha the empty cigar and watches as she licks the ends so carefully to keep it together. She dumps the weed in the middle of the dutch and begins to break it all up inside the dutch until it's evenly spread across the cigar. Then she licks one end and another and ever so gently wraps the opposite ends of the cigar, and licks it shut using those beautiful luscious lips of hers. Perplexed Lid just watches and imagines Samantha using those lips on a specific part of his body which is rock hard at the moment after watching her roll the dutch. "You better stop poking me with that thing, here hold the L and let it dry. Now what the fuck did you want to talk to me about in person?" "Listen Sequita there's no way something like this happens we have the best intelligence on earth, best national security, the stealth fighters can get anywhere in ten minutes. Those buildings imploded like a demolition sight, the steal beams should've melted and folded over. Why da fuck did the other buildings around them start collapsing? And I still haven't seen any footage of an actual airplane hitting the pentagon. I don't even think an airplane hit the pentagon?" "So hat you saying the news is lying?" "Yeah it's Forty Three yo they did this so we can go to war." "Yeah the fuck right! The government ain't doing no shit like that." "They stole the elections and put Forty Three in the White House so they can go to war, this is the new word order yo?" "Tru that they did steal the elections, but I believe the news I think some crazy muslims did this and we are going to war and going over there to kick some ass." "To each his on but I am going to get my fucking evidence." "Then what you gonna do Impeach the president like they did Forty Two ?" "I might!" "Is the blunt dry yet dummy, because you crazy" "Yeah don't be calling me no dummy Quita" Lid gives Sequita a love push on her shoulder "I'm no dummy." Sequita picks up the dutch and lights it when all of a sudden Miko pulls up with Teana Marie blasting. She double parks the expedition and gives Sequita a cold glare. She does not like anywomen hanging around the house, especially hot teenagers. Sequita puts the dutch down trying to hide the weed but they are already busted when Miko see's the guts from the dutch on the ground. "Hi Miko this is my friend Sequita" Sequita waves at Miko but Miko will have none of and explodes at the site of the dutch insides on the ground and loudly she says "Y'all niggers better get that blunt shit up off the ground, that triflent what's wrong with you man? The trash can is right over there, as she point to the side of the house. "I'll get it up right now Miko." "And don't be smoking that shit around my kids because I don't want them seeing that your in college what are you doing to your brain?" Annoyed he replies "I'm stressed plus it's the end of the world as we know it" Sequita adds "Yeah the government killed those people and it's time for the New World Order." Sequita giggles and Miko walks up the steps and leaves with an arlarming statement "I wouldn't put it past them." Lid and Sequita continue to smoke, when it's her to turn to smoke he nibbles on the sides of her ears and whispers to her "You taste like chocolate candy." She shoves him away but he gets what he wants and that was only to see her smile. Still puffing away they hug on the steps as the sun begins to set. Naim and Khadejah come to the front door and begin to tease their cousin with the age old song "LID AND HIS GIRLFRIEND, SITTING IN A TREE K-I-S-S-I-N-G!" Making things more hysterical they start dancigng while they are singing, and adhering to Miko' wishes he tosses the dutch into the street at the sight of the kids, and as they sit on the steps laughing at the kids Sequita gets up and fixes her clothes. "Yo you got a piece of gum?" "Yeah, here ya go" He pulls out two pieces of big red and hands Sequita a piece and after a few chews Sequita adheres to the wishes of Lids cousins and lays a kiss smack dab on the lips of Lid. Shocked he just mumbles "Thank Quita" The romantic moment is broken up when his cousins bang on the living room front window teasing them K-I-S-S-I-N-G! The two turn and just laugh at the kids "You want another one?" "Yeah" and he grabs Sequita by the waist and slides his hands to her but and this time in full control he slowly presses his lips against hers and they French kiss and towards the end as he pulls away he hangs on to her lower lip almost bitting her as they both pull away.

"I'm home , this is way too much for a first date, you better get a car and stop trying to start a revolution." As she walks away he say's "I'm getting a car, but we can always just go to the park." I'm not doing you in no park, it's smokers out there!" "I'll get a car but I'm still starting a revolution "VIVA LA REVOLUTION!" Sequita smiles "by Lid" "By Sequita, they wave to each other and from the window Khadijah and Naim are still laughing, and after picking up the blunt guts from in front of the steps Lid stops by the trash can and then closes the door as he walks into the house. Together Naim and Khadejah jump off the couch and the two chant Lid and his girlfriend sitting in a tree kissing, "I thought a jedi was not supposed to fall in love?" Come on y'all leave me alone she's not my girlfriend and who said anything about being a jedi I could be on the dark side." Naim ready runs to the kitchen and quickly comes back with a broom stick from the kitchen and Lid grabs a mop stick in the living room and as they exchange blows throughout the living room and dining room a very pissed off Miko screems "You fools better stop destroying my brooms now!" The boys immediately stop and Lid ask "Can we come upstairs and fight in Naims room?" "I don't care" the voice from upstairs yells, but Naim has a different idea and says "Man we not going upstairs and messing my room up." Miko and Lid start laughing and soon Lid heads upstairs to his uncles lab and parked in front of his computer he's designing away. Lid soon gets on the web and goes back to his job "I should start from the beginging with the elections." Sounds like a plan" And Lid prints out the supreame court decision for Forty Three  v Gore, and articles relating to the voters turned away in Miami-Dade county. "Yo voters were turned away on election day in Miami, but here's the twist the list was compiled by CBT and the company did not make distinctions based on middle names and some of the people were not supposed to be on the list in the first place. For example Earnest Leroy Jackson was included even though Earnest Jackson was the one with the felony, and on election day Earnest Leroy Jackson was the on sent away. Then there's the case of Wilma Thompson who was notified a few weeks before the elections that she was not able to vote, but hears the kicker Mrs. Thompson is on the Miami-Dade elections commission!" Uncle Sha bust ouit in lauphter. "The state of Florida paid this company one million dollars to make the list, but there's more the state of Florida used a felons list from another state to exclude more voters on election day, guess what state it was from?" "I don't know Missisippi?" "Close Texas!" The company that made the list the previous elections was only paid two hundred thousand dollars." "Sounds like a conspiracy, Uncle Sha stops what he is doing on the computer and swings his chair around "Count me in". Lid's phone rings and it's his friend Omar. "As-Salaam Alaikum Omar" "Wa-Laikum Salaam what happened the other weekend you never called me?" "Man I was out in West Philly and dude from around the way got rocked coming out the social club that was too much action for me." "That's the way it is these days in Philly it's like the wild wild west. I know that didn't scare you in the house?" "Naw what you got planned?" "I have to make some runs out west aint that where you at?" "Yeah at my Uncles house around the corner from Brook." "I'll be there in like twenty minutes As Salaam Alaikum." "Wa Laikum Salaam" Lid hangs up the phone and begins to get ready washing his face, hands, and brushing his teeth and when he returns from the bathroom his uncle disappointed to see his nephew giving up on the quest so early in the night "Calling it a quit already?" "Yeah I need to get out and see the city man get loose." "You didn't have enough last time when Damon got popped?" "It's cool Omar keeps a burner on him, I'll be alright." "You don't have a record you better get your permit and keep a burner on you." "I need an address you going to let me use yours?" "No way brother you ain't raising my car insurance." "Are you going to be awake tonight so I can get in?" "If the lights on then I'm up here, if not just call me and we will let you in." Minutes later a familiar two honks of the horns alerts Lid and he looks out the window and music thumping it's Omar's car, "Alright Unc I'm out  As Salaam Alaikum" "Wa Laikum Salaam, be careful out there." He darts out of his uncles lab, downstairs and out the door, sitting on twenty inch rims Nafi's oldmobile ninety eight  is extra clean and Omar calls out from the tinted window "Get a move on with those Fila boots I don't have all day." Both start laughing and Lid replies "These ain't fila boots, they timberland hiking boots." Once inside the car still laughing they exchange a quick greeting "As Salaam Aliakum, Wa-Laikum Salaam" and shake hands "Remember those Fila boots you had back in the day?" "Yo! We were boycotting timberland man they were owned by the KKK." "You was boycotting I don't care who makes them aint nothing like a fresh pair of timbs." "Nas said it the best suede timb on my feet makes my cipher complete." "That's all it takes to get these bitches they see a fresh pair and it's like cha –ching$. So what's going on I haven't seen you in like a year?" "Shit's the same I'm dead broke, in school Donte was right college students stay broke but I will make the sacrifice now. You looking good I see those twenties out there, and a fresh pair of Mike's as usual." "It's nothing you know I'm a boss. You still going to school to be doctor?" "Naw thinking about law school, that chemistry shit kicked my but." "I didn't like that shit either, I been taking part time classes at Temple but you know what I noticed that college bitches don't nuffin about what you know just like out here it's all about the money. I got this stupid case when I was at Delaware state so they kicked me out of school. But you a nerd so you gonna do well down there most of the students are about grinding, getting high, and fucking." "So what happened with the case?" "Cases I two of em I was grinding plus I had to pop a nigga on campus because he owed me money." "Hold up you shot a nigga on campus?" "Yeah right around the corner from the girls freshman dorm. He owed me a couple hundred bucks so catch this nigga coming out from seeing some bitch and popped him right in the leg." In disbelief Lid just shakes his head, "I would've gotten away with it but some loud mouth bitch from Jersey snitched and pointed me out to the campus police, then the state cops showed up and they ain't playing no games locked my ass right up. Then I went up Wilmington and got into some beef with them nigga's cause I was moving crack on this block, and had to shoot it out with them, you ever been to Wilmington?" "I drove through it, once" "You know how the downtown is right in the middle of the hood so we shooting it out right by all the stores that's open while them white people are going to work it was crazy." "So how did you beat the case, well Delaware state was like just get the fuck outta here, and my people pulled some strings in Wilmington and they was just like get out the state and don't come back. But the judge was like I had to go to some anger management classes and back to school that's why I'm at Temple taking classes." Omar parks in front of some row homes in Wynnefield and pulls a pistol from under his seat, he tucks it away in his waist band and gives Lid some orders."Get in the drivers seat and call me if anybody comes to the front door, I'll be right back." Lid does so and as  he sits and waits and thinks about his friendship with Omar going all the way back to elementary school at Sister Clara Muhammed, and later attending high school together like brothers the two would rip and run the streets of Philly in their high school years born ten days apart they almost look like brothers and when ever out at a night club, a strip club or just shopping downtown girls would frequently ask them "Are y'all brothers?" Just as smart as Lid Omar started husting in middle school and by the time their senior year of high school rolled around Omar was on the verge of dropping out because he would miss weks of school at a time. Lid used to stop by his house in the morning and wake Omar up, and a regular things was saying hi ti Omar's parents as they went to work while Lid was tapping on the garage door window to wake their son for school. Believe it or not without his diploma Omar would've been in a whole lot more trouble mixed up in the game, you get your first felony early and you have no options "Some niggers went for there's flipping coke is their careers." At least now he can still hustle and try to better himself going to class and get away from a life of crime playing right into the hands of the oppressor. A few minutes pass by and Omar finally emerges from the house, he pulls out a city blue plastic bag and says "Here take a whiff of this shit." He grabs the bag and it with one inhale he smells and smiles "What's this it smells like crunch berries?" "That's what it's called to blue berry, a regular nickel bag of this stuff goes for like twenty dollars. Shove the bag in your pants because you know I got no insurance and we gotta get back down north." He does so "So I'm going to have run if we get pulled over." "I'm not getting pulled over and if we do don't run because the haters will shoot you in the back and plant the gun." Coming out of Wynnefield they cruise through St. Josephs university even with twenty inch rims the white girls will have no time for them as they are stopped at a red light and Lid glances over at two white girls in the next lane, h smiles and they both look and with no reaction just pull off when the light changes. "Some things never change." "I know you getting upset about  that fuck them biches!" Omar pulls off and in a few minutes they are in North Philly nestled just inside of the campus of Temple university lies Nice town and it's anything but nice riddles with homicides, drug sales, and drug use it's amazing that one of the worlds most famous universities could sit in the middle of such carnage, and like at Saint Joseph's the mostly white student  base wants nothing to do with the people who just happen to live in the neighborhood. The first stop is to the high rise projects like sardines thousands of African American's are packed into these little apartments that atop each other and with little to no money to move out and little to education to find better jobs they seem stuck in a cycle of drug sales, drug use, incarceration,  and death. "Yo my cousin live in these jawns he got the whole jects jumping with this blue berry shit." "I believe it at twenty dollars a pop", and together they walk into the high rise buildings passing a few different groups of hustlers stationed out front and exchanging head nods, inside the elevator is broke and they take the stairs, "Come on man start jogging cause we have to go to the fifth floor." He does so and finally they get to the apartment and Omar pounds on the door and when it opens the smell of weed smoke hits them like a ton a bricks and the women greets them "What's up Omar Terrel is in the kitchen, they enter and Lid closes the door behind them music blasting from the radio in the kitchen the living room is filled with children and girls lying on the couch passing a blunt around. "Yo this is my cousin Terrel you remember Lid from dances?" "Yeah you were there the night Omar got shot up for his Versace jacket I knew those niggas was up to something they kept looking at us all night long." "Yeah I remember you Rell you had that Pelle pelle leather, and the airbrush timbs before anybody was doing that." "Yeah now everybody and they momma got airbrush shit's you ahd them Moschino pants and ya cut was shiggidy sharp like fire was coming out of your beard." Following Omar they move into the kitchen and sitting around a round table playing spades four men sit passing blunts around next to their feet are scissors, empty weed bags, and latex gloves all essential tools to cutting and bagging weed, and once Omar says "You guys gotta to get to work" And on Que Lid pulls the city blue bag from underneath his pant and drops the weed out onto the table. Immediately they stop the spades games and one of the players hollers "Yo Tanisha go in the other room and get me some more bags!" "Hold up wait until commercial this is my show." The man rolls hi eyes and raises his voice even louder this time guaranteeing Tanisha will get up or face a beat down for showing off in front of company "BITCH GET  THOSE MUTHAFUCKING BAGS OFF THE DRESSER RIGHT NOW!" "Oh no he didn't, the girls all cry, "Don't be hollering at me nigga!" But as she protest she is off the couch and on her way to the bedroom getting the bags. And seconds latter she emerges from the bedroom and drops the bags on the kitchen table side by side with the weed. "Don't be hollering at me nigga, let me get some to smoke?" And he pulls a piece off and tosses it to her. Like a production line the men cut the blue bery up weigh it on digital scales and bag over and over again. Omar grabs a few bags for himself gives Terrel a hug and the two are out the door. "What where you and my cousin talking about?" "That night at dances night club when they shot Omar up for his Versace jacket." "Yo those niggas where on that jacket all night I told him don't wear it out in the streets, just lucky they aint hit us because we where all together." "I know but that was the last time we caught the septa bus down there you know gotta get a ride or drive, cause that shit was crazy he almost died and it turned him right out because he been off the hook every since." "Some people are going to take that as a lesson and some are going to think they cheated death, O been running the streets ever since." As they waited for the bus standing with about a dozen other club goers two guys driving just opened fire on Lid, Omar and the group they were with aiming for Omar jelouse he had such an expensive jacket before they left they had the audacity to get out the car and remove the jacket from the shot up bleeding Omar, the jacket was riddled with bullet holes, yet and still they took it anyway as Omar all of fifteen years old layed on the ground bleeding to death. "This city is crazy cuz" "Yeah welp it's all we got, so where you wanna go tonight cause I just some quick cash on the delivery I gotta stop by the house real quick and change clothes and then may be the strip club, you got money for that college man?" "I can go to the atm, why you gotta change." "Come on man putting my fresh timbs and a throwback, don't be mad cause you got on space boots." Laughing "Yo these is timberland hiking boots." "Yo you don't want to put in this blue berry it's easy money, plus down D-Ware you can sell this shit for a quarter they will by it "Put in on wax y'all buy it, put it in bag and y'all try it y'all niggas can't deny it." Lid shakes head "Naw man I'm cool I gotta buy a car and I'm waiting on this refund check to do that then I gotta get started working somewhere." "Yo those refund checks come in handy I took my first one and lipped it moved off campus we lived in this house yo fucking new bitches everyday, waking up in the morning blazing that shit was so much fun." "Yeah college is the best yo." They pull up to Nafi's house and once inside sitting at the kitchen table is Omar's father brother Sami. Always thrilled to see Lid he smile and gives him the greetings "As Salaam Alaikum" "Wa Laikum Salaam" and as Omar trots down stairs to the basement Lid has a seat at the kitchen table. "So what brings you to north Philly I heard you were in the big easy good brother?" "I tranfered up to Delaware state I wanted to be close to my family, ran out of money, there's this girl, plus I had a bad feeling about this Forty

Three stuff." "Looks like you were right this government had only one path to go down and that was imperialism they were the only superpower left. No other country can check America's power and with Forty Three in charge anything goes." Brothers Sami's runs his own realestate business and he's always been a pretty clean and cool brother never in the streets and involved in any illegal activity the college graduate shares Lids vision of making an honest buck and being a good muslim."Brother Sami I'm thinking about starting a web site giving up the goods on what's going on." "Well you have to be careful Mikahil you don't want to get blacklisted." "Come on everybody keeps saying that but this is America we have the first admentment the right to free specch." "That's what is written but not what actually is. Look at Dr. King, Malcom X, Stokley Carmicheal, and Bobby Seals al truth tellers in their day black listed and assassinated by this government, and these people who genuinely hate us. What kind of information do you have?" "Well everything begins in Florida did you know Forty Three only won by like five hundred votes and thousands of registered democrats African Americans were turned away the day of the elections?" "Yeah that whole debacle is shady, but they've been doing that for years the questioners on election day, we had to fight and fight hard people died just to make sure we had the right to vote and we were counted." "There's more though have you ever seen an actual airplane hitting the pentagon?" Brother Sami stops and thinks "You know you are right you always just see smoke front the building and nothing more you generally assume an airplane crashed into it and that was the wreckage burning. Sounds like you are on the right track what are you going to call the web site?" "Since we make up the majority of the worlds population we are going to call it the Majority Experience Network." The conversation is interrupted when Omar emerges from downstairs "That's enough of that revolutionary Malcom X talk whatever happened in D.C. and New York has nothing to do with what happens here in the ghetto. It's always been about and it always will be about money." "Omar what happens when we get targeted the government is already running commercials linking drug sales to terrorism." "Lid it's always going to be about money the white folks brought us here turned us into slaves to make them money, we built this country the corporations, the rich class all that, this country is only about money." "Your right but this is different having an Islamic name makes us a target, being muslim makes us a target, we are going to loose control of the streets, control of the tri state area, whats going to happen when we can't get legitimate jobs, and we are forced to hustle and the prisons are filled with the brothers swept off the streets under the guise of stopping terrorism, while everyone else just hustles. You see what I am saying a line has been drawn in the sand this ain't about the rat race anymore not only do we have to duck and dodge police but we are going to be the lowest on the totem pole forced to do dirty work for the catholics, and shoot it out with our own people the Baptist just to put food on the table." "So what do you propose brother Malcom?" "Inform everyone and get past this confusion and propaganda it's time to take to the streets Omar." "Are you crazy there're going to lock you up in the nut house." "We have to make a stand against the elections and this 9/11 stuff, it's being used to confuse us and divide us I have'nt connected the dots yet but there is more to this." "Man you are tripping I bet you like this dad don't you?" Brother Sami just smiles "Get this money man women don't care about what you know or what you want to change they want money, you need money. You better take your refund check and flip it. Wake up the muslims runt he streets it's never going to change we been running the streets since the gang war days, we run the prisons, an we run the work, get in the game and stop complaining whatever happened in D.C. and New York got nothing to do with Philly." "Omar I would'nt touch the game for nothing the beast has a taste for muslims right now, the public is turning against us. I just want to finish school get a job, and get married. I've seen this path before this is exactly what happened in Germany and this time we are the Jews, based on lies they are confusing the masses and unless we get the correct information out to the masses we are going to slip into a fascist society, ruled like a military state based on money and not principles that's how Rome burnt." "You keep saying we I've got nothing to do with your revolution, I'm out here taking this money for me." "Well I guess that sums it up then, the world revolves around you." Mikahil gets up from the kitchen table, still smiling he gives brother Sami the greetings "As-Salaam Alaikum good brother." "Wa-Laikum Salaam, keep up the good work." As they walk out the door brother Sami gives Lid some more words of encouragement "One mans freedom fighter is another mans terrorist." Before he could answer Omar pushes Lid out the door and says "Yeah and the rich man is laughing at both of y'all. Come on it's party time lets get out of here." "I don't know why you get my dad started your gonna have in out in the streets marching with a fro and you know he's bald." They both laugh and Omar pops a cd into the sterio and skips to number ten and with a familiar thump you here "It all about the benjamins by Puff Daddy." "I get the point Omar, o.k. I get just call me a closet idealist." "I call you fucking crazy lets go to the strip club on Erie avenue, put some gas in the tank and give a dime for to smoke this blue berry and we will be even." "I gotta go to the atm I don't know why I gotta pay for the smoke though?" "You weren't listening when I told you its all about the cash and there will be  no cash for you college man lets go to the Sunoco, gotta grab a dutch too," And with that they pull off to the Sunoco gas station on broad street and Lid gets out and opens the door for some young ladies who are yapping to themselves as they enter the store. He takes a look a their better assets and walks in behind them straight to the atm, when he finishes he rolls his eyes at the balance of only two hundred and thirty dollars and gets in line, the girls that walked in is checking him out and when he pulls a few dollars out his pocket to pay for the gas and the dutch one of them says "He's cute and he got money too" Lid turns and smiles but before anything is said he's out the door. Once inside the car he grabs the blue berry and starts rolling the dutch as Omar is outside pumping the gas, and he gets some attention from the girls as they leave the gas station "Nice twenties light skin" "Yeah well give me your number and I'll come pick you up on these twenties blow some smoke and blow ya back out." And with that she strolls right over to Omar and finished pumping gas he meets her half way. Lid steady in the car rolling, as Omar adds the chicks number to his phone. Once inside Omar ask "Why didn't you holler at one of girl friends?" "I aint feel like it plus I just pulled this young jawn out west by my uncles house that's enough for me." "Man I'm picking her up tomorrow and blowing her back out look at that ass" And both of them look at the girls as they walk away, "Yo you finished rolling that dutch?" Lid not finished yet begins to lick the dutch dry. "Amatures" and they pull off from the gas station and head up broad street, when Omar notices. "Yo how much you put in the tank?" "Like a dub, Lid takes a look at the gas gauge and its only three quarters of the way filled. "Shit I remember in ninety eight twenty dollars would fill the tank up." "Yeah shit's crazy" they drive up Broad street listening to Jay-Z blue Print until they make it to their destination and like a car show the front of the club is lined up with Benz, Beamers, and trucks all          sitting          on          twenty          inch          rims, to most brothers in the hood the strip club is close to paradise half naked women walking around dancing naked on stage, and there's no games a dollar will get you a hug, twenty dollars will get you a lap dance, and for a few hundred the whole package, and at the end of the night no connections no feelings, no drama no flattened tires, no busted window, no lies one thing about strippers they are honest and the only language they want to understand is the dollar bill. As soon as they walk in the door the music is thumping and after paying dollars for the entry fee they get searched for weapons and then walk up the stairs and as soon as they reach the top of the stairs they catch the eyes of a few dancers standing at tables being tipped with dollars, they have a seat at a table and enjoy the shows as on three separate stages dancers perform whipping their clothes off and sliding up and down poles as club goers stand at the bottom of the stage throwing dollars at the dancers. And as they sit and watch the nakedness all around the nasty scene is interrupted when a women ask "What y'all brothers or something?" They look up and standing before them are two ladies wearing thong panties, bra's, and high heel boots, glistening with glitter on their face, neck, and breast Omar and Lid take a second to admire the view and then Lid says "Naw we are cousins, what's your name?" "Caramel and this my friend Pinky." Pinky waves and takes and stands directly in front of Omar, and he immeidiatly begins to whisper in her ear.  Caramel takes a seat on Lid's lap and say's "Boy you just got here how do you get like hat already?" "Lid just smiles and just for the compliment he pulls out a few dollars and begins to stuff them into Caramel's thong panties, with her hair died blond, caramel is exactly that with light brown skin and filling out her bra "So you gonna get a lap dance from me?" "I don't even know you what part of the city you from?" "South Philly" "Why don't you get us some drinks and we can talk about the lap dance when you come back." She rubs his dick and plants a kiss on his cheek and Lid hands her a twenty, "You better bring back my change!" Pinky sees her friend leave and ask "Where is she going?" "To get some drinks" "I want one and she takes off behind Caramel. "Y'all got close real quick cuz all up in her ear like that." "I think I fucked her before that's why she came over here so fast. So no matter what goes on I know I'm getting a free lap dance but I've got my eyes on the bitch on stage. And together the glance over at the stage and dancing on stage is the original women deep black leather chocolate piece of ass just shaking away all that her mother gave her, her pink lip stick matches her pink bra and panties which reveales the imprint of her pussy as she sweats away. "Damn cuz everybody is in front of the stage on that, she gonna want like five hundred." Omar says nothing and keeps watching when Caramel and Pinky return with drinks. Caramel is locked on Lid as she just found out that Pinky's already fucked Omar and immiediatly jumps back in his lap. "So you gonna get a lap dance with me baby?" "Where's the change?" Rolling her eyes Caramel pulls out a few ones and Lid says "Just keep it" Omar gets up and following Pinky leaves for the lap dance room and Caramel ask "Aren't you gonna get a dance too?" Lid cheap as ever brushes Caramel off as sitting and drinking is free and there's no point getting a lap dance from a chick h is not going to take home for  the night." "Look Caramel I'm going to check the scene out and watch some more dancers, may be a little latter." "Alright boo" and she walks off, checking the scene out is exactly what he does as he systematically rotates between the three stages, and quickly glances at the other strippers making there rounds. The plush couches, mirrors all over the walls, the dj spinning, and the brothers just enjoying themselves no hard looks just a real good time perfect break from the madness that ensues once he steps out the doors of this hood sanctuary. And he sits drinks and watching women use there god given gifts of titties and ass it's a sight to see as he is thinking which one of these girls he want to take home with him when he is interrupted by a soft voice that ask "You gonna tip me sweet heart?" Lid turns to his right and what do you know it's miss chocolate that Omar had his eyes on earlier. Shaking his head "Yeah you did a nice job up there dancing you belong downtown cause you a real dancer." She exhales "Thank you I used to take dancing lessons when I was a kid, I worked all over the city but it doesn't matter there's no money downtown for a sister they want the white girls." "Yeah well they out theyre fucking minds." He pulls out a few dollars and puts it in her g-string and ask "So what's your name?" "My stage name is CoCo but my real name is Chantell." "You not from the city are you?" She shakes her head no "I grew up in Upper Darby" "That's why your voice is that way too, look my cousin is in the other room getting a lap dance you got a boyfriend or something?" "No, why?" He puts another doller in her g-string and pulls her closer and whispers to her "Look why don't you leave with us and make some money when you get off?" "What you talking about because I really don't feel like two dicks tonight." Lid shakes his head naw my cousin was on you first so you got a girlfriend or something that will leave with you?" "Yeah Sparkle, she's ready to go up on stage now." Omar returns from getting a lap dance and Mikahil says "Look who came over cuz" "Whoa I was just looking for you." Excited about seeing Omar Coco turns around and shakes her butt making her ass cheeks jiggle like jelly, and Omar without thought puts a few ones in her g-string, and Omar grinds on her for a few a seconds but since it is a business Coco moves on lets Lid know before she leaves "I'm wit it, but get friendly with Sparkle I think she will like you red" She blows Omar a kiss and both of them watch as she walks away. "Look man she said she's with it, but I gotta go close the deal with her girlfriend that's on stage now." And on Q  Sparkle hits the stage as the dj is playing Akinelle "put it in my mouth" the place erupts at the sound of this club and underground classic and Lid just watches as Sparkle begins to make love the pole and as th song unfolds so does she taking off her black bra, and teasing the crowd as she pulls her panties away revealing her pussy. The place is bonkers as mountains of dollar bills up on the stage and the light skinned long black haired raven dances away. "We sould just have a party and fuck both them at the same time SWITCH!" Lid and Omar laugh thinking about old memories and Lid says "They both bad but I already plugged you in with chocolate cake plus she likes you, when she is done collecting her money I'm on it. But he doesn't have to do anything as Coco walks up to Sparkle as she leaves the stage and the girls laugh and simoultainiously look over at Omar and Lid as they giggle. "Yo Coco butt just closed the deal, you ready to go to my house and fuck these bitches?" Mocking Marv Alberts Lid says "YES" Sparkle does her rounds through the club and finally she gets to Lid and Omar's table as they sip on some beers and bluntly ask "You want a dance?" Like a child Lid just nods his head and says "yeah". Omar begins to crack up laughing as his childhood friend is completely hyponotised by Sparkle and who would'nt be as she stands before them with a body like therobread horse, her big brown eyes look right through him and like a slave to half naked women Lid just gets up gulps his beer down and puts his arm out as Sparkle leads him to the lap dance room. Linned with leather couches against the walls Sparkle sits Lid down and says " Lets wait until the next song comes on, Coco said you had something to talk to me about." Sitting on his lap Lid is only thinking about what it is going to be like fucking her later he replies "Is that your real hair?" "Yeah silly I'm mixed Puerto Rican and black." Lid mouth just drops as Sparkle brushes up against him and tosses her tities in his face "You going home with me tonight?" "I don't usually get down like that is Coco going with your friend?" "My cousin yeah, so I need a date so what's up?" "You're a cutie too, one fifty." "What! Come on I only got a hundred yo!" "We getting a room or something y'all got some blow?" "Naw we got some blue berry we was going to go to my cousins crib down north." "Yeah one fifty" The next song begins and Sparkle does her thing grinding up on Lid at first and then she grabs his dick in his pants and lines it right up and jumps on him without actually fucking this the closest two people can get and and the friction alone has Mikhial gone but before anything cums out the song ends. "You want another dance?" He pulls out a twenty and hands it to Sparkle, thinking it's ten dollars a dance when Sparkle begins to put her clothes back on as the next song plays Mikahil says "I'm another dance?" "It's twenty dollars a dance boo." "Shiitttt I remember when they was a dime inflation man." Shaking his head he says "I'm going to fuck the shit out of you tonight!" Surprised Sparkle exclaims "You gonna pay me one fifty? You must really want some pussy?" "Naw I just really want you." Flatered Sparkle smiles "Well if that's the case one twenty five, see you later sweet heart as she blows him a kiss. He leaves the lap dance room dick rock hard poking out of his jeans he joins Omar at the table as he entertains another dancer. "So what she say?" "It's on when they get off. We going to your house?" "Yeah cause I aint paying for no room." "How much Coco charge you?" "I promised her some bags of blue berry so she was like seventy five, the bitch went for it." Embarassed Lid ask "Yo let me hold like fifty dollars?" Aggravated Omar say's "I thought you said you had money." "Its in the bank man plus I gotta keep some cash stashed I'm not working." "If stop bitching and grab some Blue berry then you wouldn't have this problem." "Where am I going to hustle at I don't have no base man, we lost the house uptown." "Fifty dollars? Im talking to you about again pay me back at the end of the month. " Still aggravated as he hands Lid a fifty dollar bill under the table "the only reason I'm doing this is cause our birthday's is in a few weeks consider this your welcome home slash birthday gift." Very grateful Lid grabs the fifty and humbly says "Thanks cuz." The night goes by and Lid pays for a few more rounds of drinks Coco emerges from the back dressed in regular clothes with her rolling suitcase, and hand bag. "Sparkle is coming out in a second she really likes you red." "I cant wait." Coco entertains Omar backing her soft ass up on him and all of a sudden Omar grabs Lid and tells him "Strippers always look funny in regular clothes, I be ready to tell them take your clothes back off." Lid starts laughing and Coco turns around from dancing "What y'all niggers talking about?" They shak their heads and say nothing, angry Coco is about to go off when just in time Sparkle comes from the back dressed in regular clothes dragging her suitcase bag, he stelleto boots and skin tight black jeans only solidify's the fact that she is a superstar which is printed boldly in neon pink on her shirt. "Y'all ready?" Hype Lid says "Yeah waiting on you to come out." "All that lip is not called for One-fifty." Shattered Lid knows h can't afford One fifty and gives Sparkle a devastated look. She smiles and says smiling "I'm just playing red." As they walk out the club Coco says "We got separate cars what y'all riding in and on Q Nfis hits the alarm on his whip sitting on twenties the girls go off as the lights flash. Baller! Mikahil just shakes his head as Omar raises his eyebrows and tells Lid "I told you so." The dancers whip around the corner in their cars pushing an acura legend Coco is first, and right behind her Sparkle's pushing a jaguar. "Fucking twenty dollars a lap dance man, I'm in the wrong business cuz." "You me too, shit they just take money." Three cars deep they follow as Omar leads the entourage down Broad street, the street lights reflecting off their cars as they pass temple hospital Lid looks out the window and catches a glimpse of the cars as they roll to their destination. Still playing the blue print the group pulls up to Omar's house and shoot down stairs to the basement  and before they split up Omar says "You use my dads office the leather couch is still in their, and you better fuck the shit out that bitch.  Omar leads Coco into his room and closes the door, Lid leads Sparkle into the front room and he begins to peel off twenties he ask "Yo you got a condom?" "Naw sweetie, and I'm fucking you without a condem!" "Yeah I aint fucking you without no condom, I thought you had one go next door and ask him if he got any condems yo I gotta do some push ups." Sparkle laughs as Lid drops to the ground and does some push ups "Twenty one, twenty two, twenty three, and Sparkle comes back in the room "Get up boy he said you better fuck the shit out of me, that nigga already tearing that pussy up." "Yeah he really liked her at the club, didi he give you a condom?" "He gave me two but you gotta work to use the other one." He moves closer to her and drops the fee of one hundred an twenty five dollars in her pants and like a vampire he bits right into her neck. She pushes him off and he falls onto the leather couch, excited Sparkle begins to take her clothes off, and Lid does so too while he is rapping "Cheap lubrication life style protection." Unzipping his pants she puts the condom on his hard dick and like a work horse starts sucking onhis dick. He stands up off the couch and takes his shirt off as she sucks away on his dick like the cocoa cola commercial Lid just keeps AHHHH as Sparkle jaws away on his dick he runs his hands through her long black hair and ever so gently pulls back on it, and this makes her move her even faster, and he scream in enjoyment as she twirls her tounge around the tip of his dick. All of a sudden they hear Omar and Coco as the walls from the next room begin to make a slamming niose rythematically paraleel with Omar as he pounds up against the wall. Still on her knees Sparkle looks up at Lid and without saying a word she jumps on Lid dick as he falls back into the couchshe grabs his dick and shoves it in her dripping wet pussy and exclaims ummm "Good dick." Riding him Lid grabs her hair and pulls back on it as she bounces up and down  arms wrapped around him and Lid nawing on her neck they just fuck like animals with every heart beat, with every breathe she rides his him making music with the song of lust. Farting away her pussy is talking as Lid does his best to please Sparkle, then he turns her around on her back and starts to make his own music as he pounds her up against the wall no smiles in this serious business as they lock eyes and Lid screams Ahhhh as he climaxs into the condem.  Lid quickly pulls out of her and rolls off Sparkle breathing heavy, and sweating she says "I want some more?" " Lid adheres and pulls the condom off and grabs another one off the computer desk. And goes back to work digging into Sparkle this time laying parallel on the couch he just pounds away on top of her until he climaxs. Exhausted he rolls off her on to the floor, when a knock knock breaks the heavy breathing. Coco peaks in fully dresses "Y'all finished making all that niose?" "It's him bitch not me" "Yeah right we could here ya pussy farting through the walls, all that drama y'all crazy." Sparkle begins to put her clothes on and Omar soon emerges into the room smiling, Lid smiles too "You a drama king you know that?" "You in their doing demolition work nigga I thought y'all was gonna bust through the wall." Fully dressed Sparkle gives Lid a hug "Thanks boo" he gives her a head nod feeling cheated because he just spent a hundred dollars and some change to bust two nuts, and just replies "Thanks babe" Nasir leads the girls out and comes back into the back room "I guess you spending the night huh?" "Man I'm already asleep you better believe it." "I'll take you home in the morning ." "Yo you got a radio in here?" "Why everybody is asleep upstairs?" "In the morning Sundays with Sinatra" "You crazy you not listening to no Sinatra man you in North Philly down here we listen to power 99 ya fake as Italian." Lid laughs "As Salaam Alaikum" "Wa Laikum Salaam cuz." Lid falls asleep as a grim emerges from his face and he thinks to himself its good to be home.  The sound of footsteps on the floor from upstairs wakes Lid up and he slowly moves out of the office and walks by Omar's room, the door closed means he is still and quietly he moves up the stairs and into the living room. As expected brother Sami is making Fajr prayer and quickly goes back down stairs and makes wudu in the bathroom. He then joins brother Sami in performing morning salat and since he was late, he has make up the two rakas. When he finishes brother Sami is waiting in the kitchen and he quietly says "As Salaam Alaikum" "Wa Laikum Salaam" "You brothers had some company last night I heard y'all upstairs." Lid smiles and apologizes "I'm sorry brother Sami just having a little fun, we went to the strip club and took the party home with us." Laughing brother Sami says "Couldn't get enough of them walking around half naked you had to bring em home and see what they loked like completely naked." Both of them laughing "She was badddd man, I had to do it." "Well it's good to have fun every now and then just make sure you are not hanging around in those places when you are my age, because you are missing the point the point is family and raising children. Eventhough mines drive me crazy I love them and the memories we've shared together are truly blessings from Allah." Brother Sami gets up from the kitchen table and Lid thanks him again, and ask "brother Sami you got a radio in the office Sunday's with Sinatra is on." He laughs and replies "You in north philly aint no Sinatra jumping off in house." And with that together they shake hands and laugh as brother Sami goes upstairs Lid thinks about what he just said to him and decides to gives Jasmine a call feeling guilty about just tricking last night and thinking about having a family one day he gives her a ring, and as usual even six o clock in the mornig she doesn't answer and Mikahil leaves a message "As Salaam Alaikum Jasmine this Lid call me back, please." He ahngs up the phone and sits dejected at the kitchen table. Soon Omar emerges from the basement and tells his cousin "I'll take you home in a few hours let me some more sleep." "It's cool the sun is up I'll catch the subway and then the trolley I aint rode it in a while yo, plus I need time to think." He gets up from the kitchen table goes downstairs and gets his things, waiting at the front door Omar say's "I'll take you home later?" "I met this girl down south cuz her grandmom lives around the corner from the playground super bad" Omar stops him mid sentence "I know who you are talking about way out of your league" "But I came up here for her?" "Then get her man but don't tear youself up over some bitch." "She ain't no bitch cuz." "They all bitches, but you know what you right and I'm wrong keep chasing As Salaam Alaikum." "Wa Laikum Salaam" they shake hands and hug and Lid walks out the front door and thinks about his conduct over the past few weeks Sequita, the stripper,  if he's so commited to Jasmine why is he cheating and not being a good muslim by performing abstinence and getting grounded in life? When he gets to his uncles house the television is on in the living room and Khadejah and Naim are watching cartoons, he gently taps on the glass window and Naim opens the front door, and lets his cousin in the house.

Since September 11th the United States of America has gone through many changes. The Patriot was passed on October 26th, 2001 only weeks after the attacks on 9/11. The new laws allows law enforcement officials new powers to conduct searches without warrents, monitor financial transactions, eavesdrop on American citezins, and detain or deport American citizens secretly. In the early days following the attacks over 1200 people Americans were detained for months without access to lawyers or even being charged with any crime. During the state of the union speech Un-Elected President George W. Forty Three called North Korea, and Iraq part of an axis of evil. "We must take the battle to the enemy, disrupt his plans, and confront the worst threats before they emerge. "You can't distinguish between Al-Queda, and Saddam when you talk about the war on terror." This is his first steps towards villianizing Iraq and saying in speech that Iraq is a imminent threat to the United States of America. And if his plans to confront this axis of evil was not approved by the  United Nations then he would act on his own. Uncle Sha and Lid are still gathering information and meeting with various leaders within the African American community. Lid going to school at

Delaware State University, working for Circuit City, and spending his nights in his uncle's lab trying to build a web site dedicated to telling the truth when the cable news, and news papers have been flooded withn propaganda. Even though Iraq has been under United Nation Nations sanctions since the first Gulf War and disarmed sixty two ,percent of Americans wanted to go to war in Iraq. As usual in the lab Lid is astonished when he reads the details of the patriot act "Wow Uncle Sha this is heavy stuff it reads just like the act Hitler got passed after the Reichstag fire in thirty three. Check out section 201 "authority to intecept wire, oral, and electronic communications relating to terrorism" Uncle Sha says they do that anyway" "Yeah to crimminals not regular people, so if we protest and in our case because we are muslims and have muslim names then then we fall under the stipulations of these laws." Lid continues "Section 202 reads authority to intercept wire , oral, and electronic communications relating to computer fraud and abusive offenses." Uncle Sha replies "Then I guess we are screwed because all these computers are stolen." Lid laughs, "look at section 213 authority for delaying notice of the execution of a warrant. You don't need a warrant to go into somebody's house or arrest them, that's the secret police." "Yeah nephew that's scary because if you make too much noise then they just flush you out the system like the matrix." Since the passage of the Patriot Act the department of Homeland security has been created, a prison has been created in Cuba not within the borders of the United States of America Guatanimo Bay was established to avoid granting the enemy combantants rights under the Geneva convention. Henceforth torture tactics have been used, the rights of these people have been taken away as people were held with out being charged, without seeing a lawyer, without contacting their families. Like Germany the United States has gone into full police state and the city of Philadelphia followed suit as a tremendous drought has swept the city and there is no weed, cocaine, heroin, or anything else for that matter as the police department has completely shut down the city. Uncle Sha and Lid has gotten deeper and deeper into the grass roots causes attending meetings in center city, Drexal University, and the University of Penn, making connection with technology savvy college students from Gorilla News Network, and Democracy Now. "Uncle Sha did you talk to the white boy about designing a web page?" " I have to meet with him this week, the way I see things this should nit just be a web page, but an internet service provider our place in cyber space. This country going to fall into pieces and we our going to provide our members, our community with a way out." "What do you mean it's going to fall apart like the stock market crash?" Uncle Sha shakes his head "No nephew it'ss going to be a two class system. The elite and extremely wealthy and the poor, the key is that we will also have a spiritual change." "A sprritual change what everybody is going to start worshiping buddah or get like on Demolition man don't do this or don't do that, come on man this country is made by the middle class, we are Americans your beleifs are your beliefs and that's it as long as I am not hurting anyone it's cool." "No your thinking wrong who was this country founded by?" Lid naturally says "Columbus!" "What I know you don't believe that how much money are you paying for college again, is that what they are telling you in school?" "Naw the native Americans were here first, and the Africans, the Vikings, and Amerigo Vespuci were all here before Columbus." "But you still did not answer the question the protestants founded this country." "Ahhh" responds Lid, "The protestants were the extreme Christians in Engalnd so extreme that the English were like y'all gotta go. So they came here escaping persecution in England, but they also brought there extreme views on how to practice Christianity, then you have the Jews the zionist jews, and now the Saudi's who ccontrol the oil, the zionist jews control the banking system, and saudi's control the oil and now they are force feeding this extreme doctrine on the mases all the while lining there pockets with money getting richer and richer. That's why the nation of Islam was the most dangerous threat to national security back in the day, the though of doing for self, doing for your commnity separating from this society that's what the nation of Islam did for us for african  americans, ex slaves without the influence of the foriegners and their worship of Muhammed." Islam itself threstens this Judeo/Christian society and September 11th drew a line in the sand." "So the mass population is being fed propaganda criminalizing Islam, one of the only monotheistic religions, at root some Christianity sects are polytheistic beleiving in the holy trinity or three Gods which is a practice derived from the Greeks and Romans, who got that from the Egyptians." "The Jews only believe in one God so were do they fit in?"  "The jews represent a culture of montheistic practice that's just survived for centuries. That's why I've never been really religious because it does not unite people it divides people." "You know Unc. Forty

Three  said something about the terorist hating our way of life? It's not the terrorist that hate our way of life it's the extreme factions of Jeduism, Islam, and Christianity this new holy war will divide us create a two class system rich and poor, very religious or deviants." "So the web site will be our way of reconnecting the masses, the information we've gathered plus my position papers will give clear proof that we are being played as fools." Uncle Sha leans back in his chair "Yeah, I mean how many brothers your age have the information we just went over  the Forty Three  family, the Bin Laden Family, are all friends in the illuminati, and the Committee of 300 and the Carlye group a military contractor who is about to get paid off this war in Afghanistan, and if he goes to Iraq Iraq!" "So religion is being used to divide us? And when this is all done the only thing left standing will be the godless corporations.  Remember the 5th Element? Blade Runner?, or just look at Tokyo, Japan the whole city is a commercial for corporations." Yeah I remember those movies, yeah" Lid shakes his head as he begins to understand " Damn the United States is turning into Nazi Germany right in front of our faces!" "It's your country nephew I've been checked out of here, I've been everywhere but to work." "So why are you doing this then Unc." "We've umcovered a lot and this is a unique oportunity to pull people away from this failed democracy and get our people ready for the future, because one thing is for sure Black folks are not included in this equation no matter how you look at it. Plus I was a revolutionary back in the day me, your moms, Iman Malik the old nation of Islam crew you know you guys have it nice but I remember the days when we had to ride in the back of the bus or swim in the pool in different days, getting beat up and strip searched by the police, and you could forget about a job. That's why I never felt inclined to get a job because they didn't want us working with them anyway, and no law can ever change people who are hell bent on hate." The black panthers, the nation of Islam, all that was our people trying to help our people and take care of our communities. Because the government was not going to do it, so I tell you that to say this nephew think about what we are about to do because you will be black listed and you will live a life full of trials and tribulations because we are speaking out now in the beginning when it's not the poltically correct thing to do. Is fighting for community, your constitution, worth sacrafising your future, your career for because you will be black listed." Lid sits there for a few seconds, he could back out now and probably check back into the status quo, save his money start hustling, but that's what is expected of him. Growing up without mhis father Lid always believed in the promise of the American dream, that he lived in a fair and free society that was based on Constitutional laws to see things all fall apart this way Lid knows he could not live withhimself if he remained silent. Shaking his head no Lid replies "No way Uncle Sha let's do this someone has to stand up against this monster." Uncle Sha smiles and turns his chair back around to the computer screen. "Then lets continue on this quest as the truth seekers of Majority Experience Network. Now we have a meeting with the black baptist clergy on Saturday the best way to reach our people is co-operation with the church so we need to present them with all this information and see if they want to add content to the web page and if they want to sign people up to get the service." "What about the muslims, you know I am an outcast and have no way of getting incontact with them." "Well nephew may be a situation will present itself, the only reason I got this meeting is beacause I ran into black Bart who is the pastor over there at Sharon Baptist, when we went to that Tavis Smiley stuff he was there, and hooked this meeting up." "Good friend huh?" "Better hustler nephew, better hustler."

"Yeah with regards to crimminals but terorism is such a broad term the first time it was used in English was in the Times on January 30th, 1795 describing the colonialist and the struggle for independence against the British. "There exist more than one system to overthrow our liberty fanaticism has raised every passion, royalism has not yet given up it's hopes and terrorism feels bolder than ever." So the colonialist were considered by the British as terrorist." "One mans terroist nephew is another mans freedom fighter" "Now I was reading this book called "Silent No More" by congressman Finley and it's about the emergense of Islam in North America mainly talking about the foriegners and not us it still gives great examples of how muslims are influencial throughout all parts of government." "I bet it's not like that anymore?" "That's my point this book was published in March of 2001 that's when it hit shelves, you think some one or some group read this and like the British was like Islam poses a threat to the Judeo/ Christian society and we must do something to stop its progreesion, and make it reviled?" Uncle Sha shakes his head "Yeah that could happen not only to regain control of America but the powers that be would definetly stage an attack like that to prevent this from ever being a Judeo/Christian/ Islamic country.  But we all know one thing for sure THE BEAST DON'T WIN IN THE END."

Saturday rolls around and its time to meet with the Black Baptist clergy and Lid and Uncle Sha are decked in suits. Ready to leave they stand in the lab admiring each other out as it is a rarity that Uncle has on a suit. "Your not going to court man what do you got a suit on for?" "We're going to meet with ministers, I have to be as sharp as them, plus you got a suit on." "I'm the lawyer unc, I gotta be on my Tom Hagen." Lauhing out the door they head out the mini van and go to the meeting. Stashed behind the Philadelphia Zoo, sits one of the oldest churches in Philly three row homes now make up the church which provides daily worship, Sunday school, and church services twice on Sundays. When they pull up remincent of the outsides at Donna's this is a cadaliac convention as the best models of America's premier car maker are lined up in front of the chuch all with the licence plate CLERGY sitting in the back window. "Damn Unc, this is like a caddy convention." "Sure your right this is the real caddy club, that stuff down north philly got nothing on this. Once inside they are greeted by an elderly women, her hair covered in a veil she politely ask "How are you brothers doing today?" Uncle Sha smiles and exposes his missing teeth from all the years of cigarette smoke and says "Very Well sister how are you?" Lid does the same waving his hand and quietly saying fine, thank you." The elderly women replies 'I'm getting along doing just fine praise and glory to our savior Jesus Christ." Once again Lid warmly smiles and then he gazes upon the insides of the church which is a true sight to see. Plush wooden rows decked out with fine red appoustery, there is gold bar which seperates the pulpit from the people and the wooden frame work is spectacular as three seats sit in front of the congregation. Like the thrown of a king there is one seat where the reverend sits, and two other seats below for a minister and a deacon. With pictures of Jesus all inside the establishment and a full band drummer, guitars, and organ, like everything associated with the ex-slaves music plays a very big part in worship. After watching everything Lid immediately goes to the front scattered about in the seat are some older women worshiping , and Lid walks by them as he falls to one knee and begins to pray. Once finished he gets up and walks back to Uncle Shamo as he is being greeted by one of the male members of the church. As they shake hands he says "God bless you son my name is Ezekial Hudson we spoke over the phone. I'm from Triumph Baptist church at 21$^{st}$ and Norris. This is reverend Phillip Jackson he is the reverend of this establishment" Uncle Sha says smiling "This is a very fine establishment you have here." "Thank you Mr. Jackson replies and they all shake hands, Lid says nothing and more lile a shadow he just follows the group of older men downstairs to the basement. Once downstairs about thirteen other members of different churches are already seated the representatives from various churches throughout Philly all greet and shake hands with Uncle Sha and Lid, finally they sit down in very modest fold upchairs and they elderly women begin to bring out plates of food classics from the soul food menu Fried chicken, collard greens, macaroni and cheese, and biscuits and over lunch the clergy opens the meeting. As they clergy members go over the weeks usual business Lid and Uncle Sha sit patiently and pay attention to the meeting and topics of discussion, when in the middle of the meeting one of the clergy members sitting next to Mikail ask "Son have you found your lord and savior Jesus Christ?" Lid politely responds "I'm muslim and Christ is with me as well." The preacher just nods his head and says "May God bless you" and the meeting still going on as the ministers eat food and get seconds when finally its Uncle Sha turn. Reverend Hudson says "As you all know we have some guest here today from the Majority Experience Network and brother Sha is here to speak to us about there internet site." The group claps and decked out in his full grey three piece suit uncle Sha gets up with a speech prepared by Lid and address their host. Public speaking is new to Uncle Sha and out the block he stumbles and stutters his first words "PPPPeace and blessings to you all and may God bless us, I would like to thank you and" remembering that this the church he's talking to he says "And thank GOD for bringing us all together today." And he soon finds a rythem "Gentleman we are in very very strange times and religion is being used as a tool to place veils over our eyes and confuse the masses. There is no established religion here in America, we all have the right to exist together and we, we all share a common bond as decendants of slaves who till this day live in communities that are shaped from that inhuman experience." Uncle Shamp has the clergy's full attention as they all stop eating, look up and listen Lid just smiles because he knows he ahs them hooked and Uncle Sha continues. The Majority Experience Network is an internet service provider "Our Place in Cyber Space" giving our community information needed to move forward in this strange land and age of propaganda. An airplane did not hit the pentagon, thousands of Jews did not show up for work the morning o September 11th, most of the highjackers were from Saudi Arabia a country hell bent on imposing the Sunna of the Prophet on the world, and I too can attest to that as the muslim community struggles from within. Our people have to know that the Forty Three family, and the Bin Laden families are business partners in the Carlye group a company which profits during war time. If we don't stand up now the world as we know it will no longer exist and hell will be the destination for generations to come because poverty will leed them to sinful things in order to survive. The music, the television, the billboards all carry subliminal messages that advance the adgenda of our sworn enemy the devil and this false war will do nothing but polarize our people. The oldest trick in the book brothers this divide and conquer tactic and it will leave our communities and our city in ruins. Uncle Sha takes a second to exhale and he continues "We are moving in the direction of a facist government a two class system. Finally a reaction comes from the listeners "Facism here in America no way!" Yells one of the ministers, another minister ask "So does this web site make money for the community?" Uncle Sha smiles "Why are we paying Microsoft, or Verizon for internet service America On Line? They don't cater to us these corporations don't address our needs the Majority Experience Network will do that and like the ISP's mentioned we will have a monthly membership fee, it's the advertisement the ads promoting our own business and services is how money will be made. This keeps us all linked together a network, because the way things are going this propaganda will just divide our community and lead to our extinction. This America is going to fold like a house of cards and we have to ready to provide for our communites or we will destroy each other trying to survive. Thank You, the clergy members gather together and take a few moments to talk amoungst each other when their host reverend Hudson finally speaks up. "Thank you good brothers for coming down here today, the information and foresight into the future is very much appreciative, however they have promised us jobs and money with this faith based initative, Lid hasn't said anything the entire time but he holds dear this subject and finally break his silence interrupting reverend Hudson mid sentence "It's unconstitutional and it will never pass the congress." Reverend Hudson gives Lid a harsh look offended that the young man interrupted him and finishes his sentence. "Well this faith based initiative will bring much needed jobs and money to our community. Now we all know there is more to the story but we must all adjust to these changing times and have faith in the lord Jesus Christ for he will save us from the lifestyles of deviants and sinners." One thing is for sure Lid and Uncle Sha are far from holy and no matter how right they are in their quest they are wrong when it comes to the new adgenda two classes rich and poor, two kinds of people holy and deviants. They all shake hand and as they leave one of the reverands pulls Mikahil closer  and says "You should come down to our establishment the church needs strong young men like you." Lid replies "Thank you sir, but I am muslim." And as they walk back upstairs the daily services have started and from the pulpit a young man in his early twenties is preaching to a semi filled crowd, "LORD! I SAID LORD! JESUS! JESUS!" Lid watches as the young man possessed by the spirit preaches in front of the people. "This is one of our decans he's amazing isn't he?" Mikail replies "Yeah so much energy it is amazing." "Well gentleman I'm sorry we could not reach an agreement but feel free to stop by and praise the lord with us on Sunday's, especially you young man." Minister Hudson leads them out the door, and Lid and Uncle Sha silently leave and get into the mini van and once inside Lid breaks the silence. "DO YOU BELIEVE THAT!? We are basically alone." Still silent Uncle Sha just listens as he pulls off, "I mean he basically just said in exchange for jobs and money then we are willing to misinform hundreds of thousands." Uncle Sha breaks his silence "You got a good look at the cars sitting out front Cadalac this, and Lincoln that I don't know why I expected anything else, they probably calling the FBI right now as we speak. That nigga had the audacity to flat out say "yeah we will exchange souls for ritches and pray that god will save us." "Yo Unc we gotta meet with the muslims yo they will stand with us." "But how Lid, and if that's what the Baptist are saying I don't think its going to be much more different with the muslims the revolution been beat out of us since we assassinated Malcom. What was up with you and the faith based initiative thing, you really got mad." "They can't pass it Unc its unconstitutional for one thing religious organizations are root discriminatory you don't see any Jews and Muslims having Sunday school together? My point being to be included in the program you have to be part of that specific denomination that's discriminations that's why religious groups get grants, but government programs no way dude it's unconstitutional plus it's the beginnings of established religion. What about people who are not that religious, it's not America anymore!" Jamming to Louis Louis on oldies 98 fm they head home.

The next few months go at it alone is what they do and with the help of a web designer Uncle Sha and Lid start up the web sight Majority Experience Network. As the site grow they begin to get invited to the Philadelphia Anti War Network, or PAWN and attend weekly meeting in society hill, the meeting are made up of old hippies, people who want to legalize everything from marijuana, and all drugs for that matter, the communist party is also represented and this rag tag bunch now represents the rebel alliance the one problem I that Uncle Sha and Lid are the only African American males at the meetings, and their efforts to enlist brothers go on deaf ears, but they continue and as military actions begin oversees they have play rolls in planning and attending peaceful protest. Lid is still attending college and finding it very hard to meet new friends as he is commonly disliked and it doesn't help that he wears the most provocative tee-shirts to date. With the help of his Uncle' graphic design skills and the t-shirt printing press shirts that read "To STOP TERRORISM U.S. MUST STOP TERRORIZING" "The first step to a facisism is a merger between corporations and politicians and it includes pictures of Donald Rumsfield, Dick Cheaney, Condelezza Rice, and the corporations they either used to work for or hold shars in. The shirts spark interest with the students but no one has the heart to wear them and Lid is constantly told how brave he is for wearing them. The spring semester ends with Lid bein honered and inducted into the alpha chi honor society for his achievements the past year his three point eight grade point average placed eleventh on the deans list and only one other African American male had a higher grade point average that year. But at semesters end he finds himself out of a job, with without a girlfriend, but getting ready to take on the Forty Three administration as he and Uncle Sha continue their quest to seek out the truth.

Lid and Jasmine cross paths for a day in the summer as she invites him to her grandmothers birthday party, and introduces him to her new boyfriend who looks just like Lid except he's jewish, a new Yorker, and rich. Finally after moving, and changing her telephone number and basically disapperearing on Lid for almost an entire year she makes contact. Paybacks is a muthafucker and boy did she have the last laugh, all the talk of being together was just a lies she was still hurt because he cut her off the previous fall it was all a ruse and as he gets himself together to finally face her, Lid thinks about what his Uncle Sha told him when he first moved back home "Don't put all your eggs in one basket because women change like the wind." And so decked out in brown slacks with baby blue pin strips a baby blue shirt, and blue tie he walks into the party with gift and card in hand. Let awkwardness begin as he takes a seet next to her brother Ibn and and sister Shani and watches as Jasmine tears up the dance floor with her new boyfriend. "I can't believe this he looks just like me." In disbelief the three of them sit at the table and just shake their heads, until finally she gets up from her table on the other side of the party and goes into the guest house. He follows her and waits inside the pristine white dinning room filled fine china and silver wear, and waits until she emerges from the rest rooms in a baby blu sping dress she emerges and startled the site of Lid stops her in her tracks and he softly says "Hi ya doing?" caught off guard no acting real talk she says "I'm doing fine this acting is kicking my but Issac is their in New York with me helping me out." "I don't even want to get into that right now, you invited me to show off your new boyfriend who looks just like me?" She laughs " No honey I just wanted you to be here." "So why did you just cut me off back in September what happened to all the don't get me pregnant talk, what happened to Frank and the summer wind?" "We can still do that, I still love you." "No just say it you where and you still are paying me back for two summers ago and that's what all this is about, I came up here for you." She smiles "You can still have me but now you just have to wait." She edges closer to him and Lid takes a step back with heart pounding fast not knowing what to do his thoughts betray him as yurns for another kiss but knows the grave consequences that now follow once she has control of his heart. "Why are you backing up, what's wrong?" "I don't want to get to close you might hurt me again." "Come on Lid we are still friends that's why invited you." "I don't deserve this was it not me that suggested to you to become an actress when you where weighing your options about being a track star or going back to New Orleans and start having babies with some country bunkin?" "And when I win an academy award I'll be sure to thank you." Lid just smiles "Your crazy can I hug?" "Yeah come hear silly." And they hug still upset he doesn't show it and understanding that what ever happened happened he lets her know "I don't love you anymore." "Stop lying, your always going to love me." They let go of each other and she leaves attending to the party Lid does the same, but with plans of his own he jumps in the car and calls Sequita. Her grandmother answers the phone. "Hello?" "Hi is Sequita home?" "She's getting dressed." "O.k. I'm around the corner I will be there to pick her up in a few minutes." "Excuse me son but who are you? And were are you taking my granddaughter?" "I met Sequita a few months ago, I used to live around the corner with my uncle he still lives there, I have a job and I go to college. Suddenly Sequita screams in the background "GRANDMOM!!!! STOP!!! Your bothering him and get off the phone." She sharply replies "This is my phone I pay the bills here and I would like to know who's taking you out." And she continues with her interigation of Lid "What time are you going to have my granddaughter back home?" " Well the show is over around eleven o'clock so anytime after that." "O.k. it was nice to talk to you y'all have fun tonight." "Cool I'm out front so could you tell her I am waitng, please? Bye, bye Mrs. Jackson." He hangs up the phone and waits outfront and when she finally emerges through the front door once again she proves that it was well worth the wait as she stuns Lid with her perfectly pressed and curl black hair that flows down to her shoulders, the bang that hangs over eye and down to her luscious lips just drives him bonkers as he stares in awe. Her skin tight black pants fit like skin and evey curve in her legs, her thighs, her butt, just poke out with every motion of her stride. With a extra small pin stripe button up and ruby red lipstick Sequita will be the talk of center city tonight as she smiles when Mikhial opens up the passenger side door of his oldmobile ninety eight. "You look beautiful Quita." Blushing she smiles and says "thank you" giving him a hug and soft kiss on the cheek." "You don't even match what's with this baby blue shit?" "I had to go to this birthday party ealier and I just came right over, I have a change of clothes in the trunk it matches I can go around my uncle's and change real quick. I mean we are not going to be late the show doesn't start until like nine so we still got time." "Could you please change because I am not feeling that Carolina blue shit." "Yes Quita." He does so and pulls around the corner to his uncle's house and as she waits in the car fiddling with the radio station Lid impatiently rings and knocks on his uncles front door and finally he answers decked out in his bath robe puffing away on a cigarette. "You better have a good excuse for this one brother." "As Salaam Aliakum, Franks comedy show is tonight I'm taking my young girl." He motions to the car and Uncle Sha takes a look at Sequita sitting in the passenger side, she sees him and waves high, he waves back and as he lets Lid into the house as he does he asks "You aint hit that yet?" "Naw man you know I take my time plus she's probably used to niggaz taking that pussy from her I'm different just have a good time and let it happen." Uncle Sha starts laughing "You better hury up before she gets legal and all the fun is taken out of the whole thing." Lid smiles as he goes into the dining room and changes clothes. "I forgot all about Frank having the show this weekend, this is his last ditch effort to save that restaurant." "What's going on he's going to loose it?" "He keeps firing cooks every week and it doesn't help that its next door to the academy of music. You know them white folks is not going to support no brother and to top it all off half the city is stopping thru there picking up work twice a week." "He's moving coke out the restaurant?" "Were else is he going to store it, at home?" "You right never have your stash house as your crash house." "How did you hook with him anyway?" "I was downtown at training for that job that Miko put me down with." "Did you thank her for that?" " Yeah we had a late night randivous last week." Lid begins to giggle "Nigga I know you crazy, smoking too much of that pot." "Naw Unc you know I'm playing I mean I told her thankyou and brought her something for her birthday." "Oh yeah you did get her that watch, you better thank your lucky stars because that was right on time." "Who you telling I still can't believe Circuit City layed me off, but its cool slid right into a new gig. So I'm down town and on my lunch break I go over to the restaurant I remember you told me were it was at and had a few drinks." "In the middle of the day?" "Hey I woke up this morning and I had myself a beer! So Franks like he's throwing this comedy show so I picked up two tickets and tonights the night. I saw your Christmas gift today?" "Who the movie star?" "Yeah she in town, shows up with some jew nigga that looks just like me." "Get the hell outta here." "What really makes me mad is that when we did our thing she always used to say that she doesn't even like light skin niggas and would never date someone that looked like me." "And she shows up with a look al like bitches is scandalous." "Yes they are but I listened to your words of wisdom" and as he emerges with black pin striped pants and black button up shirt, with a red tie that matches Sequita's lipstick, and red and matching belt alligator slip on shoes " don't put all your eggs in one basket, because no matter what happened at that party I was taking my young girl to this comedy show tonight." Fed up with waiting in the car Sequita begins to impatiently burp the horn, and yell "Come on bugaboo we are going to be late!" "Good thing you were listening, you better hit that before I do?" "Thank Unc" and Lid quickly takes off out the door, and darts down the steps. "That's better, we look like we are going on the prom." "He smiles and slides across the hood of the car and into the the front seat as Sequita has unlocked and opened the front door and they are off. "You changed my radio station?" "I'm not listenin to no rock and roll crap when are you going to get a cd player in this bucket of bolts?" "This is a classic babe if I change anything it takes away from the vintage look they make songs bout this car." "You got an answer for everything, what songs out there bout this jalopy?" "PE, chuck D my ninety eight oldmobile." "That olds ass shit nigga you tripping." She flags him and listening to power 99 they cruise down Chestnut street and descend into center city both looking spectacular "I want ed to thank you for taking me shopping in the spring time I really wanted all those clothes you brought me, and thanks for taking me to this show, most niggas aren't nice like you." "It's nothing I really like you Quita and I just wanted to do something for you with no strings attached I said I was going to take you shopping in the winter so I just wanted to keep my promise." They exchange glances the whole way down as rain begins to drizzle down from the sky. They park on the third floor of the parking lot across the street from the restaurant and as the rain begins to come down harder Lid grabs the umbrella from the back seat, while Sequita finishes puffing on her cigarette. He sprays a few sprits of cologne to cover over the tobacco smell and pops in a piece of gum. "You got another one?" "Yeah" and he passes her a piece of big red gum and together they walk doen the flights of steps he opens up the umbrella and holds it for her as they cross the street. Awaiting at the door is Franks wife Sharon light skin with black hair she looks like an Arabian princess more than a sister and accordingly Lid greets her as they walks up to the entrance of the restaurant. "Hi ya doing Mrs. Sharon?" "Hey it's Shamp's nephew your uncle called down Frank put reserved on the seats right up front for you. Who is your friend she looks beautiful." Smiling Sequita replies "Thankyou" "This is Sequita" "Sequita meet Sharon she owns the joint." Sharon laughs and replies "now you know if Frank heard you say that he would have a fit." "But it's the truth" he hands her the tickets and they walk into the dimly lite restaurant the from the shinny hardwood floors to the glistening silverwear and glasses the place is emaculate. The wood grained bar is packed with people as it sits atop the dining area, and a man plans Sinatra on the piano. They are quickly greeted by Frank who is decked out in a black tuxedo looking more like asecret agent than the owner of this fine establishment and he throws a quick jab at Lid, who blocks it and then they hug. "What's up Uncle Frank it looks good it here man, this show is going to have the whole city buzzing about this place before the night s through." "I hope so." All talk stops as he finally takes a glance at Sequita who is checking out the restaurant and taking in the atmosphere, "Who's this?" "My friend Sequita." And she gently shakes hands with Frank "what is such a fine young lady doing out with this knuckle head?" She smiles "He's alright, I like him." As Frank continues to flirt with Sequita Lid looks over at the front door to Sharon who accordingly calls her husband over. Busted he just smiles at Lid and tells him "You guys table is up front right over their, have fun and spend some money tonight stop always acting like a jew your Uncle told me about you." Mikhial smiles and they take a seat. The night moves on as the show begins sipping on vodka cranberry, and apple martinis, they both order seafood alfredo and share cigarettes as the comedians keep the place in stitches if their was any doubt about how they liked each other it was all put to rest tonight as they stay locked in a love stare that only ends when Sequita sarcastically ask "What are you staring at?" Both smiling he replies "you" Frank checks in with the couple throughout the night and as the last comic brings the house down he once again checks on the status of the young couple. "So how do you think we are doing?" "I mean the place is packed Frank, nobody has on any jeans or boots there's no drama everybody's having a good time you hit a home run tonight. Now you gotta keep the momentum don't fire the cook this week." Blame it on the liquor but immediately Lid knows he's over stepped his boundary joking about Frank firing all the cooks, and accordingly Frank puts the young man back in his place. As he gets close to Lid and whispers in his ear still making eye contact with him"This is my place if I want to fire the whole staff I could and run it alone. Listen up whipper snapper! I don't need you to tell me how to run my place I've been doing this before you were born stick your kneck out sometime and get ahead of the game and if your lucky then you can own your own place and hire and fire who you want, understand?" "Yes sir." And with that he moves on back to flirting with Sequita "So how are you young lady is he getting on your nerves yet?" "No I'm having a good time." "Well let me get moving cause Sharon is eyeing me up from the front door." "Sorry about that Frank." "Don't be sorry just remember I'm the boss because I paid the cost." With that Frank walks off and Lid a little embarrassed lights a cigarette as the pianoist plays Sinatra's "that's life". Soon they leave and Frank and Sharon tell them goodbye and thanks for coming out as he is shaking hands with the old timer Franks takes the opportunity to cheer Lid up "Don't get down it's written all over your face, look around you're the youngest guy out here tonight you doing alright kid, now drive home safe and close the deal." Lid smiles as Sequita is leading him out the front door, and still raining she doesn't even use the umbrella as they run across the street to the parking lot. Inside they walk up to the third level as Lid from behind just watches as her booty jiggles with every step she takes. And all he can think about is should he make a move or not just grabbing her arm and taking a kiss is exactly what she is used to, so he stays true to his word and once at the car he opens the door and lets her in and accordingly she unlocks and opens the driver side door for him. Just as he is about to put the key in the ignition she stops him and says " Wait I want to thank you for taking me out tonight as always you've been a real gentleman tonight" Yurning for a kiss he just stares at those luscious red lips as she applies more lipstick using the vanity mirror, she ask for a piece of gum and he hands her a piece, and when she finishes he finally heres the seven words he's been waiting for "Come here and give a kiss boy." He leans over and wraps his lips around hers and they kiss and all doubts are layed to rest as indeed they do taste like strawberries mixed with a little newports as he pulls away he hangs on to her bottom lip and gently pulls away. Face to face he quietly ask "Are you ready?" and bitting down on here lip she just nods her head as he lunges towards her and endulges in those strawberry laced lips. Heavy breathing fiils the air as the windows of the car begin to get foggy and taking no mind to the sterring wheel in front of Lid she just jumps into lap locking his legs together with hers as they continue to kiss. She grabs his rock hard dick and quickly unzips his dress pants and he slightly pulls down her pants just enough to get those panties that's hides her pussy and he begins fingering her as he bites away on kneck. The lust is broken up when she breaks the silence and ask "You got a condem?" and without a word he reaches in his pocket and pulls one out, "Oh you knew you was getting some tonight huh?" He stops sucking on her young and ripe  titties and replys "always prepared." She grabs his dick and slides on the condem still kissing she stands on the front seat over top of him avoiding the roof of the car and using his thumb he finds the hole against the holes and slides his dick inside her. "Ahhh she moans and Lid just leans back as he finds paradise inbetween the legs of young lover. Clinging to each other with clothes still on they moan and moan as he quickly tosses the slim girl up and down as his dick goes in and out of her the friction and body heat has completely fogged up the windows as the car bounces back and forth. He continues to kiss kiss away and passionately pull onto her bottom lip when suddenly she puls away and just goes to work on his dick. Lid abliges places his right arm just above booty and presses down as she bounces up and down, faster and faster until one last thrust up and "Ahhhhh! He moans and she immediately slides off him pulling up her pants and then fixing her hair, Lid pulls the condem off and throws it out the window as finishes what he started by turning on the car "You got a newports?" Exhausted he says nothing and just hands her the pack as the car begins to defrost the silence is broken when she says "Don't be thinking I do this type of shit all the time I just really like you." "I know thankyou Quita." And with that he pulls off out of the garage paying the attendant and passing the restaurant as the rest of the crowd begins to usher out, into rainy night they cruise home Lid holding Sequita in arm, and completely satisfied with the night he smiles as they head home.

It's just another day at VSI Lid as usual is working hard taking as many incoming calls that he can. His co-workers are up to their usual antics falling asleep at the computer, or taking incoming calls and hanging right up on the customers. Seeing his supervisor Tammy the no nonsense white lady is marching down the hallway and Lids manager Debbie is asleep. Quickly Lid shrugs Debbi "Yo Debbie Tammy is coming this way wake up." Debbie pops right up from her sleep, and begins to pretend to type on the computer. "Thanks sweetie I was out light partying all night." "Yeah well you better wake because if Tammy sees you sleep" Mocking Harry Kalas Lid goes "You are outta here!!" As Tammy turns the corner Lid goes back to working as usual the computer generates a customer name and telephone number and it's Aaliyah Abdul Malik, he thinks nothing of it as he waits while the phone rings and finally a man answers the phone "Yes" Lid goes into his scripted speech "Hi, good afternoon my name is Lid Islam I'm calling on behalf of Peco energy. Our records indicate that you have not schedueled an appointment to get your electronic digital meters installed." The voice on the phone on the other end of the phone sounds very familiar as he replies "We have a gated security around the house that's why the installers have not been able to gain access to the house. I guess you are calling to schedeule an appointment time?" "That's exactly why I'm calling to set up an appointment to make sure someone is home sir." "O.K. what are your appointment times?" "We have three hours windows between nine and twelve, twelve to three, and three to six, breaking from his usual routine Lid ask "Excuse me are you Iman Abdul Malik?" "Yes, who is this?" As-Salaam Alaikum this is Lid Islam from Sister Clara Muhammed School my mom is sister Haleemah and my dad is Rashad Islam." Immediately knowing who he is talking to Iman Malik returns the greetings "Wa Laikum Salaam, how's your parents doing?" "Mom's alright she's living in Delaware not wearing her hijab though, my dad's up here in Philly at a housing complex for men in north philly, I usually go by there to see him on Saturdays and take him to dialysis. How's everything with you?" "Everything is going well all praise due to Allah, I'm sure you read the papers but that's comes with the territory it's a struggle to get anywhere in this country and once you attain anything Satan and his calvery, and his army will do anything to take it away from you." "I've been reading and I don't put too much stock into it." Refering to the ongoing FBI investigation at Sister Clara Muhammed School the feds is investigating Iman Malik using grant funds for himself that was supposed to go to community college classes being held at the school. The real story that Iman Malik is the chief supplier of all the narcotics to the black muslims in Philly, the throwback to the days of the nation of islam, Iman Malik is caught up in the changing times as Kieth Risk is moving in on the narcotics game with the support of the FBI and the Arab Muslims as they adhere to the new sunna of the prophet teachings. To complicate things even more Iman Malik has been dealing with internal issues as the sunna of the prophet movement have been causing trouble on Friday prayers at Sister Clara Muhammed School, trying to get them to comply with the sunna of the prophet, walking out during jummah, not letting people enter the masjid, really bad stuff. The FBI comes into the picture because the federally funded grants, which were always intended as a front for payment to Iman Malik for being the chief supplier of narcotics to the community. That's how he got paid, provided the work for his people and the FBI and Police department pick off who they want to, it's entrapment but when your caught in the devils lasso shit is and a hassell. "What have you been up to Mikahil?" "Things are going well thanks to Allah, I've been protesting with my Uncle Sha in Philly, and in D.C. against the Forty Three administration and the preemptive and illegal war." "Say no more why don't you come down to the masjid later this week and we can talk some more about everything?" "Bet brother Iman, do you have a cell phone or office number?" "Yes take the cell phone number it's two one five seven four six nine six one three.Feel free to call me Lid and let's scheduale the PECO things for Wednesday." "No problem brother  Iman so let's scheduale the installation appointment for Wednesday between twelve and three? " O.K. in-shah Allah Lid I can't wait to speak to you in person As-Salaam Alaikum." "Wa Laikum Salaam." After work Lid goes to is his Uncle Sha house and tells him the good news. Out on the porch with Dee Lid pulls up, Dee handles the credit card fraud thing he has the girls who work the in restaurants and stores and they use the swipe machine to steal the card numbers. Dee is a veteran in the streets and when he was an up in starting young boy he shot up some rival hustlers in a school yard when school was letting out, in Philly you automatically get a reputation after that. Going for a cash pick up Dee's cousin Reese was robbed by this rival gang, he immediately told Dee who was on a mission to find the guys, around 2:45 he hit the jackpot and they ensued in a high speed chase/shoot out until Dee rams the car into the school yard. Still enraged he gets out the car and pulls two hands guns out and begins to unload on the car and its two passengers. The middle school was letting out and Dee swears that all he remembers is kids running towards him not knowing were to go, he says that kids were brushing up against his pants as he still was firing taking aim at the hustlers who robbed his cousin. These days Dee operates a little more under the radar as he bust prescriptions, moves syrup, occasionally is a hit man for the Italians. On the porch Lid shakes hands with Dee, and then his Uncle Sha "As-Salaam Alaikum" "Wa –Laikum Salaam Nephew what's this good news you have to tell me?" "Guess who I talked to today?" "I hope it was that white gorl Miko keeps telling me about, so can stop hanging around here watching porno's?" "HaHAHA Yo here but is way too big to be a white that shit is crazy, but naw Iman Malik!" "Are you serios? Did you tell him who you were?" "Yeah he remembered me and everything ask how mommy and daddy was doing?" Smiling Uncle Sha say's "Yeah he married them two back in the day." "I remember he tried to tell me how to pronounce my name because everyone kept calling me Micheal, so we go into his office and he's like it's pronounced Mik-Hail. I'm like seven so i'm like look brother Iman can people just call me Micheal because I like the way that sounds." Uncle Sha and Dee both bust out laughing "You would always say some grown up stuff out of your mouth when you were a kid. So what did he say?" "He was cool about it, like you know I was just trying to help." "What did your mom say?" "She whipped my ass as soon as I got off the bus from school. All the way home I thought she was going to stop when I got in the door but in the living room was a prayer rug and she just whipped me and made me make prayer all day, I had to write a letter apologizing and everything. " "Stop lying Halimah did not beat y'all spoiled brats." "Yo you crazy it was like Indian Jones the way she swung that belt around up 961." They all start laughing "So I told them what we were doing and he wants me to come down to the school and talk to him." "When y'all gonna do that?" " I don't know may be this Saturday when I am off I'll call him." Surprised Uncle Sha ask "He gave you his number?" "Yeah" "Be careful with that number and don't give it to anyone else, you know them boys are on his tail." "Yeah I read the papers so I have to watch what I talk about because I don't want any trouble from those federalies." "He's a big fish and it's candid camera up there in Norristown so be careful." Lid nods his head in agreement "Yes Uncle Sha, I need all the paper work about 9/11, the Patriot act, and the elections." "O.k. but be careful because ehe has what I like to call the Vulcan mind trick and you will go into the office thinking about starting a revolution and leave with a whole new agenda with cocaine on your mind." Laughing Lid says "Thanks I'll try to keep focused." Dee changes the topic and ask Lid "Yo I have to go do something and I need an extra hand because it's kinda heavy ya think you can help me out?" "I don't know man what you talking bout?" Not wanting to get mixed up in any of Dee's illegal activity Lid inquiers first, and Dee assures him that "It's cool man it's just this humidifier man its gigantic and I can't take it out the back of the F-150." "Cool man you gonna bring me back here, cause I'll stay parked and ride with you, you gonna be here Unc?" "Yeah I'm not going anywhere today." "Cool I'll be back tonight to work on the web stuff." "Sounds like a plan black man." They shake hands and Lid is off with Dee, inside the truck, which is decked out with leather interior, and a sterio with a booming system Dee elaborates on the job and other plans certain parties have for Lid. "Look man when are you going to get in game and start hustling?" "Man never that's not my department if I wanted to hustle I would've been dropped out of school and started that, I'm almost finished college yo." "That college shit is for suckers man the only money out here for us is out on the streets." "Yeah well I already made my decision and it's stupid to drop out now I still have to pay those loans back." "Yeah well what we moving in the back is a humidifier it's sets the room temperature right when you growing weed pants. They wanted me to ask you because they need someone to watch the place and make sure the weed plants are growing right and just look over the place." "Were is it at?" "Out the north east, it's a two story store front but the second floor would be your apartment and the weed is all down stairs, there's no windows in the place because you have to use the inferred lights plus you don' t want nobody looking seeing all that." They both laugh "Yeah picture that shit neighbors walking by and the whole place is a weed factory, good thing you told me I'll make sure I keep some gloves on when I help you move this thing." "So that's a no?" "Yeah man I'm not taking part in it it's intrapment Dee the object of the game is to put us behind bars and systematically wipe us out. Every since we were kidnapped and brought here they have been trying to eliminate us, through breeding us out, murder through hate crimes, and lynchings, nowadays they get us to kill each other over dope money, or they simply discriminate on us in the job market. The truth of the matter is they are devils as they continue to try and wipe off the planet the first man us Adam, and the only one who had and issue with Adam was Satan who refused to bow to Adam." "You know I don't believe in that shit." "Yeah well I do and God is real so is the devil, and I'm telling you the Irish, British, and the Italians are devils as they try time after time again to keep us in check, behind bars, broke, and without our women who they promote and let live as citizens as they continue to try and breed us out." "So with all that the fact remains that you have to eat somehow so how are you going to do it, cause I know you ain't trying to be no bum in the streets?" Mikahil shakes his head "Naw I'm not but If I finish school, and stay out of trouble then hey get a job and get married it's simple for me I'm not greedy, it's trying to deal with the systematic oppression of the white man that's driving me crazy, they will do anything to prevent me from succeeding because I am not the weak, homosexual, jive talking nigga they want me to be,so I have to keep fighting but believe me hustling is not an option because that's what they want you to do, make your money destroying your own people. I always like the God Father when he says "We will sell it to the niggers and the spicks they are animals anyway let them loose their souls to it." Dee agrees and nods his head "I remember that part." "That's a real statement and that's a belief held by all the European immigrants the British, Irish, Spanish, and the Italians, they came here to conquer and destroy Adam period." "So that's a no?" Nodding his head Lid says "Yup". Soon they get to the location in the North East and Lid searches the insides of Dee's truck for some gloves "Come on man I know you got some in here." "You are too paranoid man." "Yeah well I would rather be safe than sorry." He finds some gloves behind the seat and puts them on, the humidifier is heavy and they struggle for a while as they move it out the truck and inside the store front row home. When finished they get back in the truck and pick up on the conversation "When was the first time you got arrested Dee?" He laughs "I don't know I've been locked up so many times I think I was like fifteen." "That was your first felony huh?" "Yeah I had some rocks on me, and something told me this guy was an undercover because I didn't see him before, but I sold it to him anyway." "Wanting that money huh, you know that's a felony and from that point on you lost your right to vote, from that point on you've been labled as a criminal and that has effected every attempt you've made to be a citizen. I know you never worked but don't you get tired of looking over your shoulder, don't you get tired of feeling like you just ran off the plantation and they are hot on your trail eventhough slavery been ended, we are still in chains." "Good point so since you are not getting in on this weed stuff may be you could help my dad out, he has this propane business on Graysferry." "It's legitimate huh?" "Yeah and no" Lid laughs "I'll keep that in mind right now I am working with Miko out in Ashton so I'm going to stick to that the money is good and it's easy." "Alright but if you grab a couple of ounces you could flip that money." "Yeah but then I am on the radar." "You can't play it safe forever?" "I'm not playing safe I'm doing the right thing." Dee pulls up to Uncle Sha house and they shake hands

"Thanks for the help." "No problem let me get back in here and start the revolution viva la revolution!!" Dee laughs and pulls off and Lid walks up the stairs and into the house. Like most nights Uncle Sha and Lid surf the internet on multiple computers. They also have the television on watching comedy central and a rerun of Saturday Night Live, the musical guest is Joe Cocker and he is singing "Need a little help from my friends." "I'd be lying if I told you I remember everything from this episode but I remember Joe Cocker being on Saturday Night Live it was a big thing back then to be on television remember we did'nt have video's back then. In the background Joe is still singing Need a little help from my friends as Lid pulls out on Q a half smoked blunt. "I know exactly what he is talking about" In a deep voice mocking Nate Dog he says Hey,Hey,Hey Smoke weed everyday." "I never liked that stuff these days you guys get way too little for way too much, we used to have vaniella envelopes filled with weed man for only five dollars." Lid pulls out a nickel bag from his pocket "Yeah well this is what a nickel bag looks like these days." "Hahaha Shamp bust out laughing." "I wished I lived in those days." "They getting over on y'all plus the government puts all kinds of chemicals and shit y'all stuff." "I believe you, that's why I get" Suddenly interrupted Uncle Sha screams "Whoa" as Joe Cocker is still singing Need a little help from my friends." Antisiapating Uncle Sha stumbled onto some classified documents, or a web site they are not intended to see Lid slides his chair over to his uncles desk and says "What man?" "I'm doing this search of companies Condellezza the skeezer,Cheaney, and Rumsfield got stock in or used to work for when look what came up on the search screen" He points to the screen and Joe Cocker is one of the search results listed, an erie feeling goes through the room as Joe Cocker is still singing in the background. "I got goose bumps Unc" "That's them boys Lid, what does Joe Cocker have to with Shell Oil company?" "Nothing they just letting you know they are watching all lines the television and the computer." They both start thinking about what kind of survielence they are under "I'm going downstairs to smoke this is way too much." Uncle Sha lights a cigarette and says "Stop lying you were going down there anyway." "Well considering how everything just got real I think I need a little help from my friends." Turning back to the computer screen Uncle Sha proclaims "I'm not scared of no federalies it's time for a revolution." And Lid screams "VIVA La revolution!!" As he walks out the lab and downstairs on the porch to finish his blunt and he looks up at the sky and the starry night thinking to himself that we are not alone.

A few days later Lid decides to give Iman Abdul Malik a call "As-Salaam Alaikum Iman Malik did everything workout with the installation?" "Wa Laikum Salaam, yes they did very well good brother they got here early and everything. When are you going to be the manager and start running the place?" "I don't know may be after college if I don't got straight to law school." "Oh a pre-law major huh?" "No I'm a political science minor, and public relations major I'm taking all the classes needed to get into law school through. This job is really to hold me over until I graduate." "Well always keep Allah in mind and keep the faith, why don't you come down to the school on Saturday around Zhur time and after prayer we can talk about politics, political science man." "Then it's set In-Shah Allah brother Iman I will see you on Saturday mid day thanks As-Salaam Alaikum." Saturday rolls around and Lid is ready for his meeting with Iman Abdul Malik, at the legendary Sister Clara Muhammed School. Embedded in West Philly atop a creek that still causes floods in the basement the school used to be the old Saint Thomas Moore catholic school. But at one point it was the center of all Islamic activity in the tri-state area. Filled with Muslims for the five daily prayers, and Jummah prayer on Fridays the combination of working professional Muslims and their children who attended the school made Sister Clara Muhammed the epicenter for all progression of Al-Islam in Philadelphia. But in recent years with the opening of hundreds of smaller masjids, and a disgruntal community some who wanted to break ties with all criminal activity, and some who wanted to follow the sunna of the prophet membership fell and now as Lid looks outside you start to see the effects of change. Looking at the outsides of the building the green paint is fading away and in desperate need of a paint job. The race track and the school yard needs to be mowed and the fence surrounding the school is falling apart as part of it is completely collapsed and lying on the track. Lid rings the bell and hears nothing, so he then knocks on the door, after a knocks with his hand clinched in a fist someone from the inside finally comes to the door. In a deep voice he ask "Who is it?" and Lid replies "As Salaam Alaikum this is Lid Islam I have a meeting with Iman Abdul Malik today." The voice replies "hold on a minute" and from the inside the door is unlocked and then opened. Lid does not recognize short chubby dark skinned man but the warm smile and hug he receives lets him know that this man knew him as a child, and he greets him with the words of peace "As Salaam Alaikum" "Wa Laikum Salaam brother come on in." As they walk into the school the brother ask Lid "How is your family?" "Everyone is fine my mom's in Delaware" "You don't remember me do you?" "Lid shakes his head and replies "No" "I was gone by the time you started going to school here, but your mother sister Haleemah used to run the treasury back in the day." Lid smiles and now he knows exactly who he's talking to "Brother Karim!" He smiles and aquainted with each other they shake hands again, brother Karim is a college graduate who joined the nation of Islam looking for change and equality in response to the blatent racism, hatred, and bigotry African Americans have suffered at the hands of our European oppressors. He and Iman Abdul Malik had it out on time because the masjids treasury was being used to hide drug money the constant conflict faced is this jihad or struggle your constantly discriminated against and treated as second class citizens on the work force dealing with being paid unequally, and being treated differently eventually many African American males just tap out and turn to the streets to make a living. Then you have the brothers who already tapped out and found Islam in prison like Iman Malik who have been engaged in criminal activity for years. Then there are the brothers like Karim who've graduated college and would like to see the religious community free and clear of any illegal activity. Things came to a head when Lids mother sister Haleemah confronted Iman Malik in front of the entire community at jummah Friday prayer. Holding Lid in her hands she ask that the books be opened up and that all illegal activity cease and dissest with regards to the school's tuition, and the treasury. This brought about death threats and a falling out between Iman Malik, brother Karim, Sister Haleemah and other members of the community in particular the working members who stayed away from illegal activity. Eventually they all split and opened Masjidallah in Germantown and the professionals all went to Masjidallah and the criminals all went to Sister Clara Muhammed School. That was years ago and as the Islamic community faces the threat of being wiped out by a more stricter and more Arab version of Islam it's good to see Iman Malik and brother Karim together back on the same page. Once up the stairs brother Karim ushers Lid towards the doors of Iman Malik's office when he stops brother Lid and tells him "I have to go make my two rakkas because I just entered the masjid." Smiling and happy that Lid still is practicing and not all mixed up in the momement remembered the tradition, and replies "Go ahead brother." Mikahil takes off to the wash room when brother Karim lets him know that "the water is cut off in the wash room and you have to go downstairs." Lid can tell by the tone of his voice that he is very embarrassed but Lid responds "It's cool, don't worry about it." And jogs downstairs to the basement. As he remises about being a youth and running up and down these stairs when he gets downstairs the kitchen area, and lunch room looks like a tomb of an Egyptian king without the treasure completely dark, with a smell of mildew, cob webs are all over the place and appauled Lid just goes into the bathroom head held low and turns on the lights. Half lit Mikail tries to find stall to use as the first three are stuffed up and filled with piss and toilet paper, finally he flushes the fourth stall and it works and he uses the bathroom, once he's finished the sinks are turned off except one as he washes his hands, and makes wudu for prayer. Its takes him a while because the sinks are timed and you cannot just run the water, so he struggles as he tries to keep a free flow of water and make wudu  the mandatory washing before making salat or even reading the holy Quran three times right hand to the wrist, three times left hand to the wrist, three times water into the mouth, three times water into the nose, one time face all the way to your neck and behind his ears three times right arm to his elbow, three times left arm to his elbow, three times right foot to his ankle, three times left foot to his ankle and he's done . When he is done the air dryers don't work and Lid uses toilet tissue to dry himself. Once back upstairs and after taking his shoes off its into the prayer room Lid is at a loss for words as the largest prayer room in Philadelphia what used to hold hundreds of muslims is in complete dismay, the paint is chipping everywhere,you can see termites eating through the walls, the ceiling is falling down as insolent is hanging from above and Lid does not even want to imagine what it looks like behind the stage.  Lid makes prayer and when he salaams out he asks Allah, God to help out the muslims in Philly and help the school get back together. As he exits and puts his shoes back on brother Karim is waiting for him with an embarrassed look on his face. He escorts Mikahil to the office of Iman Malik and reminds him "Take off your shoes, and try to listen this time young brother." Referring to the whole name pronounciation thing Lid just smiles, takes off his shoes and enters the room. If the rest of the school is falling apart then Iman Malik's office is the quarters of a general taking his last stand. Imaculate! the wall to wall green carpet is flawless, two leather chairs and an oak wood desk, the book shelf sits four different versions of the holy Quran, the hadith of Prophet Muhammed and a King James Version of the Holy Bible. Behind the wooden desk sits Ima Malik, and as his voice says "Sit down Lid", he turns around in a tan three piece suit, looking a little older his beard had gone grey but time does that to everyone what remains is this glow of piece that engulfs the Iman and radiates throughout the room when he completely turns around and says "As-Salaam Alaikum Lid" It's good to see that one of our old students has come back home." "Wa Laikum Salaam brother Iman." "So how's your family?" Lid exhales "I'm worried about my mom because she is not practicing the religion, or wearing her hijab anymore. I think the death of my step father really shook up her faith." "Have expressed these concerns with her?" "A few times but she equates everything to female independence or feminism she says Islam is oppressive to women. She's still working as a nurse on weedends at Christiana hospital and some weekdays she works out here in West Philly at Misericordia hospital." "The illusion Lid is that it's feminism but actually it's Iblis tricking your mother and so many of our women that independence equates to transgressing all bounds and loosing the practices and principles of the religion." "Wow that was awesome! Dad's finally back in my life he's on dialysis and I usually take him on Saturday's. My sisters are both in college down Delaware, my other sister is up here working, and my brother is locked up again but it's o.k. that's Allah's will. How about you brother Iman how's the family?" "Very well, all praise due to Allah." "So your working for PECO?" "No I work for a telemarketing company subcontracted by PECO, this is the end of the project and we are trying to get the last of then new digital meters installed. The customers I call are the last of the bunch, most of the times as in your case we can't get on the property because of a gate."Standing in the doorway brother Karim adds "So they call in the good brother to get the tough customers taken care of?" "Yes brother Karim I don't play around, I can't mess around I have o work extra hard one because I am African American two because I'm muslim and that's like being in the communist party these days. My uncle's wife is a manager so she plugged me in with the job it's tough trying to find a job with the name Lid Islam these days." "I know changing times we live in Lid, muslims in particular African American males are the enemy of the state these people are trying to wipe Islam off the face of the western hemisphere and the entire planet for that matter, its no coincidence  that most of the developing countries in the world are Islamic and African nations. And soon in the near future they will be faced with plagues, more hunger, and a lack of fresh water. But Allah knows best and he has already assured us victory over Iblis." "My Uncle and I have been working on this web site I write most of the position paper, we also spend a lot of time going to these protest and meeting about ending the war in Afghanistan. It's weird but my generation is so under represented at the meetings they usually consist of old hippies from the sixties, or real real left wing groups, but the eighties babies are nowhere in sight." "What about at the protest?" "The protest are different my generation is represented but its more of a social gathering when you start talking to them about the problems and what possible solutions they seem at a lost for words and really only want to complain and then party afterwards." "What are some of your sollutoions Lid?" "The first thing is global warming and adapting to the new climates, why try and change first developed nations who already have led us down this road through industrialization and the mass consumption of goods, why not provide the third world countries with the wind, and solar technology first so they are better equipped for the changing times, and then give it to us. But it world make sense to give it to them first so those countries are set as we march into this new century." "Well you know why Lid because it's not cost efficient for the corporations." "I know everything is profit over people these days." "No it's always been like that think about slavery Lid, that was all about profit." Lid pauses and there is a brief silence in the room and then he brings up the meeting he and Uncle Sha had with the leaders of the Baptist community. "You know we had a meeting with the Baptist ministers at the church right behind the zoo, after presenting them with the information about the elections, the war, and 9/11 they said "That if they remained silent the government had promised them jobs and money through faith based initiative." "Silent about what?" asked Iman Malik. Understanding that the office is wiretapped Lid takes this opportunity to let the federal agents listening know how much he knows "Brother Iman Forty Three  only won Florida by five hundred and thirty seven votes. A company called data based technologies compiled a list of felons that were wiped off the voting rolls henceforth when voters went to the polls they were turned away. The list was so broad that if your name was Leon Jackson and you were a felon then Leon Thomas Jackson, Leon Harold Jackson were also denied the opportunity to vote when they showed up at the polls that day. Thousands upon thousands of African Americans registered democrats were denied there due right of voting on election day." Iman Malik shakes his head in agreement and Lid continues on "Now check this out the FBI and the DEA both cancelled there contracts with DBT because the owner was involved in cocaine trafficking out of the Bahamas but the State of Florida who's then governor was Jeb Forty Three , W's older brother. Florida awarded the company with a four million dollar contract to compile the list, when the company before that made the list the previous elections was paid a few hundred thousand. This country has always written or said one thing and done another what takes the cake is that this 9/11 stuff would not have taken place if Al Gore was President. Why did the twin towers implode like a construction site? They should've melted over because the steel beams were heated from the jet fuel? No one is speaking about these issues, brother Iman and that's what we intend to do at the Majority Experience Network get the right information out to the masses." "That's a very noble and Islamic coarse of action, you know that's how we got started in the Nation of Islam standing up for civil rights, and our dignity against hate these white who claim to love the Prophet Isa yet enslaved us the first African the first man on earth. And since that time we have been faced with many challenges from slavery, to segregation, to our own self destruction brainwashed by the television, radio, and now internet to hate ourselves and our women. Who is Adam's avowed enemy Lid?" Without hesitation he answers "Satan" Iman Malik nods his head and only an agent of Satan could construct a society that lives and breathes off the sins of man, that was initially created on the backs of the original man. I see the same spirit in you just like your mother who ruffled a few feathers around here in her day, a spirit of truth and justice you should thank Allah because so many people your age are disinterested in truth and wellbeing of this nation, for we are victims of the greatest hollocost ever and this is our home until extinction. So hows your uncle doing?" "Uncle Sha he's getting better at first he was like no way was he going off on some revolutionary quest with me. But after a few weeks of talking about it he was on board the information was so overwhelming. It's nice to see him get passionate about a cause and now he's more involved with this thing than I am. Scheduling the meetings, designing the web site, all I do is write and gather information for him to post up on the website." "Well Lid this is a beautiful thing to see so many of our past students go off which way and never come back to Sister Clara Muhammed School this is where it all began." "Well you know brother Iman this is truly the will of Allah, I mean what are the odds that the computer selects your name at my work station and I end up calling you? Wow! So lets do the best we can to make something happen here." "In-Shah-Allah Lid, I myself have been doing some writing as well I recently wrote evangelical pastor Jerry Falwell regarding his comments about the Prophet Muhammed may peace and blessing be upon him." "What did he say?" "That Allahs final prophet was a demon possessed pedophile." "Wow, that's rude." "Here take a look at my reply and tell me what you think." Iman Malik reaches over the desk and hands Lid the letter. And he begins to read it.

"In the Name of Allah the Most Gracious The Most Merciful"

Dear Mr. Falwell,

I recently viewed your statements about Islam and the final Prophet of Allah the most gracious Muhammed may peace and blessings be upon him. I would like to remind you that we live in America and the first admentment gives us the right to practice our religion of peace Islam. The holy Bible which we too consider a holy book speaks about the coming of the Prophet Muhammed in John 14.26

John 14.26
"He shall teach you all things, and bring all things to rememberance, whatsoever I have unto you"

John 16.7 to 13
7) Never the less I tell you the truth, it is expedient for you that I go away for if I go not away the Comforter will not come unto you; but if I depart, I will send him unto you.

8) And when he is come, he will reprove the world of sin, and of righteousness and of Judgment.

9) Of sin because they believe not in me

10) Of righteousness because I go to my father and ye see me no more

11) Of judgment because the prince of this world is judged

12) I have yet many things to say unto you but ye cannot bear them now

13) How be it when he the spirit of truth is come he will guide you into all truth for he shall not speak of himself but whatsoever he shall hear that shall he speak and he will show you things to come."

Mr. Falwell these exerpts from the Holy Bible explain the coming of the Prophet Muhammed Allah's final messenger the seal of the Prophets and his miracle the Holy Quran. Allah's words unchanged and his final instructions to mankind regarding how to achieve paradise and escape the hell fire. The Prophet Muhammed could  not read or write the spirit of truth guided him Gabriel and Prophet Muhammed repeated what he heard.

Such ignorant, racist, and hateful comments sir are exactly what I expect from a true agent of satan confussing the masses using fiction to drive people away from each other and hate each other only a general in the devils army could do something like that and call it God's work. I will leace you with these exerpts from our Holy book unchanged over time the Holy Quran a book of peace, a book of laws, a book of Allah and a true gift to mankind.

Sura XLI The Made Plain ayatt 54
Ah Indeed! Are they in doubt concerning the meeting with their lord?

Ah indeed! It I He that doth encompass All Things!

Sura XVI The Bee Ayatt 111

One day every soul will come up struggling for itself, and every soul will be recompensed (fully) for all it's actions and none will be unjustly dealt with

Sura XXXVI Ya-Sin Ayatt 8

We have put yokes round their necks, right up to their chins, So that their heads are forced up (And they cannot see)

Ayatt 9

And We have put a bar in front of them and A bar behind them And further, We habe Covered them up so that they cannot see.

Ayatt 10

The same is it to them Whether thou admonish them Or thou do not admonish them: They will not believe.

I pray that Allah helps you to believe sir but please refrain from preaching hate and lies regarding the religion of Al-Islam.

Best Regards
Iman Abdul Malik

Lid hands the letter back smiling. "Wow, you through a cinder block at him, makes me feel like I'm throwing stones. First you broke down the coming of Prophet Muhamed in the Holy Bible I didn't even know that. Then you emphasized that if you don't believe that's o.k. because in God's plan some will not believe. I bet he won't know what to do with that?" "I hope he picks up a Quran and learns more about Islam before he starts taking shots at us." "Well brother Iman I don't see any grammical errors and all things considered I would not make any suggestions to improve it good job." "Thank you Lid it's almost time for Zhur prayer, lets go make prayer but before I let you go I would like to extend an invitation to the monthly Majils ash-shura meeting. I think the information you have will be very useful and educational and in-shah Allah the brothers will follow the lead of you and your uncle and take action." "Your inviting me to the governing council meeting of the entire tri state area?" "Yes" "I'm honored, but I have one request could I please bring my uncle with me?" "Yes, I think that's a good idea Sha will be able to speak with the brothers you are still considered a youth and they know your Uncle sounds like a plan. We will call you with the location sometime this week, it's after Fajr so you have to get up early and get to the Masjid before fajr. "It's him I'm worried about he doesn't wake up until twelve." Together they all laugh and then go into the masjid to make salat after salat Lid shakes hands with Iman Malik and is escoted out the school by Brother Karim, "We need more brothers like you and less gangsters out here, In-shah –Allah we will see you at the meeting and please stop by the Masjid some more." "I'll try brother Karim As-Salaam Alaikum Wa-Laikum Salaam."

A few days later Lid gets the location of the meeting from brother Karim the location will be at the Masjid in Frankford after Fajr prayer so the trick is going to be keeoing Uncle Sha up all night because waking him up early enough to leave for Fajr is mission impossible. And that is what they do the night before they stay gathering information on the web tonight though Uncle Sha has a surprise for his nephew. "Remember when you first told me that you wanted to be a lawyer?" "Yeah" "I said look up UCC" "Universal Commercial Code yeah I did that the laws that regulate all commerce transactions." "Yes and no, it's more to it than that after the stock market crash of 1929 a new system was made creating a state of continuous debt with the IMF and World banks, they are the creditors. They make the currency and dictate to us how much we have to compete for." "Wait a second we don't run off the gold standard?" "Were you been oh yeah in college, we haven't run off the gold standard since FDR and the Britton Woods system but that's all related. International banks set the standard based on population each of our social security card carrying United States citizens are insured to up to one million dollars to be engaged in capitalism. Based on our population that's were the numbers come from each social security number has an identical treasury number on the back written in red." Lid pulls out his social security card and takes a look at it, "wow, I never noticed that before." "So instead of common law being the supreme law of the land it's commercial law, money what is your net worth that dictates if you get away with murder or spend life in prison." "Hold up I thought the judge and lawyers determine that?" "On television Lid only in television, look at it this way if you are worth a few million dollars than you are worth more to the leviathan out on the streets engaging in capitalism than behind bars." "So because I'm worth more to the leviathan not living from pay check to pay check but and on E-trade but stocks, bonds, money in escrow, property, cars things like that?" "Now your catching on what this creates is a state of poverty alays needing the government or a hand out, and that's what the new deal represents how are we going to hand things out to the poor class, or the middle class. UCC is the law that governs all these commercial transactions and that's all America has become is a giant money making machine a leviathan who's true kings are interest driven bankers from here and around the world, and we the people have become slaves to a system that makes a million dollars off each one of us plus interest." "So what if you make more than a million dollars your worth more to the treasury department you then become part of the elite class." "Correct-A-Mondo nephew now your thinking." "So what about Fort Nox?" "There's no gold in Fort Knox Lid there's only the illusion of money houses, cars, books, and clothes, the international bankers have the real money." "Who are they?" "The shareholders of the major corporations, the big bankers, your friends down at the science center, the Jews, noble families from Europe, China, Japan, members of the Russian army and old communist party, illuminati, the Saudis, a select ten percent of the worlds population." "So they control everything?" "The whole world nephew." "This is heavy I gotta go smoke some pot yo." Uncle Sha just shakes his head as Lid leaves the lab and goes down stairs, to the front porch were he finishes his blunt and ponders what was the point of going to college or doing anything for that matter if the laws, the money standard has been designed to work in favor of the already wealthy? What's the point in doing anything at all if he's just a battery in a machine a sequence of numbers to the treasury department and nothing more. Then he thinks about his upcoming meeting with the Islamic Council and his faith his belief in Allah and the last days and no matter what secret societies, organizations, and groups may plan Allah is the best of planners and his faith will guide him and humanity through. Once back inside Mikahil quickly hits the shower and puts on his clothes once he's done in the shower he walks by the office and peeps in to check on his Uncle Sha and to his surprise the office is empty and then Uncle must've went to sleep in his room. He goes down the steps and taps on the bedroom door this early in the morning is a major no no because Miko is sound asleep and waking her up is unforgivable. With no answer the first time Lid taps again lightly and his worst fear is realized as Miko wakes up and screams "What's wrong with you man!!" Lid gently whispers "Miko wake up Uncle Sha we have to go to a meeting at the masjid in like a half and hour." Surprisingly Miko adheres and starts to wake uncle Sha up "Sha, Sha wake up." And after a few tries he gets up, Lid whispers through the doorway "Come on man, we are going to be late." Grumbling Uncle Sha replies "Alright man I just wanted to get a few minutes." Talking to Miko he calls her a "traitor" as he gets up and rolls out of bed. Lid goes downstairs and patiently waits on the couch about fifteen minutes later Uncle Sha strolls down the steps "Yo I'm going to get you back nigga for waking me up this early." "We are already late man, come on." It's a big thing getting there on time one getting to the masjid and making fajr is a big thing it shows that at home you wake up for fajr and getting up before sunrise is a routine event as muslims have to wake up and make fajr. The next thing is how do you exspect to be creditable amoungst muslims if you don't even properly practice the religion? They hop in the mini van and head towards Frankford it takes awhile to get to the edge of the city and they don't get there until around five o'clock well past the time for prayer. Inside the brothers are gathered in a circle like all masjids they have there shoes off in the masjid and Lid greets all the brothers "As-Salaam Alaikum" rolling their eyes disappointed that Lid missed salat they reply "Wa Laikum Salaam" It's obligatory to make two rakas when entering a masjid and Lid does so, Uncle Sha follows and they also make up the two rakas for Fajr prayer. Once finished they are greeted by Iman Malik. "As-Salaam Alaikum" "Wa Laikum Salaam I'm ready to speak brother Iman, apologies about being late but Uncle Sha fell asleep. " Uncle Sha throws his ahnds up in the air and smiles and then the two of them hug and shake hands, these two haven't seen each other in years and the warmth and genuine goodness is in full view as this reuniting is long over due. Lid, Uncle Sha, and Iman Malik all sit down in the circle, and with brief case in hand Lid just listens and watches as business is taken care of. In the beginning the Islamic Community was made up of the old members of various city gangs in a day and age were you couldn't leave your own neighborhood without being at risk of loosing your life the Nation of Islam put all parts of the city under one umbrella and ended the gang wars that had plagued Philly since sharecroppers started moving up north during the time of the great depression. Recently with financial backing from the Saudi's the prisons have been flooded with arab immigrants who convert brothers over into Islam and the African American community ha been locked out of gaining access to the prisons the problem arises because the new converts completely denounce the Nation of Islam Farad Muhammed, Elijah Muhammed, Wallace Muhammed, and the most famous muslim leader from that era Malcom X. The nation was pro black and instilled a sense of dignity to a defeated people it cleaned us up, taught who we were, and taught us dicipline this new movement strickly follows the sunna of the prophet Muhammed may peace and blessings be upon him. They dress just like the Arabs and take on the culture of the Arabs as depicted in the Hadith a collection of written works from the people closest to the prophet. The problem is that it's no difference than the Baptist who worship a white Jesus, following the ways and culture of the Arabs is not Islam, many Islamic African nations do not take on the culture of the arabs yet they are still muslim's, it is very important that we keep ties to who we are as African Americans and not fall into the same trap as to worshiping another white man, but as time passes we seemed destined to repeat history. Finally after each Masjids representative brings up their specific topic, when Iman Malik is called representing Sister Clara Muhammed School he introduces Mikahil and he begins to speak "As-Salaam Alaikum first of all I would like to thank Allah, Iman Malik and all of you for inviting us to speak with you this morning. My uncle and I represent the majority experience network and since the elections of 2000 and the tradjac events of 9/11 we have been on a quest with the help of Allah to uncover the truth and look beyond the propaganda that is being fed to us by the government, and the news media." The brothers all become very attentive, they nod their heads and give Lid there full attention. "This begins with two figures one and Egyptian engineer Sayyid Qutb, and conservative Leo Strauss. Qutb spent time here in the United States over in Colorado and his evaluation of American society was that the for face value Americans seemed like good God fearing, hard working Christians. But underneath the layer lied America's true face that behind closed doors Americans were anything but loyal to their Christian beliefs fornicating against spouces, drinking, and commiting excesses in sins. Strauss started this neo conservative movement through his teachings at University and instead of being the silent majority the neo conservatives would b interventionist and dictate across the globe and within these United States conservative and for face value American values throughout the world in global conflicts. Look at history and see for yourself the leaders assassinated, or overthrown during the biggest example being the assisination of President John F. Kennedy. Now when Qutb went back to Egypt he tried to spread these beliefs that western society was sinful and that the only way to a just society was strict interpretation of the Quran and the sunna of the prophet. Qutb and Mousari believed that western society had already spread and corrupted Islamic society and that the muslims deserved to die because they abandoned their beliefs. The Egyptians rejected this idea especially after this group of radicals assassinated President Sadat. As a reaction to this the Egyptian army arrested all members of the group Islamic Brotherhood including Mousari but this sparked the rise of domestic terror attacks. On our end the neo conservatives led by students of Staus Paul Wolferwitz, Donald Rumsfield, and now Vice President Cheaney all held key positions in the White House during the unelected term of Gerald Ford and this marked an increase in American pro activity interviening in global conflicts around the world." M ikhail is interrupted by brother Kieth Betts "As Salaam Alaikum" "Wa Laikum Salaam responds Lid. "Your putting all this information up on a website?" Lid shakes his head "Yes" and continues "Fast forward to the mid eighties and Afghanistan is at war with the soviet union, and this neo conservative intervention program was used to help the Afghans to beat the Soviet Army. In 1984 President Reagan called the Afghans our friends, and then Egypt began releasing the prisoners from the Sadat assaination, theyh went to Afghanistan to fight the Soviets and that's how Mousari and Bin Laden crossed paths. With the help of the CIA they defeated the Russian army but when that was over we just left them there with all that training and the group from Egypt started enforcing strict Islamic law on the people of Afghanistan. Nine eleven was not an attack by Afghans it was an attack by extreme ideologies remember the protestants were considered extreme in their days in England, this combination of radical Islamist, Jewish Zionist, and Neo Conservatives is reshaping the globe into this faith first world and those that do not get in line will be cast off into the wastelands." Uncle Sha finally speaks up " We are being manipulated into believing that this is a battle over ideals when in fact it is a diversion to keep us divided. An airplane did not hit the pentagon, four thousand jews did not show up for work that day, and most of the reported highjackers came from Saudi Arabia. Our website is an attempt to cut through the lies and present facts to the masses, because the mis information we are being fed will only lead to a divided America with extremism and isolation by all religions." Once again brother Kieth Betts asks a question "What wrong with that a society that adheres to it's religious beliefs is a more just and peaceful society." "It's not America brother Betts, if faith based initiative is passed which I don't think it will because it's unconstitutional material gain and faith will be merged, not experience and qualifications to get a job but what church do you attend? We will become a nation that lives out of fear, and a nation that lives out of strength the strength that our way is the right way freedom and personal responcibility for ones actions." The brothers discuss a few things amoung themselves and then they speak up with an answer, "We will think about it, but supporting something so radical is dangerous and rebellious and Allah dislikes the rebellious." "Fine" replies Lid call us or look us up on the web." "As Salaam Alaikum" The group replies Wa Laikum Salaam. Lid and Uncle Sha get up and shake hands with the brothers and Iman Malik comes over and hugs Lid "Well done brother well done ." Upset about the response Lid just sadly says "As Salaam Aliakum" "Wa Laikum Salaam, call me good brother and please come down to the school." Lid and Uncle Sha leave and still tired he lets Lid drive them home. "They pretty much said the same thing as the Baptist leaders?" "Yeah they just said they will think about it" "So I guess we are really on this mission alone?" "Yeah nephew but I would'nt have it no other way." As Uncle Sha sleeps Lid is looking through the rear view mirrors and behind them is a blue mini van and Lid, "Someone is following us" Uncle Sha turns around and takes a look and in the passenger side of the mini van sits Brother Kieth Betts with one of his cronies driving. "they're probably writing the license plate down to tell the FBI." "You better believe it nephew." Listening to the sounds of Sinatra over the radio they continue to drive as Uncle Sha falls back to sleep.

# One Man's Terrorist is another man's Freedom Fighter

AND GO AT IT alone is just what they do, the next year Uncle Sha and Lid would form the Majority Experience Newtwork and organize meetings along side the Philadelphia Anti War Network or PAWN the city of Philadelphia would be the battle field in a war of truth verse fiction. Truth the United States of America attacked the soverign country of Iraq on March 20th 2003, under the lies that were told by President Forty Three and Secretary of State Colin Powell. In front of the United Nations secretary of State Powell told the world that the country of Iraq had weapons of mass destruction and using a Microsoft power point presentation he told a tale of how eighteen wheeler tractor trailers housed labs in which chemical weapons were being developed in. He also showed visual evidence taken by the United States Military of locations that housed bio chemical weapons and sites for nuclear weapons. The only truthfull voice coming out of Washington D.C. was that of a true patriot former ambassador and now state department employee Joe Wilson. With over two decades of experience in the region Mr. Wilson contested on all the Sunday talk shows "meet the press, face the nation, and even Larry King Live" that United Nations inspectors were in deed correct and the soverign country of Iraq did not have weapons of mass destruction. Like so many of the Forty Three administration's political opponents Joe Wilson was black listed and smeared by the administration, to top it all off his wife Mrs. Valerie Plame was risking her life for God and country when at the orders of the Republican party the very top being President Forty Three and Vice President Cheaney leaked classified information to columnist Robert Novak. In his Sunday Op Ed Mr. Novak revealed that Valerie Plame was indeed an overseas spy for the central intelligence agency or the CIA. Reavealing such classified information can only come from the top and is indeed an act of treason because Mrs. Plame at the time was working undercover for the United States of America. Because her husband Mr. Wilson stood up for truth her previously classified identity was revealed and in the words of Vice President Cheaney Mrs. Wilson was indeed "Fair Game" as the Forty Three administration ruined the career of an American hero commiting high treason and continuing their onslaught into the middle east. The nation went on with the propaganda and after the events of September 11th America still wanted blood, and based on false facts the United States of America, with its commander and cheif George W. Forty Three went to war against Islam and went to war against the soverign nation of Iraq. In response Lid and Uncle Sha fresh off organizing and participating in demonstrations in New York, Philly, and Washington D.C. stand on the heels of their biggest triumph as they stand in front of the headquarters of Majority Experience Network in awe of the quest they are about to undertake.

"Can you believe we are about to do this?" Standing in the breezy April wind they look up and admire the blank billboard. "Well nephew its too late to turn back now, just to rent this sign was five thousand dollars, go get the supplies from the expedition and you and Rashad can get started because we are leaving around eight o'clock brother." "We are all driving down together right with the people from PRAWN?" Uncle Sha chuckles "Yeah the rebel alliance said they where going to travel down with us, but when they see what we are cooking up they might think twice." "Shit we might not make it down there!" Lid screams as he pulls the supplies from the expideition. "Now this blue roll is sticky on one side?" "How are we going to get this stuff all the up to the top?" Lids question is answered as a familiar voice emerges with Naim behind him carrying broom sticks from inside headquarters. " See you two dummies us the these broom sticks to play Star Wars but if the both of you stand underneath the roll and press up on it with the bottom half of these broom sticks then we can cover the billboard from bottom to top. You can use your blade to cut it at the top just be careful you know that's a threat to national security!" Laughing as he follows Uncle Rashads instructions "Ahhh hahahahahaha they highjacked the planes with bo cutters yeah the fuck right." As he laughs passerbyers just shake their heads as they continue to construct the billboard. Half way through rolling it horizontally Uncle Sha emerges from the expiditoin "Naw, Naw, naw that's all wrong roll the paper vertically use the push broom sticks to flatten out the paper and make sure there are no bubbles. Lid you are supposed to be handling this man how you gonna let Rashad tell you how to create this, college man?" Screaming loudly as if they are on a construction site Lid ask? Where are you and Miko going?" "Mind your business!" Lid just smiles as uncle Sha answers "We have to get some spay adhesive from Home Depot we will be right back." And they pull off ,Lid looks at Uncle Rashad and says "Hey I thought it was a good idea." They begin to roll vertically and much easier Lid cuts the ends of the blue paper once at the end of the board. "Naim use the yard stick and you and Khadejah start tracing out the letters. As Lid, Boo, and Uncle Rashad paste up the blue sticky paper "Cuzzo your mom coming down with us?" "I don't know she said she might meet us in Delaware on the way down. But that's if we make it to Delaware." "Yeah they locking us up as soon as we hit the streets with this thing. But I was wondering were your mom was at becaue this is right up her alley she was a frigin hippy back in the day." "What about you Unc?" Puffing away on a cigarette he replies "Naw nephew I was robbing the neighbors, banging all the girls in the neighborhood by the time the seventies rolled around that whole thing was a distant memory." after about a half of hour latter the build board is completely covered in blue paper, and Khadejah and Naim have successfully scetched out and cut the letters, they wait as a small crowd gathers to see what these strangers to North Philly are creating on this windy morning. When Miko and uncle Sha pull up and Uncle Sha tosses his nephew a bag and a offer "You get the donuts and coffee when this done." "Dunkin Dounuts coffee?" Uncle Sha nods "Yup" "Be back in a flash and Lid begins to spray the backs of the yard long letters and applying them to the billbards as Miko, Uncle Sha, Uncle Rashad, and the small group gathering stand and look while Khadejah and Naim hand their older cousins the letters to spray and then apply. And soon the message is seen by the onlookers and smiles emerge as finally someone is bold enough, crazy enough to stand up against the tyranny that has taken grip of America and the world as well.

"STOP THE WAR,
START THE IMPEACHMENT"

## Majority Experience Network

And in white letters on both sides the sign is finally completed, some people clap but most of the onlookers just ask "Y'all going where with that sign?" "D.C. Lid proudly replies" "Good luck" The children exclaim "Wow" , and Miko only attached because the expidtion pulling the billboard was rented on her credit card just shakes her head smiling in disbelief saying "You guys are crazy." And Uncle Sha replies " If everybody is sane right now, then I would rather be crazy because one thing I know as a fact is that an airplane did not hit the Pentagon." "I cant wait until we get down their Viva La Revolution! Lid screams loudly. "You always were extra excited when you where a kid like you had way to much sugar." Sipping on his coffee and munching on a dounut Lid just smiles, with a full mouth. Miko and Uncle Sha take the lead in the black expedition with Miko, and the kids. Following in the green expiation is Boo, Lid, and Uncle Rashad using the Nextel walkie talkie Lid and Uncle Sha are in constant communications. The quick sound of Brrrzzzt and they communicate with each from the two trucks, and the first thing on Lids mind is Brrzzt "When are we leaving here?" Brrrzzzt "I'm waiting for your people from the rebel alliance, they said they will be here around eight thirty." "Looking at his gold Gucci watch Lid sees it almost half past eight, and for good measure he gives his mother a call to see if she will be joining them. "As-Salaam Alaikum mom are you going with us to Washington D.C. or what?" " Wa-Laikum Salaam when are you guys leaving?" "At like eight thirty we are waiting for the other protesters they will be here any minute." And right on time two cars pull up filled to capacity with old hippies, white people foreign to this part of town just stare in awe as they pass the billboard that reads "STOP THE WAR START THE IMPEACHMENT!" And they park "They just pulled up, so what are you going to do mom come on its going to be fun?" "Alright meet me at the rest station right before y'all get to Maryland at the edge of Delaware." In the background Adesha is saying "I want to go, I want to go!" "Alright then so Ruqquayya is going drop you guys off?" "Yeah you know she is not going to any protest that's not her thing." "Alright I will tell Uncle Sha and we will stop off at the rest station to pick y'all up." Lid gets out the truck as the protesters from PRAWN are talking to Uncle Sha from the passenger side of the Expidition he approaches and greets his comrades. "Y'all ready to start a revolution!!!?" still shocked by the billboard the balding middle aged white man simply says while shaking his head "We have to wait for a few other people to give them rides down the protest don't start until around twelve." "So y'all not going down will us?" Uncle Sha bluntly asked. Still shaking his head the man replies "No, but we will see y'all down there be safe driving down and good luck." The other protesters stand in amazement as they look up at the billboard, the power of the message resonates as to date no one has been so bold to flat out say it's time for an impeachment, yet as they smile in agreement they are not crazy enough to drive to D.C. so boldly and condem the current administration especially when the majority of the country still believes we were attacked on September 11th by teerorist and not our government. Such a bold and fearless dislay could only be conjured up by people with no fear, people who have only felt the stomp of America's foot as decade after decade they are stepped upon like insects by the leviathan known as the United States Government well today those insects have spikes attached to their backs and the government will feel the pain of truth as its most endured right is being expressed 1st ademnedment of the United States Constitution"Congress shall make no law respecting an establishment of religion, or prohibiting the free exercise thereof, or abridging the freedom of speech, or of the press, or the right of the people peaceably to assemble and to petition the government for redress of grievances."

And they are off down broad street as onlookers just look up at the billboard and shake their heads in disbelief. Its on to seventy six and then ninety five south and leaving Philadelphia the public outpoar is of jubilance as drivers passing by just look up and some even roll their windows down to give the thumbs up sign as they burp their horns in approval. Bzzzrrrp! " Yo Unc.do you see this man, they are feeling the sign man." Bzzrpppp "You know it nephew we gonna start a revolution with this thing!!!" They continue down ninety five south and as they leave the city limits the atmosphere grows tense as the family realizes the journey they are about to embark on. " Yo y'all can take the fuck back home I didn't sign up for all this." "Come Uncle Rashad its just a couple of people giving us the finger as they pass by, you heard it when we were leaving Philly the people are behind us." "I don't know bout that cuzzo its harder and harder to keep up with them as these cars try to swerve in and out of these lanes." Bzzzzrrrp "Yo Unc. y'all gotta slow down cars keep swerving infront of us trying to break this thing up."

Bzzzzppp "Tell Boo to just speed up we are the ones carrying this heavy ass shit now stop two waying me because I have to concentrate on driving you don't see it up here but muthafuckers is driving infront of me hitting their breaks that's why the sign keeps swerving." Bzzzzzrrrp " We gotta stop to at the last Delaware rest stop, to get mom I hope they don't try to lynch us." Bzzzrpppp Uncle Sha just laughs. " They taking pictures of us right now we are all going to be ruined and black listed, take me home." "No turning back Uncle Rashad welcome to the terrordome ahh hahahahahahahaa!" Lid just laughs hysterically as they continue dowm to meet sister Halimah and once they get there her Adesha, and Ruquyya wait in the parking lot Bzzzrrpp "There she go Unc in the blue hyndai." They pull up in the parking lot and Sister Halimah, TeeTee and Ruquyya all have their eyes wide open and mouths dropped as they look at the billboard. "STOP THE WAR START THE IMPEACHMENT!!" Excited they approach Uncle Sha as he sits in the drivers side and she puts all sibling rivalry behind her and says in full astonishment "Wow I can't believe y'all did this the sign is gigantic I thought Lid nwas talking about a a poster or something this is unbelievable." "Hahahaha yeah they are going to have a fit when we hit D.C. with this." Lid gets out the passenger seat of the expedition and greets his mother with the words of peace, and Miko gets outs of the first expedition and gathered around Uncle Sha sitting in the drivers seat they catch up on old times and figure out what the next moves are. "I'm driving my expedition, too many close call back there I was watching from the mirrors these muthafuckers are crazy." "Yeah well ya gonna have to fight Boo for the keys because he was getting comfortable up there." Miko gives frowns her face and immediately goes to her truck and Boo gets out the drivers seat after a few seconds of pleading his case. "Alright you coming with us Riquyya?" "No way you know I'm not into this protest stuff they taking all y'all to guantanimo bay and I'm getting all moms life insurance pay." The group bust out laughing and Lid tells his mom and TeeTee look y'all go in the expedition with Miko and Boo, tell Uncle Rashad to come up here with us here take this Nextel and give it to Miko so we can keep in contact, and they do so. Seconds later Uncle Rashad emerges from the expedition and Lid jumps in the passenger seat with his uncle Sha. "Y'all all right leaving that nigga with my niecy poo, sister in law, and sister?" Uncle Sha replies "They will be fine, I'm worried about on of these crazy muthafuckers running us off this road. As they pull out of the parking lot in Delaware the mood from the crowd is the polar opposite from that of Philly as travelers give them the finger as they read the sign, or hog spit in the direction of the family as they pull off and back unto ninety five south enroute to the nations capital Washington D.C..” The ride down only gets worse as more and more drivers continue to derail the impeachment express by pulling in front of the leading expedition and slamming their breaks or trying to cut in front of the tailing expiditon but at no time do they separate for more than a few minutes as Miko being the rider that she is quickly catches up to her husband and using the nextells they coordinate a time when Uncle Sha pulls forward and she slides into the lane once again seeling up the Impeachment express. Once they get to the toll booths in Maryland after nearly escaping a major crash with every waking moment the state police wait at the first toll booth. And flagging the caravan he orders them to pull over before they cross the booths and go any farther. “What is this Unc? They better be offering police escort down to D.C.” Uncle Sha says nothing and nervously he just sits as he knows full well he doesn’t have a drivers license and that’s the first thing the cop is going to ask for. The older white man dressed in a polo shirt and slacks with graying hair comes up to the drivers side window as the Maryland state trooper begins to examine the billboard and how it is attached to the expedition. “Do have your drivers license?” Uncle Sha says nothing and the gentleman continues “We got a call from the other toll way up in Delaware that y’all were distrupting traffic on the way down here?” Lid estatic says “What! People were trying to run us off the road the whole way down I thought you guys were going to give us a police escort or something.” Uncle Sha knows he is in trouble and the whole shin dig might be over, if he has to produce a license and he mumbles as he says “Yeah man I’ve been dodging maniacs as they hit their breaks in front of me, we’ve trying to stay in the slow lane.” “Well what organization are you guys from y’all not with Al Queda are you?” Lid just cracks up laughing and his movements exposes to the white man the video camera he’s been using to film the entire trip. “What a second guys that’s not filming is it?” The tables have turned as he is no longer in power, he knows this stop was unwarranted and this whole traffic stop could leave him liable for a civil suit, so Lid replies “Yeah I’m filming the whole trip, you gonna be in the documentary, smile for the camera.” Siezing the moment Uncle Sha tells Uncle Rashasd“Yo go get the rest of the camera's!" And Uncle Rashad quickly goes into the back of the truck and pulls out another camera. With the state trooper beside him now the man quickly gets very nice and mild mannered. "You guys did not film any of the administration building?" "No" replies Uncle Sha "Just been taping this conversation and the crazy people trying to run us off the road on the way down here." "Were are you guys going again?" "To the capital for a demonstration can you guys escort us down there." The trooper speaks up humbly "No way we can't commit a cruiser to that but what we can do is call down until you guys get to D.C. so we can be on the look out for people trying to run y'all off the road." "Thanks" replies Uncle Sha, "But try to stay in the slow lane away from the speding traffic, and good luck." "Thanks man" Before they walk away the man asked one more time "And y'all didn't film any of the tolls or administration building?" "No sir replies Lid. And after patiently waiting a few minutes Uncle Shamp two ways his wife Miko "Alright I'm ready to pull off." Brrrzzzp "What happened Sha?" Brrzzzp "When they found out Lid was taping all this they started acting like we were paying for their salaries and treating us with some respect." "You must mean the rest of us because you aint worked since the Ford administration." "Hahaha you right I've been everywhere but to work." And they continue on their journey through the state of Maryland and into Washington D.C. were the crowd is more receptive as they converge to the family like in Philadelphia filled with exuberance, and excitement they continue to drive into the capital down Pennsylvania avenue pass the White House were the hundreds of daily protesters begin to cheer at the sight of truth in words "STOP THE WAR START THE IMPEACHMENT!" "This is crazy man, they really feeling this." "Yeah but it aint over look ahead" and as they pull into the capital circle were the demonstration is taking place they are met by thousands of protesters on one side of the street, and hundreds of police officers dressed in full riot gear on another side of the street. Blasting the beatles "Revolution" they slowly split the sea of protesters and cops as Lid leans out the window taunting the army of cops on one side the crowd is energized at the truthful words "STOP THE WAR START THE IMPEACHMENT" and on the other police only get angry as they pass and Lid hangs out the window taunting "Look there's police chief Ramsey!" dressed in full riot gear the top cop just looks and strares at the family as he pounds away on his night stick and as they pas through you can see the tension in the air, and the family just cuts through it with words that are more evident to the days and times "Start the Impeachment" And as Naim and Khadejah begin to scream "Atticka, Atticka, Atticka fromt the back seats they pull into a parking lot followed now by federal agents in and police officers in unmarked crown victoria's and chevy impala's Lid comments to his Uncle "Did you see Ramsey I can't believe a black man looked at us that way, it was as if any false moves and they were going to bash our brains in!" "That's no black man nephew, he's just another agent of the apocolyspe!" And as the doors open the family a nurse, a nursing student, a college syudent, three grade school students, and three black men that have felt nothing but the wrath of America emerge from the expiditions dressed in everyday clothes not violent kids of Seattle, not the militant black panthers of Oakland, not the militia of the deep south a family from Scotish descent, brought here as slaves and then migratred to the north, some of their fathers served for the military of this once great country, some of their fathers benefited from social justice programs like affirmative action, some of them vote, some of them engage in crime to stay aflout, but they are mothers, fathers, sons, and daughters, tav payers, voters, protesters, and Americans and the situation is quickly disfused as the police and federal guard get a close up view of the people bold enough to confront the new empire that has taken the country and the world by storm. As soon as he gets out Uncle Sha goes to Miko not runnig because his weight simply will not allow him too, when he finally reaches her they hug, and kiss. "That was insane, what did those cops want in Maryland?" "They said we were disrupting traffic." And Lid adds "But once we showed them that they were being taped they let us go and changed right up on us." The trucks and the billboard stay parked in the lot and as they usher in with the crowd of protesters they are greeted with hugs, handshakes, and smiles of approval from the protesters, and visitors of the many historic buildings and museums that come to our nations capital. And they march joined by other Americans with signs that scream the fury and anger felt by millions across the nation

## "THE REVOLUTION STARTS NOW!"

## "WHY IS THERE ALWAYS MONEY FOR WAR BUT NOT FOR EDUCATION"

## "FORTY THREE  LIED THOUSANDS DIED"

## "ANTI FORTY THREE  ANTI IMPERIALISM"

## "COLLEGE NOT COMBAT"

And as they march the end of the day nears and unlike the trust fund kids in Seattle, and unlike the police brutality that struct the civil rights protesters everything this day is peaceful as we gather to express our first adment ment right, and right before they leave and head back up north they take a spin around Washington D.C. once again into the ghetto and and receive a hauting realization. "Look at our people Unc.?" "I know they look so dejected and disenfranchised. The passer byers just look up at the sign and shake their heads and walk along the streets the walking dead plagued with drug addiction, discrimination, and poverty so close to the viens of the worlds most powerfulest nation yet and they move like zombies with heads lowered in defeat and are some of the most poverty stricken people in the lands. "They look like they have no hope at all." "That's because they don't the one thing I noticed in all the meetings in center city was this none of those organizations give a fuck about what happens to us, and our people." That's why nephew I am really starting to second guess this whole thing and start focusing strickly on the state of O.U.R. community." "Well I'm with you but I have to stay on this Forty Three  thing at least until after the2004 elections." "You really believe that Forty Three  is going to lose, you know this is an eight year plan stop ignoring the facts the electronic machines are rigged the Die Bold system isn't hack proof and who ever they want to win will win, period." "So do you want us to do have a real revolution?" "Brother its time to check out of this system, look at our people they are like that in Baltimore, New York, Boston, and Philly it doesn't matter like the anti war meetings we don't fit into the equation and at the end of the day we are going to have to do for self because the government will not help us do anything to uplift ourselves." "Well this whole shin dig doesn't really help you know they tagged us, qand tomorrow morning we are going to be on every terrorist list out there." "Yeah but you knew the consequences to your actions this morning right?" "Yeah" "But you went ahead and came down here though why?" "Because ten years from now I want to look back and say I spoke out and stood up for truth, I want to be able to sleep with myself at night knowing we presented the truth to the masses and if they listened or didn't listen we gave them a choice." " Alright but now its time to take things to the next level and really separate from this beast because you better believe there are going to be some major repracusions for this one but believe me when I say it as we drive through the ghettos we are entrapped like mice in what takes place around the corner in Washington D.C. has nothing to do with the systematic genocide, that goes on here in the ghetto, you better wake up nephew this isn't your country and they don't want you here."

# "College Graduate"

"As-Salaam Alaikum uncle Faruq, can we talk?" "Wa-Laikum Salaam Mikel what going on?" "My moms just kicked me out we had a fight and she gave me the boot, now I don't have a job, and a place to stay. I'm over Uncle Sha house trying to get things together." " Well it's not that bad you gotta a place to stay, what I can do to help?" " I talked to Uncle Razin he said your job was hiring what's up man can you plug me in?" "Yo? Didn't you just graduate from college what happened to your job at the bank? You are making some bad decisions Mikel, what's going with you?" "I've been runnig hard for years now you know that man the web site, school, work, I really just wanted some time off from work and finally have a vacation. I was only three days into it and look what happened." "What happened at your moms?" "Alright it's like this she let one of my sisters girlfriends move in." " Who" "Danielle, this bitch is baddd! So you know I went bonkers when I came home from work and she is sitting on the couch with her blue eyes and caramel skin, I was like the wolf in the old WB cartoons going right through the ROOF!" "Hah hah hah I hear that nephew, did you hit?" Mikel quickly responds I didn't even have enough time man, I'm on my distinguished gentleman thing taking her to work in the morning, waking up making chocolate chip waffles in the morning for breakfast. My moms and my sister started getting mad." Uncle Faruq is on the other end of the phone cracking up and just says " keep going, you know they were going to trip". "So Ruqayya hating ass tells my mom that I was coming at Danielle and making her uncomfortable, Come on man I'm letting this bitch sit on my couch and watch t.v. when the Phillies are on." Uncle Faruq is on the phone laughing away "You know she is not supposed to be there in the first ain't no none believing women supposed to be in the house anyway running around with her big ass titties hanging all out bouncing around the house with Winnie the pooh bajamas on, WINNIE

THE POOH!" "You crazy nephew so how did y'all start fighting?" "So when she confronted me I was like I never put a hand on her, and I never came at her we would just sit across from each other in the living room and lock eyes staring at each other." "You good nephew, that bitch was falling in love with you" " You better believe it im good I know what I'm doing. So I took it to another level and said since I did not have any decision as to whether or not she could move in, it's none of your damn business what we do in here." "You crazy, you said that to your mom?" "Yeah man I wasn't drunk, I was just hot yo she is not supposed to be there and I did not make any moves." "That's where you made your mistake the girl was all messed up she started really having feeling yo, that bitch knew if she called your bluff you would react and be outa there no more goo goo eyes, she has the couch all to herself now and I bet she will be bringing niggas in the house and everything." At the same time they both say "BITHCHES ARE SCANDELOUS!" Look I feel y nephew bitches are crazy, look I will talk to the owners they need a new porter and maybey they will hire you but you are way over qualified for the position so they might not. But I will keep you posted call me back in two days and I will let you know." "Good looking out Uncle Faruq As-Sallam Alaikum." Mikel hangs up the phone and retreats to his Uncles office on the third floor, he turns all the lights off and the computer screens are the only things that are keeping the room lite. Mikel reflects on things how could he be rejected by Danielle like that and then kicked out of the house by his mom's after graduating college? He's failed and in need of drastic change Mikel focuses on the music the chief influence in Black culture it glorifies sex, material wealth, drugs, hustling, self destruction and dumbs down the Black community. And since Mikel is not a hustler and refuses to deal drugs to his own people then Mikel is out sucker free Sundays is taking on a whole new meaning, and as he sits in the darkness of his uncle's office he begins to download songs from a different era off the site Morpheus. Classic rock and roll songs of the sixties and seventies, Monster by Steppenwolf, War Pigs by Black Sabbath, Sympathy for the Devil by the Rolling Stones, Helter Skelter by the Beatles, and Kashmir by Led Zeppelin, and many more hundreds of songs all the classic rock n roll songs he can think off and for the next two days he just polishes off a case of gueiness stout and smokes cigaretts with the  lights out, and music blasting.  Uncle Sha routinely comes upstairs to check on his now deranged nephew " Mikel! Greatest man alive!" "Yeah right all I wanted was a vacation man I've been working non-stop for like six years since ninety eight! I feel betrayed." Uncle Sha tries to give Mikel some fatherly advice " Don't sweat it, what matters now is how you get back up that is what makes you. What are you doing?" "Downloading classic rock songs I'm completely turned off by the new rap its dumb down and all they talk about is killing, sex, and drugs, it's stupid." "Going back in time huh, did you get any War yet?" "How did I know you were going to ask that? Of coarse I did "The World is a ghetto." "I remember when the anthology came out at Tower records on South Street and you listed to that jawn all night long Unc." "What else you got on there?" Iron Maiden, Steppen Wolf, The Stones, Zepelin, CCR, The Beatles, Black Sabbath, The Doors, I got my jawn on there "This is the end" my only friend the end, I'll never look inside your eyes again." Uncle Sha begins to laugh and say's "You are really taking this hard going all Brando on everyone, "The horror, the horror." Mikel laughs yeah I'm gonna start my own record company call it hood stock records Take Stock in Your Hood!" "Go ahead nephew but don't things get you down keep fighting and don't give up in the Quran it says no obstacle is put before a man that he cannot handle." "I'll keep fighting you better because when you stop that's when you loose." Uncle Sha leaves the office and Mikel takes a break from the computer. Since he is back in the neighborhood he decides to give Sequita a call, her number still in his phone he dials and after a few rings he is greeting by the voice of an old lady, "Hello?" Very modestly Mikel says "Hi Mrs. Jackson can I speak to Sequita?". "Who's this Mikel" "Oh yeah bugaboo" They both laughs "how you doing Mrs. Jackson?" "I'm fine thanks to God, that grand daughter of mines is upstairs I think" mrs. Jackson yells up the stairs SEQUITA!" And a few seconds later She picks up the phone and with just one word you can here it in a voice how much she just wants to get out of the house." "Hello?" "What's the deal Quita?" "Who's this?" "Mikel" "Where you been at, just popping up out of nowhere?" " I'm around the corner at my Uncle's come sit with me for a while? I'm going through something come on over Quita?" "You still got that Taurus?" "Yeah, so" "Naw homie my boy friend is coming around in a few minutes, and he's got a truck with twenties on it." Mikel says nothing but is really hurt on the other end of the phone. "Alright then, guess I will keep knocking off this case of Guiness" Sequita  hears the low tone of Mikel's voice and like a friend she comes up with a better plan. " You still drinking that nasty stuff later on tonight after he leaves why don't you take me out to the bar for a drink, remember the one we watched the all-star game at?" "Yeah, so you gonna call me later on?" "Yeah boy now stop sounding like your dog just died, and don't drink anymore beers !" "Talk to you later Quita." "By Buggaboo." Mikel hangs up the phone he knows Sequita was just saying that to make him feel better so he turns up the Doors "This is the end, my only friend the end." Paying no attention to Sequita's advice he pops open another guiness stout and turns Jim Morrison up and listens in the darkness as it gets deeper and deeper into the night.

The stress is staring to where Mikel down and he's almost broke, expecting his last pay check from old time bank and when it does not show early Friday morning livid he decides to give customer service a call. After a few minutes of waiting on hold he finally gets an operator and already upset Mikel lets his former employer hear it over the phone. "Why hasn't my paycheck been deposited into my account?" The operator responds "What day does your paycheck go into your account?" "Its usually in there Thursday night" "From what company does the pay check come from" "Upset Mikel sarcastocly replies from y'all I used to work for old time bank." "You used to replies the operator? Giggling the operator replies "Well we hold the last pay check so you won't be getting paid until next week." Mikel's heart just drops and all at once he thinks I have to pay Miko rent, I have to buy groceries, I have to have some money in my pocket. And that sinking feeling in his heart begins to burn up and all the rage from being kicked out the house, to loosing his job, to being all alone just comes out and he yells in a fit of rage and anger "Y'ALL BETTER GET MY MONEY DEPOSITED NOW!!!!" The usual calm and collective Mikel has completely lost his cool and you could hear the echo of his voice travel all the way down the block, neighbors rush to their windows and look outside and some even wander out to their porches. The operator hangs up the phone. All that anger for nothing it got him nowhere, now Mikel has to wait a week to get paid and with only thirty-three dollars in his account it's going to be a long week. Later that day he does get's the visit he was waiting for from his Uncle Faruq sitting out on the porch with his cousins playing in front of the house Uncle Faruq pulls up with old Ice Cube blasting dressed in his all white work uniform, blunt hanging out of his mouth he just double parks and hops out of the all white Chrysler concord. "As Salamm Alaikum, nephew." "Wa Laikum Salaam Uncle Faruq. What the deal man?" They shake hands and hug Uncle Faruq has a blunt hanging from his mouth and as they hug the aroma from the blunt is all the air. "I got good news for you, you got an interview on Friday around eleven o'clock here's the number" He hands Mikel a business card from the bakery don't be late man and put a suit on." "You know I know all that business attire from working at the bank." Uncle Faruq steps back and ask " Yo what really happened mat the bank though because that was a good job?" "Alright like a year ago for class I was reading Micheal Moore's book "Stupid White Men" I took the cover of the book off so no one would get offended because he had plastered all over the cover Stupid White Men. I wasn't quoting anything out of the book  at work, I wasn't even talking to people about it. So then I go on a cigarette break and when I come back this white boy Bob the head teller is all inside my teller station. Now he know he's not supposed to be there, but just because I was reading a book he was so nosey he had to see what the book was about. I can only imagine his surprise when he looked at the spine and read the tittle." Uncle Faruq starts cracking up in laughter, "You know how they get beat red" "Was he this nigga is all red faced and his mouth salivating, and he's like he needs to talk to me in the back office. So I'm cool as shit like whatever lets go. Inside the office he's all tough in my face talking about he's offended by the book and that I can't read that book or any books at work anymore. I'm like yeah right, the book ain't even racist its political, then I'm like im in college I need the down time to study for class and up to this point their wasn't any problems. The I said well I'm offended because the other night when I was closing April could not find the temporary checks and said I must be out mof my cotton picking mind, and then said pickin ninny too. "What you ain't say nothing then?" "That shit don't bother me for man she aint say it to my face so who cares." So Bob's pissed off now because I called April on that bull shit and he calls the sector manager Ben Jones this real live fagot. This muthafucker takes off his coat like he is the duke of earl or something every time he comes into any bank I just start dying this white boy thinks he's a duke he takes the coat and just tosses it off his back and across in one motion, talks all sweet man I can't stand it. However Ben is fair when it comes to rights, or so I thought." So we set a meeting up with all the staff from the Bear Delaware branch and we all going to address all our grevences, in particular how the blacks do all the work handle all the clients and the whites just chit chat all day like they off work. It's Bob and the branch manager April two hours to change the cash out on the atm machines. What the fuck man!" So all week the black people are like piping me up the chick Gloria, keeps coming to me all week with list of complaints talking about we gonna bring this up we gonna bring that up. Right Shaun and Kyle the other two blacks guys doing the same thing too, so I'm thinking bet on Friday it's on we gonna turn this thing around and get some equality around here." Uncle Faruq and Mikel are now sharing the blunt and as they pass the blunt back and forth Mikel is continuing with his story, while Uncle Faruq is just nodding his head. "Friday comes along and that's the busiest day of the week because it's pay day but some how we all get in there at the same time, don't ask me how but it worked out that way. Sitting across from management Bob and April , and Ben Jones this mutherfucker pulls out a dictionary and looks up the terms cotton picking and pick a ninny." Uncle Faruq stops Mikel "Hold up they have a dictionary with those words in it?" " Yeah it must be the abridged KKK version" They both laugh "But hold up it gets better after he reads the terms he ask if anyone had anything to say? So of coarse I raise my hand and was like yeah I'm offended by those terms because my ancestors worked and oicked cotton fro free as slaves, and we were brought here kidnapped" Mikel starts laughing "I took the line from public enemy Robbed of our language, robbed of our families, robbed of our God, robbed of our culture" They were really unimpressed so I took it to the next level." Uncle Faruq is in stitches laughing at Mikel for using the classic opening lines of Public enemies fight the power song, and Uncle Sha comes out of the house to join the conversation "So I was like furthermore I'm offended because I got bleached and put my hands up in the air like look at these white hands." Both uncle Sha and Uncle Faruq are cracking up and Mikel goes on "Yo them white folks got super beat red like red cool aid or ketchup and they had this look on there face like we got a problem. You them white folks do not like no rowdy out of control nigger who out works them, is educated, muslim, and a militant especially after September 11th that was supposed to suppress people like us." "So what happened?" After all that talk all week none of the blacks said anything they no Mr. White man we don't have any complaints." "God damn Uncle Tom's you in Delaware Mikel what you expect?" "I know Uncle Sha so the books got banned all books because it was security thing about theft. 911 man when all else fails call it a threat to security and you can do anything you want why wouldn't it hold true in a bank setting the country is nothing but a big bank for the rest of the world?" "I had to go through hell the last month I was there trying to transfer down to Dover, and everybody was against me." "The only good thing that came out of it was that I got a date from Salma Cruz." "Who's that?" Ask uncle Faruq "I'm about to tell you if you pass the rest of that blunt." High as a kite now Mikel gets into the story of Mrs. Cruz, Uncle Faruq grabs a colt 45 beer out of his car, and Uncle Sha lights a cigarette. "Yo when she walked into the bank the whole place would just go nuts, the men in line, the women in line would just gasp I mean this is Delaware it's not Philly, N.Y. or a major city most people we se e are over weight white bitches. She was perfect long black hair, medium titties, this brown skin that looked tanned but it wasn't that was here natural skin color." Uncle Sha cuts in as he looks around to make sure Miko was not around. "I had one like that spanish jawns like that will fuck you all night." "I know hairy arms and legs, they all agree and Mikel continues with his story. So me and Bob would face off at the teller stations like who was going to get to her first as she stood in line. And of coarse I would win everytime and I would just making love to her with my eyes as mshe stood in front of and she would play along too flirting right back checking me out it was crazy, you know Bob was mad as shit that was his highlight of the week when she came though." "Hold up this bitch was probably busting bad checks in their." Interrupts Uncle Sha, "You better believe it cause they weren't any payroll checks and after a while I stopped asking for ID anything you want baby want some extra money?" They all start laughing " So one day I was like you wanna go out on a date? First she was like no, she was married then I gave this look with my eyes like please, and she was like yeah. Uncle Sha and Uncle Faruq look at each other like how did he pull that off. Then Uncle Faruq clears things up she must've been going through something with her husband, and needed a break they do that sometimes." "All I know is that it was like a dream she was in her thirties but looked like she wasn't older than twenty five, like Miko." Mikel quickly looks at Uncle Sha who quickly gives him this what you looking my wife for? Mikel just smiles and goes on with his story Nice ass, hips, no waist arburn streaks in her long hair just super bad." Still pissed about the Miko reference Uncle Sha pushes Mikel to finish "So were did y'all go lover boy?" "We went to the movies it was when they first opened the Bridge down by Penn and saw terminator three. We shut the bridge down, that's when it was just Penn students and those wild ass niggers. But she brought drinks for me, sat on m lap in the lobby the ushers kept walking by like how did you get her? And smiling at me like you did good yo." "Shared popcorn, I hugged up on her, she hugged up on me during the movie I really don't  remember the film because we kept looking at each other you know that eye contact gets it's done." After wards we drove home back to Delaware I turned on the Sinatra" Uncle Faruq interrupts "Nice and Easy does it every time" They shake hands and Mikel continues the story "So she but her head in my lap and I stroked her hair as we drove home listening to Sinatra. When we got home she was parked at my house I walked her to her car and she gave me a hug and when we pulled back we just kissed for a long time my dick was already hard that shit was busting through my pants now and she let me palm that booty and we kissed for a long time like passioniate she would stop pull away and we would start again. The kids who live next door were outside and they kept saying damn how did he get her? She was done after that." Uncle Sha corrects his nephew "No you were done after that." Mike just smiles and replies "yeah you right, I'm never going to forget that date it was one of my best." The three men stand in front of Uncle Shamp's house watching the cars try to avoid hitting Uncle Faruq's car as it remains double parked.  Uncle Faruq breaks the silence "So what happened after that?" "Yo I saw her only one more time we talked outside the bank in her F-150 for a few minutes and then I got transferred." "Yo you messed her up though, I bet she was trying to figure out how it was going to work?" "Yeah well Uncle Sha Ik saw her husband a few months later at another bank he had their daughter with him and he gave me this look like "I should kill you nigger!" They had the same last name Villa-Cruz and the baby girl looked just like her, I just cashed his check  and told him he didn't have to show me his id the next time, yup those were the days old green eyes himself." They all just start laughing , "You haven't explained why you lost the bank job?" "I wasn't in control of anything I had a teller difference of like eight-hundred dollars which is insane because anyone with a difference of over five hundred dollars gets fired. So they did me a favor? No way, the new teller stations are computerized like the die bold voting machines that rig all the elections. On Fridays my machine would crash out like completely crash and when I booted it back up I would have a difference at the end of the day. The only thing I know is that I gave one hundred dollars to this Puerto Rican chick one day, she was cashing a welfare check, and I accidently gave two hundred dollars to this Italian man one day he was cashing out a check off his parents account and it was for six hundred dollars and I gave him eight hundred dollars because the six looked like an eight. I called his parents who only spoke Italian all week trying to get him on the phone and get that two hundred dollars back, no dice but that's it. Three hundred dollars in two years that's pretty good.  A few months before I quit the sector manager another white boy was like how would I like to get a full time position at my North Dover which was my favorite bank. Now for the past two years I've been floating around filling spots at sixteen different banks, so when I asked about the opportunity to work a the North Dover branch I was excited yo. So he offers me the position and everythings a go, when allmof a sudden Debbie this older white lady who left her job at another branch in customer service to go teach at the prisons, like that's going to last picture the mom on that seventies show in the prisons teaching inmates." "They all start laughing, then Mikel gets back to the story "Yeah the fuck right, so she comes back and he gives her the job he offered me at North Dover." "Damn nephew they want you to go crazy." "Naw uncle Faruq they want me to go crazy in the bank or steal money so I will never work again." Uncle Sha adds his two cents I've told you time and time again I've been everywhere except to work." Uncle Faruq chuckles and adds but you used to work at that construction sight remember when you was the forman and helped the whole neighborhood get jobs?" "Yeah but I stole all the tools from the sight before I left, so I was on the job so that really doesn't count." Uncle Sha starts laughing before he finishes the sentence and the three of them just laugh together in the land of the thieves it feels good to get away with something once in a while especially since white folks get away with everything in America. The momement is broken up when Uncle Faruq reminds Mikel " Look this business is owned and operated by our own people and eventhough they are pains in the ass it's still better than working for whitey. So be there on time in a suit or business attire and don't let me down." Thanks Uncle Faruq they shake hands and hug and Uncle Faruq does the same with Uncle Sha, he gulps down the rest of the forty five, jumps in his still double parked car and pulls off. Uncle Sha takes this moment to elaborate on a few things the reasons why he never worked "That white man will drain everything out of you until you have nothing left, no more fight nothing, and then still stomp on you, or use your own people to stomp on you. Be strong nephew but break free from slavery you will never be rich or find peace as long as you live in occupied, oppressive lands controlled by the devil this European." Mikel sharply responds in disbelief "come on now Uncle Sha that's a little racist." "No it's a lot of racist because he is the devil, they have no melonin in there forehead it's calcified they have no connection to nature. They have no connection to God money, and power is their God everywhere they go they have done nothing but masacur the lands original inhabitants and destroy the natural environment they are the devils own." Mikel paying full attention to his uncle responds "So the first will be last and the last will be first?" "Exactly" responds Uncle Sha.

Lid arrives for his interview around ten o'clock in the morning entering through the front door the smell of the pasteries is like a slice of heaven. The place is filled with giant cupcakes, cookies, dounuts, danishes, and Lids favorite cakes. He's quickly greeted by one of the cashiers, the older women has this grandmotherly smile and politely says " How can we help you today sweet heart?" Nervous about the interview Lid says "I have an appointment with Mr. Randel Gates." Surprised the women ask "For what a job?" dressed in a suit and tie Lid looks way over dressed and over qualified to interview for a job at the bakery but humbly he replies "Yes I am here for the porter position" Taken aback the older women says to the rest of the staff "This boy is going to be a porter check him out" The rest of the female cashiers stop what they are doing replenishing the glass encasements of snacks, helping customers, and on quew they take a look at Lid and giggle. One of them says while smiling "She is gonna have a fit when she sees him." Lid paitently waits as one of the cashiers goes to the back of the bakery to get Mr. Gates. I the mean time he checks out the hotties on staff and there's really only one a brown skinned women named Lana who has not time for Lid and his stare down as she looks away from him, he thinks to himself "she must be married." Then suddenly a set of big brown eyes emerges from the back of the bakery. The brown eyes belong to Markita at least that's what her name tag reads, and light skinned girl has long black hair and an adorable face. As soon as they make eye contact the both of them blush and for a moments they seemed locked in a star down as she pretends to be helping the cashiers and he pretend not to be looking at her. The moment is suddenly interrupted when an older gentleman slim and dark skinned approaches Lid and with eyes wide open ask him "You're here for the porter position?" Quickly Lid gets back into professional mode and answers "Yes Sir, Lid Islam" As he extends his hand, the two shake hands and the gentleman say's "Follow me to the back." The two travel through the insides of the bakery which smells even better than the front as the aroma of the pies is the first thing Lid smells, the dounuts are next as they cool on racks, next to hundreds of danishes's. The women working in the back all take a look at Mikial and smile, he smiles back and as he passes the first oven for the first time he feels the heat of the bakery the combination of the hot summer day makes it unbearable inside. Mr. Gates laughs and joke with the employees as they travel through a small hallway into the main cooking area, were Lid sees a familiar face, Uncle Faruq looks up and smiles "This is it nephew" "As Salaam Alaikum unc" "Wa Laikum Salamm" they shake hands and Mr. Gates reminds Uncle Faruq "I found more beer cans in the men's bathroom y'all better cut that out!" Uncle Faruq just laughs and Mr. Gates walks Mikhaik into a small room in between the cooking area and a cake decorating room, were he begins the interview. "So what's a sharp dressed guy like you doing down here interviewing to be a porter?" "I just moved up here from Delaware and I really need to start working, I just graduated college and I would like a chance to work and help out the business while I'm here." "You have a college degree and you want to work here?" "Yes I really need to start working Mr. Gates I have bills to pay and I have to make rent sir. But more than that I really just want some peace Mr. Gates this is a black owned business and I've been through a lot out there a lot of injustice and racism and I just want the opportunity to come work, work hard and get paid an honest buck." Mr. takes a look at Lid's resume and then ask him a few questions about his work history "Say's here you used to work old time bank what happened there?" So this I how I got the job I was volunteering at the special Olympics out the north east and my mom starts talking to white guy and telling him how I was looking for a job" Lid thinks for a second and remembers Yeah his name was Bill Fisher real nice guy and he's like come on and apply with us, gives his card a few days later I call him. Now during the interview I told them straight up part-time because I was in college I go up the bank in the North East and crush the test, they hire me on the spot. I started working at the old time banks by Pathmark, and on Haverford avenue out west Philly, then my car broke down right at the very top of the Platt Bridge they called the paramedics and all." Mr. Gates shakes his head "No they didn't" "Yes they did the paramedics knocked on my window and was like somebody called and said I was going to jump, in the meantime I had triple A and they were on there way to tow me. But know I'm all messed up because I was driving my car to Dover for school twice a week, while I was living and working up here. So I had to move back home to Delaware and while I was Delaware a few days later I just bum rushed a old time bank by the school another white guy Mr. Clark was the bank manager and I just came into the branch and was like "I work for old time bank in Philly I go to school across the street and I need to transfer down here to Dover?" Smiling Mr. Gates ask "You just walked into a old time bank in Delaware and you worked in Philly?" "Yeah, I know but Mr. Clark is cool he's like call the sector manager I get everybody on the conference call sector manager in Delaware, Mr. Fisher who had just hired me a few weeks before explain the situation and everybody was like cool. The next week I was working for old time bank in Delaware transferred. " Mr. Gates just smiles so what happened?" "Well Delaware is not Philly Mr. Gates so they had me floating teller so I was going to all the bank in Delaware my mom would give me rides to and from work until I saved enough to buy a new car, but it was crazy one time up at a bank in Newark and the chick goes "We thought you were here to rob us." I'm like I'm the floating teller, you  knew I was coming stop playing. But I went through a lot of that in Delaware especially in Smyrna Mr. Gates those people would get mad when I asked them for ID, like aint no nigga asking me for no ID, and would get the bank manager and all in the drive thru messing the line up, it was crazy I didn't expect that man you know we deal with Kennsington, South Philly, and the North East but down there they are like the deep south." Mr. Gates adds well you know Delaware was on the side of the confederates during the civil war man and some things stay the same." "I believe it now, but things were going good I was all over the place and then I got stationed at the branch in Bear Delaware and had some real live racism issues with the staff, see dealing with the customers is one thing but the staff has to know there place, needless to say I brought these things up in the meeting , Mr. Gates cuts him off " Let me guess you been black listed ever since?" "Yeah"  Shaking his head Mr. Gates explains "Young people, I don't know when you guys are ever going to learn anything goes nowadays my niece Alisha had a management job with Discover card, took a stand and now she works in here over qualified and the poor girl is going insane over working herself trying to keep busy. Look you seem like a nice young man, and you are way too over qualified for the position but your uncle Tony has been working here for a long time so on the strength of that I will run your application by my wife Daphney, and well give you a call in a few days.  But lets take a tour of the place and I will show you the things you have to do." Mr. Gates leads Lid into the prep area were once again he sees Uncle Faruq, and Mr. calls Faruq by the name his mother gave him "Toney I mean it about those cans in the bathroom!" All the cooks bust out laughing and keep working "We have two sinks the small one you passed on the way in across the from the oven and the big sink." Mr. Gates points towards the back sink and there are hundreds of dishes pilled up and Lid nods his assuring Mr. Gates that's its not too much for him to handle but inside Lid is cringing at the idea of having to wash all those dishes. "The porters rotate each week per location, now the dishes and trays have to be washed constantly because the cooks go right through them.  They proceed into the storage area "When the cooks ask for them you guys have to bring out these bags of flour and sugar, those guys are pretty old so stop what you are doing and bring the flour or sugar out." "How many pounds do they they look like they come the land of the giants?!" "Hahaha your funny yeah those bags weigh like fifty pounds each that not heavy for you." Mr. Gates pats Lid on his shoulder and leads him out of the storage area, "Now everyday you have to sweep and wet mop this area, move those cans of pie fillings around, but everyday sweep and mop the floor, this is a bakery and cleanliness is a must to keep our rodent friends out." "I see the traps all over the place y'all gotta keep this place spick and span because of  license and inspections?" "Yeah they closed a Chinese restaurant down around the corner, so this place has to always be clean. When the deliveries come in you have to unload the truck we usually get two deliveries a week the suga, flour, and pie filling all come in the same shipment." As he walks through the prep area Mr. Gates begins to point out different machines these mixers, all have to be clean, spick and span as soon as your uncle and the other bakers leave around three you have to sewwp and mop the entire room, now this wont be your job every day because you guys rotate weeks but if its your week to be on the floor this is what you have to do" leading Lid to the walk in freezer Mr. Gates takes a deep breathe and says "Its cold in here so get ready" Lid just nods his head and they walk into the freezer, the door shuts and it's frigid inside filled with cold air smoke Lid begins to shiver and Mr. Gates smile, he talks loud because the airconditioner inside the freezer is loud "This my friend is the walk in and as you can see the bakers leave this place a mess" pointing to the ground there is icing, cookies and pieces of cake all on the floor, "They come in here and just ram these racks of food all around and things falls off the racks, I loss more money here than anyother part of the bakery." "Can I turn the freezer off when I come I here and clean?" "Mr. Gates just laughs hahaha "No way son there is a coat in the bathroom you have to put that on, but Larry is going to show you how to clean the freezer it's hard work man but you are young you can get it done." They leave the freezer and head to the cake room, still chivering the bakers laugh and tease Lid as he walks across the floor. Inside the cake room he here's a familiar sound as the classic rock band the who is blazing live on the television. The cake decorating crew is a mixed bunch, and the place goes crazy with smiles as Alisha is in the cake room and for the second time today Lid and Alisha see each other. Talking to on of the decoraters when Lid and Mr. Gates walk in she they make eye contact and she immediately turns around. "This is the cake room, these guys and girls decorate all the cakes there's Cliff, Cliffs a white guy in his mid forties and from the looks of things h's the one respncible for the Who on the television as he rocks out wearing a Who bandana over his head. "You like the who yo?" "Yeah man they're the best" "Yeah I know I like Zepellin though but my favorite who jam is "We don't get fooled again. I hope we don't get fooled again with these elections coming up." Then another voice enters the conversation "You really think Kerry is going to beat Forty Three ?" "That's Mrs. Shirley Lid approaches her says "Nice to meet you mame." "Ah a gentleman that's so rare these days." Mikahil blushes and Mr. Gates introduces him to the other cake decorator who is younger than the older Mrs. Shirley and the pretty good looking like most women in Philadephia she takes the opportunity to speak to Lid as he wanders in her direction "So what's your name cutie?"

"Lid, and you are?" "Rasheedah I don't kno what you did but you got my girl Alisha over here blushing like crazy, Imma call you green eyes."He smiles and say's "O.k.", as Mr. Gates continues to talk with the other cake decoraters Alisha and Lid take the opportunity to chit chat with each other. "So your that's your uncle he told me that you graduated from college what school did you go to?" She grins and replies "I went to Penn State main campuss, it was easy majored in business and minored in finance." Her response is very cool and confident and Lid wonders what the hell is she doijng here in this bakery? "I just graduated too from Delaware State University top of my class, Political Science minor, Public Relations major." "Did you pledge anything and cross?" "Naw" She lowers her head very disappointed as Lid begins to explain. "First of all I was surprised to even be in college growing up I always wanted to just be a cop, but I get cool with these bluppies (black yuppies) and they are like yeah yeah go to college. The next thing I know I was going down Luoisiana to be a doctor." "So what happened?" "Chemistry and Biology" Laughing she says well you need them to be a doctor." "Who you telling, I had to change my major the next thing I knew I was paying like twenty grand to year on the ivy league side of things, and not even going to school for what I started out for.So then the pledgning thing a few groups wanted me in the Kappa's of course."She smiles "Yeah you would've made a great Kappa with those eyes." He just laughes it off, "Then it was the Alpha's too, my major issues were one just finish college I was the first male to graduate in my family and I did not want to be sidetracked by anything else especially since I struggles at the beginging of college." "All you would've made it its hard it's the hardest thing I've ben through being on line but I made it though and Lord knows being on call at anytime of the day, not being able to tell your friends anything, and other stuff I cant talk about is a struggle.But in the end the connections and the life long sikster hood was well worth it." "I couldn't get down with it I really wanted to be a Kappa but they had faggots in the jawn, and I was like I'm from Philly it's no way in the world I was going to get belittled by some faggots to be part of something especially since I had to survive the city just to make it this far, you know we don't play that shi, I mean stuff her in the city. I used to run those fags out of high school back in the day." "Well you can always pledge graduate level or just as a professional." "Yeah well I gotta get out of this jam because it's no way they ngonna accept no dishwasher." She laughs just keep looking there's something out there for you and who k nows may be you stay aboard and run this place with me one day." At the sound of that they make eye contact and he nods his head to say that he is feeling that idea, but just as the conversation is about to go a little farther Mr. Gates comes over and breaks up the little love connection. "All right Alisha leave the new porter alone. He's married." "No I'm not!" He quickly replies, and Mr. Gates ushers Lid out of the cake room and sits him back down in the small room and with a sigh of disappointment he finishes the interview with Lid holding up his resume. "Look son you are way over qualified for this position, and I usually just high guys from the neighborhood who had some trouble with the law, but your Uncle Toney has been with us for years and he says you are a good guy so I will check things over with my wife Daphne and get our guy to do a background check on you. No promises but we will let you know in a few days." A little disappointed he did not get the job on the spot Lid humbly makes one more attempt to wow Mr. Gates "Look Sir I'm been orking since the late nineties, I'm a real hard worker and for m its all about making an honest buck so I know you have to talk about but you will not b disappointed in me if you hire me." "Alright I believe you now its time to convince the misses." They both laugh and shake hands, and Mr. Gates is ready to escort Mikhial throught the front door when he says "I'm gonna wait for my uncle Toney he said he was going to give m a ride back home." "Alright, talk to later." And Lid waits in the back of the bakery taking in the sweet smells but also exchanging eye contact with Alisha as she walks back and forth from the front of the bakery to the back. "I hope I don't mess this job up screwing around with the owners niece he thinks to himself, good grief?"

Everything is everything as Lid has been working at the bakery for a few months and as the elections of 2004 come to a close and George W. Forty Three wins with more votes in the history of all Presidential elections he comes to a grave reality that people care more about the three hundred dollar tax breaks as opposed to whats right and whats wrong and eventhough he tried driving around the streets and roads of Delaware the night before the elections doing his best Paul Revere inpersenation playing the Who's "We don't get folled again" and voting for John Kerry the next mornig non of it made any difference as Forty Three was still President. So as the year wines down still working at the bakery and still living at his grandmothers house

Lid is at a lost for words regarding the direction the country has gone and the direction the city of Philadelphia has gone down as murder and mayhem has sticken the city street.

"Grandmom I'm coming in late tonight I'm going out with a friend of mines from college." "Who you going out with boy you know nobody wants to hang out with your crazy butt?" "I'm not crazy grandmom you know the rest of the world is." They both laugh "Naw I used to mess with her sister in school she's a twin, we going out to the strip club." "You know that's what my crazy father used to say but they locked his butt right up in the funny farm after he killed those two white boys down in South Philly.… Wait a minute kiddo you said your going to the strip club with a girl?" "Yeah I know I told you the rest of the world was crazy. They're twins one of em is straight, the other one likes girls go figure." She cracks up laughing "Hahahaha, I don't know what to say about young people today so you two are going to the strip club and she's going to stand around watching other girls take their clothes off?" "Yup I figured I worked all day I mean I worked real hard all day, and I need a break so what the heck." "You gonna waste your hard earned money in some strip club boy you are stupid." "Hey ya gotta have fun sometimes. I remember your father used to live a few door down he looked just like me I used to stare at him from the porch." "Yeah he brought that house after I told him he could not live here with me, that fool thought I was going to take care of him after they let him out of the nut house." "Didn't he buy this house?" She gets very serious and says "Yeah, so he wasn't going to talk to me any kinda way it was horrible the way he used to talk to me." "I hear that, I remember him though he used to sit out on the porch and we used to stare at each other when I used to play out there, he looked just like me." She laughs "Yeah both of y'all nuts looking at each other." "I'm not crazy grandmom!" "Yeah it's the rest of the world you better get quiet down because my numbers are ready to come on." And on that note Lid looks up at the clock and sees that it is a few minutes to seven and he accordingly gets up and leaves for the living room. "Where you going?" "I learned from uncle Rashad years ago get out the room and hide under the table when the numbers are ready to come one." "Oh hush up boy, I'mma get you for saying that." But h continues to head for the living room when right on time his phone rings and its Lana the twin that he's supposed to go to the strip club with tonight. Both sister beautiful the caramel skinned dimes where two of Lids few friends at Delaware State University. Of coarse Lid had to date one of them and Lacy the more girly of the two was hi cup of tea. It's funny how together they make the perfect women as Lacy is super girly bajama parties, baking cookies, she was a cheerleader, and member of one of the all female sororities on campus. While her sister Lana was the exact opposite she and Lid used to split six packs of beers, Lana's cusses like a sailor, and will belch and fart at will while watching the basketball or football games with you. But weekends at their apartment were like slices of heaven as he had the perfect women eventhough it was two of them, around as he watched football on Sunday, and movies all day on Saturdays. Since graduation in the spring she's been trying to make it in the big city removed from Philly for like the past fifteen years living in Delaware, Philly can be a whole lot different as an adult as opposed to a child. But the way the city has changed with the DTO or "Dikes Taking Over tattooed all over the city this town has become very friendly and open armed to homosexuals especially females over the past ten years, so Lana shouldn't have any problems making in Philly.

"Whats the deal Lana?" "What up Lid are we still going to the strip club my girlfriend said that place be popping." "Where's it at because I am not trying to be going all over the city tonight?" "Naw hommie you in west right?" "Yeah right off Girard avenue." "Yeah its right off city line avenue behind the pathmark." "You sure because I used to work at the PNC bank there and I never saw any strip club and believe me I would've known about that." "Yeah you would've been there on your lunch breaks?" "Yes indeed." "Just come get me nigga and I will show you, but my girlfriend said it's off the hook in there." "A ight I'll leave around nine thirty." In the background his grandmother starts going off as the lottery numbers for the night are being pulled. "Shoot I hate these stinking numbers, I'm never going to play again!!!" "Lana I gotta go the lottery numbers just came out and my grandmom is about to start throwing things." Lana laughs, "Don't turn your phone off nigga or I will never speak to you again." "A ight we going out tonight I'm getting ready now." He hangs up the phone and goes back to the kitchen were his grandmother is jotting down the numbers from New Jersey and after a few minutes of deep thought she breaks her silence "I had a dream about your cousin and played her birthmonth and year 583, you know what those stupid numbers came out as on the pick four?" "No grandmom what?" "5983 the whole stinking date. I cant believe this !" As she tosses the pen to the table. "Its always tomorrow mom mom" "I need a hit today." His grandmom rarely shows any emotion but around seven the lottery comes on she lets it all out, the funny thing is that she usually hits four or five times a months thanks to her math, which is combination of adding and subtracting the numbers from Delaware, New Jersey, and Pennsylvania and her hits from the illegal street numbers. But upset about this near miss today she exclaims loudly "Lid call gamblers enonomous I cant take it anymore" and she raises her hands in the air. He says nothing and just watches as she performs and a few hours later after he's showered and changed his clothes he's on his way out the door and lets his grandmom know that he is leaving for the club as she is in her room watching television. "Alright mom mom I'm out, I'll try my best not to make any noise when I come back in later." "O.k., just make sure you lock the door." "Alright mom mom I love you." "Alright kiddo stay out of trouble."Always in need to get the last word in he replies "That's hard to do when trouble is my middle name, but I will try."He trots downstairs in his grey and red academics sweat suit with his fresh pair of timbs and grey Roc –A-Wear jacket and gets on his way uprtown to pick Lana up. Jamming to the sounds of classic rock and roll on the imfamous WMGK 102.9  he darts throught the traffic and gets to Lana grandmoms house giving her a call to let her know he's out front. The good thing about Lana being a time boy is that she's on time and in seconds she emerges from the house with baggy jeans on a loose fitting shirt, and a classic black fight jacket.Lid just shakes his head "fucking dikes" in a perfect world Lana would be his best friend and his girl friend, too bad he's already been in a relationship with her sister, too bad she's gay for that matter, but as he watches her stroll to the car he can only ponder the possibilities ahhh sisters as he leans over and unlocks the door to let here in the car. "What up Lid? You ready to check some bitches out?" A smile comes across his faca as just the sheer company of Lana brings joy to his soul but the feeling is bitter sweet because Lana should be getting into his car to go out on a date. She's perfect in a way a girl who is your best friend who acts like one of your homies without all the high maintenance of a regular female, but at the end of the day she still has titties and pussy to suck and fuck on at anytime anyplace. So as he begins to speak his words are semi broken because secretly he's in love with Lana too. "I don't even feel like going tot eh strip club lets go to the movies?" "It's a week day nigga aint no late shows, come on I really want to go to the strip club. Here spark this L up and come on I'll buy the first round." And with that he grabs the blunt from Lana's hand and begins to spark it, but before he does with it hanging out of his mouth he lets her know "You know I don't be blazing shit that I aint rolled up myself!" "Go ahead with that nigga you know I aint put nuffin in it." "Yeah I guess I can trust you." Both smiling he sparks it and pulls off from the block, she's cool as she just reclines her seat back and turns up the classic rock and roll and as they puff away passing the blunt back and forth to each other Lid breaks the silence "So whats up with your sister I aint talked to her in a few weeks?" "She's cool I talked to her this morning I told her I was going to the strip club with you tonight, and she was jealous." "I miss her Lana, Lacy is so sweet" "All nigga don't be getting all mushy with me come on nigga we are about to drink some beers and watch these fine ass hoes get naked." For whats it worth Lana acts tough but that's just the top layer, she wasn't always like this at some point in time some dumb ass nigga had to break her heart and she gave up on giving her heart to any man, but Lid just can't get underneath the surface and everytime he tries she changes the subject.So tonight he tries another coarse of action, a few years ago while waiting for tickets for the homecoming game Lana was standing a few spots ahead of him with Lacy's sorority jacket on, and she was hugged up with some guy like a teenager bitting on his kneck. With her back turned to him she would just look up so seductively at Lid and make eye contact with him. He knew right thnen and there it wasn't Lacy its not in her to such a vixen and twins always share clothes so  nine times out of ten it was the girls just sharing clothes. "You wasn't always into girls Lana, a few years ago I saw you standing in line for homecoming tickets with some guy you were all over him like a vampire." "That wasn't me, I don't remember that." "Come on yo you were looking right up at me, don't give up on us there are still some good men out there." She starts to studder, it worked he cracked the surface "Nnnnn Naw that wasn't me I don't like guys did you ask Lacy?" "It wasn't Lacy she would've said something to me plus the way you looked at me, she's too nice to look at me that way." "Nigga this weed has got you going it wasn't me." Upset about Lid getting under her surface she makes an even bolder claim to put all things to rest "I bet you that in four years Lacy is going to be into girls likem me!!" "Naw!!! Fuck outta here bad enough we already lost you we cant lose her too." "Watch I bet you a dub she's going to be into girls too." "U know I don't gamble, but I think you are wrong Lacy just has to find the right man." Lanna says nothing and as they pull onto City Line Avenue she begins to give him directions to the strip club when then pull into the parking lot she reaffirms her statement with on word "Watch!!". They get out the car as he reads the name of the strip club "Sables huh?" "Yup come on nigger lets go" and she quickly runs to the front door. "You know I would've never found this hole in the wall joint on my own and I've been back this way a hundred times." The cherry wood front door opens just as soon as they get close to it and a well built stocky body guard dressed in all black and conrolls comes out with a metal detector and a mean face. As he scans Lana and Lid he ask to see there id's and once inside they pay the ten dollars entrance fee. With the small store front space that the club has they did a great job of maximizing it, because as soon as you walk in there's the stage equipped with the usual bras pole in the center, with some new school rock and roll playing Bon Jovi living on a prayer to be exact Lid feels right at home. As they pass onlookers standing up against the wall drinking beers Lid watches the dancer on stage and also checks out the other dancers walking from table to table collecting tips. As usual nothing is better than watching women already in their lingerie asking for dollars to take even more off, and Lid just smiles as he checks out all the girls in the club. They continue to the back of the club were the bar sits in the corner, and true to her word she tells Lid "Look go over there to that bar stool by the wall, and what are you drinking cause the first round is on me?" "Yo see if they got any Guiness if not just get me a Corona." And she does so patiently waiting for the bar tender, he watches as Lana is indeed out of place and a little intimidated she waits as the guys throw their weight around ordering out of place at the bar "golden rule in the city if you don't have a buner, take Sinatra's advice "Nice and Easy does it every time" And she does so and waits patiently until the bar tender calls on her, and to his surprise when she returns she has a Guiness in hand. "Thank Lana I'm surprised they had this because most places in the city especially the hood don't carry em." "I tried drinking one time it's way too strong, think I'm gonna stick to my coronas." And as they makes a cheers, there's nothing like Saint James Gate, paradise for me is a place were the streets are lined with broken Guiness bottles. Is your girlfriend here yet?"

"Lana looks around "Naw I don't see her, she might be in the back changing." Lid nods his head and they move a little closer to the stage, it's a strip club so he's going to spend some money but to this point he's only dropped ten dollars and just when he begins to think that he is up, two dancers come over to them. One white girl ith long blond hair and blue eyes wearing a next to nothing in a pinl thong and bra, the other one is mixed because she has the brightest hazel eyes he's ever seen in his life and they just glow off her light brown caramel skin, her long black hair is highlighted by a blond streak that drapes down over her face, and Lid can only think of Stacy Dash when he lays his eyes on her. He quickly pulls out some money and tips both of them placing dollar bills in their thigh panty hose. As he places the money in Mrs. Caramel he whispers in her ear "I like those leopard print thongs." She laughs and whispers back "I left my work bag in my other car and this is the shit I had on under my regular clothes." And together they just cracking up laughing "What's your name?" "Nirobi and that's Star" "Hey look this is my friend Lana we went to college together so Star show her a good time she's new to the city." And accordingly Star goes over to Lana and begins to bump and grind on her, on what only heaven knows because the one thing Lana doesn't have is a penis, but to each his own or her own. Intrigued by Nirobi Lid has no time to worry about Lana and he picks up her conversation with Nirobi. "So when do you go up and dance?" "I don't know I hope I am not next, let m go check with the DJ, don't go anywhere cuttie. But before she leaves she ask "So are you gonna buy me a drink or what?" He was up, and a slave to those light hazel eyes he whips out a twenty and hands it over to her. "Here bring be back my change." "O.k. don't let me find out you are a cheepy." "I am" "We gonna have to change that I'll be right back." As she walks away Lid can only smile as he has really really hit the jackpot with this one perfect waist, and a bubble butt that just puts an exclamation point on her entire body, yet falls right into her thighs. Standing on those heels takes a lot of strength and it shows as her calphs and thighs are all flexed and as she walks away it all comes together as her soft ass cheeks just bounce in perfect harmony. He just smiles and then takes a look over at Lana who is basically pounding Star who is bent over her face down and ass up Lana is really enjoying herself smaking the girls ass with one hand and totting a fist full of dollars in another, stuffing ones into her panties and pantyhose. Lid just looks and smiles as he takes a sip of his Guiness and thinks to himself "Fucking out of towners."

Most of the crowd in strip clubs are hustlers with so much money they blow it on the girls everynight, pimps who are carefully watching their hoes, cops who are so over aggressive they cant have regular relationships, and losers who don't make enough  money to get the girl they want so they go to the strip club, nothings illegal about dreaming. Being a conasor of strip clubs in the area Lid has really taken a liken to watching the girls just perform on stage. Its hard work getting up there on that pole and as he watches the dancer wrap her legs around the pole and hang upside down he thinks to himself "Women are crazy, they will do anything for the love of money." When Nirobi comes abck with drinks in her hand  "I got you another beer, the bar tender was shocked because nobody drinks this stuff." She hands him his change and Lid says " Thank you" as he maintaines eye contact with her. "Good thing I checked to because I go up the dancer after next." "I guess you are not staying too late tonight with only one change of clothes?" "Naw this is a slow night it's the middle of the week, the good money don't come until Friday, Saturday, and Sunday but what the hell I could pull in a couple of hundred or sit at home on my ass and watch TV all ight." "And what a nice ass it is, but your right babe take the money and run" They both laugh "So I have to get ready to go up on stage you gonna watch me up front?" "Yeah, I'll toss ya some money." She blows him a kiss as she walks away, but before she gets too far he grabs her arm and swings her back to him. "Where you from?" "South Philly" "Cool I'll see you on stage and he blows her a kiss back she blushes and smiles and walks to the back jingling that soft ass the entire way, he takes a swig of his beer as he watches and then begins to pick up conversation with Lana. "Looked  like you were having fun with the white jawn over there?" Smiling she just replies "Yeah you  know I be pimping those hoes." "Yeah the fuck right! You gave her your money right?" "All Lid I know you not talking you already in love I can see it in your eyes and you just met that bitch."  He quickly puts his pointer finger to his mouth and tells Lana to shhhhhhhsh. "Don't be talking bout her like that, I never call y'all bitches it's a derogative word plus some people get bad breaks in life and she has to do what she has to do, that doesn't mean she doesn't deserve a good man." "Damn nigga you come to all those conclusions just from that one conversation?" "Its in the eyes Lana, it's in the eyes." Here, he hands her the ten  and some ones that Nirobi just brought back to him "This rounds on  me."Lana takes the cash and goes to the bar as a few more dancers try and squeeze a few bucks out of him asking for tips and he accordingly gives qa dollar each and moves to the front of the stage and takes a seat to watch Nirobi dance. Flattered when she sees him she just blushes but as Usher and Lil John's "yeah" begins to play she blocks the outside world out and begins to dance. "I have no idea how they swing around that pole so many times without getting dizzy" and just for that Lid digs in his pocket and tosses a few dollars onto the stage for good sport, this must be a classy place because halfthrough the song  she still has her thing on, and as she slides forward and leans back her legs open wide enough and the combination of sweat and estrogen completely expose her secret garden and like her it breathes heavely and her other set of lips are in plain view. But when she looks up her hazel eyes lock right in on his green eyes, and one thing is for certain it might not be tonight, it might not be tomorrow  night but sooner or later he is going to be knee deep in her pussy. The front of the stage has gotten jam packed and what started as just a few ones scattered about on the stage has morphed into a pyramid of greenbacks and Lid just leans back in his chair watching her dance away. When she's finished club goers flock the stage and Lid gets up rock hard and goes back to his spot against the wall the bad news is that Lana is no where in sight, the good news is that the beer that she promised is. He looks around for her when fresh off the stage Nirobi approaches him. Hot and sweaty she ask "Did you like my dance?" "Yeah you used to be a real live dancer I can tell?" She smiles "when I was younger my mom had me in ballet and dancing school the whole nine yards I really like dancing." "I can tell" "Where's your friend?" "I don't know I went up to the stage to watch you and she disappeared." Together they look around the club, when Nirobi spots Lana going into the lap dance room. "Look there she goes and she's with my girlfriend Toy that hefer better not be trying to move in on my chick, that bitch licks my pussy right" and mocking the classic Little Kim song she goes "Don't want Dick tonight, eat my pussy right!!!" "hahaha" Lid just rolls his eyes and finishes off his beer "Look babe I have to walk around and get tips this is a business you gonna get a dance from me later?" "Yoou gonna charge me?" "Oh God you are so cheap I don't like that, its twenty dollars come on you a baller that's nothing for you?" "I work for a living but o.k. come get me when you are finished with your rounds." "I'll make it worth your wild" She blows a kiss at him and walks off into the crowd, and in a flash another dancer comes up to Lid she's dark brown skin with black microbraids "What's up red?" "Nothing I need another beer what's your name chocolate?" "Amalia!" He tips her placing a few one ollar bills into her panty hose and ask "Thank you boo." "Look I need to get another beer and the bar is packed could you go over there and grab me a beer and get yourself a drink?" "Yeah you get a lap dance from me when I come back?" He shakes his head "Naw you see Nirobi over there" He points her out to Amalia, "yeah that's my girl what you her boyfriend or something?" "The verdict is still out on that but we are putting it together now ." Amalia smiles "she needs a good man, someone to help her with her son he's so cute." Nirobi starts looking over at Lid and Amalia talking worried about another girl moving in on her territory and as Mihail hands her the money to get the drinks, Lana emerges with Toy hand in hand from the lap dance room, dike love this has to be bizzaro world. Lana and Toy soon come over and Toy is stunning chocolate skinned dine piece toned in shape and well built her jet black hair is ut short, and she has the perfect pointy nose. Boy does Lana know how to pick em he thinks to himself as they approach. "Lid this is my girlfriend Toy." They shake hands and with the voice of a teenager she says "Nice to meet ya" she and Lana go back to chit chatting as Amalia comes back with the drinks "Thanks Babe" "All Lid you aint order us nuffin?" "I didn't know what y'all was getting" Amalia snaps "well I'm not going back over there, I have to dance soon." "Cool its my fault I'll go back over and get them" "So you gonna get a dance from me boo?" Shaking his head no, Lid is not going to mess up the good thing he has going with Nirobi and he quickly says "Naw" "Alright then, thanks for the drink." And right on time as Amalia walks away enters Nirobi "What was that bitch doing I cant stand her always trying to dance to my songs before I do, you still getting a dance?" "You better believe it" She grabs his already hard dick which is poking out of his sweat pants and pulls him through the strip club at the shock and awe of the crowd who basically just stop and stare as they walk to the lap dance room. Where Nirobi sits him down in the plush leather chairs and she flately says "Wait till the next song comes on" and jumps into his lap kissing him on the kneck, but she tries to kiss him on the lips he pulls away "Naw you working" Upset she gets up off his lap and gets ready to dance as Lid shifts his dick up and when the song drops its "My goodies" by Ciera and after a little tease dance the fun begins when Nirobi bunny hops into Mikahils lap and perfectly places her coochie on his dick and begins to bounce up and down pushing her titties in his face all along with the rythem of the music. A real professional because Mikahil has nothing to say as his eyes and his head just roll back looking up at the ceiling. "Oh the joy, the joy" he thinks to himself and she continues up and down, the worst thing about it is that she is never going to make him cum but as all true professionals do she gets him right to the point of almost ready to bust and slows down. "You like that boyfriend?" he's speechless and he can only look into those hazel eyes and weakly reply yes by nodding his head. She smiles Nirobi has Lid right were she wants him and when the song ends he quickly pulls out a twenty dollar bill and gives it to her because every second of that dance was well worth it. "You want another one?" Still weak he softly says "Yeah" "This ones on th house boyfriend" And she does her thang again this time to rock and roll as Pappa Roachs "Last resort" fills the air he sits paralyzed, his other head is in charge tonight as he just keeps his head to te sky and zones out. When she's finished and the song is coming to an end  she takes a seat in his lap "So your gonna have to leave your girlfriend for me?" "I don't have a girlfriend" "Stop! Lying nigga that's what all y'all say then I got bitches coming up her keying cars and looking for fights." "I don't lie I really don't have a girlfriend here's my phone." He hands her his phone "Put your number in it." And she does so "So what time do you get off?" "I'm leaving early tonight aint that many people in here spending any fucking money, plus I told you this is my only outfit I have for the night." 'I hear that you don't wanna be the funky dancer?" They laugh "So I will call you tomorrow after work, cool?" "Yeah well you better not have a girlfriend cause I really like you." "I don't lie, and I don't have a girlfriend trust me."

She quickly gives him a kiss on the cheek as the bouncer also looks into the back room to let her know that the time is up. They get up and leave the lap dance room but when they hit the floor of the club she disappears into the club he finds Lana who is sitting up front watching Toy dance and tossing dollars onto the stage. Lid stays put after spending sixty bucks he's way over his budget and on a porters salary he is way out of order, but to pass the time he orders one more beer and gulps it down as Lana soon joins him finished from watching Toy stripping on the stage. "You ready?" "Yeah I spent some money in here tonight, but you did to." "Hey ya gotta have some fun sometimes, what's going on with Toy?" stuturing Lana says "SSSShe has to stay late and do some other things with those niggas over there." "Don't worry about it Lana it's a business she has to make her money." He puts his hand on her shoulder, don't worry bout it, "I'm not. Toy and your girl are good friends may be we can all get together and go out sometime?" "Yeah May be." He takes one last look around the club and takes everything in and then puts the hood from his sweat suit over his head and tells Lana "Yo we off this campus." And with that Lana and Lid are out the door. The drive home is far from quiet as Lana goes on and on about Toy but Lid just listens and when he gets to her grandmoms house he has just a few words of wisdom for her "Yo you just got back up here so take it easy be cool because Philly is real ruff town, and most of these chicks are hustlers yo?" She smirks and with a look o confidence "I got this Lid, you always acting like somebody's big brother "yeah that's my job plus I love you, she says nothing, "Good night Lana" "Night Lid" she gets out the car and he watches as she goes into the house and then pulls off, easy part check.

Now here comes the hard part sneaking back into his grandmothers house without waking her up a its getting close to two o'clock in the morning. He creeps into the house and before he hits the stairs he takes off his boots and begins to tippy toe up the wooden steps as they creek and creek away with the slightest touch of his toes. Relieved that her bedroom light did not come on he exhales when he gets to the top of the steps and just before he makes his turn to his bedroom the whole mission is blown when a voice comes from the back bed room "Did you waste all your money?" "No grandmom I still have enough money to last me until I get paid, I'm sorry I was trying to be quiet." "I heard you when the key hit the lock at the front door." "Wow I'm going to sleep on that note, sorry for waking you up." Drunk when he sees his bed it's like a swimming pool and he just jumps right in and passes out for the night.

The next morning it's off to work and as usual he's jamming to WMGK classic rock and his favorite DJ Debbie Calton feeling good about his conquest last night he decides to give the radio station a call and to his surprise after a few rings he gets through "Hello MGK?" "What's up Debbie" "I don't know you tell me?" "You the best DJ ever yo!" She laughs "Hahaha, thanks who am I talking to and what can play for you?" "Yo this is Ali, I'm on my way to work so could u play me some Zepellin?" "All Ali you didn't even have to ask it's never too early to get the lead out!" "Alright Debbie I'm a listen to you guys all day at work peace yo." "Talk to you later Ali and thank's" They hang up from each other and as promised she cranks up the Zepellin and Lid does so to blasting it to the max as he blazes through north Philadelphia "It's been a long a time, been a long time, been a long lonely lonely lonely time."

When he gets to the bakery its handshakes and hugs from the early morning staff which includes his uncle Faruq. "As Salaam Alaikum Unc" "Wa Laikum Salaam, yo I gotta talk to you?" "What happened?" "Later, man but you fucking up though." Scared about what his uncle could be talking about Lid quickly changes the subject. "Man I was at the strip club last night" The rest of the guys stop what they are doing mixing cake mix, pounding dough, and laying out cookies to bake and all gather around to hear about the strip club. "I pulled this bad chick yo her name was Nirobi, she gave me a free dance and I got her number." "Nigga stop lying you know you aint get her number!" "For real Pete wait I'm going to call her later today watch and see." "You going to be calling the party line stop lying!!" Everybody cracks up laughing and Lid begins to start his day of work. This week he is on the back sink and he spends most of the day washing dishes, and listening to the radio dancing as he quickly knocks off the hundreds of dishes. But around one oclock when the morning shift is about to leave Lid determined to prove that he was telling the truth gives Nirobi a call. Ring Ring Ring "Hello?" "Hi, could I speak with Nirobi?" "Speaking who, who's this?" "It's Lid you met me last night at the club what's the deal?" As they are talking Lid spins around facing the day shift in the prep area and motions to Uncle Faruq and the others "I got her on the phone now" pointing to his phone as he smiles away. The rest of the staff starts to smile and laugh and yell "Go head playaaa!" when all fun stops as Alisha comes to the back from the store area and at the sight of the boss Lid spins back around to the sink talking on the phone while washing dishes when all of a sudden the phone slips from his shoulder and his ear and falls into the  soapy sink water. Disconnected from Nirobi Mikahil screams "Ahhhhh!" and quickly tries to recover his cell phone out of the soapy dish washing water. His uncle and the rest of the fellas just start cracking up laughing when he finds the phone its completely useless, and he just falls to one knee. "I cant believe this yo the number was in the phone!!!!" His Uncle Faruq comes over to him "Yo I'm ready to leave man take a lunch break and come out to the car, cause I have to talk to you." He does so and inside his uncles car they puff on a blunt as his Uncle Faruq gets very Frank with him "Yo what the fuck is going on with you and Alisha??" "Nothing man, I told you I just met a girl at the strip club." "Don't lie to me nephew what the fuck is going on with you too because you know that's the boss's niece and her grandfather will crush you and all of us if you break his granddaughters heart!!!" "Alright, she be hounding me all day if I'm in the basement doing inventory she's in the basement doing inventory. If I'm in the freezer cleaning the floor, she's in and out of the freezer, she b all over me man." "So what did you do because I've been here for like ten years and I am not trying to mess this up, or have you mess this up for me." "Alright a few weeks ago I had a dream about her" Uncle Faruq just falls back and rolls his eyes, "here we go man you gonna get the whole crew fired you know that?" "So when I came to work the next day I told her what the dream was about. I dream'nt we kissed in the small freezer across from the oven and small sink. So later that day she comes over to me at the small sink and ask if I could help her grab something off the top shelf in a small freezer? So my dumb ass goes in there and gets some pie crust off the top shelf for her. She comes in there with me too and when I handed it to her she just pushes the pie crust out the way and steps forward and kisses me on the lips, I kissed her back and we had a semi make out session in the freezer." "In the freezer, man you crazy. Let me tell you something break that girls heart and we are all getting fired. So since then you've been ducking her?" "Yeah man she's the bosses daughter I cant be doing that, plus she said something to me when I was over her house one day." He slipped up and he knows it "What the fuck nigga you where over her house?" He cant continue to lie to his uncle and with a big exhale he begins to tell the truth. "Alright look I went over her house, she had an X-Box man with all the old Nintendo games on it. You know I went crazy when I saw she had Contra man Contra? Come on man up,up,down,down ,left,right,left,right,b,a select start, and the code worked! It worked!" Uncle Faruq begins to crack up laughing in the car, as Lid begins to continue the story. "So she cooked dinner for me and that shit was good some stuffed chicken breast, rice, and asparagus, and I don't be eating no vegetables but everything was grrrreat!" Uncle Faruq begins to shake his head "I know you didn't man" "Let me finish, we had some red wine, I checked out her DJ equipment, everything felt right man and then she went for the jugular and just came at me. I should've stopped her, I don't know I guess it was the wine but the next thing I know she was unbuckling my belt and sucking me off." Shaking his head in dismay Uncle Faruq is speechless as Lid continues "so she sucked me off raw dog, raw man that shit felt so good, naw that shit was grrreaaat!" "You crazy you know that, for one thing she's rich and on another note them niggas from out west partied her and her girlfriends raw dog, you know Pete told you that shit! So how could you do that without a condem on?" "I don't know it was the wine, "Spill that wine and dig that girl!!!" Uncle Faruq can only laugh, at his nephews antics "But after I bust, I started feeling quilty like in a flash I started feeling real guilty thinking about Jasmine out in L.A. and I just got up and left." "WHAT!!!" "I know I just started going on and on about Jasmine an I just rolled." "So you aint been over there since then?" "Naw" "That's why that bitch is walking around on a mission in here, and especially with me you fucked up man, you know that's the boses niece. How could you fuck things up for all of us too you didn't even think about that?" "Naw I didn't, its just when we where talking I asked her about her father and she was like "he's a bum" and I was like well that don't bother you? And she was like no, he shouldn't have hurt her mom! Then she was like he even passes the bakery pushing his shopping cart and she started laughing. That scared me Unc like if she could be that cold to her father imagine what she would do with me?" As he puffs away on the blunt "Good point but you should've came to that conclusion before she sucked you off because I cannot imagine what she is planning in that peanut head of hers so you better watch out. Alright nephew?" "Yeah" they shake hands "I'm sorry" "Don't be sorry just think about everyone else before you pull a stunt like that, I don't fuck with none of those hoes at work. You ever hear the term don't shit were you sleep?" "Yeah" "Well right now this is your money until you find something better so be smarter Casanova brown, and apologize to her man that's ruthless." He agress by nodding his head and gets out the car "As Salaam Alaikum" "Wa Laikum Salaam"

With that off his chest he goes back into the bakery and finishes his shift. And for the first time he begins to thik about the way Alisha must feel as she comes back and forth from the front of the store to the back, she's been pretty cool giving Lid room, but Lid continues to lust and lust after

Nirobi and all he can think about is getting back to the club tonight to get with her. But to a man the smart decision would've been to boo boo up with the trust fund kid millionaire Alisha, but inside Lid has this hero complex and Nirobi needs a good man in her life nothings been handed to her, she had to fight for everything even if it included taking off all her clothes and losing dignity to eat, to live, to make it He finds greater good in struggling and enduring a relationship with a stripper instead of making the smart move and getting into one with a millionaire. So as the day ends and Alisha tries to approach him Mikhial turns cold and instead of letting down his guard he sticks to his professional demeaner suffocating any spark that they shared between each other. Its hurts him to do this but in his confused mind filled with weed smoke and his lust of this world Alisha doesn't deserve his love she's always gotten what she wanted so as he drives home heart broken about breaking the heart of another Lid is also fixed on getting to Sables and finding Nirobi to let her know what happened.

After stopping off at his weed connects crib, and then going home to his grandmoms to grab a bite to eat, he darts off to Sables around nine thirty. He's on a mission tonight so there will no wasting of money on tips or lap dances but to mingle in with the rest of the crowd he grabs a beer, and looks around for Nirobi. And when he spots he immediately knows that she was not lying last night about leaving her work bag because tonight she looks even hotter. Dolled up from head to toe in a sky blue fish net outfit with pink thong and bra on and matching pink and blue boots. The blue mascara covering her eyes says it all as the two colors just glisen off the sparkle that randomly placed on her breast and face.

He waste no time because the longer he stays the more money he is going to spend so after she's finshed flirting with a few thugs he quickly comes up to her from behind and grabs her by the arm and accordingly Nirobi turns around with an attitude like who the hell is this grabbing me? But she sees its Lid she breaks out into a smile and jumps up blessing him with a hug and warm kiss on the cheek. "What happened to you I thought you just banged on me? I tried to call the number back when it went straight to voicemail." "You not going to believe this but I dropped it in the sink at work and it got all wet so I have buy a new one because that jawn is a done deal." "So you came here tonight to tell me that?" "Yeah I didn't want you to think I just hung up the phone on you, that's rude dude." You would swear she was floating on air as she blushes and smiles, without even knowing it Lid just swept the poor child right off her feet. "Come here" she grabs his shirt and pulls him closer as she whispers in his ear. "I get off at two, the place is busy in here tonight and I need to make some extra cash? Are you going to stay?" "Not on my salary." "Then be here around two and don't come in so you aint gotta pay again. What kind've car do you have?" "A burgundy Mercery Sable" "What!!! I gotta get you outta that and upgrade you to an import. But look boo just come home with me tonight?" He just smiles "OK" and mimicking the classic Foxy Brown song "gotta get you home with me tonight he says "Uh oh uh oh, ooooh baby gotta get you home with me tonight." She laughs "you are a mess so are you going to stay a while and at least watch me dance?" "Naw I want to but I was just here last night I gotta get out here right now before I'm bbbbbroke." "We gotta work on that, just come back at two and you better be here or I'm never going to speak to you again!" "I'll be here" "You better be" she blows him a kiss as he walks out the club and impressed the bouncer at the door shakes his head in approval as in two trips he ahs sealed the deal with one of the hottest dancers in the club."

When he gets back home to his grandmothers she is already upstairs and ready to go to sleep, but from the top of the stairs she ask "Is the police still out there?" "No I didn't see any cops." "They where out there a few minutes ago the muslims across the street were fighting the husband went off on his wife you should of heard the way he was speaking to B-I-T-C- this and M F er that it was horrible but she must've called her brothers because they all came around and then th cops came it was crazy." "No shooting huh?" "Nope" "And I bet nobody even threw a punch just a bunch of yapping and yelling." "Niggers, kiddo what can I tell you." "So you had a front row seat in stealth mode with all the lights out peeping throught the blinds? Heh heh heh." She frowns her face and admits to her peeping "yeah so what this is my block I've been here for thirty years I want to know whats going on!" "Hey cool with me if I was her with you I would've been right next to you peeping out the window." She laughs "You are so silly boy I'm going to sleep after the news I missed the Delaware lottery and I have to stay up and get the numbers." "Grandmom you didn't even play the numbers in Delaware?" "So what I still want to know the numbers for my math." Three or four hits a month she must have some type of system that works, alright goodnight mom mom, I'm going into the kitchen and making a sandwich I have to go out later." "Here we go boy don't start going out here all types of times in the night waking me up or I will be calling your mom right up and kicking your butt right out of here." "or you will shoot me" "You better believe it kiddo." "Don't worry about me coming in tonight I will leave from her house for work in the morning." "I bet it's some stripper?" "Oh lord yeah, but she's hot grandmom" "Your sick you know that!" "I can help her grandmom" "Help yourself and get out of my house, yeah you better not come in hear tonight because I will shoot you." "Hey that premeditated, night mom mom." "Good night" she goes back into her room as he goes into the kitchen and turns on the television the eleven o'clock news on NBC 10, but as he sits down to eat his sandwich and watch the news tonight there is something special in store for him "the Philadelphia police department will be clamping down on speeders and giving tickets out to drivers who don't wear there seat belts, or are driving over the speed limit." And as the anchor goes on with the story the news flashes his mercery sable zooming in on his uniquie bumper sticker of the Cuban flag. "Whoa!, what the hell is my car doing on the news?" But before he could even digest what he was seeing NBC ten moves on to the next story "The Gay Pride Parade is coming back to the city this weekend and like last year thousands of men and women will be their to show support and some to even come out of the closet." The next image shakes Lid to the core right down to the bone as it sends chills up his spine but before he could even digest the previous story he sees himself from last years parade on the news??? People gathered for the gay pride parade, but as he takes a deeper look into the television screen he cannot believe what he is seeing its truly astonishing as he himself him Lid!!! Is walking through the parade alone wearing a black hoodie not touching anyone just walking right throught the middle of the parade I mean it really looks like the footage was pasted and cut into the scene, no it had to pasted and cut into the scene because there is no way Lid was at the gay pride parade. And the biggest reason of them all he's not gay!!!! I have to call somebody and see if they saw this too when reality hits him…. "He doesn't have his cell pone!!" As he sits in the kitchen perplexed he begins to analyze what could've led the news or the powers that be to do such a thing. When he protested the media coverage with Uncle Sha way back in 2003? Or is this just part of the bigger picture that those who do not serve in the military are gay and this an attempt to discredit his credibility especially considering the reasons he refuses to serve? Unanswerable questions that just leave a thick fog in his mind for the next few hours as he waits for two o'clock to roll around and his late night randevous with Nirobi, and around one forty five he leaves and goes to the club and sits out in the parking lot of Sables. While the crowd leaves he anxiously looks at everyone trying to make sutre he doesn't miss her as she leaves work but on the dot right at two o'clock she emerges from the club dragging her work bag like a small puppy and accordingly he flashes the head lights on his car to let her know he's there. She comes to the car and gives him a hug "See that worked out just right you came out as soon as I pulled up." Smiling happy to see Lid she says "I didn't think you were going to show up, talking that my cell phone shit." "I said I was going to show up, talking that my cell phone shit." "I said I was going to show, so you wanna get something to eat?" She flatly replies "No I wanna go home get in the shower and go to bed…you coming or what?" Mikahil just nods his head as they stay hugged up outside his car. "What you driving" "That white Maxima." She hits the alarm on the new model Maxima and gives him a kiss on the cheek and says follo me boyfriend." And he does so as they travel down 76 and into south philly and to the infamous Tasker street projects. Nirobo opens the door to her house Lid steps into what could be his future home decked out with paintings on the wall a big screen television and a shit load of dvd's, the plush black leather couches blend in right with the black and white area rug, and impressed he still checks out the living room as she leads him upstairs. He follows as she goes into her sons room and turns on the light. "This is Nesheem, he's eight and as much as I hate myself for it sometimes I have to leave him here alone for a fewe hours because the girl can only stay until twelve she has to go to school in the morning too." "That's crazy Nirobi anything can happen to him especially down here in the jects." She cuts him off "I know but what the fuck am I supposed to do the lady next door has the key and she checks in on him too. But I have to male money and its not like I have another choice unless someone is going to stay and watch him at night." She looks at Lid with nher ever changing hazrel eyes, those lips, and that pointy nose and he just lunges down and kisses her lips, and as they shuffle out of Nasheem's room and into her bedroom she just climbs Lid like the pole at work as he lifts her up off the ground reminiscent of newly weds they cross the threshold of her bedroom were he gently lays her down on the bed but just before things go any farther she blows the whistle and stops everything. "Stop!!!" "What?? I'm going to have blue balls yo come on!!!" "Wait nigga I just got off work let me take a shower and get this sparkle off of me, wash my face and do my women things." "I like that sparkle" she smiles you are so funny" She grabs her leopard print robe and runs towards the bathroom as she is running she yells "Get the bag of weed out of my pocket book and roll up a dutch!" Surprised she is trusting him already especially after only meeting him the night before, he carefully grabs her purse and opens it, and what do you know only his days at PNC bank could rival the amount of money sitting in front of him. "WoW!!!" from the bathroom she asked? "Did you find it?" And sarcastically he replies "I'm trying gotta get past all this money!!!" "Yeah it's a lot, and its still the weekday wait until the weekends." "Found it!" And Lid begins to do what he does best and roll up some pot, and when he finishes he just stands in the doorway of the bedroom looking at Nirobi who is finished taking a shower and is in front of the mirroe pressing her hair her caramel skin is glowing and those Hazel eyes glance back at Lid simply to ask? "What!!!" "I'm just enjoying the moment it's rare for m to see a women getting dressed and being all up in ya'll house like this, I kinda like it." "Yeah the fuck right you know you be getting all the bitches with those pretty eyes." He shakes his head "Naw you'd be surprised my count is pretty low, but I really like you Nirobi." She smiles "I like you too, because I just don't be letting any old body in my house." "I know I can tell, can I spark it?" "Yeah nigga, your like a knight or something with all your manners spark that shit up." He does so and takes a few puffs then he walks to the bathroom and passes it to her. "Now go in the bedroom and let me get ready for bed, get comfortable and take your clothes off you haven't even taken your boots off go ahead and I will be in there in a minute, I cant stand you looking at me right before we get ready to fuck!" And with that he quickliy goes into the bedroom and begins to undress down to his boxers, wife beater, and sox." And he lays up on the king size bed and waits for her to into the room, like a child waiting for their Christmas present and soon she it arrives. Nirobi walks into the room with her hair pressed and pink lipstick on with that leopard print robe. Turning out the light she jumps right into bed and usually in control of situations like this, Nirobi surprises Lid as she too just sits on top of the covers and like newly weds they wait to see who going to make the first move. When the silence is broken "O.k. I'm ready" and Lid leans over to kiss her on the lips as she presses her lips into his and for a few minutes they kiss while making a heart shape in the bed as their knees and lips touch. But as he pulls away taking her lower lip with him he quickly just gets on top of her, she's tired from dancing and giving dances all night, Lid figures the least he can do is put in work tonight. He begins to kiss at her kneck, while he unwraps the present she has for him underneath her silk robe. "Damn I'm lucky" the pink lipstick matches her pink bra and panties and he quickly gets down to business of unwrapping the bra and like a seasoned vet it only takes one snip to unlatch her bra as he's already begun licking and nibbling on her breats and nipples as he moves down into her garden kissing stomach, licking her belly button, but not going as far as eating that coochie,as he sniffs Nirobi's panties after pulling them off, he finds his entry point using his thumb and a smile comes across his face nothing is going to stop him from pouding that pussy, and he slips his dick right into that slice of heaven that lies between her legs. All the love making the forplay, comes to a halt as he burries his face into the pillow. She's in for a treat tonight working at the bakery has Lid chilsiled and only when he left New Orleans could rival the shape he is in. And as he finds his rythem and Nirobi's back wall he begins to unleash all the frusterstion and anger about being a dish washer after working so hard to graduate college, and working so hard at PNC bank the failure the disappointment is all unleashed on her pussy, and she graciously accepts it wrapping her hands around his back and taking a page out of his book leaning her head back to the sky and moaning, and moaning with every thrust. His upper body is just an anchor for her his lower body is possessed as it moves in and out finding the right g-spot and pounding away, the only noises being made is the sound of clapping skin, mouning, heavy breathing the only talk he wants to hear is from her lips and not the ones on her face. When she reaches her max she digs her nails in his back and without making a sound he raises his head up from the pillow and screams, but he countinues to pound until finally he cums and shoots the last of his sperm into the condem with a few violent thrust for kicks, but as soon as he exits his dick yearns for that warm pussy he pulls the condem off and throws it on the floor. Exhausted she just mumbles "you better get that condem off the floor" "In the morning" "Whatever my coochie hurts" "I want somemore"

She exhales and he falls over next to her Nirobi falls asleep on his chest and with her mouth open exhausted snors the night away, Lid falls asleep soon after with a faint smile painted on his face.

# "King of the Hill"

THE DRIVE TO WORK is the best thing about Lid new gig at the propane and ice station. He has to be awake by four o'clock in the morning and out the door showered, and shaved by four thirty. Any other time the drive takes a half an hour to fort five minutes but this early in the morning there is no one out on the express way and it takes Lid about twenty minutes as he fly's up the highway to Philly his favorite part is the exit into south Philly as he turns the sharp corner at like seventy miles an hour and the car literally goes on two wheels. Lid still at dangerous speeds darts past the dun kin donuts filled with cops and goes straight through the lights and turns left and then makes a u-turn on Grays ferry avenue all in one motion and parks on the street outside the propane station. The owner Mr. Sampson is already there unlocking the front gate, "I thought I was going to have to call my son because you were not going to show" Anticipating the harsh treatment my Sampson Lid politely responds. "No I'm here Mr. Sampson it's only five past five it's my first day I will get better." Mr. Sampson quickly responds back upset and loud "I TOLD YOU SON FIVE O'CLOCK, AND IN THE SUMMER ITS FOUR THIRTY!" Lid just shrugs his shoulders and just walks towards the tanks; Mr. Sampson goes into the main office which sits atop the yard, which is more like a junk yard than anything. There are two broken down trucks with junk, and old tools hanging out, trash and two Lincoln town cars a black one and a white one with the windows busted out, it's a mess. On the second level were the propane is housed, there is an army of propane mini tanks scattered all over the place and Lid thinks too himself the fire marshal would have a fit if he saw this, any puncture of these tanks would cause an explosion." Lid's thoughts are interrupted by the voice of angry old man "THIS AINT NO MUSEUM TURN THE TRUCK ON AND GET THOSE TANKS LOADED! USE THE STRAPS TO GET THE TANKS LOCKED IN

ON THE TRUCK AND GET A MOVE ON SON WE HAVE TO GET OUT OF HERE!" Lid has no idea what Mr. Sampson is talking about but he sharply replies "I don't have the keys to start the truck." Mr. Sampson exhales and goes into the office he quickly comes out and tosses Lid the keys. Lid doesn't even bother to ask what key it is, that would probably drive Mr. Sampson to the limit. He just checks for the key with the ford truck logo and goes for it. After a few turns the truck turns over and the diesel smell emits from the muffler in the back. Lid gets out and begins to load tanks up on the truck. He starts with the eighty pound tanks which are extremely heavy the metal tanks which look like missal's are hard to get a hold of and you have to lift them from the top. Lid pivots the eighty pound tanks to the edge of the second level and with all his might lifts the filled up tank and slowly lays it down to the ground level. He does this process dropping down about eight tanks. With the truck warmed up Mr. Sampson backs up to make things a little easier for Lid. Lid rolls the tanks to the edge of the back of the truck and from the bottom he lifts up the tanks and slides it into the truck. Inside there is a set of black rubber stoppers, like giant size door stoppers they are used to keep the eighty pound metal tanks in place in the back of the truck. Mr. Sampson yell's from the driver seat of the truck "Grab those stoppers put one set on one side of the tanks and the other set on the other side, and get a move on son it's almost five thirty we have to get out of here!" Lid tries to move quicker but it's freezing outside and the cold air Philly hawk mixed with the heavy and freezing tanks is not a recipe for moving fast. Lid tries to move quicker rolling the eighty pound tanks to the edge of the truck and lifting them inside of the truck, after he gets all eight inside of the truck he begins to grab the smaller lighter thirty pound tanks. "Just bring ten of those and come on man stop moving like you are still sleep were late man!" Lid rushes and grabs two tanks at one time which is still five trips up the steps and down the steps, once the tanks are on and everything is tightly strapped on and in place, Lid goes up to the passenger seat when Mr. Sampson ask him "Did you put the forty pound tank in there?" "No what's that?" Loudly Mr. Sampson exclaims "Come on man! I told you to put one of those forty pound tanks in the truck too!" Lid does not remember Mr. Sampson asking that but he quickly jumps out and goes to the second level to get the tank, because he does not want to get fired on his first day. He quickly grabs a forty pound tank off the deck slightly shorter and slimmer than the eighty pound tanks without thought Lid grabs one off the deck and notices that it is really light compared to the eighty pound tanks. Lid pays it no mind and catches up with Mr. Sampson who is already half way outside of the yard. He jogs a little bit to catch up to the van as Mr. Sampson yells "Come on man, hurry up we are late!" Lid puts the tank into the truck and closes then locks the front gates. Once inside the truck Mr. Sampson upset just says "You have to get here on time man, its five forty five and we have to be outta here by five thirty son this is a real tight schedule." "Yes sir" They are off to the sound of KYW news on the am dial and with a left over the bridge and on to the University of Penn they are headed to their first set of stops.

"You have to get a move on son in the morning we have to leave out of the station at five thirty no later. I want to leave at five in the morning but that's pushing it with you. Years ago I was out of the yard at five o'clock by the time we get to Temple it's seven thirty and in the summer that's what we have to do because we will have the ice on board." The first stop is at the University of Pennsylvania the Ivy League school is one of the first Universities in America and still one of the most prestigious Universities in the country. Lid sees the small lunch truck carts, the small carts sell breakfast and lunch to students , faculty, and the workers in the area powered by the propane tanks an age old habit in Philly is eating off the trucks yeah its unhealthy, yeah its not the cleanest place on earth but the greasy food is great. Mr. Sampson pulls the truck over and gets out he approaches a man the white, slick black haired man is well built and looks to be in his forties. "Hey there Gino?" Gino continues to work as he is unloading sodas from his van putting them into the lunch cart. Very modestly he responds "Hey Mr. Sampson" They two men shake hands and begin to talk for a few seconds and then he yell's to Lid. "Young guys sleeping on the job the first day hey wake up son! " Go and grab two of those thirty pounds tanks! And get a move on!" Gino and Mr. Sampson laugh as Lid quickly jumps out the back of the van with tanks in hand. At the lunch truck Mr. Sampson shows Lid how to unplug the tanks. "Always make sure the gas is turned off because you don't want any gas explosion and you don't want any gas leaks." Mr. Sampson unplugged the tank which is empty and drops the new filled tank inside, after the new tank is in and the line secure he opens the valve for the propane tank and let the gas flow into the grill lines of the truck.

Lid puts the other tank next to the tank that's burning and closes the cart, with empty tank in hand he follows Mr. Sampson back to the truck, but before Lid gets inside Mr. Sampson ask him "Did you get the money from Gino?" Before he could answer Mr. Sampson goes on "You trying to put me out of business!" Lid says nothing and just turns around to collect the money from Gino who haves some fun with the young man "How much is that?" "I don't know it's my first day" Lid turns around and ask Mr. Sampson who is livid because this is taking too long and he's letting Lid know as he screams "Come on Man! It's twenty dollars per tank!" Mr. Sampson begins to pull off Gino is smiling holding two twenty dollar bills in his hand and gives it to Lid. Don't worry after a few days you will get used to it." Lid grabs the money and say "Thank you" and dashes off to the truck to catch up with Mr. Sampson.  Inside the truck Mr. Sampson is ranting and raving about how long Lid took, as Lid hands him the money, and unfazed he changes the subject "I used to go to Penn for this summer program we studied people with brain damage from car accidents we gave some of the subjects gingko biloba and at the end the end of the study the patients that used Gingko had significant memory repair. It was with Dr. Britton Chance he invented the CAT scan machine and the machine we used to read the brain waves and changes in the memory parts of the brain. His laboratory was right there in that building Lid points out the window.  Mr. Sampson is speechless and just focuses on the road, taken back by the fact that someone who used to work at Penn is working for him now? Furthermore why isn't this guy working for someone else? The rest of the day is filled with Lid getting out the truck installing the tanks and Mr. Sampson a lot nicer now introducing Lid to all the truck owners. "Hey this is my new guy, we are going to start bringing the ice back too when the weather breaks." He tells the truck owners throughout the morning after a few cubs of coffee Lid and Mr. Sampson are doing o.k. and as the streets of Philly clear up from school kids heading off to school and begins to fill up with blue collar hard working Philadelphian's going to work. The trucks begin to have crowds of people waiting in line and as nine o'clock rolls in they are at Lehigh Avenue. "Get that forty pound tank off the truck and replace the old one with the new one." The truck owners are a Pilipino couple, and they give Lid a very tough look as he jumps up to the back window. A lot more comfortable than this morning Lid announces "Gas man!" "I called you guys a few days ago I'm almost out of gas" Lid begins to quickly shut off the gas line and then turns off the tank and removes it from the truck. He puts the forty pound tank into the truck and connects everything, replacing the old one with the new one. The truck owner gives Lid the money and tells him "That tank better be filled to the top because you guys give us half filled tanks and then I am out of gas tomorrow." Lid apologizes "well I'm sorry for that mistake, I just started and I filled that tank up myself all the way to the top." Lid slaps the tank and says "Thank you sir, and have a nice day" as he collects the money.  He hops back into the truck and gives Mr. Sampson the money, the morning shift is over and Mr. Sampson begins to explain to Lid "Look my son Joe is going to go out with you in the afternoon shift, he still in high school but they let him out early since he is about to graduate so he can come down here and work." "You guys have to go down the garages in South Philly so don't be playing that music all load and drive this truck slow man real seriously." " I got you Mr. Sampson no problem" "I mean it son the fire marshal will be right on y'all tail and I do not want any trouble I have to pay two hundred dollars a day in insurance to move this propane in this truck, you know we are supposed to have an open air truck!" Lid responds "You know I was wondering what was going on" Mr. Sampson begins to laugh "One of those tanks start leaking son and its ka-boom!"  "But I would have to light this cigarette though Lid pulls out a cigarette and pops it in his mouth then he pulls out his lighter just messing with Mr. Sampson. Not amused Mr. Sampson just says son your crazier than I thought but I'm crazier because I would let you light it and blow us both the hell up, my family needs the insurance money." Lid and Mr. Sampson start laughing and puts down the cigarette. "Now Joe knows how to get to the garages on Ninth Street, the garages in South Philly, and the garages around the corner when we get back to the station unload all the tanks and start filling up the thirty pound tanks." Once back at the station Lid quickly gets out of the truck as customers are outside the gates waiting to get propane tanks filled up.  Lid quickly gets out the truck and hustles over to unlock the gates and, he lets the customers inside and grabs a tank from one and immediately begins to fill up tanks. Mr. Sampson parks the truck and begins talking to his customers as they wait. Always familiar with his customers Mr. Sampson starts to go on and on about how he is bringing the ice run back in the morning and buying a new truck expanding the business. Lid sits atop the platform and fills tanks up for customers and collecting money. Once the yard is cleared out of customers Lid begins to line up all the empty tanks, on one side and he begins to fill them up. He puts the thirty pound tanks on the weigh scale and when the scale tilts he knows to pull them off. Avoiding leaking gas as he fills up the tanks Lid is taking the full tanks and lining them up on the other side of the yard. With his back turned he waits for the tank to fill up he hears a voice say "Ya don't need no scale wit the small ones" Lid quickly turns around and a young dark skin man stands before him hair fixed in corn rolls and dressed in carat overalls he hands Lid some gloves, goggles, and mask and says "You better put these on because soon your going to be dumb as a shit breathing all this gas." "What you mean?" "He didn't tell you? Come on man! Bad enough you are going to smell like this stuff, but if you inhale this stuff it could kill you." 'You must be Joe huh?" "Yeah you the new guy Dee's friend, you made it here for the morning run?" "Yeah like five o'clock this morning" "You got here at five o'clock?" "A little late like five o' five in the morning." "That's good most guys don't make it at all in the morning and they show up late trying to go out on the afternoon run." "He goes out on the truck in the morning alone?" "If he has to but sometimes he would just call me up." "Well he said I could get off when we come back from the afternoon run, I'm already tired." "Well were not getting back anytime soon fucking traffic and it does not help that we can't take the truck on the e-way. The problem is that we have to wait for the fucking trucks on Ninth Street to back in off the street and that what takes forever." There conversation is broken up when Mr. Sampson emerges from the office livid MIKEL! MIKEL! Did you sell that china man up on Lehigh Ave an empty tank?!!!!" Joe just exclaims "Good Grief", and Lid walks over to Mr. Sampson to Mr. Sampson outside the office "Are you high son" Lid tries to clear things up "Well you were rushing me this morning so I just grabbed a tank and kept going remember?" "Well the tank was empty and now he does not have any gas to run his truck and he just called here curing me out and no little China man goanna curse me out, I'll shot some suckers in Nam!" Just livid he calls for Billy. "Billy! Get those tanks in the truck you go fill up two forty pound tanks and give him one for free. I'm taking it out of your pay check kid." "Lid says nothing and just turns around and jogs back to the platform taking the smaller tanks from the platform walking down a flight of stairs and loading them one at a time. Lid does this a few times attempting to be safe he only takes on tank down at a time. Billy is the truck sitting in the passenger side of the truck as if he is about to drive, when the noise from the truck's radio and the traffic noise is interrupted by Mr. Sampson. "Yo what you only one tank down at a time, I told you bout lolly gagging! Take two tanks at a time and tell Joe to get off that phone and turn that radio down!" "I was trying to be safe I did not want to drop the tanks and cause an explosion." Mr. Sampson smiles "Boy you got an answer for everything." He goes back into the office and Lid grabs two tanks and loads them into the truck. "Yo Joe Mr. Sampson said get off the phone he is trying to two way you and turn the radio down." 'Lid knows this is going to get him nowhere, but he does what his boss tells him to do. Joe just rolls his eyes and turns the radio up loader. Lid says nothing and finishes loading the tanks into the truck. The tanks sit side by side and about fifty fit into the back of the truck and at twenty five dollars a piece that's twelve hundred dollars and some change a day. Lid finishes loading all the tanks into the truck and straps them in. Finally after chit chatting on the phone Joe gets up and helps Lid straps the tanks into the truck. Using basic towing straps the boys lock all the tanks in making sure none of them can move once the truck is motion and after a few minutes of working together the tanks are all locked in. Joe and Lid go to the office and Joe marks on the board fifty tanks, and takes off to the truck. Lid looks at Mr. Sampson and they both exhale he can't drive the truck can he?"Mr. Sampson smiles he'll tell you he can but don't let that boy drive that truck because I will find out an as soon as you get in that yard I'm a fire your ass, here me buddy?" "Loud and clear Mr. Sampson aright." Lid walks out of the office door and takes a look at the truck were Joe is sitting in the driver's seat, and wonders to himself how am I going to get control of this situation?" He walks to the truck and standing outside the driver's side door he calmly asks. "Joe you don't have a driver's license do you?" Looking at Lid as if it does not matter he replies "No" "Then you can't drive yo." "Come on man stop being a girl and get in the passenger side of the truck I can drive this truck better than you plus you don't know the route." "Naw Joe this is propane and I am not getting locked up if we get into an accident, we are supposed to have this on an open flat bed truck this stuff is not supposed to be in a closed truck. This is a fucking bomb ready to go off man no way." "I'm not getting out this truck" all of a sudden Mr. Sampson comes out of the office, "What the hell are you two doing!" "Joe get out that truck and let Lid drive y'all goanna be late and hit traffic and ya know you gotta go all the way up broad street, get out of the driver's seat!" Lid just looks at Joe and raises his eyebrows; Joe exhales and quickly slides over to the passenger side of the truck getting on his cell phone immediately. Lid jumps into the drivers side and Joe instantly turns up the radio power 99 is on and the rap music is blasting Lid says nothing and just pulls out of the yard but before he makes his right turn onto the street you can here Mr. Sampson yells from out side of the office "TURN THAT RADIO DOWN". Mr. Sampson gets on the two way radio and again tells Joe to turn the radio down and get to Lehigh Avenue. Both boys laugh and jump onto the expressway. On the way up Joe stays on the phone talking to one of his girls and Lid concentrates on driving he's very nervous because this is his first time driving the truck, once at Lehigh avenue the Pilipino truck owner is livid and as soon as Lid gets out of the truck he hears it from the man and his wife in their broken English they go on and on. "Out of business you are trying to put us, all of our customers we are losing. I have no gas and can't cook; if I can't cook then I make no money. His wife decides to join "You lie you said tank was filled" Joe talks to the truck owner, "It's his first day yo, he aint know the tank was not filled. We goanna give ya one for free." Joe's very confident with the customer and Lid just apologizes "I'm sorry yo it's my first day." They shake hands and get back in the truck, and whatever issues Joe and Lid had on the way up it's strictly about business now.

Everything is going well at S&L propane until one Friday Lid decides to ask Mr. Sampson for a raise. It's pay day and Lid's been on time and working hard for about three months now. School is almost out and Joe is about ready to graduate from high school, he and Lid have been on the afternoon run just about everyday and when school gets out Billy will probably be taking over for Mr. Sampson on the day shift. Inside the office the guys Mr. Sampson, Dee, Joe, and Lid go over the total amount of tanks sold for the day and Lid is waiting to get paid so he can get on with his weekend. "Alright that's a rap for me" You missed a day this week" exclaims Mr. Sampson "No sir I haven't missed any days since I started in February." "Oh alright it was like you missed a day when you did not show up on Monday and was just dragging around HAHAHAHA." The family breaks into laughter, Mr. Sampson counts Lid's pay out and Lid just ask "Mr. Sampson I only make like four fifty an hour and I work like eleven, twelve hours a day yo. If I could have fifty cents raise it would really help me out and I think I deserve it." Mr. Sampson's eyes get wide and he just erupts in laughter Hahahahahahaha! Dee why didn't you tell me this boy was crazy, Dee just smiles he knows Lid deserves a raise but he's not going to get it. Mr. Sampson knows Lid deserves a raise but he has to stick to his guns and explains "It's a flat rate son three hundred dollars for a weeks work, I can't afford to give you a raise I have to pay for gas in the truck, the propane in the tanks that's going up every week with these crazy gas prices because of this war, I have to start paying Joe in a few weeks you know he hasn't been paid all this time he's been working here? But when he gets out of school I have to pay him I can't afford to give you a raise son not even fifty cents." Not surprised Lid just shrugs his shoulders and says "O.k. I had to ask, I'll see you guys on Monday." Lid shakes hands with everyone and heads off to his car. Once inside he turns on classic rock WMGK 102.9 to the max level and pulls off into traffic and off to the expressway back home to Delaware."

On Sunday Lid is in Philly and as he drives across the bridge to get on the expressway when he notices that the gates are open and two trailers are out in front of the yard. There's a fork lift running and as he waits at the light Lid thinks to himself if I stop and help out the old ma is not going to pay me, on the other hand these guys are like family and even though he refused to pay me a raise helping out would be the right thing to do. At the light on Grays ferry avenue Lid makes a right turn and then a u-turn right outside the gates. Dee is relieved to see Lid and when emerges from the yard driving the fork lift a smile comes across his face. Dee is inside of the Peterbilt truck and he is tossing ice bags onto a piece of cardboard lying on the ground. "I'm glad to see you" "What's going on? I was driving home and saw you guys open what happened?" Dee exhales from exhaustion "The fucking freezer on this truck broke you know how it makes that humming noise all day?" Lid shakes his head in agreement, "We come down here this afternoon and it's not making any noise so when I opened it up the ice had already started melting up front. It gets colder in the back, so Joe is already took the melted ice and put it in the freezer in the yard. Now we have to break up the ice in this truck and transfer it to the truck over there because the freezer works on that one now. To make things worse it's only the two of us and we been doing this for like three hours now." Lid takes his shirt off and grabs a pair of gloves Dee hands him a hammer and explains. "You have to break this stuff because it's frozen together and we can't move the skids. Lid just listens and nods his head. It's very tight inside of the trailer as it is filled with skids of ice and Lid and Dee squeeze through the trailer as Dee gives him the run down. "The problem is this stuff that's already a little thawed we have to break these bags up and put them back on the skids because they are already frozen together. Once we move these bags and put them on the new skid outside Joe picks them up and puts them into the new trailer." "Who's moving the skids once they are put in the new trailer?" "Dee smiles his front chipped tooth in full view that's our job too." Lid just shakes his head and replies "I should've kept going home." Joe is rapidly driving back and forth with the fork lift, as Lid and Dee break the ice bags apart, then they carry the bags to the end of the trailer and jump out the trailer fifty pound bag of ice in hand. Lining the bags up perfectly until there is a total of twenty five on each skid the number as the ones inside the broken trailer. The men don't speak much as the trailer is still cold and the task at hand may take a few hours but the longer they take the more the ice in the back of the trailer begins to melt. After a few minutes Mr. Sampson comes out of the office and hollers "Close that trailer door Joe you're going to let all the cold air out of the only trailer that does work!" What are you doing here son?" Lid responds as he continues to work "I saw the gates open on my way home and stopped by to see what was going on, thought I could help." 'Your still not getting any raise so you better talk to Dee about getting paid for today!" Lid looks at Dee, and just says it's cool, "He is hot today!" Dee reassures Lid that "I got you man I have bust some scripts tonight don't worry about it." Lid says nothing and continues to work." Soon Mr. Sampson himself is out side driving the fork lift and Joe is inside the working trailer with a pallet mover taking the melting pallets of ice to the back of the trailer which is much colder than in the front. The four men work tirelessly Lid begins to grab at his back and Mr. Sampson comments "I don't health insurance so don't be claiming any workers comp" Lid just smiles and continues to work after a about two hours of endless work they are finished the working trailer is full the broken trailer is empty, and Lid takes a rest, when his phone rings, it's Omar "As Salaam Aliakum" what's the deal?" "Wa Laikum Salaam Lid  I need some help were you at?" "I'm down south Philly;

I'll be down North Philly in like ten minutes." "Bring a bag of backwoods though" "As Salaam Aliakum" "Wa Laikum Salaam". Lid hangs up the phone and gives Dee a hand shake I'm out I'll see y'all tomorrow, but I don't know because my back is killing me from carrying all that ice." Mr. Sampson is really concerned because Lid really looks in pain "Just go home and soak in some water son I'm goanna need ya five in the morning tomorrow.  "I'll be here" Lid gives pounds to everyone and gets in his car completely ignoring Mr. Sampson he lights a cigarette and pulls off in his car towards Drexel university and onto Spring Garden street almost mirroring the route the propane truck takes he zips onto 13th and Spring Garden making a quick U-turn and gets back o broad street. Lid is blasting old Kool G Rap and D.J. Polo "Now you felt the power of the devils gun, another brother on the run." In minutes he's at he is at Broad and Jefferson and in front of Omar's house. He picks up his cell phone and turns down the music to call Omar. "As-salaam aliakum" "wa-laikum salaam" I'm out front, Omar quickly comes out the door and jumps in the car. They shake hands and Omar begins to give instructions "Alright we have to go down Puerto Rico land deep down like on J Street." "Yo you I don't like going down there to it's getting dark man."Omar pays Lid no mind they have been friends since grades school and one thing he is used to is Lid complaining, he just shuffles through the cd case and changes cd's. And even though he complains about it there is no way he's backing out of this and they travel down Jefferson past tenth street, past fifth street, and into the alphabet streets. "Man I gotta get home my back is killing me I had to move a truck load of ice today." "You still working hard getting paid table scraps to make an honest buck?" "That's the only way I know how to get paid it does not feel right the other way." "Lid there is no other way the only way is get as much cash as you can before you die by any means necessary. I'm bout to make five grand real easy that's more than you make in a month!" "Yeah but I can sleep with myself at night I know Allah is watching and I know right from wrong." "Yeah well I go to sleep real good after I toss out some back shots to my girl for half the night and spend the other half watchin her suck my dick off until I fall asleep hahahah." Omar life is not always about the joy you have to have principles." "You went to college you got your degree where's your job? You still living with your moms, that's what I found out when I went to Delaware State everybody was hustling and getting high. I realized that getting this money is the only way out here it's all about the cash yo I'm moving a pound a day. That's five hundred a pop brother Malcolm!" "You still making five hundred a paycheck. I wish you would wake up and get down with this cash and get back out in the streets." "Omar you know I protested against Forty Three , against the wars, I been blacklisted, the FBI terrorist watch list the whole nine yards. It's going to be tough finding a job for a while and maybe forever, but I did what I did because the elections were stolen, 911 was an inside job, and I don't like the direction the country is moving in it's like hell on earth yo, I had to make a stand somebody had to." "Yeah well did that stand get you paid?" "It's not about the money." The sun has gone down in Philly and as they pull up onto a small block Omar ask Lid to " Park right here the house is around the corner, turn off the lights but the car running , put ya seat all the way back so nobody can see you." "Good looking out because my back is killing me I need to relax for a second." Omar just laughs he gets out the car and heads around the corner completely out of sight. For the summer time it's pretty empty out in the streets, but Lid doesn't think too much about it and sits in his car. Omar walks up the stairs and rings the bell to the row home. The door opens and he greeted "What's up Omar?" "What up Mall" There's no smiles and Omar just walks into the house. Inside the house is decked out with a forty inch screen play station two and a surround sound system, the works, the marble floor and mirror that takes up the living room makes the low rent row home look like something out of the movies. "Have a seat Yo?" "Naw my cousin is outside waiting for me so this gotta be quick, Omar pulls a city blue clothing store shopping bag out of his pocket and Mall just grabs it, here's the money he hands Mall a wad of cash and Mall takes off for the basement before he goes he tosses the wad of cash on the dining room table "I'll count that when I come upstairs. Its business as usual for Mall but things take a drastic change when Mall is heading on his way up the stairs and Omar puts on his gloves and surgical mask. The basement door is sits on the other side of the living room and Omar just waits right between the two rooms he pulls out a black automatic 9 and listens as Mall moves up the stairs and as soon as Mall reaches the top stair, both hands on the gun Omar lets loose two quick shot right to the dome piece of Mall. As he begins to fall backwards down the steps Omar grabs the now filled city blue bag out hands of the now dead ass Mall. Boom, Mall crashes down the basement steps and Omar grabs the money off the dining room table. He opens the door and jogs his way back around the corner. Lid hears the shots but no one comes out on their porch to see anything and the streets remain empty and silent. The silence is broken when Omar opens the door and calmly says "keep the lights off and drive fast but don't speed." Understands and zips off the block and out of Puerto Rican land as fast as he could, fast enough that no one could stay behind, and cars going the other direction couldn't see who was driving he wasn't speeding but moving fast than everyone else on the road. Lid has a feeling that something just happened but he says nothing to Omar and they continue driving listening to Jay-Z's Black album Lucifer's song is playing, as they cruise back to Omar's part of north Philly. They stop and Lid parks on the side walk in front of the playground, street lights enlighten the basketball court and the two take seats on the benches. Omar burns the mask and gloves with his lighter and calls one of the young boys over who is playing basketball. "A yo you come here?" The kids stop playing basketball and one of them comes over to Omar and takes a seat next to him. "You still want that nine young boy?" A smile breaks out on the kids face and he nods his head yes. "I need that jawn out here niggas be trying to regulate my sales I'm not having it." "Two hundred you got it?" The young boy gets up and goes to the trash can and lift it up from the bottom underneath is a wad of cash and he comes back with fives, tens , and twenties that equal two hundred dollars. They make the exchange "I don't ever want to hear were you got it from." The young boy says nothing and just nods his head, he knows if he ever utters a word about were he got the gun from he is as dead as Mal who just got his wig pushed back only minutes ago. Omar counts out a hundred dollars and gives it to Lid here man a few hours of driving and look you made some cash that was good whip game yo." Lid takes the cash "Thanks man I gotta get rolling though Delaware's calling, I have to get to sleep plus my back is killing me." "Aw man you not going yet you the same you were in high school I can't stay I gotta go home. I just rolled a back wood filled with that sour diesel." If any thing the soothing power of pot will help with his aching back, plus this exotic brand of pot is new to Lid as regular nickel bags of weed go for like a dub with this stuff. Lid sits back down and Omar sparks the blunt, he and Lid pass the blunt to and from each other as they watch the young boys play basketball. The silence is broken when Omar begins to enlighten his child hood friend on the changing times. "You see that earlier that young boy is only twelve and he getting money out here, that burner is going to open a lot of doors for him in the future. Niggas mom is on crack and got the whole house to himself he be fucking the young jaws all the time in his crib." "Looks like he's has a promising career until he's shot up in a few years." "It's the young boys time Lid they run this shit now all we can do is supply them with work." "Yeah well it's not my cup of tea, this sour diesel is an acid trip though it's like a Spike Lee movie everything is moving in slow motion." They both laugh and after a few more puffs Lid gets up his back not hurting as bad and gives Omar the salaams. "As salaam alaikum old friend" "Wa laikum Salaam cuz" they shake hands and Lid leaves the playground getting into his car and rapidly pulling off. Riding home everything is in slow motion the lights shine brighter, the music is loader, and Lid is like Travolta in Pulp fiction just cruising down broad street until he gets to rave and vine were he makes a left and jumps on 76 towards the airport, once he merges onto 95 south via the airport the cruise turns into Nascar as Lid dominates the fast lane, he is home in like twenty minutes he goes right upstairs and falls to sleep.

Bzzt Bzzt Bzzt! The alarm goes off and as usual it's four in the morning and Lid knows he has to get up for work. But when he rises his back flares up, he quickly grabs it and falls back down. He falls back to sleep and wakes up around four forty five. Quickly he tries to get back up but his back is still flaring in pain, he grabs his cell phone and calls Mr. Sampson he's been working at the yard for five months and he hasn't missed a day yet. "Mr. Sampson this is Lid, I can't make it to work today. I'm sorry man but my back is killing me from lifting that ice yesterday." "Aw come on man how you gonna do this to me I just left got to the yard, and I left Joe at home this morning, now I have to go back and get him. I told you to take it easy alright then I will see you tomorrow you better be here on time." "Thanks Mr. Sampson, my back is really killing me." Before he hangs up Mr. Sampson adds his two cents in "give that girl a few kisses for me." Lid laughs as he hangs up the phone and falls back to sleep. Mr. Sampson hangs up the phone and gets out of his classic 83 suburban to lock the gates. He gets approached by three smokers out on a mission in the early mornings, all of a sudden one of the smokers ask "Yo you got a light old timer?" Mr. Sampson sharply responds "Naw man I don't smoke." As soon as he finishes his sentence the three bums charge at Mr. Sampson. One of the three men pulls out a pistol and Mr. Sampson immediately goes for him first. The old but strong man grabs at the gun and with his left hand and pushes the arm away, then with his right hand he pokes the mans eye out with his thumb. Immediately the gun falls to the ground followed by the would be shooter agonizing in pain screams Ahhhhhh! The other two men move forward and one of them punches Mr. Sampson right in the face and the other man follows with a punch to the gut and the to tee off on Mr. Sampson until he falls to the ground. They go into his pockets and take his cash; the third man still screaming in pain gets up and retrieves his pistol. Over top of Mr. Sampson he screams "I should kill your ass old man!" Mr. Sampson is facing death but it's not his time as he gets a reprieve from the sounds of police sirens. "One of the junkies grabs the man with the gun and say's "Come on we have to get out of here the cops are coming" The three men run off and Mr. Sampson is on the ground bleeding as the cops arrive.

Lid is in his bed still sound asleep when all of a sudden he awaken by the sound of his cell phone ringing the tone is Camron's and Kanye west "Down Low" and Lid picks up the phone and sees it Dee and screams "I'm off today!" Dee calls right back and Lid answers the phone. "What's up Dee I'm off yo, what's the deal?" In a very serious and dark tone, forgetting all the formalities Dee say's "Why weren't you at the yard this morning?" "I hurt my back yesterday moving that ice, I called your dad and he said he was going home to pick Joe back up." Dee is relaying the information to whoever is in the room with him, and then he says "So you called him this morning? Because something does not sound right, nobody did the morning run." "Yo I called my back is all messed up, what's going on?" "My dad is in the hospital some smokers robbed this morning at gun point." "What!" "We want to know where you were because you were supposed to be here and something is not adding up. You need to get down here because you have some explaining to do." Unfazed sure of his innocent Lid ask "How is your father?" "He's o.k. some cuts broken ribs and his face is busted up. What time are you coming up here?" "Give me an hour my back is still messed up I can hardly move." "Yeah well we will be waiting." Worried Lid hangs up the phone Dee was very serious and you can believe that Dee and the rest of the family is eying Lid for having something to do with the botched robbery and it does not help that he asked for a raise a few days before. Lid thinks deep and contemplates who would have the best reason to hurt or kill Mr. Sampson? First up is Dee if something happened to Mr. Sampson then he would be looked upon to take over the business, run the yard the trucking business, and the ice business. That means everyday he would have to wake up four in the morning, stay late at the yard and have real responsibility? Taking of things like payroll old invoices, hiring and firing people, and taking care of the day to day operations of the business. That simply does not sound right for a career criminal especially if more money on the streets a lot faster and with a lot less effort, committing robberies, strong arm, the occasional murder, and check cashing scams up an down the east coast. The life of a clean hard working American seems a little far fetched, plus the way he sounded on the phone was not that of a man acting concerned about the wellbeing of his father he was really concerned about the well being of his father. The next suspect would be Mr. Sampson's wife Claire now Mrs. Claire has a nice paying job but if anything happened to Mr. Sampson legally she would take over everything because she is his wife. Now she defiantly does not want to be at the yard all dayand night but showing up to collect her share of the pot sounds exactly like a women. Plus she could always just have Joe and some guys run the day to day operations. Then that leaves Joe, he's about to graduate high school, he is not going to the army, college, all he has to do is hustle and or work at the yard. Joe's very ambitious and knows more about the business than everyone, and how is Mr. Sampson going to pay Lid and Joe in a few weeks? No one expected Lid to last this long what if Mr. Claire and Joe planned the attack? What if they really intended to hurt Lid? These days he is at the yard before Mr. Sampson what if the would be robbers were waiting for Lid, he is the one that smokes? It sounds evil but money is on the line and money changes people. And finally it comes down to Lid what if he just missed his assignment and as fate would have three smokers decided to rob Mr. Sampson? But who would do such a thing everyone in the neighborhood knows Mr. Sampson is not to be touched? What if those people gave the o.k. on the hit of the old man, Dee, Lid, and Joe can handle everything and from the outside it would as if one old man is holding back the ambitions of three young guys? There are hundreds of different possibilities and Lid replays some of them through his mind but those answers he may never find what he has to do is get to Philly so fully dressed he leaves his moms house jumps in his car and head for Philly. In like thirty minutes he's there greeted by the whole family. Mrs. Claire, Dee, Joe, the sister Vicky, and standing looking like a giant very angry is the oldest brother Jerry. Jerry is like six five three hundred pounds easy and he is completely upset to Lid's surprise sitting in his usual spot behind his desk Mr. Sampson's face is all bruised up and his arm is being held up in a sling. The old battle axe is using a plant in his office taking the juice from the plant's leaves and applying it to his wounds. Lid immediately goes to Mr. Sampson and asks "Are you alright?" "Yeah I'm fine I have a few cuts on my face but I think I did more harm to them than anything." Joe jumps in the conversation "Yeah pop pop poked one of those smokers eye's out yo." Lid shakes hands with Mr. Sampson and hugs him. "My back man I'm sorry it's still killing me, and I need to rest." Mr. Sampson frowns his face and says "Yeah I know you had some girl over there." They both start laughing until Joe breaks it up and ask "Come on where the hell were you?" Lid sharply turns around, "I was home yo I told you my back was hurting from moving that ice." Dee backs Lid up "Yeah you were complaining about your back yesterday." Mrs. Claire interrupts "Well you are supposed to be here in the morning and you were not that makes you unreliable." "I'm sorry it was the first day I missed since I been here" Jerry finally speaks up "well pop maybe you should start bringing Joe with in the morning if the new guy is not going to be dependable?" Lid raises both eyebrows amazed that Jerry even has opinion since this is the first he's seen him ever at the yard, then he turns around to Mr. Sampson and without saying a word he moves his eyes around the room and Mr. Sampson picks up on things anyone in this room could be the responsible for what happened this morning, and Mr. Sampson acknowledges by giving a smile and a slight head nod and then he continues with the meeting. "Well I was going to start bringing Joe in the morning because he is almost out of school? Plus I need to be here in the morning. I'm sorry I missed my assignment today but my back was and still is killing me." Dee walks Lid to the door "Yeah well you almost caught a Paulie from Godfather one" They both laugh "Yeah I know I was thinking about that shit on the way up here in his best Italian accent Lid goes "Leave the gun, take the **cannolies**." They shake hands and both laugh, relieved Lid gets into his car and heads home and thinks to himself that the Mrs. Claire and Joe combination is not out of the question and Mr. Sampson knows so too.

Once home Lid's mom is getting her things together for work, they don't see each other that much because he works in the day and by the time he gets home she is already gone for work to make the night shift at the hospital. Since Lid did not go to work they have a rare opportunity to talk. "Fancy seeing you here baby what you got fired?" "No mom, I called out because my back is killing me from lifting all that ice yesterday." "Did you get paid?" "No I was on my way from Philly and saw the guys unloading ice and decided to help." "So you worked for free yesterday and hurt your back that caused you to miss work today and not get paid? Go figure baby you are doing something wrong." "It gets worse moms my boss was robbed this morning and almost got shot by some smokers." She gasps "Oh my God is he alright?" "Yeah I just came back from the yard and of course everyone thinks I had something to do with it cause I called out." "Oh you have a Paulie situation on your hands "Take the cannolies" she says with here best Italian accent. Lid laughs you're the second person today to say that." "You have to find another job, I know its tough being Muslim but you have to keep applying." "I have mom it's the same thing though I've applied for thousands of jobs no response or they just send me a stupid letter saying I don't have the qualifications." "Just k keep applying baby" "I'm not your baby mom." "I carried you in my stomach for six months preemie; you will always be my baby." She comes over and gives Lid a hug and a kiss on the cheek. "I have to go and get to work my feet are killing me all that running around at work." "You need to take a rest, you work too many hours and days." "If I stop working who will pay the bills? Y'all rent don't even cover the bills around here when I do get rent money. By the way where's your hundred dollars it's due this week." "I will put it on your night stand; do you have anything for my back mom?" "Yeah there's some Benadryl or some ambien upstairs in the medicine cabinet just take one it will put you to sleep and rest your back." "Thanks mom" She leaves and Lid goes upstairs to get his money, in a shoe box under his bed he grabs some tens and twenties and goes downstairs and puts the money on his mother's night table. In her bathroom cabinet he grabs the prescription jar of ambien and takes one, he washes it down with sink water and heads upstairs and passes out for the night.

Lid's sleep is interrupted when his sisters come home, after partying on a Monday night with them are there two cousins Tatyana and Khamilah, their load voices carry all the way up to the third floor and Lid tries to go back to sleep. Downstairs the noise continues and then his sister Ruqayya comes upstairs, on her way to third floor she turns on the hall light and the light shines directly into Lid's room making it harder for him to fall back asleep, the other three girls are still making noise as they continue conversations with Ruqayya while she is on the third floor. "Turn the light off when you go back down stairs; I'm sleep yo y'all making too much noise! I have to go to work in the morning!" Ruqayya laughs and yells go back to sleep sucker!" Downstairs the girls all laugh and when Ruqayya gets finished in her closet upstairs she goes back downstairs stomping down the stairs and leaving the hall light on. Lid gets up and turns the hall light out and tries to go back to sleep. One of the girls runs upstairs and turn the hall light back on and immediately Lid jumps up and yells down the steps "FUCKING BITCHES!, I have to sleep!" "Oh no he didn't? And Lid and the girls start yelling back and forth at one another until Lid goes back to his room closing the door Lid lays back down. All of a sudden the door busts open and its Ruqayya charging at Lid. With a head full of steam she exclaims "I know you did not call me a bitch!" Lid can hear the other girls rumbling up the stairs as Ruqayya jumps and throws a punch right to Lid in the face, caught by surprise he just takes the punch, and swings back at her. They exchange a flurry of punches and soon Ruqayya is falling to the ground, when all of a sudden in comes the smaller Tee Tee with Khamilah and Tatyana right behind her. "Get your hands off my sister." Tee Tee cries as she comes into the doorway but before she can even throw a punch Lid nails her with two shots straight to the face and she is dazed falling back into the closet Tee Tee is hanging up like one of Lid's winter coats. Coming up the stairs you can hear Khamilah saying "get your hands off my cousins" but at glance of the carnage Khamilah, and Tatyana turn right back around and take off down the steps Tanya yelling all the way down  "I'm calling the cops." Lid goes to follow but Ruqayya has gathered herself and grabbed some rope the kind used in double dutch she jumps on Lid's back and wraps the rope around his neck choking the life out of him. Lid falls to the bed and Ruqayya continues to pull trying to kill her brother with what the little of strength he has left Lid puts his fingers, then his hands underneath the rope around his neck so he can breathe and he begins to rise up and now completely enraged with the rope off his neck he screams "Y'all better not call the cops! I'm going to fucking kill y'all bitches for trying to kill me!"

Completely defeated Ruqayya takes off out the room downstairs Lid grabs his sword and follows. When he gets to the top of the stairs the New Castle county police department is already at the door. Lid puts his sword by the stairway and comes downstairs. Khamilah and Tatyana are talking to the female Black cop saying "He has a sword". The female cop takes the lead on the situation and in a stern voice she says "Where's the sword?" Unfazed by their presence Lid trots down the steps and answers "It's a dull edge sword used for practice, I was not going to use it." "What happened?" Ask the male officer, "We started fighting my sister came upstairs after we started arguing and she came upstairs bust through my door and hit me first so we all started to fight." Ruqayya stands in the kitchen with the female officer and gives her statement. Lid gives his statement to the male officer, and Adesha finally coming downstairs with the house phone in hand say's "Mommy is on the phone you two are in trouble." The male officer grabs the telephone and has a conversation with their mother. After a few minutes on the phone they come up with a conclusion "Look you two have to sign this statement and it says that neither of you will press charges on each other and there will be no record of what happed here. Ruqayya and Lid both agree to sign the paper and Lid then escorts the county cops to their cars, he then goes back into the house the girls huddled together in the living room Exhausted Lid goes back upstairs, his back is flaring up, his blood is burning, and he hasn't got any sleep, and has to be at work in like four hours. He takes the moment to pull out his prayer rug and make Isha'a prayer, after nearly being chocked to death by his sister prayer is the only thing that could bring some peace into his life after such a wild night.

Since the robbery Dee has been spending more and more time at the yard and Lid's new job is after the morning propane and ice run, he has to go all the way to the Northeast which is like a half and hour drive on 95 north, but a two hour drive coming back down 95 South caught in the early morning traffic as thousands of commuters travel from the suburbs to Philadelphia. Like a bat out of hell Lid rips through the drivers on ninety five north and ends up getting off at the Woodhaven road exit. Tucked away in a gated community sits Dee's two story condo. Lid parks outside and gives him a call, "Yo Dee I'm outside you ready?" Come on in I can open the gate from inside its address 4-B" Lid drives up to the gate and it opens, he parks and finds the address 4-B. The door is open and Lid rings the bell and waits,

Dee comes to the door and lets him in. "The door was open you could've walked right in the door." "Naw man Islamic customs don't enter someone's home unless they let you in, especially if you have a dog." On queue the giant dog jumps down off the couch, and comes towards Lid. "Whoa see what I mean" "She's cool man just smelling you" Lid raises his hands and the dog sniffs him, "What kind of dog is this?" "A Siberian husky" Dee calls the dog "Come here Sheba" "I have to take her for a walk look around and wait up here." Lid walks around the house "Can I go upstairs?" "Yeah check the upstairs out, but if I told you how much the deposit and the rent is you would say I'm getting robbed, but this is out of the way and no one knows how to get here." "You can trust the location with me." Lid goes up the winding stairs and it leads to the bedroom. Decked out with a flat screen laser television and a California king size bed, clothes everywhere and the newest video games Dee is living well. Lid screams down the steps "You just bring the girls right upstairs and it's on." "Yeah and most of them can't figure out how to get back up here after they leave so its fuck em and duck em." Lid comes back down stairs "No foreplay, no questions, straight to the show." Dee laughs and Sheba approaches Lid as he comes down the steps. "The dog doesn't bite does she?" "She wouldn't be a dog if she didn't, come here Sheba." Dee takes the dog outside and Lid stays in the house. In the kitchen there are dirty dishes, weed bags and blunt guts all over the counter. On a small plate there's white substance scattered about it's probably coke, Lid really wants to try it but doesn't remembering the "Pulp Fiction rules stay away from other peoples drugs." A few minutes later Dee and Sheba return "Are you ready? We gotta get back you know the traffic is going to be a mess on the way back down ninety five." "Yeah let's go." "You leave the dog in the house?" "Yeah were else am I going to take her day care? She knows not to go upstairs and she just lies on the couch most days." They leave and on the way to the car Lid brings up the robbery. "You know I usually get to the yard before your dad now, any other time it would've been me at the yard first being asked for a light." "I thought about that my dad's been coming to the yard at five in the morning for the past twenty five years and never had any problems and all of a sudden he gets robbed. Everyone in the neighborhood knows not to mess with my dad. "So anything that happened, some one or somebody gave the order and maybe it was to get me." "You think its Joe and your Mom's?" Dee gets really serious and says

"Hold up a minute you out of order my moms had nothing to do with it." "If anything those people got to Joe and convinced him that you were cutting into his money. And that conversation could've happened because he is down South Philly a lot." "This is all so crazy I've been thinking about that scenario a lot, but I didn't know who to run it by." "Yeah well Dee I've been thinking about it too. Those people don't want me down there because it's no half stepping and the money and the service is the best it's ever been." "They don't want me down there because I trying hard as hell to get out of these streets and out from under them, and the yard is the perfect escape, plus with the two of us down there they loose less control, they have no leverage on you. Plus Joe is money hungry and they can still get to him." Lid agrees "Correct-A-Mundo! I don't know when they are just going to fall back and let the new generation take over?" "If it was up to them they would try and hold on to power forever." Lid turns up the classic rock and roll and traffic starts to break up and they head on into work, if anything that conversation confirmed that even legitimate business could be deadly in the city of Philadelphia.

After work Lid gets a call from his Uncle Sha there relationship has swayed over the past few months especially since the Ohio incident. When Lid was working at the bakery he took a day off his only day off and went on a trip with his uncle and two cousins. On the way back from Ohio loaded with six industrial sized laser printers in the mini van, in the rain the left front wheel exploded and in second's metal was grinding against the road. The highway was only two lanes and Lid was in the fast lane one the left of him was the edge of a mountain and in the inside a tracker trailer Lid had to hold the mini van from sliding off the side of the mountain and wait until the tracker trailer passed him. To make things more complicated Lid had to use his AAA card to call for a tow truck to help service the flat tire. Once the tire is changed Uncle Sha finally comes clean about the trip explaining that he has been using fake credit cards the entire time to pay for gas. He saved the lives of his uncle, and two cousins, and the thanks he gets from it is that the mini van is now connected to him, since he used his AAA card. There was no way Uncle Sha was going to drive the trip back home he had just drove there none stop, so Lid had to go and in going he probably just saved their lives. Once back in Philly the two shook hands, but their relationship has strayed ever since and with a stunt like that Lid might be washing dishes for the rest of his life because the feds will eventually catch up to you. Today however he takes the call, "As Salaam Alaikum Uncle Sha what's the deal?" "Wa Laikum Salaam could you stop by the house black man? Could you stop by the house after work?" "I'm getting off now on my way." Lid leaves the yard and as usual he jumps into his car turns on the classic rock and pulls off. Going up to uncle Shamp's house Lid takes crosses the bridge and jumps on Walnut Street all the way up to sixty Third Street and makes a right, he takes sixty third until he gets to Oxford and then pulls up to his uncles house. Once parked and inside he gives his cousins hugs and speaks to Miko as she emerges from the kitchen. "Long time no see stranger." "I've been working" They both smile at each other and Miko continues the conversation "I heard you finally got a job." "Yeah I've been working hard with Dee's dad and after work I just go home and pass out, lifting that ice and those tanks is hard work the hardest work I have ever done. "I heard he is a mean ass" "Yeah he's tough but after a while he grows on you." Uncle Sha comes into the house "You down there with the legend that man has done more dirt for those people than any other blackman in history." "I don't know what you are talking about." Mikial quickly smiles and shakes hands with his favorite Uncle. "I need you to drive me to Chester, but we are going to take the red Cherokee." "That old thing come on man the plates are not even right on that truck." "Just come man you're the one with the license, drive it down and I will drive it back." "Another suicide mission for speed racer, nuff said. Why am I always the one called for the mission impossible stuff way beyond the call of duty?" Uncle Sha smiles "You know you love it." They get into the red truck equipped with his lap top bag, they pull off from his uncle's block. "Aw man there's no radio in this thing what am I supposed to do whistle?" "Concentrate on driving 007" " So how are things down at the propane station?" "I missed work a couple of weeks ago and Mr. Sampson got robbed in the morning, the crazy part about it is that a few days before I asked for a raise and he told me no. So you know that looked suspicious I call out and he gets robbed the same morning." "That's is crazy You had a Paulie thing going on "Take the cannolies" they both start laughing "Seriously I talked to Dee this morning about and both of us have come to the conclusion that the little brother had something to do with it, or it was those other people, I really don't want any problems with them." " Wise man and so you shouldn't because they don't play any games why do you think the little brother had something to with it?" "In a few weeks he graduates high school and he has to start getting paid maybe the robbers were there for me and when I did no show they went after Mr. Sampson?" "I don't know you think that kid could come up with something so elaborate? Your giving him too much credit. I mean this is Philly crime happens all the time around here could just be a random act?" "Everybody know not to mess with Mr. Sampson the only way something like that could happen is if it was ordered." "Then you might be on the right track it might be those people with you, Dee, and kid that's enough and they now see the old man as just taking money out the pot. You know nephew they only think in terms of dollars and cents." What exit?" "Get off at Chester man and bear to the left in one of those houses at the end of the block here." They cruise down the street until "This one with the garage pull into it." Mikial does so and the garage door immediately opens up as instructed he pulls inside. There are four men waiting in the garage Uncle Sha greats them, Mikial does the same As-Sallam Alaikum" dressed in orthodox Islamic attire black disha dasha's with black cuffi's. The men are a little skeptical when greeting Mikial and his uncle back, and they lowly say "Wa Laikum." The tense moment is broken up when Uncle Sha sees the person he came to see. "Saleem!" "As Sallam Aliakum blackman!" "Wa Laikum Salaam Sha come on in to the living room with me the baseball game is on the Phillies are playing the Red Sox in that inter league stuff." Three of the men stay inside the garage and start taking apart the Cherokee from the inside, the side panels of the truck doors, lift right off and underneath are bags of cocain and underneath the back seat which lifts completely out are more bags of coccain. Mikial just shakes his head and goes into the living room with his uncle and brother Saleem. Inside the house the place is decked out with cream leather sofa's, an immaculate white rug, black and white lamps, and a giant television screen which is controlled by a projector. In the dining room Uncle Sha and Saleem are counting out cash and when the lap top bag is completely filled  they join Mikial in the living room as he has taken a seat and is enjoying the game. "You like baseball huh?" I like the Phillies sir, the yanks too so I really want the Red sox to lose." "Ask my Uncle and he will tell you it's Harry Kalas and the boys all summer long on fifty seven.  "I think they are going to make the wild card this year." "High hopes kid but Bowa's no real manager that was a public relations move, and they still need some pieces." Uncle Sha breaks the baseball talk up "nothing but a bunch of white boys running around getting paid millions I never understand any of the sports seems like a waste of time." Surprisingly Saleem agrees "You are right the sunna of the prophet says this is all a distraction from rememberance of Allah." " Yeah well that's a little extreme you still should have some moderation, all that sunna is worshiping the ways of a man, the Quaran is the word of God revealed through the angel Gabriel and that's enough for me." "Well in shah Allah you perspective will change in the future you are still young." As Sallam Alikum" they shake hands and Uncle Sha and Mikel are ready to leave when Saleem grabs Mikial whenever you are ready to really become muslim Let your uncle know you can come out here and I will show you the ropes." "O.K. but I'm muslim now Brother Saleem." Saleem replies Lakum Deam nakum wa uladean, Mikial understands the Arabic it's from sura kafirun and translates "to you be your way and to me be mines." Not impressed Uncle Sha is already out the door, and Mikial soon follows. This time around Uncle Sha gets in the drivers seat, and puts the lap top bag of cash on the ground in front of the passengers seat. "That's the last guy you want to hang around he has no sons and he needs an apprentice." "He must not know I am a jedi and there's no hustling for me." "Yeah right you get out here with those Chester girls who love Philly dick." "That's the issue they're all on that sunna of the prophet crap that comes out of Saudi Arabia there's no moderation, it's insane pushing Islam to the limits will do nothing but fail here it does not work. This is a free society with man made laws I can wake up tomorrow and say I want to be jewish and no one better have a problem with it. Just like he used the last part from Kafirun that's for non believers those guys are all wacked out yo." Uncle Sha is speeding on seventy six he cannot wait to get home with the suite case of cash when trouble comes behind them. The blaring lights of red and blue followed by the familiar sounds of police sirens woooo, woooo, Sha pulls over there is no license or paper work for the jeep and things could get very hairy if this cop pulls them out of the jeep and finds the suit case of cash. "You know this car doesn't have paper work?" "That's were you are wrong, Sha goes into the sun visor as the cop approaches the jeep and pulls out some papers. The officer approaches and Uncle Sha gives Mikial one last message "If things don't look right grab the suitcase and run for Fairmount park you will have to jump but don't loose that suitcase." Mikial is speechless and just replies "o.k." the cop gets to the window license and registration please, he takes a look at Sha and kind've recognizes him, since it's a black cop things just sifted in their favor but they are not out of the woods yet as he still has run the paper work. " I left my license at home officer?" "Is this car insured?" "Yes replies Sha." The cop takes the paper work and goes back to his car he runs the paper work and the plates. "It's alright I don't think he's going to lock us up?" "How do you know, Mikial grabs the suitcase and puts it between his legs." "Because He goes to the after hours spot in west philly I seen him there a couple of times." Mikial laughs, a few minutes later the cop comes back to the jeep and hands uncle Sha the paper work, the cop rolls his eyes and ask "Hey kid do you have a license?" "Yes sir" replies Mikial. "Well your going to have to drive" Sha looks at Mikial and Mikial gives the cop his license. The two men switch seats and the cop hands Mikial his license back. Mikial puts on his seat belt and they pull off. "What just happened back there?" "I don't know and I don't care let's just get home now." On the way home they continue there discussion on Islam and the African American community connection with crime. " I don't understand it Uncle Sha the whole community is involved in crime but that completely contradicts the teachings of Islam yo." "You have to understand what we came through, my father and his brothers served in the military, faught in the Korean war and after they served this country they came home and could not find jobs. They put there lives on the line for strangers for this pagan white devil and when they came home war heroes they were still discriminated against. So for us Islam, the nation of Islam for that matter was our separation from this devil called America. The nation cleaned us up we put suits on were clean shaven and had dignity we respected ourselves and changed our conduct no smoking pot, or using any drugs, no drinking we respected our women. Up to that point we were a lost peoples most of us Baptist Christians who did not know what that meant and we had no guidelines or peramiters about life. After the Nation nephew we were like an army." Do for self by any means nessecary!" "So it was our job as the next generation to shed our ties to that criminal activity, becoming part of mainstream society with the dignity and self respect that Islam instilled in us?" "Yes y'all are supposed to take it to the next level, this 911 thing has completely messed everything up  because now muslim means terrorist and you guys like us are forced to engage in illegal activity because once again you are being discriminated against." So I am out of luck huh uncle?" "Young brother unless you want to sacrifice that college degree I suggest you hold on until things change because you don't want to end up in prison and a felony on your record completely erases that degree and you education." They pull up to the house and Mikial parks the jeep, "Are you staying I have to go up to Norristown to make a run, I'm going to take the Benz?" Excited about riding in the Benz Mikial quickly replies "Count me in." Uncle Sha tosses Mikial the key to the Mecedes, and Mikial quickly jumps into the passenger side. A few minutes later Uncle Sha emerges from the house lap top bag in hand and jumps into the drivers seat. On the way up to Norristown they pick up the conversation from earlier. "Uncle Sha we are muslim yo we know what's right from wrong selling dope to our people we our destroyingourselves." "Mikial ot has nothing to do with what's right and wrong, you are seeing things in black and white and this is a very gray world we live in. JP Morgan used child labor, the Kennedy's ran liquer from Canada, and the Forty Three family sold guns to the Nazi's in World War II. It's the same thing that's why muslim immigrants call this place the big satan because the winners have loss their souls to the greenbacks, and the losers die poor." "So the wicked inherited the earth?" "In America yes that is what they do, look at slavery billions were made as these so-called Christians enslaved us robbed us our language, religion, culture and because of the original terrorist group the Ku Klux Klan we lost our minds. They can't get rid of us so they give us the drug game to be the instrument of our on destruction." "So what have you lost Uncle Sha?" "I lost my family, my son mixed up in the game my son lost his life in South Carolina the same place our ancestors used to pick cotton from that devil hundreds of years ago." Mikial is at a loss of words tis is the first time his Uncle Sha has ever admitted to being part of his sons demise. A few years ago Uncle Sha and his wife at the time Veronica agreed that they were moving to South Carolina. She left the city with their two children Idris and Raja. Uncle Sha was side tracked trying to court Miko and never made it to South Carolina. Idris fell into company with the wrong crowd and one day three yound men all of them teenagers decided to rob a local convience store. Two of the three walked in and the gun man some kid Idris had only known for two weeks gets into a scuffle with the store owner. The gun goes off killing the store owner a well liked, and avid Nascar fan the "Peanut Store man" as he was called by locals died instantly and Idris ended up being trialed as an adult and sentenced to twenty five years to life in the state penitentiary. He was only fifteen when this happened and for the first time ever Uncle Sha has shown some grief concerning the situation. The rest of the trip is silent until they get their destination and park and Mikial speaks up "Nothing good can ever come out of something built on crime." "Tell that to Forty Three , because he is President and they have done nothing but crime fucking devils Elijah was right. You better wake up and hold on nephew because 911 just pissed away your future and this war on terror is an endless war." "Uncle Sha gets out of his car with the lap top bag of cash in hand, Mikial just sits and waits. There is a closed sign on the front door of the restaurant, but when Uncle Sha gets the front door and knocks on the glass someone answers the doors and the two men shake hands and Uncle Sha is out of sight. Mikial takes a look around the small town of Norristown there's old fashioned store front shops, a classic bank, but directly inside the parking lot of the bank there is an all black ford crown Victoria with tinted black windows. Mikial thinks nothing of it and sits and waits for his Uncle to return. About fifteen minutes go by when Uncle Sha emerges from the restaurant. "You are not going to believe who's in there?" "Who?" Mikial sharply responds "Iman Malik! They in there reminicising of the old times, they wanted me to stay but I told them you were in the car and I had to leave." "I guess that explains the black crown vicoria then?" Mikial points to the car sitting in the black parking lot. Uncle Sha takes a look and pulls off out of the parking lot, that's no cop that's the federalies, and that might be why they let us go on seventy six earlier because they have bigger fish to fry." chapter

# "I like punching a clock"

THE PROBLEM WITH NOT having auto insurance is that in the event you get into a car accident you can't just go to a regular mechanic one it's going to cost too much if your working, if your poor then you have to find a jack-leg mechanic and hope that he or she can put your car together for a few hundred bucks. Following the cheerleader meltdown Lid had to move back to Delaware and in with his mom with no means of transportation and no source of income searching for jobs on the internet was the only means Lid to get out of this horrid situation, until one day after work Ruquyya comes home with a proposition. "Your still sitting around on the web looking for jobs?" "Yeah I wrote a few Senators and State Reps about helping me find a job but I have not received anything back yet." "They aren't a hiring agency you need to send letters to some temp firms, but look I have the business card of a lady who does the hiring at banco international?" "Working with you?" "No way I'm ready to quit and I don't want anyone knowing you're my brother." Hurt by her comments just says "Damn I've only been unemployed a few months." "Well you if want to start working again here's the lady's business card she's the President of this professional club for women but it doesn't matter she will point you in the right direction I think you have to start as temp with Randstad and then if you don't fuck that up they will hire you full time at Citi." "How much do they pay an hour?" "I think it starts off at like ten dollars but when you get hired full time it goes up to thirteen dollars and hour. What do you care beggars cant be choser's. In her snobbish way she then says "Look my friend Sandy wants your help." Lid shakes his head "No way I told you last time she came over here and asked no you guys are not messing up my chances to be president, plus I don't want to do it's lying and I'm not with that. I mean yeah I could go in front of the feds and act like we are married but I don't want to lie it's a good thing." "She says she will pay you five thousand dollars." "The money don't matter I can't believe she hasn't found anyone yet." "Lid they are going to lick her out of the country." "What country is she from?" "Ghana, if she doesn't get married they are going to kick her out the country, you are the one always talking about slavery and ending white oppression come man step up to the plate and help a sister out." "I don't know why she wants to stay here, but I will think about only on the strength that after coming here in shackles no African should ever be denied the opportunity to become a citizen in the United States whatever happened to give me your poor, weak, and oppressed, o hold up they are picking up the phone finally." Lid's been trying all morning to call C-Span in response to the protest taking place across the country after news papers decided around the globe to publish a hate filled cartoon making fun of the prophet Muhammed. At the behest of the state department newspapers across the country took it upon themselves to still print the derogoratory cartoon. Muslims across the country are out protesting in front of various newspapers Lid is a little split because the Mislims refused to take a stand against the Forty Three  administration at the beginnings of this war on terrorism, and now they organize to protest a first admentment right o freedom of press. An avid C-Span watcher the topic of discussion this morning is reaction to the protest and finally after calling hundreds of times he gets through. "My Name is Lid Islam I am a registered Democrat, I live in Delaware, Well this is what I have to say how can the White House call this the freedom of press and expression when just months ago Cindy Sheehan was escorted out of the capital building right before the State of the Union Address and all she was doing was wearing a t-shirt that stated how many soldiers were murdered in Iraq?" Lid hangs up and the guest interviewer smiles and replies "The caller made a great point." "I know you are not calling C-Span?" "Yeah" You are such a loser, call that lady today and get a job."

He does so and the following week he has an interview with Randstad dressed in a gray suit and red tie he is ready to leave, when sister Halimah stops him "let me take a picture, honey?" "Mom please stop calling me honey and no you cant take a picture I should be dressing like this everyday mom all that hard work to graduate college so I can wash dishes huh?" "Lid be content with life as it is don't harp on what was look forward and try to make the best out of that." "Well all I know is that once I get in there I am out working everyone, everyone." "You don't even know what you are going to be doing." Immitating the Rock "It doesn't matter what I'm doing I know I'm out working everyone I have to catch up." "Hows the car running?" "It sounds like a Harley when I start it up and something is wrong with the engine heads but it will make it to Wilmington." "But will it make it back?" "That's the question my thing is the hood it doesn't look like its on there right but hey what can I do." They both shrug their shoulders well I'm off I love you mom. He gives her a hug and a kiss and leaves. Jamming to classic rock and roll 102.9 blasting extra loud to block out the horrible noise the engine is making.  When he gets to Randstad a little nervous he walks in the door with everything on the line almost two years after graduation top of his graduating class, near miss getting into law school, washing dishes in the bakery, working at the propane station, demolition at the federal building and now finally he has a shot to work for one of the fortune 500 companies again, receive health benefits, and try to move up in the corporate ladder, save his money and move along in life. With all this riding on this one interview Lid takes a deep breathe an opens the door, to what could be the beginning of his comeback from the wastelands. "How did the interview go?" "Mom I crushed it, she said she would call me back later this week, I it only starts at ten dollars an hour but its something." "So when do you start?" "I have to wait until she calls me back, but probably next week." "I'm proud of you honey now you can start paying me rent and move out." "In a couple of months let me get some money saved first, As-Salaam Alaikum mom I love you." Excited Lid calls classic rock MGK and his favorite DJ Debbie is in the air, the phone rings and rings and finally she picks up "Hello 102.9 MGK ?" driving on the expressway heading  back home and excited he loudly says "Debbie I'm back in the race can I request a song?" "Who is this Ali?" "You know Debbie, could you play me a song please?" "What do you want to hear Ali?" "Rock and Roll by Led Zeppelin." "I love getting the led out congrats Ali bye." Smiling filled with joy he drives down the expressway and as requested rock and roll comes on, and while he is jamming to the music the wind begins to pick up and the hood from his car slightly rattles still jamming to Zepelin speeding in the fast lane swwmmmppp!! The hood from his sable flips up and crashes into the front window shattering the glass. Completely blinded Lid has to think in split seconds to avoid crashing into any cars and hurting other people. Without any car insurance he's in a lot of trouble if some one gets hurt and driving in the fast lane he has to exit off the expressway three lanes over to the right blind without seeing what's in front of him. He quickly hits the breaks trying to get the hood to fall down but to no avail it doesn't move but there is a crescent only millimeters he looks out the front and sees that he's far enough away from the traffic in front of him and as he checks the mirrors the cars are far enough away from him and while rock and roll is still playing he grabs the wheel and with all his might turns it to the right and in one motion the car just darts across two lanes. Finally it's the hard part getting off the exit dealing with the curves he hits his turn signals and slows down using the crescent to see he slowly gets off the exit ramp turning slow and once he's clear he pulls over and in perfect harmony still blasting loud the drum break is on and Lid gets out the car and slams the hood down, the windshield is totally cracked but that's secondary compared to the near death experience relieved he gets back in the car and thanks Allah for getting him through such and event, new job, survived attack of the phycho hood, hey today was a pretty good day he thinks to himself and heads back home.

Next week rolls around and its orientation day at Citigroup, with the wind shield cracked on his car, Lid ask his always helpful mom to give him a ride to work. Dressed in full suit its remiscent of the first day of school. As his mother drives him to work "I cant wait after all this time I'm finally back in corporate America." "Well I hope you learned your lesson from the bank job about just up and quiting." "Come on mom they had me down for like being short eight hundred dollars if your short five hundred you are supposed to get fired." "Well they really liked you and gave you a second chance." Shaking head no "Naw mom they was stealing money out my cash box that's why they don't have floating tellers I would go to different branches all month long and then I when I would come back to certain branches in Milford, Middle Town, and Smyrna my cash box would be short, then the computer would crash at certain banks." "You sound like my brothers everyone is out to get you." "Its not everyone it's the white man mom its good white people and bad white people but at the end of the day when it comes down to money they will ruin you if it means they are going to make an extra buck I have no doubts about the eight hundred wasn't even the half of it, they probably took more. Then you gotta look at like this even if I would've stayed mom I couldn't get promoted or post for any other positions that means I could never move up in the company take or leave it nigga, because the truth of the matter is we would rather have you dead, hustling, or behind bars. The prison population is almost three million people and that another conversation for another day but sixty percent of people incarcerated are African American eventhough we only make up thirteen percent of the total population, one out every three African American males will be incarcerated in our lifetime. If that is not Nazi Germany I don't know what is. So yeah I made it out the cracks the pit falls of the hood, but now they will sabotage their own system to make sure I'm never promoted and make no progress at my job so minus taxes, the five to six hundred dollars I work for every two weeks is all the corporations are wiling to pay me for my services, this take it or leave it mentality is nothing but Nazi Germany or Apartide in South Africa. Basically telling me go ahead take your chances hustling but remember locking you up is the objective of the game." "Lid you have to overcome that and keep fighting." He quickly cuts her off "But when is the fight going to end when I die?" "Yeah" "So spend the rest of life trying to stay above water against this beast who is hell bent on locking me up, stomping me out like a roach, or dying from a gun shot at the hands of another brother?" "You have to keep fighting son don't give up." "I won't but I am getting real tired mommy real tired, but anyway thanks for letting me back in the house I really wanted that fire fighter gig but I couldn't find any jobs in Philly and I wouldn't of made it up there without having to hustle, or steel to pay rent." "Stop talking like that, I didn't raise my children to be like that." "Its like nothing has been right since I graduated from college, I wish you hadn't kicked me out like that I only wanted a break for a little while I was burnt out." "Well you should've never talked to me the way you did, and stop bringing up the past. You have to learn how to move on Lid." "The things that happened to me in the past mom makes me the man I am today. I'm not blaming you its just that you picked an outsider over me. How could you open our house up to outsider and kick your only son out on the streets, after I graduated from college?" How do you think that made me feel about myself?" Very coldly she replies "Wellyour acting like a child bringing it up now." "It doesn't sit right with me mom and I'll never forget that." "Don't then boy that's on you!" The rest of the trip is silent and when they pull up to the corporate headquarters of Citigroup she has a parting shot "Move out boy you are too old to be living with your mother." Dejected he walks through the front doors and up to the security desk. Arlarmed by Lid's presence she immediately stands up and ask "How can I help you?" "Hi my name is Lid Islam I am here for orientation." A little shocked her eyes open wide and she hands him the sign in list "Well you are early so just have a seat over there on the couches." "Thank you" he proceeds to sit down and from a conference room around the corner he hears a very familiar voice.

"The American Economy is the fastest growing of any major industrialized nation in the world. Productivity has been growing at the highest rate in decades. An economy that is productive is one that will help increase the standard of living for the American people."

It's President Forty Three  being played live and Lid can only think of 1984 as like his shirt predicted so many years ago the first steps to a facist society is the merger between politicians and corporations. Inside the corporate headquarters of one of the largest banks on the globe the President's mornig speech is being played and as citigroup employees walk by and give him the look of fear as they at first glance see Lid sitting down on the couches they just as fast look up at the security officer and plead, the eyes say it all please protect me from him. Feared because he is African America, feared because he is also muslim Lid nonchalantly listens to President Forty Three  as he continues on with his speech and waits as new employees roll into the waiting area and sit in the chairs and on the couches.

"We've added jobs for thirty one months in a row, and that's totaled 5.1 million new jobs for the American people. Home ownership recently reached record levels. That's important I mean I love the idea when somebody opens a door to where they live, says welcome to my house, welcome to my piece of property. It is good for our society to encourage ownership."

The first to walk in is a little white girl built like she just got out of high school her tight pin stripe pants brings out her little but and clearly shows the in print of her coochie. Her long shoulder length black hair and white top which slightly exposes her  titties takes a seat to the left of Lid and she tries to look away but eventually turns her head where Lid greets her "How you doing?" She smiles and whispers "Fine" and Lid continues to listen to President Forty Three  as he reads the name tag she is wearing it says Karen an older lady comes in looking like she is of Arab decent the slightly tanned lady takes a seat and says hello to Karen and Lid, then together to overweight African American women come in very loud they are very friendly as they get some chit chat started with the Arab women and Karen and Lid continues to listen to President Forty Three 's speech

"One of the most important explanations for this strong economy is low taxes. Drowned by applause. When I came to Washington taxes were too high, and this economy of ours was headed to a recession."

It's almost nine o'clock when a women comes to the security desk, and ask "Am I late they did not leave yet, I had to take my kids to school." He cant see her face but from what is revealed she's dark brown skinned and has a very unique voice. Finally she comes into the waiting area and he finally gets to see the women causing all the commotion and he is not disappointed. Simply breathtaking the caramel skinned women starts to sit down directly across from Lid dressed in a black shirt and black business pants she looks up right at Mikahil and he thinks to himself "We have a winner!" Her pointy nose and curly long black hair, a white girl butt, and big titties busting out her blouse are tell tell signs that she is mixed. The most alluring thing about her is her lips better than Sequita's, fuller perfect both upper and lower iresistable would be her name is the name tag on her shirt did not read Angelina and like lightening Lid and cannot stop looking at her as she conversates with the other females. A little past nine o clock the Ranstad representative shows up  chipper from her morning coffee she reintroduces herself to everyone "Hi all I'm Shannon from Randstad remember me? I need everyone to sign this check list just to make sure everyone here is supposed to be here." Everyone signs the list and its off upstairs to human resources the group forms a line and Angelina and Lid drift to the back of the line. "This is just like school huh, for this early in the morning she sure as hell is chipper Todd must've hit that flat ass right last night." Lid smiles "Yeah you know how they get on that coffee, drink cups of that shit and it does nothing, just really excited about starting a new job, Lid." He extends his hand for her to shake. "Angelina I'm not from around here." "Yeah me either I'm from Philly" "Yuck its so dirty trash all over the place." "hey don't be talking bout Philly miss that's my town, so where you from?" and with a air of confidence she says "Texas" "Don't mess with Texas." She giggles and with that its up the stairs and on to human resources  where they are greeted by a full time citi employee a less excited than Shannon she's way overweight and carry's an eyre of arrogance the sister is African American and she's defiantly muslim then she must be

Christian. As she hands out the paper work when she gets to Lid she rolls her eyes thinking nothing of he politely says "Thank you" and begins to fill out the forms. Its been a long and thousands of job applications in between PNC bank and now the only thing going on in Lids mind is get started, get hired full time, and get promoted as fast as he can. When he finishes the paperwork he immediately goes to the citigroup employee and gives her the paperwork and rudely she holds the folder up with just her middle finger and shocked he looks up at her and she smiles hurt more anything he just walks away and takes his seat. And so it begins the five point million new jobs added origionated from the faith based initiative program, and anything goes when the national agenda is to stomp out muslims and in particular the black muslims. Once the rest of the orientation class is finished their paper work its off Shannon lets everyone know "Its time to go up to the other building where you all will be working." Angelina ask "You mean we are not going to be working here?" Shannon shakes her head "No you work for Randstad and will be working up the hill." The Human resources rep jokingly says "its like a circus up there you guys are gonna love it have fun." And with that they leave the corporate headquarters and walk there way up a long and narrow hill and into the public sector lock box. Shannon has to wait as an representative comes to get them and let them through the secutiy check. "All this security is necessary because you will be working with sensitive material." She's referring to the Wakenhut security guards that greet you from a security station as soon as you walk in. Then there's the rotating door which can only be activated by identification cards, which leads to a room that fittingly has the citigroup logo on the wall, the group is locked in the room until someone comes and lets them in using there security card. "There are no windows here because it is a risk to security once again this is a secure lock box, as we handle sensitive government material. Greeted by a dark haired women they enter the production floor and the first thing Lid sees framed on the wall are copies of the United States Constitution and the Bill of Rights hanging next to the American flag and he thinks to himself maybe there is hope for us after all. The production floor is lined with tables of employees opening and sorting mail, to the left of him is a laberithy of computer work stations as the air is filled with the sound of finger tips tapping key boards. Towards the back of the production floor is a room encased in glass and lined with machines, Lid cant see what is going on in there but the noise resenating from the room also fills the air. They follow Shannon into a small room right next tot eh cpu area, where they are introduced to a short stocky arab man who greets everyone "Hi my name is Anwar, the data entry people he begins to read a few names off the list, and Lid is praying he doesn't say Angelina's name, but to his dismay Anwar says "Karen, Tracy, Wilameena, and finally Angelina." Disappointed it looks like its just going to be Lid and the older arab women Salma, in the batching room. Angelina waves Lid by as Anwar leads them back into the production floor. Lid and Salma arre greeted by the full time citi employees a brown skinned African American women, pleasantly smiling she greets them "Hi my name Chantel, I'm going to show you all how to operate these machines." Then Lid is greeted by an African American man who looks a little older that him he's brown skin and has a real smooth demeaner about "What's up man David, this stuff is a breaze its just not getting Anwar upset and getting here on time." Lid shakes his hand, "Lid, oyu from around here?" "Yeah I grew up around here, you into hip hop cause I be spitting mad bars." Not really into the rap scene Mikhial says "Not anymore man I used to live by it but I don't like the new stuff that's been coming out all that down south crap and the stuff from up here is no better, we really had a chance to speak out a few years ago but we took the money and all the stuff you here on the radio is stupid dance music, and watered down hip hop I miss Nas, Az, Biggie, KRS -1, and those guys they educated and still gave us club bangers." "I hear that I'm like then man my stuff is to educate our people, why don't you spit?" "Don't feel like anymore lost my love for the music years ago, its not like they will ever play any of it on the radio, its all nonscense like when did it become more important to sell products than deliver the message?" "My lines are different you check me out on myspace that's where I sell my cd's." "Oh you got a cd out?" "Yeah my name I flamethrower." Lid shakes his head "never heard of you, you said you from down here?" "Yeah" "Then that's why Philly has trouble marketing its talent how you expect to get famous down here, you ever hear of another rapper from Delaware?" He shakes his head no "Exactly you gotta go to NY that's where its at." A little embarrassed he replies "Yeah well I having a party a this club in Philly and my lines is hot." Getting a little annoyed as the conversation is going nowhere people get upset about constructive criticsm but facts are facts and after letting David know what steps he needs to take to further his career Lid changes the subject back to whats relative the work at hand. "So I guess you're the fastest in here on these machines?" "Yup the fastest ever, plus I scan on the big machines one day I batched twenty thousand orders in a shift." "That's the record?" "Yup, I'll keep that in mind give me a few days." David smiles and they continue to chit chat as Chantel continues to show everyone how to operate the machine. When lunch time rolls around to his surprise Angelina comes into the room and ask Lid "Did you bring your lunch." "Naw I didn't have time to make one I'll probably just eat some butterscotch crimpits I saw them in the vending machine." "Well come on I brought mines you can have some." "Alright come on." Following Angelina out the door and onto the production floor they walk through the hallway past the rest rooms and Lid stops at the vending machines and buys a pepsi and krimpets. "That's so not good for, you know your teeth is going to fall out with all that sugar." Paying Angelina no mind they sit across from each other as they eat there lunch." With eyes locked she ask "You want some?" "What's that?" "Fish, and some vegetables." "If its not fried I don't want it and I really hate vegetables" "You sound like my son, that's not good." "You have a son?" "Yeah a daughter too, and got another one on its way." Shocked that a women on her third child could look so good and be so freelance its obvious she has plans to make a forth with Lid. "Where's your baby's dad?" " I left that nut in Texas he's in the army and all army guys are fucking crazy." "Well that's what happens when you're a mercanery going to war for money and not a cause." "What are you talking about they crashed into the trade centers they started this." "That's not what happened but I'm not going to start anything here at the corporate headquarters of citigroup this is my first day." "All no way don't chicken out now what happened, I want to know?" "That's classified so your other two kids all have the same father?" Embarreased the strong willed Angelina humbly says "No, that loser lives in Dover and washes cars, I know I sure know how to pick em." "Does he help out?" "What I had to go down there to his job and fight him about child support." "You went to his job, that's a little extreme don't you think." "I think these weak as black men need to step up to the plate and break off some money." Lid shakes his head in agreement "My mom raised all three of us by herself, its tough on your own with no husband, but I think a pregnant women should be with the father of her child during the pregnancy." "I'm not alone I have the church helping me out." "Oh your Christian." "Excited she shakes her head "Yeah how do you think I got this job with my work history all over the dang country." Mikhial laughs "Come on have some of this fish its good?" He takes a look at it and smells it and not impressed with the way it looks and smells he tells Angelina "Naw I'm cool." "See that's what's wrong with black men y'all never want to try anything new." "I'll try new things but not that fish." "So are you Christian?" "No, I'm muslim" disappointed she says "I should've known from the name Lid don't you have to pray five times a day?" "Yeah, but I don't pray like that anymore having a little questions about everything considering what's going on around the world." "Why don't you come to church?" "No way the church believes that Jesus is the son of God and I can't get down with that, God is bigger than that and to attribute human qualities like child birth or even having a wife is wrong and remincitcent of the ancient times of Egyptian gods, and the greek roman gods." "Well my lord and savior is Jesus Christ" "Be that as it may my conduct is recorded by angels on my left and right and the things I do here on earth dictactes if I'm going to heaven or not, and I have to stick to that." "Well just to let you know your o.k. because Jesus died for all of our sins." "That's your opinion Angelina, I'll stick to mine." "So are you married or have a girlfriend?" "No just checking things out but I will let you know when I do." She smiles and the saying is certainly true that time flys when you are having fun as the half and hour lunch is finished. "Time to get back to work Angelina, I guess this interview is over?" Full of energy she says "Oh don't say it like that we where just having lunch, bye Lid." He gets up and goes back to work and the rest of the day is filled with what kind of possibilities could erupt with Angelina, but at the end of the day his mom picks him up from work and finally after being clean for a months he can enjoy a much earned and deserved weed break, provided by Tee Tee's boyfriend Baron Lid rolls a dutch and sits in his broken Mercury sable and puffs the night away.

The work at citi is easy and quickly Lid breaks David's record and begins to establish his own presence at work as he does not engage in too much jibber jabber with his co-workers, true to his word however he meets with Raqquya's friend Sandy about possibly marrying her so she could be a full citizen. After work Ruqquya picks him up and they drive over to fox run apartments. "You know I really don't want to do this sis." "Why because she is dark skinned you never know things could work out and y'all will have kids give mom some grand kids cause you sure as hell know I'm not." "That's the problem I don't want this to be like no relationship you know I still got Jasmine out in California." "Hahahaha when was the last time you talked to her? That was your girlfriend like six years ago, listen you gotta get over her loser!" "I'm still dreaming huh? Well see" "Look just here her out but your always the one talking about how everything was stolen from when they took from Africa do an African a favor and let her stay here." "That's the only reason I would do it, I just never liked the way she came over the first time remember when y'all brought pizza hut and she looked around the house like we where poor or she wasn't impresses I don't know it just rubbed off on me the wrong way." "You think too much into things, but you are right some of them do come off like they are better than us, excuse me you where living in a teepee before you came over here eating food airlifted to you guys with our taxes." They both laugh and and pull into the parking lot of Sandy's apartment complex. Once inside the building the smell of fried bananas fills the air, "See they always talking shit about us, she in there eating bananas like it's a delicacy, fucking African monkeys" Holding back her laugh Raqquya says "Shut boy are so ignorant." And Sandy opens the door black and beautiful she smiles and exposes her perfect white teeth. "Hi, come on in." "I finally brought him by to talk to you, he's house trained so don't worry about him stealing anything." Lid sharply looks back at his sister and then takes a seat at the kitchen table. "So what's the problem Sandy Raqquya tells me they are going to kick you out the country?" She sighs "Yes my student visa is up I graduated in May and I really want to stay here." "So why don't you just apply for citizenship?" "It takes to long and they will send me back." "Alright I'm not really sure about this because I don't like lying to any federalies, plus this messes up my chances for being President." Sandy and Raqquya bust out laughing "I told you he was crazy." "I will pay you five thousand dollars to do it." "Its not the money Sandy it's the principle I'm a pretty clean guy, why do you want to stay here?" "Are you crazy I never want to go back to Ghana everyone is so poor and desolate, its so much I can do here, make so much more money, night clubs all over the place its different women are free to be who ever they want to be, at home we still have to serve our fathers, our brothers, our husbands it not equal." "I don't really want to do this." "Please Ruqqaya said you would do it." Tears start to flow down here eyes and she starts to cry as she reaches across the table and grabs Lids hands. "I don't want to go back there I love it here in America, I love it so much." Going against his natural instincts insdie Lids heart dictates to him his next move as Sandy's crying and he thinks to himself it's not fair to send any African back home, especially given the facts of how we got here shackled, whipped, sold as personal and corporate property, breeded to be servents, hunted down and murdered, lynched, persecuted what ever happened to send me your tired, your poor and your hungry and he agrees "O.K. Sandy I will do it, but you have to get this citizen stuff taken care of as soon as possible because I'm getting out of here and going to California." Sandy looks at Raqqaya and his sister say's "He trained but he's crazy chasing some dream" "Lets just get this started as fast as we can so that I can be done with this, I don't know why you want to stay here but no one will ever tell me an African cannot stay here, no one." And with that he agrees to the terms. "O.k well the first thing we have to do is set up a date to get married." "Were not having any ceremony or nothing?" "No we just go to downtown Wilmington and sign the papers, before a judge." "Alright then lets it done." "I will have the money for you then we can open a joint account at commerce bank." "Whatever I could use the cash and get a new car I have few hundred saved and that could help me out." They agree to the terms with a hand shake feeling a little split he knows this is not the right thing to do, but he also knows Sandy is in desperate need and nothing makes him feel more like a man than being needed.

Work is a struggle as he finds it difficult to make friends and everyone is clicked off into their church groups Lid spends most of the day working and becomes good friends with on of the Vice President's at Citi Mr. Jack Warner, these development s don't make it easier for him to make many friends but everyday Jack comes by Mkhails cubical and they talk about Phillies baseball a subject they both hold dear. "So what do you think their chances are this year?" "I remember when Brett Myers was our best chance to win, I like Hamels but he is real young and its going to take a few years." "Your right they don't have the pitching, what about the kid Howard they moved Thome out of town to get him in the line up?" "I don't know why they signed Thome to all that money in the first place because they knew Howard was coming up in Reading, but he strikes out a lot but he can sure hit the home run ball, they are just missing a few pieces to the puzzle to really make a run for the wild card spot and the playoffs." "So how's everything here?" Lid shrugs his shoulders "well the contract is almost up with Randstad and I still haven't been offered a full time position all the other temps event the ones who came on after me are hired full time and I don't understand what's going with that. It really doesn't help because Anwar left and that was my only connection to management so I don't know." Laughing Jack says "Well about me?, they haven't made you full time yet huh? But you are on top of every list statistically, I know I look at the list everyday." "That's what I am saying Mr. Warner and our six months are almost up." "Well I'm not going to make any promises but make sure you stay on the top of the statisitical list and keep applying for full time positions." "Thanks Jack, they might make the playoffs this year as the wild card but I don't know they are still missing something." They shake hands and Lid takes a look around at the day shift managers who all have a look of anger and distaste as Mikhial has gotten very cozy with the vice president of operations for the public sector. Later in the day he's assigned to search for some missing docments and he ends up in the cubicles with Angelina, Chantel, and David and they begin to engage in conversation. "So I see you been getting real friendly with Mr. Warner Lid?" "Yeah we be talking about baseball yo that's it the Phillies." "So you think they gonna hire you full time?" "I don't know David, I would like to because the work is easy, but we will see what happens." Angelina joins the conversation and says my pastor thinks sports and such are distractions from performing service to God, like how much time do you guys waste on watching and playing sports? When you could be out at church doing good?" "Angelina just because it has to do with religion does not always mean it is good." "Your right you need to take your but to church and give up that muslim stuff because y'all aint nothing but a bunch of terrorist." Lid just shakes his head and David helps out "He's right Angelina the church has done nothing but suppress independence, creativity, and free thought for thousands of years, plus look at what we worship the image of a white Jesus, when the bible says it and history proves it that Jesus had dark and wooly hair. Plus look at all the pastors, and ministers they take that money man none of that goes back into the community they just line their pockets with it it's." David shut up! You know that's not true" "yes it is, I just go because that's where my momma took me as a child and it's a habbit now, plus I love me some church girls." Chantel starts to laugh and Lid still in shock that Angelina called him a terrorist adds his comments "Angelina I really don't like what you said." "Well its true y'all the ones crashing planes into building kidnapping reporters and cutting their heads off, its barbaric we have to stay over there and save those people with the love of Christ." And now engaged in what he has trying to avoid during his six month tenure at Citigroup Lid begins to lay Angelina out the Texas native who seems to be misinformed like the mass population or just too ignorant to seek the truth and the old protestor, the old truth seeker declassifies previously classified information. "First of all Texas Forty Three  did not even win the two thousand elections, and if Al Gore was president nine eleven wouldn't of taken place." "That loser who wants a nerd as President, Forty Three  went over there and got Saddam for trying to kill his father." "Listen to what you are saying they lied to the United Nations Secretary of State Colin Powell went before the world and told us Saddam was creating weapons of mass destruction on eighteen wheelers that where driving through Iraq and constantly in motion. Do you know how dangerous that is? If one screw is messed up the whole things could explode and a nuclear blast would go off in Iraq? That's crazy then he said that Iraq posed an imenent threat to the security of the United States of America, Angelina we've been disarming that country since gulf war one so for the past eleven years we have policed the air, had troops on the ground, and had UN weapons inspectors all over the country. The state department's own people Joe Wilson was over there and he said they don't have any weapons. This is the first time in history that we have conducted preemptive attacks on any country and its all based on lies, so what he tried to kill Forty Three  senior that still doesn't give him the right to invade and occupy another sovereign nation. They all begin to nod there heads in agreement and for a brief moment Lid has a flashback to his days at Xavier just before the 2000 elections and how everyone was misinformed about who George Forty Three  was. "Listen nine eleven was an inside job so that we could go to war, has anything of that magnitude happened since? No because it was allowed to happen when looking at a crime always look at the party that benefits as your primary suspect. Iraq hasn't benefited, Afghanistan hasn't benefited they are getting blown to pieces I have the pictures I used to present them in college yo people incinerated just ash and the shadow of a body on a wall, women and kids missing limbs, stop lying to yourself you know exactly what this is the new crusades a war against

Islam against muslims for no reason other than greed and control of oil, and look at the gas prices high as shit paying three dollars a gallon, the rich get richer, and the poor get misinformed and divided. How you gonna call me a terrorist? Let me tell you something I met with the Baptist leaders, and the muslim leaders in Philly and both groups basically said they would rather take jobs and money than stand up for truth, the truth is I will never say Jesus is my lord and savior and I will never believe in any trinity that comes from the Romans and their beliefs in the gods polytheism, I'm muslim there is only one god and he has no son. Who beneifited from this the military is back in action and President Eisenhower warned us this would happen, who benefits the church, the radicals on all sides he Zionist, the extreme muslims, and the ultra conservative Christians this is not right we are nation of laws and if those laws are broken to achieve greater goals that on paper seem like the greater good, we will fail, we have failed where's Bin Laden that was five years ago." "He's in the mountains hiding and we are going to smoke him out?" Lid shakes his head he's having lunch with Jeb Forty Three in the United Arab Imerits and they are laughing away as the Carlye groups stocks soar through the roof, think y'all we've been played." Angelina still defiant until the end says "I don't believe that you better go to church and get baptized because you need your soul cleaned." "Never this is not a Christian nation we have the freedom of religion and if I want to wake up tomorrow and be a jedi and call that my religion I have that right as a tax paying social security card carrying citezins." "So you don't support the vets I bet you cheer when you see the body count comes on the news?" "No I don't cheer because they should not be there and its sad people are dying to lace the pockets of the super rich throughout the globe, and I do support the vets bring them home this is not the path we should be going down." "Well you better get with the program because this is a Christian nation and we will stomp out terrorist so says Jesus." "So when are you getting married Angelina because that baby looks like it is about to bust out of your stomach?" She frowns her face and replies "I don't know there are no available men all the good ones are taken or to selfish to commit to anything." Mikhial gets ready to respond when the day shift manager Rene comes over as the conversation has gotten pretty loud and ask "Lid what are you doing over here with Angelina?" "I was looking for some lost checks and this was the only department I hadn't checked yet." "Did you find them?" "No" "Well come on and get back in the US mint room, and Lid gets up and goes back to the mint room, on his way over he is met with evil looks from his co workers as they roll there eyes and suck there teeth at him. Later in the day Renee lets him know that "Your going to be hired full time, the only opening we have is on third shift." "Come on Renee third shift all the other temps where hired on first shift." "What can I say they have children and mothers need to be at home with their children at night Lid, the only thing we have open is third shift." "I'll take it ." "You have to go back down to human resources tomorrow and you can start on Monday your new manager will be Kenny the shift is from ten until six thirty." Still smiling she shakes Lids hand and happy but disappointed it's third shift Lid clocks out for the day and as the first shift leaves the managers and his co workers all laugh and snicker at Lid because this will be the last week he is on first shift and the last time they have to work with him. But as he leaves Angelina will also be leaving to have her baby and when Lid opens the door for her as they head off the production floor she says "Well I guess I wont be seeing you anymore except in the morning during shift change." "I guess not good luck with the baby thing you come up with any names?" She strongly says "Yeah Christian!" "Good name, see you when you get back Angelina."

# Sura 2 Ayat 225

"God will not call you to account for thoughtlessness in your oaths, But for the Intention In your hearts And he is oft forgiving most for bearing"

WHEN HE GETS HOME he lets his mom know the good news "I'll be on the night shift like you mom." "You don't want to be on the nigh shift honey it drains you the Quran says God made the night for slumber and to get rest, and that is what you should be doing." "Well that's all they offered me so I took it, it didn't help that I got into a discussion about the war and religion today either." "Why would you do that you know they could fire for that, are you trying to get fired tell me now because I will just kick you out know and stop beating around the Forty Three ." "Aw mom they started it this chick." She cuts him of "Who's a chick you mean this women." "Yes mom this women from Texas called me a terrorist she is so Jesus this and Jesus that, but she's pregnant on here third child and not married." "You sound like you like her." "I don't like she gets on my damn nerves." "Watch your mouth" "She does remind me of you though having the three kids and trying to make it on her own I just don't think a pregnant women should be away from her baby's father." "So why don't you step up to the plate?" "I don't know I'm married now how's that." "hahahaha" she laughs as Lid and Sandy have already gone downtown and made legal their marriage by swearing before a judge. "So how did that go and what's it like being married?" " was exhausted because I stayed at work late the night before, but we went don there and what she didn't tell me was that I had to swear on the bible." "You don't have to do that!" "For real!" "No you can just request to sign the papers you didn't have to swear on the bible." "Well I'm not worried about it because the whole time I was thinking I'm doing this so she can be a citizen, I'm doing this so she can be a citezin, that's where my intentions." "Don't worry about it honey so did y'all kiss?" "Yeah and that's when I knew I was in trouble because as soon as I was finished she had that glow in her eyes sparkling, I hope she doesn't think too much into it I'm just acting." "Why don't you give her a try Lid I really want grand children?" "Not like that mom that's not how you get me, she specifically asked me to do this because they where going to kick her out of the country otherwise I wouldn't of done it. I don't feel like lying to the feds yo that's a lot of acting." "And you are such an actor I understand that's deceptive so how long do y'all have to be married the whole process takes about two years and believe me I am counting down the time I cannot wait for this to be over." "Well may be in the mean time you can get to know this girl at work?" "Angelina yeah right I told you she gets under my skin." "Your just afraid because she's a powerful women." " Yeah well she better use that power when she's shitting that baby out because her belly is gigantic its like 4-D or something." Sister Halimah laughs "You are so funny, you should be a comedian." "I'm a lawyer mom I just didn't go to law school." "Well you can still try again just your working now just take the prep coarse and bring up that score." "I know I've been saving and looking at law schools again, two years later and I am still shocked I did not get in." "You know why you didn't get in you're an Idealist Lid, they don't want people with strong convictions they want robots and money hungry leaches." "Well Uncle Sha lawyer Mr. Davidson wrote me a recommendation to go to Temple so all I gotta do is take the test again." "Well stop talking about and do it, by the way when are you going to move out of my house boy I'm sick and tired of living with a grown man." "Give me a few months once they make me full time to get some more money saved I just brought a car from the grand Sandy paid me, now I have to save again you know I don't want to stay down here, I can't stand it there's no action." "You would rather go to Philly where four hundred African americans males are murdered every year?" "Yup that's my home and my city they need me." "Your crazy well to each his own you just better get out of here soon or one day there will be a U Haul truck parked out front and you know what that means." "Yeah I'll be living alone again."

The next week he starts full time with citigroup and on the night shift. The crew is different with a lot less people on the production floor and mint department is even thinner, made up of six people two couples Rick and

Gwen and Micah and Vivica, the assistant manager is Sophia and the manager is Kyle. Kyle and Sophia are Italian the U.S. veteran is pretty down to earth and a cool customer, Sophia a lot younger than Lid lacks self confidence and her eratic behavior is only quelled later in the night after she takes a few of her multiple prescription drugs for depression, and scerzaphania, Gwen and Rick are the pretty practical both high school graduates long ago they accepted the fact that poverty was the sentence dictated to their generation and the love they share is what they hold on to more than anything. Micah is an ex ball player who cannot stand authority and constantly gets into verbal arguments with Kyle and Sophia his girlfriend Vivica probably played ball too because she is pretty tall but if she doesn't stop eye balling Lid when ever Micah leave the room or turns his head Lid senses there will be big problems. But things are a lot better than on first shift with the mint department the problem arises when Lid is selected by the Manager of third shift passports division Kevin to work in the scanning room with the rest of the passports department. To this point Mikhial would knock out the incoming orders for the mint department, do a little data entry for the mint department, and then some scanning for the mint department only when things really got busy for passports did he help out and that was still dealing with the much older first shift, the night shift is a different story. This rag tag bunch immediately starts to dislike Lid the first night he comes to the scanning room. Thomas the ring leader former ball player and now part time referee for the local high school teams he's in his late thirties and there is deinetly something going on between him and the assistant manager Jill the manager Luke is a white guy red with red hair probably a scot form the old days and he's cool as he appreciates Lid helping out with the scanning especially nowadays when the work load is the heaviest, the other employees for that matter don't because he has no ties to any of them he simply works away not talking to anyone once he begins the shift. Nene is African American and a little younger than Lid she's from Philly though she now lives in Delaware, Terance and Darren work together on scanning machine Terance and both went high school together Darren's jewish and they bust on each other all night, behind Lid is James who wears a cooks aprine as he works, the usual passports crew all have partners and sometimes they are pulled off the production floor, Mikhial works on the scanning machine for the mint department and because the mint traffic is slow he scans US passports works all night. Thomas and the others joke and play all night and eventhough he tries to make friends with them they will have none of that, but the good sportsman in him always shakes hands with everyone before the shifts and he puts on his music and dances the night away. He and Micah go through some things after Micah goes away from vacation for a week. Whatever Vivica told Micah it wasn't good because the first night he is back every time he passes Lid he cracks his knuckles, this night the mints workload was heavy and Lid is doing data entry when Micah and Vivica sit directly across from they spend the night whispering to each other and at the end of every conversation Micah looks at Lid through the glass window and gives him a very grimy look and says "I was only gone a week and light skin was pressing up on my girl." Trying to ignore Micah Mikahil thinks to himself what is he talking about? The first day Micah was gone she just falls out on the flat bed yeah she had on tight jeans on put she swung her legs right open you could see her pussy imprint and all, and she did this right in front of Lid, besides that nothing else happened, but whatever the story this has to stop because Lid will not be terrorized on night shift as well. So when Micah goes to the bathroom towards the end of the night Lid a little scared gets up and follows. He waits inside as Micah uses the toilet and when he emerges Lid is standing next to the door. "What's your problem? Micah smiles caught off guard he knows he is skating on thin ice already and any altercation would mean immediate termination. "What you talking about man there's no problem." " So why you talking shit about me all night man cracking your knuckles when you walk by me?" "You know Kyle said if I get into anything else they are going to fire me." "So why you barking up my tree?" Someone tries to come into the bathroom and blocking the door Lid says "Come back later, oppupied." "Are you going to answer?" "Its nothing man she just said you where trying to come at her when I was gone." "Are y'all not together? Every night y'all sit next to each other and talk why would I come at her do that seems like the actions of an intellengent person?" "He shakes his head no, "Naw that seems like something a jock would do stop with the bullshit man I don't need it." And Lid turns around and walks out the bathroom, he stares down the guy waiting outside in the hallway and goes back to his seat. Micah comes back and they continue to talk and giggle for the rest of the night but Micah doesn't crack his knuckles and Lid thinks to himself four hundred dead a year and two hundred of the homicides is because of these stupid as bitches. At the end of the shift Lid has to hang tight for a while and get his new identification from corporate headquarters down the hill. This gives him a chance to see the old first shift David, and Karen are still there as Angelina is still maternity leave. He chit chats with the old crew but stays to himself but before he leaves around nine oc'clock he expresses his disagreement about having to stay so late after working night shift. "This is crazy David I'm exhausted and I gotta stay three more hours to get a stupid ID I don't understand why I cant use the old one, then I gotta get right back up an come in here tonight." "Yeah man I hear you Angelina is coming back this week." "So she had the baby? What did she have?" "I don't even know, hey Karen what did Angelina have?" Smiling Karen replies "She had a boy." Karen is rolling when they first started she looked like she was just out of high school, but the whole first shift has been messed up since Anwar quit and Renee returned from disability leave, one morning Lid took a handful of sugar packs and poured them into a paper cup, he sits the paper cup by the computer and when Renee walks in and sees the paper cup she gets really excited and uses her index finger to taste the sugar, the arrogance, the constant red noses, and pinching of nostrils Lids lived in the city long enough to know Renee has the whole first rolling on coke and since she's a pretty wise girl its more likely than not. He's on third shift now and it really has nothing to do with him, but as he leaves he says goodbye to the old crew an walks down the hill. Inside citigroup for the first time since being a temp employee he's recieced different by the full timers they don't fear him like before, and things are pretty nice as the security guard greets him after he signs in its down a hallway and then a left into another hallway. He can see inside the security area filled with monitors and such, and he waits for someone to answer the door, upset about having to stay late dealing with the bullshit from Micah a few hours ago everything just stops and Lid's heart just quakes as he turns to his right and sees a love walking his way. Decked out in her Wackenhut uniform she tries not to look at him as that is all he can do, struck by lightening his mouth just drops as he watches her long black hair just bounce off her shoulders, her white security guard uniform is doing a great bad job holding back her breast as they seem ready to bust out at any momement and full figured all the way down to feet looking like Sophia Loren  her form fitting pants shows her pussy imprint with handcuffs and all she walks by Lid who is still a mess and glances right into his green eyes stunned at the sight of a matching pair of green eyes he just stumbles to the wall and falls completely to the floor. And that is exactly were is stays mezmorized his heart burning what ever he was complaining about seconds ago meant nothing, what mattered was getting another look at those green eyes, and still sitting on the floor she comes out the door and ask "You Ali?" Lid says nothing and just nods his head, unimpressed with his childish behavior she says with authority "Get up and come to get your new id!" And he does so once inside a far less attractive guard takes over as Mrs. Green eyes is watching the monitors. She has the toughest time getting Lid's finger prints to scan as he is non complient constantly trying to look into the the next room and see Mrs Green eyes. Once they are finished he is issued his new id card, and he walks by the room she is in and once again their eyes meet and he just waves his right hand and air whispers "hi". She quickly turns back around and checks out the monitors, Lid goes leaves and goes home, with his heart still pounding, sunken in, his blood is boiling and the simply act of closing his eye lids for a split second is tourtous as the memory of Mrs. Green eyes haunts his soul.

A few days later as advertised Angelina is back from maternity leave a whole lot thinner from the look of things she's waiting for this day since she first started back in May. Since this is the busiest time of the year for passports everyone has to stay overtime for mandatory three hours a shift, and Lid decides to get his time in doing data entry. Angelina and Karen take seats right next to him and unfazed by her beauty despite the rosy red lip stick on those perfect lips, her hair done up, and her grey gator print boots with matching pants and sweater he continues to key away listening to his earphones until he is taped on the shoulders "Do you want to see a picture of my new son Christian?" "O.k." and Angelina pulls out a picture of cute blue eyed baby boy "Ahhhh Angelina he has eyes like Sinatra, he's going to be a heartbreaker." The two women giggle "You and that Sinatra Lid you are like an old man." Lid goes back to keying and Karen ask "So Angelina what are you going to do now that you've had your baby, move back to Texas?" "I don't know Karen I want to stay here but things are so tough for me now with three kids being a single mom I've been handling it but the bills are pilling up because I was out for a whole month." "You need a man girl somebody needs to step up and say something before you find someone else or move back home." "Yeah well Jenny I can't wait forever." He listens to their conversation as the two of them look over at him when they say somebody. Lid really doesn't want to get involved with Angelina she has three children by two different baby fathers and she is a real man eater! But he takes the bait he's always liked Angelina from day one and even though she has a strong personality he enjoys the batter they've engaged in over the past six months and just this one time he could mess with somebody at work considering the circumstances three children he makes his mind up. After keying for about an hour he gets up and bids Angelina goodbye "Angelina the baby is beautiful , I'll see you tomorrow bye." He gets up and clocks out once he gets home he breaks out his bible and his Quran and finds two passages to merge into the love letter he's going to write Angelina.

Dear Angelina,

Since the first day we met I think there's been some type of chemistry between us. I've had my reservations because I am not the type to play games and once I make a decision to be in a relationship with anyone I mean it. This world has changed so much over the past six years and I respect the fact that you are a believing Christian women, I myself am a muslim and in this day and age such relationships are complicated and not popular. Enclosed are excerpts from the Holy Bible and the Holy Quran one explaining the way I feel inside after so many trials and tribulations alone and without love.

Lamentations 3

I Am the man that hath seen affliction by the rod of his wrath.

He hath led me, and brought m into darkness, but not into light.

Surely against me is he turned; he turnnith his hand against m all the day.

My flesh and my skin hath he made old;

he hath broken my bones. He hath set me in dark places, as they be dead of old.

He hath hedged me about, that I cannot get out; he hath made my chain heavy

Also when I cry and shout, he shutteth out my prayer

He hath enclosed my ways with hewn stone, he hath made my paths crooked

He was unto me as a bear lying in wait and as a lion in secret places

He hath turned aside my ways and pulled me in pieces: he hath made me desolate.

He hath bent his bow, and sent me as a mark for the arrow

He hath caused the arrows to his quiver to enter into my viens

I was a derision to all my people; and their song all the day

He hath filed me with bitterness, he hath made me drunken with worm wood

He hath also broken my teeth with gravel stones, he hath covered me with ashes

And thou hath removed my soul far off from peace; I forgot prosperity

And I said, my strength and my hope is perished from the LORD

Remember my affliction and my misery, the wormwood
and the gall

My soul hath them still in remembrance, and is humbled
in me

This I recall to my mind, therefore I have hope.

Angelina this passage represents the way I feel inside deep down inside,
I've been through a lot these past few years life has been very difficult for
m as I have done some very tough jobs and my life is not turning out the
way I thought it would be. But I have an opportunity now to make things
right and my past failures have humbled me and made me remember God
and my commitments to God.

I grew up in a single parent household with two other siblings, and it was
a true struggle and balance was not established until my mom remarried.
Being a step father is a very important job and you would really have to be
ready to settle down. There is something I would like to share with you now
I am legally married and I had to do so in order to help a women in need out.
However I am Muslim and like the Mormons I can have multiple wives. But
I would really like to do this right in the eyes God so that we don't make the
same mistakes we made in the past. The trials and tribulations of the past
have made me a different person I'm a family man now and if we do things
right then may be when the kids are sleep, the homework is done, we can
enjoy each other like drinking champagne from the tips of your toes as you
pour it down those great legs of yours?

Sura XXIV Ayat 32
"Marry those amoung you who are single or the virtuous
ones among your slaves, male or female: If they are in
poverty God will give them means out of his grace: For
God incompasseth all, and he knoweth all things."

Sura XXXV Ayat 2
"Verily God knows all the hidden things of the heavens
and the earth verily he has full knowledge of all that's is in
men's hearts."

Sura XVII Ayatt 32
> "Nor come nigh to adultery it is a shameful deed, And an
> evil, opening the road to all evils."

So lets try to do things right so we can be to each other that hope talked about in Lamentations and lets refrain from any sin because it is not a good thing in the sight of God as revealed in the Holy Quaran.

He buys a card from the local drug store and after the night shift, he stays three more hours for overtime and when he is done Lid approaches Angelina and says good morning "Morning Angelina how are you today?" "I was late because those kids are getting on my nerves not getting up for school on time, its rough being a single parent." He smiles and says "May be things will get better. Here's a card and a letter please just take heed of my words because I mean what I say and what I write." Surprised she ask "What's this?" "Just read it, and I will see you tomorrow morning." Exhausted from working and standing on his feet all night Lid leaves nervous about how she might react to the letter but confident that he did the right thing he glances over at the Constitution as he walks out the door. The rest of the day he's restless and axious about how she might react he doesn't sleep well and is up earlier than usual. He gets work a little early and the night shift is business as usual Thomas and his bunch crack their jokes all night some geared at Lid but he just outworks them and dances the night away as he scans. In the morning when the first shift comes in Lid is still scanning passport work when Angelina and David walk into the scan room. And right in front of the scanning machine he's on for his eyes to see they grab each other and French kiss. The scanning room erupts in laughter and shattered Lid's heart is simply shattered as Angelina lets him know what she thinks of his feelings, speaking as if he is not even there or doesn't exist she says "He's going to write me with that Muhammed crap, sounds like he is going to jump off a building or something I'm Christian! Christian!, Lid walks out of the scanning room and as soon as he hits the production floor the rest of the building erupts in laughter and inside he can feel his heart just shatter, shatter into pieces, his mind is having trouble processing the embarrassment and he begins to fight tears back. He just looks at the people astonished that so many people have found enjoyment in his pain. These people who he thought where his coworkers, these people who thought where just jealous of his work habit, the actions today revealed something more something hateful something wicked and as he walks by managers row and clocks out they too have lost all sense of proffesionality and snicker and laugh away. Lid holds back his tears and with his head low to the ground he glances up at the Constitution and walks out the door, to head home devastated and crushed. There's no music on the drive home and like a sped demon he darts off lightening fast zig zagging in and out of traffic on the verge of crashing into cars once he gets home he calls his cousin Boo and grabs the wooden Louisville slugger from his back seat "YO I NEED A BOX TRUCK!!!!" "Whats wrong cuzzo why are you hollering?" "I NEED TO QUESTION SOMEONE NOW!!!" "You got him in the car with you?" "NO HE'S AT WORK BUT I KNOW HOW TO GET HIM THEY GET OUT AT THREE!!! SOMETHING HAPPENED AT WORK AND MY HEAD IS ALL MESSED UP." "Lid you gotta calm down." And with bat in hand he slams it to the ground shattering his twenty year old baseball bat and at the top of his lungs screams "I'M A FUCKING KILL THAT NIGGA WHEN I SEE HIM!!!!" and hangs up the phone, he rolls a dutch and pops open a bottle of champagne and sits in his car he doesn't cry but he does shed tears as he is stricken with disbelief that so many people could find enjoyment out of his pain. Playing Sympothy for the devil in the back ground finishing off his dutch and bottle of champagne, the tears start to flow down his face and he comes to the grave realization that this is not the America he grew up in, how the mighty have fallen and the wicked have inherited the earth.

Just when everything was going well, this Angelina and David stuff hits the fan and now the night shift has something to tease him about, and that is exactly what they do. But it doesn't stop there as he's constantly laughed at while at the mall, the local wallmart, even at the Wendy's drive thru. This Angelina and David sure spread pretty fast coming from the city he's not used to personal business being out there like this, and humiliated he doesn't feel comfortable or safe in any environment outside of his home. During the night shift he just turns his music up and blocks out everyone, but everytime he turns around the ruckus is going on as his co-workers point and laugh at him. "Hell is truly a place of amForty Three " To make things worse every morning Angelina trots David around by her side when they come into work and just the sight of them bruises his heart, his only way to combat the terror is through silence and as Angelina continues to confront him in the morning he says nothing to her or the entire 1ˢᵗ shift. Until he is confronted by the 1ˢᵗ shift manager Renee she's Italian and a real hard worker and as she request Lid to have a sit down in the lunch room its obvious by her friendly demeanor that she doesn't not understand the gravity of the past events. "How you doing Lid, is everything alrigh?" "Yeah Renee I'm fine." "Well it really doesn't seem that way you are not your usual up beat happy self and you aren't speaking to anyone on my first shift, as the manager of first shift I am very concerned about that." "Look Renee if 1ˢᵗ shift was concerned about me then they shouldn't of behaved the way they did a few days ago." Smiling she sits back in her chair "What are you talking about that stuff with Angelina? She said you are the one not speaking to her, I was not here that morning so I have nothing to do with it, but you have to start talking to 1ˢᵗ shift." Still smirking she is not taking Lid serious until his eyes get beedy and he bluntly says "Renee I'm not going to be the same, they messed my wiring up in here" and shuffling his fingers at his brain he continues "You don't know how long it took for me to get my wiring right upstairs and now it's all messed up! I don't know what that means or what I'm going to do! But what I do know is New Castle, the state of Delaware, and Philly for that matter better watch out! Because I'm not in the right state of mind which means I am in the wrong state of mind! Shocked Renee sits up and looks directly into Lid eyes who has yet to blink and now she begins to fully understand the pain he is feeling as the smirk is wiped off her face. "THIS MEETING IS OVER!" Agrilly he gets up and leaves the cafeteria confused, hurt, he takes his frusteration out on the road as he recklessly speeds down the highway.

The next night at work the jewish kid Darren comes to Lids defense as the scanning room is once again laughing at him throughout the night. "Y'all need to stop messing with him man he's not going to take too much more you shouldn't do that to people." Darren says it loud enough for Lid to hear over his earphones and he turns them down to thank Darren "Thanks man I appreciate that" But as he thanks Darren Thomas reply's "Well we can always start on you Jew ManFoo." And they all bust out laughing. Lid just shakes his head and turns up his earphones and continues to work. During the final cigarette break Lid as usual standing alone, and Darren standing alone feeling the pain of the comments made by Thomas have a few words "It gets kind of tough in there huh?" "Yeah its like being in the yard back in school you gotta keep throwing punches laugh with them and tell funnier jokes." Naw it shouldn't be like that I don't understand how grownups behave like that it's like Pinnochio and everyone all the kids are on that Island and while they are turning into jack asses and don't even know it, it's the same thing here." "Yeah well that's a little bit of a deep comparison for me but I see what you are talking about. So do you smoke weed?" Not saying a word he just replies with a head nod "Its alright man you are not going to get busted it's legal in Denver, Maryland, and California it's cool these days." "I blaze I usually get regular green from this Jamaican they got all those chemicals in the other stuff out there you have to careful who you buy from I don't wanna get slipped no PCP and start flipping out." "I have some hydro and purple haze at the crib, plus I use this challis weed bong to smoke it in man the high is real clean none of that tobacco paper mixed in." "Man I never smoked out of a bong before they used to do that shit in college but they used an old two liter soda. My first year I was staying in the dorm and we all decided to have a session inside don't ask me why but we just did knowing there's no smoking inside. So it's like twelve of us packed in this room with a shit load of pot blunts all in the air the lights are off this nigga from Cali got posters on the walls that glow in the dark and we are tripping, then all of a sudden somebody bangs on the door. Now we cant open the door because its all taped up with towels and shit underneath it, he's talking about he can smell the shit all the way down the hall blowing everybody's high. So my nigga Craig who don't be smoking starts getting paranoid." Darren starts to laugh "So he's a little guy and I don't know what came over him but he just takes off for the door and with all his might rips it open with the tape and everything and takes off into the hallway. But he doesn't go to his dorm room, busted cause if their was any question about the smoke in the hallway its all throughout the dorm now, so we all just take off out the room. He's standing there in the hallway motioning us to go like he's directing traffic. I always tease him because he was like Moses and we all darted out of there like the Hebrews escaping from Pharaoh." "Hey hey hey man I'm Jewish that's serious stuff Moses saved us." "Come on Darren way back then the jew's looked like me and like Thomas in their." With a look of shock Darren says "What!" "Yo man Y'all European Jews man Jesus, Moses, Ibrahim, Adam and Eve were black man all human life origionated in Africa they found a female skeleton with no belly button." "So what does that mean?" "Everybody has a belly button except someone who wasn't born connected to the ambilical cord and only Eve could be like that they found it in Africa you gotta check out the history channel." "You really believe that?" "Yeah over time the people who origionated from Africa migrated across the globe but the farther away from the equator and the suns rays the lighter you become and the less melanin you have in your system. I'm talking about thousands of years migrating so yeah the jews at one time were just as dark as Thomas." Still looking at Lid in shock with his mouth open, there's so much misinformation, and distractions these days that people really never take the time out to find out the truth yet and still they hate and are bigots, any type of racism shown towards African, or darker skinned people is phycotic in nature because you are hating yourselves man origionated in Africa and like most white people Darren is in shock as Mikahil relays to him the truth of his origions. "Alright that's enough for today my brain is ready to explode, why don't you come over this Saturday and blaze some weed with me?" "Alright man but you not gay or anything are you?" Darren looks at Lid and ask "Are you?" Shaking his head he says "Naw man but you gotta check these days its crazy out here, get up in your house and you go all gay on me and I jumping right out the window." "I got a girlfriend man." "Wish I had one" "Be patient man it'll happen" they walk back into the job and its comforting to finally speak to someone on his cigarette break and share a few laughs the isolation has been driving him crazy but tonight he got some relief as a muslim and a jew made friends after the jew stood up for him against the hatred that sprewing out of the employees at citigroup.

Saturday comes along and Mikahil gets to Darrens house around one o'clock. "Yo I had trouble finding this place, I've never been up this way before." He sarcastically relplies "Really because I have never have trouble finding this place." Lid bust out laughing "Yeah because you live here smart ass." Like many of their generation Darren lives with his parents, and the three story house is very nice. They march up the steps to the third floor and the first thing Lid sees is Darren's comic book collection as he walks into the room. And naturally he takes off towards them, "Hold up just don't take them out of the plastic!" "Ah man you got the Avengers, Spiderman, and the X-Men old school X-Men when it was just Scott, Jean, Bobby, Hank, and Warren. I used to have a collection but I lost them when I went to college yo and I still cant find the dude I let hold those comics." "Bummer yo" Darren pulls the weed from his dresser and bunched up in a plastic bag Lid sees the brightest neon green weed on earth illuminating though the bag. "You've never seen weed this green before they grow this shit under water dude!" A few seconds later Darren has the weed inside the challis weed pipe and boom they spark it and begin to pass it back forth to each other taking deep inhales, and then exhaling. "Yo this high is different" Lid's mind begins to think of multiple things at once. The beef with Angelina, how people found joy in his pain, people laughing at him at wal mart, the super mart, all the turmoil in his life, yet he is still holding conversation with Darren as he rambles on "Yeah she's a school teacher, I'm thinking about moving in with her, but I need to get a better job." Lid nods his head in agreement, but this weed has got him going as he continues to think about multiple things at once, when all of a sudden he thoughts get focused on one conclusion "I need to buy a gun, I am under attack by these Christians in Delaware." And that thought resonates in his mind as he and Darren continue to pass the weed pipe back and forth. They continue to chit chat about sports and their common dream to go to California and surf, and then Lid just gets up and says "I have to go" "So how did you like the weed good shit huh, hungry aint you thinking about some food?" Lid shakes his head "Naw I have to go buy a gun. You got some weed to sell?" Darren shakes his head no a little startled by Lid's last comment he just say's "Naw man you sure you are alright?" Coldly like a robot he says "Yeah man, thanks for inviting me over." They shake hands and Darren walks Lid out the door, "Take it easy man don't do anything I wouldn't do." Mocking Jay-Z he says "I'm focused man, and laughing as he gets into his car he takes off down the highway heading straight for the gun store.

Playing AZ in the car and replaying his line "Have you ever smoked a challis weed pipe that shit will have you right" Lid is jamming to the music and as he is parked in the parking lot of Millers gun shop he takes a few drops of visine to clear the red out o his eyes sprays some cologne and walks into the store. Filled with white people buying every gun they can get there hands on. Its like toys R us on black Friday as even the elderly are picking up pieces to strap onto their walkers and wheel chairs. Being the cheep skate that he is Mikahil goes right to the used gun section and takes a look at the different guns they have for sale a few thirty eights, a nine, a beretta, getting an up close and personal view he is on one knee when he looks to his right at the new gun display and smiling right at him is a barrel he remembers from the nights running the streets with his uncle. He gets up and walks over to the new gun case and what do you know its his old .45 that he stole from his Uncle Sha girlfriend house never forgetting the barrel, he stands at the counter and patiently waits for some help. Once the sales is finished with a customer someone tries to skip in the line, but the cashier politely says "He was here first", and waits on Lid. "How can I help you?" "How much is that gun" pointing to the .45 He pulls it from the glass casing and shows it to Lid as he runs down the specifics, "This German Ruger .45 calibur hand gun is four hundred and twenty dollars it holds eight in the clip and one in the chamber, but you can go to the gun shows and get the clip that holds twelve or more." "I'll keep that in mind" "You also get the case, two free boxes of bullets, and the trigger lock. Here check her out." Lid picks up the gun with his left hand and then places his right hand over the left, he checks the chamber, and the clips, then he cocks the empty gun and pulls the trigger shooting at the wall away from everyone. "This isn't your first gun you know what your doing." He says nothing and just casually shakes his head. The entire store is looking at Lid shocked at his cool demeaner. He knew when he first saw the gun that he was going to buy it and flatly says "Can I put two hundred on my credit card? And pay the rest in cash?" "Sure no problem I just need your Delaware drivers license and the credit card." "Here you are sir." "I have to run background checks and ask you a few questions "Do you have any criminal convictions?" "No" "Do you use any drugs?" "No" Lid has to hold back a smile as he thinks to himself "Muthafucker I'm high right now!" "Are you going to harm anyone?" "No" "alright I have to run background checks with the state and the FBI, this might take a few minutes so check out some more guns and accessories I'll be right back." He takes a look around the store theres a wall dedicated to shot guns, and automatic weapons I don't know who would use an M-16 to shoot down ducks but to he each his own as he admires the Tommy gun on the wall another customer informs him "You can buy the roll drum on the internet or at gun shows and make it look like the one from the nineteen thirties, like Capone and Elliot Ness." "Mikahil just shakes his head and the salesman returns just in time with the look of disbelief because Lid passed the background test with flying colors. "Alright guy you passed it with no issues." " I know I stay out of trouble and out of the way." He pays the cashier using cash and a credit card and just that fast he is ready to walk out the store with a brand new gun, when he ask the cashier one last question " What are the rules here in the state regarding carrying a firearm?" Well you can carry it on your hip preferably on a holster unloaded." "So I can carry my pistol on my hip and keep the clip in my back pocket?" "Yeah" Lid just smiles and replies "Cool". He walks out the store high as a kite, with a brand new gun that at close range will cut limb off a person and as he walks to the car he says out load "Damn I love America."

On cigarette break the place is abuzz becaue the night shift has a new employee and to Lids surprise its Mrs. Green Eyes from weeks ago, and he stands alone in the corner smoking he listens as the goup chit chats on the smoke break. The women of the hour is speaking loudly "So I just came back from fucking "Toys R Us"and spent like six hundred dollars on Christmas toys for my daughter. But its Christmas so I figure what the hell." The crowd nods their heads in agreement, and someone else adds "Yeah Christmas shopping is a mess, I spend so much money on holiday gifs but I figure it's the holiday season and that's what Jesus would want me to do." She adds "I wish Jesus would someone to spend six hundred dollars on me damn it!" As she speaking she seductively makes eye contact with Lid as he leans against the wall. The crowd continues to chatter until the group begins to go back inside from break, and as Lid begins to light another cigarette she strolls over and ask "Can I have a light?" "No problem" and he lights her Newport as she leans over once again they make eye contact and like a reflecting mirror their matching sets of green eyes meet and naturally they both smile. "So your working up here now?" "On third shift yeah I used to work day shift but some bitch said something to me and I had knock her the fuck out. So the manager firied me, but I know the third shift manager he's the pastor at my church and he hooked it up so I'm on third shift." "Y'all must be real close friends you got fired from here and they hired you right back?" "Everybody in here keeps saying I slept with Kevin just to get my job back but I'm no slut and I don't care what they say." "Yeah me either I'm like public enemy number one in there but I just gotta keep moving and out working everyone." "I see you in there your like part of the machine the way you move and be dancing its like a show." "I be having my music on just dancing the night away after that stuff went down with first shift I just wanna get out of here and get home, it still hurts because people still be snickering and laughing at me. So what's your name?" She quickly replies "Teresa" "I'm Lid" "Like Micheal?" "yes and no its Arabic for Micheal but you pronounce it Mik-Hail in muslim." "I used to know some of them off ogontz avenue." "I used to go to that masjid when I was younger." "What did you call it?" "The masjid, its like a church we just have our sevices on Friday." "Well I don't like it they make you wear those things that cover your hair and face." "oh the hijab well you don't have to cover your face all the way up just your hair and that's optional its only required when making prayer or when ever you are in the Masjid." "Church is cool just as long as you are a believing, practicing Christian. I mean don't just go or be part of something because it is the popular thing to do." She rolls her eyes and looks away for a brief second. "When I was in high school everyone wanted to be muslim because it was the in thing to do nowadays your considered a terrorist if you are muslim and that's crazy but what kind of person would I be if I just abandoned my name and faith because it is no longer popular?" They get closer and Terresa is looking right up at Lid as he speaks "That's not what is about its your personal faith not a social thing or club, because on judgement day its just going to be you and him." "Well I don't have anything to worry about because Jesus died for all my sins, so I'm forgiven and I'm going to heaven." "That's where the part about living as a believing Christian comes into play. The bible has laws and rules rules regarding how you should conduct yourself the ten commandments not fornicating until you are married those things. Now the ten commandments come from the book of the dead written by the Egyptians but that is another story for another day." "Well I need to get married because I am sinning way too much." Flattered by her honesty Lid smiles "Nobody's perfect but try to do the right thing." Finished their cigarettes they both walk back into the job and as they go into the production floor past the flag, and the constitution he glances at it as he walks to the back and into the scanning room and as he walks back his co-workers scowwer and whisper as he goes into the scanning room. At the end of the shift he grabs his coat from the coat room and Teresa is waiting for him she quickly walks by him and passes him a piece of paper and air whispers "Call Me". Lid nods his head and as he I putting on his coat and walking out the door he thinks to himself maybe this time things will work out. It's raining cats and dogs outside but that's not going to stop him from moving today as sister Halima has already arranged for him to move today, with the u-haul truck already reserved shes been packing his things up for days now and nothing short of the end of the world will stop this from happening. And he pulls up to the house what do you know the U-Haul truck is already parked in front of the house. Inside the house sister Halimah is boxing up his things, "Hey babe, here's most of your stuff boxed up you can start taking them over now." "Mom please don't call me babe, I really wanted to wait a few weeks until I saved some more money up, plus its raining outside and the radio said its only going to comedown heavier today." "No excuses you have to get out of here today, I have some trash bags of clothes that are too heavy for me to take down the steps could you bring those down?" "I just got of work mom you know how it is working all night I'm exhausted can I get a few hours of sleep?" "You can sleep at your new apartment when you finish unloading everthing. Come on Lid I have to take the U-Haul back in the morning and you have to be at work tonight at ten." Against the whole move thing this is all the doings of his mother who picked the same apartment complex Sandy is staying in, and put the contract and everything in her name. Not taking into consideration the fact that he's worked all night or noit even caring to top it all off its pouring down raining but to his dismay exhausted he starts taking boxes out of the house and putting them in the truck. Marching through the mud and rain he takes all the boxes in the living room and dining room, and then ask "Is Adesha's boyfriend Baron coming over to help?" "Yeah he said he will be over around twelve, but in the meantime you can start loading the bags I have upstairs for you, and take a load over to the apartment now you don't want to be overworking Baron." "I don't have much stuff mom we should be able to knock this out in one trip." He goes upstairs to get bags out of his room but when he gets upstairs out of sheer exhaustion he just passes out on the bed.

# "Green Eyed Lady"

"WAKE UP BOY, I told you I have to take the U-Haul back in the morning, plus Baron is down stairs he doesn't have all day to be waiting for you he and Tee Tee have to go to the movies tonight." A little rested he takes a look at his clock and its almost twelve o clock "Mom I had to get some sleep I'm on my feet all night I'm exhausted." Once downstairs he and Baron shake hands their relationship is as good as it can be considering he's the guy sleeping with his baby sister, but considering boyfriends of the past Baron a pretty stand up guy. The last few before him especially Tariq who got Adesha pregnant she aborted the baby but when he tried to talk to the guy in front of the house Adesha went off and started throwing punches at him, and against ever fiber in his body he had to slam his little sister to the ground, as her jerk off boyfriend just stood there watching. Barons different and even though sister Halimah treats him like the king of the world, and its always "Oh yeah my son the loser." Lid and Baron has found some common ground in NBA live on playstation and watching sports on T.V. plus they occasionally escape and smoke pot together at his cousins house. Decked out in a fresh roc a wear sweat suit with Jordans, and a fitted hat to match "Oh Baron give me a another hug?" And smiling he does so Lid breaks the love fest up "I know you are not going to move in that man it pouring down raining nice sweat suite though." "Thanks B I got these custom Mikes of the internet they match the suit and everything I gotta keep up with y'all Philly niggaz." "Y'all can have the Mikes Sweade timbs on my feets makes my cypha complete." "Nasty Nas, I got a change of clothes in the trunk that usually ball with, how much stuff you got?" "The television, the sterio, and the speakers, the entainment set, the bed, the head board, that's going to be the tuff part. Then I got some books, clothes, the kitchen table, the computer, and the computer stand."That s the big stuff that goes in the truck, the rest I can put in the car." "Alright let me change my clothes and lets get cracking." Lid starts grabbig boxes and going to the truck, the rain is coming down harder and now lightening and thunder fills the sky "I don't know why I have to move in this weather man she's tripping but that's life." They continue to move things when Baron apologizes to Lid "Yo I'm sorry about that stuff at your job man you know these people down here hate ya'll Philly niggas." "Damn you know about that?" "Hell yeah the county be talking about it this girl I know who works there told me." His heart drops and he replies "It was pretty embarrassing especially when I walked in wal mart and everyone was laughing at me, fucking wal mart I can't even shop in peace. I gotto food shopping at night to avoid the crowds its crazy you would think I'm public enemy number one!" "I cant call it but with so many people hating on you you must be doing something right." "That's what I keep telling myself." The rain is pouring down but everytime they come back from the truck and into the house sister Halimah has brought down more and more stuff. "You can have this toaster, and these cups, and this knife set, your going to need all this stuff." "Thanks mom, I still don't know why we are moving today." "Because you are too old to be living with your mother." The truck is about full and they drive over to the new apartment only a few blocks away, the problem is that it is on the third floor and with no elevator they have to struggle up three flights of stairs. Its pain staking moving everything in the rain, and then up the stairs but Lid and Baron get it done and while Lid is trying to arrange things they chit chat "yeah I keep missing those games when Cleveland comes to town I know you get free tickets behind the bench I mean what's up man can I go?" "Naw man I cant have you sitting behind their bench cheering for the sixers when you know LeBron is going to give it to the them triple double time." "I miss A.I. already and he just got traded a few weeks ago, they should've fired Billy King he built the team its his fault they are losing." "Well I got you the next time they come to town now we can talk about this and that but you know you don't want no work from Bronny and the Cavs on the game?" "Man LeBron is not trying to see Kobe and the Lakers  and oyu know that. Baron gets real serious "you win a couple of games now you think you are the live king huh? Nigga I remember when I was blowing you out by like twenty and thirty points and you had to quit on me." "I didn't know how to play playstation two man I had to get used to the controllers." "Stop lying it's the same controllers as playstation one" "I mean we can always just hook the game up right now you know Its Kobe time!" "Maybe tomorrow I have to take your sister to the movies" "I thought so, I gotta get ready for work anyway so how you two doing?" "Everythings good we had a an argument a weeks ago but I break her down, and every things cool." When he says break her down he imitates bumping and grinding and Lid quickly reminds him "Remember who you are talking to." "See you my homie man I be forgetting you her brother." "Yeah well here's a reminder are you going to marry her?" Baron gets real serious and his voice gets low, "I really want to finish school first but yeah, I only have a year left and my job already said it's a done deal and they will hire me full time after graduation so the money is there." "The money ain't the issue I just want to know if you have some intention of marrying my sister she really likes you, we all like you your nice to her and I know she can be a hand full at times, but she's a good girl, just don't ever put your hands on her." "Lid I would never do that" "I know but I gotta mention it older brother hand book." They pull up to the house and shake on it, "Thanks a lot Baron I called a lot people from home and nobody showed up or they didn't answer the phone, so thanks man. Baron gets out the truck and Tee Tee opens the front door they hug and kiss, and Lid looks at them in the doorway and thinks to himself I wish I had someone in my life to love."

He makes one more trip and this time alone unloads more things into his apartment, and fueled by the site of Baron and Tee Tee together he decides to give Teresa a call. "Hi Teresa this is Lid from work, I just moved into this apartment and already I'm feeling lonely." "Awwww you want some company? I'm trying to get my daughter to sleep so I can take her to the babysitter before I go to work, she cries when I leave but if she is sleep it's a lot easier." "I just finished moving all this stuff in the rain I'm exhausted I really don't feel like going to work." She sharply replies "You don't want to see me?" "Yeah I do that's why I'm calling now you going to take your breaks with me tonight?" she flatly says "No" and the always sensitive Lid lowers his voice and replies "Why not?" "I'm just playing you know I cant wait to see you tonight. Where were you living before?" "I was staying with my moms I had to move back in because I couldn't find a job in Philly and make rent." "Everybody in Philly hustles why didn't you start hustling?" "That's not the plan the object of the game is to incarcerate as many African American males as they can, and its double bonus because I'm muslim so hustling is out of the question." "Your crazy" "I would rather be crazy than be sane in this world especially if all the sane people believe an airplane hit the pentagon or Forty Three won the elections." Uninterested Teresa ends the conversation "I have to get this little monster to sleep I will see you tonight at work bye." Cutting the conversation way short she hangs up the phone exhausted with only a few hours of sleep Lid starts to iron his clothes for work. With no sleep for the day its business as usual as he outworks everyone, his co workers still snicker and laugh when he walks by them throughout the night rubbing things in about the whole Angelina debacle. But at lunch break he gets relief from the persecution, and as clocks out and looks around for Teresa she is no where in sight and thoughts of standing alone outside begin haunt his soul until he turns the corner and what used to be his smoking corner stands Teresa underneath the light, with a thin leather jacket on and blushing red cheeks from the cold they make eye contact and freezing she says " It's cold as fuck out here, do you want to go over to my car and sit in it?" He is so thilled to see her like a child he cant even utter words and just nods his head. And together they walk down the hill to the parking lot finally after spending the past six months in that corner alone he has someone to keep him company and his heart just pounds away as they get into her car. "I used to know this girl who had a gold Honda like this." "Baby I'm ready to trade this crap in and get a truck with TVs in it." "The insurance and gas on a truck is going to be through the roof how are you going to afford those payments at this job?" "Oh no baby I hustle in Wilmington, gotta flip that check that's why I was like you crazy talking about you don't hustle." "I never wanted to hustle I've seen the way that story ends time and time again. Trash bags of designer clothes in the attic, all the fancy cars seized because you miss a payment or cant make payments. How many hustlers you ever met finished the payments on those fancy cars and now own the car?" Teresa takes a few seconds to think and looks over at Lid "Your right they always have a story of how they lost it." "Its not a good lifestyle to raise children in, and on top of all that its not the right thing to do!" "Your tripping I know cops that sell drugs anything goes these days." Lid begins to break out in a Sinatra song "Heaven knows anything Goes" "Whats that?" asks Vanessa? "Sinatra yo, I always listen to Frank on Sunday morning before the Phillies game." "Hold up you don't hustle you watch baseball, and listen to Sinatra what are you gay or something?" "No! my mom says I came twenty years too late, because I enjoy all the things that used to be pop culture. These days the whole generation is lost because of confusion and lies. But did not win Florida be shouldn't be President, plus they lied about Iraq just to go to war. Silence is a form of agreeing to a contract, the contract was money, jobs, and a green light in the dope game in exchange for silence about the 2000 elections, 911, and the war in Iraq." "But the terrorist hit us first they attacked us?" Shaking his head Lid flatly says "No if Al Gore wins the election 911 doesn't happen, you probably wont get rehired at Citigroup after they fired you the first time but Forty Three is the anti Christ and this whole thing  the whole country is going to fall apart. The dollar will lose its value, the banks will collapse, and the fortune 500 companies will go bankrupt." "Wow you are heavy, why are you working here?" "Because I was blacklisted for protesting back in 2002, 2003, and 2004, I mean they where peaceful protest we where not destroying public property like the trust fund kids in Seattle, but the government does not want you telling the truth. Eighty five percent of the population is preoccupied with material possessions and keeping up with the Jones's meanwhile the country is getting flushed down the toilet while ten percent of the population controls ninety percent of our wealth, and me the five percent are trying to educate the masses." "You sound like the fucking President or something, but your wrong Jesus died for our sins so we can do whatever we want to do this is his gift to us just as long as we say our lord and savior is Jesus Christ." "That's the rhetoric coming out of the church than we are in a lot more trouble than I thought." "I don't even know why I'm sitting down here with you Terrorist." Hurt he simply replies "One man's terrorist is another mans freedom fighter." Keeping eye contact during the conversation Teresa says softly "Lets get back up the hill boo before people start spreading rumors that we are sleeping together, they get the fuck on my nerves boo." "That's the idea, who cares about what they think." She just purrs, come boo lets go." They get out the car and walk side by side up the hill under normal circumstances they would've never crossed paths but a twenty two year old mother, felon, and part time hustler and a college graduate, with a spot less criminal record, and over twelve years work history, and no children seem inseperatable as they walk back into work. The building is buzzing as Lid and Teresa walk in together, and once he goes back into the scanning room the manager Jill has a scow on her face when she bluntly ask Lid " met a new friend huh?" aware of her presence he turns his earphones down and says "I didn't hear what you said my earphones where on." And with a devilish grin of disapproval she asks again "met a new friend huh?" "I don't know what you are talking about I just had a conversation during lunch trying to make new friends." "Well you better watch out cause we are watching you." "What's that supposed mean?" Jill says nothing and just walks away, African Americans like crabs in a barrel they are and as Lid continues to work the night away the scanning room is a buzz  but instead of the usual side jokes and teasing that's directed at Lid the work room is kind of in shock as Teresa keeps finding reasons to get up from the batching area and walk by the scanning room and very briefly she draws Lid in with her gaze of desire and he falls head long as he watches her walks by and begs for her to turn around again, for just one more look. Jill soon comes into the scanning room and begins to talk to James who is operating the scanning machine behind Lid. Jill and James begin to talk and through the reflection of the computer screen he sees James angrily nodding his head, still pretending to have his music up Lid air whispers the lyrics to a song as he listens in on their conversation and over hears "Don't worry I got something for him." His heart drops as h continues to work, a little shaken up he doesn't say anything. James continues to make mockery and laugh and Lid sees everything through the monitor screen on the scanning machine, once he's done his work he turns around and lets the grown man who is acting childishly know  while pointing to his earphones "Yo my earphones aren't on I heard everything , you have something to say to me?"  Embararrsed, he manages to break a smile and he replies shaking his head "No, I don't have anything to say." Lid turns around and goes back to work the rest of the night is quiet, and in the morning as they leave to go home Teresa and Lid meet up at the crowded time clock and she ask him " could you turn car on and defrost it?" To be needed he quickly says yes and grabs her keys. As he leaves through the front door Angelina and David are coming into work on first shift and they've been going through some issues but as Lid walks by them for the first time his heart doesn't drop he can look at them and feel no pain, and surprisingly he speaks to both of them ending his vow of silence.  "David Angelina goodmorning?" Astonished both their eyes get wide and they say hello and keepon into the building. In the parking lot Lid starts Teresa's car, and waits a few minutes. Once the car gets warmed up he leaves the car unlocked and on his way to his car he sees Teresa coming down the hills and she says "Thank you Lid!" "Your welcome Teresa!" and he then gets in his car and lets it warm and then pulls off. As usual Lid blazes through traffic like a sprint car driver but today he stops off at the convience store close to his apartment. "Daily news and a strawberry dutch please?" Its different in the stores now there's no one snickering or laughing when he walks into the store, his waist bulging because of his pistol there is a different feel about things, especially when Lid pays for his dutch and newspaper and the cashier takes his eyes off of him, he gives him the change and ask him in a broken Arabic accent "Why you know buy News Journal, you live in Delaware?" "Because there isn't any action in the news journal, plus I like to keep up on everything that's going on back home." He smiles and goes out to get in his car but in the parking lot he is alarmed as a dark blue Delaware state trooper cruiser is parked in the lot and up near the window pointing Lid out and speaking to the cop is the security guard from the job who works for Wakenhut. Lid says nothing and just looks as the the security guard points him out. From shear exhaustion h passes out as soon as he walks throught he door, and does not wake up until his phone rings and its Teresa. "Hello?" "What's up babe, was still asleep from last night." "I was thinking about you and I wanted to hear your voice boo." Annoyed because his sleep was disturbed yet excited because he is so close to getting the love he's desired for so long he wakes up and ask "So what's on your mind Teresa?" "I would really like for you to come over for New Years Eve? AMANDA stop it!!!" She loudly screams over the phone. "What is she doing?" "This child is a mess she's throwing her lunch on the floor and then picking it back up and eating it." "Sounds like fun and typical kids stuff." "Hahahaha well she can't be wasting any food because it cost too much money, they stopped my food stamps boo this stuff cost money now. So you gonna come over for New Year's?" "You better believe it I never go out for New Years I usually stay in the house and watch my cousins for my aunt and my uncle. I'll bring some Moet and we can bring in the new year together." "Alright I'm having a party so get here early because I want you to meet everyone." "I gotta get some sleep Boo I'll see you tonight?" "Yeah see you tonight." She blows a kiss to him over the phone Lid smiles and hangs up. When the night falls its time to go to work but tonight is going to be a pretty slow evening because they passports division is having a Christmas party. So everything is business as usual until around three o clock and work is stopped everyone lines up and starts to make plates chit chatting amoungst themselves Lid not being to popular and having many friends just lingers around until the third shift manger Kevin approaches him, Kevin is gigantic around three hundred and fifty pounds and well over six feet, the member of omega psi phi greek fraternity or better known as the Q dogs Kevin also has a masters degree in theology and is the minister at a local church. Searching for Teresa he doesn't even notice Kevin coming his way until he says "Hey Lid you work good in there man I be checking you out your always tearing away at everything on that scanning machine with your headphones on moving to the music its like poetry." "Thanks Kev I have to stay hard at work man I'm way behind and I need to catch up." "Keep working hard and you will have no problem getting ahead here. Did you eat?" He shakes his head "No I was waiting for everyone else to eat then I was going to grab something." "Don't be like that man, here take a turkey leg." And Kevin cuts out a huge turkey leg and hands it to Lid. "Thanks Kev" It must be the holiday season because all year he has felt a sense of loneliness and exclusion but tonight everyone is so pleasant and nice and after his talk with Kevin he is really starting to feel accepted. Then out of the corner of his eye he sees a women in a pink sweater, and as he turns still chomping on the turkey leg he sees Teresa and his heart automatically begins to pound away through his chest, he automatically gets up and goes to her. "I was looking for you earlier then I started talking to Kevin and lost track." Teresa does not have time formalities and ask "Do you want to get out of here?" Lid just nods his head and says "Yeah" he follows her as she leads him out the door and down the hill to her car, thinking they are just going to sit in the car like always he is shocked when she starts the car up. "Where are we going?" "To my apartment I figured since we have a longer lunch beak we could go home and spend some time together." "Where's your daughter" "I told you I take her over my moms house at night." She lives only a few minutes away and once inside she leads him up the flight of stairs and into her home. Inside there are pictures on the walls of her, Amanda, some Puerto Rican guy who amazingly looks kinda like Lid. Teresa is so beautiful when she is pregnant and her smile is awesome she was so happy pregnant that must have been very good times Lid thinks to himself. "Who's that in the pictures?" "My ex Hector, he's Amanda's father. I used to love him, I mean I still do. But he's been locked up for like two years and he has some more time to do." Lid takes a seat on the couch as Teresa stands in the kitchen and begins to tell the story. "He and his brothers were getting money big time change in Wilmington moving heroin, but like most hustlers he started using what he sold and he started changing." "How did he get locked up?" "I snitched on him to the cop!" "You did what?" "I told the cops what he was doing, I had to he was going to destroy himself." You can forget about all the fears he had up to this point, Teresa's last statement really bothers Lid and her actions go against all the rules ever established in the drug game never under no circumstances ever snitch on your man, one because you're the only person he can trust out there and two because you reaped the benefits of the game when the money was flowing and things where good, and I bet at not point during that time did Teresa think about snitching. Her last statement leaves a empty feeling in his stomach but nothing appeals to Lid more than a falling angel so he continues "Teresa the man you loved how could you do such a thing your baby father?" "That's why I did it because I loved him, but the heroin was tearing us apart it was changing him he was turning into a junkie." "Well that's no excuse, where is he at?" "Locked up in Smyna I go to see him every week on his visiting days." "So you still with him?" "No its just for Amanda I don't want to be with him anymore." "So what's the deal with you are you a hundred percent Puerto Rican?" "Puerto Rican!" she smacks her lips insulted by his implications and reveals the only thing that would give him amnesia and forget about the whole snitching on her babies fathers thing and with full confidence and prestige she says "Honey I'm Italian." Still on the couch h opens his eyes wide and takes a double take of Teresa and within seconds he's up off the couch and standing right next to her holding her hand. "Don't hurt me Teresa, I'll a good man and I will be a good man to you." She looks up in the sky and when she brings her head back down their foJasmineds meet "I won't" their foreheads lock their hands intermingle and they kiss away from the job the natural attraction completely takes over the lust, the love, the passion as they just kiss lips interlocked and as he pulls away from her lips and moves on to her neck and ears she breathes heavy as the air from her nostrils gives rise to the hair on the back of his neck as she too nibbles away at his ears, and back to the lips again until they both pull away and stop. "We have to get back to work" they both exclaim "All right one more kiss please?" She agrees and pecks him on the lips and as they walk out back down the flight of stairs this time down the steps he grabs her arm and snatches away kisses trying to be careful and not fall down the steps Teresa begs him to stop but when they finally reach the ground level they once again become locked in a kiss and again before they get into the car, and again when they get into the car until finally she exclaims "That's enough" and they head back to work. The holiday season brings the calm of peace as this time no one seems to upset about Lid and Teresa coming back to the Christmas party together and for the rest of the night he plays Frank as he dances the night away scanning thinking about the love he just found. Once again Teresa gives him her keys to start up her car, and the both of them cannot wipe the smiles off their faces. When he gets home he plays Frank on his stereo sits I his recliner and sparks a blunt in love, overwhelmed by the feeling he just falls to sleep and can only think to himself I can't wait for work tonight. Around three thirty he is awaken by his cell phone and thinking its Teresa he answers but to his surprise it's an old friend's voice on the other end "As Salaam Alaikum?" "Omar Wa Laikum Salaam , what's the deal man?" "I'm in Delaware and I wanted to see what was up with you." "Nothing I was trying to get some sleep you know I'm on the night shift man day time I'm no good." "Look I need some help why don't you come up here and bring ya burner." Alarmed because Omar of all people knows not to talk about burners on the phone and Lid quickly responds "Man I don't know what you are talking about." He thinks to himself how does Omar know he has a gun? But always ready when needed he replies "Your in Wilmington I will be there in ten minutes." He gets up throws on some jeans, a t-shirt and grabs a jacket, before he goes he takes an extra clip and walks out of the apartment still sleep he stops off at the liquor store and grabs a small shot of Hennessey. Downing it before he gets to the car he quickly darts up the highway into Wilmington. Whatever the problem is he needs to be wide awake and functioning because he may have to use his gun, and on the way he thinks of the possible senerios this could a robbery because niggas from Philly are always doing that shit in Wilmington and New York niggas do the same in Philly, but when he gets to Wilmington Omar tells him to meet up at the projects blocks away from the police station. Lid parks and waits pushing his seat low so no one sees him, a few minutes later Omar taps on the window, Lid gets out and they exchange the greetings "As Salaam Alaikum" "Wa Laikum Salaam" he follows Omar to his car and takes a seat in the passengerside. "So what's the plan here?" He points to the back seat where some young boy is half asleep and says "We are going into this apartment and rock this nigga, I need to use your gun to get this done though." "How much are they going to pay you?" "Im going to pay the young boy two hundred. Im getting paid twenty five hundred though." Disappointed that Omar would take a murder for hire job for so cheap he says "That's nothing North Philthy I tell you. That's a five thousand dollar job you gotta extra guy here that's a witness and the Wilmington police keep hovering around here in those unmarked crown vics." Annoyed Omar insist "Yeah well all I need is your burner." Lid shakes his head "No way this is my gun registered in my name the serial number and everything if any bullets get pulled from the scene it comes back to me, that's not worth twenty five hundred number one number two the cops are going to be looking for me." Frusterated Omar stills pleads his case, but Mikahil is like stonewall Jackson and will not budge. Ready to go home and sleep Lid changes the topic "Yo I met this girl at my job she's half black and half Italian super hot, I'm going over her house for New Years." "Did you hit yet" "Naw you know me I take my time." "Well you don't want to be hitting someone that everybody's hitting." "You know her?" "Naw but if she is as bad as you saw she is a couple of muthafuckers must be hitting, and that's all I'm going to say." And with that they give each other the Salaams and Lid gets back in his car and ponders what just took place his best friend from grade school just called asked him if he could use his burner to kill somebody? Omar been killing people for years and never needed one of Lid's weapons he has guns for that? So who's pulling his strings? And who would think Lid is that stupid or gullible to do something like that?" And how does he know Teresa? And why is speaking in riddles all of a sudden? Their friendship is based on trust, Lid knows that no matter what he can go to Omar and ask him anything and get a straight answer from him that's what their whole friendship is based on trust? Still tired from working the night before he heads back home with a lot more questions than answers he thinks about an ayat from the Holy Quran "Hell is Truly a Place of AmForty Three "

Citigroup is different the sight of Teresa just eliminates the pain felt from the constant laughing dished out by his co-workers. All night long he performs while scanning dancing away still processing more applications than anyone else. What used to be lonely cigarette breaks are different now as he engages with his coworkers with Teresa right next to him both co signing on each others statements. But it's all about her as she holds court happy and full of joy, and every few seconds they share a glance a glance so powerful it halts all conversation. During their lunch breaks they go down to her car and pull away to a secluded part of the parking lot and just kiss and kiss, and kiss she like pink and he likes AZ and during the lunch break they rotate songs from each artist cd when they do take a break from lip service Lid lays his head in her lap and just looks up into her eyes. New years eve is quickly approaching and Teresa is so excited she begins to go down the line of things that she's serving at the party. "I'm making a cake, cookies, and frying chichen. Could you bring a few bottles of champagne?" "I'll try to bring a bottle babe." He gives her a kiss and she starts going on about the trouble that she is in "I owe James some money, last month the cops took some crack off me when I was selling it up Wilmington. I didn't r get the money back for those rocks and the shit was his he wants the money or may be something else." "What are you talking about? James is a correctional officer right? He's hustling too that's a contradiction of values." "Huh what are you talking about what's that?" "A contradiction he's in law enforcement like a cop he must uphold the law." "Who said he was a correctional officer?" "That's what I heard in the scanning room." "Naw he's a narcotics op in Philly!" "What and he's moonlighting here, and hustling?" "I don't know what kind of reality you live in but these days its just about the money its all the benjamins baby!" "Yeah I know don't remind me we will stay silent because they promised us money and jobs." "What are you talking about?" "Just something some preachers told me back in my revolutionary days." "Naw but James moves major weight in the tri state area the state trooper who put me down with the security job at Wacken Hut, them niggas move major weight in the tri state." "Teresa it sounds to me like he's not going to be upset about a few rocks now it's up to you if you are going to do anything else that's your decision but you got a good job here a high school graduate making good money don't be greedy." "I'm not leaving any money on the table I want it all." "Lawlessness it's all Forty Three 's fault his own ambition led us down this path Gore won Florida we didn't stand up we took those three hundred dollar rebates and elected him in 2004 and in exchange we lost our souls, greed the people who are supoosed to uphold the law broke their oaths for money." "That's a little extreme your starting to sound like a hater or a terrorist." "Sweet heart one man's terrorist is anther mans freedom fighter. I sound like a man with integrity who wont put money over principles. But I failed too, I'm married Teresa." "WHAT??!" She pushes him off her lap "oh hell no nigga get off me and your married." "It's not like that" "Then how is it?" "She's African and they were going to kick her out the country. She asked me to do it a few years ago and I was like no way because it's wrong and it was going to mess my chances up of becoming President." "You want to be President?" "I can't anymore because I married her but she was crying to me fearful that she was going to loose her job and get kicked out of the country and I was like o.k." "So how much did she pay you?" "It's supposed to be five grand over two years, but she already paid me a stack and I used that to buy my car.?" "That cop car?" "Yeah I had to swear on the bible but when the judge was administrering the oath I just kept tellinh myself I am doing this so she can become a citizen and not for the money." "Your going to hell" "Don't say that God is closer to all of us than our jugular vein he knows what my intentions were and that's what counts." "the bible says Good intentions are the pay to hell. I don't know about you you're a married man I cant be fooling around with you you're a married man, and I'm no slut." "And I'm not married" sitting up in the passenger seat he says "Come here" and he pulls Teresa closer and ask " If it makes you feel any better you can have the rest of the money, and as soon as its over I'm getting a divorce and I am really thinking about marrying someone else." "Who?" Teresa ask, "Did you hear an owl in here or was that me?' She laughs as he continues "But I don't know I have to think about it." She taps him on the face now laying in his lap "Stop playing you know you want to marry me because I am so beautiful." "Yeah you are T, can I please have a kiss?" "No" and she turns her face away from him. "Please?" She turns back towards and pulls him down to her grabbing the front of his shirt and they kiss with heart racing they sit in the cold car just staring up at each other until its time to go back to work.

Its New Years Eve, and Lid is estatic because for the first time in years he has a date for new years. Most of the time he is babysitting Naim and Khadejah because Miko and Uncle Sha are out on the town. But this year is different and eventhough he's only ten minuted away in his new apartment he misses having Breakfast over his moms. With Raqayya moving to Las Vegas and Tee Tee hanging out on campus or with over her boyfriend Baron's house its become very lonely for sister Halimah as this is the first time's she had an empty house, after making some photaotoes, turkey bacon, and waffles they sit down and Lid fills her in about the girl he just met. " She's amazing mom, she has a matching set of green eyes like mines but she's street smart too tough to find that out here in the suburbs everybody is all "One life to live, or General hospital with the drama. I like her though because she's from this new generation and I missed out on a lot of things mixed up in my revolutionary days." "You only think you missed out on things, it was already written that life would play out  the way it has Allah is the best of planners." Lid looks at her in dismay, he still does not understand how she can quote Quran yet still at times behave like a scorned women in her plight for women's right. It's like dealing with two people at times and the other sister Halima is so foreign to Lid because she behaves like a teenage girl, as he sits across the table he thinks about an ayat in the Quran "Verily if I grant you old age you will be reversed in nature." "Does she have any children?" "Just one, a baby girl named Amanda and she is adorable." "You've been over her house?" "Yeah its on the other side of the New Journal building close to Wilmington." "Oh honey I call that bottle O beers land." Shaking her head in disapproval "What do you mean?" "Its poor white trash that lives back there, I don't want to sound like a bigot but be careful because its dangerous like Kennsington is back home in Philly." Upset about his moms disapproval he immediately goes on the defensive. "I don't understand y'all I mope around the past few years with nobody , and when I finally find somebody its this and that." "Just be careful back there sped racer and use protection you should see the mess these girls come into the hospital with, still having babies." "I always do mom that's why I don't have any kids." And with that said hi phone rings and its Teresa like a zombie his unfinished breakfast still on the table he gets up zombie like and walks out the front door. "What up babe?" "Whats up with you?" "I'm eating breakfast with my moms right now and waiting for the liquor store to open so I can pick up the champangne." "Tell your mother I said hiiii." "Do you need me to bring anything else?" "Bring some cards because we are going to play spades tonight." "You gonna be my partner?" "Yes Lid see you later." He hangs up the phone and walks back into the house. "She's that special you can't even talk to her around your mother?" "Sorry mom I just need to concentrate its been so long since I felt like this." Adesha comes downstairs and asks "Whats going on?" "Your brother has a new girl friend." "Where does she live?" "Right before you get to Wilmington." "Oh God bottles of beers." And they both laugh "What about your wife Sandy?" "That don't count she's not my girlfriend or wife I'm doing this because she want to be a citezin, and that's all." "Well you should at least give it a shot because I want grand children." "Well that's not going to happen because that was not part of the plan, Its after nine I have to go because the liquor store is opened and I gotta pick up some Moet." "Ooh get me some?" Tee Tee says, but paying her no mind he just storms out the door and to the liquor store were he picks up two bottles of peach Moet, and some vanilla ditches. Later in the day he makes a quick stop off to buy some weed, and then heads over to Teresa's house. She has a few people already there and she introduces him to everyone. "This is my friend Tamoo  slim and dark skinned she's beautiful with her full set of lips and if Darren was here Mikhial would point Tamoo out as a shinning example of what Eve really looked like, "and her daughter Aaliyah" "Hi ya doing?" he ask as he shakes hands with her. "She's going to be staying with me for a few weeks because her baby's daddy is tripping up in Philly, I don't know what wrong with you niggas up there." Lid just shakes his head in disbelief. "This is my friend Chad but call him C-Dog, and his girl friend Janet." Mikahil shakes hands with Chad who is a pretty husky dude well over two hundred pounds but he notices a tattoo under his left eye of a blood drop." That gang related anyone with that tattoo is an official member each tear drop represents a murder, wearing his red C-Dog says "Yo you look familiar man you from Delaware?" "Naw man I'm from Philly. And finally he is introduced to Janet she brown skin and has the sexiest dimples on earth but she favors James and is probably his younger sister, which means Teresa is a lot closer to him than she led on to. The night goes by pretty fast they drink and play spades Lid and Teresa teaming up against all comers they only loose one game and C-Dog finally places where he knows Lid from "That's why you look familiar you got Mobb Deep second album?" "What infamous who doesn't?" "Naw man that was their first album, Hell on earth in the insert you look just like the boy." "Oh the leader of the bloods up in New York? Yeah somebody showed that to me years ago, but for real Infamous is the second album they had a first album that nobody was feeling." "Yeah well you look just like him." "Yeah well that shit is corny we don't need any bloods in Philly, we don't need any gangs for that matter, that's why we got so many killings up there because its not organized anymore." No matter how you slice it with the fall of the nation of Islam and the old masjids, the feds busting up the strong Philadelphia Mob, and the flood of money and drugs into the black community by way of the Baptist church, gangs have spread up and down the east coast in particular the blood gang origionating in Los Angeles this is totally different than brothers banning together to fight for their neighborhoods. This is the Baptist Christians believing that they are the blood of Christ, and that they are in a war with anyone who is not from the church whom they consider crypts, or to get more specific the police department. So lets recap black Christians have the green light to hustle, they are already getting plugged into jobs that they have no qualifications for from networking at the church. Flooded with new money, they start investing into the now debunked drug game as the feds have crushed the black muslims under the guise of fighting terrorism, and the Philadelphia Mob has taken a back seat after the bosses where sent up for decades at the end of the nineties. So now you got the black Christians running things as law enforcement cops, correctional officers double as drug dealers, distributing the work to the community, a community that's no longer united as the lowest level the hustlers are now becoming members of the blood gang which started in Los Angeles? Confusing as it is that's why 450 people prodominetly black males are murdered every year in Philadelphia, and to make things worse all wearing red has done is give the white boy Irish catholic cops targets to look for as they patrol the streets.  Lid was under the impression that the city had yet to fall and the gang related activity had just been in the outskirts in the suburbs of jersey and in Delaware. C-Dog gets quiet and for the rest of the night he really does not hold much discussion with Lid. But as they whip up on the competition Mikahil cant hold back the fact that he is so happy and he covers his face when he blushes or laughs at Teresa as she entertains guest. He doesn't want anyone to see his joy and happiness as he just smiles away with his face in his hands. Nevertheless he continues to go along with the flow playing cards, drinking, and laughing away, close to Midnight they open the bottle of champagne and between the two of them they sip away as they watch the ball drop from times square. And around one o'clock the visitors begin to leave and it's just Lid and Teresa finally alone sleeping in her mother's bed Amanda is knocked out and as soon as the last guest leaves and for a few minutes in silence two start cleaning up avoiding the fact they are finally alone, drunk from wine and wine and spirits and ready to let go of all inhibitions until breaks the silence "Can I go to the bathroom?" "Its in my room be very quite because Amanda is asleep." And he tippy toes through he room and into the bathroom rock hard from the alchohol, and Teresa hugging and kissing him all night he checks the medicine cabinet for any prescription drugs or anti biodics used o fight HIV, and he sees nothing just over the counter things and as he begins to zip his pants up he hears Teresa on the other side of the door, which he intentionally left cracked open. He quickly open the door just enough to get her through grabbing her jeans by the waist and simoutainously turning off the bathroom light as passionately kiss he closes the door completely she grabs his pants button and thrusts her hand down his pants underneath his boxers and just starts to jerk away on his dick. He continues to kiss her on those lips, her neck, and he naws away neck nippling and bitting as she bites on his neck and jerks his dick off. And as he unbuttons her jeans nothing is going to stop them from fucking tonight right her, right now, nothing accept Amanda that is she begins to cry from the bedroom. All contact sport comes to an abrupt halt and Teresa says "She must've heard us and said Oh no Y'all not going to make another me." Lid laughs "Oh yes we are sooner or later." He washed his hands as Teresa attends to Amanda, and then goes to sit on the couch. She comes out a few minutes later "So you really want to have a baby with me?" "Yeah I like you physically you meet the qualifications of the type of women I'm attracted to. Long black hair, matching set o green eyes, and you built right. Mentally you represent the new generation of chick bike rider, you hustle, your funny, center of attraction come Teresa there's a lot of things to love about you." "So what do you want to have a boy or a girl?" "I want a little girl." "Oh no Amanda will have a fit!" "Well then I guess a little girl your Italian I need that flame inside my son that intensity, flare for life Italians have." "O.k. I'm with it lets have a baby." "Alright then I have to take care of this fake marriage thing." "For sure you have to get a divorce because we need to get married." "I know" The kiss and the rest of the night they make out on the couch falling asleep and kissing each other until day break, when he leaves grabbing the half empty bottle of Moet and strolls down the steps. Outside he blows a kiss at her and she screams from the window "I Love You" and blows a kiss back at him for the first time ever he just spent the New Years with his girl, with a new love in the new year things are looking up for Lid as he cruises home.

After seven months of stress at Citigroup, a year of hauling propane tanks all over the city, and six months of washing dishes, and heart break after heart break Lid finally gets the much needed vacation that he longed for after graduation in 2004. The new year brings in a full week of paid vacation the second week of January. With things rapidly heating up between him and Teresa and the madness in general that is Citigroup the week long vacation from work is just what the doctor ordered. Energized by his new love, Lid breaks out his recording tools and begins to reconnect with something else he holds dear to his heart hip hop and rap music. He locks himself in the bathroom and using a kareokee machine and microphone he writes, records, and mixes songs reminiscing on his days as a member of the rebel alliance with his missed Uncle Sha, the assult he's come under at the hands of the black Christians, and all the turmoil surrounding the war and the new agenda America has embarked on Lid holding nothing back Lid takes his listeners on a history trip that has led up to the ugly situation over seas and that has ripped the soul right out of America.

"A yo Nixon got crossed by the Neo cons/Ford tripped in it was the perfect timing/ Un elected king kept the right wing smiling/ propaganda tapes on present danger/lobbying groups that trying to change ya/ the embassy attack made Carter whack them Reagan came in things got on track/ War with Iraq sold guns to Iran/playing both sides I see through that scam/ Christian extremist and your racist plans/ the eighty four doc closed a lot of doors backed Bin Laden and ya covert wars/ enslaved us with crack like ya did before/coalition was made and everthing just changed/politics and faith became one in the same based on false facts took the world by storm/exporting freedom like its our to give American empire this country's dead/

"I use it for protection when I walk into hostile areas/ its getting scarier the streets will bury ya, shit the cops will bury ya/ It's war out here in the streets so I keep ma four pound on my hip/ the pine box is coming if you cross the beast/ the protestants lost control of the golden leash/now sit back and listen while I school my peeps/ ya see Mikes have inflated to two beans a piece/ And Spike is getting paid by the boy Dwight /Its like everythings changed since they took those flights/the rights of the people have been strippen away/ the congress sat back and just stamped it away/ and I would say the courts but the been brought out/ M & M's in Forty Two  days what you pouting about/ minimum mandatories you will never get out/ the judges don't want to change them they don't want to be out/the city's under siege we need the fighting to stop/Philly streets they bleed when the pistol goes pop."

Excited he calls up everyone and spits some rhymes for them, and they all acknowledge "It sounds good" but as reality would soon settle in He's almost thirty and the rappers these days are being bred as teenagers and with so much emphasis on free style battle rap Lid stands no change of getting his music recorded or even out there until he calls Omar up spits for him. "Yo you should come to the studio with me on Wednesday?" "Where at downtown?" "Naw man boy got the studio in his garage out the northeast just call me before you come up here from Hellawere." Lid laughs alright man As Salaam Alaikum." Wednesday rolls around its visiting day for his brother Ra-Zen at the federal prison in center city Philadelphia, recently transferred up from Virginia, Ra-Zen is awaiting a resentencing hearing as he appeals the courts decision, this all coincidently happened right when Lid purchased his gun and was going through that stuff in Delaware with Angelina and David. For weeks he was out on the hunt for David in New Castle and Newark Delaware. And on a few occasions he even got his wish or at least part of it catching David off Citigroup property. One night while leaving his moms he's parked at the light when going south David pulls up in his girlfriends white expedition. Taking a double take and seeing a boy in the passenger side Lid makes his own lane and looks over at the expedition he well the glance David got of Lid he darts off through the red light almost crashing into turning vehicles. As soon as the light changes Lid gives chase and David takes off even faster down the road with his son he has to going over ninety because is up at eighty, needless to say Lid eventually stops giving chase as David recklessly runs red lights to get away from the man he betrayed and laughed at inside the cozy confinds of Citigroup. A few weeks later there paths would cross again as assistant manger of third shift Sophia threw a birthday party at her house. Built up as the next rumble in the jungle it turned out to be nothing more than a scare out in bear Delaware.

Invited guest included David and Angelina, and for the first time ever Lid was invited to a party with his co-workers outside of work. As he told Renee weks before his wiring is all messed up and it showed as he smoked a few bags of weed and drank a six pack of Guiness before even leaving the house. Driving eratically down the highway strapped with his gun Lid pulls up to Sophia's house music blasting AZ and knocks on Sophia's front door, with no answer and no sound of music he goes around back where the garage door is open and passes a brand new white Pontiac and just as he is about to open the garage door and go into the basement he thinks to himself, Sophia has no problems mouthing off at work how she is in the mob and her father was so and so before he died a few years back. Understanding the way that world works Lid knows that if he walks through that door looking for trouble with his pistol in his waist there is someone waiting at home, in his living room waiting for the phone call from Sophia's mom to move out on Mikhial for such a blatent violation, so he chooses not to but inside his car right in front of the house he plays AZ to max volume and waits for David to come out don't fuck with me under at work lets settle this right here and right now, but to his dismay no one ever comes out, Sophia doesn't answer her phone, and Lid high as a kite and drunk just goes back home.

But that was the past and coming up here to visit his brother for the second time since his transfer Lid is dressed down in jeans and polo shirt and boots. The last visit was cut short. Coming straight from work he was dressed down in his black slacks, black shirt and tie with his cashmere trench coat. They don't share the same mother's so they have different last names. Clean cut an well dressed he waits in the waiting area underneath a picture of unelected President Forty Three . When he is finally ushered in by the correctional officer being the gentleman that he is he lets the ladies sit down first and now there are no more seats in that specific area. Not saying a word he throws his arms up to the guard. I guess the guard took that as Lid asking him "Are you going to sit me here?" "The guard reads into it and says "Please come with me sir. And leads him into the attorney/client room unprecidented because the closest Lid came to law school was getting rejected by all the schools he applied to and bombing out on the LSAT getting a 139. But Mikahil takes a seat and waits for his brother to come downstairs. The visiting room continues to get crowded as the real attorneys are filling up the meeting rooms and as the odd lawyers look into the room Lid is sitting in scratching their heads wondering "Who is that?" After some tense moments Ra-Zen comes back downstairs with all his legal paper work. This is the first time they have seen each other since Lid stopped by Ra-Zen grandmothers house right after September 11, 2001 and he told Ra-Zen then to "Stay out of trouble." Excited to see his younger brother sitting inside the lawyers room, they break out into big cool aid smiles and hug giving the greeting of peace "As Salaam Alaikum Lid!" "Wa Laikum Salaam Ra-Zen. "You went to law school?" Lid shakes his head no, "how did you get in here?" "The guard put me in here." They take seats and Ra-Zen lays out his legal paper work across the table and as Lid looks at the work, he is acting like he is reading and discussing Ra-Zens case while they catch up on old times. "So whats going on what you doing up here?" "I have my appeal in progress and I need you to get in contact with my lawyer." "What's his name?" "Jerry Blakwell call information or something to get his number because the one I had is disconnected." "So you did your whole appeal thing by yourself?" "Yeah , and I got them with there hands tied and they have to educe my sentencing." "How's everything with the family?" "Everybody is ok on paper but mom is still working, and the girls are all working finished college." "Well that's good?" "Yeah but they lost their Islam man they lost it." "Well I know you haven't?" "Naw man its still their I just need to mkake my salats more, especially now I'm going through it at work." "What's going on people messing with you?" "Yeah our people messing with me every night. I went through this stuff at work with this girl and its just been horrible." "Lid don't mess with any chick that you work with." "So whats going on out their in the streets?" "I don't know I don't be out there I work, but they been using this 911 crap to polarize us and its working and we end up doing is landing back up in here." I see you didn't but your right most of brothers in here is in here because someone from their team snitched on him, but the new guys aren't nothing like the guys I was in prison with in Pennsylvania. Most of them don't belong here, they just not tough enough then they be telling me about the houses, new cars and the girls, and I'm like if its easy like that I cant wait." Shaking his head in disapproval "These days crime does pay, but that's the object of the game its to keep us incarcerated man and take away all our rights, why do it." "Because we have to get paid man, and if I don't do it somebody else is going to take that money." "You haven't learned, and the conversation is cut short as the guard from the front desk opens the door,

Mikahil drops his papers and the guard says "This visitation is terminated!!!!" Not sure what to do Lid stands up with his down now worried about being arrested for some fraud stuff or inpersanation, Ra-Zen gets right up and the two brothers walk out of the visiting room with their heads as they enter the main visiting room. The guards takes Sharref right upstairs and Lid not sure of his fate goes to the front desk where he is interrogated by the prison guard. "Was this a social or legal visit? Telling the truth is the only way to get out of this mess, so he explains what happened "The guard put me in the room." He repeats again "Was this a social or legal visit?" Sticking to his story he says "The guard put me in the room." The prison guard shows Lid his visiting form which clearly states that this was a social visit, but for the third time Lid just says "The guard put me in the room." He's escorted out of the building relieved that they did not lock him up, but if he would've lied and said that this was a legal visit they could've locked him up for perjury because inside a federal prison the correctional officers are federal agents. As he walks out grinnig retrieving his i.d. the guards remind him "You know we could've locked you up!" This time is different though the waiting room is filled with the finest looking women of all races, Blacks, Whites, Latina's, Italians, Jersey chicks, super fine you would think you were in a club or something if everyone wasn't sitting down. But that's the benefits of a drug related life style, with the hot cars, the fast money, comes the baddest women. No one in the waiting area pays Mikahil much attention as he sits in the front row, but after a while he gets some unwanted attention from the feds. The prison warden escorted by two feds, and probably home land security dressed in their cheap suits stand right in front of Lid and begin discussing some type of construction that will be going on inside the waiting area. When all of a sudden they turn facing Lid and the warden says loud enough for Lid to hear "I want him right there in here." Lid just looks towards the ground and after a few seconds they just walk away. He has to wait and again like last time he takes his seat right under Un Elected President Forty Three and they stamp his left hand, then they use florescent light to see what they stamped, and the guards escort him into the visiting room once seated in the regular visiting area Ra-Zen soon comes downstairs, they hug and greet each other. "As Salaam Alaikum, "Wa Laikum Salaam. "How did you get in here last time like that?" "The okeedoke white boy guard put me in here." Ra-Zen starts to laugh but its not genuine there's nothing funny about being locked up for nearly twenty years. "So whats going on lil brother?" "I got a new girlfriend." "Is she muslim?" "No she's half Italian and hot." Ra-Zen shakes his head as Lid goes on and on about Teresa. "You better make sure she doesn't have a boyfriend." "Your right we spend a lot of time together at work but during the day we only talk on the phone for a few minutes." "You ever think about that?" "I'm blinded by love." "Love Allah Lid your blinded by lust and you wasn't listening last time I told you to stop messing around with girls at your job, don't piss were you sleep that's your money." "Its been a long time since I had a girlfriend I just one bad." "Need Allah Lid, love Allah the sunna of the prophet Muhammed is the only way." "I don't believe that Ra-Zen, it's a very extreme interpretation of Islam." "How is the correct way of practicing Islam extreme, Muhammed is the final prophet of Allah and his miracle the holy Quran and his sunna is the only blue print needed to survive and attain paradise out here against Satan who has a hold on this country." "I don't agree with that on the day of judgement its just going to be you and Allah here are your good deeds and here are your bad deeds nuff said." The rest of the visiting room gets quiet as now the two brothers square off on what has become a very hot topic between muslims across the globe. Mikail represents the second generation of Muslims, black muslims in America. The first generation being the deciples of Elijah Muhammed, Malcom X, and Wallace Muhammed from the Nation of Islam, after the death of Elijah Muhammed and the assassination of Malcom X, there was a split and many of the followers sided with the son of Elijah Muhammed Wallace Muhammed who preached a more global teaching of Islam the way Malcom did just before he was murdered. Wallace Muhammed emphasized on reading the Quran, learning Arabic, but more importantly building a strong African American community. It wasn't until the mid ninety's with the emergence of Arab immigrants that a new way introduced to the African American community, a way that mirrored the Saudi's called the sunna of the prophet which is strict application of Islamic doctrine the sunna of the Prophet Muhammed. This may work in the desert with kings and a royal family that operate a modern day caste system but in America which is not an Islamic country to look at non-believers as wrong doers and practice shutting yourself off from society is Un American, and non progressive. So the second generation of African American muslims faced off with the extreme sunni muslims for almost a decade with the help of the federal government the teaching of Islam was done exclusively by Arabs who pushed this doctrine of application of the sunna. So the city was flooded with inmates from up and down the east coast September 11th was the catalyst that brought to the for front thousands of ex cons endoctrinated to hate America and push forth soley the sunna of Prophet Muhammed. But that is not the only application of Islam there are Sufi's, and the Shiattes. The more moderate muslims feeling betrayed, disenfranchised, and displaced left the city or were murdered in the streets of Philadelphia by the hands of a the new muslims, or by the hands of the black Baptist who carried a get down with Jesus or die attitude as they gained more power after being flooded with jobs and money post 9/11 through faith based initiative. The ones who did survive moved to the outskirts of the city, or changed religions, or relocated to another part of the country. To complicate things more New York started to raid Philly buying up property and setting up drug front, and drug houses with no one left to defend the city the gangs came back inparticular the bloods which came down from New York and now teenagers brought up in this madness see the gang as there only way to eat and in many ways it is. The public system has collapsed with hundreds of smaller charter schools opening, and the colleges Drexel, Temple, University of Pennsylvania, La Salle, Villanova, and St. Joeseph's do nothing but profit as they deny students from Philly admission and on the flip side buy up property to house more students, the corporations don't hire Philadelphians and that is how the city has been sacked ransacked, and taken over. The fault falls on the African American community the black muslims kept things in order balance within the city, the Baptist cannot do that because at the root of their beliefs they believe that Jesus died for their sins so they have no sense of right and wrong or doing good because they are already promised heaven. Its different with the black muslims as our deeds are counted and everyday we wake up striving for paradise doing good, and being fair and balanced. This confusion all started with the incarceration of John Malzanno, the Republican national convention in 2000, and September 11th in 2001.

This visit by Mikail is rare opportunity as two sides of the Islamic community sit downand discuss things and the other inmates know it because they are glued to the conversation. "Anything built from a foundation of lies is wrong Elijah Muhammed is not the last prophet of Allah, Muhammed may peace and blessings be upon him is." "Look man that was like sixty years ago, it helped convert people but we you and I are the fruits of that struggle, many of us can read Arabic and teachings of the Prophet, but it's a transition I see the way you all behave dressed up like we live in the desert. That's not Islam how you look and how much Arabic you know means nothing if you are a criminal that makes you a hypocrite. If every time you open your mouth you swear, or if underneath all that garb you are an ugly person, if your heart you hate the society you live, the community you live in, hate will never hate yo." In disagreement Ra-Zen says " Your wrong we have to survive because without the streets we would be finished." "Get out of prison go to school, get a job and live on rations and be thifty. I see y'all long beards sheik this and sheik that all y'all doing is imitating the arabs, Islam is not an Arab thing, you guys have disrupted our natural evolution as African American muslims and played right into the hands of the true enemy Satan becoming terrorist extreme Islamist who are anti government criminals who nobody wants here except the feds because it fits the lies and bullshit propaganda they run across the television screen everynight." "You will see for yourself little brother when you are under full assult and you wish you were living the ways of the prophet." "Well when that day comes I'll make salat and ask for forgivness for the sins I committed but once again on judgment day it will be just you and Allah Ra-Zen. The conversation shift as Ra-Zen gives Lid instructions on who else to call, "I wrote you a letter you got  those numbers you have to call my mans Paul, Manuel, and Ishmial, ask them to put some money on my books. Look there's another lawyer too he represented me in the begingin of this case Ryan Washington I wrote him and he  wrote me back he was like for twenty five hundred he will trepresent me on this appeals hearing." "Man I aint got no twenty five hundred yo and it would take me months to get that kin of money up. You were locked up with Malzanno though in Kansas why don't you just ask him?" "Man I don't wanna ask Johnny man then everybody is going to b like Johnny got me out." So what don't you got the address?" "I know this girl who has it her number is in that letter I sent you call her and ask for it write him and ask him, but don't be writing no crazy stuff man please don't embarrass me." "I wont, Yo I been writing let me spit some bars for you." "Man you a joker you ain't got no lines for me?'

I feel like a black puppet man/all this college and studying / I did it all for nothing man/ almost spent a hundred grand/ stepping up for the brother man/ on college campuses across the nation/come on dog / you know we ndanger/perfect strangers/ classrooms will try to change you/jobs don't want to pay you/so I move that yeyo and ride out/go head and cop new guns like Neo/ its unbelievable but I aint mad yo/he's a DSU drop out and I'm DSU grad/ and he makes more cash than me and my dad/ the whole worlds gone mad/but that's what happens/ post world war take these guns and keep clapping/ xporting freedom like its ours to give/American empire this countries dead.

Hype Ra-Zen balls his hand into a fist and puts it over his mouth, "oohhh little brother that was nice" he leans back in his seat smiling, "You coming right at them what was that you said at the end?" "Exporting freedom like its ours to give, American empire this countries dead." Jackson, Ramirez, Crump, and Sheldon your time is up." The guard called Ra-Zens last name Sheldon and the visit is over, they hug and give each other the Salaams Ra-Zen gives Lid instructions send the letter to Johnny. As Ra-Zen sits waiting to be taken back up stairs, Lid yells over to him across the room "She's Italian yo!" Ra-Zen just smiles happy to see his brother is in a good mood and doing well. Lid stands and wonders if this is it and finally after spending much of his life behind bars will he an Ra-Zen finally get a chance to run the streets together? Now its time to get up with Omar down north Philly, out in font of his house Lid pulls up "Yo As Salaam Alaikum?" "Wa Laikum Salaam" You still going to the studio tonight?" Standing out by the house are a few other friends from the neighborhood one in particular Will who went to middle school with Lid. Standing behind Omar as he approaches the car, Will gives Lid a stone cold look and just shakes his head no. "You want to go to the studio? Its going to cost you light fifty dollars? What you been writing?" "Yeah man I'm professor pissed wait until you hear this." Lid opens the passenger side door and lets Omar in the car. "Come on cuz we have to get a dutch from the store, Mikhial stops and Omar runs into the corner store to grab a dutch, and on their way to the studio they spark some green up. Lid hands Nasir the money for the studio and when they get out the north east they park and walk down an alley way, and into the back of someone's house. Omar knocks on the door, and a dark skinned brother answers the door, happy to see Omar he smiles and says "What's the deal Omar?" They hug and shake hands and as they walk in he holds the door open for Lid "Yo this my cousin Lid he said he has some shit written down I can't wait to here it." He closes the basement door and once inside the place looks like the hip hop hall of fame framed on the wall are classic records from the greatest of rap artist. Jay-Z, Biggie, Nas, Big Daddy Kane, Kool G Rap, Public Enemy, MC Lyte, EPMD, and the Wu-Tang Clan. "So whats up Donte I see you have new equipment in here." "Yeah nigga I told you I was getting new shit, check out the sound both." At the control board he flips a switch and turns the light on to the sound booth. And the sound booth is state of the art with fresh sound panels on the walls, a microphone, and the room is illuminated with lights everywhere. "Alright who's first?" Excited about having the chance to rhyme Lid gets up with rhymes in hand and goes right to the studio. He stands at the microphone and takes a few seconds to gather his thoughts with his rhymes memorized he drops the papers on the ground, Donte gives him the go ahead pointing at him through the glass, the beat drops and Lid begins to spit

We the type of niggas ya better believe that/ stash heat in the back of the e-class/niggas wanna flip I flash the heat fast/jake got the city as hot as a heat rash/undercovers making deals with federal marked cash/left town last year and watched my doe stack/N.O. to P.A. set up shop in V.A. the only time you see Lid is Lid is if ya sleepy/ I'm a let these chicks know if ya fuck up my doe hoe I'm a kick ya to the curb and go to the go go/ "Hold up hold up, let me do this again. Lid pauses the beat stops and Lid gathers his thoughts. And Omar comes into the studio "Yo you have to break these verses up into 13 bars man." "Alright I didn't know, I just started."

"A yo Nixon got crossed by the Neo cons/Ford tripped in it was the perfect timing/ Un elected king kept the right wing smiling/ propaganda tapes on present danger/lobbying groups that trying to change ya/ the embassy attack made Carter whack them Reagan came in things got on track/ War with Iraq sold guns to Iran/playing both sides I see through that scam/ Christian extremist and your racist plans/ the eighty four doc closed a lot of doors backed Bin Laden and ya covert wars/ enslaved us with crack like ya did before/coalition was made and everthing just changed/politics and faith became one in the same based on false facts took the world by storm/exporting freedom like its our to give American empire this country's dead/

"I use it for protection when I walk into hostile areas/ its getting scarier the streets will bury ya, shit the cops will bury ya/ It's war out here in the streets so I keep ma four pound on my hip/ the pine box is coming if you cross the beast/ the protestants lost control of the golden leash/now sit back and listen while I school my peeps/ ya see Mikes have inflated to two beans a piece/ And Spike is getting paid by the boy Dwight /Its like everythings changed since they took those flights/the rights of the people have been strippen away/ the congress sat back and just stamped it away/ and I would say the courts but the been brought out/ M & M's in Forty Two  days what you pouting about/ minimum mandatories you will never get out/the judges don't want to change them they don't want to be out/the city's under siege we need the fighting to stop/Philly streets they bleed when the pistol goes pop."Lid leaves the studio and Donte is hyped "Yo boss that shit was like that don't anybody be talking about no shit like that." Omar gets up all right its my turn, its my turn and goes into the studio.  Omar has to take a few reps to get started he doesn't have any paper its all free style and memorized but once he gets started he starts off saying "North Philly niggas stand the fuck up!" Lid stands up eventhough he's not from North Philly and Omar goes off on a tear "I got pounds for five, its do or die in these streets and I'm staying alive so if I spark you in da face please don't reply/ Don't even try to grind on my blocks I'm ripping off limbs with the noise from my glocks/ hip hop was dead but we raising it back up dump trucks of dat raw turning it into dem brinks trucks/ Its our town and these clowns better pack up and get loss/ the new boss is coming through with my crew and we don't front

Off the top of his head Omar just drops a quick verse but then he stays in the studio as he listens to his recordings, he doesn't like it and stays in the studio to record again. Mikahil gets angry because the half and hour is almost up and Omar has been in the studio for way longer than fifteen minutes. Lid thinks about the warning he got from Will earlier and chooses not to cross Omar. Omar eventually gets out and Lid quickly jumps into the studio he drops one more verse and when he emerges Donte lets him know that his time is up. "Yo you didn't pay for another half and hour?" "Naw" replies Omar I got what I wanted recorded." "Yeah but you took fifteen minutes to drop just one verse!" "Who da fuck is you hollering at!" Lid calms down they've been friends for too long to get into an argument about nothing and he puts arm on Omar's shoulder and says "Its cool man I just wanted to spend some more time in the studio." "But Omar doesn't smile back he glares at Lid with a look of hate and ask Donte "Yo you done with the cd's?" "Yeah" and Donte hands him two cd's. They leave and on the way back down North Philly they play the song with the two verses together and it sounds great. "Yo I want to go back up there next week I'm going to go back up home and write some more rhymes." "So what got you writing?" "That girl I was telling you about she's like an inspiration." "Well you better not get hung up on somebody's else's girl." "What you talking about, are you going to stop with these riddles and tell me what's going on do you know these people or what?" Omar says nothing, the basis of their friendship is trust being friends for long Lid truly wants to believe that Omar is the one person in the world he can trust for advice and the truth especially when the current situation directly effects Lid. But no dice Omar remains tight lipped and says nothing the entire way back to his house. When he gets out the car h simply says "In two weeks after you get paid may be we can go back up there. As Salaam Alaikum" "Hurt more than anything Lid just replies "Wa Laikum Salaam." On the drive back to Delaware he contemplates what just happened its always been about the money with Omar and if he wasn't willing to give up any information bout Teresa, James, and the Delaware crew than his money must be directly connected to them more than ever Lid feels alone and realizes the term "trust no one" even applies to your best friend.

The rest of his vacation week is spent working on rhymes, cleaning up his apartment, smoking weed, drinking, and watching movies. He hasn't seen Teresa all week but they routinely check in each other over the phone, eventhough its not the on the phone all day and night crazy in love thang, Lid is willing to settle for anything after being so long without any love. But when Sunday comes along and he returns back to work, they immediately are drawn to each other, and in front of everybody for the first time face to face they just start talking inside the job. "I missed you all week Lid" "I missed you to Teresa, you should've came over to my apartment though." "I have to pick Amanda up in the morning plus I don't know were you live. I don't want to get lossed." "What ever I would've gave you direction." " So what are doing after work today?" "Going home and going to sleep." She looks at his eyes and without blinking says "Can I sleep with you?" Shocked by her straight forwardness he stumbles as he replies and before he could the words out defeated he just nods his head and then replies "Please" For the rest of the night Lid hustles extra hard and jams to his classic rock jams Zeppelin , the Stones, Journey, and Springsteen tracks grinding, groping, and playing the air guitar on the machine as he scans away. In the mornig she as usual she ask him "could you warm my car up?" and hands him the kys, Lid does so but today he leaves a note, "Follow me but if you get lost I live in Fox Run apartments builing C apartment 301." He takes the Pink and AZ cd's and using a paper clip from work he connects the two together and puts the note underneath it in the drivers seat. After warming up his car he pulls out the parking lot with Teresa following him and in about ten minutes they are at his apartment. Both nervous when they arrive they restrain from touching as he leads her up the stairs, and she ask "You stay here by yourself?" "Yeah that's me I hate being alone but most of the time I usually by myself." "You to get out more." "Its crazy out there I need peace been through to much bull shit." When she walks in the door the first thing she sees is his forty inch television siting atop an entertainment center loaded with a sterio and hundreds of DVD's lined up next to the television, and play station two games. She walks around and takes a look his dining room table which is filled with cd inserts of the hundreds of hip hop cds scattered about like a puzzle across the table as she sees artist she likes she begins to pick it up and then ask "Can I touch it?" "Yeah go ahead" "I used to love this CD back in the day" "Yeah Act like you know was the shit, I love her hair, and that around the way girl point." "MC Lyte's voice was the truth." "That's that New York accent only get that up there." Sitting in his recliner Lid sparks a blunt up and begins to puff away as Teresa comes back into the living room and sits on Lids lap "I used to love rap music back in the day but these new guys messed it all up they don't talk about anything and the genre has regressed too much violence and talking about women and sex, this is not the time for that because hip hop influcenes our culture, just like our culture is expressed in hip hop but all the mainstream music played on the radio is shoot em up shit, then the streets are going to be on some shoot em up shit, If all the music played was on some fight the power shit we would be fighting this apartied going on today." "What's apartied?" That's when a system is put in place to keep a specific race over top of all other races, basically its legal racism like the Nazi's, Austailia, or South Africa." "These days I listen to classic rock most of it is from an era when young people stood against the establishment and protested the Vietnam war, our generation has failed us because we went for the money, and left principles and morals on the table. It cost us our integrity, it cost us the country we should've started burning this mutha fucker down when Forty Three stole the elections." "Its eight o clock in the morning and you are already sounding like the President." She giggles and gives him a peck on the lips and he continues with his Monday morning speech. " A lot of people had to step up and be president go the extra mile to do good for others, if its just opening the door for elderly or some women, helping lady's across the street, just going the extra mile to do good because that balance was disrupted and as a nation we are way too aggressive right now and violent." "Well Mr. President relax and take a break." She gets way serious and locks her eyes onto Lids eyes and without blinking she grabs the dutch from his hand and takes a puff and says "You smoke to much." "It's a stressful job." "Lets relieve that." She puts out the blunt and begins to softly kiss Lid one the lips first, then his cheeks, and finally she moves onto his ears and nipples on his earlobes. In his mind al he can think about is finally getting Teresa after all the bullshit at work, after first seeing her and basically passing, and this life long dream to find a women with matching eyes, who also half Italian and dripping wet with sexuality. They continue to kiss erotically back and forth he kisses on her kneck and bites into it as she unbuckles his pants, he pulls back on her hair and endulges in her breast sucking on her nibbles like a baby craving for milk, but to no avail nothing comes out but her moans of pain and joy, she starts rubbing his now rock hard dick slowly stroking it, still kissing his forehead and face she stops and gets up "What going on?" She says nothing and just continues walking to the bedroom and in one motion she drops her pants, and panties and her nakedness reveals a tattoo of a red dragon above her ass cheeks, butt as naked she walks to the bedroom, and right behind her Lid follows tossing his clothes off and by the time he gets to the bedroom he too is naked and they continue were they left off. Standing up and kissing he picks her up and tosses her on the bed this is serious and she just look at him directly in the eyes and says "come on" He grabs a condom off the dresser and puts it in and jumps into the bed using his thumb to guide him he slides his right into to her wet pussy and her eyes roll back and he begins hammering away at her pussy. Still kissing on top he tries to make eye contact with her but she turns away and with faces cheek to cheek he continues to pound away as the two crosses she is wearing begin to inprint onto his chest. Both of them are gone and like poetry in motion he doesn't even have to pull his dick out as they change positions, and he begins to smash her from the back and with soft ass cheeks bouncing of his stomach with every thrust he grabs both of her arms and begins to pound harder when his lower back begins to ache and cramp up. The pain forces him to let go and he pushes her face against the wall just hard enough to let her know how his back was feeling and finally a spoken word is uttered "Let me get on top." To his dismay he pulls out and she grabs his dick and sits on top of it, the joy is unbelievable as all five walls clamp down on his dick instanyly warming Lids insides shes riding away but because he has three mattresses she's barley missing the ceiling as she bounces up and down. Still the make no eye contact as she looks down at him he turns away, and when he looks up at her she does the same, but shame would not in this day as they boh fall victim to more animal instincts. She leans in and her crosses are once again pressed up on his chest, and after kissing and she takes a breather and then begins to really work away no more up and down its circles as she sucks on the tip of her finger and he cannot do anything but fall back and enjoy the ride with arms spread. He smacks her ass and just as she is thrown up into the air she takes the condom with her, and in a fraction of a second he falls back on his dick and Lid quickly throws her off him. "Whoaa!" they both start laughing as she pulls the condom out of her pussy, and tosses it on the floor. "That was close" "get another condom you aint cum yet id you." "Good dick" he grabs another condom and she puts it on his still hard dick and she just clamps down on his dick and rides away. Tired she ask "you still haven't cum yet?" riding hard and fast he looks up at her and ask "Are you cool?" finally they lock eyes and she says "Yeah" "U going to having my baby?" " yeah" and she continues to ride as the walls of her pussy clamp tighter and tighter onto dick, when in a flash Teressa yells not in joy and pleasure but more vicious and monsterous "AHHHH!" and pulls the condom right of Lid dick, then starts riding his dick raw and in seconds he finally bust inside her as she falls onto his chest he thrust deeper inside her and unloads all it exactly where its supposed to be inside of her. They take a few heay breathes as she grabs a cup of water off the carpet and then kisses him on the lips. And all of a sudden she gets up and rolls off him and starts gathering her clothing from the hallway and putting it on "where you going?" "I have to go home, before Mikail can get the energy to get out the bed she's already in the living room putting on her top as he walks out the bedroom in his boxers. He walks her to the door and they kiss but whatever magic they had I gone as she just pecks him on the lips. "I'll call you later" and she walks out the door with mixed emotions of joy and distress he closes the door and gets back in the bed "what just happened he thinks to himself, and why did his new found love just dart out the door, and why does this seem vagually familiar? Was this love, or did someone just set him up from behind the scences? In need of comfort he grabs his comforter from one of the moving boxes and low and behold an old mystery is unraveled as his old cell phone at the bottom of the box. Filled with all his contacts from college, and Philly, Lid remembers that's the phone that Jasmine's number is in and still confused he grabs the rest of the dutch and and puffs away until he falls asleep in his bed fulfilled yet confused about the actions of Teresa, and worried about the ramifications of his.

Going to work has become a drag for Mikahil Teresa is on the second shift but most nights she stays for overtime, after breaking up with him over breakfast at IHOP she doesn't answer his calls or even give him the time of day as he tries to talk to her at work. His last ditch effort was making reservations at Maggionoes in Philly and planning to just propose to her but denied that request and would have nothing to do with him. His new promotion is anything but that. He doesn't know how long he can hold on to his sanity, but with every passing night he gets the feeling that he is going to erupt into a furious rage at citigroup or just walk out the doors and never come back. To complicate things even worse Teresa has moved on to another boyfriend, a veteran, a soldier, a white man, and there love is the new talk of the town at citigroup. What really pisses Lid off is that h pulled Clark off the batching floor because he does work just as hard as Lid, not saying much to anyone and scanning away applications but the fact that Teresa started messing with him is nothing but an arrow right through his heart the truth verse fiction, who the real war hero? The military attacked the United States of America on September 11th, the military just went over seas and attacked without cause the soviegn nation of Iraq. Only in this bizarre, bizarre world would the hero be called the terrorist, and the terrorist be called the hero. And as he tries to hold on to dignity, to his pride, this night however would mark the beginning of an onslaught of new offenses that transgress all bounds.

While on cigareete break he decides to confront Teresa's half sister Tammy who now works in the scanning room with Lid eventhough she does not do any scanning she taking up book keeping, the problem is that she is intentially not speaking to Mikahil for the entire night, so standing outside puffing away in newports he says "If we are going to be working back here we have to communicate and talk, now I don't know what your sister told you about me but it shouldn't get in the way of work and getting things done at work." She says nothing and continues to listen as Lid goes on " Your sister told me you were still getting welfare checks like two grand a month even though you are working now, she was like that wasn't fair, but I told her that she should never speak out against her family especially guided by envy and she should not speak out against you. Now I don't even know who you are but I stood up for so I don't understand why you are not talking to me?" As he speaks Tammy looks at Lid right in his eyes,  and sharply replies with the snapping of her neck "Well my sister did not say anything about you except for the fact that you had a small dick." She giggles and walks off back into the main building. In complete shock Lid just stands there and puffs away on his cigarette, when he finally goes back in from his smoke break confused with all kinds of thoughts "that's all Teresa had to say?" "She been knew my dick size because we almost got it in on new years?" "When the fuck did work shit become personal and I guess Tammy doesn't even respect enough to give me a straight answer." But as he enters the main floor respect or lack there of is in full view as the entire staff his co-workers, managers, even the temps are in an uproar as Teresa dressed in her army fatigues runs up and down the floor showing everyone the size of Lids dick. His heart just drops as tears begin to flood his eyes, while he watches Teresa run up and down the production floor like a buffoon, completely out of control and completely humiliating Lid. As he walks alone back to the scanning room his co workers point, look, and laugh as he passes them carrying the shame of such embarrassment he looks at the managers who just laugh, he looks at Tammy who is just cracking up, and finally looks over at Teresa who is still running around like a buffoon and just shakes his head, as he turns on his earphones to the max level to everyones surprise he clocks back into the scanning machine holding back tears, his heart sucken any all self respect and sense of dignity gone he just falls back on the music. Soon she sits back down and the place begins to get quiet and once again the ball is Lid court. He selects MTV's unplugged Jay-Z album and turns it to max level and with the words "Welcome to Jay-Z's poetry reading" Lid performs the entire album as he scans away, then it's nas illmatic, then it's AZ's pieces of man every song, every lyric, every hook, for the rest of the night as some coworkers try to harp on the antics of Teresa the place is silenced as unfazed he scans faster and more accurate than anyone, while he stills performs his favorite artist ignoring the snickers, ignoring the devilish smiles, ignoring the pain, the hurt, the embarrassment. By the end of the shift Teresa cant even look up at Lid as he gives her a deranged look of hate, and after holding back tears Lid leaves when the shift is over and hurt he ask the Wakenhut security guard as he walks out early this Friday morning "On a Friday?" the says nothing and with a devilish smile he grins and just nods his head yes. Lid head home driving much slowly looking dejected and in shock, what did they expect him to do a sane person would've went crazy in there? What are they trying to get out of him, do the want to see him cry, why did he have to go through that just weeks ago he and Teresa were madly in love, now she hands to date his greatest defeat, why does everyone hate him so?, what did he ever do to deserve to be terrorized in such a manner? When he gets home he heads straight for the fridge and grabs a bottle of champagne, he opens it and sparks a blunt as he falls into his recliner and opens the flood gates as tears that's been building for hours begin to spill down his face defeated, and devastated he only the weed and the alchohal can help him cope with the horrible acts of people destined to burn in flame. Lid finishes the bottle, the blunt and the crying but he cannot go to sleep as his mind echoing a thought cutting though the memories, the confusion, the pain two words pound away at his mind "Make Salat" "Make Salt!" and finally he gets up and grabs his prayer rug from the closet and for the first time in along time he calls the athan for prayer and makes salat. When he finishes on his knees he makes dua to God, Allah and ask "Please Allah help me defeat our enemies, and please forgive me for my sins." With tears subsided he arises and goes to bed feeling much better he goes to sleep.

# "Exodus"

DISGUSTED, HURT, AND ASHAMED how could a man endure such a devasting punishment from the mouths of his co-workers he walks out the front doors of Citigroup finally in tears and in a fit of rage. In what started as a simple conversation with a white women during lunch break, morphed into the most hateful, acts of vengeance to date. May be they really believed they were fighting terrorism, may be they really believed Lid their coworker was a terrorist, and may be they just enjoyed torturing him but whatever the reason he's had enough and is not going to take the abuse anymore. Without a word to a single coworker Lid hops in his car, pops open the glovebox and puts his gun in his lap, "I should just blow my brains out right now?" He thinks to himself, but I can always go home to Philly they will help me at home. As he speeds in and out of traffic glaring at the Delaware drivers as he passes them, in a fit of madness he violently pulls into his apartment complex and takes off up the stairs to his former abode as today will be his last day in Delaware. He quickly grabs a plastic city blue bag and fills it with some clothes and toiletries, and with his gun barrel first he opens the door, looking like a secret agent he moves down the steps, full of fear, and insanity as the ayatt from the Quaran rings through his mind "Truly Hell is a place of AmForty Three " and at no time can he let his guard down at least until he reaches home Philly. Once inside his car he speeds off thinking to himself that he will set in foot in Delaware again, but before he goes he stops off at the Shell gas station to grab a daily news, and on his way out he is greeted by a tinted grey crown Victoria with front plates that read "GET OUT!" "No argument from me" and in the blink of an eye he is on the highway the music expresses his feelings as his shattered heart, soul, mind cannot concentrate on anything else but revenge, "I'm calling Omar we have to ride out on these muthafuckers in Philly", he thinks to himself. Playing "Lawyers, guns, and money" he pleads with God hoping that the music will reach the heavens. Completely insane he screams to the top of his lungs the words to the song, as the rain begins to fall from the sky, and like a man possessed  by a demon he recklessly speeds in and out of lanes tempting fait with each and every move. As he leaves Delaware the new castle county police ride with him all the way to the Pennsylvania border. Ignoring the fact that he's speeding in the rain the message was clear "GET OUT" and as he enters Pennsylvania the anger only  increases and he changes songs "Get down with the sickness!" as he screams the lyrics to the music, the look of fear encompasses the faces of the other drivers, as he continues to blaze up ninety five north, when he finally touches down in Philadelphia he speeds up as he exits and fly's through red traffic lights. The best way to explain it are in these terms spiderman has always been one of Lids favorite super heroes, and he has a dark half when he puts on the black costume. The living alien symbiate is in a constant struggle with Peter Parker for control, it has no conscience, it is only anger, evil, dark, devilish. And as he pulls up to the house of his cousin Boo's in the pouring rain he finally finds the strength to say something and he yells representing the anger felt for not doing something before things got this far, before his fate was handed to him by false Christians, before the beast had stomped on him with his cold reptilian claws of hate, envy, and pride, before the things that took place at a job designed to just make profit from interest changed the man he was and the man he will be for the rest of his life, Lids black costume had taken over and in the pouring rain he yell's "PARKER!!!!!!!!!!!!!!!!!!!!!" as reality begins to slip away from him." Always the fan of the marvel hero Spiderman, the only way he's able to express his anguish, anger, fear is letting go of this reality and creating a new one, let the black costume take over, let his anger take over, let his rage be his guide in Philadelphia and let the world take heed it is time to get down with the sickness that has over taken the world. He walks up the stairs to his cousins house and bangs on the door, but the dog just barks away  at the front door. He stands alone contemplating all things with thoughts just racing through his mind. What kind of world do we now live in where peope find joy in the pain of others?" "Do I really have AIDS?" "Did Teresa take pride in telling people she just murdered Mikahil because she was fighting terrorism?" "Why didn't anyone warn him before hand?" "Did his coworkers keep silent because they where fighting terrorism as well?" What kind of people makes humor of such a situation?" "and if the whole knew about how many other people know about it?"the moment is broken when the next door neighbor opens the door and leaves for school. Still in middle school the young chocolate baby is filling out her jeans and as she looks up to give Lid some news, his eyes open wide and he lustfully he looks at her as if he was going to devour her at that very moment. "They just left, he had to drop her off at work." "Thanks where you going?" with book bag on and everything he already knows but setting her up for the next question the young and dumb girl replies "To school" and sharply he says "Why don't you just cut school and hang out with me?" she smiles and ask "where we gonna go?" "I don't know just get lost or something." "he knows he is dead wrong but right and wrong have nothing to do with it he wants revenge, and exploiting a child, a minor is the perfect place to start. "So what you in high school?" "Yeah I go to Brook, im in the 9th grade." Just before things go too far she's saved by the bell, or the honking of the horn as Boo pulls back on the block. "Ugly! You better get your butt to school!" Lid smiles "See you later babe." And flatered by the attention she smiles and says "goodbye" "What the fuck are you doing up here cuzzo? And know you wasn't talking to my neighbor don't tell me you turning into Sha man." They shake hands "Naw man" but before he says another word Boo looks at his cousin who was obviously crying and the red tint of his eyes tell the story. "Whats wrong?" Lid lowers his broken head and just and looks back up at his cousin directly into his eyes holding back tears and camly says "This whole world is going to hell." "Oh lord they still fucking with you at your job, I told you to quit man!! Come on and lets gets beers man?" Mikhials follows his cousin to the car and gets in the passenger side, "You know I was messing with that girl?" he pauses and jumps to another thought "Yo those fucking Christians were teasing me at work last night." "Grow up people are always going to fuck with you." "It wasn't like the usual cuz." He pauses "They were saying I got aids from that bitch and I was going to die, calling me a terrorist and laughing and pointing at me, one mutha fucker even started saying Charles teasing me about my step father you know he die from AIDS man." Driving Boo's face turns completely red and in a fit of rage he just smashes the front window and screams "Ahhhh!" in the middle of the street he slams on the breaks "What the fuck are you telling me they were teasing you about it?" "Yeah" "Why the fuck did you tell me something like that?" "It just happened a few hours ago, I don't know what to do my mind is all messed up." "Did you get tested yet?" "Naw this all just happened." "What the fuck is wrong with people, what kin of people would do something like that?" "These people are crazy yo, Delaware was the only colony that you had to be Christian in, these people are fucking crazy calling me a terrorist and everything." "Did you tell your mom?" "Naw I went over their this morning and she just kept saying "don't believe the hype like she already knew about it or something." "Why the fuck did you tell me?" "I want to go down there and fuck these people up just shoot the whole job the fuck up and ride out." Shaking his head Boo just replies "You need to relax and chill man, I have to take my wife something up at the school." 'She's going to mad about the windshield." "Fuck that windshield I'm going to take you back to the house o you can chill out." Irritated his cousin did not adhere to his call arms Lid becomes rebellious and says "No I'm going ot the masjid there was a time when shit like this was not tolerated." "This aint the days of the nation what the fuck are they going to do, this is your problem." "Whatever I will be back later yo." He gets out and slams the door, looking through the half wayh rolled down window he just says "As Salaam Aliakum." "Wa Laikum Salam Boo replies and he just gets in his car and pulls off. With Iman Malik ready to go to prison Sister Clara Muhammed School and he really doesn't have anyone in authority to go totalk aobut what just happened at his job, so its off to north philly to see his old friend Omar, if there is anyone who will ride out with Mikahil for vengeance its Omar and shaken, erratic, and completely out of sorts from his normally cool demeaner Lid pulls up to the playground and greats Omar "As Salaam Alaikum" in full tone as he parks on the concrete, glaring back through the fences of the playground he replies "Wa Laikum Salaam" Its election day so the normally empty recreation center is full of people waiting to vote and campaigne adds old people, much different than the usual pick up basketball games, and the neighborhood hustlers parked on the benches. Lid jumps out the car and slames the door, giving cold glares to the elderly as they standout side awaiting to vote crosses hanging from their knecks and clean cadillacs parked out front Lid lets Omar know what's on his mind as he approaches his old friend "fucking Baptist are all gonna go to hell." "What's wrong with you Lid you look crazy? They fucking with you at your job? I told you to quit." Fumming from last nights lynching he cuts right to the chase "Lets go I am going back down there to shoot up the whole fucking place." All things come to ahead as he gets louder and shouts "AND NOBODY DOING THAT SHIT AND GETTING AWAY WITH IT!!!!" "Calm down yo, what happened?" "These MUTHAFUCKERS!!!" Everyone waiting to vote turns around and starts to look at the commotion. But he can't utter the words, the stress, the pain, the anguish all take their tolls and he just falls to onto the steps leading to the pool area and in ruin he puts his face in his hands as Omar takes a seat to the left of him and begins to whisper. "If you don't get a grip they are going to 3-0-2 you." "What's that?" "When they take you away to the nut house." Shaking his head "Naw not me we gotta go down there." "What happened, hold up roll this up while you explain." Omar reaches in his pocket and pulls out a bag of weed, and a dutch. Mikahil takes it and instinctively begins to crack the dutch open and the weed into it. With his head hung low he begins to tell his best friend friend the horror that just took place only a few hours ago. "So I'm at lunch break right and the shit just hit the fan these mutha fuckers can't beat me, or break me in their so they just went to the extremes trying to get me to snap in that muthafucker. The shit started earlier in the day when I came up their to talk to the white boy vice president, he's in charge of the whole thing Mr. Thompson. Now when I first pulled up mother fuckers were laughing at me as I walked into the building." "That's your problem because I would've punched one of those squares from Delaware right in the fucking face." "Yeah and you wouldn't be working anymore, but the only person that said anything nice as I walked into the building was this chick Faith, who believe it or not went to Parkway." "For realdid we know her?" Naw man she's ancient but she walked up to me and was like "I'm sorry." "Catholics man you gotta love em. So I go into to see Mr. Thompson and ask him if I could transfer out to Cally you know Jasmine is out there in L.A." "Omar turns around and looks across the street at the homes, Jasmine's grandmother lives their and the neighborhood has always been infactuated with the quarter piece who only used to show up for a few weeks out of the summer. "You still chasing her, you know she is way out of your league!" "Yeah well she asked me to come out there and stay with her, and the white boy is cool about it, he's like yeah let me make some calls and it's a done deal. But somehow they must've got word of it because that night them niggas was crazy in there. The white bitch just walks up to me on my lunch break, here" He passes the now rolled up dutch to Omar, "and I'm smoking she just walks up to me and is like" "I heard you got raped like a bitch by Teresa!!" She's laughing and shit" "You aint punch that bitch in the face?" "Naw cant work anymore plus they gonna lock me up down there." "Nigga you crazy I would've beat that bitch the fuck up." It gets worse though when I go back inside the whole place is cracking up pointing at me laughing saying" He cant utter the words but Omar pushes him on, "what happened man speak up" He leans over to his left side and whispers "they said she gave me aids." Omar's reaction is even more shocking as a smirk comes across his face and he says "from the italian bitch you were telling me about?" "Yeah I got her pregnant and she aborted the baby." "How do you know the baby was yours?" "What else aren't you telling me about this, how do you know these people?" Omar says nothing "You know Lid you gotta control these bitches man that's why I never had problems with my bitch I be giving her back shots all night putting her ass to sleep." He looks and smiles at Lid as he puffs away on the dutch horrified Lid thinks to himself "how the fuck is Omar making a joke about all this?" "How you making a joke about all this come on man lets just go down there and spark that place the fuck up?" "You really want to do that college man?" "Yeah" "Alright let me go get the verdict." And on that note he passes the dutch over to his childhood friend as he gets up to consult with the old heads in front of the recreation center. He listens in and watches as Omar chuckles with the old heads and for a few moments look over at the poor and unfortunate soul slumping over on the steps and trying to pull out the last of the weed from the roach before he tosses it away. Soon Omar rejoins Lid shaking his head no "Naw man there was a muslim sister that worked there too right?" "Yeah Jasmin" Omar hruggs his shoulders, there you have it you muslim why you aint with her?" "What! That's it!" "How do you know the Italian bitch even liked you man?" "What! Fuck this shit I'll do it myself." Enemies as he arises from the steps and they glare at each other with a scowl of hate that engulfs both their faces, abandoning the usual handshake as he walks to his car with back turned to Omar he says "As Salaam Alaikum" and Omar replies "Wa Laikum Salaam. Calm down man or they gonna 3-0-2- you!" Hahhah!" Mikahil says nothing as he heads to his car coldly staring at the old heads who just sealed his fate and as he arrives to his race horse a stocky dark skinned nigger black as the night just leans on the hood of his burgundy dodge magnum and just stares

Lid down and air whispers "You got played, she's mines" Lid replies with a whisper "Yeah right" and gets ino his car pulling off from the playground that was once his second home the site of summer league basketball games, blunt sessions, and fun pulling from his old friend and in desperate need of sanctuary as hell is truly a place of amForty Three . Boo's running arons for his wife, Omar just showed his true colors, and Uncle Faruq is at work in the bakery with his self confidence shattered inside the best thing he can do is look good on the outside, so its off to the barbera shop "Who's Next on 5th street and so he travels up broad street and then onto the always packed 5th street were he finds a parking space a few blocks down from the shop. And as he walks passes the elemtary school yard and watches  the children playing during recess and reminicess on how he and Omar used to play the same way in the old days and wonders how such a friendship could be broken? When he looks up at the passing cars and glistening he spots a clean BMW coming his way and as it slows down he thinks to himself I know that car. And on Q the driver steps out of the car and its his old friend from Sister Clara Muhammed and from around his old neighborhood Khaliq. Khaliq and Lid went to school together but they also shared driveways with each other Khaliq on Rittenhouse and Lid on Price street, from sleep overs, bbq's, birthday parties, church yard football, baseball and backyard basketball they hung out together as children until Khaliq moved away. Always in contact with each other Lid even moved into Khaliqs bachelor pad a few years ago until things went sour. Khaliq is like Lid's big brother two years apart he detesses the fact that Mikhial smokes pot and one day after warning Lid aobut smoking pot in or near his house he sucker punched Lid has he emerged from the basement. And in a split second Lid had to make a decision, if he fights back the friendship is over, because in rage Lid is capable of doing anything. So he doesn't swing back and proceeds to move out a few days later. Since that time they had not seen each other, but the friendship was saved as clearly Khaliq has something important to say to Lid. Double parked on 5th Street they exchange handshakes and the greetings "What's the deal Liq I see you got the rims spinning on the beamer, this thang looks nice." "Yeah I'm getting tired of it man ready to check back down and save some money plus it draws too much attention these young boys are crazy out here they have no respect for nothing." "Aint that the truth If I had the money I would take it off your hands but you know the deal no risk no reward." Khaliq ends the small talk and gets straight to the point "Look man I don't know whats going on down Delaware but them niggas are about to move out on you." "What!" "I'm going through some shit at my job but that's about it." "Naw your fucking somebody's girl and them niggas are ready to take you off the chess board." "She been broke up we me months ago." "Yeah well you know I be down there because I have to pick up my mail, but that's what I heard that you were under fire man so be careful." "Yeah well thanksfor saying something that's why I got my burner in me." And without showing it he grabs his waist. "Yo you got a permit for that?" "Naw you don't need one in Delaware." "Yeah well you in Philly and you know they are roofing niggas for that these days." " I gotta be safe plus I got insurance on the car so there is no need to pull me out the car and search me, it's a traffic stop." "Yeah well be careful" "I had to get the fuck out of Delaware that shit started getting crazy down at the job. I gotta get a new one Septa hiring?" "You ca apply just put me down as a reference but that shit takes time in the mean time go check out the telemarketing place up on the boulevard my man Jimmy works there and they hire right on the spot." "The jawn off cottman avenue huh?' "Yeah just fill out an application its only like ten dollars an hour but it's a start." "Thanks for the information, I'll check it out this week." "Stay out of the way Mikahil and stop messing with other niggas girls man." "I didn't know it was like fire and desire for like three months then she just called it off, broke me right up." "Well be careful man alright?' "Thanks Liq" they shake hands and give each other the greeting "As Salaam Alaikum" "Wa Laikum Salaam." Khaliq pulls off blasting the hit song "We taking over" as Lid is buzzed into the barber shop, leaving all the stress from theoutside world as he enters holy ground a safe place for both Muslims and Christians as they talk politics and shoot the breeze waiting to get hair cuts, and like days of old everyone is equal. He speaks to the barbers his Khalid, Kieth, and the legend Najee, but as Khalid hold court telling funny stories, and inpersonaing Martin Lawrence Lid has trouble leaving the stress of the world on the outside today as he cannot turn off his mind as it continues to ramble on, and on. Why didn't Omar tell him things were more serious and just by the graces of Allah he ran into Khaliq on the streets who informed him of the grave danger he was facing. Who was that guy at the playground? All this time he thought James and his crew had something to do with Teresa, confused all Lid knows is that he was ready permit or no permit he had his light saber and if any bullets come his way he was ready to return them back. Another good thing about the shop is that he can go into the basement and make salat finding even more sanctuary in the basement of the shop alone just he and Allah. Salat which has now become a mainstay in his life after risking everything to have a child with Teresa and losing, and then having to deal with the possibility of only having ten years left in his life, the entire situation at banco international has been nothing more than the trials and tribulations of life and to deal with it without restablishing salat would be stupid, and may be Allah will hear his pleas and save his tortured soul. When he emerges from the basement it is time to his hair cut and his barbera Khalid sees that Mikhial is obviously in a bad mood he ask "What's going on good brother?" "Just going through some stuff at my job and down Delaware people are crazy calling me a terrorist man its crazy out there." And with words of wisdom Khalid replies " the Quran says that there is nothing Allah puts in front of you that you cannot handle, so remember Allah Lid and remember that you can handle what ever is put in front of you as long as you keep Allah first." "Thanks Khalid" And with that Khalid continues to cut Lid's head and lik a half and hour later Lid is shiggity sharp and ready to take on the world. As he pays and gets some words of wisdom from his barbera " Be cool man and stay out of trouble." "I'll try man but it is no fun being Neo and no fun constantly under fire." They shake hands and exchange the greetings "As Salaam Alaikum" "Wa Laikum Salaam" The break from reality is over and as he pushes open the goes back into the dunya(*Dunyá* literally means 'closer' or 'lower'. In the Qur'an, *dunyá* and *ākhira* represent oppositions in temporal, spatial and moral dimensions: now and later, below and above, evil and good, respectively.)

Next on the adgenda is the big question where is he going to stay? And since he is uptown he stops by his grandmothers old house now inhabited by his aunt Clareese and cousin Gabbana with just the two of them there are plenty of rooms available and as he hits Gratz street right off of ogontz aveneue he passes the old ice cream and candy store on the corner, which is now closed down after the owner was shot do death by robbers, closing up the store one night. There was a time when something like that would never happen but things change as the new generation the children of the apacolypse take hold of the streets. He parks and trots up the front stairs looking at the garden and the disarray that it is in and picking up the mail as it sits in between the screen and front doors. His rings the bell and awaits as someone must be in the house because the television is on full blast nad seconds later the front door of the house swings open. "What's up?" greeted by his half naked cousin Gabbana decked out in a revealing halter top and boxer shorts, she's light skinned and her blond weave hangs to her shoulders. "What you doing here?" She stares her older cousin down and he replies "Can I come in?" Smacking her lips "yeah" and she fully opens the door letting Lid in he puts the mail on the radiator adding it to the already stacked pile of unopened mail, and follows Gabbana as she walks into the living room . Dead wrong he checks out his cousin as she jingles away while walking in front of him and plopping herself on the cream leather couch and continuing to watch the Tyra Banks show. "I heard you were down Delaware what are you doing up here?" "Them niggas down there are driving me crazy stupid ass girl yo!" "Awww you got girl trouble cousin?" "I need a place to stay where's Aunt Clareese?" "She's at work your dad's old room is empty, but you still have to pay rent you working?" "Naw I'm not going back there, they gonna have me on the news if I go back down there, but I got a couple of leeds and next week I am going to check out this telemarketing gig up on the boulevard, plus I got some money saved to pay rent until I get back on my feet." "Well she should be home any minute now, she gets off at like three thirty." "Can I wait?" "Yeah if you buy me something from the Chinese store?" "Alright just order it." "I love you cuz." Gabbana gets up and grabs the phone to order, he checks out the infant lying asleep on the couch, the baby boy is huge but its reassuring to see a new boy in the family with everyone having so many girl. "Don't wake him I just got him to sleep." He sits down in the recliner and looks around at his grandmothers old house and besides the sixty inch plasma screen television nothing has changed the red wall to wall carpet, the living room set, the dining oom set, the drapes, even the pictures on the walls of family are all the same as they were fifteen years ago. "Y'all didn't change much in here it looks the same." "I know we just moved back in, we had to break into through Tammy's back porch next door, you see the door lock on the radiator." "Damn y'all wild." "I don't care bout no fucking bank aint nobody going to tell me I cant live in my grandmothers house." "Yeah aint nobody tell y'all to take all those loans out in the house either this thing was paid for when grandmom willed this to your mom." "I know that's her fault listening to them fools at the church taking a loan out on this house, runnig around the city like she is rich wasting all that money." But as Gabbana is just about to go on the skreach from the screan door fills the air as keys begin to rangle and Aunt Clareese opens the front door and Gabbana quickly shuts her trap. "The mail man didn't bring any mail today?" Dressed like Laverne and Shirley in her work uniform overweight decked out in jumbo braids she exclaims "Did the mail man bring any mail or what girl I'm talking to you!!!?" "Hey aunt Clareese, I put the mail on the radiator." LID!!! What are you doing here?" he gets up and gives her a big hug exhausted he rest his head on her shoulders and she immediately ask "Whats wrong?" "Aunt Clareese I need a place to stay." "What's wrong with Dealware?" He shakes his head no "I had to go this girl I was messing with" She cuts him off "She worked at your job?" "Yeah" she knocks her nephew across the head softly "Just like your father chasing those girls around, so what happened that she made you just pack up and move?" "She goes around the job telling everyone that I had a small penis." Gabbana just starts cracking up laughing in the living room. "That's not funny because I don't ! It's more she is telling everyone other stuff too I don't want to talk about it but if I stay down there anylonger I'm going to go crazy Aunt Clareese and just snap!" "Well come here nephew" and together they walk into the living room, Gabbana grabs her son off the couch and Aunt Clareese breaks out her holy bible, and together they get on there knees and begin to pray.

"In the name of the lord Jesus Christ please lord Jesus answer our prayers and help my Nephew Lid beat the devil and overcome all obstacles placedin front of him! We call upon you lord to help him ind sanctuary, to help find a good wife so he can raise a family and please lord Jesus take away any seen and unseen afflictions that may be hanpering him please lord Jesus. Here me out lord Jesus I am your humble servant Clareese please accept my prayers. Lid do you accept Jesus Christ as your lord and savior?" Lid hesitates is he says no will Aunt Clareese still let him rent a room? But he sticks to hi guns and replies "Allah is my lord and savior and Jesus, Isa is the humble servant and prophet of Allah master of of the universe and lord of all things seen and unseen." Aunt Clareese finishes the prayer up with an "Amen" and they hug an she asks "Feel a little better don't you?" Lying Lid says "yes" as he nods his head but inside he is still cold and gray. "Alright nephew you have to find a job, but you can stay here I don't know how long we are going to be here but I havew an accountant and he says we can save the house. My mother your grandmother left this house to family and this time of need the doors are always open, just don't be brining no girls in here." "Thanks aunt Clareese, I have some money saved up so I can pay rent so how much are you going to charge me?" "How much can you afford nephew because you still have to save money to move out you cant stay here forever." "Like three hundred a month." "Well that's more than what your cousin is bringing to the table so it's a deal." Smiling together they both hug, "Alright I'll start bringing my stuff up, and tonight I will just call when I come in the house." "O.k. we will be here I'll probably be slep because I have to work around five in the morning, but Gabbana will be awake.And you can help us I could really use a man around here lifting things around and throwing some o this trash out in here." "I love you aunt Clareese I'll come see you later, I have to go out west." And with where he is going to stay checked off his list, its on to find out if his gut feeling that some one else some other group is behind all this?" So as he continues farther uptown into the Germantown area to an apartment that he spent only one night at home to an od co-worker,an old lover,  he patiently waits out in front of the apartment complex listening to his rock and roll when suddenly a familiar face emerges from the front door and shocked at the sight of seeing Lid the member of the female sorority Delta, the trust fund kid, a Philadelphia princess confirms all of Lids suspicions when she air whispers in shock "Damn!" and turns around back into her apartment at the sight of Lid. Alisha was behind it all along and with that Lid darts off, this was all set up the way Teresa just got up and walked out the door after sleeping with Lid, mirroring the same way he just walked out on Alisha, she has enough juice to pull that off how else could so many people know about it, and the rumor that he had aids spread so fast and as he heads to west Philly all things are connected as Lid thinks about and makes sense of the situation "The we stick together line" "Being asked by Mrs. Dorothy from first shift  about working at the bakery. " Pulling up to his Boo's crib Lid is greated by the twins Kendra and Kia and as soon as he gets out of the car they hug him and scream his name. "Lid!!" But changes begin to take effect as his cousin gives him a cold, fearful look as he wraps his arms around then two girls, and mat first sight of that Lid quicky lets go of the girls. Exhausted both physically, mentally, and emotionally he strolls up the stairs and Boo ask him " You want a beer cuzzo?" " Yeah who won the elections?" As Boo tosses Lid an ice cold colt forty five he says "Nut as Nutter is winning for mayor, and from thneks of things around ya boy Robinson is gonna win." "Y'all going to campaigne heasdquaters to celebrate?" "Hell yeah all that campaigne shit every Saturday that nigga better hook me up with a job or something. May be he can help ou out you poor unfortunate soul." "Yeah I hope so because I need all the help I can get, its no fun being Neo and its no fun being under fire." And as they sit out on the front steps sipping away on brews the day turns into night and it becomes official neighborhood legend Ken Robinson has won the city council elections and with that information Boo and Lid travel to campaign headquarters around the corner from Uncle Sha on sixty third street. Filled with people inside and outside crowding the sidewalk Boo almost crashes into the outside pedestrians as he parks on the corner and drunk as a skunk gets out to go celebrate. "You coming in cuzzo?" "Naw man I'm exhausted." "Suit yourself", and with that Boo pushes his way through the crowd as Lid lays in the car with his chair leaned back trying to rest physically, mentally his body and soul drained as he reflects on the past horrors he's experienced and the horrible future that soon awaits him. The momement of clarity is broken from tapping on the window of the car, and as he is awakened he rolls down the window, and casually dressed a dark skinned brother says a few words "You must be doing something right good brother for so many people to hate on you." Exhausted Lid just replies "Thanks man" as the brother walks away he rolls the window back up and closes his eyes to rest.

Up early with the sun rise to make Fajr prayer, Lid takes a few moments to read from the Holy Quran given the circumstances now more than ever to find the answers he is looking for as he walks through this inferno Lid needs and turns to Allah. Why is he going through so much pain and turmoil and why do people find humor and folly in his pain. He opens the Quran and it opens to Sura 30 Roman ayatt 60,

> "So patiently persevere:for verily the promise of God is true:nor let those shake thy firmness who have (themselves) no certainty of faith."

He closes it and opens it again to Sura LVIII Ayat 13
"The evil one has got the better of them losing the
rememberance of God. They are the party of the evil one.
Truly it is the party of the evil one that will perish."

He closes it and opens it again to Sura LXXII the Jinn or the Spirits
"Say: It has been revealed to me that a company of Jinns
listened to the Quran they said we have really heard a
wonderful recital."

"It gives guidance to the right And we have believed therein,
we shall not join in worship Any Gods with our lord."

"And exalted is the majestry of our lord:He has taken
neither a wife nor a son."

"There were some foolish ones amoung us, who used to
utter extravagant lies against God."

"But we do think That no man or spirit should say aught
that is untrue against God."

And with thise words of wisdom he gets up and hits the shower and gets
fully dressed for the day, he wanders to the back room were still sleeping is
his cousin Gabbana and when he sees this he turns to leave when she
surprisingly says "Why you waking me up early in the morning?" "Sorry
Gabbana but I wanted to make breakfast what do y'all got in the fridge?"
"I don't know but I want some bacon, eggs, and pancakes". "I don't know
about any pancakes but I will check the fridge and see what I can cook up."
"Lid hold up." Now fully awake she arises from her bed in just a t-shirt and
probably panties underneath and bluntly says "Lid could you beat my baby
daddy up?" "What!" "he doesn't do anything for Samir, he doesn't give me
any money for formula, or pampers nothing he doesn't even come around
to see his son." "Well is he working?" "No he hustles" "Who doesn't these
days, where does he live?" "Around the corner" "So why did you have a baby
with him Gabbana? Hustling will only get you so far and even then you
need some type or skill to fall abck on because the fast money will always

slow up." This early in the morning she is in no mood for a lecture and she once again bluntly ask him "So are you going to beat him up or what?" "No I am not beating him up, did he put his hands on you?" She breaks out in hysterical laughter "Who Jay? Please I be punching him in the mouth" "You shouldn't hit a man Gabbana" "That boy aint no man please." "Then think about that why did you have a baby with a boy?" There is a brief silence and then she flags Lid off "forget you anyway that's why when my brother Lester gets out he's gonna beat that faggot up himself." And on that note Lid walks out the room and goes downstairs to the kitchen, and like every other part of the house the kitchen looks exactly the same. The brown refrigerator from the seventies still with the Jackson 5 stickers from the kelloges corn flakes giveaway of years past, the same wooden cabinets and old stove, but when he opens up the refrigerator he sees the new school of waste. As the refrigerator is filled with unfinished take out bags from McDonalds, Wendy's, and the Chinese store, and while he searches through the refrigerator looking for some eggs and bacon to cook up for breakfast he reminisses on Christmas over his grandmothers house and how the whole house would smell like sweet photato pies, pineapple upside down cake, turkey, ham, fried chicken, and his favorite macaroni and cheese." How his fathers mother fresh out of south Carolina would slave in the kitchen for days leading up to the twenty fifth of December cooking food for her entire family, her foster children, and the unfortunate members of her church. How he used to steal candy canes off the Christmas tree, gone are those days when his grandmom was the matriarch of the family and everyone would come to her for help, and being the saint that she was she would always say yes to any request. Grandmom Dot was one of a kind but here now are the days of greed and wastefulness. Disgusted with the waste in the refrigerator and unable to find any eggs, or bacon in the fridge he slams the door and heads out to the Puerto Rican store to buy some groceries. A dozen of eggs, one pound of turkey bacon, half pound of American cheese, some bread for toast, and a pound of corn beef for hot sandwiches later." The mommi at the register is bad and with her jet black hair and big titties Lid can do nothing but think about Teresa as he stares into her brown eyes. He thinks to himself "All Puerto Rican women look perfecto" As he maintains eye contact with her the entire time he pays for his groceries and smoothly he says "Thanks Mommy" the older women cracks a smile and with full latina pazzaz she says "Your welcome Papi" and then licks her lips. Lid smiles and then walks back around the corner and on the block he passes Mr. Scott and elderly man who was friends with his grandmom and with all due respect Lid speaks to the old timer Goodmornig Mr. Scott!" "What's up there young fellow?" "Staying alive sir that's it." He notices the red Philles cap the old man is wearing and accordingly ask "So what do you think they winning the series this year?" "Who the Phillies young man what do you know about the Philles?" "They need more pitching and Howard has to stop striking out, you know that's my team I was born the day they won the World Series back in 1980." The old man's eyes open wide "Yeah I remember your Grandmom telling me that you were in the hospital they didn't think you were going to make it." "Yeah I pulled through though so I always have had a special conection with the Phils, I don't know about this year they need another pitcher but we will see come October if they make the playoffs." "Alright young man, you guys back in there for good?" Mikail shrugs his shoulders "I don't know we will have to see if things work out?" "Well its good to see you back around here." "Its good to see you too Mr. Scott." Lid tips his red Phillies hat and walks up the steps and back into the house. Gabbana is downstairs with her son Samir and they are watching television. "You brought us some breakfast?" "No  I brought some food so I can make breakfast." And with child in hand she follows him to the kitchen "Alright when I come back later we are going to clean the fridge out and throw this old stuff in the trash." "I know its disgusting my mom keeps all those left overs in their, if grandmom Dot was alive she would never go for anything like that." He says nothing and just continues to prepare the breakfast not engaging in any back bitting especially since Gabbana is just as guilty as aunt Clareese. "Do you know how to cook? Because I don't want to be eating no nasty food!" "Look Gabanna one thing I know how to do is cook that's what you pick up living alone and on your own. "Alright then call me when its ready." Cooking is onething he really enjoys so as he cuts the photatoes into small pieces and jams to Led Zepelin on his ipod, he zones out forgetting about his problems and issues scambling eggs and turing bacon over to keep it from burning. And in like twenty minutes breakfast is ready and together they sit down at the dining room table lit by sun light and say grace and then dig in to some home cooked food. Relaxed and safe Gabbana acts silly like a child as she say while scarfing down the food "This is good cuz which one of your girlfriends taught you to cook like this?" "Nobody Gabanna I just picked up different recipies over the years." "Yeah right" and when they finish Lid gathers his things his keys to the car, his rings, and money off the dining room table and ask "Y'all gonna be home tonight because I'm probably not coming in until later." "yeah I'm not going anywhere just call before you come home though." "Alright". He leaves to tackle the first thing on his adgenda going up to Roosevelt Boulevard and fill out an application at the telemarketing firm and as he speeds through the city and onto the Boulevard the eight lane drag racers dream is empty as most of the traffic is going from the northeast south bound and into the city, Lid zooms off at every light as it changes from red to green still fuming from his defeat in Delaware he takes his anger out on the road just beating yellow lights as they change to red until he finally reaches his destination of Grant and the Boulevard and making a left into the side street of Grant. A few blocks down he finds a small mini mall and parks gathers himself for another interview as a sad sense of repetitiveness overtakes him just before he goes into the front door he takes a look at his reflection, and ask himself how many times is he going to have to do this? How many times dressing up in a suit and tie pretenting to be normal, when he always comes out on the short end of the stick, these days even the square jobs are filled with criminals, when is he going to get with the program and start hustling? Because there is no justice and nothing fair in the corporate world, why is he still doing this? And as he goes to open the door to his surprise its locked and he thinks to himself "give up now and just go back to the car and go home, go back to Citigroup, go back to Dealware go to work and live with the shame of being humiliated every night, and coming back to work because of how good the money is?" But he cant and so he travels to the back entrance of the building and onto the front desk and opens with a line that he has used so many times in the past "Excuse me my name is Lid Islam and I would like to fill out an application."

Sitting in traffic after leaving the interview  a little perplexed about what to do yesterday he was middle management at one of the largest banks in the world, then in a flash he is interviewing for some run of the mill telemarketing company. With a Septa bus picking up passengers in front of him there is no way he is going to make the light and being young and restless he releases his foot from the break and slams down the gas changing lanes trying to beat the traffic light as it just begins to turn yellow as he enters the intersection. BAM!!!! Out of nowhere a yellow buick le saber slams into Lids car and if he hadn't hit the gas it would've taken off his whole front end. "Damn it almost seemed like she was aiming for me as the yellow buick did not even try to stop as she plowed through him." But that's the last thing he will think about because the air bag rapidly releases and Lid slams up against it and passes out for a few seconds until he awakens and still woozy from the accident Lid gets out of the car and begins to pick up debris from the accident which is scattered all over Roosevelt Boulevard. When the female driver gets out of her vehicle she approaches Lid and says "I didn't even see you buddy you came out of nowhere." He meets her halfway and they shakehands and continues the conversation "You o.k.?" "yeah I already have a bad back, how about you?" "My airbag deployed and the powder burned my hands up a little bit, my back is starting to hurt too, you got insurance?" "Yeah its in my husbands name you?" "Yeah let me go get my paper work." Confidents about being in the right this time after not having insurance after the cheerleader incident, a few hours before Jumah prayer on a Friday Lid was driving his cousin Boo home from down the way coming up Lancaster avenue stopped at the red light a few cars back full of lust at of the dismay of his much older cousin Lid was perplexed checking out the cheerleaders from the world famous Overbrook high school. As they practiced outside in the school yard with those skimpy cheerleader outfits, the high skirts, and the brief glimpse of panties and legs as they are tossed in the air intriqued to the point where he had to just show off for kicks he had to rev his engines up as he exchanged eye contact and smiles with the very very young girls "Oh thank heaven for little girls" but all good things must come to an end and when the red light turns green and the cars in front of him pulled forward showing off he slams down on the gas still smiling at the cheerleaders as they comply and smile back when all of a sudden SLAM!!!! Boothe abrupt stop is only osteracized as Boo slams his head through the front windshield almost going right through it, and Lids airbag ejects as the rouring of the engine was silenced and the giggles of the cheerleaders filled the air as he's crashed into the car in front of him. Taking off the bumper of the car infront of him, and giving the old lady driver in front of him one heck of a case of whiplash, with his front end and hood completely smashed in the front windshield broken, the Boo bleading from his foJasmined Lid gets out the car and just waits for the police to arrive, no insurance, no fix and it would take months for him to recover from this screw up.

So as he sits on the Boulevard patiently waiting as the black and white takes the info from the women driving the car that hit him, Lid just takes the time to call his company Gieco and let them know he was in a major accident, and when given instructions to take down all her information and that he is fully covered Lid smiles as his luck is changing and finally doing the right thing is going to pay off. The bible says be a good Samaritan and still bruised and battered from the accident he gets out once again greeting the older women as she chit chats with the tow truck driver. Accidents happen on the Boulevard all the timeand tow truck drivers just sit like sharks in the water waiting for accidents to happen especially at Grant and the Boulevard. "How you doing?" "I'm fine just worried about my car the whole front end is crashed up." "Yeah almost did the same thing to me good thing I sped up it would've been a done deal you would've taken off my entire front end." "Good driving you should've tried out for nascar, the cop said she is just running the paperwork but she is not writing out any tickets on anyone." "She better not, I didn't do anything wrong, my insurance company wanted me to get all your information because they will be contacting your insurance company." On the hood of the womens car he begins to jot down her information as he ask her questions. "What company do you have?" "AIG" "What's your name?" "Deborah Lions" "What's the make and model of the car?" "The car is a 1997 Buick LaSaber" "Whats your policy number?" "Uh I don't know it but let me see if the cop is done writing down all the information." And Mrs. Lions goes over to the cop car and inbetween a few light laughs with the female officer she comes back with her paper work and surprisingly his paper work too. "She was done with your paper work and so here ya go." Pissed off the cop had the nerve to give his insurance information to Mrs. Lions Lid frowns his face from the lack of respect, he angrily says as he hands Mrs. Lions a piece of paper "Here I wrote everything down already, Gieco told me to give your company a call so I'l do that when I get home." They shake hands and the tow truck pulls away with Mrs. Lions and her car, as Lid waits for the AAA tow truck to come puck him up and when it does the driver tries to talk him into junking his car, but Lid will none of that. And as they drive back to his aunt house exhausted depressed, and dejected Lid just rests his head on the passenger side glass and looks out the window his lower back flaring up from the accident and his left hand bruised up from the deploying airbag dust he takes notice as the young boys from his aunt's neighborhood smile and grin as he passes by with his horse busted up on the back of a flat bed, it's rabbit season and they cant wait for the seasoned veteran to be on foot in the night time or even the day time as anything goes these days in Philly. What else could go wrong the bullshit in Delaware, and now this on foot in the murder capital of the country, without a job and money running low what else could go wrong? His back stiffens as they pull into the block and his entire left side begins to swell up beaten Lid just parks the car in front of the house and goes inside were he is met by his cousin Gabbana. "What happened to your car!!!?" "Some crazy ass white lady just crashed into me up on the boulevard like a missle." "Hahaha you got bad luck loser!" "I aint no loser, she crashed into me and this time I have insurance so either I'm getting a new car, or they are going to cut me a check to get my baby fixed and I will up and running in the next two weeks." Lid grimises in pain and Gabbana ask "What's wrong with you?" "My whole body is hurting from head to toe, I got this headache that I cant shake, my shoulder, ribs, and back are killing me." "You better go to the hospital and get checked up you could get paid she had insurance didn't she?" "Yeah" "Well I don't know what you waiting for you better get down to Einstien!" "I can catch the C bus down there huh?" "Or wait for my mom to come home from work and she can drive you." "Naw I'm just gonna go before it gets dark outside." Limping badly he leaves the house and begins to walk around the corner and then onwards to broad street it only about ten very short blocks but as he looks ahead the corners and the stoops are populated with young boys just salivating at the mouth to take a shoot at Lid this is his first time on foot in years and already underfire the situation has gotten only worse as he is knee deep in the line of fire without any allies in the tough town of Philly or known these days as simply Kiladelphia. Only one block into his odessy he afraid he turns around and limps back into the house were the giggling Gabbana ask "scared huh? you gonna wait for my moms college man?" "Yeah them young boys out there all got burners." "You aint never say no lie, you a punk though they aint worried about you." "Yeah right I'm a high profile kill Gabbana, old timer yo from the nineties." "Please you act like you flipped a few keys of coke or something you better get back out there before it gets too dark because that's when you better worry." He goes upstairs and in his room he makes salat grimissing in pain with every motion and after he salaams out he ask Allah for some help "Allah could you please protect me from satan and protect me from his army these children of the apocalypse as I am hurt and need to travel by foot to the hospital." He then takes a seat on the edge of the bed and contemplates taking his small twenty two caliber pistol the tiny pearl handle gun can fit in his back pocket without anyone knowing it. The downside is that unlike his peacemaker the .22 is not registered and spent some time in west Philly with his uncle which means it could've been used in a shooting or worse a murder, and if caught with it on him Lid could be facing major jail time. But as the sun lowers and day becomes night he knows what he must do and he grabs the pistol and puts it in his back jeans pocket and limps down the steps and on his way out the door Gabbana ask "You going out there now? You stupid its dark outside dummy, why don't you wait until my mom comes home?" Shaking his head he replies with confidence "Naw im cool I'll just walk down to Broad street and catch the C down to Einstien." This time as he walks around the corner he continues past one block and unafraid strapped he maintains eye contact with all that he passes on the street, and what seemed like an impossible journey only minutes ago is a quick ten minute walk to Broad street absent of fear eventhough glaring cars pass him buy and drivers and passengers stare him down. In this town you are more likely to be robbed by some nigga driving a car as opposed to another pedestrian walking the streets. The unknown soldier waits for the C bus and it's a different feeling when cops pass by and you are doing something wrong or illegal. Turning away is a sure fire sign of guilt and your best bet is to look at them right in the eyesor before they pass act like they are not even there and pay attention to something in the distance. So as the cruisers pass him on Broad street he focuses on the car dealership across the street and pays them no mind and when the bus finally arrives he takes his seat on the back row and looks out the window praying that the .22 doesn't go off as he is sitting right on it, relieved as the bus gets to Einstien Lid gets off and limps to the front door, and to his dismay it is locked and the security guard tells him " This entrance is closed you have to walk around the back and come in through the emergency room." Lid follows the signs and limps around to the back of the hospital, best case scenario theyh don't have any cops guarding the emergency room, worst case scenario they do and there's a metal detector. And as luck would have it its worst worst case scenario as he greeted by a small platoon of Philadelphia's finest and in perfect harmony they all look over at Lid as soon as he turns the fucking the fucking corner. Breaking his own rule he just turns away as they look over at him and limps into the emergency room doors, as the police get back to breaking up a fight between two families in the parking lot of the emergency room, relieved that they did not stop him he doesn't even notice the metal detectors guarding the hospital as he enters and as they go off out of knowhere dressed in the sunna of the Prophet Muhammed white cuffi, jeans cut to his ankles, and a long beard the muslim brother walks in at the same time as Lid. Together side by side as the metal detector goes off the now standing security guard is confused as to who to stop and Lid taking control of the situation looks the security guard right in the eyes and ask "where do I sign in at so I can see a doctor?" Initiate the conversation and control the situation the guard immediately resorts to his natural duties "this chart right here sir, sign here and then have a seat in the waiting room over there." He points to a small room and Lid signs and then goes to have a seat. And patiently he waits while watching an NBA game on the television figiting around in the seat trying not to directly sit on the pistol God forbid this thing goes off in here. Still in pain and now completely stressed out he nervously checks the front entrance for any actions from the police or the security guard and as time slips by fifteen minutes turns into a half and hour, and then hour Lids turns creeps closer and closer as he oveJasminers a nurse or a doctor from the back say "He's not coming back here with that!!" "THEY KNOW!!!!" his heart just drops and he continues to wait he's confused about what to do if he gets up the cops can lock him up right outside in the parking lot. The new stop and frisk program is in full effect and at the any given moment without any probable cause cops can just grab you and search or even hold you in custody indeffinatley. This is a complete contradiction of the fourth amendment of the Constitution of the United States which states "The right of the people to be secure in their persons, houses, papers, and effects against unreasonable searches and seizures, shall not be violated, and no Warrents shall issue, but upon probable cause, supported by Oath or affirmation, and particulary describing the place to be searched, and the persons or things to be seized." But if he stays he is trapped in the back area, what if they keep him for the night and he cant control his clothes and a nurse finds it? None of these scenerios crossed his mind when he walked out the door his only concern was just overcoming the fear of walking a few blocks but now the flip side has him fearing the consequences of packing heat without a permit in a public facility. As he turns around to once again check the entrence another muslim brother who Lid recognizes from days at Sister Clara Muhammed School Raqmon the well built dark skinned brother is also dressed adhereing to the sunna of the Prophet his pants cut to his ankles a long beard and white cuffi, Lid takes note as his cab is pulled up directly infront of the front door, and he watches as Raqmon helps his fare check into the emergenc room and as he turns to leave in one breathe Lid is right along side as he once again walks through the metal detectors, as they exit the front doors Lid says "As Salaam Alaikum." "Wa Laikum Salaam" making eye contact and relaying only through that the seriousness and desperation involved Lid ask "Brother could you please give me a ride to my house on 66th and Gratz, I need to come home and drop something off then come back here." He says nothing and focuses on the desperation on the face of Lid and replies "Alright I will drive you but you have to find another cab to take you back I have a fare I am supposed to pick up now." "Thankyou brother" and Lid jumps into the plush leather black back seats. "That was close this is the first time I've been without a wheel uphere since I was a sophomore in high school, I had to bring it out." "Just be careful it's still dangerous for us out here brother but you off the hook bringing it in the emergency room. He watches as the meter on the fare box goes up and after a five minute ride they are in front of his grandmothers house but as he is about to hand Raqmon a ten dollar bill, the brother says "that's o.k. brother, no charge just hurry up and I will drive you back to the hospital." "What about the other fare you had?" "Just hurry up and don't worry about it." Lid jumps out of the car and runs into the unlocked door sitting on the couch is Gabbana and Aunt Clareese "You gotta move that car out back I cant have it outside broken down in the street." "O.k.' he replies as he darts up the steps ignoring his anguishing shoulder and leg he runs into his room and puts the twenty two in between the box spring and the mattress and then takes off back down stairs and out the door. "Thank brother for taking me back" "Your welcome" Still exhausted bruised and battered Mikahil is driven back to Einstien hospital's emergency room. "Thanks again brother As Salaam Alaikum" "Wa Laikum Salaam" Without any fear this time, no pistol, no police, he walks into the emergency room like a law abiding citizen signs in at the front desk and takes a seat as he patiently waits to until his name is called "Lid Islam?" "Yes" the blond haired blue eyed white jaun tells Lid "Please come with me so we can get you checked in." Exhausted he arises and limps to the back area following the nurse. In the interview room they sit across from each other and before he is asked about what is ailing him she asked him "Do you have any insurance?" Proudly Lid pulls out his health care card from his former employer citigroup and replies "yes" "thank you sir, now whats wrong with you tonight?" "Some lady hit me on the Boulevard she crashed right into me, and now my back is killing me, plus my arm is all burned up from the air bag, plus my whole left side is hurting me." "Well you look mentally and physically exhausted when was the last time you ate anything?" "I had breakfast this morning but…." He struggles to get out the rest as embarrassing as it to tel people Lid has to speak up because what happened in Citi was a hate crime and if doesn't speak up now he better forever be in peace. And he looks at the nurse who is pretty hot he looks right in the eyes and embarrassed ashamed of his defeat in Delaware he tells her what happened. "It was a real real rough week at work, the whole third and second shift was laughing and pointing at me saying I had AIDS because I slept with this girl at the job." She gasp, and says "Oh lord, have you been checked yet?" "No, Im a mess right now my mind is going in all types of places and I cant shut it off, now this accident" He grabs his head and just starts to ramble "I need to rest please I'm tired." "No problem Mr. Islam from the sound things you have been through a very tramatic experience and you need to rest, we are going to check you in for the night bandage you up and in the morning I seriously suggest that you go to out HIV clinic and get a free check up, its 99% accurate and we have help for you regardless of what the outcome is. That's horrible for people to talk to you like that at your job, this happened at Citigroup?" "Yeah I left out of there yesterday I couldn't take anymore them people in Delaware are crazy yo." "Well your in Philly now so take off your clothes and relax on the stretcher we will fix you right up." Lid contines to fill out the intake form and then undress and put on the hospital gown his heart aches as once again he's relayed to someone the awfull news about what took place at citigroup the humiliation at the hands of the Christians from Delaware, Delaware the only state within the thirteen colonies that mandated you had to be Christian to live there, those people in Delaware. Then he comes to grips with reality its nobodys fault but his own, he didn't have to sleep with Teresa he chose to. Its nobodys fault but his own no one forced him to smoke weed he chose to, its nobodys fault but his own no one forced him to miss his prayers he chose to. Yeah the whole country's turned upside down , yeah Forty Three is the anti Christ, yeah he didn't win the 200 elections, and yeah if Al Gore wins 911 still remains just the number you dail in an mergency. Yeah he was right about a lot of things, yeah the world has treated him pretty unfair but at the end of the day sitting on the stretcher exhausted mentally, and physically he listens to former President Jimmy Carter's book "Peace not Appartiad" on his I-Pod Lid knows this was all in Allah's plan and he has only been an instrument for God so whatever the outcome of his HIV test in the morning, whatever the future may hold the final goal is the return to his lord. So as he lays there finally resting after years of pushing himself to the limit, from dishwashing, propane, demolition, to out working even the machines at Citigroup the peaceful voice of a Georgian Peanut farmer fills the air as he explains the unholy situation going on in the holy land of Jerusalem and how each party can fix it. The hospital pass by and stare at the exhausted revolutionary who almost looks njust breathes away from passing into the next world.

In the mornig the humbled staff who has attended to Lid hand and foot throughout the night gets him ready for discharge as the shift changes. "Here's a prescription for some aspirin and an extra set of bandages for your arm. Once again it might not mean much but no one should have to go through anything like that and I am so very sorry." "Thank you, you guys have been great like angels all night thank you and may God bless you." The nurse smiles and she leaves, Lid begins to put his clothes back on and when he is fully dressed he goes out to the front dest to be discharged and ask the ordily at the front desk quietly "Where's the clinic so I can get tested for HIV?" Respecting his privacy the odily quietly says "On 16th and old York road they are about to open, go on over man, and we are sorry about what happened to you, get some rest man and stay strong." "Thanks" He leaves and his drops as soon as he walks out the doors and onto the street here comes the moment of truth. The gun, the cops, that was all the prelude because whatever the outcome of the test determines if Lid is going to quietly go into the night or start burning down building angry and upset about the cards he's been dealt or better yet the cards he dealt himself. What if the test comes back positive? What am I going to do? Alone without Teresa it was worth contracting the disease if he could be with her to keep that love to have that feeling of joy all the time it was worth even it meant just spending the next ten years together on earth. He shakes his head and wakes up from the dream and gets to the truth Teresa never liked him, this is Alisha's doing and her reaction the other day proved it. Confused he imagines taking the same twenty two from last night and just blowing his brains out in response to a positive test, but suicide in Islam like Christianity is a one way trip to an enternity in hell fire so as he walks into the clinic the already filled up waiting area is limbo as he signs in and paitently waits to find out his fate positive? or negative?

While sitting with the batteries on his I-POD drained he has to face the world and as he looks at the rest of the room filled with women and children and a few scattered men, he wonders to himself "do all these people have HIV?" "Should I start looking for a girlfriend in here and find a chick who has HIV?" "There are a lot of people in here wow" and after waiting he name is fanillay called the hospital representative is a chubby white jewish women with long brown hair and considering the gravity of the situation she seems very chipper fucking coffee he thinks to himself "Goodmorning." She puts her hand out for Lid to shake and he does so "Hi ya doing?" he follows her into the back and they have a seat in a small examination room. They sit across from each other and he gets straight to the point "The emergency room says that I can come here and get an HIV test?" "Yes, why do you think you contracted the HIV disease?" "This girl at my job, I messed around with this girl at my job at banco international and the whole place started teasing me saying I had AIDS." Shocked she just drops her mouth you can hate or love em but the one thing most Jews will not stand for is hate and if anything the holocaust is the perfect example why. "Are you serious this whole world is going to hell, I cant believe people your co-workers said anything like to you." "Yeah I'm kinda all out of sorts right now, so I went to the ER" she cuts him off "becaue you think you contracted the HIV virus?" "No because some crazy lady smashed into my car yesterday on the Boulevard." "Oh you have just been through it, well I hope things get better for you." "I pray they do to, so how long is the test and how long do I have to wait to get the results?" "No time at all, the test only takes a few minutes and you get the results right then and there its like a pregnancy test." So she pulls out and opens a test which is housed in a bag the size of the peanut bags on the airplane and says "O.k. no information from this test will be made public and if your test does come back positive rest assured you are not alone and the facilities here at Einstien hospital is here for you at all times." "Alright lets get this over with." "Very well" she takes the q-tipped shaped swab and places it in Lids mouth rubbing around and around collecting saliva. Then she places the swab on a plastic base and says "Alright the results will show up soon a line means the HIV virus was not found in your system, if no line shows up then you have contracted the HIV virus, but rest assured we are here to help you." They wait and Lid waits for what seems like an eternity his life is over if this thing comes back positive. I'm gonna kill Teresa, Alisha, and anybody else for that matter I can't believe this shit!!! And as he contemplates his fate she finally looks at the test and exhales and then looks up at Lid smiling. That could mean anything crazy ass white chick does this everyday a smile could still mean I have AIDS come what the results just say it?" And in slow motion the words roll off her tongue "NNNNNEEEEEEGGGGGEEETTTTTIIIIIIIVVVVVVEEEEE." Stumped he doesn'tknow what to do so he just smiles, as she once again professionally says "The results from your test are negative see take a look at and she turns the test around to show him "see there's a line you don't have AIDS so forget thousand e loser down Delaware." Lid laughs and he sits back in his chair a little relieved, and after a few seconds of just breathing without that dark cloud hanging over his head he graciously thanks the women and after disgards of the test in the trash they shake hands. Lid leaves and as he walks back into the waiting room a smirk cracks his face as he tries not to look at the people waiting, and as he walks out the door with some confidence restored, and some energy back from his night at the hospital he strolls along to the bus stop, when all the turmoil comes to a head this was done by the church, the Baptist who tried to break Lid the Angelina thing, the Teresa thing, and now this somehow they believed that he was a terrorist or that they were doing something for the American cause since America is over seas fighting Islam killing muslims I guess being quiet qand watching as Lid fell in love with Teresa was part of there plan. I guess teasing him about having AIDs was part of the plan to break Lid into finally saying the most sacreligious phrase ever for a muslim that Jesus

Christ was GOD or the son of God, all this done in the name of JESUS and as he walks alone down to the bus stop it comes to a head and he screams in broad daylight at the top of his lungs full of might and anger "ISAAAAAA! ISAAAAAA! ISAAAAAA!" what has happened here all that was done was done in his name in an attempt to destoy a muslim in an attempt to destroy a true American the one who stood up against terany, all that done in the name of Jesus, or Isa as the muslims call him Arabic. So as he walks to the 6 bus stop in the daylight he shouting to the heavens for the Prophet Isa to help him as he was under fire and thanking Allah for protecting him against the same disease that took his step father the same disease that has taken millions of people around the world, Lid continues to shout to the heavens "ISAAAAA!" Pleading for some help in this struggle, this jihad against good and evil.

Sura XIV Ayat 30
"And they set up idols As equal to GOD to mislead (men) from the path! Say:Enjoy your brief power but verily ye are making straightway for hell!"

Sura XL ayat 66
"Say: " I have been forbidden to invoke those whom ye invoke besides God, seeing that the clear signs have come to me from my Lord; And I have been commanded to Bow in INslam, to the lord of the worlds."

Sura LXI ayat 6
"And remember Jesus the son of Mary, said "O Children of Isreal! I am the apostle of God sent to you, confirming The law (which came) before me, and giving Glad Tiding of an Apostle to come after me whose name shall be Ahmad but when he came to them with clear signs, they said this is evident sorcery!"

Chapter

Lid awakens with the sun and he calls his cousin Boo, its been a few weeks after the car accident and after buying all the parts to get his fixed. He's been looking forward to this and he's enlisted the help of the neighborhood grease monkey Squater to fix his baby after Mrs. Lions smashed into him on the Boulevard. "As Salaam Alaikum?" "Wa Laikum Salaam what's your problem calling me this early in the morning messing up my Saturday morning cartoons!!!?" "Come on man you know I gotta get my baby fixed today, yo I got all parts, come on man I know you told Squater right?" "I sold those parts." "Stop playing man." "What's my motivation?" "Alright I'll pick a six pack of beers for you and we can grab some green too." "Now you talking I just saw Squater this morning he's ready to go you just better have his money right because he'll fix it and then when your half way down the street it will fall apart as soon as you hit the road." "Naw I got his money I have to get this thing fixed it's no fun being on foot and its about to get cold outside." "Alright so when you coming down here man, lets get started" "I already called triple A, and they are on there way should be here any minute now." "Hey cuz why didn't the the insurance company pay for it, didn't she crash into you?" "What! I aint tell you? Gieco and AIG fucked me over, on the day of the accident Gieco was like everything's cool right. So when I called them back the day after the accident they tell me I don't have any coverage." "WHAT!!" "Yeah these  muthafuckers redeposit my payment into my account, then take it back out when I didn't have enough after money in the account. So I talked to them days before I got into the accident and made my payment, then they gonna tell me that even if I payed I was not covered the day I got into the accident." "That shit don't make any sense cuz you better get a lawyer." Still talking loud Lid goes on "But wait it gets better her company AIG is like they aint paying for it because Mrs Lions and the witness, the tow truck driver said I ran a red light." "Cuz you do be driving like a mad man, I been told you to slow down." "So what!" I still didn't run no red light, I even called the parking authority and for like an hour we went through the camera at that intersection she was like if I didn't get a ticket mailed to me then I didn't run a light. Then I stayed on the phone and she zoomed in on my car and the accident and was like I didn't run a red light." "You need a lawyer man" "No I need a fucking bazooka so I can start destroying building and shit and may be I can get some respect around this muthafucker! The sound of a truck fills the block and Lid looks out the dark red curtins of his grandmoms living room and sees the tow truck."Yo I gotta go because the tow truck is here, Salaam Alaikum." "Wa Laikum Salaam"

He goes out the front door to meet the tow truck driver the scruffy old white man jumps out the drivers seat and they shake hands. "How ya doing?" "I cant wait until I get this baby up and runnig again" "You got your triple A card?" "Yeah" he hands the truck driver his card "So what happened the whole left side is crashed up?" "Some crazy women crashed into my car on the Boulevard, now the insurance companies are saying its my fault because I ran a red light." "Well did you?" Lid shakes his head no, "Do you have a witness?" "Naw, the tow truck driver that towed her car tells her insurance company that I ran the red light." "Well I hate to tell you this man but that happens a lot in this business, how was her car?" "The whole front end was busted up" "Yeah that happens a lot in this business man she probably promised him the car so he can junk it, if he said he saw you run the red light." "Well I gotta fix this myself, the messed up part about it is that I pay for insurance and then when I need them they don't back me up." "It's not fair sometimes, you gotta make the best of it." The driver takes a look at the car and scratches his head and exhales "Boy this is going to be a tough tow, good thing I brought the flat bed." "How come?" "Youzze see the way the car is leaning because its just sitting on the rotor, and at some point I am going to have to drag that rotor up against the ground and it's gonna get stuck in the ground as I pull it into the flatbed." "Yeah I see what your saying but I had to take the wheel off, to see what was broke." "Well the best thing we can do is try, you got a jack in there?" "Yeah" "Go get it and start jacking her up." "I have a piece of ply wood in the truck after you jack it up I am going to put the ply wood underneath the rotor and try and to drag that plywood along until I get it up on the flatbed." Lid retrieves the jack from his trunk and proceeds to jack the car up when the tow truck driver places the plywood underneath the wheel in question. "I did this on a tow years ago and it worked so cross your fingers sir and may be we can get this bad boy moving." To say the least Lid is impressed the man is very helpful and considering the evil events that led him to having to fix his own car its very reassuring to see some balance in the universe. Willing to go the extra mile the tow truck driver tries and tries again until finally the car is lifted onto the flatbed. "Thank's man. Hey what's your name cause I'm going to tell triple A about the good job you did here?" "Thanks man its not like its going to make any difference they still treat me like crap but hey it's a job. The names Milt Thompson." "Lid Islam" and reintroduced they once again shake hands. "Look Mr. Thompson were taking this car down to my cousins house in wynnefield I know its supposed to go to a shop, but I cant afford that and me and the neighborhood mechanic are going to fix this thing or at least try." "Don't worry about it man just tell me the address and I will drop it off." "Cool" When they finally get rolling and onto Boo's house as promised Mr. Thompson drops the car off right in front of the house. "Thanks a lot sir" "Hey don't call me sir I work for a living." "Understood Mr. Thompson thanks a lot here's a few dollars for your troubles." He hands Mr. Thompson a ten dollar bill and at first he refuses to accept the money. "No way man you just told me about what happened with the insurance companies, plus I'm just doing my job." Lid insist "That was beyond the call of duty yo, if they send someone else the car would be wrecked or still sitting uptown if not for you." I guess the sound of the tow truck sparked Boo's attention as he emerges out his front door and sees his cousin handing Mr. Thompson the money "Well somebody better take it before I do!" "Its o.k. Mr. Thompson you did an outstanding job, thank you." "Thanks man" and he takes the ten dollar bil and gets in his truck and as he begin to pull off he honks the horn and Lid waves. "As Salaam Alaikum" "Wa Laikum Salaam did you talk to Squater yo?" "Come on cuzzo where's mines?" and he holds his hand out, "Come on man its after nine and the beer store is open, lets get that six pack." "Naw man you peeling I want two six packs." Lid frowns his face and ask again "Did you see Squater?" "Yeah man he came by the house this morning before you called he had to go work on another car he said he will be back around like ten. You better the man yo because this shit should've been done in a fucking shop!" "Tell that to Gieco and AIG I cant believe they crossed me on this one, this time when I ackually had insurance."

They jump inside Boo's Mini van and continue to talk "Damn Cuzzo it's like you got no rights if your name is Lid Islam?" "You telling me, I cant wait till Forty Three  is out of office!" "You try going to the masjid and asking the muslims for help?" Lid shakes his head "No dice, I went to jummah a few weeks ago and some weird things happened, for one thing Iman Malik was there!" "Aint he about to get sent up to the fed?" "Yeah they shipped him to Texas the following Monday so that was his last jummah.

He didn't even give the talk that Friday, dethrowned king he's been the visiting Iman all over the city after they closed the school down. The crazy part is when jummah was all over I walked outside solo and there he was standing out front solo too no entourages, no body guards, just him and I give him the greetings and then we hug. It was a touching moment" "I can only imagine with your dramatic ass, that's crazy all those bums that used to cling to him all disappeared when the shit started to fall down." "Yeah they hit the deck when the feds came knocking but it was going to happen sooner or later, Uncle Sha told me years ago when we were out Norristown and investigation was going on." "So did you tell him what was going on in Delaware?" "Naw" "But you told me?" "You family I just asked him if he had any connections for any jobs because I was out of work." "What he say?" "He told me to go down to district 33 labor union and tell the white boy that he sent me down there? So I go down there a few days later and there is a big sign as soon as I walk in "YOU CAN GET HELP FOR DRUG ABUSE!!!" and things really started to hit home." "What you mean cuzzo like you smoked too much pot?" "Yeah, but I never really let that mess me up man, so I don't understand that shit. If I didn't have any money I didn't smole, and I used to just smoke on the weekends after work." "So what the muslims say, you know its still a big thing you back, you back in the city?" "They already knew what happened with the shit at Citi, that Friday it was all these Delaware plates outside of Masjidallah and new faces in the crowd. So I'm catching up with a few people the regulars from the old days and I kept a common theme. I'm back in town I just had to leave Dealware because of some domestic terror stuff and I lost my job and my apartment I'm looking for some work. But one of the old heads brother Jamal he aint like me when I was a kid, he just flatly walked up to me and was like "We know what you are trying to do." It was a cold and icy reception so I just left but as I walked back down Ogontz avenue this women is outside her house and she started stomping her feet, now I seen that before but this time I really connected everything what she was saying was "We stomping y'all out!!" "Who the muslims?" "Yeah" "Cuzzo you think way too much into things and you don't miss nuffin. Now yeah that's gotta be a mind fuck knowing what we know, but do you really think muslims from Delaware came up to Philly and told the muslims about your situation?" "Yeah I think they told them that, its everything they first reported me and Sha to the

FBI when we first got started they know what we are trying to do, all this the stuff in Delaware, all this ficticious war did was turn the poor against each other meanwhile white folks still ranking in the big bucks laughing all the way to the bank." "Yeah I cant stand those muthafuckers you know Sha is right about that kill white people shit." Lid shakes his head "Boo I cant go for that, that's hate man" "Desperate times calls for desperate measures cuzzo look at the way your life is fucked up and played the game right and played by all the rules?" They park and get out the minivan and go into the liquor store. Only a few minutes past nine oclock and its open the Chineese, Japaneese, Koreans, Vietnamese who ever own and operate every beer store in Philly and to cope with the sheer terror of just surviving and living in lands where we are unwanted black men, with no money for a phyciatrist find theropy in drowning our sorrows in beer. "Lost in a Roman wilderness of pain, and all the children are insane."

When they get back to Boo's house before they get out the car Boo ask, "Look the boys are back from Iraq and they over my moms house if you and Squater pull off mission impossible and fix your car you wanna go over there and kick it with them?" "If no way man we are fixing my baby today, I cant be on foot so yeah when we get finished I'll go check them out it'll be good to see what there minds sets are coming back from basic training and the war, idiots overseas killing muslims for money." "Yeah well no muslims better kill them over there because I going to go nuts." "I know I don't want anything to happen to them either but the U.S. and everybody else needs to STAY THE FUCK OUT THE DESSERT!!!!" "So how much you gonna pay me for using my tools?" "I just brought you two six packs of beers right?"

They sit out on the steps and knock down beers while Boo washes another car for a neighbor up the street. "What's her story man she bad as shit and don't have no man?" "I know the other person that comes out of her crib besides her sons is that damn Nikki and I cant stand that bitch." "I don't understand how a women so fine don't have no man? She got a good job with the water department, she's already had two boys, she's bad as shit with that Jamaican accent." Boo cuts him off "You know the story man stop playing fucking undercover dike yo, she'll never find a man that makes her kinda money" "Yeah that's crazy man I'll gladly step in over there" "Nikki would eat you alive little cuz, eat you alive." Around eleven thirty Squater pulls up in none other than a clanky run down Monte Carlo that's being held together by duck tape and a prayer. He pulls up and takes a look at Lids sable and immediately says "Yo I'll sell you this thang for five hundred dollars and junk the green car for you?" The balding overweight brown skin nigga is dead serious, but as Lid stands along side the assortment of parts he's already picked from the junk yard and paid for giving up on his car is completely out of the question. "No way man, we can put this back together man just tell me what to do and I will do all the manual stuff." Squater gives Mikhial a frown and a look to say yeah the fuck right. "You really love this car don't you?" "Yeah man she's my baby, come on lets do this." Squater smiles he knows there is no way Lid is going to junk his car and he reallt wanted to see how much Lid loved it.

Together for the next five hours they work on the car, taking apart the entire wheel, the rack, and pinion, the rotors, the brakes, the calibers everything. And when its finished with minimal damage to the body it looks just like it did before the accident. "You can go down the junk yard and get a whole set of rims to match." "Man it doesn't matter I don't need any rims I'm just happy this thing is back together." "We pulled off a miracle because I was ready to call a quits when we couldn't screw that rack back into the frame, you still need to use a drill to make sure it's locked in there because if that comes out while you on the road it's a done deal brother." "Well I don't know what to say Squater but the hundred bucks I promised you is not enough so here's one fifthy and thanks again." Squater takes the money, and corrects his last statement "Don't worry about that screw coming out I locked that sucker in there it's cool." Lid smiles just as Boo warned you better have Squaters money right. "You gonna drive around the block to make sure it runs right?" "Naw me and the incredible hulk have to go out southwest so I'll how she runs on the way over there. Thanks again Squater." "No problem you came through because it looked bleek for a while yo." "Where there's a will there's a way." Sitting on the steps Boo is polishing off the last of the beers from this morning as Lid shakes shakes hands with Squater who accordingly gets into his car and pulls off. "You ready to take this baby on a test run?" Boo belches "Yo cuzzo, I can't believe you fixed your car, that jawn looked like mission impossible and I've damn sure would've quit when y'all couldn't get that shit screwed back onto the frame." "That shit hurt my hand yo, but I had to get my baby running again this my girl man." And with that he jumps into the car through the window mimicking the dukes of hazard one of his favorite television shows growing up and he screams "Yeeeahhhhh Hah!!!!" and he turns the car on. Boo gets in the passenger side using the more conventional way the door, and they pull off Melvin street and make a quick right, and then a left and then another right across the bridge and after driving for a few seconds Lid gives a diagnostic of mhis car. "I need an oil change, and a wheel alignment she's pulling to the left." "That's the side y'all were working on right?" "Yeah it's gonna cost me like a hundred and forty but all things considered all the parts, the labor puttiing her together it all only cost me five hundred dollars that aint bad."

When they get across Market street and into the southside of West Philly he pulls up to aunts house and tells Boo "Look I'm going to the gas station to get some dutches and some gas plus I wanna drive alone for a few minutes I'll be right back." "You wanna have some alone time with your bitch?" "My girl man, my girl" Boo gets out and Lid makes a wreckless u-turn on sixtieth street and takes off towards Baltimore avenue. It's nothing like driving alone just him and his car and as he cranks up the music there's nothing more fitting for the occasion than AZ's "Love Me" as he he reunited with his one true love of driving, the flattered grin, the boyish smile just resonatres of the face of a man who thought he was never going to be driving his precious car again. The joy of this moment earases the physical hurt of the day he got into the accident, and the mental anguish of betrayl from his insurance company Gieco. But on his way back to his car the brings another surprise as a familiar face lies tucked away under a baseball cap, but even the cap cant hide the walk and swagger, not even the shadows as almost simoultainiously they look up at each other and reintroduce each other…. "Lid?" "Dee?" They both smile, hug and shake hands "What's the deal man? Hows your dad?" "You didn't hear, my dad had a stroke, he cant feel his entire left side!" Shocked at the news Lid just says "WHAT! When did this happen?" "A few months ago after my brother was killed." And even louder Lid yells "WHAT!!!" and this time the customers at the gas station even stop pumping gas to listen in. "What!! Billy's dead?" "Yeah dem fucking pigs shot him down in South Philly." "I'm sorry Dee, I'm sorry for your loss." They have a brief moment of silence and Dee begins to elaborate on what took place. "This nigga was down South Street, of all the places sticking people the fuck up with them sickos from down there. I don't know what he was thinking mbut they had been doing that shit for months, so the cops set up a sting. You know you cant be doing that shit down there those white people were probably having a fit." "I'm surprised it took that long a few months shit they got a station right down there." "Yeah I know, so the cops is watching the whole area and they catch him robbing somebody, Billy runs off them niggas he was with jump in the wheel and pull off. They slow down to wait for him to get in and the cops just open fire on Billy, the car like nigga season and they just unloaded right on South Street they just shot the car up. Riddled Billy with bullets my brother looked like Sonny in the Godfather at the funeral." Lid just shakes his head "Damn" "He was running the propane yard but you know my dad don't be paying much so he got with a click and went all out." "I know you went crazy?" "Did I, I was on a rampage seriously I was on a rampage and them people knew I was about to start killing cops, so when I was on my way back from Jersey I get pulled over just before I hit the tolls and they keep me for some warrant from like 2001." "Get the fuck outa here all the times you been locked up since." "I know but they arranged it becaue they couldn't have me going to war with the police. So I just did like six months over in Mercer County! That shit is crazy I never thought I'd see the day when the muslims get beat down in the prisons." "Huh?" "Yo the place is set up wit these bubbles from A-Z. The guards put all the muslims in the back like W,X,Y,Z, then they put all the bloods in the higher letters. So to get out to go anywhere you have to walk through an army of bloods in the higher bubbles and they used to just fight like royal rumbles everyminute of everyday. Shaking his head in disbelief "for real Lid the bloods aint no joke." "The guards don't stop it?" "Man most of the black guards is bloods and the white boys don't care they just let them fight and its not a real fight because they just beat the muslims down they got the numbers." "Trying to break us huh?" "Naw they are breaking y'all." "So what happened with your condo?" "I lost it, my dog died in the place, I lost everything I mean I just got out a few weeks ago and I'm trying to rebuild everything and survive." "What's up with the yard?" "Its closed down nobody there to run it my Dad is stuck in the house messed up he can hardly talk." "That's crazy Dee I'm sorry everything yo."

"I heard about your shit in Delaware?" Surprised Dee knows anything about his trial and tribulations in Delaware he ask "what stuff?" "Some bitch said she rapped you and gave you AIDS, yo she put that shit up on her my space page, plus they got another site "Don't date him girl.com" "What!" "Your uncle showed me." If the news of Mr. Sampson and Billy was not enough to bear, the revelation that Teresa and whatever other organization probably Alisha and the Delta's have his, his personal business streaming through cyberspace for all eyes to see defeated he just slumps his shoulders and tries his hardest to hold back tears. "Well my test came back negative, I'm gonna get that bitch a swear to God, fucking church people man this shit is crazy." "Fuck it man you know what I say live each day like it's your last." "Wish it was that easy Dee, what's your number you know I'm…" he rubs his nose to let Dee know he's snorting coke. "For real!! When this happen?" "On labor day I had a few bags, Rick James is right terrible terrible drug yo. But I really want to invest some money and grab some cause I'm working out the airport and I got a few extra bucks." Dee nods his head and they exchange numbers and shake hands. "I'll call you Dee, I'm sorry about your father, and I'm sorry bout Billy be easy yo."

Shocked about the news he just got from his old boss, Lid drives back to Aunt Beverly's house with his mouth wide open, and his heart and soul shattered into pieces. His own people would sink to the level of completely destroying him under the guise of fighting terrorism. How could someone even claim belief in anything after bragging that she raped and murdered another human being, how the fuck is she even still walking the streets? As he pulls up to his Aunt Beverly's house he takes a deep breathe because now he has do deal with his two cousins who serve in the devils army and watch as they are worshiped as war heroes he holds back tears as he steps out of his car and continues the trajedy that has become his life.

# "Niggaz Can't be serious"

Sura XLII ayat 61

> "And (Jesus) shall be a sign (for the coming of) the hour
> (of Judgement) Therefore have no doubt about the hour but
> follow ye Me: this is a straight way.

IT'S LATE AND LID's been drinking the combination of Johnny Walker whiskey, a fresh blunt, and a few lines of cocaine has Lid feeling like he can do anything, and so he does. As he stumbles out of his Uncle's apartment and down the stairs all he sees is anger and frusteration, envy, and despire. And the streets of Philadelphia would now have to pay the penalty for Lids ungodly feelings. He jumps into his car and just burns rubber as he pulls off onto sixty third street towards city line avenue. Flaming through the traffic in and out of cars just missing red lights as the yellow light flashes, Lid is hell bent on getting on the expressway and letting go. Music blasting Voodoo Chile by Jimmy Hendrix Lid sees his destination and takes off when the light turns green like a drag racer he speeds ahead of the pack and turns onto the expressway. With no thought of the traffic he just presses down on the gas and like a bat out of hell he's on his way swerving in and out of lanes almost clipping cars, until he exits the expressway and gets off on Wayne Avenue. Everything like a blur as Lid just darts through Germantown violently pulling off when the lights go from red to green. He gets to sixty six and broad street and begins his descent into North Philly. Under strict orders from his brother Shereef Lid has not been down North Philly in almost a year, his meltdown and exodus from Delaware and meeting that followed with Omar was his last stint in this part of town. Their friendship has been broken since that day Lid always keeps an ear to the streets and word on the streets is that he is a dead man if he is seen in North Philly, the combination of the coke and liquer has Lid completely forgetting about fear and as he descends into North Philly past Logan, past Lehigh avenue, Erie, Alleghany the people in the street, the people driving glance at Lid and give him a ghostly stare saying without speaking a word "What you doing down here?" With music on full blast playing Nortorious BIG "I hope y'all niggas Sleep" Lid darts into Oxford county full of envy and hate. Like a child throwing a tantrum he blazes through stop signs, and street lights, as if the streets of Philly was his personal race track with no regard for anything or anyone, until he stops at the top of Omar's block, and rev's his engines. In the blink of an eye he's off and darts down the block, finished starting trouble Lid pulls of onto Girard avenue and begins to head back to West Philly. People walking by just shake their heads in disbelief because they know in a town where the slightest misstep could lead to death, actions like this have very swift and serious consequences. He makes it back to his uncles apartment and staggers up the stairs,  his head a little more clear Lid takes a seat in the recliner, and immediately a car pulls up in front of the building. From outside he hears a familiar honk, two quick honks back to back, he remembers that call but in better days it was for a double date at the movies, hang out in the clubs, or just sparking up some green and laughing it up. This was different Lid knew there would be consequences for his actions but not this fast, and with all his courage he gets up to face the ramifications of his actions. This was the show down he was asking for and he complies with Omar's demands and goes to the closet and grabs his pistol. On the way to the window he also picks up his prayer rug with pistol and prayer rug in hand he looks outside and yeah it's Omar in a car he does not recognize but as they look at each other both of them know that one of them could die tonight. Mikel puts his prayer rug up against the window, letting Omar know if it is written that he dies tonight he will pray to Allah before he takes his last breath. Lid begins to pray Isha prayer and by the time he gets to the end he's no longer scared after replaying in his mind what could possibly happen he is fully prepared to kill or be killed and as he Salaam's out he quickly grabs his gun and rushes out the door. Omar is the murderer of muslim's and people in general, not because it was the righteous thing to do but because he's greedy and worships money he's lost his soul to money and the possession of material things. As he descends down the steps Lid thinks to himself Allah has put me here to slay this demon, heart still pumping almost mocking the way he drove through the city streets just minutes before, would that be his last joy ride? As he opens the door to the apartment building and breathes the cold air produces a cloud and looks left and then right and there is nothing. Relieved he exhales which produces another cloud and then goes upstairs, his high blown, he spends the remainder of the night sitting in darkness left hand glued to his gun, and thinks to himself if "I better slow down because death is getting very, very close to him." The next morning Lid awakes with the sun, his gun lying next to him fully loaded he quickly picks it up, thinking about his little cousin Malik finding it, but its too late for that as Malik is fully awake and standing in the dinning room. Lid knows Malik was eyeing his gun and only by the mercy of Allah his young cousin thought better and did not pick up the loaded gun. "How long you been standing there?" "I don't know" "Yo don't do that again, and you better not think about touching my gun" "I wasn't going to touch it" "Stop lying man did you eat breakfast?" "No, I can't pour the milk" "Did you wash you face and hands?' " No" "That's disgusting man Lid goes into the bathroom when all of a sudden he gets a call on his cell phone. To his surprise it's Dee calling him this early in the morning something must of happened last night, Lid quickly answers. "Yo what's the deal?" Skipping the formalities Dee quickly asks "That was all you last night huh?" Surprised Lid really wakes up and ask "damn it was that deep, you know about it already?" "Man you know you are not supposed to be in North Philly, the whole city is talking about it." "Yeah well I got a little drunk and brave." Dee laughs "You were drunk by yourself like NAS huh?" "Exactly, that shit almost went down like the O.K. coral last night." "Be careful yo no need to start any trouble it's enough bullshit going on out there no point addn yo self to the homicide list for no reason." Lid uncharecteristly snaps back "No reason?! That's nigga's trying to kill me popping up all over the city where ever I am at. What do you want me to do? He knows that bitch killed my daughter and then he lied acting it wasn't my baby! That's conduct unbecoming of a muslim! But you wouldn't understand that." Taken aback because Lid is always cool Dee just ends the conversation "Lid I said what I have to say be careful and stop starting shit." Dee hangs up the phone and Lid and takes heed to the warning. Refocussing on today's events Dee puts his gun on the sink and begins to brush his teeth and wash his face when he interrupted by his younger cousin Malik's knocking on the bathroom door. "I'm hungry

Lid could you make me some cerial?" "Yeah I will be out in a second, go to your room and make your bed up." Malik does so and Lid quickly leaves the bathroom, pistol in hand he goes to the closet and unloads the gun keeping the clip in his back pocket, and placing the pistol in the box at the top of the closet, when he is interrupted "I'm finished" grinning like the McDonalds character grimuse Malik startled Lid as he just put his gun up kids are a lot smarter than they look and Malik quickly ask "What's that a gun?" " Stay out of my closet and if you touch it I am going to kill you." Malik gets somber and explains "I'm not going to touch it I don't even want to see it, that's why I stayed in the dining room this morning." "Smart kid, so what do you want for breakfast?" "Trix, mixed with Cinnamon toast crunch" "Sounds like a plan, Lid makes his little cousin breakfast and then gets ready for his day. Today is inauguration day for the city of Philadelphia the Mayor, and new city council members are sworn in, Lids cousin Boo has tickets to the day's events and he gives hima call just to make sure everything is a go. "Yo Boo are we still going down to city hall today?" "What's my motivation? Don't you have to go to work?" "Naw I already asked for the day off last week man come on you know I want to get down there and brush shoulders with the people in power." "Yeah you ain't nothing but trouble we are leaving in like fifteen minutes, I'll meet you downtown at city hall just call me peace cuzzo." Lid hangs up the phone and gets dressed for city hall, the historic building that dates back to the days when our nation was first created, Lid always enjoys being star struck when he visits city hall. In center city he meets up with his cousin Boo who is accompanied by his two twin step daughters Kendra and Kia. "As Salaam Alaikum Cuz" wa Laikum Salaam Lid" The two girl twins have crushes on Lid and as soon as they see him they blush and say "Hi Lid" Lid loves it but the girls are only twelve so he just smiles and says "What's up Kia? What's up Kendra? Y'all ready to see history?" Together the girls say "Who cares about that new just want the free food." They all laugh and make their way into city hall past the security check and into the elevators "Would you girls stop playing around!" "Come on man let them play and have some fun, nobody's here today let em have some fun." "Yeah let us have some fun!" "Yeah stop bullying us all the time!" "Kia and Kendra he's not always going to around to save y'all butts!" Lid just shakes his head as Boo continues to raise his voice like he's in the street in the horstoric these historic halls.

"These my kids Lid, you want to call shots have your own." "I tried". They continued down the hallways of city hall looking for room number five sixteen unlike most days it's pretty empty so there's no one walking the halls to give them directions or at least tell them they are going in the right way, everyone is over at the academy of music watching Mayor Nutter get sworn into office. But as they follow the room numbers to five sixteen, and as they approach the room a caramel skin very slim women walks out of room five sixteen, and as she passes by Lid he cannot contain himself from speaking and asking a question he already knows the answer to. "Excuse m" he softly grabs her arm and she attentively turns around as if she couldn't wait for him to make the first move. Taken back by her chesser cat grin, long black hair with bronze streaks her black pants are skin tight and her white blouse exposes her shoulders and neck, she just looks like trouble but Lid can't resist it. Grining she answers "Your looking for the inauguration gala?" "Yes" Still grinning at each other she politely points to the room she just walked out of. "You that room there that were you have to go" as she is turned around Lid takes a look at her assets but before she turns around he quickly looks her in the face. "And you are?" "Lid Islam." They shake hands softly "I'm here to history an African American Muslim elected to city council in this day and age." Quickly placing her finger over her lips the women makes the shhh sign and comes closer to Lid in a low tone voice she says " A lot of people don't know he's a muslim we are really not trying to get that out." Surprisingly she greets Lid with the custom greetings of "As-Salaam Alaikum brother" "Wa-Laikum Salaam" they shake hands again but this time its a lot less professional and a lot more personal. "My name is Ashanti Jackson I'm in charge of organizing this event. I was on my way out, but you make yourself comfortable and I will be right back." Always smiling Ashanti and Lid just grin at each other for a few seconds and for the third time since just meeting each other and the chemistry between the two is self evident. Ashanti walks off and Lid watches her walk away, he then turns to Boo and the girls and he exchanges a smile with his cousin thanking him for the ticket to admission because it just paid off." Inside the room is filled with history as the ceiling has a mural of all the signers of the declaration of independace and in the center sits a round table that looks like it comes right out of the days of king author and his knights of the round table. With two flat screen televisions on each side of the room the mayorial ceremony is already taking place around the corner. Lid helps seat some elderly women and shakes hands with a few familiar faces, Boo is a fish completely out of water and it shows as he mingles with party goers and constantly refers to his wife Amina. Lid just smiles as his cousin finally throws the towel in and just sits down giving up on friendly chit chat. Soon Ashanti returns and she starts running the show ordering the twins around assigning them to greet people at the door, rearranging things in the room making it look better and greeting everyone as they enter the room, really working the party  the two of them exchange eye contact and glances with each other as they pass, and Boo sees the chemistry in the air between the two and reminds Lid "She is way out of your league." " I don't have a league cuz I'm already in the hall of fame." Smiling when she approaches Lid Ashanti whispers as she walks by him "In ten minutes I'm going don stairs for a smoke break, but a few minutes later these people are so nosy." Lid nods his head in agreement and soon Ashanti disappears from view and is heading downstairs, and minutes later he soon follows. Outside Ashanti is waiting just about ready to light her new port Lid quickly pulls his lighter out and like Johnny on the spot lights her port. All the pleasentries are thrown out the window and they both go back to their rolls of being gritty Philadelphians trying to win "So what's your story?" Ashanti exhales "I'm so tired of this bullshit, I can't wait to get out of her because this shit is so fake." "Yeah well this politics this city hall stuff is all a show so just play with endurance." "I hear you, I'm always busy I run this company called rags to riches, I rap,I model, and I'm working on this movie." "Wow your busy Ashanti, are you married?" Still locked in eye contact her eyes widen and her chesser cat grin turns into a full blown smile, being tough though she leads on that she just haven't found the right person. "Yeah righ I have to find a man on my level and with my bank account before anything like that happens." Completely different from the way she was inside City Hall Ashanti, comes off like an around the way girl and not a bubble headed sorority girl Lid is used to on college campuses. She's hot blooded, sexy, and cunning. "So who are you brother Islam, roaming the Halls of City Hall?" "Me I'm nobody I'm just here for the food." They both laugh  "No really I'm a witness to this historic event and may this usher in a new era for African American Muslims in Philadelphia and America for that matter." "What are you talking about we are eating?" "No! We are eating the wrong way right across the street at the criminal justice center hundreds of Muslims are processed every day on drug related charges because that's the only way we can eat or make any money as legal jobs are given under qualified Christian job seekers and we are constantly discriminated against. Needing to eat we are forced to engage in illegal activity, we are not the only ones hustling in Philly but we are the only ones getting locked up." "I agree" "Betrayed by the black Baptist we are being manufactured into criminals and that was not the fate of the second generation of African American Muslims, I told them years ago was going to happen, this is the agenda of the federal government to incarcerate and help eliminate Black Muslims, the nation of Islam was on the FBI's list for number one threat to national security. Do you want to know why?" "Intrigued Ashanti nods her head " Because Islam is our true religion when we  organized genocide created by the federal government." "Look at you sounding like Malcom X, so what else do you do besides talk, and start trouble?" Shrugging his shoulders Lid says "That's all I do is rabble rouse and start trouble. In the in between time I work at the we do it all tower making copies, anything else no comments." "Yeah you make copies alright. With a cashmere blazer on, Here's my card, put it away fast because they are always watching." Lid puts the card in his in his back pocket. Out of thin air she pulls some perfume and gum and she gives Lid instructions once they get back upstairs after she fixes her hair sprays perfume, and pops a piece of gum in her mouth, "call me, may be I can plug you in with the right people and you can stop starting trouble. How do I look?" ""Go get em tiger" They both smile and use better judgement not to hug each other no matter much they wanted to and Ashanti takes off back upstairs. Lid waits a few minutes and fixes his tie and sports blazer, and he notices the cops going in and out of city hall paying him much attention, but thinks nothing if it. Back inside the crowd is filling up, as the police commissioner, fire commissioner have arrived, councilman Robinson's entourage has arrived and a few different state representative. Iman Mahdi from Germantown Masjid is there, and he and Lid shake hands and exchange the greetings and a few words. As he stands in line for food he bumps into Nicole an old friend of uncle Sha and she immediately sounds him on his criminal conection. "Aren't you Sha's nephew?" "Yeah I rememeber you Nicole from Wynnefield you used to work for us down South Philly." Sounded Lid quickly denounces his Uncle "He and I haven't talked in a few years." And he quickly turns around dismissing Nicole. As he continues to mingle with the crowd he comes across a very familiar face it's Nasir's mom sister Kareema. She's always been like a mother to Lid but today she is a little bothered and concerned especially considering what took place between her son Omar and Lid just a few hours ago. "As Salaam Alaikum Lid" "Wa Laikum Salaam Mrs. Kareema." Smiling she comes closer to him and whispers "Why don't you come wit me and get some cake?" "Yeah O.K. the two of them walk into the chamber room and head towards the cake, it's not cut yet plus the cake is from Daphneys as Lid recognizes it. "Hey Mrs. Kareema it's not cut yet, plus it's from Dapheneys you know I am boycotting that place." They both laugh, but the warm momement is broken up when Mrs. Kareema gets very serious and ask "What's going on with you two?" Quickly Lid thinks about his next decision if he speaks up and explains the problem he fails a very important test in manhood as a child going to sister Kareema would've been the solution but that's not the answer as an adult this is between the two men, so he looking at her lying with every fiber in his soul he says "Nothing, How's Omar doing I haven't seen him in a while?" She just rolls her eyes and answers "He's fine" They continue to chit chat for a while about politics and issues concerning the city until the crowd from the hallway ushers in as the swearing in ceremony begins. The council room is filled with dignitaries state representatives, present and former city council members, the fire and police commissioner, and acroos the round table councilman Rich Robinson and a group of friends hob knob as they enjoy the momement. With camera's flashing the ceremony starts and after every sentence eventhough nothing is being said thunderous applause erupts. Towards the end Lid is on the other side of the table and he and councilman make eye contact and he says "A new start that promises resolutions for revolutionaries!" Lid smiles twelve hours ago he and his best friend were seconds away from shooting each other to death, in the short period of twelve hours he's crossed paths with Omar's mom, met a new women plugged into City Hall, and the streets, and was just promised a new start from the newly sworn in city councilman. Mission accomplished as Lid slips out the doors towards the end, making quick eye contact with Ashanti and giving his cousin Boo a hand shake he's off to work and a cunning smile overtakes the usual somber look as he walks to work.

Saturday comes alon and Lid picks up Asanti from her mothers house in Germantown. One of the last parts of the city inhabited by white's in the late seventies African American families migrated to this part of town from out west philly, Ashanti stays with her mother and step father in a neighborhood tucked away from the crime that now riddles the area. Jamming to Mickeal Teirson in the morning on classic rock 102.9 the Saturday morning sixties show is a collection of real rock and roll from that era. And as he pulls her to house he calls her "As Salaam Alaikum, im out front are you ready?" "I still haven't figured out what boots to wear. I'm unlicking the door now just come upstairs." He does so and once he gets upstairs to her room its filled with clothes all over the place."Sorry I couldn't figure out what to wear today, so I was in here trying on everything." "Well you did a good job Ashanti" With a black skin tight catsuit orange mink vest and boots to match Ashanti looks like she is going to a fashion show instead of shooting video for here documentary. But all in good time he thinks to hiself, nervous she rambles on on making sure she has everything. "Brother could you grab those bags it's the camera and all my stuff?" He quickly picks up the three heavy bags and together they walk out the bedroom door and up and out the front door. He pops the trunk open and puts the bags in "Come brother its cold out here?" Lid closes the trunk and being the gentleman that he is opens the passenger side door to let Ashanti in and the inside panel of the door falls right off. She laughs "what's on here brother you gotta get this fixed if I'm going to be riding with you." "I stay on the drivers side so it never bothers me and I'm always solo so you know" She gives him a look shaking her head excuses excuses will not do and he quickly complies "I will get it fixed next time" She slides in the car and Lid closes the door behind her. As he walks around the back of the car she passes the test, made famous in a Bronx Tale Ashanti reaches over and unlockes the drivers side door. Lid looks up at the sky and nods his head in agreement she's a keeper. As usual he quickly pulls off "You drive way too fast brother." "Relax yo I know what I am doing" "Just don't get into an accident I don't need that shit, because I will sue your ass, you have insurance don't you?" Lid looks over at Ashanti and just frowns his face like yeah right and picks up speed. She starts to laugh "Your crazy we have to pick up my number two up Tia she lives closs to here in the jungle." Jamming to his classic rock and roll Ashanti quickly turns the radio station "Yo what are you doing?"

"No way brother we are not listening to no rock and roll." "Well I'm not listening to any rap off the radio." "Well then we are going to listen to my cd" and she digs in her bag and pulls out a cd, and puts it in the radio. "I made this when I was in Atlanta, turn right here and go down this block." Annoyed because her raps are the worst he says sharply "I know were the jungle is at I grew up around here." "What happened?" "My moms just up and left the house after I went away to school knowing that I was going to sell the house to pay back my loans, she lies and tells me she is not going to move and then inOctober just leaves." "That's mean what were you always in trouble or something growing up?" "Naw I was never in any trouble she's just a mean bitch when she wants to be, that's what happens when you forget Allah and don't submit to Allah's will, all that feminism shit is just another one way trip to hell, and its dark and hell is hot." "I don't agree with that y'all can't be using Islam to abuse us." "I never abused anyone but I will make the calls about what's right and what's wrong even if it hurts me in the long run the right way is always the better way." They pull up to block and she says "Right here this is Tia's house, are you coming in?" Sarcastically he says "No I'm going to stay out here and listen to your cd." "I'll be right back" as soon as she leaves Lid snatches the cd out of the sterio and turns his classic rock and roll back on. She soon disappears into Tia's house and Lid recalls as directly in front of him is the rec center he used to play little league football at for the North West raiders. They won the championship that year, but he had lost contact with most of his teammates but over the years you hear rumors of guys getting locked up, or murdered but that's the way it is in Philly, but as he waits for Ashanti who is taking forever he remineces and thinks to himself "damn those were the good old days." After about twenty minutes Ashanti finally emerges from the house with a delicious dark skinned piece of chocolate cake following behind her. That must be Tia he thinks to himself and as she walks down the steps her titties just bounce up and down in the air,she has a slender figure with a short hair cut, blue jeans and tube top, and doesn't look as glamourous as Ashanti but just as good looking.He can do nothing but think of having as threesome with the girls as they walk towards the car. "We getting into this, I thought you said he was a boss!?" Lid sits up in the window of the car and quotes Jay-Z "Imma baller for real no crome on the wheel." "Yea right" Tia replies and once they get inside Lid becomes just a glorified taxi driver as Ashanti and Tia just talk about nonscence. Planning their day were to buy weed from, how they are going to the documentary, and what they are going to do afterwards. "Do you know were master street is in West Philly?" "Yeah" "That's were we are going, Lid jumps on the expressway and in minutes they arrive on Master "This house right here" Lid recalls the three story house "Hey this used to a strip club and after hours spot? They used to have camera's in the alley way and that was the only way you could get in, the kitchen was turned into a bar, and the first floor had couches everywhere and dancers all the living room and dining room, upstairs you could nail in the bedrooms for a few dollars." Looking at each other in disbelief the two girls simoutainiuosly say "OK Boss!" Tia exclaims "I used to work their how did you know about that place?" "Somebody put me on to it back in the late nineties." Ashanti feeling left out interrupts "Well its different now my father lives here, they get out and Mihail grabs the bags from the trunk, Tia reaches to grab a bag when he stops her "I got this." Feeling threatened by Mikahil presence Tia tries to make herself usefull because whatever was going on before this they used to either catch a taxi or catch the bus to get to film the documentary. With Lid around who has a car and is a man Tia could soon be out of the picture so she goes the extra mile to make herself useful. At the front door Ashanti knocks and says to Lid "I hate this mutha-fucker he is always trying to feel me up." He says nothing and they continue to wait until a very large man comes strolling to the door, with a friendly smile he shows his silver teeth and just as Ashanti called it a few seconds ago he is feeling her up as he hugs her." Lid immediately recognizes him it's the pimp brother Idris, uncle Sha introduced them years ago and Idris used to hook Lid up with strippers when he used to saty in one of his sisters apartment complexes. Back in those days Lid was applying for the fire department in Philadelphia, working at his original job on 36th and Market. Put on by Leslie Abraham the CEO of PMG using his writing skills he wrote Mr. Abraham a letter explaining the situation he was in, the way things are these days its difficult to have any relation with Jews, Christians, and Muslims as the city and the country for that matter is completely polarized post September 11th. But Lid reached back in time and for a few months h made enough income to buy food and pay rent, in Philly. The final stand between he and Uncle Sha took place during this time. Idris's sister Leandra was the land lord of the building and one day she had some choice words to say about Uncle Sha. Eventhough he and Uncle Sha were already going their separate ways he always felt like he should've stood up for his family, and his uncle as Leandra went on and on about how Uncle Sha was stupid for taking Naim and Khadejah out of school and how Khadijah was going to grow up to be a stripper or something. She was basically trashing Uncle Sha, Lid was too weak to speak up against Leandra, one because she was the land lord of the apartemt two because his relationship with Uncle Shamp really swayed after the trip to Ohio, and Mikahil was suspicious of his uncle for stealing his missing passport. It all came to head when hurricane Katrina hit New Orleans and Uncle Sha was planning a trip to New Orleans. Being the white colar king of Philadelphia he was planning a trip to cash in on the relief being offered to victims of the hurricane.Lid refused to go because as he told it "The people of  New Orleans were very good to me, I can't go down there and capitalize on them its not right." And standing at the top of the spiral stairs Uncle Sha leaves the apartment and walks out of Lids life for good and since that day the two former revolutionaries have not spoken.

Idris sees Lid and smile comes across the large mans face "As Salaam Alaikum" "Wa Laikum Salaam" They shake hands and Idris ask "What are you doing here?" "I met Ashanti downtown at city hall, the rest is history its been a while." "Yeah I got new girls, have you talked to your uncle?" "Naw he and I on the outs." "Naw man you shouldn't let nothing call you guys on the outs brothers have to stick together." "You know his twist I did not want to go down to New Orleans with him those people were good to me." "Man o ideals and morals huh well out here young blood those things will get you no where." "I'm learning the hard way." They go inside the living room and looking more like a place of residence and not a strip club he begins to set up the camera as Idris and Ashanti talk about her fathers care. "So he's been on time with his rent huh?" "Yeah I have to get to the supermarket and get some more food for him but besides that he's o.k. says he likes walking to the Lincolns Fried Chicken around the corner because hes supporting the muslims." All of a sudden a brown skin old man slowly walks down the steps and like seeing gifts on Christmas morning Ashanti says with all exuberance "Daddy!" and runs to the bottom of the steps to greet him with a big hug." Tia comes over and hugs him too, smiling the thin gray haired old man greets everyone "Wa Laikum Salaam" and calmly he begins to dish out orders to Idris  "Brother could you get some lunch meat please, there's nothing in the refrigerator but water, can we go to the supermarket tomorrow." "We were just talking about that daddy." Not as casual and more attentive Idris responds "No problem brother Bains, is it all right if we go tomorrow?" he nods his head yes. "Daddy I want you to meet a brother who used to go to sister clara Muhammed school his parents used to work their too, Lid I would like to meet my father brother Alfred Bains." "As Salaam Alaikum" "Wa Laikum Salaam" they shake hands and theexcitment oozes from Lid's face as he resonates a smile. Brother Bains is a legend Mikahil would here stories of how they used to rob banks up and down the east coast in the sixties during the days of the nation of Islam. Uncle Sha would speak the world of Brother Bains who went by the nick name of Don't change Bains because even in the misdt of a bank robbery he always kept his calm, cool demeaner, Iman Malik was part of the crew in those days and Big Boss Chritopher Samuels. They ran the whole east coast and spread all the way out to parts of the Midwest, Chicago, Indiana, and Detriot. So meeting brother Bains is very exciting and Lid hangs on everyword that he speaks. So who are your parents that used to work at the school? "My mom's was sister Halima Islam, and my dad is brother Rashad Islam. He thinks for a second and says "I don't know Rashad, what did he look like?" "Dark skinned clean shaven, and he used to brush his hair backwards so it was pretty high. He shakes his head "I ont remember him." "You said your moms was sister Halima?" "Yes she used to work in the bookstore, and for the treasury department." He smiles "Light skin, and always used to wear those glasses?" Mikahil smiles "yeah that's my mom." "I remember you now they didn't think ou were going to make it, you almost died in the hospital." "Yeah that was me." "So how is she doing?" "Still working, but not good she stop making salats and practicing the religion thinks its all a bunch of male domination and abusive to women." "I'm sad to hear that she was always such a strong believer in those days may Allah habe mercy o her soul." "In Shah Allah" "The trick of Satan is to have you believe that freedom means you can do anything you want, just because you can do anything does not mean you should especially if it's the wrong thing to do and hurts others. Allah is the only controller of all things for the Quran says he is the master of all knowledge and all things in this world and the universe. So are you going to be doing the interview?" Lid shakes his head and Ashanti quickly speaks up "No daddy this is my documentary

I'm going to be interviewing you, he's just going to be working the camera." And they do so and Ashanti takes a seat next to her father and starts the interiview as Lid begins to roll the camera. "I'm here with the legendary Alfred Bains one of the original gangsters. So Brother Bains whats the difference between the old days and the guys who run the street now?" Brother Bains replys humbly "The big difference is the commitment to community in our day we commited crimes but all the spoils of the crimes were put back into the community to help uplift us and transition out of those days. We lived in a day when a black man could not get a job and it did not matter if you were a veteran or not, the blackman was and still is on the extermination list of that white devil." "What do you mean still is on the list we have programs like affirmative action, and equal rights now?" "Yeah but they don't reinvest that blessing back into the community and these days the affirmative action stuff includeds women and Hispanics. We spend too much of our time buying clothes, fancy new cars, and drinking the muslims too wasting the bounties of Allah, that money shoul be used to do good and not become slaves to these women buying material things." Another difference is the drugs being sold its destroying the community we sold reefer, that's not like this crack that has crippled the black community. Without a community we have no future." "So brother Baines tell us about your lineage and past?" "I hold up I forgot my daughter was interviewing me we came from the lineage of Geronimo and within my viens my family has been fighting this devil for hundreds of years but these days the new generation has been brain washed to destroy themselves. It's not like before when they had to chase down and hunt the native Americans, naw these days the music, the drugs, the way we are portrayed on screen all of leads to the us destroying ourselves." Lid I tapped on the shoulder by Idris and he motions to Lid to follow him into the kitchen, Lid lets Tia know to jump on the camera and she does so. "So you haven't talked to your Uncle in how long?" "Like three years now" "Wow" "How did you hook up with Ashanti?" "I met her downtown at councilmans Robinson's inauguration." "Well look we are old friends so I am going to tell you she looks good and has a lot of guys chasing her but she is a lot of trouble and will get you in a lot of trouble." "I noticed she has like two sides everything is all nice and smooth one minute and the next minute she flips out on you." "I'm glad you noticed that about her, she hasn't talked to me that way though." "Good and don't let her she's always dealing with those knuckle head wanna be gangsters out there, and I know you your always staying out of trouble so becareful." "She's warm and that softer side of her is the muslamina inside of her." "Yeah well that other side is a queen pen and the only thing to blame for that is this western society." "We messed that up when we gave them the right to vote."They laugh and go back into the living room. Brother Bains is going on about this generation "It's the music, the television, and the fast money, they don't work hard the drug game has been handed to them as a means o their own destruction. We had neighborhood gangs growing up and when the honorable Elijah Muhammed showed up with the message of Islam all the gangs converted to Islam it gave us dignity and self respect. These kids today run around they are in the blood gang, talking about they are the blood of Christ and the girls are even worse in some dike mafia most of them are harder than the boys I go outside and can't tell the difference between them the girls dress in bagy  jeans the boys wearing tight jeans its like the twilight zone." The Baptist church should be ashamed of itself we should be ashamed of ourselves in the muslim community not casting out homosexuals that's a crime against Allah and brings me back to the point just because you can do it does not mean it's the right thing to do.This is all completely backwards from what the nation taught us they have no God, no code, no set of principles we were an army set out to up lift the black race after hundreds of years of persecution all over the globe. Now we an army our own people set out to finish the job of the original terrorist group the ku Klux klan and white supremacmacy started wiping out the original decendants of Adam. A knock on the door and the ringing of the bell stops the recording. "Thank you daddy!" And as soon as the red light goes off a little bit of the queen pn comes out Ashanti as she hollers at Lid for leaving his post "What are you doing I thought I told you to work the camera, if you want to chit chat with Idris do it on your own time were trying to make a movie here!" "We were catching up on old times my bad." Idris goes to answer the door and when he does a sharped dressed middle aged man in a three piece suite with balding hair but a shiggady sharp shape up walks into the room. Ashanti jumps up off the couch and gives the man a hug. "As Salaam Alaikum" "Wa Laikum Salaam" Brother Bains arises from the couch and shakes his hand as he sees his daughter turn right into pussy cat mode, which he must be the money and that's confirmed when she introduces him to brother Bains. Dad this is State Representative Tom Waters, and this my dad Alfred Baines. Represetative Waters takes a seat on the couch and Ashanti begins to interview him back behind the camera Lid begins to roll tape "I'm here with a special guest all the way from Harisburg State Reprentative Thomas Waters, Representive Water's what are some of the problem facing our community?" Like a seasoned politician Mr. Waters like a robot begins to answer "Education and lack of young people finishing high and going on to college and finishing school. There are too many young smart children not just African American but all young people just combing the streets not in school." Lid whispers to Idris "I graduated top of my class and I'm sitting I'm broke as hell sitting in here with these losers, bizaro world Idris when are things going to turn around?" Idris looks at his watch and lets Lid know in time, in time. Representative Waters continues "This city, this state for that matter has many universities and I don't understand why Philadelphian in the inner city don't take advantage of that? What about gun crime, how do we stop the violence?" "Education is one way, another thing is strict gun enforcement laws these kids stalking our streets should spend at least five years in prison I commend the attorney general for attaching stiff laws to illegal gun possession especially if you have some type of banned substance as well. I propose the plan that implimated in Washington D.C. a complete ban on hand guns in the inner cities. We have to regulate who gets gun permits and get all these guns off our streets. In my day we fought like men and sometimes it would take a few fights a day to get your point across but everybody was still alive at the end of the day." Ashanti continues to interview as Representative Walters goes on rambling, Idris grabs Lid again off the camera who lets Tia know to take over and they go into the dining room. Idris pulls out the china closet and grabs a shot gun out. "Wow" exclaims Lid, he knows its not a good idea to buy anu guns from Idris because for one thing he is a stick up boy, and occasionally things get bloody and this gun might have a few bodies on it, but he plays along and kistens to the offer. "This is brand new young blood, I'll give it to you for three hundred." I don't know man it doesn't have any bodies on it?" Shaking his head no "Naw why would I do that to you come on brother you know we are fam." "Alright I have to wait until I get paid next Friday." "Well you don't have like a hundred now to put down as a deposit?" "Naw Iris I'm light right now, I had to pay rent this week I have wait until I get paid again." "You mean you are not hustling?" "No that's not my twist?" "Then what are you buying it for?" "Because I have to go hunting." Still blinded by revenge from what happened in Delaware Lid still has plans find James, Teresa, and anyone else for that matter involved with his humiliating defeat. "Alright I will hold it for young blood because we go back." "Thanks" they shake hands and after Idris puts the gun up they go back into the living room were Ashanti is finishing up her interview. "Well thank you very much representative Walters for your time. The two get up and they hug and as he grabs his overcoat Lid takes the opportunity to make aquainteces with Representative Walters. "As Salaam Alaikum, nice to me you sir, Lid Islam I had some questions about some of the points you raised." "Wa Laikum Salaam" Annoyed because he didn't think he was going to come across a real live reporter today Representative Walters listens as Lid ask " The gun problem in Philadelphia is about illegal guns on the streets, so how does enforcing stricter laws on gun permits solve that problem?" He rolls his eyes,Lid knows he is never going to get the real answer to this question that enforcing stricter permit laws only helps the corrupt police department, they have access to the guns, and the drugs and the police department helps fuel this war in the streets by providing these kids with the guns and drugs to spread terror in the city. Take Afghanistan for example, the CIA provided these people with the guns and taught them how to make bombs, henceforth it creates a need to go and POLICE this people. The same technique is used in Philadelphia, gone are days of one person controlling the rackets like Johnny Malzanno or Iman Malik, the police run the drug game, this keeps the financers away from any real time as the hard work storing the narcotics, and delivering it is done by the same people who swore to uphold it, when the lines between whats right and whats wrong are crossed and everyone is living in gray that's when you have the problems you have today six officers slain in the line of duty in a two year period because people don't respect the badge. Corruption spreading from the city to the state capital,but Represntative Walter will not get into that discussion as he simply says " The point is getting all guns off the streets, and letting the police do their job protecting the citizens, the students, and property here in Philadelphia, yes you have the right to defend yourself, your home and property but keep your gun in the house and if you feel safer with it stay in the house with it. Not wanting to aggravate the man

Lid moves on to his next question "One more thing I graduated college at the top of my class, and I still cannot find a job in the city that goes along with my degree, my loans are pilling up and I'm almost in default we were told in the Forty Two  era to go to college and get and education to help talke care of this city and now they wont let us in." "There are a few options you can look into I suggest the military because they are always hiring and we do have troop shortages, and I am sure your signing bonus could take care of those loans.On another note about the changing face of Philadelphia we are an inclusive city now and we look forward to extending our arms to people of all walks of life especially the gay community, and finally if things don't work out in your home town you can always move I was born and raised in Detriot and ended up here twenty years ago, so you have to keep trying." "Alright that's enough, Lid representative Walters did not come here to be grilled." Ashanti grabs Reprentative Walters and ask Lid "Could you hand me my coat off the banister?" He does so and she says "I'll be right back we have to talk business." Yeah right thinks Lid he is probably going to suck him off in the car, they leave and Lid takes the time to sit back down on the couch with brother Baines again. "You know you are right those are the same problems that exist today its like a cycle. I think it all stems from September 11th, we had a chance to step up both communities the black Baptist and the black muslims and we did not. In exchange for for our silence we lost our souls the Baptist got jobs from this faith based initiative, the muslims classified as terrorist were forced into hustling to survive or starving to death as our family cousins, sisters, aunt and uncles turned against us beating us down with the acceptance of Christ. Brother Bains nods his head "The honorable Elijah Muhammed told us the day would come when that devil would divide our people and they did it to us divide and conquer. But they also succeded in turning our most sacred and cherished gift the black women against us. That goes back to the days of slavery these days its all ecomonic if the black man is not the bread winner in the household he cant keep his castle it belongs to her, and she has the final word. That undermines our legacy our kingship and that is oppression and this is not the future for y'all. That second generation of muslims you young brothers and sisters were supposed to be professional completely away from crime. We went backwards black muslims running around sloppy dressed like the Arabs, in skirts and sisters completely covered up, don't get me wrong yes its part of Islam but what sense does it make to dress like that if inside you don't behave like a muslim, its what's inside that counts, "Allah says I am closer to you than your jugular vien! Inside is what matters dressing for show does no good if your actions contradict the teachings of the Prophet Muhammed peace and blessing be upon him." In the first we were clean cut, this is not y'all fate just hold on brother in shah Allah things will turn around for us and the truth will be reveled Allah says "We did not create this would for mere sport we created it for just ends." They pause and Brother Bains looks at Lid so light skin was your mother than your uncle is Sha?" Lid nods his head "You come from a good family, hows your uncle he was a soldier back in the day?' "He lives close by here, and I haven't talked to him for a while but from what I understand he has completely given up the religion. He thinks that religions are enslaving us and the rich and powerful are using it to turn us against each other. He's gone back to his African roots and has gone all organic, took my cousins out of school, and really doesn't leave the house. He's pushing this whole new adgenda because the food we eat is killing us, and the public schools are teaching us to be slaves and not Gods." In some ways he is right but that's why as muslims we are supposed to eat Halal food only, you don't see the jews eating anything else but Koser food that's why, the additives in the food, the way the cattle is raised is all about making money on one end and cutting cost on the other. So he's right" "Here's the busniness cards he is passing out" Lid reaches into his wallet and pulls out the business card, brother Baines takes a look at the business card pulls out his glasses and reads aloud

"I take this Oath Of My Ancestors, To Fight For OUR Restoration & Liberation World Wide. Against The Whites, Their Offspring And Collaborators. If I Fail to Devote Each Day Of My Life To OUR Victory My This Oath Kill Me And Be A Curse On My Entire Family" www.race 1st.tv

"He's right but hate will never defeat hate how did he get so far and extreme?" "When Forty Three  stole the elections in 2000 he and I became activist, revolutionaries we protested, we went to anti war meetings, one time we went to D.C. with a billboards attached to an expedition that said "Stop the War Start The Impeachment" Impressed brother Bains smiles and begins to pay closer attention to Lid as he gets excited and begins to talk about the old days and the rebel alliance. "He got disenfranchised because no one wanted to join no youn people that what was missing, the meeting were filled with old hippies or really extreme left wing groups. But the major problem was that no one was at these meeting addressing the real problems our problems. So we started our own thing and got a building down North Philly, the oigional Temple 12 on Susquehana." "Oh yeah I remember those days, your right that's were it started." "Now you would think that in the heart of Temple university college students would want to join a progressive movement but no way, they were not interested, and it was just the two of us." "They did not get involved because they were not incharge." "Right!" So he gave up his citizenship and turned his social security card in." "Confused brother Bains shakes his head and says "I don't follow?" Lid pulls his social security card out and turns it around, on the back of the card are a series of red numbers during the days of FDR a banking system was created and the gold standard was no more. Everyone in this country is insured with the Federal Reserve for up to one million dollars to engage in capitalism. Our very existence is based on interest as the loans we get from the World Bank and the IMF is based on our population how many people we have taking part in capitalism, and as we both know interest is un Islamic and sinful. He has the right idea but I wasn't brave enough to go to this extremes." He picks up the business card, "For me it was only about Forty Three  because he was not supposed to be Presiedent, Al Gore should be President because he representated the future and progreesion into the future the right way, Forty Three  has done nothing but set the country back, and the world for that matter starting two different wars and reestablishing white supremacy which was slowly fading away. I'm not going radical and extreme and I cant't give up on the country all together." "You kno the Prophet Muhamed peace and blessing be upon him said you should not hold a grudge against another muslim for more than three days.Call your Uncle brother. Do you have any children?" Mikahil shakes his head "Are you married?" He smiles "Yes but No" "It can only be one or the other good brother" "I'm getting a divorce just waiting for the paperwork, I married this African women because she cried and cried to me about getting deported so I married her so she could stay here like how are you going to deport an African after we were brought here in chains?" "So what happened?" "She aked for a divorce said because I was not Christian it wasn't working going to work out.I'm still confused because I didn't think that had to do with anything, but all the crap I was going through in Delaware with those Christians I had to leave and I was not about to stick around and ask why? But when I swore on the bible in my mind and in my heart I just kept saying I'm doing this to help someone I still believe in America, and this was not about the money." "Believe in Allah brother, and continue to make salat and ask Allah for forgiveness because the bible is still a holy book, but Allah is the most merciful. Well you are a very informed young man keep up the good work." Brother Bains just made Mihails day and the glowing smile that comes across his face is clear evidence of it "Stick around with my daughter it's rare to see Ashanti bring home a man of such good character and nobility. They shake hands Ashanti comes back into the house. "Alright people that's a rap, Tia we got to make that move. New guy break up the camera and pack the equipment up we are outta here." "Ashani could I talk to you for a minute?" "Sure daddy whats up?" "I don't get my check until next week and I have to get some food in here, could you loan me a dollars?" "Ashanti smiles no problem daddy." And fresh from the bank she pulls out an envelope full of crisp bills." She takes out two twenties and gives it to her father, "Thank you" they hug and kiss the group is ready to go. Lid shakes hands with Idris who reminds him "Don't forget what we talked about." "Next week, I got you." As Ashanti goes to open the door once again the panel falls off, and she says " You gotta get this door fixed." "I know" He puts the bags in the trunk and gets into the car Ashanti hands him a twenty dollar bill and says "Tom approved the budget, so we can continue filming and now I need to get high." "I feel her that girl" "Getting tired of fucking with that old nigga Tia you should here his ass stuttering and shit." Tia starts cracking up in the back seat, and as Lid drives Ashanti is giving him directions go downthis street an stop at this house. When he pulls up to the house and the girls begin to talk about what they are going to buy. "All right get a quarter pound of green and see if he has some blow." Lid quickly look over at her when she says powder and she quickly replies "its for Tia." "Its cool I just started snortin things get real focused and intense." Impressed Ashanti giggles and replies smiling "You are full of surprises." She gets out the car and it is just he and Tia,and as soon as the car door closes she says "So when are going to tell Ashanti that you are married?" "That's my business, you shouldn't of been listening when I was talking to her father. Our conversation was between men." "That was the fifties women are equal now." "Naw y'all live outside your roles here in America yo you been here all day with me and Ashanti who's home watching your kids?" "How do you know I have kids?" "Don't you?" "My friend, who lives with me, I'm working today." "They your kids and somebody else is watching them while you run the streets with me and Ashanti?" "We working nigga what you talking bout." "No I work Monday to Friday downtown, this is defined as running the streets. And after y'all ditch me tonight I bet y'all gonna exchange dike moves with ya kids upstairs asleep." She says nothing and has a look of shock as Lid knows their dirty secret, but he keeps going. "I see the way y'all look at each other its by design the strap ons , the sex toys, freedom right its o.k. these days to be dikes or bi-sexual right? It's the movies, the role models, the music but its not it's a crime against God. No other animals have sex with the same gender except humans, you don't see lions fucking each other do you? You don't see no female momma bears fucking each other?" Tia laughs, "because its unnatural and they cant even think about it." Ashanti returns smiling she ask "What are y'all talking about? I saw you rapping from the street I kow wanna know?" Tia speaks up before Mikahil says a word "This nigga is married!" and Ashanti snaps "What!!!" "Its not a real marriage it's an immigration thing" "Legally nigga you married?" "Yes" "These niggas is crazy first Vince wants to make me his second wife and now you talking about you married.When were you going to tell me?" "I told your dad ealier today" "You just met him?" "Look I don't like that take us home nigga!" "Look I mailed the paper work in last week this thing will be over soon and I will be divorced." But she will have nothing of it "I'm not trying to here that I'll catch a cab home from Tia's house you nigga's is crazy." Lid says nothing and just turns on and up his friend 102.9 classic rock WMGK and drives until he gets to Tia's house, he hands Ashanti and pops the trunk as Ashanti is still rambling on and on "Married what's wrong with you, black men y'all have some serious problems!" "Whatever" hand he just pulls off.

It's Sunday and cruising to the tunes of Sinatra on the a.m. Lid is on his way to pick up his cousin Lester who was just recently released from prison after serving ten years behind bars upstate. Away from his children he ask his cousin to come with him to breakfast at IHOP with his three kids, his mother aunt Sharon, and his little sister Gabbanna. It's the first time Lid has seen Aunt Sharon and Gabbanna since he moved from their house at the end of the summer and if anything the combination of the three will make for an interesting breakfast. He pulls up to the house Lester is staying at and waiting outside on the porch Lester immediately jumps in the passenger side of the car. "What's up little cuz?" "Same old shit trying to find another job and  hold on to the rope. Whats up with you?" "Still working at Bally's plus I got this new job on the way it's part time at the hospital." "Damn you just got out and got two jobs how did you manage that?" The paster at Moms church hooked me up with the gig at Bally's, the new one I got hooked up with the boy Tracy, I don't feel good about it because he's fucking Harold wife but I need the money man." "Yo you staying with Harold cuz, y'all been like brothers I wouldn't do that." "I kno cuz but I need the money" "You don't need it that bad, Harold just got locked up for slashing dude tires and they always going through some domestic shit." "I know cuz but I need the money yo I'm trying to be out here and be broke I just got out man I gotta catch niggers out here making money cuz." "You don't need the money you want the money, these niggas out here taking all that cash to show off for these scandalous bitches look at that shit Harold went to school graduated college, and graduate school nigga got a good job with the city paying the bills, food in the house, clothes on all two hundred of those kids." Lester starts laughing "Yeah it's a lot of them in there" "I know but my point is this all that he's done for his family because he been with her for a long time they was on Queen Latifa show together and she out here cheating on him and you bout to take a job with the nigga that's fucking ya cousins wife, that shit aint cool." "I know I gotta think about it, man what's this shit you listening to?" "Its Sunday man I listen to Sinatra on Sunday's" "Man I'm not listening to no Sinatra what you think you Italian or something." "Naw I just like Frank outside of prayer it's the only peace I get these days." "Lester goes through Lids cd's "You aint got no new shit? Just new Nas, corny ass AZ, that's it? Ohh I'm listening to this" and pulls out the public enemy cd, and puts it in the cd player. "The only reason I'm letting you do that is because it's the PE cd Nas got the best shit out man, and everybody is always sleeping on AZ but name one bad song or one bad bar for that matter his whole catoluge is flawless but people don't feel that they want beats and who ever the radio tells them is hot and that my friend is why hip hop is dead." "I feel you on that its been just a bunch of bullshit out on the radio." "Mind control man there will never be anything like that era again from 1992 when Def Jam re launched LL, Onyx, and Redman, then out west Cyprus Hill, Dre, and Snoop then the Wu-Tang came out Nas, Eric Sermon was hot, Biggie dropped, AZ, Jigga that whole era of rap music was real I don't even know what they be talking about these days its crazy but that's why the kids are crazy." Lester turns up the tunes and as they drive listening to the classic terminator X. They go to pick up all three children from three different baby moms and Lester tries to flirt with each one and get some quick ass even though they all have another nigga in there life. After a little fooling around the girls will have none of that and with the back seat filled with one girl age 11, and two boys ages 11, 12 they pull into the parking lot of IHOP on Roosevelt Boulevard. Already at IHOP Gabbana and Aunt Clareese are already there and as soon as they see Mikahil's car pull into the parking lot they get out the car, carrying her infant son Quadir who has gotten very big since the last time Lid saw the them. As soon as she sees Lid Aunt Clareese gives him a big hug, and ask whats going on with you, it's a good day it's Sunday O get to see my grands and my all together at once." "I know that's why I told him I would do this because all you guys haven't ben together, I'm still working trying to stay out of trouble." "I just brought a new car, the insurance is out the roof, but I needed a new car." "Didn't you just loose the house?" "Yeah I'm living in a room with cousin Tammy and her family right now." "But you just brought a new car?" Flagging her hand she says "Yeah my credit is all screwed up but we got the hook up at conicelli dodge and they approved me, it's the insurense that's the kicker." "Yeah that's why my car is paid for it keeps the insurance a little low, what kind of car is it." "The new Dodge Avenger they just came out this year." "Well congragulations" They stop hugging and Aunt Clareese goes immediately to her grandchildren and she goes from being a grownup to a grandmother and begins to talk baby talk to her grandchildren all included with big hugs and kisses on the cheeks which the boys quickly wipe away from there cheeks. Standing alone is Gabanna holding her son Quadir "Whats up Gabanna?" With all attitude she replies "Nothing whats up with you loser?" Lid shakes his head and shrugs his shoulders and replies "I'm just working cuz that's all." He opens the door for Gabanna, Aunt Clarees and the children and the once inside Lester is trying to get his family seated but this being a Sunday morning the place is packed and after waiting for a few minutes they are finally seated.

Gabanna orders first then the children, Aunt Clareese, Lid, and finally Lester. Lid makes sure to tell the waitress as she walks by "hold the meat because I don't eat any pork." She smiles and as she walks back to the kitchen she tyrns to take another look at Lid. "Yo cuz that waitress was on you, why don't you get the number?" "Yeah she got pretty eyes but I'm cool working on something right now and its no point of messing that up." "You better get over all that one man one wome thing times changing look at the table, and Lester motions to his three children all of whom have different mothers yet they are separted by less than a year. "I was all over the place cuz you better wake up." "I met this girl at city hall I like her and she's really connected, a go getter." Gabanna interrupts "yeah right, she's using you for something cuz, you aint got no money." "Do you let her use your car?" "Yeah Aunt Clareese" "Bingo" and Gabanna and Aunt Clareese laugh." "That's it cuz she needs your car. Did you at least hit cu?" "I'm not commenting on that Lester." "Come on were family you can tell us?" "Naw I got nothing to say." And with that Gabanna has the last word "Uh huh she got him whipped off one shot and now he's giving her his car." Lid just shakes his head as they all conversate the kids with each other, Gabanna and Aunt Clareese continue their on going mother daughter relationship which goes frm one argument to another while Lester and Lid sit on opposite ends of the table and Mikhial is constantly looking out the window after a few run ins with Omar he's always careful when ever out in public away from west philly when his concentration is broken up by Lester "So good brother Islam how is the job coming along?" "It's the worst cuz I hate being on the bench fighting with the white boy manager everyday, over worked under paid and going nowhere fast its like I'm running in quick sand.You only been out a few months and you've made more progress than me." Aunt Clareese interrupts "You should go to the church Lid Jesus is the answer to your problems." Shaking his head he says "I'm muslim Aunt Clareese I just don't see myself saying that Jesus is the son of God the whole trinity thing I don't agree with." "Well Jesus is the answer." Lester grins, and Gabbana and Aunt Clareese giggle with each other the fact of the matter is that faith based initiative changed the social fabrics of the job hiring thing and no longer did it matter what your qualifications were it only mattered if you went to church and were not muslim. Always preoccupied with his safety Lid constantly looks out the window his near run in with Omar a few weeks back gives him the feeling that he is being hunted, always being followed or watched. The waitress brings the food over and everyone begins to eat, he looks up at Lester and reminds him "Yo don't forget to say grace man this is your shin dig." "Everybody stop eating lets say prayer" exclaims Lester. "I'll lead prayer everybody lower your heads and Aunt Clareese starts "In the name of the lord and our savior Jesus thankyou for the food we are about to eat." "Amen!" Everyone starts to redig in and Lester and Lid continue their conversation "So what's up with you brother Ra-Zen?" "He's downtown at the fed prison, I usually go see him once a week and put money on his books when I get paid. Its killing my pockets though. Can you go down there to see him?" Shaking his head no "No way man I'm a felon I cant do it they wont let me in." "Well I'll give him your number so he can call, just becareful because once he has your number its on the fed list and they have your number." "Its cool im not into nothing aren't they gonna let him out?" "I don't know it's a fifty fifty thing we hired a new lawyer Eric Kennedy." "Wow he's pretty expensive" "How did y'all pull that off?" "He gave us a discount on the fee, and I collected money from a few different people and got major help from others." Lid raises his eyebrows to imply the major help came from South Philly. "Well that would be a good thing for you because Ra-Zen knows everybody." "Yeah I know he just better stay out of trouble there's nothing out here but fast money, women, and hustling, and all those things lead right back to jail. When I saw him the last time he was out, I told him to stay out of trouble. He didn't listen and ended right back into trouble." "When has Ra-Zen ever listened to anybody." "Your right but this time he has to get out and do the right thing." Aunt Clareese looks at Lid and says "Yeah right boy you must be dreaming." and Lester adds "Cuz the candy store is open crime pays when Ra-Zen gets out he's going all over the place." "Then may be he shouldn't get out because that's not the idea." They all finish eating and Lester ask for the check as he flirts with the waitress. He pulls out a big mit of money and puts like eighty dollars on the table "Yeah cuz I aint doing nothing." He gives his three children twenty dollars each and gives Lid a twenty "Take my kids home and I'll call ya." "Alright I'm ready to get back down my uncles and watch some basketball, wash clothes, and get ready for work." "Alright kids, daddy gotta go." Lester gets up and hugs all three of his children and Aunt Clareese and Gabbana continue to have their rolling conversation of an argument and they all leave the restaurant. Lid loads the kids in the back seat of his car, and then pulls off the parking lot listening to the sounds of Sinatra, tunes from a different day and age when America was America and Men were Men. "What's this exclaims the children?" "Sinatra, now please leave me alone." "Yeah well this sucks" "Well theres no way I'm playing that new rap stuff because its demeaning." "What's demeaning mean?" "The music y'all its self destructive, it teaches you to have multiple boy friends and girlfriends, or both, sell drugs, money, money, money. I don't listen to it." "What do you listen to?" "Public Enemy" and with that he turns off the Sinatra and slides his Public Enemy CD in and turns up the music. As he sits on fifth street the block as usual is jammed packed, the traffic from Sunday church is letting out and the traffic from the stores and shops has the traffic backed up bumper to bumper. Lid takes the time to glance to his left were he sees a Filapino girl standing on the bus stop. She's beautiful her legs fit perfectly into her pin stripped pants it's almost in 4-D the way her butt and hips just poke out of her pants. She sees Lid starring at her and in slow motion she moves almost slow dancing with the pole. Lid just is mezmorized and in awe. The light changes green and Lid in his usual fashion hits the gas on the car and pulls off, still staring at the fillapino girl. "SMASH!!!!" he crashes right into the back bumper of the car in front of him. There is a deaf tone silence for about five seconds as Lid gets his thoughts together. He immedaitly turns to the back seat, "are you guys o.k." "Shocked!!" they all look up with eyes wide open and shake there heads yes. He then looks at the car in front of him and inside there are three people, a baby seat in the back and two passengers in the front." This time his air bag did not deploy and there's no damage to the car because it is still running. He gets out the car and the driver of the car he hit is out too already talking on her cell phone. The heavy set Puerto Rican women immeadiatly asks "Are you crazy?" and Lid responds by saying "Are you guys alright?" she says nothing and she looks really mad, the passenger gets out and she is an older Puerto Rican women and Lid ask her "Are you o.k?" She nods her head yes, and he then says making full eye contact with her "I'm sorry." He takes the time to listen and the baby is not crying as she is moving around in the car seat so he concludes that it must be alright.Finally the driver of the car ask "What the hell is wrong with you!!?" "he quickly responds I'm sorry, do you have any insurance?" She says nothing and begins to dail another number on her cell phone, when he ask again do you have insurance? And once again she says nothing, Lid takes a look at the front of his car and there is no real damage they exchanged a little paint but both cars are in good shape. The traffic on fifth street begins to get back five or six blocks down and people start honking their horns as the accident has cut off all traffic going north bound. Obviously the women does not have insurance but there is no damage to either of the cars so he looks at the driver again directly in the eyes and says for the third time "I'm sorry" understanding that one back here in Puerto Rican land he might not make it out alive for hitting two women and a baby, two if the police or fire department come they are going to take Lids car because he does not have any insurance, plus he doesn't have the right plates on the car. He only has twenty dollars to his name and that's not enough money to get all those kids home to three different locations all on the bus. "I need to pull over because we are blocking traffic" proclaims Lid. He makes eye contact with the women who is on the phone, and he ask again "Pull over so we are blocking traffic, and we need to get out of the middle of the street." The women finally agrees and she gets in her car and pulls over, he does the same stopping in front of her. He gets out his car halfway and looks back to see if any cops are struck in traffic, and then looks forward. The accident has kept all the traffic going north from passing and for the first time in his memory fifth street is completely clear. Before the cars could pass, he jumps back in his still running car and without even closing the the door he hits the gas with all his might and takes off like a race car driver. "Put y'all seat belts on right now!!!" He yells to his cousins, as he presses forward on the gas "Put yall seat belts on NOW!!!" and he presses even harder on the gas getting up to 65-70 in seconds. He takes a right down a smaller street and then turns left up a side block were he once again picks up speed going like 80 he hears sirens to back and to the left of him which makes him just press harder on the gas. In a distance he sees two kids playing on the side walk and prays that they don't run into the street when all of a sudden they stop runnig along the side walk and the boy and the girl just stop and drop their mouths as a green blur flys by them and all you hear is Swzzzzooom like the wind and nothing more. Inside his head Lid has already figured his route out, as a child in middle school he used to ride the K bus and pass throough this very neighborhood. Believe it or not he used to imagine what if he had to get away from the police in this part of town, and in his mind a green and black graph just falls in place and through instincts, concentration, and desire he just picks up speed, running stop signs, and then slowing down on American street to listen for sirens. The sirens are still coming from the left and to the south of him and when he emerges from American street he goes the opposite direction to the north and to the right. But to his surprise and EMS truck is right along side of him separated by just one block and as the passenger talks on his walkie talkie Lid looks at him and smiles and then just presses down on the gas leaving the paramedics in the dust. Runnig through a red light h blazes past Cardinal Dougherty catholic school and past 66th avenue Lid races forward until he gets deep into West Oak lane he makes a left and then turns down a one way street and flys towards broad street where he emerges and it flows into Ogontz avenue, with no sound of sirens or no sight of the police he mixes in with traffic and begins to drop his cousins off. The kids are in back seat livid smiling and talking about what happened "Wow" "He was Like" You're the best cousin" the rest of the way as they sing his praises but heaven only knows how close they were to going to the department of human services and how close he was to getting locked up. As he drops one of his cousins off and the young kid gets out of the car Lid remarks "I guess you had all the fun you can handle for one day?" smiling he replies "can we do that again?" He smiles and waits for the kid to go in the house, he drops the other two off but when he drops Lester Jr. off he has to go back down into the very neighborhood the accident took place in constanly looking out for the police and driving at a frantic speed he finally gets to the kids house and tells him "nothing happened right?" Lester Jr shakes his head in agreement "My lips are sealed"Yeah right Lid thinks to himself as he gets back into his car and pulls off. He drives back down to his uncles apartment and as he goes down Landcaster avenue there are three parked police cars, and as he passes them they look over at him with very mean and dirty looks and finally the cop driving the third police cruiser looks down at Lids bumper and just smiles.Damn he thinks to himself the paint from the car is still on the bumper I'm in trouble. When he puls up to his uncles apartment and parks outside his uncles a nigger in a gold two door Mercedes gets out as soon as he does and looks down at his watch and then gets back into the car. "I'm going to pay for that" Lid thinks to himself and goes into the apartment complex. As soon as he sits down the phone rings and it's his cousin Lester "What up cuz?" Livid Lester shouts

"My son just told his mom that y'all were in an accident and you were in a high speed chase with the cops. You know she called me like what the fuck just happened cussing and screaming at me." Lid bluntly ask "Is he alright?" "yeah" and Lid just hangs up the phone and turns it completely off. For the rest of the day he just sits in the recliner he knows his days are numbered and whatever the police department, and the city of Philadelphia has planned for him is not going to be good.

# "The Devil he told me to go"

L ID WAKES IN THE morning with the sun and immediately makes Fajr prayer, Malik comes into the room and watches his cousin perform prayer and giggles throughout the prayer. When Lid finishes he confronts his cousin about his behavior "Look man if you are going to laugh when I am making prayer you have to stay in your room" "I don't want to go in my room I'm always in my room." "I know but I cant have you breaking my concentration when I am praying." "I'm sorry I promise I wont do it again, why do you do the Allahhh" mimicking his cousin Malik puts his hands on his ears like he is calling the athan. "Because I'm muslim and Allah orders us to pray five times a day." "What's Allah?" "Allah is God Malik I don't want to get into it but Allah is God, do you want some breakfast?" Smiling Malik says "Yeah", Lid lights a cigarette and goes into the kitchen, he grabs a few ego waffles from the freezer and puts them in the toaster. "Lid can I go with you today?" "No way dude I'm running the streets and that's no place for a little kid." "I'm no kid I'm a big man." "Yeah you are a pretty fat kid but you still can't go with me." "I'm going to tell my dad you called me fat." "I don't care it's the truth look at your gut busting out of your bajamas, what's wrong with you sams?" Mocking Morgan Freeman in "Lean on Me" Malik just laughs as Lid changes his voice, then pop the egos are out of the toaster. Lid fixes a plate for his cousin pouring syrup over the waffles he then grabs the ironing board and starts to iron his clothes for the day when his phone rings, the caller ID says it's Ashanti and Lid is a little apprehensive about answering the phone. He and Ashanti have not spoken since he refused to let her hold his car, right after he had the high speed chase incident, but being the softy that he is he answers. "As Salaam Alaikum Ashanti?" sounding like an angel with her sweet voice on she replies "Wa Laikum Salaam good brother long time no here from what've you been up to?" Staying guarded he simply responds "Working

Ashanti whats going on?" "I was wondering if you could help a muslim sister out you know tommorows easter they are having some events in West Philly and we would like to shoot some of the events for the documentary." His instincts tell him to say no I mean she did dump him, after he told her she could not drive his car anymore, but being in desperate need of gas money he continues to listen to her proposition. "All we need to do is pick us up from Germantown and drive us to West Philly we will find our way home from there." "Alright twenty dollars in gas money and I will be there in like an hour to pick y'all up." Upset about the gas fee Ashanti goes from being an angel to a devil in just a split second "Damn brother twenty dollars what are you trying to do rob a sister?" "My gas tank is on E Ashanti plus gas is way too high these days and this was not in my plans." "Alright be here in an hour you see who your friends are when you need them, twenty dollars in gas money." She hangs up the phone without saying goodbye and Lid finished ironing gets his clothes together and breaks down the ironing board. "I'm done Lid" The lazyness of Malik is appauling and feeling like everybody's fool Lid says "Well put the plate in the sink, what do I look like Mr. Belvadeer!!?" "Laughing Malik ask "Who is Mr. Belvadeer?" "Way before your time my point is you can reach the sink put the dirty dish into the sink man and stop being lazy." Malik gets up and leaves the plate on the table grabs the remote control and and turns on his favorite cartoon "Sponge Bob Square Pants." Immediately he starts to bust out in laughter and Lid tells him "I don't know how you watch this stuff, when I was young we had real cartoons with heros good guys and bad guys, this clown is always running its stupid man, you kids are doomed damned nation." Lid shakes his head and walks away into the bathroom Malik is not listening to anything Lid just said as he is hypnotized by the television. Like most kids today the television is raising them and projecting false images of what is good with no distinction between good and evil, subliminal messages planting seeds for homosexuality, and in the case of African Americans putting no role model on the television for Malik or any other African American male that is as all he constantly sees is himself projected as a homo or a clown but never the hero. This subliminal racism teaches viewers that the Caucasian is the only leader or hero to look up to and that at all times the minority is always inferior to the Caucasian. Emerging from the bathroom fully dressed Lid goes into the living room, the plate of syrup is still sitting on the table as Malik sits hyponotized by the television. "Can I go with you?" "What do you think I am going to say yes if you keep asking? I asked you to put your plate in the sink and it's still sitting there, come on man!!?" Hearing Lid get loud with Malik Uncle Rashad comes from his room high and smelling like pot adding to the confusion he ask "What's all this screaming about?" "Nothing he wants to go with me, and I'm like no way." Always hollering at his son Uncle Rashad tells him "No you aint going nowhere boy, now get in that bathroom and wash your face and hands!" "I told him to get his plate up off the table too." Surprisingly Uncle Rashad takes a very junveinalle approach, because the only sense of authority he gets is from ordering his son around all day he immedialty tells Lid " Don't tell MY son anything Lid he's my son I'll do it." "O.k." as he is saying o.k. Lid is also leaving out the front door he jumps in his car and begins to play Bruce Springteen as he drives to the gas station and spends his last ten dollars to fill his gas tank a quarter of the way, it used to take ten dollars to fill up his old mercury sables, but now the way gas prices have gone up ten dollars only puts a quarter tank into the much smaller v-4 Hyndai. His phone rings while he is pumping gas and its Samantha, it's not good to use the cell phone and pump gas as the combination of the electric waves, static, and gas vapor could cause an explosion so he waits until he is finished and calls her back inside the car. " Samantha what's the deal?" "I don't know why didn't you answer the phone?" "I was pumping gas, I have to talk to you though because I just applied for this job with we do it all." "That's what's you diverse to be making more money yo, I remember you used to help me with my homework." "I know but the thing is the job is in Minnesota." "What that's the middle of nowhere." "I know" "Why don't they just hire you here in Philly, they all over the place here st the stadiums, the schools, and that's the headquarters where you work at?" "Cause the adgenda they don't want any straight African American males being successful in the cities showing these kids that it's worth going to college, the government wants us to hustle, get felonies and be criminals. The only brothers that work there are either really old men, ex-cons from inside their program, or fagots." "So they will hire you but in the middle of nowhere so you don't an impact on the community you grew up in?" "Yup and fucking Jew owns the company they got some nerve helping engaging in genocide after the shit that happened to them." "So what do you want to talk to me about?" Lid pauses because he really wanted to ask Sequita this in person but he builds his confidence up and ask "Why don't you come with me?" Sequita pauses for a while and then with fear in her voice she begins to run off they reasons why she can't go." "I don't know anybody out there" "Niether do I" "My family is all here, my grandmother, and my brother." "I know just think about it, please?" Pulling up to Ashanti's house Lid lets her know what he is doing. "I'm giving somebody a ride from uptown out west, when I get back come over the house and we can talk some more please?" She softly replies o.k." And they hang up from each other, relieved Lid might be out of dodge, finally getting a descent paying job that reflects his education and being able to do get Sequita out of the city, he starts thinking about when they first met on the way to seven eleven, and how he tried to help her get educated and stay out of the streets and not fall victim to the city, she still fell and now just smokes pot and lives in despire, part time girl friend, part time hustler, and part time dike Samantha is completely lost and getting away with Lid might be there only salvation as he too is stuck in Philly lost, but with a new start together in a new town maybe there can be some story book ending to this dream that has become a nightmare. Lids daydreaming is interrupted when his cell phone rings and its Ashanti, he answers "As Salaam Aliakum?" "Wa Laikum Salaam, I see you out front that was fast I will be out in a minute. About ten minutes later Ashanti emerges from her house with that chesser cat grin, as usual Lid gets out the car and opens the door up for her, "As Salaam Alaikum brother? Annoyed already and ready to get this over with and get to Samantha Lid flatly replies "Wa-Laikum Salaam." Still grinning she says "I see you have a new car what happened to the old one?" As she is asking Ashanti turns the radio station from the classic rock channel and puts in her cd. "I was listening to rock and roll please take the cd out Ashanti." She complies and Lid begins to explain what happened to his old car. "The cops pulled me over out west, now my paper work is not right so when they run the plates you know it comes up my old Sable the red one, so they pull me out the car, and search the it, I'm standing there watching as the cop from his top shirt pocket drops the bag of weed on the floor. Then all of a sudden he emerges with this bag of weed so they cuff me and put me in the cop car. What they wanted was me to break down and confess about the Nascar stuff but that's what I get for pulling off the way I did." "How you know that is wasn't your weed?" "If it was my weed Ashanti I would've been smoked it no way a bag a weed in my car I check for that a few times a week" laughing a he finishes the sentence Ashanti starts to laugh too, as Lid finishes the story "So they run the plates and there're like either we book you for the weed, or we take the car? Well that's a no brainer I'm not getting no felony possession charge and it's not my weed, so as much as it hurt my heart I said take the car so I grabbed this jawn from my moms. I hate it but it's better than the bus." "Well that's what you get for pulling off on them like you crazy." "I'm just an urban cowboy Yeaahhhh hah!" Ashanti gives Lid directions to her girlfriends house and in a few minutes the car is full with Tia and three other girls, and as soon as they get into the car Ashanti changes and turns right into a devil as she transgresses all bounds talking loud and cursing with every other word. On the way down to west Philly one of the girls screams "I have to go to the bathroom!" On the road and not wanting to stop anywhere Lid replies "Well you have to wait we will be at Idris house in a few minutes." Like a beast and not a human being her response is "If I don't go right now I am going to shit all in the back seat." The girls all begin to laugh and Lid abruptly pulls over next to a corner store were the most disgusting act of lack of self control takes place as the girl gets out the car and cocks over like a bitch and takes a shit in broad daylight. Astonished Lid just turns his head and soon she gets back in the car to make things worst Samantha calls him and Mikahil with thought answers "What's the deal Sequita?" As soon as he says Samantha the jealous Ashanti starts talking loud so Sequita can here her on the other end "Who's that in the background nigga?" "I told you I'm picking up someone and taking them out west I'm almost done and I'll be home in a few minutes." Alarmed Samantha is pretty angry and now she has an attitude "Well you better drop them bitches da fuck off." OveJasminering Sequita say bitches Ashanti goes off in the background "Who she calling a bitch!" Lid hangs up the phone and confronts Ashanti on her rude and ungodly behavior she's almost thirty and should act better than that, "Why did you get all loud when I was on the phone that's high school shit! When your on the phone I turn the radio down show me the same respect!" "Who is Samantha, couple of weeks ago we were going to get married!" "Yeah well that was before you dumped me for the already married Vince, because I wouldn't let you hold my car?" Pulling up in  front of Idris's house Lid does not even take the time to park and sits in the street as he lets them out. Yo were is the twenty dollars for gas?" "Ashanti pulls out a ten dollar bill and hands it to Lid "What's this you agreed to pay a dub?" Grinning with her chesser cat smile she says "Well I still need a ride back uptown tonight." "Whatever" Idris approaches the car and they exchange greetings "As Salaam Aliakum?" "Wa Laikum Salaam, you still hanging out with these losers?" "She needed a ride yo , got me on the be a good muslim thing." "So this is your new ride?" "Yeah you know the police took my other wheel they planted a bag of weed in my car and was like look either we are going to lock you up for possession or take the car. I was like take the car." "Smart move, what's this eyeing the car up he points out Lid bumper sticker which says "Say no to war" You cant have anything like that on your bumper that's going to draw attention and get you on the terrorist watch list." "Man I'm already on the watch list from protesting back in the day" Not paying Lid any mind Lid pulls out a knife and begins to try and scrap off the bumper sticker, Lid immediately stops him "Hold up Idris I like the sticker on there cool out." "Alright man I was just trying to help you out." This is the first time Lid has seen since Idris called him for a ride up fifth street right after Lid got in a high speed chase on fifth street a few weeks before. Smelling a set him he refused to go and Lid has not been answering any of Idris's calls since. And abruptly he ends the conversation with Idris's knowing no good can come from any of this "Alright I'm out As- Salaam Alaikum" they shake hands "Wa Laikum Salaam". And Lid peels off to his uncles apartment and as soon as he gets close he calls Sequita axious to speak with her because the last thing he wanted to do was upset the always fragile Sequita. " Sam I'm back, you still coming over I still want to talk to you about getting out of town yo!" As she should be angry about the whole Ashanti thing Samantha flips out on the phone "Who da fuck was that in your car?" "Ashanti and her girlfriends, she asked for a ride from Uptown out west I needed the gas money so I was like yeah." "What the fuck what are you doing because something doesn't sound right" "That's it I just gave them a ride I'm on my home now waiting for you that's it I promise." Calmed down she ask "You got some weed?" "Naw" "Just pick some up before get over here and I will pay you, I'll grab two ditches from the store." "Alright, I'm on my way" After a quick stop in the corner store Lid runs into the apartment and since it's midday he makes Zhur prayer. As soon as finishes Sequita is calling him and as he looks out the front window he sees her Toyota Camry and runs out the door, on the phone with her as he walks outside Lid opens the door and lets her in. "You always look beautiful" And she does with just a pair of blue jeans on and a top and leather jacket, a little burnt from the all the weed smoke over the years her lips are still as alluring as they were the first day he met here. Unfazed by Lids complitment with all attitude she says "Save the bullshit, did you get the ditches?" "Yeah" they hug for a few seconds and Sequita stops him on the steps "Look who the fuck is Ashanti?" "Nobody I been called that thing off months ago?" "So why the fuck was she in your car?" "I told you she called for a ride from Uptown" "You lying you fucking that bitch?" Telling the truth and straight faced he shakes his head and says "Nope, I want to talk to you about leaving if I get this job we can get the fuck outta this town yo!" " How you gonna ask me to leave my family and you cheating with some other bitch?" "I'm not cheating she asked for a ride." "You got the ditches?" "Lid pulls out the ditches from his pocket and hands them to Sequita, she quickly snatches them out his hand and says "I gotta think about it I'm getting lost." With a quick peck on the cheek Sequita is out the door and Lid at a lost for words and defeated goes back upstairs. And waiting for him is his Uncle Rashad "what's wrong with you nephew you look like someone kicked your face in." "mentally exhausted Mikahil just falls into the recliner "Girl trouble Unc Sequita just walked out on me, and Ashanti coming around again getting on my nerves." "Why you still messing with that girl you know she is just nothing but trouble." "I know but she is muslim and I feel compelled to try and help and do some good plus I needed the gas money." "Yo you got some weed for sale?" "Naw brother but I got a half of dutch in the back room I'll sell it to you for like three dollars?" "Cool" Uncle Rashad gets the dutch and they begin to smoke as they continue the conversation "That's your problem nephew I keep telling you that religion stuff is all played out that bitch is a muslim as Pam Anderson, she ain't no Muslim that shit was created by white people to maintain control over the masses, look at Christianity they believe some white Jesus is God, and the muslim's worship some white arab named Muhammed. Check out this video I got from Sha it breaks everything down." Uncle Rashad puts the video in a Lid puffs on the blunt as he tries to sit through it, towards the end bored with the propaganda he gets ready to leave when Uncle Rashad attempts to question him. "See what I mean the religions were all made up it's been at least twenty five other cases of the same story of Jesus over time. This is a new age nephew two thousand one marked a new age." "I know the twenty five other cases were prophets or messengers of Allah but the seal of the prophets lies with Muhammed may peace and blessings be upon him. This new age is talked about in the Quaran , have you read it?" Uncle Rashad shakes his head and says "No", "This is the day and age that satan wins many souls, individualism people who work soley for self that's why 911 was so important, silence is a way to agree to a contract, the mass population remained silent and hell on earth was unleashed. George W. Forty Three  was the anti Christ, and from now until Judgement day the leviathan, the beast will take more and more souls into the hell fire this time than duing any other time in history. When me and Uncle Sha was doing our revolutionary thing we used to say the beast don't win in the end. But watch societies principles and morals all begin to decline, greed Americans voted for Forty Three  in 2004 because they got three hundred dollars in tax breaks now things are starting to fall apart, he went to war and we murdered millions of Iraquies after we disarmed them for ten years, we just killed millions of muslims most of them Shiite collaborating with the illegitament Sunni royal family in Saudi Arabia. All trying to push the adgenda of Sunni muslim, which is not the only application of Islam but farther more completely conflicts with Western American society. But this is just the beginning lust look all around you the women dress naked in the summer time pretty much naked nothing is left for the husband to enjoy, because they don't want husbands they want money so they can buy material things. Capitalism women will work all day neglecting their children letting the tv raise them so they can engadge in capitalism and buy things. Our whole system is based on consumption right?" Uncle Sha nods his head, "Who does the most consumption men or women?" "Women" "exactly so by becoming part of the work force you have a better participant in capitalism men not the black man because habe never been the bread winner but that's a different story, but men used to be the gateway to the cash but women their own now and they still get money from us. But to add insult to injury they don't even need us anymore and half of them have turned into dikes or get the best of both worlds being bi-sexual. Who wins there man and women were put on earth to procreate if you take the man out of the situation and just have sex then your just fucking to sin or out of lust. Read the story of Lot it's in the bible and quaran. Wrath: so now you have a population of young adults fighting for dope money, dope which is being used to destroy our own people, but end up short on some money, or better yet rub a nigga the wrong way and they will sure as hell put you in the ground, at all cost I have to keep up with everyone else, willing to kill one another for money or pride, that's satan yo he's full of pride so full of pride he refued to bow down to Adam you the African man the first man on earth, and this is his revenge the systematic genocide of his first emeny his envy drives him to lead man into hell even if means using our most sacred gift our companion the female. With Lids full attention Uncle Rashad just listens as Lid continues "If paper money was the death of Christ, then a cash less society will be the death of God as we all become consumers living for me, this age of self worship the corporations have us waste your life eight to twelve hours a day, and forget God altogether. The books are important Allah made Adam in his image, and man has a responcibility to always remember Allah or God, women are different they are emotional, impulsive, we are not equals but complinments to one another that's the beauty of Allah's creation. Now who would design a system like that which falsy says we are equals?" "I don't know the white man?" "Close, but no it's satan, iblis, the devil whatever you want to call him it's real no pitch fork and tail naw this system has been designed using our companion against us, to lead more and more souls into hell. The white man helps because he lacks melanin in his foJasmined, they were people who migrated north and lived in lands with less solar energy and rays from the sun, this caused a biological change they lack melanin. One day when I was young an old sister in a bakery told me and boy the Marlboro man that that's why we are so good in sports because we have perifural vision. Our skulls differ theirs is calcified because they grew up not exposed to sun light, that sun light is our natural conection to the planet, and to one another. They lack natural connection to the Earth that's why more destruction has been done to the planet over the past one-hundred years than all of history combined. Slavery took place for one reason PROFIT, the destruction of the earth is taking place for the same reason. Religion was created to reconnect these people with God, were different because we are the first we always will have that natural connection as long as we still walk the earth because extinction adgenda is in full effect. Greed Uncle, everywhere they have gone destruction, and the sacking of ancient lands and the extinction of ancient peoples in the pursuit of prosperity, and wealth. This society is a mess and soon we will have a God-less society based soley on self Satan he was so concerned about himself that he refused to obey God's commands to kneel making him not a fallen angel but a Jinn freedom of will and his envious heart has led him raging full asult on the first man us. It's already written Uncle, so yes the video was informative but that was not any new information for me, nothing will shake my beliefs in Allah and the promise of paradise that is the only thing I can grasp on to after going through so much barbaric persecution my entire life. A little embarrassed that his nephew just broke things down the way he did, but also shedding a grin Uncle Rashad still sticks to his guns and proclaims religion is phony man." "It's needed to save as many souls as we can, I gotta go Uncle Faruq is texting me he needs a ride from the bar." "As-Salaam Alaikum uncle." "Wa-Laikum Salaam". On his way out the door Lid gets a call from Ashanti, already pissed off with her he doesn't answer it but when she calls back after a few rings he picks up, he knows she wants a ride back uptown, but she already shorted him his gas fee from earlier being a good person he doesn't want to turn a person down in need, plus the he's pretty high from weed smoke right now and the thought that he might have another shot at Ashanti flaming Indian pussy crosses his mind and he picks up the phone. "As Salaam Alaikum Ashanti what's the deal?" Back to her calm and softly ways she replies "Wa Laikum Salaam we are finally finished filming and could I bother the brother for a ride back uptown?" " I really don't have the time Ashanti plus I got to pick my uncle up from the bar." "Come on brother I know you not going to leave a muslim sister without a ride home?" A glutton for punishment Lid agrees "Alright I need some gas money, and its going to take a few minutes cause I got to make another run." Lid hangs up and does something completely out of character almost in his car he turns around and goes back into the apartment. The odd behavior of Idris, and feeling like this might be a set up Lid goes into the closet and grabs his pistol knowing that without a permit he is not supposed to have it out on the streets in Philly he takes it anyway. Placing the pistol on his waist he tightens his belt and it's off to pick his uncle Faruq up at the bar. On his way to the bar Ashanti is blowing his phone up and Lid is not answering it, around the corner from Idris's house sits the bar Lucky's on Haverford avenue and just in time as Lid pulls up Uncle Faruq and Pete from the bakery emerge out the front door obviously drunk they both are stumbling as they try and rap to a few women standing outside. Lid waits in his car and calls Faruq on his phone, "I'm right here do you see me?" "Yeah, why don't you come out the car and come back inside with us?" "Naw man I'm staying out of the bars man nothing but trouble come on cause I have some other things to do." They walk over to Lids car and completely drunk Uncle Faruq ask " As-Salaam Alaikum"? "Wa-Laikum Salaam replies Lid he shakes hands with Pete and Uncle Faruq wants to know "Look could you take Pete home, cause I am drunk as shit?" "Man both y'all ready to dip I thought I was going to take you home?" Angry about Lid suggesting that he was too drunk to drive home, showing how drunk he is Uncle Faruq snaps at Lid "Man I can drive myself home don't be telling me I'm too nothing, I just don't want to be this nigga home way out southwest." Not in the mood to argue Lid just says "O.K., be careful As-Salaam Alaikum" "Wa-Laikum Salaam" they shake hands through the window and Lid watches as Uncle Faruq stumbles into his car. Pete already in the passenger seat pulls out two cans of coors light and ask "You drinking man" "I'm driving I'm not supposed to but what the hell." And he cracks open a can of beer and downs it quickly, then he relates to Pete what he has to do with Ashanti. "Look Pete I have to pick these girls up from around the corner and take them uptown are you going to ride with me?" Excited Pete ask "Is they fucking?" "I don't know man I nailed one of them but when they get around each other they turn into dikes like they have no time for no man, but they smoke and snort so if you got anything once they get on like all hoes they will do just about everything." On Q Pete pulls out two twenty dollar bags of coke one already with a straw hanging out the top and he quickly takes a sniff placing the end of the straw and sniffing with one of his nostrils and then the other and says "I got plenty of blow I guess we fucking tonight." They both laugh and at the red light Pete ask "Yo want some?" Lid thinks about it for a few seconds its been months since he's snorted any coke and that was when he first started it took him weeks of drinking can pepsi's in the morning to get rid of that early morning craving for a hit, but after one beer and the possibility of nailing Ashanti and Tia together Lid shrugs his shoulders and says "Yeah man" two quick sniffs later Lid is really feeling good as the coke has numbed hi insides and he is wired on a higher level. Just around the corner from the bar Lid pulls up in front of Idris's house and standing out front is Ashanti and her three girlfriends, excited Pete ask "All of them?" "I don't know the other two like that but the dark skin one and the caramel chick are coming uptown together." "Yo I don't know how y'all gonna fit in the back it's four of y'all and its pretty tight, figure it out." "Ashanti wearing that chesser cat smile is wired and completely over the top as she starts cussing Lid out for having Pete in the car "How the fuck are we supposed to all fit in here?" "Look just get in the car yo, I'm trying to get this done I hope y'all are going to the same place because I'm not trying to be making any extra stops." Then Ashanti relates some very disturbing news to Lid, these two are going to North Philly and we are going uptown." "Come on you know I don't go down north Philly yo, I need more gas money!" As always Ashanti takes the lead "We got you brother I know you are not going to make these black women walk home or get a ride from some stranger out here in the streets, what kind of Muslim are you?" As usual playing on Lids faith he folds out of guilt and the possibility that he could be nailing Ashanti later in the night, "Alright twenty dollars for gas" "I got you when we get uptown trust me." High off coke and the beer Lid pulls off and Pete turns around and takes the time to introduce himdelf to the ladies in the back seat "How Y'all ladies doing?" Together they all reply "FINE", as Pete goes down the row of who is who Lid is concentrating on the road as with such a filled car he has to look out for the cops, and since he's going down north Philly he has to look out for Omar too. And quickly he gets north Philly and tells the girls "alright y'all gotta go now, because I'm not supposed to be here." Already aware of the situation they sarcastically say "What you scared to be in North Philly?" Ashanti and the girls laugh and Lid says "If I was scared I wouldn't be down here dropping y'all off" Then why don't you stay?" "Because I have my orders!" With the two girls out of the car Lid just pulls off with the door still open and as quickly as he can gets out of north philly "Wait the door ain't closed" Ignoring her Lid just keeps driving as Pete is trying to get to know Tia a little better he offers her some coke "Yo baby you want some coke?" and before she even answers Pete pulls from inside pocket the bag of coke and in plain sight passes it to the back o Tia. Estatic Lid turns to Pete and yells at him "What are you doing I'm driving yo, put that up!" Most of the time Lid is cool about using drugs while he is driving but the comination of having his gun on him, and the fact that the police are still upset with him about the speed racer thing Lid is extra paranoid and his behavior throws everyone off guard, and Ashanti calls him on it. "What's wrong with you tonight yo your tripping nigga!" "Ashanti I told you I don't want no trouble with the police!" Then you should've thought about that before you hit some women and her child." Pete reassures Lid "Man that was like two months ago they not thinking about you." Ashanti and Tia quickly sit in the back seat, and quietly finishes off the bag of coke. Finally uptown at Tia crib Mikail parks and asks for his gas money. "Alright Ashanti were's the gas money because I have to get back out west." "Your not going to stay, your friend Pete wants to hang out don't you?" High and drunk Pete say's "Hell yeah!" In the back seat Ashanti and Tia move closer together and their faces are cheek to check just about ready to kiss each other, Lid watches in the rear view mirrow as the two of them edge closer and closer to kissing but cooler heads prevail and he sticks to the plan "Naw I have to get back out west Philly." Alright says Ashanti here's the gas money and she pulls out three wrinkly one dollar bills and hands them to Lid. "Yow whats this? I went all the way down North Philly you said twenty dollars I'm still waiting for the ten you owe me from this morning." Tia speaks up and says somebody around the corner owes me some money we can go around there and pick up a bag of weed and y'all can stay smoke and relax." "I'm cool yo let me just get out of here." Pete looks at Lid as if to say what the hell is wrong with you, but Ashanti and Tia exit the car and Lid pulls off. "Yo why didn't you stay I got more coke left we could've had a party yo freak fest with them two you see the way they was kissing each other turn around!" " I know they dikes to you, I really want to hit Ashanti again yo that pussy was the warmest shot I ever had I thought she was about to burn through the condom that's that Indian in her." "That's what it is too turn back around yo!" I have to get back home and do something after that we can go back uptown." "stop lying you know when you get out west you ain't coming back." While driving down 5th street Lid along the smaller side streets sees a woman standing on her steps yelling for help. With the air of invinsability because he has his pistol on him he decides to pull over and right up to the lady. "What's wrong?" the women shocked that someone came to help in a heavy Spanish accent the women says "There's a man upstairs in my house papi, I saw him and I just took off running." "Did you call the cops?" "My cell phone I called them on my cell phone" Immediately Lid hears the sirens coming down the street "Alright just stay out here, and don't go back inside the house." Hollering from the car Pete says "What da fuck are you doing you aint no cop, you better come on before they lock you up."Lid looks at the women and ask again "Are you o.k.?" She nods and says "You better get out of here" "Just stay out here and don't go back in" "Thank you papi" "No problem" Lid gets back into the car and pulls off as the police lights glare in the background. "You tripping tonight you pass up on a freak fest and then stop to help some women out like you Spiderman or something" "I know man but she looked so scared and in fear." "Fucking superhero" Lid phone rings and its Ashanti he immediately picks up and sounding extra seductive she says "Tia just called her friend around the corner and he has the money he owes her, so I'll pay you the money I owe you just come back up here with your friend and his friend, we can blow some green and and whatever happens happens." "Without hesitation he turns back around and heads back to Tia's house. Pete is chearing and screaming out the window "I'm fucking tonight!!" "I'm Fucking tonight!" both laughing Lid forgets about the gun he has in his waist and being smart and falls to his lesser desires thinking about hitting that red hot pussy between Tia's legs, still taking snorts from Pete's bag of coke Lid is hell bent on this freak fest and he fly's through the city and in no time he is back at Tia's house. Pete gets right out the car and head towards the front door not even knowing which house it is, and luckily Tia comes out from the front door. Startled she says "Whoa nigga you scared the shit out of me." "Pete talking extra loud in the middle of the night because he is drunk and high says "Y'all got some condoms?" Still in the car Lid just shakes his head, and Tia quickly shushes Pete and lets him into the house. Soon she cat walks to the car and Lid in anticipation of fucking her tonight too gets out the car and opens the door for her. When he walks back around the back of the car to get in his gun almost falls and he quickly adjust it in his waist slightly exposing it. When he gets into the drivers seat sitting at the corner is a burgundy Pontiac 6000 and Lid sees a person in the drivers seat talking on the phone, thinking nothing of it he gets in his car and pulls off. "Yo Tia were are your kids at?" "They upstairs asleep" "Yo we about to make a lot of noise" Tia arrogantly laughs and Lid just continues around the corner to the jungle. Cops are all over the place as two police cruisers pass them on the way over, "Somebody must've got robbed or a house broken into because the dope boys are still out on the corner." There's always something going on back here" Tia points right at the dope boys standing on the corner and says "That's were I have to go" Lid pulls over and watches as Tia gets out the car, and forgetting about the dangers of the situation he's hypnotized watching her slide out of the car, he waits paitently and watches as she walks over to the dope boys on the corner in seconds they exchange cash for weed and Tia is getting back in the car. Still with his seat belt on Lidturns the car on and is ready to pull off when he's blocked by a police patty wagon from the intersecting street, who immediately turns on his spot light a flashes it on Lid and Tia, his heart racing Lid turns on his front headlights and wait as he and the patty wagon are at a stale mate the wagon turns off the spot light yet , no one wants to make a move and finally Lid caves and pulls off what's the worse that can happen he thinks to himself I have all my paper work. Very slowly he turns up the next block and turning right behind him is the patty wagon with its red and blue lights flashing. Lid immediately stops there will be no high speed chase tonight in a V-6 it was a reach in the hyndai V-4 forget about it thinking that the worse could happen is that he would just get a ticket because he has all his paper work he pulls right over. "I knew they were going to do that" Tia says nothing and as the cops get out of the pattywagon and approach the car Lid thinks about his pistol in his waist and prays that he doesn't have to get out the car. "Hand me the paperwork out of the glove box Tia." She doesn't move and Lid quickly grabs the paperwork out of the glove box and as the cops approach two white cops one Italian and one Irish the Italian cop  and as Lid hands him his paper work he immediately and forcefully says "Get the fuck out of the car!" Startled Lid does nothing but roll his eyes, and quickly the cop ask again "Turn the car off and get the fuck out of the car!" Lid responds this is a traffic stop, I' m not getting out of the vehicle here's my paperwork." Shocked by his insubordination the cop puts his hand on his pistol and says "If you don't get out the car I'm calling backup and we are going to pull through the window, now get out the fucking car!" Tia finally says something "Get out the car." Lid looks over and sees the other cop looking into the vehicle with his flash light and says to Tia "This is a traffic stop I am not getting out the car." The Italian cop is looking into the vehicle and he says "You got beer cans in there, What you've been drinking" Lid looks over at the cup holders and sees the crushed cans of coors light.  Damn he got me he thinks to himself "I had a beer like four hours ago, that's it" "Well this is now a dui stop" Suddenly two more police cruisers pull up in front of Lids car and with hands on their fire arms steps four all white cops and Lid thinks about a few weeks ago when the Philadelphia police pulled suspects out their crown Victoria and beat on the guys with night sticks all while being video taped by one of the news stations. Contimplating getting out Lid knows he has his gun on him and if he gets out the car and the gun falls and goes off he is a goner, so he has to be very careful about how he oes about things and he continues to jouast with the officer, until the new officers start screaming "Get the fuck out the car!" Lid opens the door and as soon as he steps with one foot out of the car the cop just grabs Lid and pulls him from the car. Snatching the paperwork out of his hand and throwing it on the roof of his car. He quickly frisk Lid snatching out his wallet from his back pocket and tossing it on the hood of the car, he continues to search and finds the broken blade in Lids pocket and immediately cuffs Lid "That's a dangerous weapon". Shocked that he is cuffed eventhough he still has his pistol his 45 calibar P-90 pistol in his waist after being searched. He looks over inside the car and Tia is still sitting there amazed that the cops did not pull her out the car Lid is confident that Ashanti and Tia set him up and this is Philly's way of dealing out justice for getting away from them weks ago. With his gun in waist while he is handcuffed he is just standing there as the cops talk amoung themselves thinking that he has to be very careful at this point if he tells the cops he has a pistol they might shoot him, or if the pistol falls out it might go off and they might shoot him, so he does nothing and waits as another young cop grabs him and pulls him towards the patty wagon. Looking over at Tia who is now friendly with the cops and still they haven't asjed her to get out the car, Lid just stands and waits until a younger cop start to frisk him in front of the glaring lights of the patty wagon the cop frisk Lid again and still he has not found the gun, and as he slowly taps around the waist of Lid he dodges the gun as if he knows the gun is their and is waiting for Lid to make a wrong move, and finally he ask "What's this?" "My pistol" and the cop pulls the hand gun out of Lids waist. Just as the cop pulls the gun out the Irish cop walks up and at first sightn of the gun he goes off "Fucking Asshole!!" "All man you are a fucking asshole screams the Italian cop and Lid says nothing but he does crack a smile if they were trying to catch him with some weed they failed, and since they found the gun they have ATF issues and District attorney issues, and Lid knows his car, his drivers license, and the gun are all registered in Delaware and based on the shady circumstances that got him to this point he knows they have no case, and with the gun finally being revealed at the cops own accord hes in the clear. Handcuffed the cops usher him into the patty wagon constantly calling him an asshole!!!" But before he's completely in they ask him " What do you want us to do with the car, we can leave out here with the keys in it, or the girl can drive it home?" Lid yells to Tia take the car and tell my cousin what happened and to please call my uncle." Devestated Lid really cannot focus on the car the cops failed to book him drug possession which carries a mandatory felony sentencing and guaranteed time. The gun charge really messed things up because it's his gun, but for now Lid with worries about going to prison for the first lays down on the floor of the empty patty wagon and thanks God that he's alive because one wrong move and he was sure to be a dead man, or what if he had some weed on him or in the car he would be doing jail time for sure and could forget about getting a job ever again. He could still be facing time for the gun possession, and he thinks about what his life is going to be like from here on out and how disappointed his mother and family will be, still handcuffed he just shrugs his shoulders on the floor of the patty wagon. Its takes a few minutes for the cops to get into the patty wagon and when they finally get in the Italian officer opens the window in the middle of the barrier separating the wagon area from the driver and just starts laughing, after about a half a minute of that he closes the window and Lid still lying on the floor just listens as the wagon drives through the night. But instead of going straight to the station the wagon makes a stop and Lid thinks to himself "Oh lord I am about to have company in here and gets up off the floor." But as he listens to his surprise only one door opens and one cop gets out of the patty wagon, this can't be an arrest because only one door opened up, this must be the payoff and Lid wonders who it is paying these cops. Still uptown Lid thinks to himself who could it be Iman Mahdi from Germantown masjid or may be Hakima's grandfather? Who ever it is the cops are paid as the passenger side door opens and closes and soon the patty wagon pulls off. And a few minutes later they arrive at the 35th police district years ago he used to dream about being on the force and now he's being taken in, once inside Lid is seated and still handcuffed the cops ask him some questions about his weight, height, date of birth, and marriatel status, and finally they ask "This is yours huh?" holding Lid pistol up in the air "Yeah and I want it back too" Lid watches as the irish officer takes the gun and puts it in his coat pocket and heads downstairs to the locker rooms, and in disgust he just shakes his head. Then another cop brings in another prisoner and to Lids surprise it is a familiar face, Golden from his North West Raiders days of little league football sits down opposite Lid. Golden is a career criminal and he had a great career as a football player but he's a hall of famer when it comes to the dope game in the streets of Philly. It takes a few seconds to recognize Lid but when he does he says puzzled "THEY GOT YOU IN HERE?" Feeling defeated Lid just shakes his head and says "Yeah" "It must be bullshit charges huh?" All of a sudden the action at the intake window stops, every thing just stops to here Lids response regardless of the fact that it was his gun, regardless of the fact that his rights were violated, having a gun without a permit is illegal and the charges he's facing could carry some serious time and he replies "Naw this some serious shit gun charges." Taken back Golden just shakes his head. In the processing room he complaines about his missing things to new cops "Were's my wallet, keys to ny car, and paper work for my car?" The cops look around puzzled and the black cop makes a joke "They are going to love you up CFCF." Lid just shakes his and before he goes the white cop uncuffs him and Lid ask "Is it too late for the academy" the black cop quickly replies "Yup, with a felony on your record you can't do nothing" and Lid looks over at the white cop who looks at his file shakes his head and says "No". Lid smiles and is escorted into the holding cell area with no windows to see daylight the place is filthy, a real cesspool and the stink of piss is all in the air. Inside the cell there is one metal strip I guess is supposed to be the bed, a sink and metal toilet filled with piss and filled with empty water bottles. Lid just has a seat on the bench and lucky for him his cell mate is Golden after a few minutes of just sitting there Lid takes off his racing jacket and places it on the floor, there's one person who could get Lid out of this trouble locked away when the doors slam he cannot move at his own free will and only one person can get him out of this trouble and that's God so He begins to call the athan for prayer and just starts to pray, when Golden gets up and lays his jacket down and says "I'm muslim too" and starts to pray with Lid. When they finish the two catch on old times reminincing about their old football teammates "So what ever happened to Aaron? "Yo he's dead got into some shit with another nigger about some girl and got rocked." "What about Chance?" "Dat nigga's up state he was getting big money up state but you know how that shit go in those small towns they eventually catch up with you." "What about Randy?" "I don't know I heard a few years ago him and his brother moved down south." "Damn it's like everybody's gone man either they dead or just MIA." "I know that's why I was surprised to see my nigga in here." "What ya doing in here?" "These muthafuckers tried to kill me man, the cops pull me over in the jungle and he's like get out the car or they gonna pull me out the window." "You know they do that shit" "Do I! I saw that shit on television down North Philly, so then they cuffed me and I still had my burner on me" "What?" Shaking his head in agreement Golden says "Yeah they were trying to kill you they wanted that thing to fall out." "I know" "So what do you do hustle or something?" "Naw man I just work, that's it." Lid about telling Golden the high speed chase story but thinks otherwise Golden could be a mole or someone else could listening and he has seen people give themselves up enough time on television to know not to incriminate himself. Suddenly the two are interrupted when the cop who arrested Golden comes into the holding cell area, the young clean cut cop begins to jaw at Golden and like two school yard kids they go back and forth at each other through the bars. "I told you too put that weed out!" "Yo I was putting it out, I'm not trying to here that shit I want my money! They only checked in five hundred dollars" "The young cop grins I guess that's all you had was five hundred." Heated Golden Golden threatens the cop "I am going to fuck you up!!!" "Well come on then" replies the cop, "Open the cell and come on then." Laughing making fun of Golden he knows there is no way Golden can open the cell "I told you to put that blunt out." "I was going to I had to finish talking to that bitch what the fuck!" "You should've did it when I told you to put it out" laughing the cop walks away and Golden takes a seat on the bench. On the other end Mikail starts to think about what got him in this jam. Why did he take that gun out? Even if Ashanti was setting him up what good was it going to do? Half way home he should've kept going out west, high on that coke he was thinking about skewing Ashanti and Tia at the same time conduct so unbecoming of a muslim he should've kept going home. The combination of the coke and the alchohol blured his thoughts and made the wrong decision and just that fast he's facing time. The thing about it is that Lid has no idea how much time he is facing, and if had weed on him it would've been even more trouble, hand gun possession and narcotics possession have minimum mandatory time of three years, with a felony like that he could forget about getting a job. Hours pass by until a new group of inmates walk in some Puerto Ricans and as they walk by they lick there lips at the sight of Lid and he knows this was a set up. He thinks to himself that when he hits the CFCF the main prisons he is a done deal all because of a fender bender a few weeks ago. Worried he asks Golden about the process, "So whats going to happen next?" "Like what do you mean?" "When do I get my phone call?, they probably know already because my cousin was with me and he probably told my Uncle, who told my grandmom by now." "You were with your cousin?" "Naw I left him at this chick crib and took her to get this money somebody owed her out the jungle." "But the girl took the keyes to the car and I know he grabbed them and went straight back out west, that was his only way back yo." "Well that's wat's up, they gonna start bringing us out to get finger printed, and processed, then later they bring us out and interview us, then after the interview you see the judge, then after that you get the phone call." "So when do I know how much my bail is going to be? You find out after you see the judge, this is your first time though so you will probably be released on your own reconosince." " What's that?" "You don't get any bail, they give you a court date and trust that you are going to show up for court." "That's what's up cause I don't have no real bail money that's all my savings." A few hours pass and the cops bring back some more people, and as the cop leaves Lid ask "What time is it?" "Almost six o'clock, replies the cop and Lid goes to make wudu at the sink for prayer when he is finished he calls the athan and Golden follows suit making wudu, when to his surprise a few of the other inmates in the different cells ask "Y'all about to make prayer?", and Lid replies "yes" they follow suit and make wudu and a few minutes later Lid leads salat. Its different than before because now when Lid says Allah-hu-akbar the response that follows is not just the voice of Golden but many of the other inmates making this morning fajr prayer something special as brothers including Lid who have neglected salat for so long remember Allah in the most horrid of times. Behind bars you loose the freedom to do what you want, someone else tells you when you can eat, you can't smoke any cigarettes, no women, no driving, no music, no job, no television all your actions are in someone else's hands except on thing the worshiping of God. As he prays he thinks It's astounding that so many of the other inmates are muslim's there was a time when there entire generation was either muslim or leaning towards being Muslim, what happened? 9/11 happened Islam was not the popular thing to do villianized by propaganda and put under the thumb of local, and federal policing agencies under the guise of fighting terrorism. What became popular is being a deviant having no rule of la on how you conducted yourself and transgressing all bounds as the city has seen and rise in homicides, robberies, and spiritually a rise in homosexual behavior by men but more outlandishly women. A society that was once in order now completely in disarray and a unfair distribution of wealth as through faith based initiative unqualified workers find jobs, and qualified muslim workers are discriminated against forced to ingage in criminal activity to feed themselves, and feed their families, all the while Christians in the city have a green light to work, and hustle with fear of no consequences from the police or any other policing agency because they are giving us the means to our own destruction and saying here if you want the jewels, moneys, the girls and the glamour that we project to you through the TV and the music destroy your own people and be great but this is a war and anything goes during war time. War against your own people divided and conquered the black race this 9/11 crap is nothing but a false tale that covers up a lie, a lie that in reality this is just a means to systematically wipe the rest of the ex-slaves off the continent, and finish creating the new master race. Hell has been unleashed in the cities and the one saving grace for the African American man was the decipline of Islam that's why the nation of Islam was a threat to national security because any doctrine that empowers the first man the African man threatens the status quo and as he salaams out and hears that the most of the inmates are muslim as they too salaam out it's obvious that white's are still crusading against Islam against Africa, against the legacy of kings they dethrowned thousands of years ago and will transgress all bounds and exceed all limits to deny rights and keep them under their thumb. Once he is finshed Mikahil rises sits back down and patiently waits, for he did everything in his power to avoid ever being in this position yet still here he is behind bars, like everyone else. About an hour passes by and after seven o'clock shift change, around seven thirty Easter Sunday the new cop comes to the back and escorts two inmates from different cells to get finger printed and then interviewed. Escorted to a small room Mikahil is photographed and then finger printed, and led into a cell that has a telescreen. Looking dejected in the corner sits a clean faced young man, with his head held down low and his eyes closed he just sits on the chair in a dark corner, and as Lid sits down in a chair across from him he ask "How long do I have to wait for the interview?" the boy looks up and eyes red holding back tears he says the "The red light will come on then you have to move over in front of the screen and then the lady pops up and starts to ask you questions." Lid nods his head and says "Thanks", but before the boy lowers his head in defeat something inside Lid urges him to simply ask the kid "What are you in here for?" The kid raises his eyebrows and then shakes his head a gun charge yo." "Was it yours?" "Man I'm nineteen naw it wasn't mines plus I had a dime of weed on me." "What they say at the interview, you young you in school or something?" "Naw I dropped out like two years ago, she aint say shit was just like wait until the judge sees me." "Well listen man it's not part of the program for you to succeed." "What you mean yo?" "I mean this program here in America it's not designed for you succeed it's designed for the African American the ex-slave to fail period. Look at this way everybody back there in those holding cells is black, excluding two Puerto Ricans, white cop locked you up?" The kid nods his head "yeah", me to this whole society has been deisigned to eliminate the African male, the black male by any means nessecary. Y'all running around out there killing each other over dope money that the same dope the cops escort into the city from up state or from down south. Yeah they let you make a few dollars here and there but as soon as you do something they don't want you doing ,like a ref they blow the whistle the Italians are the refs yo, don't do something they ask you to do after you've taken work from them and with the help of the police they pluck you right out the game. Meanwhile the Irish white boy cops are chomping at the bit every morning when they go into work that they might blow one our brains out, beat us the fuck up, or worst case scernerio lock a nigga up, and we don't see the blue blood white boys they don't even interact with us if frowning there face up when they see us down south street, or at one of the games." With full attention the kid head raised just listens as Lid continues "Look don't be too hard on yourself that's my point you playing cards with a stacked deck, playing spades with one spade and they got all the spades you can't win. I'm in here cause they found my gun on me, my gun registered in my name, I went to college yo and I gotta fight everyday for my job deal with hate and get paid chump change just to make an honest buck." But their kids don't even have to graduate high school and it's easy for them everything honest is harder for us because they expect you to be behind bars. The kid interrupts and says "You don't hustle? you crazy yo!" Lid shakes his head I'd rather be a lame than make a fortune off destroying my own people even though my own people can't stand me." "Yo you crazy, you know what HOV say nigga ya munching punching a clock lunching." A little hurt Lid shakes his head and replies "Paper money was the death of Christ now all you shorties resurrect ya life it's like a cycle" A couple thousand dollars don't mean nothing to me yo, twenty inch rims and all that shit man nothing. That's what they want us to chase instant gratification and this beast will be done with you, chewed you up and spit you out and on to the next one, this your first case so think about that when you get back out here it's designed to keep you behind these bars under their thumb, always running looking over your shoulder like a runaway slave."The kid lowers his head in defeat once again and says "Naw man this my second gun charge." Lid mouth just drops, shocked he says "you nineteen?" And the red light comes up the screen and Lid gets up and sits in front of the television screen. When the television screen turns on to his surprise there is a sister on the other side wearing her Islamic hijab covering her hair. A little relaxed Mikahil says "As Salaam Alaikum!" "Wa Laikum Salaam I see here that your name is Lid Islam your muslim huh? Lid shakes his head yeah "I went to Clara Muhammed back in the day, my parents were in the first." She smiles "Me too headquarters was done on Broad and Susquehana in those days." "I know we had rented the building a few years ago my uncle and I were doing this anti war thing in the same building it was fun." "What happened?" Lid shakes his and exhales "sis he was talking about down with Isreal, no you know I can't b part of anything like that that's too extreme, don't be messing with those Jews they will call you an anti semite and ruin you." Agreeing she shakes her head and smiles and begins her interview "Now Lid you have to b completely honest with me because this is a sworn statement and anything you say that is false can be classified as perjury O.K." Lid shakes his head "O.K." "Your full name is Lid Islam?" "Yes" "Have you ever gone by any other name?" "No" "What is your address" "506 Stoney Bridge Circle, New Castle Delaware 19720, but sometimes I stay with my grandmom or my uncle out in west philly." "How old are you?" "I'm twenty six" "How much do you weigh?" "Like one hundred and eighty five pounds." "How tall are you?" Lid thinks for a second like five eleven." "Do you have a job?" "Yes" "Were do you work?" "I work for kinkos in center city?" "What's the address?" "eleven O one market street, they want to see if I can pay bail and if I would run or not?" She nods how long have you worked there?" "For like a year and a half." "Do you use any drugs?" Lid quickly thinks to himself on file he has a failed drug test, so they already know he's used drugs so it's no point in lying "yeah I smoke pot." "How long have you used drugs?" "I started my senior year of high school, but really started smoking a lot when James Baker got off the airplane during the elections in Florida." Lid smiles and so does the sister "Alright is this your first arrest?" "Yes then you should be released on your own reconisence, I'll see what I can do brother." Still smiling Lid says "As-Salaam Alaikum" and as the screen closes out she replies "Wa-Laikum Salaam." Lid gets up and takes a seat across from the kid again, still dejected he waits for the kid to raise his head and when he does they pick up on their conversation. "So what happened?" "She said they might release me on my own reconiscense and she was going to see what she could do." "She asked me if I smoked weed, and I was like yeah." The kid shakes his head "Why did you tell that, you supposed to say no." "Ain't nothing wrong with no weed that shit is legal in some states and I ain't never wanted to hurt nobody because I didn't have any money for green." "I be smoking that wet man that shit be having me gone, it's like being on another planet or something." Cause you are, on another planet, I been getting my weed from the same guy for like six years now, it's from Jamaica Lid catches himself as he remembers he is inside a cell, and says "It's good shit and I know  ain't no chemicals in it, that new stuff be having you guys tripping because it's laced with PCP. One time I was on the El in Frankford and there's this kid high on that shit on the platform and he is grinning and trying to climb under the trashcan on the platform." The kid bust out laughing "Naw it's not funny because he was on another planet high off that wet but the thing is this fifteen years ago when I used to come down that way to go to middle school it was PWT's on the platforms high on crack or pcp, tripping on the trains, now that whole neighborhood in Kensington is young African Americans, or Puerto Ricans, all the white folks moved outtta there out to the North East, and we are all the junkies back their now, that wet ain't no joke yo." So what happened?" "With my case?" "Yeah you the only one in the room" " The cops pulled us over and underneath the seat was a three fifty seven, plus we had weed in the car" "You ain't even know it was under the seat did you?" "Hell yeah I knew it was there we were on our way to go pop this nigga for fucking my girl." "She ain't your girl if she's fucking another nigga yo." The kid shakes his head "Naw man I spent too much money on her, that's my bitch." "Yo these chicks is crazy out here man everything is about money, man how long was y'all together?" "Since I was like fifteen,and she was twelve, she's pregnant and that baby better not come out dark skin because that that nigga's baby and not mines, she better visit me though I know that much." Dejected Lid just shakes his head, and the cop finally comes to take them back to the cells "Y'all done?" "Yeah get me outta here!" "Man you ain't going nowhere but back to the cell and then to CFCF the Ricans can't wait to get you up there speed racer!" On the way back to the cell Mikahil ask don't I get my phone call now?" Yeah me take this guy back to his cell" The kid speaks up and says "Yo let me get my phone call now to?" "Alright and Lid goes first,with his money checked into evidence Mikahil has to make a collect call and h calls his grandmom two one five eight seven seven three one three one.  The phone rings and rings until finally she picks up "Hello?" Why are you calling my phone collect?" "I'm locked up Uncle Faruq didn't tell you?" "No what's going on and where's your car?" "Pete has it he was with me, I figured y'all would be on ya way by now that would've told y'all or something?" "Your getting out of control Lid" "Grandmom the cops pulled me over on a traffic stop talking about they gonna pull me out the window. I don't have that much time though Grandmom I'm at the 35th in West Oak lane, I gotta see the judge to get my bail, but I got like two hours after that to get the money to the criminal justice center at 13th anf Filbert." "Well if you don't make bail what are they going to do with you?" "Take me to CFCF and I am not trying to go up there." "Well I don't have any money Mikahil" "Just call my mom grandmom I have some money in the bank so it's cool, they said I might get released on my own reconiscence because this is my first time, but I wont know until see the judge.Call my mom grandmom please and happy easter." The phone hangs up. The kid makes his call and it's not to his mother but one of his comrades from the streets, "Yo I'm locked up yo they gonna take me up

CFCF Rell still up there?" "Alright, bet I got get a public defender you know I ain't got no lawyer money.(mumbled voice on the other end) They caught me with a burner in the car, but they let Hanif go and he was driving. The cop runs our records and is like you already got a burner charge and they brought me in, Alright yo tell my moms I'm locked up im out yo." (mumbled voice on the other end.)

The cops smiles as Lid just shakes his head in disgust, once back in the cells he ask the officer "what time is it?" "Like one fifteen." "Thanks" and Lid lays his racing jacket on the ground and once again calls the athan for prayer. And once again Golden and other inmates make salat as Lid leads the midday prayer. They continue to sit after prayer for a few hours as inmates are ushed into the cells, the cop comes and gets Golden out the cell for his visit with the judge. When he the cops bring in two Puerto Rican inmates and as they pass his cell they like there lips and he's really scared as the idea of going to CFCF is starting to sink in. When the cops bring Golden back they take Lid in to see the judge. Hand cuffed he's escorted to another room with a seat and a flat screen television. And all of a sudden the television screen comes on and the judge sits before him decked out in his black robe, already beat faced red the over weight white man looks pretty upset and it's probably because he' working on Easter Sunday. "What's your name?" "Lid Islam sir" "Where do you live?" "605 Stoney Bridge Circle New Castle Delaware" "Say's here you have a job where do you work at?" "Fed Ex Office in Center City" "How long have you been working there?" "For like a year and a half sir?" "You've never been involved in anything like this, looks like your first arrest?" "Yes your honor?" "Do you use any drugs?" "I smoke a little pot" The judges face gets redder and the tone of his voice lets Lid know he is angry. "How long have you been smoking marijuana?" he smiles and says "I've been smoking marijuana ever since James Baker got of the airplane during the 2000 elections in Florida your honor." The already mad judge's face turns completetly red and in one motion he slams his mallet down and says "Violation of Pennsylvania fire arms act ten thousand dollars bail." And the screen shuts off, and to himself Lid thinks "may be I shouldn't of said the whole James Baker thing." Before going back to his cell he is granted one more call, and he's been waiting to make this call to hi mother even though she's going to be really angry she would never leave her only son locked up would she? Only one way to find out, and he carefully dials collect three zero two three seven five eight one six eight. And the phone rings once, and then twice and finally she picks up "I don't know why you are calling me I'm not going to bail you boy, what do you think this is some rap video or something? You wanna be a ganster huh? Well arevah dechia your on your way up to CFCF or DC and they gonna show what it means to be a gangster, I used to work up there I know how bad it can get." Expecting that he keeps his cool and just says "Mom! You guys have one hour to get a thousand dollars down to the criminal justice center on thirteenth and filbert please I do not want to go to CFCF, it's four to a room and I cannot take that, I'll turn into a monster and be on medication the rest o my life please." "I don't know boy you so tough want to have that fucking gun on you in the city, what did you have it on for?" "I don't want to talk about it on this phone mom but I have like five hundred saved in the bank but please get down to the CJC before ten because that's when the bus comes and I'm gone." "Were is my car?" "I don't know?, I was with Uncle Faruq's friend from work Pete I think he has it." "So you don't kno were my car is boy do you?" "I can't think about that now mom please get to thirtteeth and Filbert and please pay my bail by ten o'clock please." "Alright I'll try to get down there but I'm coming from Delaware so I might not make it time, and you better pay me back." "I will mom, just hurry please." He hangs up the phone and the cop escorts him back to his cell. Golden is gone and he sits alone in the cell waiting, and waiting getting a sinking feeling in his stomach fearful that his mom might not make in time, he makes salat, but the feeling does not escape him and time just ticks away, as the guard comes back he quickly ask "what time is it and smiling the cop says "nine thirty". Up against the cell bars  screaming get me out of here he just waits and starts to think about what CFCF is going to be like four to a room a couple thousand nigga's and the Rican's already mad at him about the speed racer stuff? How did things get like this he did every thing in his power to avoid selling drugs a engage in criminal activity but sine 9/11 things have changed and making money is the only thing that matters no matter how you get it. To make things worse there is a war going on and the Muslims are the enemies, and so not only is he not wanted in the mainstream work force, but if he hustle's he's a prime target for the police under the new terrorism laws. Religion should never be enforced on anyone especially in exchange for success or wordly possessions because you can't take them with you in the after life. The only thing that matters is the good deeds and bad deed that you put forth and to be staring down jail time the wicked have surely inherited the earth.

Shaking his head he starts doing push up's on the floor, and then the cop walks by, "Islam, you made bail" relieved and a lot more humble than when he entered the cell the idea of being able to just breathe fresh air has Lid excited to be leaving, but to his dismay as he collects his belongings there are some very important things missing. "Where's my paper work for my car, my wallet they threw all that stuff on the hood of the car the cops didn't check it?" " That's all we have replies the cop, you might want to check with the 14th district because that's who locked you up." "So why didn't y'all take me to the 14th? The cops all look around baffled and astonished that Lid made bail they don't have too much to say. "When do I go to court?" Behind the glass the cop hands Lid a piece of paper and says "You have a preliminary hearing on next Tuesday, don't miss it or the district attorney's office put a warrant out for your arrest." "Oh I'll be there, you better believe that." Exhilerated about leaving the police station Lid quickly walks out the front door and into the free world. Filthy dirty from being locked up he smiles when a group of girls walk by him and just the smell of their perfumes brings a smile to his face, and then the smell of fried chicked from the Chinese store hits his nose and like zombie he just marches into the Chinese store, minutes ago he was facing the remote possibility of never being able to utter these words especially if he had been sent up to CFCF breath stinking, his body stinking he say "Four wings and fries please." "Four twenty five please." And he pulls out four wrinkly dollars and digs through his pockets to find change and hands the man money. "How much y'all sodas?" "One dollar" knowing he does not have enough, just let me get a quarter hug" And when handed the hug Lid punctures it open without thought and gulps down the drink thirsty from yesterday just being able to buy some juice is a privilege appreciated after spending the night and day behind bars. The dinnig area of the Chinese store is too confining and he marches outside back on the street just to enjoy the open air and the freedom, when a sight for sore eyes pulls up with a license plate reading "World Best Grandmom" he thinks to himself yes she is, and the moment is broken when the Chinese store cashier says "Four wings and fries, you ready." "Thanks man" He grabs the food and rushes out the store, and humbly he goes to get into the passenger seat when he sees Naim sitting there and the back door automatically opens. "I love you Grandmom thanks for bailing me out. What's up Naim. This is the first time in years Lid has seen Naim and he is starting to look exactly like Uncle Sha, "What up man" Lid gives his grandmom a kiss on the cheek "Don't be kissing me all filthy dirty you better thank your mother because if it was up to me I would've left your crazy butt right in there." "The girl set me up Grandmom" "I don't want to hear you had your gun on you and you know you are not supposed to have that gun on you unless you have a permit I have to go down there myself and renew mines because it is almost expired." "I don't have an address but I'm going to sue the city cops going to tell me to get out or they were going to pull me through the window." "You better pay us back our money you owe me three hundred and you owe your mother six hundred, Shamp's gave us a hundred to get your butt out so you better thank him." Knowing that he and his uncle do not speak anymore Naim would be the best way to relay the message, and Mikahil ask Naim "Yo Naim please tell your dad I said thankyou for bailing me out."The very distant Naim just nods his head. "All I have to do is go to the atm and withdraw the money I have like five hundred in the bank and I get paid again on Friday, Aw Man I don't have my wallet!" "What happened to your wallet?" "The cops took it" "Where's your mothers car?" "Pete should have it I left him at the girls house then I got locked up I left the keys with the girl I was with because I didn't want the cops leaving the car on the street, because somebody was sure to steal it." "Don't nobody want no beat up old Hyndai, and Toney doesn't know what's going on." "He had to get back out west, when she came back home he probably grabbed the keys and went back out west." "So you don't know where your wallet is, or your moms car, I tell you boy your are a mess dummy." "I gotta get my stuff back, and my battery is dead on my phone so I can't do anything until I recharge my battery. Naim don't ever get locked up yo it's the worse." "Don't worry I'm not." "Grandmom I thought they were setting me up so I took the gun out." "So what was the gun going to do?" "I don't know but the cops were trying to bust me for weed so I could'nt work anymore, once you get a felony weed possession that's it your pretty much unhirarable, and I don't have a gun permit because Uncle Rashad won't let me use his address." "Then you should not've took the gun out." "Yeah right the whole city is trying to get me." "That's what you said in Delaware everybody is always out to get you, for what you don't have nothing." "I don't know I'm just different, when I first got up here on election day I was in Boo's mini van and some guy walked up to the window and said "You must be doing something right for so many people to be hating on you." "Yeah well you better your mothers car back and get to the bank because I need that money to play numbers with." "I'll go to the bank in the morning but with no id I don't know what good its going to do may b I'll take a picture." Naim laughs as his Grandmom continues to drives as Lid exhausted and safe falls to sleep."The abrupt stopping of the car awakes him and double parked in front of Uncle Rashad's apartment he kisses grandmother on the cheek and tells her "I love you and thanks for bailing me out no matter what I get paid on Friday I will pay you back, tell Uncle Sha thanks for helping to bail me out to yo, I gotta get in here shower, pray, and then sleep." "You better thank your mom should've left your crazy but up there." "Four to a room, I wouldn't make it, I'd have to kill somebody, then they would never let me out love you grandmom." Once inside the apartment doors she pulls off and up the stairs he goes to an awaiting Uncle Rashad who expecting his arrival already has the door cracked open. And as soon as he walks in the door "What the fuck is wrong with you!!! I told you you were out of control, what the fuck were you thinking bringing that gun out without a permit?" "I would have my permit if you let me use your address!" "What! You still blaming everyone else, where's your car at?" "I don't know I have to call Pete because I thought he had it, I don't know what happened but I will find out when my phone gets charged" and he quickly puts the phone on the charger. "Did you talk to Uncle Faruq?" "Why the fuck would Faruq be calling me?" "Because I was with Pete I figured Pete drove the car back out west and got home that night an told Faruq they work together." "Yeah well we gotta talk because I don't know about you staying here." "Ahh come on Unc don't do this to me know." "Look nephew Karens back plus you are out of control." Shaking his heas he just ignores Uncle Rashads last statement and says "I gotta get in the shower and figure out what happened to my car." He grabs his towel and toiletries and goes to the bathroom and the shower last so long the hot water runs out and when it does he abruptly gets out. His phone rings on the charger and he runs to answer it only to see his mom on the caller ID, and dreading this phone call he reluctantly picks up "As-Salaam Alaikum mom." "So I bail you out and you don't even have the decency to call me and say thank you." "Thankyou

I was just getting out of the shower and getting my mind together." "So when do you have to go to court?" "Next Tuesday on April 1st." "You better show up because I want my money back." "I have to get a lawyer and that's going to cost me." "If you don't have the money you better get a public defender." "Yeah right it's the city trying to take me down I gotta get a layer." "Well you are already in the hole like a thousand dollars." "Mom I cant pay all that right now I have to pay Grandmom like twofifty and pay you like two fifty because I need some money on the side to pay the lawyer, plus I can't even get the money out the bank because I don't have my wallet." "The cops stole your wallet?" "When they cuffed me they tossed my wallet on the roof of the car and that was the last time I saw it, I thought they checked it in but when I got my stuff all they gave me was my rings, some money I had, and that's it." Wheres my car?" "I don't know! I had Pete with me and I left him at this girls house and took her with me that's when I got locked up. He had to get from Germantown to West Philly so I'm thinking while I'm locked up he has the car and he's already told Ucle Faruq about what happened. But when I called Grandmom and she didn't know what was going on I was like hold up? So I don't know I think the girls stole it, now that my wallet is missing. Plus the cops took all the paper work when I was handing it to them and tossed it on the roof of the car." "So these girls have my car, with all my paper work the insurance card, owners card, and registration, and your wallet? Boy you better get out that city and stay away from those crazy niggers they are always up to no good." "Sorry mom." "Don't sorry mom me your retarted and you better get my car back now because I am calling and reporting it stolen first thing in the morning. Bye stupid!" She hangs up the phone and he gives Pete a call, the phone rings and rings and Pete finally answers, "Yo what's the deal?" "Where's my car?" "What happened man?" "What the fuck do you mean what happened, Tia aint tell you I got locked up!" "Yeah she said the cops locked you up because you had your gun on you!" "Yeah they did they were trying to kill me! Where's my car?" "I don't know I caught a cab home." "What da fuck are you talking about why didn't you grab the keys from Tia?" "When she came back she sat down and pulled some weed out of her boot, and they started rolling a joint when all of a sudden her nigga walks in the door. So you know I'm all messed up because I'm by myself way uptown and he's asking me who the fuck am I?" And with that Lid knows he was set up, "Them bitches set me up, this city just set me up." Co signing on Lids check Pete replies "You better believe it." "I aint trying to hear that shit you should've took those keys Yo, now I gotta get my car back." Mikahil hangs up the phone and immediately calls the lawyer that represented him in traffic court Bobby Giacanna. Redered to him by Uncle Sha lawyer Leslie Davidson Bobby seemed like a real goodfella the first time they met and he handled the traffic court stuff with ease, plus Lid really liked his shoes they were worn which is a clear indication that he works for a living. Still in the bathroom and clothed with just his towel he calls with no regards for the fact that its Easter Sunday land he calls and after a few rings he picks up "Hello?" "Bobby! My man I want to apologize about calling so late, but the cops locked me up early this morning and I spent Easter Sunday behind bars I just got out on bail man, and I need a lawyer." "What happened and where were you at buddy?" "I was uptown, they pulled me over on a traffic stop." "So what did they say when they pulled you over?" "Get the F out the car, or they were going to pull me through the window." "So did you get out?" "Yeah he called back up and like six white boys showed up." "Why didn't you let them pull you through the window?" Lid starts to laugh "Naw Mr. Giacanna I had my pistol on me. It was my gun registered in my name down in Delaware." "But you didn't have a permit to carry in Philly?" "No sir if I would've let them pull me through the window and that guns falls out or goes off they would've shot me." "No Biddy they would've killed you, so when is the court date?" "April 1st next Tuesday." "Alright call me tomorrow sounds good though." "How you gonna charge me?" "It's a gun case and you don't have a record do you?" "No sir" "Then like ahhhh twenty five hundred." "Alright I'm working, so I have to pay like every two weeks cool." "Alright buddy thanks for calling me first talk to you tomorrow." "Thanks Bobby." A little relieved he leaves the bathroom and throws on some sweat pants and a t-shirt, but what still looms over his head is getting his wallet and car back. Lid makes prayer things have gotten so out of control but he knows God had to play some part in getting him out of prison and neglecting salat after making salat when he was in trouble is a major sin so he performs Isha prayer looking for guidance and some type of piece of mind in this crazy world, when he finishes he just sits in the recliner exhausted and passes out.

Waking up with the sun Mikahil makes Fajr prayer and once he is finished begins to iron clothes for work in a few hours and still bothered the whereabouts of his wallet and car he calls Ashanti up. The phone rings and rings, and rings, and rings until at last she picks up "Hello?" "Yo Where is my fucking car?!!!" "Who is this?" she replies and in a louder and more serious tone he says "It's Lid where the FUCK is my car?" "You out?" "Yeah" but before Lid gets the word out Ashanti quickly hangs up the phone. He calls her right back but her voice mail picks up on first ring but Lid leaves no message and goes to the bathroom to get washed and dressed still asleep Malik is knocked out in his room with the television still on from last night, and Uncle Rashad has his door closed still asleep as well. After a quick shower h emerges from the bathroom and to his surprise fully dressed in her black rain coat and bucket hat sitting at the dining room table is his Grand mom with a serious general like look on her face right now the last thing he wants to here is any more bad news but she utters "He wants you to leave." Everything just went from bad to worst. Still missing his wallet, car, facing court in less than a week, and now unarmed in the most dangerous city in America, he has to find a new place to live. "What? Where am I going to go?" grim faced she replies "He said he's had enough and he wants you to move." Angry Lid raises his voice loud enough for his uncle to hear "Yeah right his girl comes back and he's using this an excuse." "Lid calm down you need some help boy, you runnig around like everybody is out to get you." "Well I can't do nothing right now grandmom I have'nt even got my wallet back." "Well you got one week to move before you go to court next week." "We agreed to eight months when I first moved in here, I wouldn't left Boo's crib." "He's been sayig what a lot of people have been saying about you something is wrong with you and you don't want to listen to anyone you just got into all this trouble." "Grandmom the girl set me up and stole my wallet and car the only thing that saved me was the fact that I had the gun on me." "Listen to yourself the only thing that saved you was the gun, you don't need any gun." "In this city everyone needs a gun. If I had a bag of weed on me I would still be locked up now facing major time and an automatic felon. So he's not going to come out here and say anything for himself?" "He doesn't want to get into a fight with you." "And I bet this has nothing to do with the fact his girl's back in his life?" "Lid stop it, he just wants you out of here by next week." "Alright I have to work gandmom."

"Do you have any tokens?" Completely shocked because that never crossed his mind he quickly comes to his senses about the current situation. "No I didn't even think about that" "Here she hands him three tokens and she gets up to leave and still in his towel he gives her a hug "I love you grandmom and thankyou." "Take this twenty dollars and get yourself a transpass." He kisses her on the cheek and says "Thank you" she leaves and Lid begins to get dressed and almost ready to leave for work his uncle coms out of his room after his mother has already spoken for him. Looking down to the ground and shaking his head he says "Yo man your just out of control, I can't have you in here with my son and me out of control." "Whatever man we agreed to eight months, your girl comes back and the first excuse you get you ask Grand mom to come tell me to get out." And then Uncle Rashad shows exactly how low he is and how low the entire city can stoop to in order to achieve their own personal gratification "Can we keep the direct TV in your name and I will just pay the bill?" Appauled Lid just says "WHAT! You haven't even paid me for the first two months, I'm cutting that cable off as soon as I leave, I can't believe you asked me that after kicking me out with all this shit I'm going through." "Sorry nephew life is tough" they glare at each other for a while and Lid just shrugs his shoulders and storms out the door for work. As he waits for the ten trolley wearing his rio di jinero jacket with the Christ logo he spreads his arms out along the gate and fold one leg over the other and just nods his head to the ground reminiscent of the crusifiction of Christ, until the trolley comes by to pick him up.

Everything is business as usual on the trolley but once off and upstairs in front of 1234 building things really hit home about the gravity of yesterdays events as the sidewalk is filled with cops, police cars, ATF, FBI, and homeland security agents. He walks through the melee as law enforcement stars him down, and heads south towards the we do it all towers, and once inside security has two extra people behind the desk and everyone is starring him down, the elevator ride up stairs is awkward none of the we do it all incorporated employees speak to him and when the elevator doors closes Lid the last to get on watches through the reflection as everyone looks down. When he reaches the fifteenth floor he gets off at his usual stop and heads into work. As soon as he walks through the door John greets him "Goodmorning" "Morning John" Lid replies, smiling he ask "How was your weekend?" "Cool I got locked up on Easter can you believe it?" Smiling John says "Kathy is waiting for you downstairs" "You already know huh?" John says nothing but his face turns red, "she's waiting for you." "Alright I'm going back down stairs after I just came up here." And just that fast he's back on the elevator and down stairs on the street. Not changing from his usual behavior once once downstairs hold the door open for a few ladies as they enter the building then walks up Market street to the fed ex store, once inside he goes directly in the back office where Kathy is waiting for him chipper as always she mocks an Italian accent and says "How you doing?" Not feeding into it Lid flatly replies "Good morning Kathy, what's going on?" Annoyed that Lid did play along with her mockery of Italians she gets straight to the point "What happened this weekend?" "I got locked up on Easter Sunday the cops told me to get out the car on a traffic stop and I was like no. So then he threatened me and said he was calling backup and they were going to pull me through the window of the car. I had my gun on me which is registered and paid for in my name." "But you don't have a permit to carry?" "No but I will be applying for one." Sadly she says "Gee Lid I am very disappointed in you your lucky you still have a job with Fed Ex office." "Yeah well I haven't been convicted of anything and the police had business pulling me over anyway, I can't wait to see the citations." "Well I am very disappointed in you why did you have a gun anyway?" "Its my second admendment right I bet you got guns out in the suburbs?" Kathy doesn't reply and Lid continues "How do y'all know my business anyway that's my life? The gun was mines registered in my name I earned that right by staying clear of any trouble all my life." "Well it looks like you found some trouble things are not the way they used to be Lid." "Are we done here? Already turned around and walking towards the door Kathy says " Yes, but working at Fed Ex is a privilege Lid let me know how the case turns out." Lid says nothing and walks out the office into the retail area when a fellow co-worker ask "You look heated what happened in there?" "Nothing just a bunch of nonsense 1984 crap I can't wait for Forty Three  to be out of office." "I here that, take it easy man." "Right" and he proceeds to leave the store escaping the madness that is market street Lid takes the back way through the hotel and onto Filbert street. But to no avail as even the back street are linned with police vehicles and suits clean shaven, stand in groups of three watching Lids every move. You would think he was on the terrorist watch list with all the attention he was getting but he continues inside the we do it all tower were once again the security guards eye ball up him up and down as he goes back upstairs to work. Once upstairs he clocks in and only talks to John and Zack about work related things, the we do it all employees stop by and make printing request and unable to restain there joy the African American employees chuckle as they drop off jobs. Still worrying about the were abouts of his car, and his wallet he routinely gives Ashanti calls from his phone and to no avail there's no answer, after making Zhur prayer he finally gets a call its Sharif and Lid quickly accepts the call. "As-Salaam Alaikum" "Wa Laikum Salaam" "I'm at work man I can't really talk I got locked up the other night." "ON EASTER? What happened?" "That chick I met" "Down City Hall?"" Yeah I'm not going to say her name on this phone set me up they stole my car and my wallet. I had my burner on me so the cops booked me, good thing I didn't have any green on me or I would be out of a job and looking at three years from the door." Disappointed Sharif says " I told you not to carry that thing without a permit. So what happened with the car?" "The bitches stole it from me." Sharif starts laughing "Hahahaha" "Its not funny man I have to go get my stuff back." "Yeah well when you do give Rasoul a call so he can put some money on my books. And write this number down six zero nine five eight six fifty five thirty." "Jersey?" "Yeah it's this girl Sonya she wants to come down and see me this weekend." "What about your girl man?" "Aw forget her she doesn't want to be muslim talking bout her family would not accept her.""Is Sonya Muslim?" "She used to be" "That' what everybody says these days" "Yo stick with your girl she's a  good women and she's been with you the whole time you been down man the Quran says "unchaste men are supposed to marry unchaste women and they can be either Muslim , Jewish, or Christian." "Like always whenever he makes a point Sharif does not agree with he gets off the phone and does so "Alright this card is about to hang up you better get out of Philly and get your id back As-Salaam Alaikum." "Wa Laikum Salaam" Lid hangs up the phone and continues to work when the thought crosses his mind that before he pays a Mr. Chicana any money why doesn't he check out what the public defenders office is talking about it's free and given the facts surrounding the arrest he should be in good shape, and with that he John. " Yo can I go to lunch everyone else has gone and have to take care of a few things?" And with a head nod of yes John gives him the o.k. and reminds him to "be back in a half an hour." Knowing he won't be back within a half an hour he just replies "alright" and storms out the door, into the elevators, and onto the street. Once again he tries to call Ashanti, and once again there's no answer up and into the Pennsylvania building and to the eleventh floor and the place is a mad house standing room only the majority being African American's he waits in line to schedule an appointment the girls check him out but he has none of it and after one glance he just turns the other way. When it's his turn sharply grinning behind the counter is a Puerto Rican man, "What can we do for you today?" "I just got locked up over the weekend I would like to talk to a public defender so they could explain what I'm facing and if I need to hire a lawyer or not." Still smiling he say's assuringly "you will be o.k. you don't need a lawyer." And paying those words no mind Lid replies "Alright what time can I see a public defender?" "Sign the list and one of their assistants will come out to interview you." He does so and waits, and waits, and waits well past the half and hour for lunch he calls John and let him know that he will be late. He continues to wait and finally a young white women comes out and says "Lid Islam" Lid gets up and greets the women with a pleasant hand shake "I'm Katlyn come with me please" and he follows her to the back and into an interview room, where they both take seats. "Do you have your notice to appear in court?" "Yes" and Lid pulls out the suppeana to appear in court on Tuesday. "Well that's next week and the public defender is going to need more time to look over the details of the case. What happened?" He goes through the details of the other night and finally says "So I should win this thing huh?, they had no business pulling me over." She frowns her face and replies " The maximum you could be facing is seven years for violating the Pennsylvania fire arms act. Is this your first offense?" "Yes" "Well that might help the situation you are a resident of Delaware?" "Yes" "Then why don't you go back there are way too many guns on the streets of Philadelphia." "Yeah guns in the hands of the wrong people so you're telling me that eventhough they had no business pulling me over, and threatened to pull me out of the window of the car I am still looking at time?" "What did it say on your tickets?" "I haven't received any tickets, that's what I'm saying they had no reason to pull me over." " The police department will b sending you something in the mail, and I'm not an attorney so I am not a liberty to get into the details of the case with you but I will forward your file to the attorney and please call me back later this week we will have the date postponed so you wont even have to show up next week." Ready to walk out ten minutes ago Lid shakes hands with Kaytlen and says " I will be in contact with you guys." He leaves and takes hi supeana with him and glances over at the Puerto Rican guy behind the counter before he leaves who at first sight of Lid begins to smile. As he walks back to work he decides to give Mr. Chicana a call, and let him know he will be going with him. "Bobby! How ya doing?" "Fine buddy how ya doing?" "Just came out of the public defenders office and they talking about seven years, that's crazy this is my first offense I can't take the risk of a public defender screwing this up so I'm going to go with you." "Hey Buddy I'm leaving court let me call back you back, what day is the hearing again?" "On Tuesday the 1st next week at eight thirty" "It's in my calendar Buddy, make sure you have some money on Tuesday and I will see you then alright Buddy." "Thanks Bobby." As he walks back to work he passes the lunch trucks and cooks give Lid head nods as he passes by. Opening the door for some ladies as he enters the we do it all towers he's once again eye balled by the security guards as scans his ID to get to the elevators. Getting out the elevator all he can think about is getting his car and wallet back but when turns the corner bam like a bolt of lightening he's stopped in his tracks as there she is standing at the store window, her black dress pants fit like skin and her ass is just poking out of them a pink sweater that covers her neck up and the only thing you can see is her radiant skin and jet black hair dipping down past her shoulders and Lid quickly gets a move on to help her at the window. Once inside the store he tells Zack who is waiting on Mary she looks at him different Lid notices almost unnatural like she's trying to be alluring and strike Zack attention and Lid goes to the window and takes a look at the job. Very quickly they exchange eye contact which seems to last an eternity as Lid says "When do you need this by?" Breaking off the eye contact she looks down and then back up at Zack and says end of the day would be nice because I have to review all the files tomorrow." Zack shakes his head and replies "I don't know this a whole box of work? What do you think?" "I'll have it done by the end of the day, you have another box of work down here I called you and left a message but you never came down. Locked in eye contact Zack has already sat down as Lid and Mary copy images of each other that will lye in their minds forever he picks up the box and puts it on the counter, and softly he says "you can't carry it's too heavy" She picks it up and says "I'm strong I can carry it " she struggles as she tries to walk down the hallway and Lid stops her. "Mary? Let me carry the box." "Ok here" and Lid walks out the store and side by side they walk to the elevator hiding the attraction and looking away from each other but once on the elevator it's just them two Mary leans against the wall of one side and Lid on the other side and lock in eye contact until the silence is broken "What happened?" "Everybody knows my business around here some girl set me up I spent Easter in jail" "Are you getting a lawyer?" "Yeah I'm not going in there with a public defender I might walk out with a life sentence."She giggles and blushes when she does so the elevator doors open and Mary says "I hope you learned your lesson" and goes back to professional mode as she exits and walks to her cubical, with Lid following enjoying ever second, as soon as she gets to her cubical she sits down and says "Thank you" "Your welcome replies Lid and they share eye contact and like a robot he lays the box down and walks away. Once downstairs he begins to get things in order to copy Mary's job loading up paper in the copier, and removing staples when John returns with a ream of paper form the store downstairs and lets Lid know he was just talking to Kathy regarding his extra long lunch. "Kathy said when you take breaks like that if you need to stay out you can just the remainder of the day off." "That's o.k. I just knew that I was not going to be back in time so I called." "What's this job your working on now?" "Legal just dropped it off she needs it back by the end of the day." John takes a look at the box of legal work and exclaims "What's her extention I have call her back and tell her later in the week because we can't get this done we have all this other work in here." "John I can get this done by the end of the day everything else due today is done, boxed and the mangers have been called." "The rest of this stuff is not due until later in the week or we are waiting for approvals and okays, I got this John." John hangs up the phone and sits back down at his desk, and Mikail starts copying Mary's work jamming to classic rock and roll until the ringing of the bell disturbs his rythem. Lucy and Zack stay glued to the computers and John does not get up, Lid stops his work and goes to the window and reminiscent of jaba the hut standing at the window is Linda Kale and Lid smiles and greets her "Hi Mrs. Kale, picking up those flyers I had printed up yesterday." "Yup here they go still maintaining eye contact with Mrs. Kale, who unrolls the flyers very slowly by sliding the rubber band off and then as the rubber band takes off into the air she says while maintaining eye contact with Lid "And you just slide the RUBBER band right off, pop" and giggles as she does it, completely rattled Lid has flashbacks to when Teresa just slid the condom off his dick and if his intuition serves him right Mrs. Hale was mocking that situation horrified and shaken fighting tears from falling from his eyes he waits for Mr. Hale to examine the flyers and as always she has a complaint about the way they are printed. Mikhial just turns around and ask John "John could you please help out Mrs. Hale and when he turns back around she grinning and he tells her embarrassed he says "John printed these out he's going to help you have a nice day Mrs. Hale." Understanding that even if he expressed his suspicions she would deny it and get him fired, so crushed he turns around and continues working on Mary's job which takes on an entirely different meaning as the memory of hundreds of co-workers teasing him about being HIV positive and horrific memory being raped as Teresa just pulled the condom right off his dick. He's on whatever primal feeling he for Mary earlier, he's not in rythem how did Linda Hale know about what happened with Teresa? He finishes the work fifteen minutes to five and gives Mary a call, just the thought of seeing her again would earase the aguish and pain rekindled by Mrs. Hales act of terror but when he calls all hopes are crushed as the voice mail picks up and she is gone for the day. "Mrs. Suarez, this is Lid at kinkos office the job is finished you can pick it up tomorrow." With the rest of his co-workers gone Lid is  alone and as promised he's trying to finish the jobs that are due the next few days, when as always his friend the security guard comes in the store "Hi ya doing?" Lid shakes his head "Not good I gotta get a lawyer, I should not of went out with it without my permit by my instincts told me better." "We learn from our mistakes stay out of trouble, you think the Phillies are going to make a run for it?" "I hope so they got Hamels and Myers is going back in the rotation so yeah they might make a run this season but we still need pitching and Howard has to stop striking out. When he first came up he was pulling those balls for singles and doubles." Attentively listening the security guard replies "I know he better get it together all that money they're paying after going to arbitrations." "I heard that" "Well I have to get back to work young fella, have a good one." "You too sir, and thank you." Feeling much better Lid continues to complete jobs until six o'clock and with most of the work finished he gets ready to leave when a thought occurs to him, call Ashanti on the we do it all phone line."

He does so and to his surprise she picks up "Hello?" "As-Salaam Alaikum Ashanti were's my car?" "Why you playing games calling me on some other line come on brother wit these games I don't have your car Tia has it." "I calling the cops reporting it stolen when I get home tonight the twenty four hours will be up." "Her number is two six seven seven four five thirty nine sixty seven hahaha" Ashanti giggles away over the phone." "Why don't y'all bring me my car back and my wallet too and I don't have to get the cops involved." Still laughing Ashanti says "I told you I did not have it." "Whatever" and Lid slams the phone down. As promised he stays and finishes the jobs on the table and as the night overtakes the day and city skyline lights up he closes the store and makes Asr prayer. With the confusion and madness his upcoming court date, his identification missing, his car stolen, his job in jeopardy, Lid turns on the Holy Quran on his I-Pod and just listens on the trolley ride back home. A few weeks ago he was looking forward to being plugged in with City Hall and who he thought was a mover and shaker in the city, weeks ago he was starting trouble with Omar, weeks ago he was the hunter without his pistol and an upcoming trail he was now the hunted and without his id and his car he was pretty much stripped naked in days how fast his fortunes turned and now with no place to live a very liminited budget, and possible time the only salvation Lid can find is in the words of the Holy Quran and peacefully he rides on the back row of the trolley and gets to his stop thinking how did I go from bad to worse?" Once he gets to his uncles apartment his cousin Malik is sitting in then recliner in front of the television mezmorized and glued to the seat. "What's up Lid?" "Yo you gotta get out of here man I need to be alone and figure things out." Malik huffs and puffs and gets his fat ass up and into his room, for an six year old he has so much attitude, then Uncle Rashad comes out from the back room "Why you'd tell my son he has to go in his room?" Already angry at Uncle Rashad Lid steps to him face to face and exclaims "Yo I gotta call the cops and try to get my car back and get my wallet back I need to concentrate man I don't want him listening to what I am saying." "Look brother I need you to get your shit and get out now?" "You mean after I just worked all day, I cant do it, I have to get my car back and my wallet I don't even have money to go anywhere yo plus I don't know where I'm going." "Well I'm sorry brother life is tough." "Yeah well I'm not leaving until Friday Unc that's when I get paid, the first thing I have to do is get my car back so that's it life's tough." Uncle Rashad huffs and puffs and takes a second to gather himself and just before he makes his final plea for Lid to get out he girl Lynne calls him from the back room "Rashad, Rashad the Come on I got the blunt rolled, what's up Lid how you doing!" "What up Lynne I'm going through it." Uncle Rashad agrees to the terms and says "Alright you better be out of here by Friday." He turns around and leaves and Lid thinks to himself the nerve of Uncle Rashad behaving like this when he was growing up Uncle Rashad used to spend every winter living in Germantown with his sister Halima she never charged him any rent and like clock work every spring he would leave, he has some audacity kicking Lid out in the streets especially after making an agreement with him but that's life and just another example of how hell has been unleashed on earth as on bloodlines mean nothing and the joy and pleasure, or just having power over the living arangments of another corrupts ones soul, but right now Lid has other pressing issues like getting his car and his wallet back. He does so and does something that violates all the principles he was brought up believing in and calls the cops. "Good evening I would like to report a stolen car?" "Laughing on the other end the officer ask when was the last time you saw your car?" "I was arrested early Sunday morning and the girl I was in the car with took it, the arresting officer threw my paper work and wallet all on the hood of the car, and I didn't get any of that stuff back." "You don't know who the women's name? Or where she lives at?" Lids no snitch and Ashanti is connected to Mr. Valentine, a few state reps and, a city council member, so dropping any names could mean death so he lies "No I didn't know the girl, we were up on McMahon street when it happened." "So what do you want us to do?" "Could you please send a black and white around so I could report the car stolen let them know the tags so you guys can be on the look out for it?" "Alright what's your location?" "I'm at sixty third and Oxford I'll be waiting outside." "I can't give you a specific time when the officer will be there just be on the look out." "Thanks". Lid grabs his cashmere trench coat and walks outside in the cold of the night, around the corner he waits in front of the closed Bodega, and waits, and waits wearing just a wife beater underneath his coat and timbs on his feet the cold winter hawk produces clouds of smoke with every breathe and after about a half an hour of waiting the officer pulls up in his cruiser alone they exchange eye contact and the cop makes a u-turn and pulls in front of Lid. He walks to the cruiser and goes to open the passenger side door when the officer says "BACK AWAY FROM MY CAR I DIDN'T TELL YOU YOU COULD GET IN!" Filled with dishonest cops his actions only solidify the fact that America has become bizaro world as the man with integrity and commitment to serving the public is ready to speak to a police department  that assisted in robbing him???" So given the chance to hop in the front seat of a police cruiser by instinct he goes for the door "Sorry officer" and from the outside of the door he ask "You came by here about the stolen car report?" Grinning he replies " Yes do you have the year, make, and color of the car?" "Yeah here's the insurance paper work and the tag number." The cops gets on the radio and as Lid stands outside the cop car the young boys from the block start to come outside and watch on the porch. "So I heard the call you don't know the girls name and she has your car, you just gave your car away?" Both of them start smiling the cops know who has the car but Lid has to lie to make sure he lives to see tomorrow. "No officer I got arrested on Sunday y'all took my paperwork and wallet and threw it all on the roof of the car. Then y'all gonna ask m should I let the girl take the car or leave it uptown with the keys in it?" "So you let the girl take it?" "Naw that was twenty four hours ago the car is now stolen, what am I going to do let the young boys uptown steal the car, or what yo?" Simoultainosly the cop is running the paper work as they continue their exchange.  "So you don't know the girls name?" Lid hakes his head "She's from uptown, that's all I know." "I don't understand what you want us to do you gave her the car." Frusterated Lid finishes the song and dance and says "Look you guys got the make, model, and color of the car please keep a look out for it and mark it as stolen, if she doesn't bring it back by morning some one is going to have a federal problem!!" The cop pulls off, and Lid goes back into the house and he passes a few young boys they give him a head nod of approvement and utter "He's gangsta" Back inside he makes Magrib prayer and begins to pack his things together his mind is racing about his stolen car and wallet and overwhelmed by the current situation he sits down in the recliner and begins to read the Quran, things have just gone from bad from worse with every passing minute he shake the memories of his co-workers at citigroup teasing him about having aids, he thinks about Teresa ripping the condem off his dick and bragging to people even posting on her my space page that she raped Lid. He thinks about how fast so many people knew about what happened, yet all everyone does is ridicule, laugh, and make judgment. He thinks about all the time he has spent with his brother Sharif which has got him no where, his upcoming trial and the time he could be facing, and where he is going to stay come Friday after his Uncle kicks him out. His only source for hope is to turn to Gods miracle the HOLY Quran, and as he opens it as always it reveals a verse that soothes Lid's soul.

Al-Kahf Ayats 103-108

> "O Muhammed, say to them "Should we tell you who are the most unsuccessful people
>
> Miserable failures in regards to their deeds. They are those all whose endeavours in the wordly life, had gone astray from the right way. But all along they were under the delusion that everything they were doing was rightly guided."

He closes the Quran and opens it again to
Romans Ayatt 30

> "So patiently persevere for verily the promise of God is true:
> Nor let those shake thy firmness
> Who have themselves no certainty of faith"

He closes it and again opens it to
Sura XLI
Ayatt 30

> "Whatever misfortune happens to you,
> is because of the things your hands have wrought
> And for many of them He grants forgivness"

After reading Lid makes Isha and then as usual smokes what is left of the dutch he had rolled the night before, the stress of being a victim of identity theft, and car theft at the hands of the Philadelphia police department, puts Lid right to sleep, and in the morning he awakes to the sound of his cell phone ringing. With the sun not even up yet he quickly picks up the phone. "Yo who this?" the voice of a familiar women says "Yo I'll be at 63$^{rd}$ and Wynnewood road around ten o clock with your car." Its

Tia but before he could respond she quickly hangs up the phone. Relieved Lid gets up and makes Fajr prayer once he's finished he begins to iron his clothes for work, and as the sun rises he calls John at work to let him know he is going to be late."Thanks for calling kinkos office John speaking how can I help you?" "John this is Lid the girls who stole my car my car is bringing it back around ten o'clock is it o.k. if I'm a little late?" "Yeah no problem does she has your wallet?" "I don't know I hope so because I need to get to the bank and get some money out." "Good luck and I guess I will see you around eleven?" "Yeah around eleven thanks John." As Lid hangs up the phone Uncle Rashad emerges from the back room. "What's all this noise that you are making out here, my son is sleep in his room when are you getting your shit out of here because I wanted you out of here before you got out of jail." Lid rolls eyes irritated and replies " I'll be out Friday, yo I'm trying to get my car back and my wallet and can't even go to the ATM and get any money for any tokens do you have any tokens so I can get to work." Shaking his head he replies "Naw I don't have any I gave them all to my girl. I'll ask her if she could give you some tokens but what were you going to do, how was you going to get on the trolley?" "I don't know blind faith Unc, things is crazy right now and I'm moving off blind faith these days." "Didn't you watch that video man that religion shit is bull shit." "Well I have to have faith Unc with all this stuff happening to me the shit at banco international, the city, now with you I have to have faith that Allah is watching over me as long as I do good and not transgress all bounds." "Yeah well I hope he can find you a place to stay because you are getting out of here on Friday. Let me go see if she has any tokens to sell you?" "Thanks Unc." Around nine thirty after buying tokens from his uncle Lid steps out the house and waits on the corner for Tia to bring his car back, as he waits African Americans drive by and scream out there cars "We da MOB!" as they drive by laughing at Lid, he just smiles as he once again hangs on the fence mimicking the crucifition of Christ and finally Tia pulls up a little after ten. He immediately goes to the driver side and opens the door. "Get out the car" With her face all frowning and obviously angry Tia gets out the car, and says nothing. He quickly checks the glove and nothing, then the insides of the in between the chairs and nothing, underneath the sun visors nothing, and finally underneath both seats and to his dismay nothing. "Where the fuck is wallet and paperwork?" "I don't have it" If she doesn't have it then Ashanti has it but as ten thirty approaches he has to deal with that later because he's about to be late for work. Ready to pull off Tia stands on the curb and has the audacity to ask " Could you give me a ride back uptown?" "What? No way Tia I have to get to work the sixty four is coming and the stop is right around the corner." " I don't have any tokens or money to get on the bus please." She's serious and against every fiber in his body Lid read the expression on Tia's face she's still a women and only a bastard would leave a women out on the curb that way and the goodness in his heart takes over "Come on get in, but I gotta fly cause I'm already late for work." They drive up Germantown and the traffic is empty going north as most of the traffic is heading south and into center city, this allows Lid to fly and soon he is infront of Tia's house when her phone rings and you can here Ashanti hollering over the phone. "Did you bring that pussy back his car?" Tia says nothing and Lid grabs Tia's phone "Yo were the fuck is my wallet?" "Who the fuck is this? I don't have your wallet, pussy give Tia the phone back?" Completely out of character Mihail yells "You better give me wallet back tonight or I swear to GOD!!!" "You aint gonna do shit." "Just give me wallet back you got until tonight or I'm going down 6<sup>th</sup> street." Ashanti hangs up the phone and Lid gives the phone back to Tia, she leaves and slams the door behind her, defeated she goes into the house as Lid thinks about vengeance and thoughts of fire bombing Tia's house even cross his mind. As he quickly pulls away and gets back to his Uncle's apartment he parks the car putting the club over the steering wheel taking no chances because may have made copies of the car keys, and like clock work the trolley arrives and its off to work. Ashanti has to heed to Lids warnings he's been down the federal prisons for the past year visiting Sharif, reached out to an old King of Philadelphia in Mr. Malzonno and that move definetly raised some eyebrows in the fed, and team alphabet does know about him a few years ago during the winter of 2005-2006 Uncle Faruq plugged him in with a night job working in the federal building on 6<sup>th</sup> street. The background check was stringent but being one of the only African Americans in the hood with a clean record he passed it with flying colors. Demolition was the job and they had to completely destroy the old court rooms and bathrooms in the federal building. The job was the hardest Lid ever had swinging a sledge hammer up against concrete walls and destroying toilets and sinks. The court rooms were even worse as they had to break down all the wooden benches and the gut out the carpets inside the court rooms real blue collar work but it was legal and all winter Lid worked the job with his Uncle Faruq. Team alphabet took a liking to Mikahil he was the youngest of the group and passed the background check with flying colors and more than once he was asked to go ahead and apply by a few of the agents. On his way up from the trolley stop always attentive he sees a dark haired septa employee talking to a man holding a note pad. And as he walks by them he is stopped, by the man holding the note pad. "Excuse me sir my name is Rob Martin I am with the Philadelphia Inquier, I would like to know your opinion about the man who died yesterday on the El platform yesterday during rush hour?" " I saw the crowds and the EMT's rushing down here, the news said a man died after being beat up by some kids?" "Yes he was the assistant manager of the Star Bucks right upstairs h lived in South Philly." Shocked that the man was from South Philadelphia very upset Lid just responds accordingly "I'm appauled  only monsters would do that to a hard working American." And with that statement the reporter the reporter says "Good job, what's your name?" "Lid Islam I work upstairs in the we do it all  tower for Kinkos." "Thank you sir, very good." He walks off as the reporter stops more people and once upstairs he's on his way to the we do it all tower. Upstairs a little past ten the meeting with Bobby is completely out of the question and Lid thanks John for letting him come in a little late. "Good morning John, I got my car back but my wallet is still missing." "Bummer man what are you going to do?" "I gotta wait and hopefully it turns up." John comes from behind his desk and as he clocks in he tells Lid later today we are going to have your performance evaluation and Kathy is going to come upstairs o.k.." "Yeah no problem and Lid continues to clock in and starts to go over the days work. As usual he works like a dog quickly knocking out jobs and boxing them up, jamming to classic rock 102.9 and the day flies by, when around two o'clock Kathy comes into the store chipper as ever greeting Lid with that devilish smile and says " How you doin Lid once again mocking Italians and Lid bluntly says "I'm good Kathy, ho is everything with you?" "Great" "We are finally going to have that performance evaluation today huh, get that fifty cents raise?" Kathy makes a sad face and pokes her lip out, Lid continues to work and John and Kathy go into a cubical and talk, then they finally appear giggling and smiling they ask "Lid could you com back here for your evaluation?" And Lid goes to the back cubical sitting in a round table across from Kathy and John, Kathy starts the meeting " Lid you have to finish your online training, because that is holding you up from advancing in the company." "Kathy it's tough for me for one thing I'm doing all the work in here just about every job that comes in here I'm printing and cutting." John interrupts "But I give you time to finish your training and you decide to stop the training and complete jobs." "John you like running the store like it's run downstairs" Before he finishes his sentence Kathy interrupts "You guys better be running the store up here like I run the store downstairs." "Let m finish Kathy what I mean is job jackets and the color system in the store its o.k. to give customers set times based on when they come into the store, and how difficult the job is but up here its different this is we do it all inc.and these people need these jobs right then and their, most of the time it's a real quick turn around because of meetings and people going out of town needing the work before they leave." "So what does that have to do with you not completing your training?" "Kathy let me finish this isn't Germany this a meeting let me speak please? When I'm on the computer doing training John starts ordering jobs like the store telling customers things will be done in like three hours, you should see their faces Kathy very disappointing if we are about customer service we should do our best to met the needs of the customers here at we do it all incorporated. So when I see customers having to wait at the window, or ask if their jobs could be done ASAP and they are refused I take it upon myself to stop training and get back to work. Then there is the actual training I read all the slides and take notes however when I take the quiz at the end of the section I fail the test, the multiple choice answers do not fit the questions and they don't match my notes Like I select what seems like the right answer based on my notes but the answer comes back wrong." Smiling Kathy just says "Well you have fifty percent of the online training done and your future at Fed Ex kinkos is jeopardy and you could be fired if you don't complete your training am I making myself clear?" "Crystal clear" Lid smiles as Kathy moves onto the next section "So based on that John and I agreed that you derserve a 2.95 on your performance evaluation. John interrupts "That's just less than enough to get a raise and gives you the ability to transfer or get promoted to another position." "Gee thanks you know I would like to bring up a few things." "Go ahead Lid we are like family here." "Right the online training is bias and racist and I would like to point some things out especially the fact that one of the sections even says that people in North America and Europe think one way and people in Asia and Africa think another way. That's racist Kathy and the courts found that Fed Ex ground was responsible for the same kind of discriminatory practices when promoting employees. I would also like to add that time after time I have requested training on the design programs and as my co-workers sit in front of the computer screens all day long off their feet I am constantly refused the opportunity to hands on training and when Zack or Lucy try to train me John you quickly get me off the computer." John replies "Well if you don't like it up here you can always go down to the store, we are having budget problems and in reality I need to cut the staff to two people and I looking to hire a real project manager." "What do you mean a real project manager John I have two years experience running a print center like this that was my first job. Plus I have my experience here, so I don't know what you mean when you say a real project manager." "Well Lucy is what I mean by a real project manager." "Yeah well I was here first I still don't understand why I didn't even get asked about the early shift, anyway I guess anything goes in the new America now?" "What's that supposed mean Lid?" "Kathy that means you will transgress all bounds to deny me my rights, is this meeting over?" "I don't know what you mean but, yes you can go." Lid gets up and goes back to work, he finishes the day and on his way home he gets a call from Ashanti, "As Salaam Alaikum you got my wallet cause I'm on my way back from work yo and I need my atm card." "Wa-Laikum Salaam brother meet me at the rite aid on 45th and Chestnut and hurry up because we are in the parking lot now." "Yo I just got off work I gotta go home and get my car." "Well you better hurry up then." Once he gets home he immediately gets in his car and drives down to the rite aid he calls Ashanti as he pulls into the parking lot "As Salaam Alaikum" "Wa Laikum Salaam we are in the grey dodge Durango" Lid parks and gets out and to his surprise inside the Durango is State Representative Nelson and Ashanti, and staying calm Makhail approaches Ashanti in the passenger side and nicely gives the greeting to both of them "As Salaam Alaikum" "Wa Laikum Salaam, they reply, Ashanti can I have my wallet please?" Not paying much mind to Lid she searches through her pocket book obviously angry that she has to give it back the federal things must've worked because the State Representative is present. While Ashanti searches the State Rep and Lid chit chat, "So when do you have to go to court?" "Next Tuesday I was thinking about getting a public defender, I can't really afford a lawyer." "What the charges marijuana possession?" Lid shakes his head "Naw I had my pistol on me it's registered in my name and paid for." "You didn't have a permit?" "No sir I don't have an address but I will apply for it when this is all over." "What kind of gun was it?" "German Ruger forty five caliber" "That's on that list man didn't somebody just use that to kill a cop a few months ago?" "I don't know but that's my burner man and I want it back." "Your not getting that back man you might as well forget about that." "Yeah well you know any good lawyers?" "I'm a lawyer but not a defense attorney look in the phone book and find somebody but you don't want a public defender you'll end up doing the maximum." "I know, Ashanti interrupts their conversation "Oh here it is " and pulls out Lid's wallet from her bag. "Thanks and he grabs the wallet from her hand" and begins to walk away Ashanti makes sure she's loud enough when she says to the Representative Waters " We have time to make it the seven o clock show come on lets go babe." They pull off as Lid goes through his wallet making sure all his identification is their and bank cards. Next stop is finding a place to stay and the best bet would be Idris's house he rents rooms there, and Idris already had a falling out with Ashanti and Idris is always hungry for money. Mikhial makes his way back up West Philly and to Idris's house. He knocks on the door and Idris comes to the window projecting the look of excitement his raises his hands in air, he soon comes to the door and opens it. "As Salaam Alaikum" "Wa Laikum Salaam" I told you about how Ashanti can be she got you locked up man, O I told you weeks ago that she was bad news and you needed to stay away from her." "Yeah well she called me and played me on that muslim sister stuff." "And like a sucker you went for it, so what can I do for you brother?" "Can I come in?" "Yeah come on your just in time I have company." "Siting on the couch is Caramel bright eyed, young girl real young girl and taken aback Lid just smiles and ask "how you doing?" "Fine, Idris when are you coming back to sit on the couch?" "In a second sweet heart look why don't you stand up and show my friend here what you packing?" She gets up and starts dancing shaking her phat ass booty and jangling her big tities poping that pussy like a real pro, and Idris tells Lid "she's only fifteen." Lids mouth just drops and yeah she could built like that at the tender age of fifteen she has a developed body of a twenty two year old. It's the food they eat the school lunches, the fast food, the Chinese store, and fucking at early ages and this young girl is just built her long black hair and blond streeks her body is just thick an she has a tender young face and Lid hasn't seen anything like her since high school and as she sits back down on the couch Lid ask "What's your name?" "Holly, I'm going to Hollywood and be a star." "Yeah O.k, I believe you." "Idris so look man I was wondering if I could move in one of the rooms upstairs?" "You want to move in here? The rents like five hundred, and I want first last so that's a stack up front. This will work out because I'm going back and forth to reading and you can keep an eye on these niggas, when I'm gone, come here look at this." Idris takes Lid to the dinning room and pulls out a shot gun from behind the china cabinet. "Two fifty man right now?" Shaking his head "Naw Idris I can't get it right now, my money is tight I have to pay the lawyer and get things together for rent." "Aw man you can't do me like thatcome on let me show you something" and together they walk downstairs to the basement and from behind the hot water tank he pulls out a large bag looking like sugar but its all cocain and says "I'm all ready to go I got this girl up reading at this house and I was setting up there the money for the shotgun going to buy my  ticket and I was out." "Naw Idris I cant buy that shotty right now" Determined Idris ask again "Come on young blood get the gun man?" Lid sences that something is wrong because Idris would never b so desperate and the money is not the thing, the cops control the game and for him to end up with such a big ass bag of cocaine, his assignment must be to get that shot gun in Lids car, furthermore for him to have so much coke he has plenty of money to buy a a ticket to Reading. Lid stays strong "no way Idris, moving is my first priority when I can I move in here I'll have a few hundred on Friday." "How much?" "Like six hundred" "To move in here you gonna need nine hundred from the jump and I'm dropping it a hundred after I just told you a thousand upstairs." Knowing he is not going to have the money he still agress "Alright" and they head back upstairs watching on the couch Holly sits and waits "Alright young blood could you do me this favor" Smiling "Take Holly home because I don't feel like calling a cab." "Yeah I can do that, come on Holly lets go were do you live?" "Right off fifth street on Ducannon" That's right around the same neighborhood the high speed chase occurred at, but there's no way he's going to turn down a shot at nailing this young chick. He watches to see if she passes the test and she does with flying colors unlocking and opening the driver side door for Lid. "Thanks" "For what?' "Unlocking my door" She laughs "So why don't you want to ride or smoke nigga I'm trying to get high!!" "I cant I had to change the plates on this car and they don't match, the registration plus the cops been trippig so I cant risk getting pulled over." "You act like you moving keys or something" "It's a long story babe but this is the first time I've been uptown in weeks so I'm going out on a limb for you." She smiles and as they drive on the expressway a few brief moments of silence shackle the ride home until it's broken when he ask "So do you have a boyfriend?" "No, me and this young boy I used to fuck wit broke up but I have a girlfriend though." At thisp point nothing can shock Lid and he just shakes his head in disbelief "I don't understand that its like every girl in this city has a girlfriend!" "Its better than a boyfriend girls understand you better they know how to touch us in all the righ places during sex it's more intiment." "You do understand that men and women compliment each other and our differences is what makes us compliments to each other? That homosexuality is a crime against God right?" "What are you religious or something? Nigga I didn't say I don't take any dick, I fuck niggas too but just the ones I wanna fuck your cute so I'll fuck you but its gonna cost." That's all he really wanted to hear, "How much?" Like fifty dollars, you better have some condems though, cause I aint fucking you raw." Already in Germantown Lid is not going back to West Philly gas is way too high, so he comes up with an alternative plan you know where Aubury park is at by A.D. Lewis?" "Yeah right behind king high school, we gonna fuck in the park?" "Thinkng bout it." "Come on nigga get a room at the hotel its cold outside." "It'll be fun" "Give me the fifty dollars now." Lid reaches in his pocket and pulls out three twenties and steps on the gas headed straight for the gas station. "Yo go get some condoms" With money in hand she agress, "O.k. Boo" with the sixty buck still gripped in her fist she puts her hand out and ask "Arent you gonna pay for the condoms?" "You said fifty I gave you sixty take the condem money out of that." She's young and there's no way she has a witty come back for that one so she just lies and say "I thought you gave me two twenties and a ten my bad." And with titties and ass jiggling away she jogs to the gas station, while he waits in the car he thinks about Aubury park and how every summer him and his friends used to crash the pool at night time, the classic football games on King's field, and trying to teach Tee Tee how to play basketball when she was like five on the courts up there. But most of the neighborhood crew had got there first piece of ass up in the park, but not Lid because being Muslim once he smashed something for the first time the word would get back to his sister and the flood gates would open, you did it so we can do it. So as he waits for Holly to come back to the car he's excited about fulfilling one of his child hood dreams finally getting to hit something in the park and being that Holly is young and tender it will be just his teenage years, the moment of clarity of broken when the car door opens and Holly says "I got em boo, I had to get some tampons too because my period is ready to come on." Already into that fifty dollars, "Then I better hurry up." And as usual he darts off from the gas station like a bat out of hell. It's winter time in Philly so the park is clear, but the cold air whips through the sky and Holly only wearing a tight fitting hoody ask "Can I wear your jacket because it's cold out there boo?" This bitch don't even know my name, but being the gentleman that he is he takes off his leather jacket and gives it to the pretty pretty young thang, and together they get out the car and walk against the walls of the recreation center hiding away from any passer byers. With his back to the wall they begin to rac against the cold and quickly exchange kisses and Lid just grabs up her shirt and begins to liss, nipple, and suck on her big ass titties, its col so everything going by quick and before he knows it Holly's unbuckled his pants and dropped to her knees putting the condom on his dick, and she takes those soft lips and just sucks away slowly and paralyzed from the pleasure Lid just leans back on the wall and everytime he looks down at her the feelin intensitfies so he keeps his head to the sky, while he strokes her long hair. "Ahhhh!" "Did you cum?" "No its so cold out here but inside yo its burning like a flame or something in me." "Well come on boo because I wanna get you in me." "Lets go over by the steps and quickly she pulls down her pants halfway and drops that young, ripe, wet, tender, pussy on top of Lids dick and what do you know it's a perfect it. "Ohhh Boo Holly moans and moans getting great practice for her movie career because she is way to loud for the action going on. As Lid's dick gets deeper and deeper inside her until after a few pounds the tip of his dick reaches her back wall and moans louder and louder, "Oooh Ooooh boo you found my spot, you found my spot!!!" Up and down Holly slams her pussy onto Lids dick the cold wind bustering around them and all into their open parts the combination of the hot friction and cold air make a sensation that's indescribable. But the cold is also an incentive to hurry up and Lid just grabs Holly's waist and slams into her pussy until AHHHH! He climaxs, Holly dismounds and snatches the condom off Lids dick, and together both of them hugged up on each other hurry out of the cold and into the car. Once inside Lid turns on the heat and Holly fixes here air in the mirror when suddenly she plants a kiss on Lids cheek, "yo you just sucked my dick, cool out." "he grabs a bottle of water "Here" She gargle's it for a few seconds and then spits it out the window, and they kiss in the heated car for a few minutes as he takes her home "You live here with your mother?" "Yeah and my stepfather who gets on my fucking nerves, if he puts his hands on me again I'm going to kill him!" "Call me first I'll help, can I call you when I get home back out west?" She shakes her head "I'm going straight to sleep I have to go to school tomorrow." There's something very wrong with that statement but what the fuck I paid for it. "Alright Holly I had a good time, talk to you later." "Thanks Boo I have to get my hair done and I needed that money plus you really was hitting my spot call me tomorrow." She gives him a kiss on the cheek and gets out the car and he watches as she jingles away, and goes into the house. Still paranoid about the Philadelphia police department Lid drives slow on his way back home and realizes he just accomplished a dream he had conjured up in his mind years ago when he was a teenager a vision he never shared withanother human being a vision that he and Allah only knew about.

Sura XX
>"Say "each one of us Is waiting:wait ye, therefore And soon shall ye know who it is that is on the straight and even way and who it is that has received guidance."

# "Boss With No Racket"

ITS SPRING TIME AND Lid has really kept a low profile his upcoming court date scheduled for the first week of July, work, and the Phillies are the only thing popping. The police department has nothing to go to court with Bobby handled the moving violations and with them thrown out the city has nothing to stand they had no business pulling Lid over, so the police department will do whatever it takes to bust Lid on any charges and the best bet is to stay out the streets and keep a very low profile. Today however his cousin Khadejah is going on her prom and eventhough h is banned from his Uncle Sha house nothing is going to stop him from seeing Khadejah going off to prom. Sitting in his grand moms house she explains " You know my son does not want you to come over his house." "I'll stay in the car Grandmom." "Always starting some stuff, come boy." And together they drive up in her mini van to Uncle Sha house. There are no parking spaces so she double parks and warns Lid don't get out this van, always starting trouble. Outside all of Lids cousins are outside playing when Miko and Naim pulls up and begins to walk up the stairs with a cake, it's a nice scene as Lids little cousins are now watching their children who all run up and down the street, and he thinks about his child that was murdered and Teresa and how much fun this would all be but he failed and defeated Lid sits in the car holding back tears when his cousin Nadia says "Aw why don't you get out the car Lid what you scared of Uncle Sha?" "Shut up Nadia, no I'm not scared of Uncle Sha I just cant go in the house." "Bye!" The crowd begins go into the house and Lid sits in the double parked car alone and contemplates whats the worse that can happen? Just go inside, unsure of what he was walking into Lid took his twenty two out with him and as it sits in his back pocket he contemplates If Sha gets crazy an pulls his gun I will be ready for him. That's what a pistol does to you gives you a false sense of superiority or braveness and feeling that high he gets out the car and begins to walk up the steps that for many years were familiar to him and until recent history had become hostile, and up and in through the front door and when emerges from the vestaview and all the air is taken out the room when Lid looks to his left and sitting on the couch is Uncle Sha and for the first time in three years they meet face to face and Lid says "What's up Unc?" Shocked Uncle Sha just quietly says "Hi" everyone moves into the kitchen as Naim comes down stairs and Lid gives him a head nod. Naim says nothing and continues into the dinning room. Uncle Rashad comes out the dining room and just looses his mind "Oh this mutha fucking nigga must be crazy!" and storms out side, staring Lid down as he walks outside. Miko comes from the kitchen and Lid greets her humbly and softly "Hi Miko", she breaks a smile and says "Come on in a sit down in the dining room" Uncle Sha says nothing as he just sits on the couch, meanwhile Grandmom is going off on the dining room as Lid walks in and takes a seat. "Always starting something he said he did not want you in his house, why would you come in here you promised you were going to stay in the car." "I got tired of sitting outside plus y'all can't take these memories from me this is my family too and I want to be here to see Khadijah in her prom dress and I want to be here to see all my cousins playing." Miko steps up and defuses the tense atmosphere "He can stay you too just two just try to not to be in the same room." "I like what y'all did to the house Miko it looks great." "Thanks Lid" And looks great is is an understatement the once gray and gloomy living room and dining room had hard word flooring and the walls are painted in a real bright yellow just bringing light into the whole room, with new couches and flat a flat screen television Uncle Sha has done good for himself and his family especially considering just years ago he was a hard liner that prophesized not to buy anything and engage in capitalistic or materialism related things and make a  step backwards into feeding your own people buying organic food, giving up all the technological distractions, but from the looks of things that was all rhetoric because what was once a rag tag living and dining room is now a full spread in your latest home and garden magazine.  As he sits in the dining room with his twenty two in his back pocket the situation becomes old news as Khadejah comes down the steps and everyone gets up and runs to the living room. This is the first time Lid has seen Khadejah in three years and now the blooming teenager and as she stands at the bottom of the steps in an orange gown with her long black all rolled up the entire room can agree on one thing Khadejah is breathtaking. Lid moves behind everyone as they all take pictures and she quickly sees him and they make eye contact old cousins who haven't seen each other in years from escorted walks to seven eleven to this and Khadejah smiles and air whispers "WOW" as Lid smiles back and air whispers to her "you look beautiful" and as she tries to wipe away the tear from her face Lid quickly leaves through the front door and back in front of Grandmoms double parked mini van. The rest of the family comes out of the house still taking pictures as Khadejah leaves the house. Lid follows the crowd as they move across the street and over to the house of her date Lamar decked out in a white suite and matching orange tie and orane alligator shoes as both families come together and everyone takes pictures Uncle Sha gives one of Khadijahs girlfriends a hug and from the bottom of the porch Lid looks at Khadejah and they both laugh some things never change, a dirty old man will always be a dirty old man. Lid takes the time to go make prayer as the sun is setting and it is time for Magrib prayer rug in hand he makes wudu using a water bottle, and next to Uncle Sha house while everyone else is across the street, he makes prayer  and once h is finished Uncle Rashad is coming back from walking the dog  and he and Lid star each otherdown as he puts the dog back in the backyard it's a look of hate Uncle Rashas hates his nephew and  it's so obvious Lid fresh from making prayer is in a peaceful mood as he took a chance and things turned out right and the last he wants to do get into an argument with Uncle Rashad so he says nothing and walks across the street to Lamar's house. The hate reside from Lid being bailed out of jail after only spending a few hours in jail. When Uncle Rashad was about the same age as Lid coming home from the night shift at the Blue Moon hotel he was arrested and charged with rape. Completely innocent Uncle Rashad would spend thirty days up in the detention center until the women picked the real assailent out in a line up, but no one ever bailed him out, Grandmom didn't when weeks before she put up her whole house to get Uncle Sha out of prison when he got locked up runnin coke up from Florida. Animosity has always lingered in the heart o Uncle Rashad because no one bailed him out and what ever happened up there changed him, so when his mother Lid's grandmother had anything to do with getting Lid out of prison sparked that hatred  in him his anismosity is what led him to just kicking Lid out in the streets and the fact that Grand mom allowed him to move in with him only infuriated that anger and hatred, so as Lid walks to Lamar's house he understands his uncle's resentment and dislike for his nephew but to express in the manner that he did breaking the agreement and kicking his nephew out on the streets is unforgivable and just another example of why African Americans are on the extinction bloc because its all personal and with no understandings of business we are doomed to fall victim to the hands of the oppressor.

The limo soon pulls up and Lid and Naim quickly move up to the drivers door, when he rolls down the window and to Lid's surprise it's one of his friends another real good fella who accordingly greats Lid first "How you doin?" "Family stuff nothing but drama man, how you doin man?" "Aliright, I don't usually come up this far that's why I'm a little late." " Don't worry about man she just came out the house five minutes ago its no big thing." As everyone takes pictures Naim standing next to the limo driver and Lid starts to take pictures with his digital camera when the driver ask him "You like that technology huh?" Naim nods his head and Lid laughs thinking to himself they are always on the job. The couple gets into the limo and Lid ask loudly hey is somebody going to tip the limo driver? He's broke so tipping is completely out of the question but he would never pass up the chance to put Uncle Sha on the spot and accordingly Uncle Sha pulls out a mitt of cash and pulls out two twenties and gives it to the driver Lid winks his eye as the driver smiling gets backs in the limo "See you later man, later." And with a quick head nod the driver pulls off and everyone goes into Lamar's house neutral ground in the kitchen the men stand around the kitchen and begin to discuss the state of affairs in the city last week another cop was murdered and that is the topic of discussion, as Lamar's father a Philadelphia fire fighter hold court in his kitchen. " What happened to this city, all these kids out here have guns and they are shooting anyone who gets in their way, I  don't even go out anymore I just get off work and go straight home." Uncle Sha adds to the conversation " I here that but you cant be afraid to go outside like this is the wild west, they hate themselves it's a self destructive cycle all created by the white man so I can't get mad when another one of there hired guns in the police department gets shot and killed how many of our babies, our children do they kill every night? Fuck the Police they deserve it." Uncle Sha radical perspective is no shock to the room nut Mikahil uses the opportunity to bridge both sides and find a medium. " I'm his nephew look there is no way we are going to revolt or have any revolution the best way to fix this situation is reeducate our people with factual information this all stems from the wars against Islam overseas 911 was a lie, I was reading in Joe Wilsons book who  worked for the state department his wife was a CIA operative and the white house gave up her identity as retaliation against Joe because he said time after time there weren't any weapons of mass destruction in Iraq. But in his book he's like on 911 he was leaving the state department driving on the capital rotunda when he heard on the radio that the pentagon was hit." Lid stops and allows everyone to digest what they just heard and collectively the group gives Lid a so what are saying look and then he continues to drive home his point. "If your driving in D.C. from the state department its no way you don't see an airplane fall from the sky and crash into the pentagon?" They all including Uncle Sha exclaim together "AHHHHH" So based on that lie we've gone ahead and went to war with two Islamic countries based on lies, the muslims ran the streets an we believe that, Uncle Sha interrupts "Man they all religions that worship the white man, we had great kingdoms in Egypt and Africa the original man and these religions are full of it!" "Unc let me finish, these kids don't wake up with heaven on their minds. You understand making muslims out to be terrorist and making it a taboo things has caused an entire generation to fall into the wastelands. These kids are crazy because they have nothing to look forward to. Think about it at least with Islam we had to look forward to heaven, so that dictates how I go about on this earth, these kids believe that Christ died for there sins so they have nothing to strive for nothing to keep thinking about the consequences of their actions." Another man adds "Well the church is not to blame because we don't promote violence and murder this is crazy what's going on out there." "I'm not saying you promote violence what I'm saying is that without Islam , Christianity, or any religion for that matter these kids are walking around doing anything with no thought of the consequences not from the police department, or from God for that matter. This stems from Forty Three he's the anti Christ." And with that the conversation intensifies "Come on man you gotta to be kidding me the anti christ?" "Yeah ten years ago everybody was Muslim even if they were not practicing the right way they still had some belief and fear of God, now everybody is gay, to polar opposites one is bringing you closer to god while the other is in complete rebellion to God and his laws." Uncle Sha adds "I hear you on that, but no religion is the answer all the religions promote a white man and in the end all we are doing is worshiping the white man, what we need to do is stop relying on the society that is hell bent on eradicating people of color off the face of the earth. I say start taking them out before they take us the cops provide us with the narcotics we kill each other every night, you a sucker playing in their game they not playing games and its time we stopped playing the game and start our own for our people." "Your right but we can't just walk away from America?" Uncle Sha gets really upset at Lamar's fathers statement "What has this country done but force us to the worst kind of slavery in the history of mankind, and now they have us locked in this system of self destruction as we fight over table scraps its time we just walked away from the table." "I don't agree with that were are we going to go the Irish, the English, the Italians, the Dutch, the German, everyone else can just pack up and go home we are the only people's who have no home because this is our home and just bucking out of the system is not the solution the solution is doing more with the money we take off the streets and get these kids back to believing in something other than money, we are a dammed people if we don't because this is our home and I'm sad to say it but we are living behind enemy lines as our oppressors slowly reduce our numbers and keep millions of us behind bars" "I know the preasures of the oppressor is hell living." "Well brothers both of y'all both are right in part but reality is we have to deal with things the way they are the Muslims are finished 9/11 took care of that and no matter what Joe Wilson says or anyone else for that matter the winners of wars write the history books and as far as the story goes Muslims crashed into the world trade center and the pentagon and we have to find another way to save our children brothers or we will be extinct." "Yeah but you all want to bargain and cut deal with the same beast trying to eliminate you." "What would you have us do start killing white people?" Uncle Sha shakes his head and the dejected group bust out in laughter "That not feasible Unc you know that, we just have to deal with being on the extinction list and keep surviving." "Your dreaming nephew that's like bargaining with the hunter as he stares game down with his shot gun." "Well we all can agree to disagree but sooner or later the decendants of the slaves will be no more here in America because this is a self destructive society we live in." Lid finishes the conversation "A self destructive society that preys on the first man Adam and only the devil could com up with a systematic way to eliminate his sworn enemy the first man us, adam." "Preach on brother." They all continue to chit chat in the kitchen when Lid gets a call from Dee on his cell phone. "What's the deal man?" "Hey do you think you could help me tonight with the super markets thing?" "Yeah I'm at this prom thing up my Uncles right now I was going to go to the masjid and make Isha and then I guess we could do that you want me to meet you at your house?" "Yeah just call me when you hit the block, thanks man because I am running really late and they want me to get that done tonight." The politics of South Philly runs so deep that the supermarkets will not put up the groceries of specific families on the isles, in other words management inside of supermarkets get orders from certain families not to put groceries up or to put the fresh stuff in the back of the isle and the old stuff up front, so when customers buy the products they get the older out dated cans. Crazy crazy but in South Philly they live by there own set of rules. Dee is called in by the family he is employed by to go in the warhouse part of the supermarket and like an employee restock the shelves with the new deliveries for that specific family. So Mikahil has something to do after he leaves the prom shinaticans, and as he kisses his mom goodbye and exchanges hugs with his cousins and aunts Lid hopes in the mini van with his grandmom and they descend down to her house from Uncle Sha. "I really don't have much to say to you but you are a troubled troubled boy you know that." "Grand mom I'm sorry I just when I was sitting in the van and saw everyone playing all my cousins and all their children I got to thinking about my baby that was aborted and how much it would've been to have Teresa here with my family and my daughter, I felt really bad inside and I thought to myself well I 'm not going to cheat myself out of memories these are my relatives too, and my memories and he didn't like me coming in his house too bad." "What do you mean too bad my son told you that you were not allowed in his house." "But Nadia is in their after all the junk he talked about Nadia over the years and how she has such a smart mouth she's in there that's crazy. Anyway nothing happened and everything turned out o.k." "No it didn't he's really upset and you better be careful because he might send somebody around to kick your but." "Yeah right I think the situation with the limo driver let him and everybody else know to leave me alone I belong to them." "Your crazy you know that Lid I remember when you were a good little boy now you are crazy just like my father." "Who me?" "Yup he used to sit out on the porch and I wouldn't say nothing to that crazy old man, you look just him and you are going crazy just like him too." "He brought that house didn't?" "Who? Yeah so he wanted to move in with me thinking I was going to take care of his crazy but, after all those horrible things he used to say to me, ask your mother he was horrible to us and I used to take my kids your Uncles and Aunts up there to see him at the nut house." "He did like twenty five years didn't he?" "I don't know I can't remember it was something like that." "Hey I think he got off pretty easy for killing two white boys back in those days." "They owed him some money he did some work for them down were your people are at in South Philly." "Grandmom they are not my people, they just been real nice to me since I got back from Delaware." "Whatever but you swear by them, now he was doing some work for those guys and they did not pay him when he got done the job, he did masonry work and I will never forget that day we were all in the house and he just comes in and grabs the shotgun and said nothing to anybody and walked out the house that was the last time we saw him until his trial. But he went down and shot two white boys back in 1949, and killed them two." "How did he get out?" "He was declared insane and they made him serve twenty years up in the funny farm and that's were they are going to put you kiddo if you don't get yourself together." "Alright Grand mom , sorry I didn't mean to start anything." She pulls up to her garage and he gets out to open the garage she pulls into and parks and the two of them walk up the block side by side not discussing any family business outside and Lid waits as she unlocks and open the door. Lid jogs upstairs were he takes the gun and outs it between the bed.  Its night fall and time for Isha prayer so Lid leaves and drives to Sister Clara Muhammed school and in the still darkness of the new night out front only one car waits, as usual it brother Eliajah is waiting out front in his gold Honda accord, in his late seventies since the reopening of Sister Clara Muhammed brother Elijah and Lid are the only regulars for the daily night prayers, and tonight at first sight of Lids car pulling up brother Elijah gets out and begins to unlock the front doors. "As –Salaam Alaikum brother Elijah?" "Wa –Laikum Salaam good brother how was your day today?" "Good All praise due to Allah, I got see my family today for the first time in years." "I don't understand why we so mad at each other for so long the prophet said Muslims should not be mad at each for more than three consecutive days after that It really doesn't matter who was wrong forgivness is more important than anything." As Lid open the door for the older brother Elijah his cell phone rings and its Dee, Lid turns the phone off and as Brother Elijah goes upstairs and begins to turn on the lights , Lid goes into the wudu station to make wudu preparing for prayer. Once inside the prayer room joining brother Elijah he makes his two rakas for walking into a masjid, and once they are finished Mihail ask" Can I call the athan?" He nods his head yes and says " All praise is due to Allah that you show up here at night time because before you started coming I would wait and if no one showed up I would o across the street." "I don't understand that why do we have two masjids  directly across the street from each other?" Brother Elijah laughs "The great bean pie conspiracy." "What's that?" " Search your thoughts you know what I'm saying , but that does not make them right across the street the Nation of Islam was tailored for our people and our community and I've been oversees brother and they don't all dress in traditional Arab attire, or follow word for word the sunna of the prophet. The solution is the Holy Quran brother, when ever I have a dispute or conflicts in the heart I turn to the Quran, because that is the word of Allah." The way I look at it is like this without the nation of Islam millions of African American Americans would've never been introduced to Islam and we the decendants of the slave would've never reconnected with the religion that was stripped, beaten out of us." "My thoughts exactly" Brother Elijah looks at his watch "Its time to call the athan." Mikahil gets up and makes the call for prayer, and when he finishes they begin to make salat but tonight is different and as brother Elijah recites the Quran out loud the erie old building building begins to speak when thre rusty door in the front creek open and close rapidly making a slaming boom!! Standing in silence Lid listens as Brother Elijah recites quran, but he cannot help himself to think who or whom just entered the masjid and change in the status quo as he and Elijah are usually the only two making Isha prayer at night, but tonight security has been violated and Lid cannot break prayer because he only fears Allah and would be a sign of disbelief but who could it be Omar? Has he finally just tracked Lid down? Who would miss Elijah, who ever it is could takeboth of them out while they pray but what a holy way to die, and as they continue to pray and who ever it is about in the lobby Lid tries to concentrate on prayer and he ask Allah to keep him safe, and finally the person inside the prayer room and moving right in the direction o Lid eyes closed he tries to concentrate on reciting Quaran and then a hand extends out and touches the right shoulder of Lid not fazed Lid continues to pray but he keeps his eyes closed as the person pulls him by the shoulder behind brother Elijah, and Lid resist this the last rakah for Isha and he refuses to break stride. When they finish and salaam out Lid takes a look behind him and sees that it was Yusuf, from the old days of Sister Clara Muhammed. In the bathroom downstairs, in like the second grade Yusuf and his younger brother were beating students up as they went to the bathroom collecting dues. They tried the same with Lid as he went to the bathroom during lunch time on day. He refused and was told by Yusuf and his older brother that they were going to beat Lid up for not paying. Later in the day Lid somehow finangled another trip to the bathroom were he found the custodian working in the basement of the school. Worried about getting beat up after school and mad that students were actually collecting dues from other students Lid explained his dilemma to the custodian. The custodian assured Lid that he would be alright and thanked him for coming forward. Once this information was relayed to Iman Malik the brothers were immediately suspended and that was the last of the having to pay dues in the brothers bathroom. Relieved that it wasn't Omar walking in the masjid or some non believers Lid says a prayer and then shakes hands with brother Elijah. After he makes two more rakkas following Isha prayer Yusuf approaches Lid and ask "What are you doing?" Understanding that he asking Lid what is he doing in Philly causing such turmoil the car accident thing, showing up at Sister Clara Muhammed School everyday, and basically not adhering to his exile in Delaware Lid simply responds sarcastically "I'm making salat" Yusuf gives Lid an irritated look and replies "Be safe out there brother and get all five salats in." Always having to say the last word smiling he replies "That's the idea but everything is in Allah's hands." He gives Yusuf the greetings and brother Elijah as well and walks out the prayer room. Once inside his car he notices a Philadelphia police cruiser parked on the opposite end of the school yard and Lid makes sure he puts his seat belt on as he calls Dee to make sure he is home. As he drives by the police cruiser he smiles as he straps on his seat belt. When he gets to Dee's apartment he parks and goes to the front door its dangerous just waiting out on sombodys porch as the young boys draped in red walk by. Dee finally answers and comes outside

"What's the deal? They shake hands "Thanks for helping me with this, I caught up with some bitch earlier and she messed my scheduale up." "Yeah well I never pass up the chance to help out especially when its legal work it's the illegal stuff I have to stay away from especially when the department has the hots for me." They get in Dee's truck and cruise down to South Philly and as usual they catch the eyes of the cashiers and the shoppers in line as they walk through the store and in tne back to the warehouse area. Tonight however one store employee has the balls to speak up and say something. "What are you guys doing back here? Y'all don't work here do you?"Lid says nothing as Dee walks closer to the man and says "We have to put up the grocereies for Francesca packing do you know were they are at?" "Y'all cant put those groceries up I'm getting the manager." He walks out into the store section and Lid and Dee continue to move skids of food around using the jack until buried beneath other skids he finds the skid full of Francesca's foods. "Look at this shit they sent this stuff down here days ago and its buried beneath all this shit that's why they have me come down here and do this." "I cant believe things get so petty man its just food." "Naw you aint seen shit one time I was putting the groceries up and this guy comes down the eisle and starts knocking Francesca's shit right onto the floor breaking glass its pasta noddles all on the floor the shit was crazy." Lid starts laughing and the accompanied by the store manager the guy from earlier points and shows his manager what is going on. For a few seconds things get real intense and the situation is defused when Dee simply says I'm here from Francesca packing we have to put these groceries up, you guys have all there stuff buried back here, and the old stuff is out on in the store, we have to put this new food out there." "O.k, that's the day shift manger who does that I have nothing to do with it." Then the manager replies and he and the salty employee go out into the front." "I don't know how you guys do it work for a fucking paycheck every two weeks then to add insult to injury they fucking tax y'all and steal more money from you." "Keeps me out of the way the idea is to keep us all engaged in illegal activity so that we are always looking over our shoulders yeah I don't have much money, yeah it's a drag but I am not playing in a game that's designed to keep me behind bars, and or destroy my people with that wet, crack, or crystal meph. I always think about God Father when the guy says "We will keep it in the black neighborhoods sell it to the niggers they are animals anyway let them loose their souls to it. You know it's by design man it goes against my moral fiber to take part in that especially considering I see what crack has done to our communities." "You gotta get paid man" "Yeah I do but not that way, on the other side of things taxes they have no right to tax any of us for our labor. The IRS, the Fed it's all bullshit when it comes to labor tax, there is no labor tax, the only thing that should be taxed is purchases, and goods, but they slipped all that shit in there with the new deal and the government been stealing our money ever since." "So you o.k. with that?" "No way but what am I going to do they automatically take that shit out of our paychecks you gotta pay, the only other alternative would be to start cutting hair, or hustling but like I said before you are always looking over your shoulder I don't feel like living like that plus I went to school man I made a decision to be part of the legitimate society eventhough the program changed and now I'm the enemy of the state because I'm muslim, the work place has changed from the late nineties until now and if I would've known the stuff I know now I would'nt of went to college I probably would just be a cop or something." "Yeah well I don't know nothing about that I'm like your uncle I've been everywhere but to work." They both laugh, and continue to put groceries up and when they finish they clean up and put everything back the way it was and go on to the next two supermarkets. Dee doesn't pay Lid for helping him and Lid never ask Dee for any money but on the strength of the way he's been befriended by those people he helps out when ever he has the opportunity to, once they finish Dee says "You want to go half on a couple of bags I know this spot down the bottom that has pure fucking raw." "I keep raw and uncut for all you bitches and hoes and the first time you sniff it it might hurt your nose. Yeah man let me go to the atm to get some cash." Getting close to mid night they cruise back up west philly in the tinted out silver F-150, listening to the classic hio hop group tribe called quest, as they cross over into west philly from the University of Pennsylvania they hop on Landsdown and the sight of four police cars blocking off entry into the bottom catches Lid's eyes. "You see that they got the whole street blocked off, I wonder how the trolley is going to run, can't nobody get into the bottom past fortieth street." Accordingly Dee yurns at thirty six and descends into the bottom, its called the bottom because that exactly what it is the very bottom of west Philadelphia tucked away across from the University of Drexel, and around the corner from the University of

Pennsylvania the streets are all one way and the first few are hills that usually lead to dead blocks or one way streets if you don't know where you are going you will get lost and this one part of town that you do not want to stop and ask for directions. They pull up to a set of row homes on would you believe it a one way street and as Lid checks out the scene the dark street filled with more vacant homes than occupied is pretty desolate and quiet for a spring time night. "I'll be right back." Dee goes to take the keys out the ignition and Lid ask "Yo leave the keys I might want to listen to the radio, or roll down the window." Dee does so and Lid waits some young boys walk out the corner house on the other side of the street and immediately look down at the F-150, Lid takes record of it and just watches as they stand in front of the house trying not to directly look at the truck but keep an eye on it from afar. When all of a sudden a black Nissan Maximun pulls up tinted windows sitting on twenties and they park on the opposite side of the street directly across from the truck. A female gets out the drivers side phat ass and all and Lid checks her out as he's now rolled down the window and hopped in the drivers side, she pays no attention to him and looks down as she struts up the stairs and enters one of the homes. The passenger in the car starts to talk on his cell phone very loud and Lid is starting to wonder what the fuck is taking Dee so long as what usually takes ten minutes max is well past twenty minutes. Then the passenger says "Yeah man I'm made as shit my Pistons lost tonight in the playoffs and I feel like shooting somebody, as he looks out the car and over to the truck Lid is sitting in." His instincts begin to kick in a Lid quickly rolls up the window on the passenger side of the truck if someone does decide to shoot into the window, then at the glass breaking gives him a few split seconds to pull off. He continues to check his mirrors watching for anyone to walk up on the truck and as he waits he visualizes Omar pulling what right up behind Lid. A few minutes pass when a car pulls up behind Dee's truck and the driver gets out and too far too see who it is using the drivers side mirror the driver walks in between the front of his car and back of the truck and first sight a sharp bolt of electricity jolts up his spine as its Omar looking right into the tinted back window of the truck and and Lid looks right him from inside the truck they lock eyes for a moment and there is no doubt that Omar does not see the bright red Phillies hat Lid is wearing tint or no tint and like Uncle Rashad there is a look of face written on the face of Omar and he notices that Omar is a little heavy and probably has a bullet proof vest on and his waist is bulging which means he is packing. In split seconds he has to decide does he get out the car and confront his child hood friend, does he stay put, does he pull leaving Dee?" Getting out would be very dangerous Landsdown is blocked off meaning no one can get in or out of the bottom without passing the Philadelphia police department on the other hand if anything happened the EMT truck would not be able to get in either, he knows Omar is packing and the police department took his gun and months ago so everyone knows he's unarmed, so there will be no wild wild west shoot out going down. There's at least two other shooters the passenger in the black car who's already proclaimed he is in the mood to shoot somebody tonight, and the hustler hiding in the corner that Dee shook hands with on the way into the house, out gunned and out maneuvered Lid watches as Omar goes into the house hand on the ignition heart racing Lid keeps an eyes on all things as he rotates between mirrors like clock work, there is a silence in the air as the passenger in the black car has stopped yapping on the phone, the young boys stay perplexed on the corner and Lid waits sometimes the best move is making no moves, and Dee finally emerges from the house, and into the passenger side of the truck. "You trying to get me killed?" "What you talking about look at these bags and Dee pulls out four plump bags of coke looking like chikalets." Turning on the ignition and backing out of the parking space, "You must be fucking crazy y'all trying to get me killed." "Wait I gotta go back in and get another bag." "You not going back in there" and Lid pulls off. "What you doing man why you puling off?" "Y'all trying to kill me, fucking city is crazy and as he passes through the police blocking off Landsdown avenue they smile at Lid who heads back up to Dee's apartment silence, silence, and more silence which is finally broken when Lid ask "Let me get my two bags?" "What you not going to stay and snort, what happened down there?" Lid says nothing the points already been made there is no way Dee did not know what was about to happen and if anyone he knows the drama that's been going on between Lid and Omar for it was he that called the morning after the whole drunk by myself thing. This was a set up and Dee Lids friend and associate was behind it, so was the Philadelphia Police department, and as Dee hands Lid his two bags of coke they pull up on Dee's block and Lid gets out closes the door and hops in his car. "What happened man, yells Dee from the truck not smiling and very seriously as if he really did not know what was going on. Lid just shakes his head and pulls off. Narrowly escaping death he drives back to his grandmothers and jogs into the house, quietly he creeps up the stairs and once in his room he grabs his twenty two from between the bed, and quietly leaves the house, once back inside the house he gives LaLa a call real late past one o'clock in the morning she answers "Hello?" "You coming out tonight?" "You got some money?" "Yeah I be uptown in a few minutes." Lid opens up the bag of coke and using a straw still parked on his grandmothers block takes a sniff into both nostrils, and as the powder shoots up his nose into his brain what ever fear he was feeling is gone and the numbness begins to take over his body, numb as he takes another wiff into both nostrils and his teeth and gums all go numb the coke has his whole body just numb and like a superhero there is an air of invincibility surrounding him eyes wide open he sees the message Philadelphia is sending him "GET THE FUCK OUT!!!" and rebelliously he continues on and pull off to LaLa's house. Zipping through the streets running yellow lights and onto the expressway he fly's through the traffic and in minutes is on fifth and Ducannon giving LaLa a call. "Yo I'm out front in front of the Rican store." Feeling good rolling in his coke rush Lid keeps snipping his nose and cannot wait for LaLa to come outside, and when she struts across the street titties bouncing in the air, Lid gets rock hard in anticipation, he opens the door and LaLa gives him a hug and kisses him on the cheek. "Im hungry were are we going to get something to eat?" "I don't know I gotta get down south Philly the only place that I am safe at right now." Lid pulls off and goes down Broad street as they pass fast food places LaLa insist "I want to go to McDonald's" Lid says nothing and keeps driving once he crosses into South Philly he turns off Broad street and stops at the McDonalds " I was hungry like fifteen minutes ago why didn't you stop up North Philly McDonalds?" "I'm only safe down here black folks trying to kill me." "What are you talking about you act like you moving keys or something?" " I'm not just order the food" LaLa leans over across Lid and orders the food as she is ordering Lid rolling off coke takes another snort of the new bag this is raw because his nose begins to burn and when he checks his nostrils in the rear view mirror they are burning red. When they get the window Lid pays gets his change and pulls off. Like everyone else the first thing she eats are the fries and with a mouth full of them she ask "Where we going?" "I don't know I just need to stay down here for a while this is the only place I feel safe at right now." "Well I hope you don't think I'm going to fuck you in this car, its not enough room." "I really just wanted the company, but I got some cash though." "How much money you got?" "Like fifty dollars." She looks into the back seat of the car and says "Its enough room in the back seat we alright." Lid smiles and LaLa smiles too, together they just cruise throughout south philly until they down to were the stadiums are at, and Lid remembering where he parked at for one of the Phillies games goes into the parking lot, with a chalky taste in his mouth he quickly finishes the rest of his soda, and to his surprise the desolate parking lot is not so desolate this Friday night. Lined up along a bunker are cars Mustangs, Lansers, Jetta's, and Eclipse, with there lights on and the smell of burnt rubber tires fill the air. Lid parks as they will treated to a car show and after fingering LaLa and taking a few kissed from her, they get out the car and sit on the roof of the car watching as the street racers drift burning rubber and making figure eights the smell of burnt tires just fills the air and Lid just takes it all in. Considering that just hours ago he was about to be assassinated checking out the street races is a real blessing and as the racers look down from the bunker they see Lid and LaLa sitting on the roof of the car and gives nods of approval, he might not be known down here as a street racer but everyone knows Lid has a lead foot. For the next few hours they sit on top of the car and LaLa lays her face on Lids dick and bits at it through his pants while Lid plays with her big titties underneath her shirt. When the racers drive down from the bunker they all give Lid a head nod as they leave the parking lot and now with the smell of burnt rubber all in the air LaLa ask with her finger in her mouth "what are we going to do now?" Lid high as shit and without any inhibitions quickly get ready to "Fu" when his words are cut short as a single rain drop falls from the sky followed by more as they trickle down from the sky, "Well I guess someone else is speaking for me" LaLa smiles "That's why I like you your different from other boys." As the rain falls she gives him a kiss on the lips and Lid completely aroused from the coke and the intimacy pulls away and jumps off the car, he catches LaLa as she does the same. He opens the door and lets her in the back seat were he soon follows. Lying on her back with her back up against the door she begins to unbutton her pants and pull them down, already with a condom in his pocket Lid climbs in and closes the door with his leg and reaches in his pocket and pulls out the condom he gives it to the now pants less LaLa and begins to aggresivly kiss there will be no love making tonight the coke has Lid on another level and like the "Fat Man Scoop song he's fucking tonight!" She takes the condom and puts it on his dick as he kisses away at her body her titties, kneck, he naws away at kneck and she just screams in joy, and finally when the condom is on using his thumb as a guide he finds his entry point and slides his dick right into LaLa's pussy "Ahhhhhhh oh boy you get to spot every time." Lid says nothing all the emotions felt today the drama with his uncle, the drama at the masjid, and the near assassination attempt with Dee Lid lets all his emotions and anger out on LaLa's pussy and thanks to the coke he is in another zone pounding away as LaLa screams and moans but true to her word Lid can feel her back wall as the tip of his dick touches it with every stroke and she automatically yells and moans. Pressed up in a small space the back seat Lid has no room to drift and he just pounds away until he's had enough and from back of his balls he ejaculates and it shoots right up through his dick into the condom as he is planted inside LaLa's pussy. "Ahhh" he moans and immediately sits up in the back seat pants down to his ankles he pulls the condom off his dick open the door in the pouring rain and throws the condom outside LaLa pulls her panties up and lays down in his lap gently kissing his dick. "You got some more coke I want some?" Lid shakes his head "No way babe your like sixteen can't mess you up that stuff will destroy you it takes two weeks of can pepsi's in the morning and no coke just to get rid of the yearning for it that shit messes with your mind." "That's how you beat it?" "Yeah every morning can pepsi and no coke at all yo I don't even look at any straws babe that shit will destroy you have you out here doing anything to get a few bags." "I can handle it, give me some." "No way" his refusal to share his coke upsets LaLa but as the rain continues to pour they fall asleep with her lying in his lap. Just before the sun rises in the morning they wake up and get into the front seats Lid pulls off and LaLa ask "I want some coffee can we stop off at dunkin dounuts?" With his pounding and all out of coke Lid knows he has to get a pepsi real fast so agrees and stops at the dunkin dounuts at broad and Christian, located down the street from the masjid parked in the parking lot Lid contemplates going into the masjid to make fajr prayer, and as the cab drivers all muslims, and some south philly residents walk in to the masjid Lid decides not to and inside his stomach turns as the muslims look at him and just shake their heads when LaLa walks out the dunkin dounuts. Lid shrugs his shoulders and pulls out from the parking lot even at the edge of death last night he still refused to make Fajr prayer and spent the night with some young girl snorting coke and fornicating all night long he drives LaLa back home and can only think about a verse in the Quran

Sura XLIV ayat 15 "We shall indeed remove the penaly for a while but truly ye will revert to your old ways" chapter

# "Need a little help from my friends"

T HE FALL TIME WILL finally bring some relief as Lid has been walking on pins and needles all spring and summer. With a pending case and the city cops already with the hots for him engadging in any illegal activity from jay walking, driving without a seatbelt, to just buying a bag of weed is out of the question and Lid has played the last few months accordingly he's stopped smoking weed and rarely comes out the house for and the occasional Phillies night game. But this being the city's third attempt to just hold preliminary hearing the arresting officers have to show up or the case will be thrown out. On a better note Jasmine is in town for her brothers birthday party in Old City section of Philadelphia and Lids promised to show up, but depending on what happens with this court case all those plans might hit the back burner because anything can happen when your life is in the hands of the judge especially a judge working for a system that wants you behind bars and incarcerated. "Grand mom I'm almost dressed for court, I'll be out the door in a second." From down stairs she screams "Well I cant go with you I have to watch Adesha and Sha and Miko might be bringing Kofi over later." Coming down the steps fully dressed in a blue suit, brown shirt with matching blue pin stripes, "I need my rain jacket, you going to watch both of them that's too much." "I know but your aunt Christina needs me to watch Adesha, and Miko has to work tonight." "Well good luck today kiddo" "Grandmom It's cool traffic court threw the tickets out that means the cops had no probable cause from the jump legally they have no case." "You say that Mr. know it all but anything goes when you walk into a court room white folks are not playing." "Your right grand mom God willing I will be back for the Phillies game tonight but the last thing the cops want to do is trial this case down at the criminal justice center." "Did you talk to your lawyer?" "I called him a few days ago he knows its today he said he will be there." "You better double check, those lawyers are shysters." "Bobby's a good guy he will show up I'm worried about looney tooney Judge O'Niel the last two times I was up there he was giving out time like a wrist watch it was nothing to him violation of this slam on his mallet, violation of that, issue out bench warrents laughing away it was crazy." "Well good luck kiddo." She gives him a kiss on the cheek and he's out the door. On the way up he grabs a daily news and a pack of newports and listening to the more mellow a.m. station plays classic Sinatra and big band music. Once in front of the 35th district he parks and stands in front of the police station listening to his I-Pod, classic rock is the choice of the day as the rolling stones "gimmie shelter plays" There are few people standing out front waiting for court as well but on particular a brother a little older than Lid also dressed in a suit yapping away on his telephone continues to give him hard looks, real grimy looks but accordingly he just smiles and continues to play the stones. There's also a shift change going on and as the police officers walk in for work they don't make any eye contact with Lid as usual and that look of confidence that they carried the previous two court hearings is gone. And Lid gets the feeling that things might go his way this time in court. Around eight o'clock the doors open and alone Lid takes his seat in the front row directly in front of the judge. The defendants side is packed with African Americans, and Latinos, but is the victims side poverty is the main reason for crime and the most impoverished are victims and the perpetrators represented by minorities one group kidnapped and brought here to be slaves centuries past there usefulness are just a fading minority population stricken with disease, poverty, and crime. The other the latinos escaped the third world and came here looking for better opportunities a rising minority group that is still broken down into sub classes based on color of skin, country you come from, and money you posses. In the front row on the victims side there is a real wise guy sitting with jeans on and a t-shirt. And as time passes he begins to work the room and move around at first he start talking to the cop in charge of getting the cases in order and announcing the names of the defendants. Then he goes to the back door and looks directly into the window were all the cops are standing waiting to appear as witnesses for the prosecution, then he sits back down. Lid thinks nothing of it probably a cop or something looking for his buddies and continues to sit and wait for the show to begin as its almost eight thirty and

Bobby still ahs not shown up. Checking his watch Lid begins to get worried and replays the words from his grandmom "Those lawyers are shysters." With every opening of the door Lid turns his head to check if Bobby is walking through and to his dismay its another lawyer dressed in a fine silk suit. The defendants side begins to laugh and tease Mikahil "Nobody's gonna to show for him." "He doesn't have a lawyer" then as he looks over the crowd h catches the mouth of the guy from out front who says Cecil B. Moore." Shocked because knows exactly who the man is referring to Omar, Lid air whispers back "South Philly". Taking it as a joke the man begins to laugh then the most amazing thing happens as the busy body from earlier gets up and as Lid sits worried about his lawyer showing up but now really worried about walking into a hail of bullets after trail is suddenly accompanied by a figure standing directly to his left not in front of him but next to him and he looks at the crowd of defendents with a look of death, his eyes so serious and wide open like the hero who finally help the kid that's getting picked on in the school yard he's had enough and stands with an emotionless face yet the eyes tell it all. Lid just looks down as inside he gets that butterfly feeling when someone is teaching you something new or a stranger helps you out and stands with you. And when the man walks away, he looks back up at the defendants side and with mouths wide open in shock and in fear they try to not even make eye contact as Lid cracks a faint grim and turns back around to the front. Accordingly Bobby walks right in the court room and taps Lid on the shoulder and says "Im here Buddy" and begins to chit chat with other attorneys next to the bench. The judge walks in and at first sight of the black robe Lid immediately stands but to his surprise it is not Judge O'Neil, "All rise for the honorable  Judge Salvatore" and the salt and pepper haired man of the court walks up to his seat and cracks a smile at Lid making direct eye contact with him and immediately gets serious and sits down.  The first two cases are called  the second case involves the man giving Lid dirty looks and it's a gun permit case. The district attorneys office cites that the defendant was carrying a fire arm in Philadelphia without his permit to carry. The defense's attorney lets the judge know and presents evidence that the defendant indeed has now been granted his permit to carry a firearms. The charges are dropped and then the clerk says "The City of Philadelphia v/s Lid Islam, Lid stands up and Bobby motions to him to sit down. He does so and Bobby approaches the bench with the district attorney's office and the judge the three counsel for a few minutes and the Judge ask "Does the district attorneys office have any witnesses to uphold these charges?" The DA shakes his head, and the Judge slams his mallet and says "The district attorneys office has failed to produce any witnesses for the third time, this case is dismissed" Bobby turns and smiles at Lid and walks out the court room as he passes Lid he says "Come buddy we are out of here." And Lid still not sure of what exactly took place gets up and follows Bobby out of the court room. "You know buddy they can still charge you for hurry up and get a move on out of here." Once outside the police district Lid pays Bobby still short by like two hundred dollars he says "Bobby I have to wait until my next pay check to square things with you." Bobby takes the four hundred dollars Lid has in his hand and says "Don't worry about it, nice and easy does it every time, but you have to promise to stay out of trouble." "Man they did not want to go to court with that case once the tickets got thrown out in traffic court they had no probable cause to pull me over the city knew that. What I want to know is when can I get my gun back its mines I paid for it legally?" Bobby rolls his eyes and shakes his head "you need to forget about that gun and cheer up this thing is over now, just stay out of trouble." Lid shakes his head "I talked to Mr. Davidson and he said I can go ahead and apply for my permit to carry." Now annoyed Bobby just says "They are very particular about who they give permits to capish?" "Its my second admendment right to carry my firearms Bobby this is supreme court stuff." Shaking his head Bobby says forget about the gun buddy lets call it even and you don't have to pay me the two hundred you owe, but the permit thing is going to be very tricky because they are very particular about who they grant permits to." "Alright then, I'll Mr. Davidson but I am still putting my application in, thanks Bobby I'm glad this over." "That's the spirit now relax man and have some fun" "I am I'm going to the Phillies game tonight and my old girlfriend is coming into town so that's a plus." "Whoa look at you I try to get down there like once a month myself." "Yeah about the same for me to they got a good team and they might win the series if they keep hitting." "Wouldn't that be nice buddy a championship after all these years." "Who you telling" and on that note they shake hands and before Bobby leaves he gives Lid some parting words of wisdom "Remember Buddy nice and easy does it every time." Smiling he walks off and Lid makes his way to his car smiling that this case is behind him but realizing after all this time he still has really gotten nowhere he still cant carry in the city, he's still being hunted, and he's working at some dead end job for fed ex." Once inside the car the soothing tunes of Francis Albert Sinatra fill the air and windows rolled down and his blue Phillies fitted hat on he cruises to the A.M. music and heads back home to his grandmoms.

As the key unlocks the door she moves from the kitchen to the dining room and when he emerges from the vestiview she says "I was worried about you up there by yourself" "I wasn't by myself, NOT GUILTY!!!" exclaims Lid and she quickly gives him a hug. "The cops did not show up so they through the case out, I'm going to work so I have to hurry up and catch the G bus, but look this guy from South Philly was there and I think he kept the cops from coming out." She shoos him away "Oh your crazy, boy" "Naw for real grandmom like the other defendants were laughing at me and all of a sudden he just got up and stood right next to where I was standing and gave them this look of death and when I turned around they had nothing to say at everybody was punked. Then the judge was different" excited like a child he tries to explain the circus that was a court hearing just a few hours ago "O Neil wasn't there this time it was Judge Salvatore the Italian judge and he smiled at me when he was walking up to the bench like did you really think we where going to lock you up?" "Oh boy you are crazy, but the charges are dropped?" "Yup now I'm going to get my permit, and get my gun back." "Well you are not going to be living here with it, and why do you need a gun? You just got off on this case and you ready to go out there and keep fighting." "I have to its my constitutional right plus I cant go anywhere at night time I'm being hunted." "Then stay in the house." "Yeah right I'll be home little late I'm going to the Phillies game, plus my friend is in from California they're having a party downtown for her brother." "See there you go your going out?" "That's different it old city and south Philly I'm safe in South Philly and it's a hundred cops out there protecting those white kids from anything in old city. I need to be out up here with my people." "They not your people kiddo you called them monsters." Simotainsously she pulls out the article he was quoted in "Well the only way to change them back into people is to educate and them pass along knowledge the correct knowledge and the way to get to them is at night time in the street, and the streets are too dangerous to be out there without a burner."

"Your crazy you better get to work before they fire you." "I'm walking out the door now, still dressed in his business suit Lid puts on his matching blue Phillies hat and strolls up the street and as he the row homes on the ground is a silver M madalian and to himself he thinks yeah Mr. Marzonno did have something to do with the circus that took place earlies this morning and he looks up to the sky and softly says "Thanks dad" continuing on to the bus stop waiting for the G to take him to work. Once downtown he walks from center city down the back street taunting the police department he walks by the criminal justice center and smiles as he passes city cops, when he his approached by a gentleman who could be the cousin of his lawyer Bobby. "Hey buddy?" Lid turns around and the man smiling says "You look familiar, you sure I don't know you from anywhere?" Lid shakes his head and not taking the man as a threat they walk side by side as he continues to talk "You never did any construction?" "At first Lid shakes his head no, then he remembers the federal job and says "Oh yeah I used to do demolition at the federal building on sixth street." Taken aback the man quickly stops in his tracks and says "No I wasn't talking about that see business is real slow for me right now on the account of the economy and all and we had some extra WORK and I was wondering if you could help us out and take some of it off our hands." Remembering the instructions Sharif gave him months ago not to get involved with anything "Lid immediately shakes his no "I don't know anything about construction sir, I'm sorry I can't help you." Continuing down the street to work, the man stops and Lid turns around to see the man looking up at the sky probably asking heaven to help Lid the only way he is ever going to get paid was through the game. When he gets to work theres a shocked look on everyones face as word must've gotten down to the we do it all building building that his case was thrown out and the usual silent treatment since his arrest that engulfed everyone has now changed as people begin to once again smile and greet him as he walks to the Fed Ex store. Once inside he announces to John first "Not Guilty" and John sighs and says "Good" Lid changes clothes and clocks in. A little shocked from the results of the trial the rest of the day is awkward for his co-workers John, Zack, and Lucy and the end of the day Lid gets a visit from his favorite security guard who enters with a joyous smile. "Hi you doin buddy?" Lid smiles "I'm doing great sir, how bout you?" He shakes his head in agreement "My case got thrown out this morning in court it was like a movie or something." Suddenly the security guard takes his right hand and quickly zips his lips. Lid catches on to the sign and start to talk about the Phillies game tonight "I'm going down there tonight I hope they win." "You going to a playoff game look at you?" "I know I went to the game against the Brew Crew and watched em beat Sabathia last week. It was all about the Brett Myers at bat he kept fouling off pitches fighting him, fighting him then Sabathia walked him and the place went crazy. I mean its not like a regular season game its different the electricity is all in the air. Then J Ro got on and Victorino comes up, and by this time the crowd was ballistic and on the second pitch BAM outta there grand slam." The guard smiles "I was in here working and heard it on the radio, so that must've cost you a pretty penny huh to get in there for an NLCS game" "Yeah but its my birthday month so this is my birthday gift I hope they win tonight because I'll be mad if they don't." "You think they are going to win the whole thing?" Lid smiles "yeah it depends on who they play in the series but yeah they can beat the Dodgers and as long as they don't have to play the sox they should be o.k." "I went down there to see the sox in the interleague game and they lost." "Boy you been to a lot of games "yeah ten games this season and they are nine and one only loss against the red sox." "Your there good luck charm." "I was born the day they won the series in eighty so you never know." He smiles "Alright buddy I have to get back to work try to stay out of trouble." And with that he leaves Lid soon closes the store up and rushes home he has to get his car and then go straight down to the ball park. And once he gets to south philly the place is jam packed and as he waits to get inside and park a women taps on his window and when he rolls it down she says "Here's a parking pass so you don't have to pay." "Thanks, I was just complaining to myself about having to pay the eleven bucks to park, right on time so do this tonight!" "Go Phillies she replies and Lid pulls into the stadium parking lot flashing his parking pass, after he parks and walks to roll call to pick up his ticket still dressed in full business suit with his very rare blue Philles hat, the ticket scalpers all African Americans and they gather and say loud enough for Lid to hear "We Have to Stop Him!" Lid pays it no mind and goes on to roll call the goodfella's are all around and as they pass Lid they greet him with head nods of approval and smiles at roll call he picks up his ticket and the cashier says "Alright boss have fun at the game." Lid says "Thank you sir, and continues on to his seat it seems like everyone has someone but Lid but this isn't the first time he's gone to a game alone so he's used to being Hansolo in South Philly and as he takes his seat to watch the game he thinks to himself Teresa could be right here sitting next to him, but she would rather be a deviant than be an American but I'm the one on the terrorist watch list go figure. The most alarming thing about the game is the way the crowd boos when Ryan Howard comes to the plate yeah he strikes out a lot but he's led the national league in homers and RBI's and without him there is no way the Phillies would be in the playoffs, yet and still the crowd boos and inparticular the younger crowd the people Lids age, and that alarming. The clear example of racism his generation has been corrupted from this war and the first generation of Americans who where supposed to be colorless still carry the old ways of hate. The Phillies win the game eight to five and as the excited crowd begins to leave Lid passes the gate ushers and the old man who has been working for Phillies since the days of the vet and  without saying a word Lid nods his and raises his eyebrow, yeah they are going to win it this year. On his way to his car he's stopped by a real wise guy and his wife who asked "What's the name of the street we are on?" Not wanting to be disrespectful he only looks at the mans beautiful blond haired wife and breaks a smile as he tells the man the directions "This is citizens park way, right over there is broad street." "Thanks buddy." Lid finally makes it back to his car and calls classic rock 102.9 as usual he gets right through "Ray Koob? What's up brother coming back from the game that's two playoof wins man I don't know this might be it?" "Ali whats up brother you where down there when Victorino hit the grandslam against Sabathia last week?" "Yeah man love my Phillies" "You really have to think about how special that was being in the building watching a grandslam being hit especially with regards to Phillies playoff history." "I know it was like electricity just filled the air Ray it was crazy the same tonight though they might get it done this year and end the curse of Billy Penn." "Shhhhh, you know we are not supposed to talk about it Ali, so what can I play for you?" " Bon Jovi yo Wanted Dead or Alive, I'm only safe in South Philly Ray." "Well stay down south philly brother and have a good one thanks for listening. And as he pulls out of the parking lot Bon Jovi comes on and enjoying the momement, the win, the respect and the bonous tonight of getting to see Jasmine Lid turns up the radio full blast and as he cruises through the parking lot blasting Bon Jovi he gets nods of approval from fans and heads onto  club dreamz in old city Philadelphia.

Old city is a haven for the young rich and powerful predomently white the place is packed with trust fund kids as they rave from club to club high on extacy, coke, and what ever else they can get there hands on. Lid just watches and observes as he walks to the dreamz entrance and gives Ibn a call on his cell phone "As Salaam Alaikum, I'm out front man." "Wa Laikum Salaam, alright brother I'm coming out now." Ibn comes to the door and waves Lid forward past security they check for his name on the list its on there and he's inside. Laced with framed pictures of hip hop albums and old movies Lid walks through the dimly lighted hallway and into the filled club. Only minutes in and he has already lost Ibn and from the looks of things he doesn't know anybody in the building, so he comes to the one place where he always knows someone the bar. "Y'all got Guiness" the bar tender smiles and she says "no, but we have Yuelang black and tan it's close." He thinks for a few seconds and she says "Come its good I  drink it" "alright give me a yelang black and tan." Then he hears a familiar voice in his right ear, "So you got outa that trouble huh?" He turns and its not who he wants it to be but close enough and her warm smile is just as comforting as if it was Jasmine, "Peace sister Kareema" and Mikhial leans over and gives her a kiss on the cheek. "Hi you doing sweet heart?" "Well as you know they threw that case out so I can breathe again." As the bar tender brings him his beer he pay but before she goes he ask "what are you drinking Mrs. Elaina?" " get me a cosmopolitan, I get out  here with all you young kids and I'm ready to get down and dance." He just shakes his head as he orders a drink for Mrs. Elaina "So what you going to do?, I remember when you wanted to go to law school it's not too late for that?" "Yeah well anything is possible right now I'm just going to chill and enjoy things the way they are, no point in moving too fast trying to keep up with the Jones especially if they ain't playing fair and by the rules." "Yeah but you gotta keep trying and not give up." "You right Ibn comes over with his girlfriend and Lid takes the opportunity to mossy about the crowd with drink in hand he looks for Jasmine and at the end of the bar a group of women stand and one in particular matches the siloeete of Jasmine and with all his strength and confidence he approaches the young lady and taps her gently on her shoulder. Built up with anticipation his heart pounding away the women turns around and says "Yes" but to avail its not Jasmine and deflated Lid says to the just as beautiful lady "Can I buy you a drink?" "Sure" "How you doing my name is Lid" "Sasha, you look a little lost were you looking for someone else?" "Yeah" "I'm sure you will find her?" So what you drinking?" "Get ma an apple martini, cutie." Lid order the drink and he and Sasha chit chat for a while but its obvious he's ready to get back on his mission and soon departs, to the back of the club but no sign of Jasmine. Finally he just haves a seat on the couches up against the wall, and finishes his beer, when from the back of the club the dance floor splits open and Jasmine walks through side by side with Issac the two stroll through the club until she looks over at the couches and sees Lid. Right in her tracks she stops and with such enthusiasm and excitement that only Jasmine could bring she say's "LID!" and rushes forward, he stands up and they hug Lid closes his eyes and just enjoys the moment her smell, her hair as it softly touches his lips and surprisingly she hugs back even harder without saying words the hug expresses how much they miss each other and with her glass of red wine in one hand they have a seat, she has seat right on Lid's lap and perplexed the club goers just stare. "You hanging out with us all night babe?" "Not unless its just you and me three's a crowd babe." She exhales "so what's going on what did you have to tell me that you couldn't tell me over the phone?" "Well I beat my case today the cops didn't show up and they had to toss the case out." "What happened silly, don't tell me you were hustling?"  Naw I got all speed racer with cops, I hit this lady on a Sunday yo I was looking at chinesses girl babe she was standing on the bus stop with these pin strip pants on they were like in 4D." Jasmine starts laughing "You are so silly" with her still on his lap sipping wine he continues "So I'm looking at her she's like dancing on the bus stop pole traffic starts moving showing off I hit my gas bammm and smashed right into the car in front of me." "Ohhhhh!" "So you know I aint got no insurance, she gets out the wheel and its this big old Rican chick and she is pissed. I'm like yo you got insurance? She gets on the phone and starts calling somebody." "Probably her brothers to come beat you up." "You better believe it so I look in the car and the baby is in the car seat moving like she's not crying though and then the old lady gets out the passenger side and I'm like are you o.k.?" "There was a baby in the car?" "Yeah! So the old lady is cool, I'm like are you o.k.? She nods her head and says yeah I'm o.k." "In the meantime the lady is on the phone plus she's still double parked on fifth street backing up all the traffic on a Sunday. So I'm like could you pull over so that traffic can go by? At first she is like naw but then she pulls over." "She didn't have any insurance did she?" "No!, and it wasn't nothing wrong with her car nothing she was just trying to get over. So after she pull over I pull over in front of her and keep my car running I take a look back and don't see any cop cars in the traffic going south and in front of me its empty I mean the first time ever the whole 5th street is clear and I just take off like the wind." "Ohhhh you gonna pay for that?" "I did like twenty three hundred plus I've been walking on ice for like six months." "No he's going to make you pay for that." She looks up to the sky, and Lid just shakes his head." They look at each and with every fiber in his body he just wants to ask her to please take him to California right now. But he doesn't as they both look around at Issac being a dickhead dancing with other women, and Ibn and Mrs. Elaina looking at Lid and Jasmine he DJ lets everyone know "Thanks for coming out to the Bleu Martini night club, we about to wine this thing on down but remember we are here every Friday and Saturday nights for hip hop nights." "Gotta go babe, see you later." She knows what he means later in the after life the one thing time has revealed is that cherishing those summers and the memories of what was become harder and harder to see taking place in the future. They hug and kiss each other on the cheek and just because she ask "Come on stay out with us?" Lid takes a look over at Issac and shakes his "I gotta get in the house still a hunted man, see you later." In pain she frowns her face and Lid turns to leave and this time the crowd parts like the red sea for him and he shakes hands with Ibn as he walks out, and goes to his car. Heartbroken, shattered he gets in his car and even in a V4 engine he begins to let his anger out on the road peeling off at every red light as it turns to green, dusting anything lined up with him at the light. At one light a group of white girls sit in the back of the taxi and as Lid looks at the light waiting for it change green the group of trust fund chicks roll down the window and just start laughing at Lid who once again is going home alone defeated he wheels home, makes Isha prayer and falls asleep.

Sura XCIII ayat 9-11
    "Therefore, treat not the orphan with harshness"
    "Nor repulse the petitioner"
    "But the bounty of thy lord Reherse and Proclaim"

# "The truth needs no explination"

P HINALLY AFTER TWENTY FIVE years of being barren from any championships in any of the four sports, the Phillies ended the curse of William Penn and excercised the demons of heart break after heart break in the World Series back in 93, the NBA finals of 2001, the Stanley Cup playoffs, and the 2003 SuperBowl featuring the Eagles, and the fighting Phils beat the Tampa Bay Rays in the fall classic. The only thing could top an October to remember took place a few days later when for the first time in the history of this great nation and African American took center stage and won the 2008 Presidential election, President Barack O'Bama did it in deciding fashion collecting the much needed electorial votes, from all across the nation and becoming the 44th President of the United States of America a little bit before ten o'clock easturn time.

On both nights the streets of Philadelphia were jammed packed and electricity filled the air and as Lid walked up Broad street and watched hundreds of cars filling the air with enthusiasm the atmosphere was surreal, with young people screaming Forty Four!!! Freom out of the roofs of their cars all this for the President of the United States a far cry from the debacle that was the 2000 elections, a far cry from tomatoes being tossed at the Presidents motorcade, this time around there was only joy but if the seeing him elected would bring such joy what type of anger would result in the assination of such a beloved President? A few weeks prior when the Phillies won the world series thousands upon thousands of white kids flocked the city streets and by day break center city was run a muck a complete wasteland with store front windows smashed in and street signs torn down. And all that damage was reaction to the Phils winnig the world series?? What would happen if that positive energy was turned negative? But all that forseeing is null and void as he alone walks the streets of center city, smiling happy his Phils won the world series and taking it as a sign of good things to come, with his brother Ra-Zens upcoming appeals trial, and his love Jasmine in town he walks past the federal prison and then over to Jefferson hospital and as irony would have it he' standing outside of the same hospital he was born in when the Phillies won the World Series in 1980. Lonely he calls Jadfa to see if his old friend, his old flame, his love will come downstairs to sit with him or even walk the streets with him for a few minutes. "As Salaam Alaikum" she softly replies "Wa Laikum Salaam" "It's bedlam out here the whole city is going crazy, they runnig laps around city hall, and everycar is just honking their horns." "I know babe I'm watching from the window." "Come outside, I'm walking around downtown alone." "Where are you silly?" "Coming around the corner." "Shut up!!!, you are crazy you know that." "I'm not crazy, come on and come outside?" "It's dangerous silly, I cant go out there plus no one is going to be here with my mom." "How she doing?" "She's getting better, she just went to sleep I have an idea though if you can get inside the visiting room I'll come downstairs until they kick us out." "Consider it done."

Some things are a lot easier said than done but as the security guard opens the side door responding to Lid's tapping at the glass of the hospital window the guard quickly responds "What can I do for you?"and wasting no time he flat out says "My mother in law is in there sick and I need to talk to my wife, I just got off work and this is the only time we can sit and talk because she' leaving for LA in the morning." Even full of intensity the guard will not risk his job and breach security so keeping eye contact with Lid he says "Tough luck buddy but visiting hours are over and there is nothing I can do for you." But he continues to negotiate "Look man she cant come out here it's too dangerous, I'm not going upstairs we just need to talk downhere in the lobby or something just for a few minutes, when right before he is about to get rejected again his phone rings "You wanna talk to him because he's not going to let me in?" and Lid following the orders of Jasmine hands him the phone." "Who's this I'm not letting him its after visiting hours." but after saying what he had to say he listens as Jasmine voice fills the air over the phone and a smile comes across his face and Lid knows he is only seconds from seing her, "Alright you guys got a half and hour but that's it man." "Thank brother, he replies after getting his phone back, and with that he is escorted to the waiting room and empty with no soul in sight he sits and waits until the elevator rings and out steps Jasmine. Dressed in all black and a whole lot slimmer than usual, she's had some work done to her because her once full and rosy cheeks are gone and as a smile comes across her face at  the sight of Lid they hug as she illuminates like a shinning star throughout the lobby. "As Salaam Alaikum" "Wa Laikum Salaam babe" but once they sit down like there lives they cannot help but turn their heads in opposite directons as they try to hold conversation. "So how nis she doing?" "She's pulling through you know my know my mom's strong but the doctors said it is going to take some time for her to recover from the surgery." They face each other "You know the best bet is too take her out west with you, you gonna do that?" "I would love but, she wants to stay here in Philly." They make eye contact, as he engages in double talk he's asking if he can come out to LA and she's telling him its up to you, you're the one who doesn't want to leave Philly." They make eye contact for a brief moment and then quickly turn away from each other "Yeah I can relate, I don't wanna leave either even though they are politely asking me to go, soooo you look beautiful." Used to hearing that like an actress she superficially responds "Thank you, but your not looking at me so how would you know silly?" and once again they turn to face each other and she ask "So whats oing on with you?" "My brother might be getting out, I'm ready to sue the city for my firearm permit and defamation of character Nutter and Ramsey's talking aobut I'm a threat to the city." "Honey you are dangerous." "No I'm not just don't make m mad." "Your funny." Lid rolls his eyes "But that's about it you know I'm trying to stay alive and out of trouble, whats that necklace around your kneck." Shaped like a heart in a tiny yet fine leather pouch around a plain black string its nothing he's ever seen before and very different than the run of the mill necklasses you usually see, and instantly she smiles and grabs hold of it and begins to explain its origins. "Oh this?" she smiles "inside this pouch are elements from all over the globe sand from the Sahara dessert, water from the nile river, grass from China near the great wall, my sprirtual advisor requested I collect these things as I traveled the world." "Whats that like scientology or something?" "Don't be smart stupid, you know I've been traveling the world is spacious its not all about whats going on here in America." "I know that's right, but I cant leave Philly right now my brother is getting ready to come home." She rolls her eyes "So I cant do anything until he gets out." "You can do whatever you want on your own just don't give up on yourself babe." He rolls his eyes. And for a few moments they just look at each other and so much can be said without saying a word "yeah nigga I did it, without you ha,ha,ha,ha,ha" "take me with you honey I have to get out of here" "why don't you just make it so I can see that you have it in you?" "I'm getting tired I don't have much more energy left" "you fucked up you know that rigtht?" "the test came back negative" when the silence is broken by the dreaded sound of the guards voice and what mirrors a prison visit he yells "Times Up!" and Lid to go time flies when your having fun and like a prison visit its time to go back to severring his sentence life in the streets of Philadelphia, alone, broke, and without his sunshine, his spark, his love. So sadly he lets her know "I gotta go." "You just walking out here all alone while everyone is celebrating?" "I'm always alone, can I have a hug?" Its been years since the dentist office, two thousand six hundred and twenty five days to be exact and in every way she has grown into an independent, strong, and unique women so this time when he leans forward both still sitting in the chairs no longer lovers, no longer husband and wife to be, no longer friends, just old aquaintences and as he gets up to leave Lid cant help but turn back around and take one last look as she turns away almost caught watching him walk away both having so much more to share with each both talking but not saying too much of anything the unspoken words are the ones that mean the most, she turns the other way and through the reflection of the waiting room window he sees the sickly grimise her beautiful face makes as he leaves and walks out of her life, "damn she still loves me, and gut wrentching to see him leaves.

Things are moving fast and Sharif's trial date is set for tomorrow, nervous about the situation Lid paces around his apartment until he gets a phone call from Michele, Sharif's girl. They've been together since they were teenagers and if anyone deserves it's her to once again see the love of her life freed from behind bars. "What's the deal Michele?" Always heartbroken and sad she says after sighing "I'm worried Lid what they don't let him out, after all this the appeals, the money to the lawyer after all this what if they don't let him out?" "I know that's a possibility especially considering the way things are nowadays this is not 1998, this is the new America and anything goes no matter how much evidence or how right you are." "So what did his lawyer say?" "You know I haven't spoken to him directly in a few weeks." "For real, are you serious?" "Yeah he's either out of the office and I leave a message but he still doesn't get back to me." "What if he doesn't show?" Not wanting to be pessimistic the thought had crossed his mind, but being the optimist that he is Lid as usual puts all his eggs and one basket and doesn't even fathom the possibility that Chris might not show. "I paid him the twenty five hundred he asked for, and the last time I spoke to him he said he was going to show. Now he also said that Sharif was not doing what the feds wanted him to do, and that he scared Judge Diamond." "For real that doesn't sound good." "Naw it doesn't especially considering the fact that two cops got killed fitting the description of Sharif since the last hearing. Both of them were Muslims and both of them had recently been paroled, so that really doesn't bode well for Sharif." "So what do you think you are a pretty smart guy?" "Fifty fifty Michele, I mean we had them the last time in court and Chris got up there to testify and basically cleared everything up I had never seen a prosecutor with his face in hands just shaking his head in disbelief." She laughs "well what happened?" "I mean he basically got up there and was like Sharif caught a raw deal, they made an agreement to charge him at level 20 under the federal sentencing guidelines, which he like the rest of his co-defendants would be out by now. But Chris was like after the whole 9/11 thing the information Sharif provided did not mean anything and he got steam rolled, they used an old charge from when he was inside to boost him up to a career felon and that's how he ended being charges at a level 26." "I don't understand all these levels what's that mean?" "Alright during the Forty Two  administration the feds started gong by this federal guidelines thing, so if you commit this, this, this crimes it automatically places you in a specific sentencing category. It doesn't matter what the circumstances were it doesn't matter about how the evidence was ascertained. So in Sharif's case he was buying an assault weapon, he's a felon so that's a violation, 100,000 ecstasy pills, that's contraband no body can have that so that's a felony and with so many pills intent to distribute, the same thing with the key of coke." "Damn he had all that?" "Michele, whatever he was trying to buy he was going to make a real big dent into the tri-state area." She laughs "I hear that." Now it didn't matter that the guy he worked for Deniro was a federal informant, and he basically entrapped Sharif by holding back his wages and telling him to take part in this deal." "Like yeah isn't that like against the law?" "There is no law anymore Michele, that's what I am trying to tell you if they want you off the streets they will get you off the streets he had to do his whole minimum mandatory in Pennsylvania the first time around they don't want him on the streets." "So they not going to let him out tomorrow?" "Fifty fifty Michele, I've been pretty well behaved in Philly plus everyone else in the case is out so you never know, and his public defender Gerald Hill keeps said the last time they thought they were going to let him out." "I can't stand that guy! I hate to say it but I am so happy we got another lawyer I mean I don't mean to dog our own people but every time I stop by his office its like he's high on coke and wiping his nose." "Because he is" "That's trivalent why do black people have to be ignorant then he thinks the judge is going to show him some respect in the court room I'm so happy Chris is going to be there this time." "I know it really sad to say that because once again some white man has to come save the day, but the public defenders are over worked there was a day when Gerald probably was a pretty good lawyer but this place will get to you and break your spirits. Right now what we need to focus on is that once he is released then we have a support team ready to be there for him so he doesn't have to go back to crime." "I know but these days crime pays" "Yeah I know but he messed that up going down right before 9/11 when the flood gates opened." "I know I told him to slow down but he was so off the hook when he got out." "That's what happens" "Nooo I mean he was off the hook Lid he took my car on night got drunk and just wrecked it. Then he shows up one day with another girl this monster talking about she's is a model and was going to make him one. Lid begins to laugh "You should've saw her she was all black and ugly I mean what magazine was going to put her in it Halloween weekly?" "That's not funny Michele," he remarks as he continues to laugh "For real Lid I mean it's some fine looking dark skin sisters don't get me wrong but he was cheating on me with that after he wrecked my car." "It's different know Michele, Islam plays a major role in his life and from what he writes me and from what he talks to me about the religion will keep him from transgressing all bounds like he did the last time." "That's another thing he really wants me to be Muslim? And I'm like Sharif I am not going to change my religion for you, why does act like that's the only way?" Lid exhales this has been a sore spot for some time as Sharif is adamant about Michele, converting from Christianity to Islam for them to get married and be together. "I was coming back from AC (Atlantic city) one night after this party I had went to with a friend of mines and one of the guys that went with us is assistant council down at CJC, on the way back we started talking about the city and how violent it was and how everyone seemed to be engaged inn crime." "O.k. so what does this have to do we the whole Muslim thing?" "I'm getting to it Michele, it's like this we both agreed that more Muslims come in to the criminal justice center each day and go up state, by far way more Muslims than Baptist Christians and you forget about the white boys they are lawless." "You aint never lie" "So what happened in Philly after 9/11 was that the flood gates opened up and crime really really started paying, now we the Muslims caught the short end of the stick because automatically we were classified as terrorist, and the police department and the feds for example when Chris said the whole 9/11 thing in court meant that it was open season on Muslims throughout the states." "Dag" "You ever watched the old bugs bunny cartoon and he argues with daffy about whether it was duck season or rabbit season?" "Its rabbit season and the Muslims are the rabbits so that's how you could work down the criminal justice center and be amazed at the amount of Muslims that get locked up, it doesn't help that we are locked out of the legal jobs, and basically been betrayed by or own family the Baptist divide and conquer. Anytime my own cousins call me a terrorist we have a serious problem especially if I was the one that went around with the factual information Michele, So the cops are brainwashed into thinking muslim means terrorist, the second generation of muslims like myself are forced to hustle because we cant get employment its like get down with Jesus or starve and to top it all off when we show up for court the Baptist are snitching and getting shorter sentencing, or not even getting locked up as the cops conviently turn the other cheek. So that's why he wants you to be Muslim Michele, because you guys betrayed us and you knew the truth and went along with the bullshit excuse my language that Forty Three  and them were feeding the public. Y'all turned against us your own people family friends for jobs that most of y'all are under qualified for, and money? That shit ripped the city apart it ripped the country apart divided we fell Michele,, he wants you to be Muslim because just by y'all actions you guys have proved that most of it is a bunch of bologna." Michele has had enough and she stops Lid dead in his tracks "hold up wait a minute the church has done great things for the community and black people as a whole, I mean everybody is eating." "Yeah but you tossed us into the pit of snakes, was it worth it? He wants you to be Muslim because Islam is the way to paradise, because he believes the sunna of the prophet Muhammad is the only way to paradise, because who would want to live in a household with a Christian after all that I just told you? I mean look at the shit I've been through!" "You ain't never lie." "And how do you know all my business, that's not cool Michele,, that's evil and hateful the church should never be like that, Jesus wasn't like that Jesus was love so how can you say that Jesus was the son of GOD and he was a messenger of peace but then wage war on your family, your kin over money and jobs?" "Yeah well my family would never let me turn Muslim they would have a fit, they don't even know I be going down there to visit him." "How are old are you Michele?" "Thirty four" and you're sneaking around your moms back? That's what he means women are not supposed to be running the show ya'll are emotional beings and y'all don't play fair, in Islam the man runs things the husband." "You see I don't agree with that stuff the male dominate thing I see the way Muslim so called men be hollering at their wives like they are slaves or something I'm not with that." "That's abusive and not the way of the prophet but Michele, the male is the figure head white girls know it, they wouldn't dare cross their husbands." Michele, interrupts "Yeah because if they do they gonna end like what's her name Lacy Peterson, or that other cop who killed three of his wives." Lid laughs "Yeah only the African American women think they are the heads of the family and that goes back to the days of slavery when the black was crucified by the slave masters humiliated robbed of dignity and it continues on today, what Islam does is re affirm the black man, the man for that matter contrary to popular belief we are not equal yo we compliment each other and until we find some common ground we will continue to have dysfunctional families that will self destruct and only assist in the this extinction agenda." "I don't agree with that It's time for black men to step up and be men even if he gets out what is Sharif going to bring to the table I'm a nurse and will always make more money than him." "Elaina what does making more money have to do with it? So what you make more money you have a dream to have a family and a household but at the head of the family in order for it to work there has to be a black man in order for their to be the correct balance there has to be a black man, its by design that one out three of us will see prison time, its by design that the only black faces you see working in the corporations are gays, weakness they present us as weak, so we don't pose a threat to them, they are o.k. with you being the head of the household because you pose no threat." "I hear what you are saying but black men need to get yourselves together." "We need the help of the black women stop trying to bring us down and start helping to uplift us bad enough the whole is against us how do you expect us to get anything accomplished is y'all are bringing us down to, that's were Islam comes in money means nothing faith and practice of faith, leading the family in salat and practicing the ways of the Prophet Muhammed is what counters this hell on earth that's been designed by both of our enemies satan, you know that's what you want Elaina a man that doesn't use drugs, lies, drinks, or fornicates." "Yeah I hope when he gets out he will follow all those rules." "They are not rules they are agreements with God." "You ain't never lie Lid." She sighs "Alright let me get off this phone." "You coming down tomorrow?" "Oh no we have this thing were I just cannot see him cuffed up like that its so demeaning I cant take I would just erupt in tears and get all emotional in the courtroom." "See what I mean Elaina emotional creatures" She laughs "Yeah I understand." "Alright I'll call around twelve tomorrow I should know the verdict by then inshah Allah he will talking to you from my phone." "That would nice I going to just go crazy." "I gotta finish ironing my suit talk to tomorrow Elaina bye." They hang up and as he irons his suit Lid thinks to himself about the chances of Ra-Zen getting out and the words of his brothers attorney Chris Warren rings in his ears "He's not doing what the fed's want him to do?" Sharrefs serving his time, and yeah he's appealing his sentencing but that is well within his constitutional rights. And then it occurs to Lid they still have not broken him, they still have not broken his older brother, and that's what Chris means Ra-Zen is still fighting, he still refuses to even acknowledge the judge in the court room, he still fights with other inmates, and he still plots and plans with his cohorts over the phone and by letters to the outside. Even up until last week when he asked Lid in the visiting room to get a message to one of his friends on the outside, is just further proof that Ra-Zen will not be broken by this system. At the behest of his younger brother Ra-Zen informed Lid that someone was snitching on the inside the federal prison walls, and a secret grand jury was assembled to trial and convict a muslim sister for assisting in a fire bombing that happened a few years prior. She basically drove the guy to the house that he firebombed because the people there were slated to stand as witnesses against the guy.

The worked and convicted the man for murder but the city and the feds wanted more so they conviened this grand jury and were ready to charge the women with second degree murder, Ra-Zen got wind of it and quietly he whispered the information to his brother in the visiting room. He gave Mikhial specific instructions not to mention any of this over the phone, and not to leave any trace of it on paper or even verbally say anything to the his old comrade Big Keif . Lid takes the information and calls Big Keif as soon as he gets home and pleads with him to come by his apartment and please, please speak to him, please. After a few hours of paying Lid any mind Big Keif finally agrees to meet Mikhial. In the cold Philadelphia winter Lid waits outside on the street corner and when Big Kief finally pulls up with a female in the car he gets out and they exchange the greeting of As Salaam Alaikum, and Lid opens up the Holy Quran on a small piece of paper he states "There is a secret federal grand jury out on your baby's mom get her out of town now!!!!" Big Keif looks at the paper and in full shock, he is startled by the news as no one on the outside had any idea about the grand jury. "Thanks, she's in the car right now!!!" And takes off for the car, probably to get his baby's mom out of town, and as far away from the tri state area as possible. So even after spending a decade in a half behind prison Ra-Zen will not play ball and that is just another example of how far he is willing to go to help out another even it means sacrificing his own appeal.

The next morning Lid awakes early and makes Fajr prayer with his suit neatly pressed and ready to wear he gets dressed, blasting Billy Squires "Lonely is the Night" Lid prays that this will be the end of his plight to make it Philadelphia, to run the streets with his brother, and feel safe in a city that has his childhood best friend hunting him, had the police taking his identity and his car from him, has basically boxed him in to this corner in a unfamiliar neighborhood, holding on the rope. When he emerges from his apartment umbrella in hand the bus stop is packed and he patiently waits. His friends from south philly shake their heads no as they drive by the bus stop, and Lid knows what they are implying but he will have none of that today. The bus takes longer than usual to get there and the corner begins to get full with transit riders, and finally he sees a 17 bus coming up 19th street. As usual he lets the women and elderly get on and finally when there very little room left on the bus he is the last to hop on. But this morning the bus ride is different a lot faster as the driver skips stops and leaves passengers waiting in the rain. Soon the riders get a little frantic and begin yelling at the bus driver to "Slow down" or "You passed my stop" and bam the frenzied daily commute comes to an abrupt halt as the driver hits the mirror right off a car, and she has to stop. "I have to pull over y'all, there's another bus right behind me so you guys will have to get off and wait." "Yeah a bus filled with people you just left behind." Lid looks at his watch and it is almost nine o'clock no where near center city or even the federal building for that matter he begins to panic as he walks off the bus. In the rain he begins to walk in the direction of center city and a thought hits him, catch a taxi. And so he begins to try and haul a cab, and even dressed in full business suit with his cashmere coat cabs just pass him by as hails them from the curb. He continues to walk southbound in the direction of center city, when he sees parked out in front of a church a cab. "Yo could you get me to six street man I am going to be late for court?" The cab driver takes a good look at him and replies "I would give you a ride but I'm waiting for a fare now." "Cool" he replies and just as he is about to continue his trek in the rain another cab pulls up just in the nick of time. He jumps right in "Could you get me to sixth street, in like ten minutes I am going to be late for court." "Yeah, no problem" and the taxi driver pulls off and as promised in less than ten minutes he's out in front of the federal building. Years ago he was demolishing the bathrooms in this place now it holds the key to his salvation will they finally let Ra-Zen out? And as he pays the fare and jogs into the building he is greeted by the security guards, who once he presents his id go the extra mile patting him down and making sure he doesn't have any contra band on him. "Your good to go sir." "Thank I thought I was going to be late, and he quickly goes to the elevator passing the crystallized United States Constitution, and the Bill of Rights. Upstairs on the six floor he waits, and waits anxiously looking out the window and glancing over as the elevator doors open to let people out. Is it Chris he wonders is it Chris, when finally the elevator opens and to his dismay its Gerald Ingram. "Where's Chris?" "I don't know he was supposed to be here?" "Yeah I paid him the money" "Well I think they are going to let your brother out this time, I thought they were going to let him out last time but then he asked Chris to cme and testify for him so they postponed it he should be o.k." "I don't know I'm calling his office" and Lid does so but no one answers and Mikahail goes into court room. The court reporter comes out and says

"How ya doing?" Making him feel comfortable and when some of Ra-Zens friends show up and family even his grandmother made the trip, they quietly wait as Ra-Zen is walked into the court room in shackles. "What's up Cuz" Smiling he turns around "Whats up y'all. Were's Chris at?" he bluntly ask his little brother "I don't know" the last time I spoke to him he said he was going to be here, but its alright, its cool." Pissed off Ra-Zen looks over at his friends and says "Y'all better get that money from Chris!!!" "I wouldn't worry about that right now" Ra-Zen gives his brother a cold glance and if he wasn't cuffed you better believe he would be whipping on his little brothers ass in the court room "All Rise the honorable Judge Paul S. Diamond" and with that everyone stands up and when the fat pig of man sits down so does the rest of the court room. "Alright this is a resentencing case and we did not have the parole board from Pennsylvania present last time but here she is Mrs. Thompson, so we can go ahead with this resentencing hearing. If you will Mrs. Thompson, the blond haired, blue eyed bitch begin to speak and everyone just zones out as she begins to list the past record of Ra-Zen aggravated assaults in 84,85,86,87 possesion of illegal firearm in 88,89, aggravated assaults inside the prison system, and then the current charges he was found guilty of possession of controlled substance, intent to distribute, possession of assult weapon by a felon, the list just goes on and on when finally she says the state of Pennsylvania finds that the defendant Mr. Shelton was correctly sentenced at level 26, along the lines of the federal sentencing guidelines. And with that judge Diamond ask ask the family if anyone has anything to say and Lid gets up with a prepared statement

"Good morning your honor, I believe in God sir and I still believe in America. This is a land of great opportunity and second chances and with the family sitting here behind me and myself we have a good support team in place this time to ensure his success. I've seen him change sir, and he is not the hot tempered man that he was years ago, his presence in the community is needed to help these young men understand the consequences of their actions and the horrors that await them behind prison walls. The city of Philadelphia needs him we he turns around and points out everyone in the court room his family needs him so could you please release my brother your honor, please. He made a mistake because he thought he was owed something that cutting corners is alright that doing wrong is ok as long as no one sees you. He understands now that cutting corners will only lead to a small room with a small window and dreams of being in the real world, he knows this your honor he's remorseful about his actions because he knows he's lost so much of his life behind prison walls and more importantly he knows that if he was to ever get into any trouble again its that the three strikes and your out rule is in effect and he doesn't want to spend the rest of his days behind prison bars, he's older, and his family and support staff are much more secure and able to provide excellent support for him in his time of transition. On another note the last time we conviened here your honor our father stood before and as tears began to fall from his face he pleaded with you acknowledging the mistakes he made while raising Raymond, he's dying sir he doesn't have his kidneys anymore and a transplant may be the only thing that sustains his life, the only thing that makes sure he is still here on earth to see his grandchildren and to see his sons together, such a selfless act Judge Diamond is just another sign that Ray has changed. I still believe in America your honor so could you please release Ray my brother, his cousin, her brother, her grandson, his nephew, his best friend, our family your please, thank you sir." "Judge Diamond smiles "Heart you for those heart felt words young man, but with a devilish grin Judge Diamond lets Lid know that kiddie time is over "And now based on the testimony of Pennsylvania's parole commission and the record I have in front of me I can only agree with the federal sentencing guidelines and recommend that Mr. Shelton continues his sentence of 168 months in federal custody, followed by five years probation in the state of Pennsylvania . . . .

Since the streets got news of Sharifs fate, life has taken a quick real quick nose dive for Lid and he's nothing more than a bird on a wire, unable to sleep at night time in his studio apartment in South Philly the heats been turned up tremendously especially over the past few days post Christmas. And as he sits in her truck trying to explain what's going on to his mother, she coldly lets him know "Well I you think somebody is going to kill you you better call the cops before they do." Mom the cops!! They are the ones behind this, I need a gun." "That's what you don't need how do you know they are after you?" "Everynight this truck drives by my apartment and it just slows down and then pulls off real fast." "You need some help son. You need to check into the phych ward and get evaluated." "No I don't, I need a gun I owe that money, the lawyer took that money and now he's incogneeto, they want that two grand back that's what this is all about." "Look boy I don't know what kind've of mess you got yourself into or what kind o mess your brother got you into but I'm not buying you a gun and you are not moving back to my house! Be a man and get out my car because I am late for work." "But mom they are going to kill me!" "Too bad now get out!" And automatically eight words rings out in his head "Now I realize I'm on this earth alone." "Alright mom As Salaam Alaikum" "Be a man Lid you had plenty of time to find a place to move to deal with it Wa Laikum Salaam." He gets out her truck and glances up at the small church on the corner as the septa bus rides by "Zion first Baptist church."

As he crosses the street the first thing he notices is a skinny young boy standing at the bus stop with a red hoody on and a menancing grin wrapped across his face. Smiling at Lid as he crosses the street they stare at each other and Lid comes to the conclusion that he is indeed being hunted as the bus just rode by and the kid did not get on. And as he continues down Dickenson street he notices in the reflection of a parked car that the kid is following him "fucking bloods" he thinks to himself as he quickly turns down his block and checks the mail box and then unlocks the door as the kid walks behind him. Once inside his apartment a long exhale is the prelude to him trying to secure the apartment as he grabs the refrigerator and pushes it all the way towards the front door. If anyone is going to come in here they are going to hell one hell of a time, and then its off to the bathroom to make wudu and then salat.

But soon the sun sets and the day becomes night and the yong boys begin to hover around Lid's apartment and for most of the night all he hears from the outside are threats fearful that he will be caught off guard he gets into a defensive position on top of the stove, armed with his sword in one habd and his billy club in another in stealth mode with all the lights turned off in his room Lid watches from the cracks in the blinds and listens as gun shots riddle the night air and the madness feels like its getting closer and closer to him. "That nigga aint got nothing in there!!" a voice yells from the street, "pap pap pap pap pap ahhhhhhhhhhhhhhhh!" mimicking the sounds of getting shot as they walk by his apartment time and time again, he just sits croached on top of the stove like a gargoyle waiting for anyone to try and come through his door, if anyone does come in here they better be ready for a fight because they are going to have a hell of a time getting past the refrigerator. His only break from this chaos is when it is time for

Isha prayer and once he is finished it's right back to his post. He knows soon that black tinted out Dodge Ram is coming back to run laps around the block and torment him throughout the night. Again and again the young boys walk past his apartment and this time all fears are comfirmed as a voice from the outside says "he's trying to bring down the church!" and another voice mimics the sounds of a gun "Pap,pap,pap,pap,pap,pap! And then screams Ahhhhhh!" Scared Lid just continues to sit on the stove, trying to call everyone and anyone who will answer him on his cell phone but to no avail no one picks up and he waits as two o'clock rolls around and the nights entertainment begins.

The sound of a hemi engine is very distinct like rolling thunder it stalks the streets and revs its engines, and revs its engines, and then finally it hits the bottom of his block and violently pulls off up the small block until it passes Lids apartment and slows down, then speeding up again and turning the corner and around and around it goes like the craftman's truck series lap after lap, round and round. This has gotta be the cops no one else on earth would spend their time tormenting Lid time is money, plus no one on the block has called the cops, its gotta be the cops. He thinks about when he first moved into his apartment and the graffiti on the ground said big and bold "Welcome to Hell" and truly hell is a place of amForty Three . As the truck continues to circle the block Lid turns to Allah at any time the driver of the truck can open fire and cut right through the paper thin walls and take him right off this earth. Without a pistol he's defenseless against a shot gun blast to the door and a gang of young boys once inside these children of the apacalype will do anything raid his apartment, slay him, or even worse they could just send a professional and Omar could show up with one of his young boys like the time they met up in Delaware two shots to the head spinkle coke on the floor and make it drug related and with all these dooms day scenerios and the five daily prayers all finished for the day he turns to the glorification prayer the rememberance prayer. Like all salats he begins with the Al Fatihah and then he repeats thirty three times subhana Allah may may be glorified and exalted, Allah Akbar Allah is the greatest, Ahumdulallah praise to Allah, and La Illahah Illah Allah there is no diety but Allah. The salat is painstaking as it begins like any other but as he moves into the different positions of salat holding himself in these positions his body begins to hurt being bent for an elongated time, but that's the challenge his faith is strong especially as he fears death, and being so close to death Lid seeks to become closer to Allah giving up on the salat because it hurts too much is like giving up on Allah and he cannot do that as in a matter of time it seems like their meeting will commence, as the Black dodge ram continues to circle the block. Another challenge with this particular prayer is that it takes over thirty minutes to complete and as Lid blocks out his fears fifteen minutes turns to thirty and tears begin to flow down his face. How did things get to this point just weeks ago he was riding high as the Phillies won the World Series, things were looking good with Sharifs appeal, and after being denied his right to carry in Philly for being deemed a threat to the public 2009 was looking like a real good year with an upcoming civil suit against the city, a new democratic President who was of African descent, and a new apartment in a prime location in South Philly? He continues to pray as the truck circle and circles the block slowing down with every pass of the apartment and then pulling off, yet he continues to pray louder and louder La Illahah Illah Allah! La Illahah Illah Allah there is no God but Allah! That is what it comes down to no three Gods, there is and always will be the one God and finally after he salams out and his prays drown out the sound of the rouring engine the truck stops and disappears and silence overtakes the street As Salaamu Alaikum wa Rahmatulaah, As Salaamu alaikum wa rahmatulaah peace and blessings of God be upon you. A voice from the outside breaks the silence that had overtaken the street and Lid hears "Be Muslim". When down the street the door to the truck violently slams and the voice of a white man says in all rage and anger "SO!!" with sword in hand h rises from prayer and takes his spot on top of the stove, looking out the blinds and trying to rest his eyes as its almost four o'clock and the sun will be rising in less than two hours.......

"GET UP!!!!!!" The terrifying yell from the same white voice awakens Lid as the sunlight encompasses Philly illuminating his one bedroom studio apartment. He jumps down off the stove and immediately goes to the bathroom to make wudu. Exhausted, tired, beaten is the story his reflection relays to himself as he looks into the mirror. After wudu he makes Fajr prayer and then begins to get his clothes together for work and early way early he steps out his apartment and into the same street that terrorized him only hours ago. At the bus stop two squad cars sit parked across the street from him and when they get out one asian, and three white cops they start cracking up at Lid, with his earphones on h hears nothing but the he clearly sees their smiles, and he knows the infamous Philadelphia police department is behind his current torment, Nas says it best "the cops are the demons." After all this time they finally have him isolated alone, away from people and his family, but desperate times calls for desperate measures.

So the usual goodmornig to John is replaced by a frantic plea as Lid leaves all pleasantries behind and desperately approaches John, the tall red headed white man the poor English man is all ears as this morning the usual run of the mill chit chat is replaced by "I need to apply for family medical leave John, my dad is sick in Florida and I need to leave town and tend to him." No mention about the bullshit sports games over the weekend fuck the Eagles, the Steelers, or any other NFL teams, fuck the Flyers, and the Sixers this is serious and John is completely caught off guard by Lids request and as he watches the young man go to the computer without even waiting for a response he takes a seat next to him. "What do you mean you are leaving? What's going on?" Mikhial turns his chair to face his manager over the past year and a half their working relationship has been filled with all types of ups and downs they bonded with classic rock and roll, sports, and stories of the crazy things that happen within the confines of family life. But whenever Lid begins to leadership and management skills within the walls of kinkos office he and John have always clashed. Lid reflects back to when John tossed a chair across the room because Lid was able to do some designing better and faster than him, or how he had to stand and do all the physicall labor while his white co-workers sat at the computer stations all day, he knows he cannot tell him the truth so he lies and like a broken record he says " My dad is sick in Miami he has dialysis and I need to leave town." "well it takes a few weeks for everything to go through, so your going to have to wait." "I cant wait here's the FMLA application could you please sign it?" And Lid hands the forms over to John, and goes back to the web where he's found the telephone number for the recruiter Randy Rochevick for the south Florida region. And as John shakes his head the good man in him understands Lids request so he signs the forms while Lid gives Mr. Rochevick a call. "Good mornig Mr. Rochevick, its early man sorry about calling you so early but I'm kinda in a jam and I need some help." "O.k. who am I speaking with?" "My name is Lid Islam I work up here in Philly for kinkos office at an offsite location inside the we do it all tower. I've been here for like a year and a half and my father is ill down in Florida, he has dialysis and its pretty bad for him, I wanted to transfer down to Miami?" "Well I'm sorry to hear that, are you in good standing with the company?" "It's like this I my manager right now signing the FMLA forms, and I was going to take a leave and come on down there, are you guys hiring in south Florida?" "We are always hiring in spite of the economic situation, are you eligible to transfer?" "No, but my evaluation score was 2.95 so I was only five tenths of a point from getting a raise and being able to transfer. Look Mr. Rochevick my dad is sick and I really need to get down there, I'm a hard worker, and that's why my evaluation score was not at a 3.0 because I did not complete my online training, but that's hard to do because I'm running around the store doing everything always busy working on a project. Our location is different because its inside the we do it all tower so we take care of all the printing they do and that's a lot, as you we do it all incorp is all over the globe. So we don't have job jackets and specific times our clients need their work asap. You wont be disappointed I've had like five years running a printing center and I know what to do so please man open up a door for me so I can help take care of my sick father?" Mr. Rochevick hears the call to action as the tone of his voice changes, what ever Lid just said has got him motivated and he takes charge "Alright look do you know how to go online and internally apply for open positions, what are you an in store production assistant?" "Yes sir" "Alright I'm looking online there's a few open positions for in store production assistant apply for all of them, what location were you looking at?" "I was looking at the Alton Road branch?" He laughs "hahaha in South beach? Good choice I know the manger over there Armondo Teheda, look here's his number give him a call and apply for the position and let him know about the situation with your father. Lid take my email down and give me a call after you've talked to him and applied for the position." "Thanks Mr. Rochevick, I will not let you down sir." "You better not, have a happy new years and I hope to se you working at one of our stores down here in Miami, but call Armando now take care man." "Thanks" They both hang up the phone and its well past nine o'clock he waits as John is on the telephone probably talking to Kathy. Relieved because the hardest part securing a job is finished Lid begins to apply for jobs online through the internal web page for fed ex office employees only. And when John hangs up the phone he ask "What happened, you must've got some good news I see you over here clapping. Is your dad feeling better?" "Naw John, I just spoke with the recruiter don in Miami Mr. Rochevick and he was like they have job openings down in Miami, I told him what was going on with my dad he gave me the number to the store manager in south Beach and told me to call him." "What do mean so your leaving and not coming back you don't even have a high enough evaluation score to get a raise let alone transfer." He would know, "On the FMLA forms you just signed you see were it ask for a return date, I put in writing I plan on living in Miami and working for kinkos office I need to stay in Miami to take care of my sick father. I told Mr. Rochevick everything that was going on and he said under the circumstances things could be worked out." John takes a few deep breathes and his face which now beat red but before he can utter a word Lid quickly picks up the phone and dails back to South Florida "Good morning could I speak to Armondo Teheda?" Lid holds and patiently waits to speak to the store manager, as John grabs the phone on the other line and to someone probably Kathy again. "Thankyou for calling kinkos office Armando Teheda speaking how can I help you?" "Good morning Mr. Teheda my name is Lid Islam, I work for kinkos office here in Philly and I would like to come down to Miami and care for my sick father." "Well we currently have a hiring freeze right now because of the economy." "Yeah I know, but I'm on FMLA and I just got off the phone with the recruiter Mr. Rochevick, and he basically said things could be worked out, because of the medical situation plus its not like we are hiring a new employee, we are just changing the locations of an employee from one part of the country to anmother." "You already spoke to Randy?" "Yeah, he advised me to call you and see if you could help me with my situation since you guys already have posted the in store production assistant on the intraweb. The problem on my end is that I don't have a evaluation score high enough to transfer." "What was your score?" "Two point nine five." "All that's no problem why though?" "Because I did not complete my online training, but like I told Mr. Rochevick I'm runnig around like crazy in here all day I don't have time to complete it, I cant stay for overtime to finish it and during the day I'm runnig around here like a chicken with head cut off. The customer comes first and we are an offsite location so we do it all incorporated comes first and they keep us busy all day in here." "Yeah I started at an offsite location I do have a production assistant position open and I was planning on filling that spot soon. Tell you what when will you be down here you said your father is sick are you coming to visit him?' "Lid mhas jo idea when he is leaving but he knows he cant go back home to his moms, to his apartment in South Philly so it has to be right here, right now, so he quickly responds to Armonda's inquiry "Man he's sick now I'm on my way down there tonight." "Tonight!" "Yes sir I'm catching the bus down and will be in Miami for the new year." "Wow that's right on time because I need to fill the position tell you what I'll give Randy a call, and what I need you to do is take my number down." "Pen ready" "thre zero five five ive five thirty seven eighty one, and call me as soon as oyu get down here." "Thanks Mr. Tehada" "Look Mikahil you sound a great person to work with and I look forward to you joining the team here at kinkos office in Miami. I hope your dad gets better and I hope to hear from you when you get down here." "Alright Armando, thank you sir, and I wont let you down have a happy new year."

After hanging up the phone reality begins to sink in "I don't even have a bus ticket? I haven't even cleaned my apartment out? How am I going to leave for Miami tonight?" For that matter I haven't even talked to my dad? His thoughts are interrupted when John comes over and ask "Mikhial, Mikhial? When are you going to clock in because I have to go down to the store and meet with Kathy?" "Hold up John I'm thinking, I need to call my dad" upset Lid just dismissed him John walks back to his desk, and Lid picks up the phone and calls his father. A few times a month the two of them speak to each other, and in their relationship one thing has always been clear brother Rashad was never in the business of raising children so as he picks up the phone and Lid greets him "As Salaam Alaikum" "Who's this?", "It's Lid dad" the introduction alone lets him know that this might be a harder sell than convincing kinkos he needed to move. "So what's going on son I spoke to Sharif the other day he was pretty upset about the lawyer situation." Where's the money son a lot of people put in on that, I know I want my hundred dollars back." "Dad I cant think about Sharif right now, I need to leave Philly right now" "What happened Lid are you alright?" "Yeah but I wont be if I stay in the city another night, there's this truck that keeps circling the block" "Where you staying at?" "Down South Philly." "Why did you move out of your grandmoms house?" "We had an agreement I only had a few months there and my time was up so I got a studio down

South Philly and everything was cool until Sharifs case and then the whole place just went bananas, I don't have any protection it's like duck season right now." "Lid what really going on you sound like you need to talk to a doctor, have you spoken to your mom and about moving down there and back to Delaware?" "No I'm not going back to Delaware, seriously the city's trying to kill me I got this civil case against them because it's a second admentment thing about my gun permit and defamation of character." His father interrupts him "Slow down Lid, you think the city is trying to kill you because you have a civil case against them?" Lid begins to speak lower into the phone he doesn't want John to oveJasminer him "Dad there was this black dodge pick up a ram circling the block all night long. The young boys been walking by my apartment acting like they are going to bust in their and shoot me I haven't slept for days." "You soun crazy son have you talked to your mom about this?" "Dad look I don't have anywhere else to go, I need your doctor to send kinkosa letter explaining your medical condition so I can get final approval for this family medical leave. But Wa allah hi I swear by Allah dad that this not just a neighborhood thing, when I was living with grandmom the phone used to ring all night all kinds of times at night and it wouldn't be anybody on the other end. They were terrorizing her until I moved out because I asked her and it doesn't happen anymore." "Look I'm just holding on to the rope son and I cant carry you so you better have the job situation together, how are you just going to leave your job? And please give me a few weks to get things together down here when do you think you are coming down here?" "Dad I'm leaving tonight!!!" and without giving his father a chance to respond he simply says "As Salaam Alaikum" and hangs up the phone, quickly going to John at his desk.

"John!!!" I need to leave for the rest of the day." Jo0hn shakes his head I already gave Germain the day off it's you and me because it's the day before New Years's eve!" "John there aint any work in here, I cant stay I have to get ready to leave for Miami please?" John gets up from his desk and puts his hand on Lids shoulder and looks him directly in the eyes. "Lid, we have been through a lot here, but I always respected you as a person and without a doubt you are a hard worker and good friend what's really going on?" Lid reflects and thinks about the memories he has with John, the Phillies finally making the playoffs, then the next season winnign the world series, how throughout the season everyday they would give updates whether or not the Phils won, the eagles, the flyers, the NCAA tournament, Johns family coming to visit for Christmas his wife and three children, Lids court situation, the battles at work about management and how the store was going to be run, all the laughs and all the conflicts. He knows regardless of what corporate John is thinking, John the human being is really concerned and to lie to him at this point at this moment would reduce Lid to nothing better than the scum that are running him out of Philly, the scum that ran him out of Delaware. So he looks at John and exhales and begins to tell the truth. "Remember the other day when I was here early in the morning?" "Yeah" "I slept in here all night long I couldn't sleep at home, I'm being hunted and I have to leave town, they I ont know who it is the cops, my people, the mob, the military, I don't know but I'm being hunted and they are going to kill me if I don't leave town right now, I have to go." And a truthful answer equates a truthful response as Lid has breached the surface of corporate John and got to the huma being. "You know I live out Willow Grove it's safe out there you can stay in my house with my family for a few a while don't leave." The quakers used to hide runaway slaves almost two centuries ago in the same area and Lid no choice but to think as John along those lines, he knew John the human being was a good person, but Lid also knows Willow Grove is not far enough to escape the domestic terrorism the hate that's been chasing him so he refuses Johns act of goodness. Shaking his head "John thanks but that's not enough I have to get far away from here until this stuff settles down if I ever come back at all." "You sure?" "Yeah" "Do you need anything any money or anything?" "You already did it by signing the FMLA, now all I really need is for you to let me go for the day I have to clean my apartment out while its still daylight." "Alright it was nice to work with you, and I hope your dad feels better and things work out for you in Florida." "I'm never coming back John, thanks man just call me if there's any problems with the FMLA and I will fax you up the paper work from my dad's doctor." They shake hands and John takes his seat back at his desk while Lid solidifies his move when he goes online and purchases a bus ticket to Miami, the greyhound ticket is one hundred and eighty one dollars one way and with an investment like that it's a dine deal he has to leave and once h is finished printing out the E-ticket he bids John one last goodbye. "I'm out John, see around man tak it easy and thanks a lot." And with a bitter face John knows there is nothing he can do to persuade Lid to stay he's gone so he just says "Take care Lid." And waves his hand.

Mikhial storms out of the fed ex kinkos store and into the hallways of the we do it all incorporated tower, and thinks about what he is leaving behind no more Mrs. Puerto Rico and her boxes of legal work and those big brown eyes lighting up at the sight of him. No more skyscraper view of city hall and center city Philadelphia, no more lunch in center city rubbing shoulders with the real white colar criminals and holding court with the hard working blue colar Philadelphian's. No more "hi ya doing?" from his south Philly friends, no more hall seats at the Phillies game, no more sky box seats at the sixers game, no more cheese steaks, soft pretzels, water ice, or tastykakes, no more of the love affair with the city he fell in love with as a child no more Philly.

Sitting on the ten trolley his mind cannot turn off all the events that led up to this point, and he has one last place to go to and file an appeal for old times sake may be he can get him off the hook, and get him out of this trouble. It's been months since he stepped through these doors after helping to bring back to life the epicenter for all progression of Al-Islam in Philadelphia, and his strategy was if the cops were going to watch him while he was charged with the fire arms violation, then guess what they were going to watch him at the masjid especially considering the fact that it's the cops who supply the old head muslims with the work in the first place. And right on time the historic Sister Clara Muhammed School was reopening its doors in March and Lid spun a good web entrapping the department, and the city while he was being watched under the microscope. But as soon as the case was thrownout at the behest of the brother he is sitting in front of at this very moment h disappeared and resorted back to his old ways.

"As Salaam Alaikum brother Karim" "Wa Laikum Salaam Lid whats going on I haven't seen you around the past three months ever since your case was thrown out?" "Its cold outside brother Karim you know everyone stays in the house in the winter that hawk man, plus I just moved out of west Philly and down South Philly just trying to settle down." "So have you been down to South Philly masjid with brother Betts?" "No, you know I don't mess with them." "So how can I help you?" He exhales "I'm being hunted brother Karim and I don't know what to do, this black Dodge keeps circling my block everynight, the young boys are walking by my apartment acting like they are going to bust through the door and kill me." "What makes you think that?" "They keep making gun shot sounds and one of em said that I was trying to bring down the church." "Brother Karim laughs "heheheheh" "It's the city brother Karim I have a civil case against them because they denied me my second admendment rights to carry a firearm." Brother Karim quickly interrupts "Now what did we tell you about that Lid they don't like giving the permit to carry to just anybody." Lid gets very angry as a law student he sees everything in black and white whats legal and illegal, constitutional and unconstitutional but in Philly, Philly is nothing but a gray area, and depending on who you know and what you can do for the people pulling the strings you can end up in the winners side or the losers side and the Boss put so correctly "Don't get caught on the wrong side of that line." by no means is brother Karim Iman Malik so as he sits behind Iman Maliks desk in power and Lid shows his discontent "its not there call!!! That's a constitutional right in no way am I a threat to the public and the only due cause is because I am muslim point blank period!." So I'm appealing the decision and later on its going to be a civil case because that's defimation of character, I gotta keep fighting but I cant go back down there tonight because you might be doing my janazza Islamic funeral tomoorow." He doesn't get bothered by Lid raising his voice out of respect or just acknowlagment that in another reality or may be in the future you will be sitting behind this desk and quickly tries to come up with a solution to Lid's problem. "Well the first thing you need to do is get out of that apartment now, give me your number and I will look up some brothers I know who rent apartments but get out of there now!!!" "Alright here's my number two six seven five five four seventeen thirty six." Lid knows moving to another place is out of the question he just paid his land lord a thousand dollars just to move in back in October, he doesn't have any money to move to a new place and the fact remains this isn't about where he is living or what part of the city he is living in, this is Philly telling him to get the FUCK OUT!!! This is the Sunni Muslims telling him to GET THE FUCK OUT!!! This is the police department telling him to GET THE FUCK OUT!!!! This is the Baptist telling him to GET THE FUCK OUT!!! So as he shakes hands with brother Karim and smiles he knows inside underneath that grin he's getting on the bus tonight for Miami and his next move is going to his grandmoms and asking if she can house his things that represents whats left of his shattered life.

"No solilitors or jahova witnesses" Grandmom's never gonna change, he rings the bell and waits and as usual she peaks behind the shade on the fornt door exposing just a glimmer of her face "ooh what are you doing here?" And as she opens the door the frightened and fearful Lid greets her with his usual kiss on the cheek, "Grandmom can I please put my stuff in your basement?" "Boy you crazy didn't you just move in there?" "I have to leave, I have to leave the city, I'm going down Florida with my dad." "When? What? You need to get some help boy come on in." He walks into the living room when to his surprise his little cousin Aquil is playing with his toys, his Uncle Sha newest addition who some reason looks exactly like Lid red hair and all. "What's up man?" He kneels down to shake hands with his youngest cousin who ablidges but then their Grandmother breaks up the love fest and starts to grill her troubles grandson with some serious questions. "Now what is this you are talking about?" "Grandmom I have to leave I can feel the heat coming, if I stay another night down south Philly I'm a dead man, I already brought my ticket and talked to my dad in Miami he said I can come down, I just brought my ticket for greyhound and I have to leave tonight." "Boy I'm say it again you are crazy just like my father, did you talk to your mom?" "Last night I told her what was going on and she said I cant come back to her house and basically told me to get out of her car, so I'm out." "What makes you think someone is trying to kill you?" "I just got this feeling it happened again when I was on the ten coming up here. I'm siting down and these two guys get on at city hall, dressed in the one piece carhart sets one light skin and one dark skin both of them had these big old shades on like I couldn't i.d. them and with the one piece sets on they could easily have a change of clothes on underneath so any witnesses are giving descriptions of the guys in the wrong clothes." "So what's that mean, that don't mean they were after you." "Grandmom the trolley started to fill up like on 30th street but there was plenty of seats and they just stopped right in front of me and kept looking at me as they rambled through this duffle bag that was open, they wouldn't pass me and kept looking at me. Then when we got down the bottom on Landsdown avenue it was this baaaaddddd young girl walking up the street and all the guys on the trolley just turned their heads and was looking at her I mean she was baddddd, everyone except them two I saw them through the reflection in the window and they were looking right at me the whole time, they never turned to look at the girl, they just kept looking at me." So I was shook so I throw them off and just get up from my seat and start moving to the back door of the trolley. They followed me and when my stop came up one stayed on the trolley and the other followed me, so I just backed up towards the beauty shop and we just starred each other down, the he turned and walked away as I crossed the street to go over to sister clara Muhammed school." "That is odd, let me call your mom." "Thanks grandmom I love you" "Now I don't want any dumb stuff because his father has to come pick him up so you just calm down and after Sha comes we will go down to your apartment and get your stuff. What about your job?" "I talked to the recruiter in Florida and the store manger down there too, I'm out on FMLA and they said they have a job for me in Miami, I told them about my dad being sick so the job thing is cool, I just need to get my stuff out of that apartment."

So Lid waits as his grandmom calls his mother Halimah and she informs her daughter about the bad news concerning her grandson. "That what I told him he needs to get some help you should see him Halimah he's just all over the house pacing around and talking about people are trying to kill him. Here's your mother on the phone she wants to talk to you." And Lid grabs the phone from his grandmother "As Salaam Alaikum Mom" "Don't As Salaam Alaikum me boy!! What the fuck is wrong with you bringing you crazy bullshit to my mothers house. She is not going to let you move back in with her and you are not moving back in with me Tee Tee and her boyfriend are living upstairs on the third floor and they are getting ready for the baby." "I didn't ask if I could move back in there, you already said no last night remember? I need to clean this apartment out now and put my things in her basement" "Boy you just moved in there? What about your security deposit?" "I'm going to loose it, I have to get out of here." "Lid don't lie to me are you smoking crack?" "No mom, Ive never smoked any crack and I get my weed from the Jamaican dude just to make sure its not laced woth anything, but I haven't even smoked since they locked me up back in February." "No mom its nothing like that I told you last night what was going on, and they did it again as soon as it got dark mom I'm rattled, I just need to get my stuff and leave mom." Lid there is something wrong with you, your doing the same thing you did in Delaware don't you see, you stuck me with the apartment in Delaware you said the same thing they are trying to kill me, they are chasing me are you sure you did not use any PCP in your pot because there is something wrong with you?" "Mom I don't know whats going on this time if it's the military, the cops, the mob, I don't know but whats happening now is nothing like what happened in Delaware that was because I beat them down there and they went to extreme measure at Citigroup but yeah its kinda the same thing because they just want me outa here. I need your help moving please come up here and help me get this stuff outa this apartment, so I can get on the bus tonight?" "You said it I may to spend some time with dad, but what I don't want to do is die without falling in love, what I don't want to be is assassinated and it gets classified as a hom invasion, without my gun to defend myself. The bus leaves at ten mom we have a few hours of daylight get some sleep I'm going to grab the first load with Grandmom as soon as Uncle Sha comes here and picks up Aquil." She exhales shes tired you can hear it in her voice, "You need some help son, may be your dad can help you. You know I worked last night I have to get some sleep, I'll be up in Philly around three." "Alright mom I love you." He ahngs up the phone and sitting in her black recliner his grandmother just watches and looks at her grandsons every motion as he sits on the steps in shambles, in ruin, when the silence is broken by the opening of the screen door, and the subsequent ringing of the door bell. "Aquil get your coat your father is here." She gets up to answer the door as Aquil looks over at Lid and just smiles his father is here to pick him up, and as he waits for his Uncle to emerge into the living room Lid thinks about his split with his uncle. How he refused to go to New Orleans with Uncle Sha back in 2005 after hurricane Katrina devastated the city of New Orleans leaving hundreds of thousands homeless, hungry, displaced. He decided then the apartment, and his application with the fire department was more important than anything else, especially considering this all took place after the 2004 elections forget the revolution, forget fighting the power at that time all Lid wanted to do was check back in. But there is no checking back in after you had stood up to the leviathan Uncle Sha knew that Lid on the other hand is learning the hard way. He should've kept on the quest that he and his uncle started years ago post September 11th, but as he sits on the his grandmothers steps the same steps he used to play GI JOE, Transformers, and Spiderman on as a child as an adult he is ruined, with all his civil liberties violated, the police, the Baptist in Delaware, the Muslims here, the Delta's, the Baptist in Philly, the whites pulling the strings from behind closed doors Lid can only think that he made a bad decision, a life altering decision by speaking out against Forty Three , that he should've never spoke out with the truth,  should've never wrote a disrotation about the stolen elections of 2000 for his senior project, never applied for law school as an opn idealist, never protested, never marched, never called c-span, never voted for Kerry, never wore those t-shirts, because being the enemy of the state is no fun at all. "I know the pressures of the oppressor is Hell living feel like I'm Mel Gibson."-AZ

So as Uncle Sha comes into the living room and his son runs too him and he picks him up, Lid thinks about how he desired that so much from his father growing up but never got it, and knows going to Miami will be a good thing for him. He continues however to sit on the steps with his face in his hands until "Whats up blackman? You still trying to make it a country that does not want you, that's trying to terminate you like you are an insect?" "Ohh hush up Sha and don't get that boy started he's already talking about people trying to kill him." "Because they are mom, and they wil." Lid finally speaks up "I'm fine Unc., you gotta gun I can hold, they got me pinned down in South Philly." "Shut up boy you don't need no gun." "Seriously unc the white boys the police, the military, the devil I don't know but they keep riding around and around my block all night long, its driving me crazy." "So what is a gun going to do but get you shot? You know the number one rule nephew UNDER NO CIRCUMSTANCES GIVE YOU A GUN." "Come on man I'm older now, they doing this because I'm muslim Unc. I hired Mr. Davidson for my appeal because I was denied my permit to carry its because I'm muslim I cant get these Christians man they are trying to destroy me." "You sound kuukuu kiddo everybodys always out trying to get you and you don't anything there's something wrong with that picture." "Grandmom I'm serious." And finally the former king of white colar crime, the over weight lover, finally speaks up "No mom he's right they are trying to kill you and they will kill you as long as you play their game, let me explain a few things to you your not muslim, your Africanu and there is no such thing as Islam or Muhammed they made all that shit up."

"Come on Unc you know Islam is the way, Allah never had a son and the trininty is just made up nonesecense by the catholics, when Nero was emporear of the Roman empire he just fused all the pagan gods into the belief of jesus and the loop hole was creating God in three parts saying he was one in three." "Stop it right there nephew, everything you was told blackman is wrong it's a lie a fable, listen to me and listen to me carefully. Its not history or his story, its true story and my words Lid the son of my sister will heal your tortured soul." "I'm getting outta here you then got my son started, I forgot you two are terrorist." And true to her word she gets up and goes into the kitchen as Uncle Sha continues, with his eyes wide open full of intensity and passion excited about the truth he is about to relay to his nephew.

"Ra is the name of the of the designer of the world, Ra-Et is the name of the goddess who is the creatise of the world. Together they represent the spirit of the supreame being they represent the energy that moves throughout everything that exist, the sun, the moon, and all the animals, you, me and Aquil interrupts "Me Too dad?" "You too son, and together the three of them share a rare laugh together. Ka and Ka-Et is your soul, they are the soul in all living creatures, the divine consciousness, our intellence its present in all that is created. Amen and Amen-Et represent the spirit of human beings two halves that compliment each other, together they make up the great being the God in all of us." Lid listens and attentively watches as his uncle is full of fire, the same fire that fueled Lids soul so many years ago when their quest first started. "So hold up thiers Ra and Ra-Et that represent the spirit, Ka and Ka-Et that represent the soul and Amen and Amen-Et that represent the being?" Excited his nephew is paying attention he nods his head "yeah now the black energy substance that gives us color is derived from the blackness of space and was inherited from the primordial black heel of the earth. Amen and Amen-Et created Ka-muu and Ka-nuut they allow our physical bodies to function to receive and transmit the full divine energy from above." " In everything, that's the melanin in human beings?" "Its in all things it's in the plants nephew see our divine connection to all living beings all living things have souls and through respect for there existence their function in the world, the earth we maintain balance between each other." Lid is pretty learned in a vast amount of subjects but he is in awe of the information being relayed to him "This is what they need to teach in college, so I still don't get it what's wrong with Islam?" "Im a get to that but think about it nephew there was no need for an extinction list until they started killing off animals, destroying and killing plants, for that matter killing us for profit, for money destroying souls in order to make money? Demolishing habitations, the rain forest living things that have been here on earth for tens of thousands of years some plant life since the beginning, they do this because they have a dysfunctional soul, because they lack the proper levels of melanin because they lack the divine connection to the ancients. We live under their thumb this system is contradictive to our divinity our souls, our spirit, our physical body is all in disorder, your soul nephew is in malfunction in this new world that the whites created.

This entire system is a system of disharmony, its in disorder, theyh have a spiritual disconnection to the earth because they lack the divine way of living." "Hold up Unc everyone knows that white people are light skin because they migrated from Africa and the separation from the long sunny days, the cold weather in northern Europe, and Europe caused them to evolve and adjust to their surroundings" "See that's history but not the true story they did not just pack up and leave Africa they were banished because that group rejected living within the divine laws, they chose to pursue a life driven by lust. They were forced out of the African tribes and families, they were outcast who pursued lust and through sexual activity with members of their own clans, and families they embraced self destructive, dissexual activity, homo sexual activity, incense their offspring had no external skin color we call it Albino, but they also had genetic mutations like light eyes mr green eyes, and blond hair this is the true story nephew the origins of the people we call white people or Caucasians today."

These are the ones who rejected divine law, and embraced disorder, this is the culture of the whites they cannot tune their bodies like we do to respect the souls of all living things because they lack the proper levels of melanin because they lack any connection to divinity. That's why its possible in this day and age that all things can be destroyed in the blink of an eye, the nuclear bomb can destroy everything, the pollution and rape of the earth will eventually lead to the changes in her that will destroy everything we love here, this isn't the natural order of things, disorder nephew is not the opposite of order." Lid looks at his uncle confused until he finishes the statement. "Disorder is the perversions of order the only true evil. So that's why we have so many gays and dikes because they have embraced this white culture of disorder!! We shouldn't be acting like that, this entire culture of disorder is designed to exterminate the Africanu man, take our women corrupt there spirits and give birth to more offspring with these dysfunctional souls. This makes them our enemy because they are the ones who were rejected and they are destroying us, and this earth because they are dysfunctional to the natural order of things the divine laws" "That sounds like hate yo, I cant get down with that." "Oh why because Jesus said love thy neighbor? "he laughs I'm going to get back to that but its not a hate thin, it's the right thing because if we allow them to exist in this manner or any manner for that point they will continue to spread disorder throughout the planet bacuase it's who they are." "Yo I cant get down with that, I cant hate white people." "Then you're a fool because as sure as shit they hate you and the divine connection you have to the spirits, now listen nephew because I'm getting to your precious Islam and Christianity for that matter"

"After spending thousands of years in isolation in northern Europe the whites came back and made contact with us the Africans in southern Europe, North Africa, Asia, and Asia Minor driven by the lust of conquest they started a series of wars against us. But they failed and were driven back until they changed strategy and attempted to corrupt and control the culture of the Africans, by settled near and close to our kingdoms and civilizations, they interacted with us through trade, visiting our lands and introducing corruption as a way of living a lust dominated culture. They played on the immature and young of our culture just like its done today, exposing poisons that corrupted their body, like the pot you love so much." "Hey hey hey man I haven't smoked since the cops locked me up." "Good, the pot, the pills, the beer, the cigaretts all poisons you allow to enter your body all have negative affects and push you away from divine law and towards evil and disorder." They used this rift between the young and the old to farther disassemble our culture creating fictional white charecters as alternatives to the Gods and Goddesses for the rebellious youth, trying to establish that those who were once outcast had some divine connection with divinity. They stole the names of the Gods and Goddesess and created false life stories of these fictional white charecters living near Kamet which is falsely called Eqypt, they learned some of our language and perverted it creating a false bloodline and a fake heritage, false ancestery making us believe that the whites were chosen by God to rule the earth and show us how to live! Are you listening to what I am saying? Abraham,Issac,Ishmeal, Judah, Moses, David,Sheeva, Buddah, Yaweah, Eloheim, Muhammed, and even your precious Allah are all made up charecters created by the exiled ones who rebelled against divine law, the one who rejected our culture and chased after their own lust.Thats why you are headed for self destruction because you keep trying to exist and achieve success in a culture that conflicts with your natural divinity a culture that rewards disorder and corruption!!" Lid shakes his head in disbief, there is no way after twenty seven years of believing that there is only one God but Allah is he going to believe what his Uncle Sha is telling him that the lineage of the Prophets all twenty five of them mentioned in the holy Quran is false its preposterous especially coming from the king of fraud himself, Mikahil just shakes his head rejecting the words of his uncle but that will not Sha who is now on a role and he continues "You don't believe me do you? Listen to this, the name Moses comes from the language of Ka-met it's derived from the word Mau-Shire, Mau means truth, and Shire means word, true word, is this making sense to you becauseits easy to understand?" "Yeah, im following." His brother Aaron is another false prophet his name aqnd his character was taken, no stolen from the name Anaan which is the spirit force in creation, he is the divine assistant of Tahuti he comes to us in the form of a baboon. Remember the Lion King how many times did we watch that with Naim and Khadejah? Who was the wise ma, the ancient, the relayer of information from above?" Lid eyes open wide as light bulbs begin to turn in his head "The baboon!" "Exactly listen to this Habweah another ancient God had the body of African man and the head of a bird this name was corrupted into Yaweah. Issac and Ismial all false they were stolen the names were derived from Sheik and Ismeool, the story of Seth and Hiro, Seth means evil spirit, and Hiro is the good spirit, Hero??? You understanding what I'm saying nephew?" "So that's why the arabs and the jews are always fighting?" "No they are always fighting because it is in their nature to fight and shed blood period. What I'm saying is this why would you start a story from the middle you start stories from the beginning and this language, this true story, our lineage, and divinity is the true story." "So what about Isa, or Jesus come on man the whole world recognizes him." "He's a fictional character created in there quest to have some identity with God they created this fictional character lying to themselves that as long as they believe in this fictional character lying to themselves that as long as they believe in this character they are forgiven no matter what they have done to us the Africanu it's o.k.

they are rightly guided by God. Think about it, the story of Jesus teaches us that we should love all our neighbors, this is nothing but a means of control to accept invasion of course you are going to preach love all your neighbors if you've been defeated centuries before and they failed to breach Ka-Met." "You losing me Unc. Jesus was made up too and the teaching of love your neighbor was just a means of tricking us into letting our enemy get close and live amoung us?" "Yeah listen to how they stole the story, another tittle for Hiro is Shaansu, she meaning child and ansu meaning royal divine king. Hezeus, Jesus the name is derived from Shaansu, the story is made up.." "That makes sense because Allah has 99 attributes or names mentioned in the Quran." He laughs nephew your mind, its all in your mind you have to unlearn what you learned, the whole story of Asar, ans As-Set the King and Queen of Ka-Met they represent the divine balance, other names are KA and KA-ET, think about it that A in Adam, and the E in Eve its all right there you just need to look closer, but back to the story Seth murdered the King Asar or KA and took over Ka-Met and his government and his rule was corrupt in disharmony. Forced out of her role as Queen, Aset or KA-ET found the body of her husband Asar and through their divine spiritual connection she became pregnant, she now had the tittle of Mariet Asar or the beloved of Asar." "Damn Unc they had to really be in love to have a baby and he was dead." And for a brief moment Uncle Sha goes back to being the old Uncle Sha "Yeah he had some good dick knocking her up when he was a spirit, but listen that's were Mary or Maryum came from Mariet, but her son through this divine birth Shansu the son of Aset and the spirit of Ansar, they corrupted this story into the immaculate conception and virgin birth. Shaansu will grow up to re-establish order, the divine order and dethrown Seth. Seth is another name in which the whites corrupted and turned into Satan making him responcible for all evil. The story of the Mahdi and Jesus returning to restore order and overthrow Satan was stolen from the story of Shaansuu." "Makes sense Unc. Makes a lot of sense but for me Islam and the prophet Muhammed makes sense too." "WHAT!!!! That's because your brainwashed Muhammed never existed the term was stolen from the name God of the Nile, how many people were named Muhammed before Muhammed? You ever ask yourself that?? The nile river of Ka-Met which we call Happ or Hapi, rikset means south, and met means north, the word for water is moo. Moo Happ Met, Moohappmet or the spirit of the river nile flowing north. Think about it these religions have all been spread through war the calipha's it was get dowm with Islam or die, and survivors still had to pay a heavy tax if they did not get down with the message of Muhammed, that doesn't sound like a religion of peace, that sounds like thugs saying get down or die. Look at Christianity nad the crusade, even our experience here in America with slavery put in shackles, beaten, murdered, while our women and children watched our women raped while we watched but they were good southern Baptist Christians right? This was done in the name of God cthe God created by the rejected ones."

"What about the books Unc. I read my Quran and my bible yo, the Quran is perfect everytime I open it it reveals to me a ayatt that fits with what ever I am going through." "That's because whatever you are going through is not that difficult to remedy. Listen it's all stolen and made up lies, the Bible is a series of stolen works from KA-Met, Egypt from the book of the Dead and other scrolls its only 1600 years old, while the stories I just told you are over 20,000 years old. The English term Holy Bible is derived from the Helios Biblos, Biblos is derived from Papyrus that's the plant used to make paper. The term helios is the greek perversion of the name of the God Ra it really means the paper book of Ra." In the language of Ka-Met the Tior like Christian Dior means worship, the term Torah means worship of Ra. In the ancient language of Ka-Met Akoo means illuminated or wisdom, the ancestrial spirits are called Akoo meaning the illuminated or shinning ones or those who have embraced divine wisdom, Koo-Ra which means divine wisdom of the creator Ra it was corrupted to Quran, this why the Quran is called the book of wisdom." Shocked Mikahail realizes that everything his uncle is telling him is making sense and he shares some doubts that he has always had about the Quran. "You know in sura Lahab I always thought it was way too personal, you mean to tell me angel revealed to Muhammed a sura about Lahab a member of the Quararish tribe who torment Muhammed and how his wife used to torment Muhammed too, that's just way too much for me the all powerful God master and sustainer of the Universe revealed that to Muhammed??? I never got that, but I never questioned it because I didn't want to lose faith or lack faith." Smiling Uncle Sha says "Question all of it now brother, you've been blessed with the divine knowledge pass it on, peace black man,come on Aquil you ready to go home." "Bye Lid" "Alright Aquil peace out hommie." And like that their conversation is over, and like that Uncle Sha just blew Lids mind opening doors upon doors that were once sealed with belief in Islam, his faith and everything that he has learned to date, all of it his belief in the hereafter, good deeds and bad deeds, the stories of the prophets, and considering all that' been hanging over his head Uncle Sha true story makes complete sense as to why things are the way they are.

As his grandmother emerges from the kitchen to say goodbye to her son, and grandson "You fools done talking about nonscense?" But before his Uncle walks out the door Lid has one more topic of discussion with his Uncle and he speaks up "Forty Four's going to bring change Unc. watch, he's the Mahdi, the one who defeats Seth and brings order back to the world." Uncle Sha smiles "Lid you know just as well as I do what he's there to do, the extinction adgenda is in full effect." "King Alfred plan huh?" "Come on man that's your field of expertise political science you know damn well Mcain or Forty Two should've won the the White House, but you know all that stuff is rigged the Diebold machines. Naw black man you are the Mahdi the black man figure it out nephew." "Beginning of the second term, or during campaigne trial?" "Yeah and I bet he'll have a middle name it's the same game." "I told my bother the same thing, thanks Unc." Lid gets up and shakes hands and hugs his uncle his one time mentor, his father, his uncle, his brother, his friend and as they look face to face, eye to ey relaying a message without uttering a word the message "I'm sorry", as he walks out the front door with his son. "Alrigth kiddo your mom is on her way, I'll be right back let me talk to my son outside." Lid takes a seat on the steps and the classic words of Nas rings, and rings through his head "Taught Greeks and Romans but the legacy was Stolen."

# "Send in the Clowns"

This town is a lonely town
Not the only town like-a this town
This town is a make-you town
Or a break-you-town and bring-you-down town

This town is a quiet town
Or a riot town like this town
This town is a love-you town
And a shove-you-down and push-you-'round town

This town is an all-right town
For an uptight town like-a this town
This town, it's a use-you town
An abuse-you town until-you're-down town

This town is a losin' town
It's a miserable town
It's a nowhere town
And I am leavin' this town
You better believe that I'm leavin' this town
Man, it could never be uptown
It's bound to be downtown

This town, bye-bye
Bye, bye, bye, bye, bye-bye

"Thanks Grandmom for taking me down here and holding my stuff,
I really didn just want to leave all my things down here, that's my life."

"It's  nothing boy you just better get yourself together you cant keep telling everybody that someone is out to kill you, you sound crazy Lid. I'm with your mother on this one you really need to get some help." "No way Grandmom I'm not going to any doctor I am not checking myself in toany hospital and losing my rights, I cannot afford anything like that on my record, I could never buy a gun no way." "That's all you think about buying a gun there is something seriously wrong with you. Well you better do something you cant keep going from this place to that place you are going to be a nut on the corner or even worse behind bars because you killed somebody." "I know, I know I just need a break that's all , right here on the corner grandmom I'm on Garnet street." "I know I've been down here before" "What!!" "Yeah when you first moved downhere your mother told me where it was." "So you did one of your famous drive bys huh?" "Hush up boy and get your stuff." "You not coming in?" "No way, Im not going out there with those crazy folks." He laughs as he walks out the door and spits a line from his brief rap career "Hahahahaha, the whole worlds gone crazy but that's what happens post world war take these guns and keep clapping." He gets to the place which only a few hours ago was ground zero for fear and unlocks and opens the door the refrigerator out of place is the first thing he sees as the tough task at hand lies in front of him. The first thing he grabs is his laminated collection of Daily News Photos and covers  off the wall highlighting the Philles playoff run beginning the season before when they got swept by the Rockies and ending this season when they won the whole thing. At the time it seemed like a good omen, but now as he retreats to Miami it was all just the pipe dream of a teenager to be king in the town that he loves so much, a town that doesn't even want him around. And after packing most of his things up he starts to load up his Grandmoms mini-van, and when its full he sits back down inside hiding from the frigid winter cold.

"Alright grandmom I don't think anything else can fit in your van did mommy say if she was going to come down here or meet you at your house?" She just called when you were inside she said she was coming straight down here." "Well I'm taking a lunch break because I don't think I can fit anything else in your car." "No you  not you better start packing the rest of that stuff up so when she comes all you have to do is load everything in her car, Lid your mom is tired she worked last night." "Alright, alright" so he goes back inside passing the refrigerator with the picture of Sharif and

Mr. Malzanno together in prison, boy how things have changed it was all so close, to touch the dream. He could taste victory in his hands and just that fast it all slipped away." Soon his mom pulls up and as begins to pack everything up into the her suv the neighbors come out side to see whats going on. "Listen to me boy you need some help and you cant come down my house until you get it." "Mom I'm leaving for Miami and I am never going back down there to Delaware after what happened to me down there." "So your gonna stay in Miami with your father?" "It beats a blank plus I don't wanna stay in a place that don't want me I'm out yo." She comes into the apartment and begins to help him pack everything up "So what time does the bus leave?" "I gotta be there by ten thirty, we leave around eleven." "Alright lets fill uo this load and take it to my moms house its no point in having her sit out there all day she's wasting her gas trying to stay warm. And I want her out of here, and for that matter I want to be out of here before the sun goes down and it gets dark.

Once at his grandmoms they unload everything and store it in her basement and being the saint that she is using her last she offers to give her troubled grandson her last. "Here take this its only a hundred dollars but it will help you out on the bus trip. I had to take that ride to get Sha out of trouble when he got locked up in Florida so I know it's a long bus ride." But his mother rightfully intervenes "No mom don't give him anything he's o.k." "Excuse me?" Taking the lead from his grandmother he humbly refuses "That's o.k. Grandmom I have some money saved up plus I start work on Monday and I get paid next Friday." She still insist and puts the money in his hand, but when he goes to give her a kiss on the cheek his quickly slides the money back into her coat pocket. She needs it more than him, and he knows that. "Come on boy lets get you to the bus station." "Alright mommy I don't know what to do with these crazy kids?" "If you got any sense you better do what I am about to do and that's lock my door and not answer it." "Thanks for helping him out." "No problem but he's gotta get checked out, something wrong withn somebody who thinks someone is after them and trying to kill them." "I know, may be his father can help him out."

They leave and drive down to the bus station a few hours early but it gives them plenty of time to talk and try to figure out what went wrong. "Mom you shouldn't ve of left the house uptown, that was everything for me all I wanted to do was move back home after college, live in the house

I grew up in fix it up sell it after a few years and move just outside the madness of the city." "I know you are not going to throw this all back into my face? Boy it wasn't even your house to begin with, so this is all my fault that's what your saying?" "No Im just saying you shouldn't had lied when I asked you if y'all was moving that summer I would've never left philly and just transferred school." "Well you should be over that by now it was almost ten years ago." "But you didn't stick to the plan mom." "Things change honey." "I'm sorry mom it's everything your brother just schooled me on some things over grandmoms earlier like why did y'all become muslim in the first place?" "Because it was the in thing to do the fish man rounding everybody up off the corners, all the gangsters were turing muslim from the gang wars it was in style." "Cause he was saying some stuff that made a lot of sense about Africa, about all the religions stealing all its origins from Africa and Ka-Met or Egypt about all the religions Jeudaism, Islam, Christianity, and the Buddist stealing its origins from Africa and just making there stories up along the way. I mean I just went through hell down in Delaware and up here in philly because these people think I'm a terrorist because I protested against the FORTY THREE  shit and your telling me the only reason I'm not Christian is because being Muslim was the popular thing to do??!!" "So again its all my fault?" "No its my life, its my fault, I just don't want to leave Philly and its breaking my heart." "Then don't leave." "But I cant go back over there, they gonna kill me I can feel it, please just buy me a gun mom down Delaware it's cheaper I'll be o.k. then." "No I'm not buying you anygun, I think you need to go down south withn your dad now what really happened because you are not telling me everything?" He exhales knowing that he took a vow to his brother to not tell anyone about this but he has to explain to his mom whats going on. "Alright Sharif asked me to tell one of his friends out here int the street that the guys girls was under secret grand jury investigation because one of the guys he's locked up with is snitching about what happened with that fire bombing." "What fire bombing?" "Remember when the brother fire bombed the house killing the family of the the witnesses the women and likem four children well this chick was the driver of the car. And the feds had put together a super secret federal grand jury and they were about to pick her up off the streets. Shafif tells me because he got word of it on the inside, and I have to tell his friend on the outside needless to say the feds, the Philly police department at that point had enough of my espionage games and pushed the button on getting me out the city by all means, plus I owe two grand to you know who, the high speed chase, it's a lot of things. But this is the first time I've in isolation away from my family, alone and they just running me out of town, but they will send someone to kill me if I don't leave."

Lid I did the best I could but a women cant raise a man you need to stand on your own and if it's one thing your father knows is how to take care of Rashad." They both bust out laughing "Yeah he's got nine lives mommy" "So go down there and pick up a few things from him and get to know your dad you never had that see how he lives and survives yeah in a lot of ways he's still that nineteen year old kid who got locked up but most importantly honey he's a survivor and he can stand on his own and that's the key." "I just feel so rejected mom like all the things Uncle Sha was saying made so much sense mom like I went to this Halloween party with the white boy Zack from my job and you could feel the divide between us when he got around his white friends. When it's me and him he's cool when the numbers change, its this air of arrogance or superiority, then the sait paulie's girl" "What's that?" "It' a beer chick but this girl was dressed up as the Saint Paulies girl, she was hot too." "I don't wanna hear that." "Sorry but she sees me at the party later on in the night and she is like "You still here?" "But I felt like she wasn't asking me if I was still there at the party, it felt like she was saying you still here on earth!" that's what my intuition my gut was telling me and right now its telling me to get out of town." "Then you should go, but listen son my brother is who he is a freaking con artist and even if the information he told is correct which it is because you know I have entire book shelf of our history, that doesn't give the right to go around telling people to kill whitey, I bet his ass aint gonna do it himself?" They both bust out laughing "However we all came about on this earth son we have to learn to live together and we cant socialize together then a simple goodmorning or ho ya doing should good enough but hate can never defeat hate honey you know that, and I didn't raise my children to be like that." "Your right mom" "I know and you know my brother isn't all the way correct because you are not with him. You just got to figure things out son here's a hundred dollars, don't spend it all on junk food just getting down there save your money because you never know about these jobs they could still burn you." He takes the money and gives his mom a kiss on the cheek. "I love you mom" "I love you too but don't make the same mistakes in Florida don't be calling me talking about they are trying to kill me because I am just going to hang up the phone." "Yes mom, I think I am just going to take it slow and not mess with anybody just going to sit in the shade and focuss on Lid." "Do that but learn from your father because he knows how to survive." "Thanks mom I love you." "Love you too honey." Mikahil gives his mom a kiss, on the cheek and then grabs his bags from the trunk and walks to the bus station but before he turns the corner he looks back to say goodbye and she has a look of fear on her face, fear of the unknown its always the scariest, so as he turns the corner it might be the last time she sees her oldest, her only son, the only one who has yet to figure life out and find his own way.

But he's not in the clear yet as a septa cop walks towards Lid, who's hands are tied carrying both bags and whats makes things even scarier he's an ITALIAN cop so Lid can only think to himself that yeah it might be going down right here, right now and watches as they both maintain eye contact squinting his eyes in anger as they pass each other. It's only two grand, the trick was getting away without them holding any leverage over him, pulling your strings is their game and even though they showed much love during his stint in Philly getting away scott free without any type of injury is a rare occurrence in homicide heaven kiladelphia, but the mental scars are there, plus its not his fault he doesn't know what the lawyer did with the money or where he's at for that matter, but sticking around to find out what they had planned for Lid to pay off that debt was out of the question.

Once he gets on the bus he takes his usual seat on the back row and waits and watches as the charecters get on this pre new years eve trip, until to his surprise a stunning slim chocolate sister gets on and continues to walk to the back of the bus it's a long trip to Miami and she is just a prelude to the wild nights and latina lovin he's going to get down on South beach. Jackpot!!! She sits in the seats directly in front of him, but what in the world is a professional women like her doing on this bus, this late? She didn't even have a carry on bag just her black leather prada purse and as she takes off her winter coat revealing an all to tight pin stripe business suit Lid can only stare at those perfect legs, nice legs, she throws her coat mover top of the aisle seat and Lid takes a quick whiff of the air never passing up the chance to take a smell of the lovely scent of a women and sits back and waits as the bus pulls off and the journey back down south begins.

"Excuse me do you want to watch a movie with me I have my portable DVD player?" She looks over at him with cat like reflexes and her big brown eyes just glimmer, her shoulder length black hair, he thinks to himself God she is beautiful yet but her answer while smiling and showing off pearly whites is heartbreaking "No I'm sorry I have get off soon and I don't want to start a movie without finishing it." But like a true professional she him right back up after knocking him to canvus "Do you have any music?" Back in business "Yeah I got some Teena Marie, Sade, and Boys II Men." "Do you have any Jazz, when a man doesn't have any more words for the worls he listens to Jazz." "You know I do have some Miles on my MP3 player so you wanna listen?" "Yes I do, we can share earpieces just wipe it off because I don't want of your cutties." "Yeah cause I got'em. So where, hold up I didn't even ask you your name?" "Its Ciara" "Like the singer?" "No Ciara like me." "Lid I'm from Philly how bout you?" "Military brat so I've lived all over the country all over the world for that matter but origionally I'm from Chicago Forty Four!, and I went to school in D.C. at Howard and I've been working in Washington since graduation." "I went to Delaware State" "That's a party school" "heheheh yeah I know but I didn't do much partying I was in the library trying to get into law school, but I didn't get accepted anywhere." "You should try again never give up." "Your right its just the past few years have been a mess for me personally and with this country for that matter to see the Constitution trampled on by FORTY THREE  and his cronnies its discouraging because we were so close to world peace and fulfilling the dream our forefathers had when they signedin Philly." "Your passionate about America, that's good." "I have to be cant go anywhere else, I was real passionate about the old America, its different now." "Its going to change we have a new President now you'll see, its like a cycle." "I hope so." They listen to Miles Davis live from Manchester,and then the classic live album from Carnegie hall its simply uncanny the way that man plays the trumpet but when they get to D.C. she lets him know when they get to D.C. "this is my stop. Ruining a good thing would be asking her for her phone number she's way out his league but what the hell it's a new year "Hey look Ciara could I uh get your telephone number?' She smiles a tell tell grim like brother you are pushing your luck but in a professional manner she says "I'm sorry

I don't give my number out to just anyone do you have facebook?" "Naw whats that?" "Look it up on the web but it a social networking site, but here's my full name and she jots down her name on a small piece of paper "Alright then Lid you have a good time in Miami, it was nice to meet you and don't get discouraged things change." "Thanks Ciara, take it easy miss and thanks for being so nice its hard to get that out of people these days." She smiles and hands him a piece of paper folded in four ways and walks off the bus. That was nice he thinks to himself and as the bus pulls off and continues to descend the last one on the coast, opening the note (peace symbol). Its like pure kinetic energy immediately an earth-shattering shot chill engulfs his spine:

*"Campane annuls, sigillum fractum, nes, spirituum, excitavit, finis, agere Descendere in graliam." True believes . . . . .*

*Author: Lid N. Ali*

*Love + Truth = Peace*